CW01500857

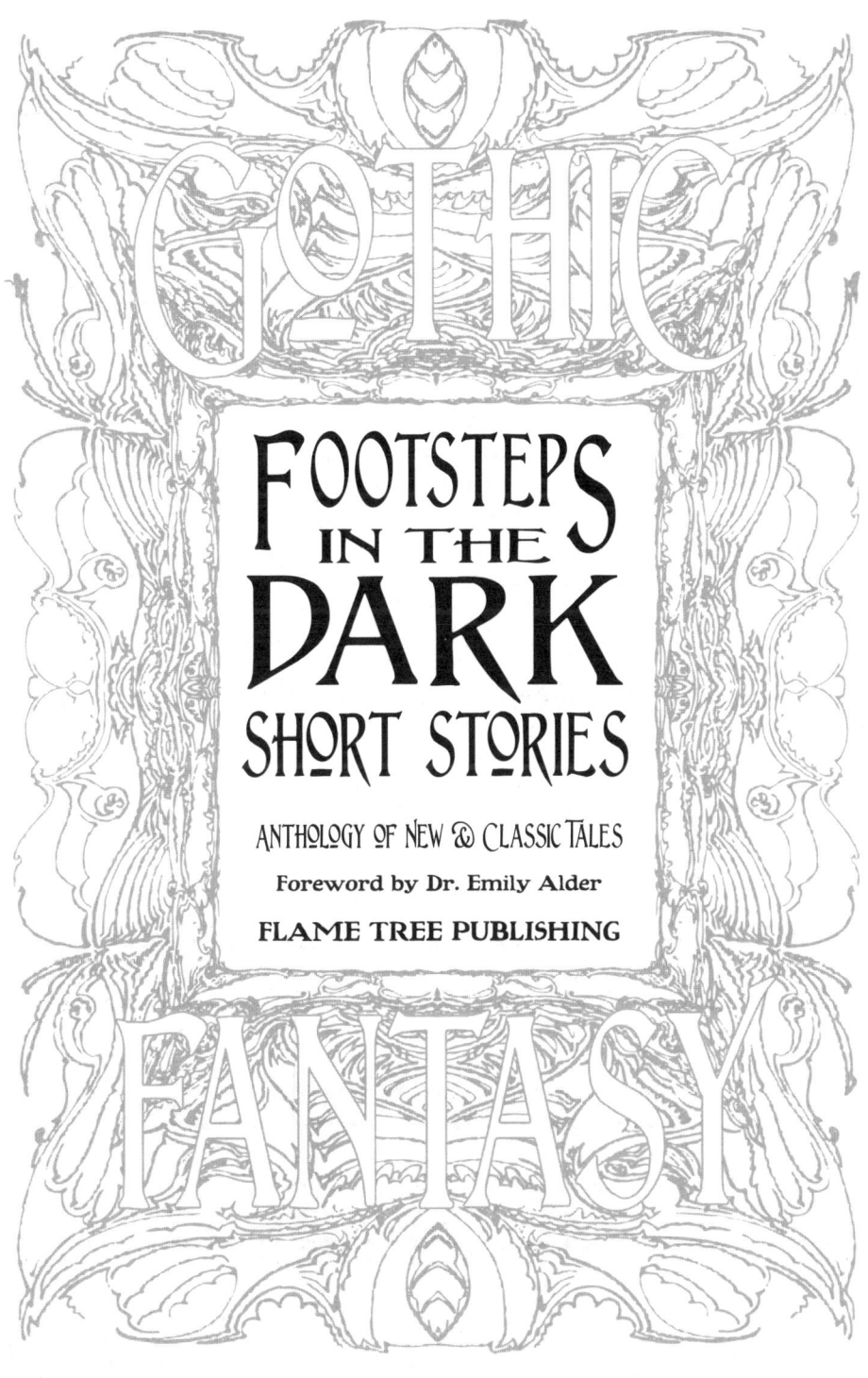

GOTHIC

FOOTSTEPS
IN THE
DARK
SHORT STORIES

ANTHOLOGY OF NEW & CLASSIC TALES

Foreword by Dr. Emily Alder

FLAME TREE PUBLISHING

FANTASY

This is a FLAME TREE Book

Publisher & Creative Director: Nick Wells
Project Editor: Gillian Whitaker
Editorial Board: Josie Karani, Taylor Bentley, Catherine Taylor

Publisher's Note: Due to the historical nature of the classic text, we're aware that there may be some language used which has the potential to cause offence to the modern reader. However, wishing overall to preserve the integrity of the text, rather than imposing contemporary sensibilities, we have left it unaltered.

FLAME TREE PUBLISHING
6 Melbray Mews, Fulham,
London SW6 3NS, United Kingdom
www.flametreepublishing.com

First published 2020

Stories by modern authors are subject to international copyright law, and are licensed for publication in this volume.

20 22 24 23 21
1 3 5 7 9 10 8 6 4 2

ISBN: 978-1-83964-187-9

The cover image is created by Flame Tree Studio
based on artwork by Slava Gerj and Gabor Ruszkai.

A copy of the CIP data for this book is available from the British Library.

Printed and bound in China

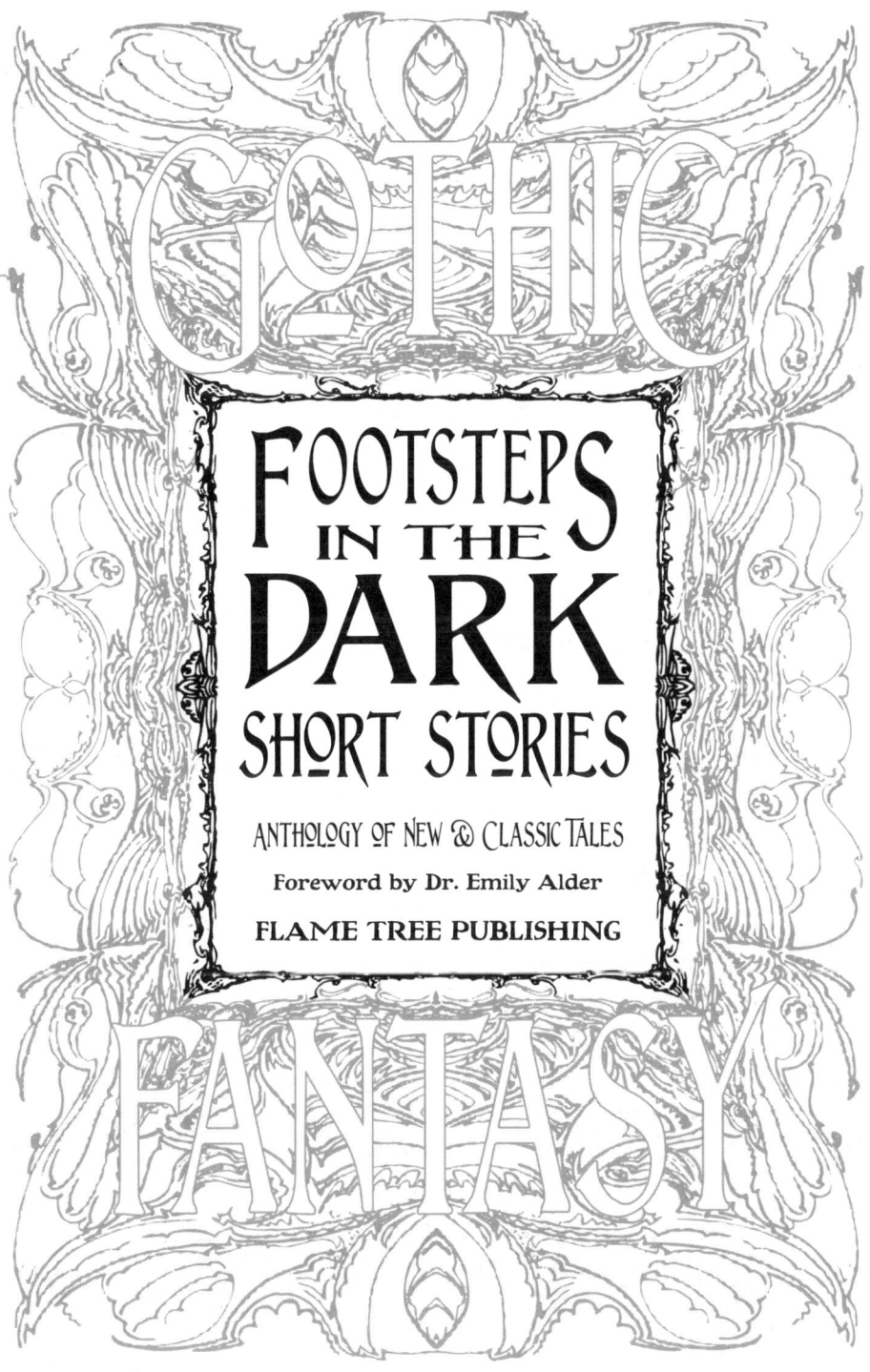

FOOTSTEPS IN THE DARK
SHORT STORIES

ANTHOLOGY OF NEW & CLASSIC TALES

Foreword by Dr. Emily Alder

FLAME TREE PUBLISHING

Contents

Foreword: Footsteps in the Dark Short Stories

A JANGLING BELL in the middle of the night. A cloaked companion on a moonlit walk. Swift footfalls on a deserted London street. A honeymoon menaced by a mysterious mesmerist. A bony hand creeping from an ancient book.

Gothic tales dwell on fear of the past's resurgence in the present. Repressed memories, personal crimes, family secrets, and cultural anxieties take form as ghosts, monsters, or shadowy doubles. They haunt the pages of Gothic literature as warnings, symptoms of psychological stress caused by intense desires, fears, or guilt, reminders of a past that won't go away or is doomed to repeat.

Mysterious doppelgänger figures mirror central characters in many of the best-known Gothic novels. In Mary Shelley's *Frankenstein* (1818), Victor's creature is the second self he can never shake off, but their story ends with Victor in pursuit, trailing his creation across the Arctic on foot and sledge. Forty years later, Anne Catherick walks the moonlit road to London in Wilkie Collins's *The Woman in White* (1859). Laying a chilling hand on Walter Hartright's shoulder, she inaugurates the novel's central mystery that operates through her physical resemblance to Laura Fairlie. And short stories specialise in elaborating these moments, conjuring the dread of things that follow.

In his famous 1919 essay, Freud associated unsettling repetitions and the figure of the double with the experience of the 'uncanny', which he described as 'all that arouses dread and creeping horror'. The feeling of 'creeping horror' we enjoy as we read Gothic short stories is as much a consequence of narrative construction as it is of the glimpse of a ghost. It is no surprise to discover that Dennistoun should have left Canon Alberic's scrapbook well alone in M.R. James's 1895 tale – rather, our pleasure comes from anticipating that something horrible will happen but we don't quite know what. Exploiting night-time atmospheres, usually dark, moonlit, or stormy, Gothic short stories play on readers' expectations. Their structure builds gradually, so that each scene or phase deepens the mystery, heightens the suspense, delays the denouement, and intensifies the protagonist's psychological misery. In Joseph Sheridan Le Fanu's 'The Familiar' (1872), a haunting that begins as invisible 'footfalls, pattering [...] two score steps behind' Captain Barton repeats and intensifies with 'diabolic perseverance' into a confrontational figure that even other characters can touch and speak to.

Doppelgängers hover on the edges of the real. Robert Louis Stevenson's 'The Strange Case of Dr Jekyll and Mr Hyde' (1886) closely associates Hyde with the city and with walking. 'Odd light footstep[s]' warn Utterson of Hyde's approach and recall to us his callous trampling of a child; Hyde's realness is deadly, yet he vanishes without trace whenever Jekyll takes the antidote. The ghost of Emma Saxon, the presumed ringer of Edith Wharton's 'The Lady Maid's Bell' (1902), appears only to the narrator, as a warning of a dangerous liaison whose consequences she fails to prevent.

Gothic tales grapple with the consequences of transgression, especially transgressions of the norms that make up their society's moral foundations: of the just exercising of power, for example, as the punishment Captain Barton dealt the sailor under his command is revisited upon him, or of sexual behaviour, as Harriott Leigh's affair with married Oscar Wade traps her perpetually in its worst moments in May Sinclair's 'Where Their Fire Is Not Quenched' (1922). Either way, to hear footsteps in the dark is to recall that there is no escaping the past. It stalks the pages of the Gothic from early romances to modern horror, driving its victims to the limits of what the human mind, body, and soul can bear.

Dr. Emily Alder

Publisher's Note

FOOTSTEPS IN THE DARK offers a particularly tantalising strain of horror: while with 'footsteps' you may think yourself on safe ground at the thought of a recognisable, human agency, this becomes ambiguous or uncertain when combined with darkness, obscurity or secrecy. The results are often something that is not quite human, and yet sufficiently human to disturb in its uncanny likeness. As such, there are all sorts of almost-humans, double lives, and chilling transformations in the pages of this book. Werewolves, vampires, ghosts and creatures from folk horror abound, but there are also those footsteps conjured by the mind, whether through guilt, with past sins resurfacing in startlingly real forms, or through grief, as in 'Death and the Woman' and its sense of death's approaching footsteps. From the cabin in the wood in 'The Eyes of the Panther' to the deep dark underground of 'The Mines of Falun', this anthology's focus is in many ways the 'intangible and unseen pursuit' that Captain Barton feels threatened by in 'The Familiar'. It's both something we try to escape from, but also find ourselves drawn into. The characters in this book may not all feel like Mr. Utterson in 'The Strange Case of Dr. Jekyll and Mr. Hyde', whose need to see Mr. Hyde to 'lighten' the mystery does nothing to assuage his concerns, only to heighten them. But they do all become involved with some sort of creeping force, malignant or otherwise, lurking just out of sight.

As is customary in this series of anthologies, we have sought to choose the very best new and recent fiction from a tough submissions process. We're delighted with the results, and have tried to select stories that sit comfortably alongside the classic fiction while offering new takes on an intriguing theme. We hope, therefore, that this anthology proves a fascinating and absorbing collection, where you'll find all manner of potential horrors brought on by the cover of darkness.

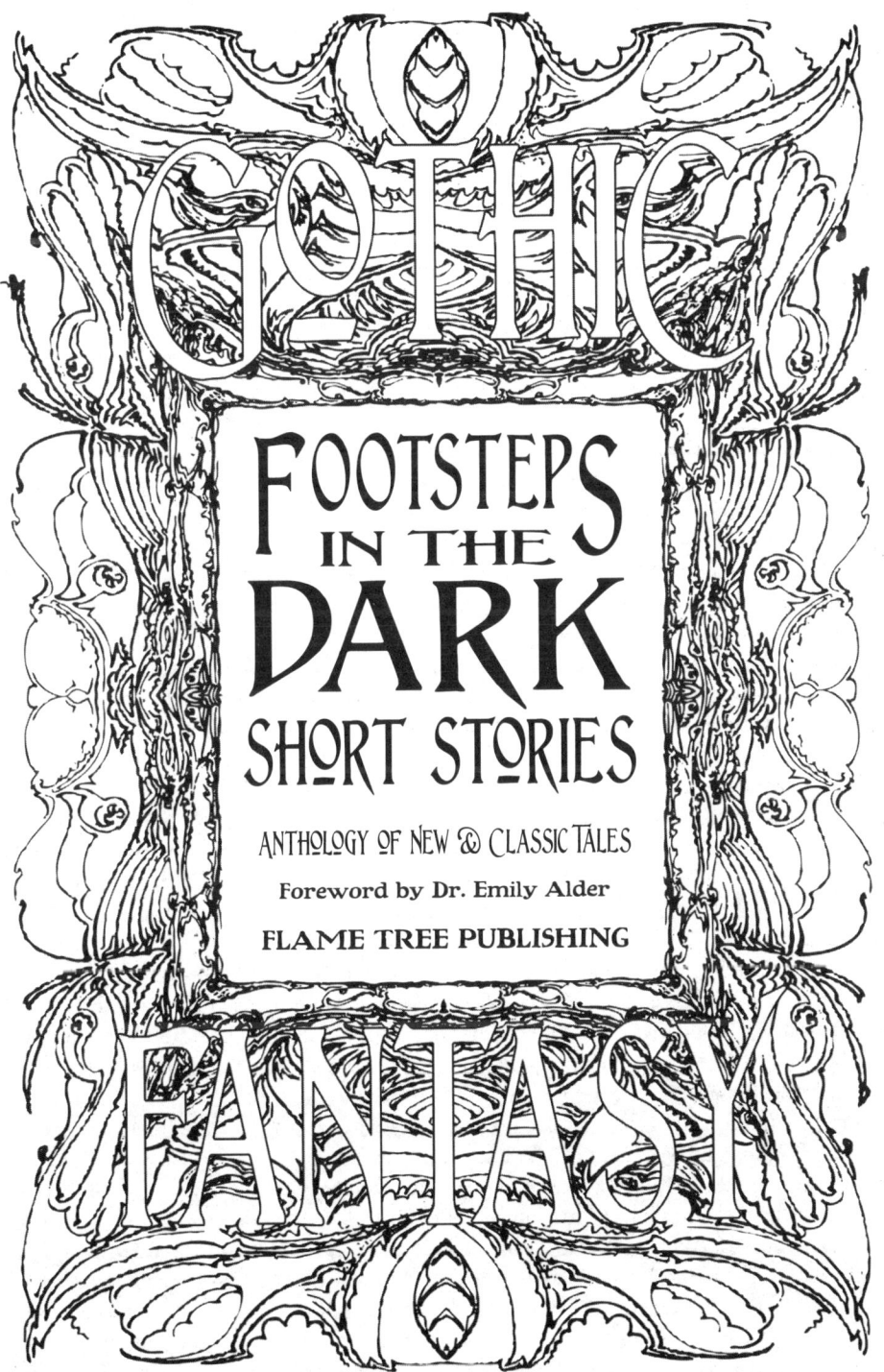

GOTHIC

FOOTSTEPS IN THE DARK

SHORT STORIES

ANTHOLOGY OF NEW & CLASSIC TALES

Foreword by Dr. Emily Alder

FLAME TREE PUBLISHING

FANTASY

My Adventure in Norfolk

A.J. Alan

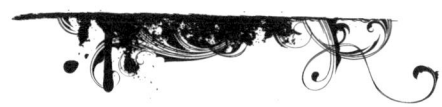

I DON'T KNOW how it is with you, but during February my wife generally says to me: "Have you thought at all about what we are going to do for August?" And, of course, I say, "No," and then she begins looking through the advertisements of bungalows to let.

Well, this happened last year, as usual, and she eventually produced one that looked possible. It said: 'Norfolk – Hickling Broad – Furnished Bungalow – Garden – Garage, Boathouse', and all the rest of it – Oh – *and* plate and linen. It also mentioned an exorbitant rent. I pointed out the bit about the rent, but my wife said: "Yes, you'll have to go down and see the landlord, and get him to come down. They always do." As a matter of fact, they always don't, but that's a detail.

Anyway, I wrote off to the landlord and asked if he could arrange for me to stay the night in the place to see what it was really like. He wrote back and said: "Certainly", and that he was engaging Mrs. So-and-So to come in and 'oblige me', and make up the beds and so forth.

I tell you, we do things thoroughly in our family – I have to sleep in all the beds, and when I come home my wife counts the bruises and decides whether they will do or not.

At any rate, I arrived, in a blinding snowstorm, at about *the* most desolate spot on God's earth. I'd come to Potter Heigham by train, and been driven on – (it was a good five miles from the station). Fortunately, Mrs. Selston, the old lady who was going to 'do' for me, was there, and she'd lighted a fire, and cooked me a steak, for which I was truly thankful.

I somehow think the cow, or whatever they get steaks off, had only died that morning. It was very – er – obstinate. While I dined, she talked to me. She *would* tell me all about an operation her husband had just had. *All* about it. It was almost a lecture on surgery. The steak was rather underdone, and it sort of made me feel I was illustrating her lecture. Anyway, she put me clean off my dinner, and then departed for the night.

I explored the bungalow and just had a look outside. It was, of course, very dark, but not snowing quite so hard. The garage stood about fifteen yards from the back door. I walked round it, but didn't go in. I also went down to the edge of the broad, and verified the boathouse. The whole place looked as though it might be all right in the summertime, but just then it made one wonder why people ever wanted to go to the North Pole.

Anyhow, I went indoors, and settled down by the fire. You've no idea how quiet it was; even the waterfowl had taken a night off – at least, they weren't working.

At a few minutes to eleven I heard the first noise there'd been since Mrs. What's-her-name – Selston – had cleared out. It was the sound of a car. If it had gone straight by I probably shouldn't have noticed it at all, only it didn't go straight by; it seemed to stop farther up the road, before it got to the house. Even that didn't make much impression. After all, cars *do* stop.

It must have been five or ten minutes before it was borne in on me that it hadn't gone on again. So I got up and looked out of the window. It had left off snowing, and there was a glare through the gate that showed that there were headlamps somewhere just out of sight. I thought I might as well stroll out and investigate.

I found a fair-sized limousine pulled up in the middle of the road about twenty yards short of my gate. The light was rather blinding, but when I got close to it I found a girl with the bonnet open, tinkering with the engine. Quite an attractive young female, from what one could see, but she was so muffled up in furs that it was rather hard to tell.

I said:

"Er – good evening – anything I can do."

She said she didn't know what was the matter. The engine had just stopped, and wouldn't start again. And it *had*! It wouldn't even turn, either with the self-starter or the handle. The whole thing was awfully hot, and I asked her whether there was any water in the radiator. She didn't see why there shouldn't be, there always had been. This didn't strike me as entirely conclusive. I said, we'd better put some in, and see what happened. She said, why not use snow? But I thought not. There was an idea at the back of my mind that there was some reason why it was unwise to use melted snow, and it wasn't until I arrived back with a bucketful that I remembered what it was. Of course – goitre.

When I got back to her she'd got the radiator cap off, and inserted what a Danish friend of mine calls a 'funeral'. We poured a little water in… Luckily I'd warned her to stand clear. The first tablespoonful that went in came straight out again, red hot, and blew the "funeral" sky-high. We waited a few minutes until things had cooled down a bit, but it was no go. As fast as we poured water in it simply ran out again into the road underneath. It was quite evident that she'd been driving with the radiator bone dry, and that her engine had seized right up.

I told her so. She said:

"Does that mean I've got to stop here all night?"

I explained that it wasn't as bad as all that; that is, if she cared to accept the hospitality of my poor roof (and it *was* a poor roof – it let the wet in). But she wouldn't hear of it. By the by, she didn't know the – er – circumstances, so it wasn't that. No, she wanted to leave the car where it was and go on on foot.

I said:

"Don't be silly, it's miles to anywhere."

However, at that moment we heard a car coming along the road, the same way as she'd come. We could see its lights, too, although it was a very long way off. You know how flat Norfolk is – you can see a terrific distance.

I said:

"There's the way out of all your troubles. This thing, whatever it is, will give you a tow to the nearest garage, or at any rate a lift to some hotel."

One would have expected her to show some relief, but she didn't. I began to wonder what she jolly well *did* want. She wouldn't let me help her to stop where she was, and she didn't seem anxious for anyone to help her to go anywhere else.

She was quite peculiar about it. She gripped hold of my arm, and said:

"What do you think this is that's coming?"

I said:

"I'm sure I don't know, being a stranger in these parts, but it sounds like a lorry full of milk cans."

I offered to lay her sixpence about it (this was before the betting-tax came in). She'd have had to pay, too, because it *was* a lorry full of milk cans. The driver had to pull up because there wasn't room to get by.

He got down and asked if there was anything he could do to help. We explained the situation. He said he was going to Norwich, and was quite ready to give her a tow if she wanted it. However, she wouldn't do that, and it was finally decided to shove her car into my garage for the night, to be sent for next day, and the lorry was to take her along to Norwich.

Well, I managed to find the key of the garage, and the lorry-driver – Williams, his name was – and I ran the car in and locked the door. This having been done – (ablative absolute) – I suggested that it was a very cold night. Williams agreed, and said he didn't mind if he did. So I took them both indoors and mixed them a stiff whisky and water each. There wasn't any soda. And, naturally, the whole thing had left *me* very cold, too. I hadn't an overcoat on.

Up to now I hadn't seriously considered the young woman. For one thing it had been dark, *and* there had been a seized engine to look at. Er – I'm afraid that's not a very gallant remark. What I mean is that to anyone with a mechanical mind a motor-car in that condition is much more interesting than – er – well, it *is* very interesting – but why labour the point? However, in the sitting room, in the lamplight, it was possible to get more of an idea. She was a little older than I'd thought, and her eyes were too close together.

Of course, she wasn't a – how shall I put it? Her manners weren't quite easy and she was careful with her English. *You* know. But that wasn't it. She treated us with a lack of friendliness which was – well, we'd done nothing to deserve it. There was a sort of vague hostility and suspicion, which seemed rather hard lines, considering. Also, she was so anxious to keep in the shadow that if I hadn't moved the lamp away she'd never have got near the fire at all.

And the way she hurried the wretched Williams over his drink was quite distressing; and foolish, too, as *he* was going to drive, but that was her – funnel. When he'd gone out to start up his engine I asked her if she was all right for money, and she apparently was. Then they started off, and I shut up the place and went upstairs.

There happened to be a local guidebook in my bedroom, with maps in it. I looked at these and couldn't help wondering where the girl in the car had come from; I mean my road seemed so very unimportant. The sort of road one might use if one wanted to avoid people. If one were driving a stolen car, for instance. This was quite a thrilling idea. I thought it might be worthwhile having another look at the car. So I once more unhooked the key from the kitchen dresser and sallied forth into the snow. It was as black as pitch, and so still that my candle hardly flickered. It wasn't a large garage, and the car nearly filled it. By the by, we'd backed it in so as to make it easier to tow it out again.

The engine I'd already seen, so I squeezed past along the wall and opened the door in the body part of the car. At least, I only turned the handle, and the door was pushed open from the inside and – something – fell out on me. It pushed me quite hard, and wedged me against the wall. It also knocked the candle out of my hand and left me in the dark – which was a bit of a nuisance. I wondered what on earth the thing was – barging into me like that – so I felt it, rather gingerly, and found it was a man – a dead man – with a moustache. He'd evidently been sitting propped up against the door. I managed to put him back, as decorously as possible, and shut the door again.

After a lot of grovelling about under the car I found the candle and lighted it, and opened the opposite door and switched on the little lamp in the roof – and then – oo-er!

Of course, I had to make some sort of examination. He was an extremely tall and thin individual. He must have been well over six feet three. He was dark and very cadaverous-looking. In fact, I don't suppose he'd ever looked so cadaverous in his life. He was wearing a trench coat.

It wasn't difficult to tell what he'd died of. He'd been shot through the back. I found the hole just under the right scrofula, or scalpel – what is shoulder-blade, anyway? Oh, clavicle – stupid of me – well, that's where it was, and the bullet had evidently gone through into the lung. I say 'evidently', and leave it at that.

There were no papers in his pockets, and no tailor's name on his clothes, but there was a note-case, with nine pounds in it. Altogether a most unpleasant business. Of course, it doesn't do to question the workings of Providence, but one couldn't help wishing it hadn't happened. It was just a little mysterious, too – er – who had killed him. It wasn't likely that the girl had or she wouldn't have been joy-riding about the country with him; and if someone else had murdered him why hadn't she mentioned it? Anyway, she hadn't and she'd gone, so one couldn't do anything for the time being. No telephone, of course. I just locked up the garage and went to bed. That was two o'clock.

Next morning I woke early, for some reason or other, and it occurred to me as a good idea to go and have a look at things – by daylight, and before Mrs. Selston turned up. So I did. The first thing that struck me was that it had snowed heavily during the night, because there were no wheel tracks or footprints, and the second was that I'd left the key in the garage door. I opened it and went in. The place was completely empty. No car, no body, no nothing. There was a patch of grease on the floor where I'd dropped the candle, otherwise there was nothing to show I'd been there before. One of two things must have happened: either some people had come along during the night and taken the car away, or else I'd fallen asleep in front of the fire and dreamt the whole thing.

Then I remembered the whisky glasses.

They should still be in the sitting room. I went back to look, and they were, all three of them. So it *hadn't* been a dream and the car *had* been fetched away, but they must have been jolly quiet over it.

The girl had left her glass on the mantelpiece, and it showed several very clearly defined finger-marks. Some were mine, naturally, because I'd fetched the glass from the kitchen and poured out the drink for her, but hers, her finger-marks, were clean, and mine were oily, so it was quite easy to tell them apart. It isn't necessary to point out that this glass was very important. There'd evidently been a murder, or something of that kind, and the girl must have known all about it, even if she hadn't actually done it herself, so anything she had left in the way of evidence ought to be handed over to the police; and this was all she *had* left. So I packed it up with meticulous care in an old biscuit box out of the larder.

When Mrs. Selston came I settled up with her and came back to Town. Oh, I called on the landlord on the way and told him I'd 'let him know' about the bungalow. Then I caught my train, and in due course drove straight to Scotland Yard. I went up and saw my friend there. I produced the glass and asked him if his people could identify the marks. He said: "Probably not", but he sent it down to the fingerprint department and asked me where it came from. I said: "Never you mind; let's have the identification first." He said: "All right."

They're awfully quick, these people – the clerk was back in three minutes with a file of papers. They knew the girl all right. They told me her name and showed me her photograph; not flattering. Quite an adventurous lady, from all accounts. In the early part of her career she'd done time twice for shoplifting, chiefly in the book department. Then she'd what they call 'taken up with' a member of one of those race-gangs one sometimes hears about.

My pal went on to say that there'd been a fight between two of these gangs, in the course of which her friend had got shot. She'd managed to get him away in a car, but it had broken down somewhere in Norfolk. So she'd left it and the dead man in someone's garage, and had started off for Norwich in a lorry. Only she never got there. On the way the lorry had skidded, and both she and the driver – a fellow called Williams – had been thrown out, and they'd rammed their heads against a brick wall, which everyone knows is a fatal thing to do. At least, it was in their case.

I said: "Look here, it's all very well, but you simply can't know all this; there hasn't been time – it only happened last night."

He said: "Last night be blowed! It all happened in February, 1919. The people you've described have been dead for years."

I said: "Oh!"

And to think that I might have stuck to that nine pounds!

Death and the Woman

Gertrude Atherton

HER HUSBAND was dying, and she was alone with him. Nothing could exceed the desolation of her surroundings. She and the man who was going from her were in the third-floor-back of a New York boarding-house. It was summer, and the other boarders were in the country; all the servants except the cook had been dismissed, and she, when not working, slept profoundly on the fifth floor. The landlady also was out of town on a brief holiday.

The window was open to admit the thick unstirring air; no sound rose from the row of long narrow yards, nor from the tall deep houses annexed. The latter deadened the rattle of the streets. At intervals the distant Elevated lumbered protestingly along, its grunts and screams muffled by the hot suspended ocean.

She sat there plunged in the profoundest grief that can come to the human soul, for in all other agony hope flickers, however forlornly. She gazed dully at the unconscious breathing form of the man who had been friend, and companion, and lover, during five years of youth too vigorous and hopeful to be warped by uneven fortune. It was wasted by disease; the face was shrunken; the night garment hung loosely about a body which had never been disfigured by flesh, but had been muscular with exercise and full-blooded with health. She was glad that the body was changed; glad that its beauty, too, had gone some other-where than into the coffin. She had loved his hands as apart from himself; loved their strong warm magnetism. They lay limp and yellow on the quilt: she knew that they were already cold, and that moisture was gathering on them. For a moment something convulsed within her. *They* had gone too. She repeated the words twice, and, after them, "*forever*". And the while the sweetness of their pressure came back to her.

She leaned suddenly over him. *He* was in there still, somewhere. *Where?* If he had not ceased to breathe, the Ego, the Soul, the Personality was still in the sodden clay which had shaped to give it speech. Why could it not manifest itself to her? Was it still conscious in there, unable to project itself through the disintegrating matter which was the only medium its Creator had vouchsafed it? Did it struggle there, seeing her agony, sharing it, longing for the complete disintegration which should put an end to its torment? She called his name, she even shook him slightly, mad to tear the body apart and find her mate, yet even in that tortured moment realizing that violence would hasten his going.

The dying man took no notice of her, and she opened his gown and put her cheek to his heart, calling him again. There had never been more perfect union; how could the bond still be so strong if he were not at the other end of it? He was there, her other part; until dead he must be living. There was no intermediate state. Why should he be as entombed and unresponding as if the screws were in the lid? But the faintly beating heart did not quicken beneath her lips. She extended her arms suddenly, describing eccentric lines, above, about him, rapidly opening and closing her hands as if to clutch some escaping object; then sprang to her feet, and went to the window. She feared insanity. She had asked to be left alone with her dying husband, and she did not wish to lose her reason and shriek a crowd of people about her.

The green plots in the yards were not apparent, she noticed. Something heavy, like a pall, rested upon them. Then she understood that the day was over and that night was coming.

She returned swiftly to the bedside, wondering if she had remained away hours or seconds, and if he were dead. His face was still discernible, and Death had not relaxed it. She laid her own against it, then withdrew it with shuddering flesh, her teeth smiting each other as if an icy wind had passed.

She let herself fall back in the chair, clasping her hands against her heart, watching with expanding eyes the white sculptured face which, in the glittering dark, was becoming less defined of outline. Did she light the gas it would draw mosquitoes, and she could not shut from him the little air he must be mechanically grateful for. And she did not want to see the opening eye – the falling jaw.

Her vision became so fixed that at length she saw nothing, and closed her eyes and waited for the moisture to rise and relieve the strain. When she opened them his face had disappeared; the humid waves above the house-tops put out even the light of the stars, and night was come.

Fearfully, she approached her ear to his lips; he still breathed. She made a motion to kiss him, then threw herself back in a quiver of agony – they were not the lips she had known, and she would have nothing less.

His breathing was so faint that in her half-reclining position she could not hear it, could not be aware of the moment of his death. She extended her arm resolutely and laid her hand on his heart. Not only must she feel his going, but, so strong had been the comradeship between them, it was a matter of loving honor to stand by him to the last.

She sat there in the hot heavy night, pressing her hand hard against the ebbing heart of the unseen, and awaited Death. Suddenly an odd fancy possessed her. Where was Death? Why was he tarrying? Who was detaining him? From what quarter would he come? He was taking his leisure, drawing near with footsteps as measured as those of men keeping time to a funeral march. By a wayward deflection she thought of the slow music that was always turned on in the theatre when the heroine was about to appear, or something eventful to happen. She had always thought that sort of thing ridiculous and inartistic. So had He.

She drew her brows together angrily, wondering at her levity, and pressed her relaxed palm against the heart it kept guard over. For a moment the sweat stood on her face; then the pent-up breath burst from her lungs. He still lived.

Once more the fancy wantoned above the stunned heart. Death – *where* was he? What a curious experience: to be sitting alone in a big house – she knew that the cook had stolen out – waiting for Death to come and snatch her husband from her. No; he would not snatch, he would steal upon his prey as noiselessly as the approach of Sin to Innocence – an invisible, unfair, sneaking enemy, with whom no man's strength could grapple. If he would only come like a man, and take his chances like a man! Women had been known to reach the hearts of giants with the dagger's point. But he would creep upon her.

She gave an exclamation of horror. Something was creeping over the windowsill. Her limbs palsied, but she struggled to her feet and looked back, her eyes dragged about against her own volition. Two small green stars glared menacingly at her just above the sill; then the cat possessing them leaped downward, and the stars disappeared.

She realized that she was horribly frightened. "Is it possible?" she thought. "Am I afraid of Death, and of Death that has not yet come? I have always been rather a brave woman; *He* used to call me heroic; but then with him it was impossible to fear anything. And I begged them to leave me alone with him as the last of earthly boons. Oh, shame!"

But she was still quaking as she resumed her seat, and laid her hand again on his heart. She wished that she had asked Mary to sit outside the door; there was no bell in the room. To call would be worse than desecrating the house of God, and she would not leave him for one moment. To return and find him dead – gone alone!

Her knees smote each other. It was idle to deny it; she was in a state of unreasoning terror. Her eyes rolled apprehensively about; she wondered if she should see It when It came; wondered how far off It was now. Not very far; the heart was barely pulsing. She had heard of the power of the corpse to drive brave men to frenzy, and had wondered, having no morbid horror of the dead. But this! To wait – and wait – and wait – perhaps for hours – past the midnight – on to the small hours – while that awful, determined, leisurely Something stole nearer and nearer.

She bent to him who had been her protector with a spasm of anger. Where was the indomitable spirit that had held her all these years with such strong and loving clasp? How could he leave her? How could he desert her? Her head fell back and moved restlessly against the cushion; moaning with the agony of loss, she recalled him as he had been. Then fear once more took possession of her, and she sat erect, rigid, breathless, awaiting the approach of Death.

Suddenly, far down in the house, on the first floor, her strained hearing took note of a sound – a wary, muffled sound, as if someone were creeping up the stair, fearful of being heard. Slowly! It seemed to count a hundred between the laying down of each foot. She gave a hysterical gasp. Where was the slow music?

Her face, her body, were wet – as if a wave of death-sweat had broken over them. There was a stiff feeling at the roots of her hair; she wondered if it were really standing erect. But she could not raise her hand to ascertain. Possibly it was only the coloring matter freezing and bleaching. Her muscles were flabby, her nerves twitched helplessly.

She knew that it was Death who was coming to her through the silent deserted house; knew that it was the sensitive ear of her intelligence that heard him, not the dull, coarse-grained ear of the body.

He toiled up the stair painfully, as if he were old and tired with much work. But how could he afford to loiter, with all the work he had to do? Every minute, every second, he must be in demand to hook his cold, hard finger about a soul struggling to escape from its putrefying tenement. But probably he had his emissaries, his minions: for only those worthy of the honor did he come in person.

He reached the first landing and crept like a cat down the hall to the next stair, then crawled slowly up as before. Light as the footfalls were, they were squarely planted, unfaltering; slow, they never halted.

Mechanically she pressed her jerking hand closer against the heart; its beats were almost done. They would finish, she calculated, just as those footfalls paused beside the bed.

She was no longer a human being; she was an Intelligence and an *Ear*. Not a sound came from without, even the Elevated appeared to be temporarily off duty; but inside the big quiet house that footfall was waxing louder, louder, until iron feet crashed on iron stairs and echo thundered.

She had counted the steps – one – two – three – irritated beyond endurance at the long deliberate pauses between. As they climbed and clanged with slow precision she continued to count, audibly and with equal precision, noting their hollow reverberation. How many steps had the stair? She wished she knew. No need! The colossal trampling announced the lessening distance in an increasing volume of sound not to be misunderstood. It turned the curve; it reached the landing; it advanced – slowly – down the hall; it paused before her door. Then knuckles of iron shook the frail panels. Her nerveless tongue gave no invitation. The knocking became more imperious; the very walls vibrated. The handle turned, swiftly and firmly. With a wild instinctive movement she flung herself into the arms of her husband.

* * *

When Mary opened the door and entered the room she found a dead woman lying across a dead man.

Mrs. Amworth

E.F. Benson

THE VILLAGE of Maxley, where, last summer and autumn, these strange events took place, lies on a heathery and pine-clad upland of Sussex. In all England you could not find a sweeter and saner situation. Should the wind blow from the south, it comes laden with the spices of the sea; to the east high downs protect it from the inclemencies of March; and from the west and north the breezes which reach it travel over miles of aromatic forest and heather. The village itself is insignificant enough in point of population, but rich in amenities and beauty. Halfway down the single street, with its broad road and spacious areas of grass on each side, stands the little Norman Church and the antique graveyard long disused: for the rest there are a dozen small, sedate Georgian houses, red-bricked and long-windowed, each with a square of flower-garden in front, and an ampler strip behind; a score of shops, and a couple of score of thatched cottages belonging to labourers on neighbouring estates, complete the entire cluster of its peaceful habitations. The general peace, however, is sadly broken on Saturdays and Sundays, for we lie on one of the main roads between London and Brighton and our quiet street becomes a race-course for flying motor-cars and bicycles.

A notice just outside the village begging them to go slowly only seems to encourage them to accelerate their speed, for the road lies open and straight, and there is really no reason why they should do otherwise. By way of protest, therefore, the ladies of Maxley cover their noses and mouths with their handkerchiefs as they see a motor-car approaching, though, as the street is asphalted, they need not really take these precautions against dust. But late on Sunday night the horde of scorchers has passed, and we settle down again to five days of cheerful and leisurely seclusion. Railway strikes which agitate the country so much leave us undisturbed because most of the inhabitants of Maxley never leave it at all.

I am the fortunate possessor of one of these small Georgian houses, and consider myself no less fortunate in having so interesting and stimulating a neighbour as Francis Urcombe, who, the most confirmed of Maxleyites, has not slept away from his house, which stands just opposite to mine in the village street, for nearly two years, at which date, though still in middle life, he resigned his Physiological Professorship at Cambridge University and devoted himself to the study of those occult and curious phenomena which seem equally to concern the physical and the psychical sides of human nature. Indeed his retirement was not unconnected with his passion for the strange uncharted places that lie on the confines and borders of science, the existence of which is so stoutly denied by the more materialistic minds, for he advocated that all medical students should be obliged to pass some sort of examination in mesmerism, and that one of the tripos papers should be designed to test their knowledge in such subjects as appearances at time of death, haunted houses, vampirism, automatic writing, and possession.

"Of course they wouldn't listen to me," ran his account of the matter, "for there is nothing that these seats of learning are so frightened of as knowledge, and the road to knowledge lies in the study of things like these. The functions of the human frame are, broadly speaking, known.

"They are a country, anyhow, that has been charted and mapped out. But outside that lie huge tracts of undiscovered country, which certainly exist, and the real pioneers of knowledge are those who, at the cost of being derided as credulous and superstitious, want to push on into those misty and probably perilous places. I felt that I could be of more use by setting out without compass or knapsack into the mists than by sitting in a cage like a canary and chirping about what was known. Besides, teaching is very bad for a man who knows himself only to be a learner: you only need to be a self-conceited ass to teach."

Here, then, in Francis Urcombe, was a delightful neighbour to one who, like myself, has an uneasy and burning curiosity about what he called the 'misty and perilous places'; and this last spring we had a further and most welcome addition to our pleasant little community, in the person of Mrs. Amworth, widow of an Indian civil servant. Her husband had been a judge in the North-West Provinces, and after his death at Peshawar she came back to England, and after a year in London found herself starving for the ampler air and sunshine of the country to take the place of the fogs and griminess of town. She had, too, a special reason for settling in Maxley, since her ancestors up till a hundred years ago had long been native to the place, and in the old churchyard, now disused, are many gravestones bearing her maiden name of Chaston. Big and energetic, her vigorous and genial personality speedily woke Maxley up to a higher degree of sociality than it had ever known. Most of us were bachelors or spinsters or elderly folk not much inclined to exert ourselves in the expense and effort of hospitality, and hitherto the gaiety of a small tea-party, with bridge afterwards and goloshes (when it was wet) to trip home in again for a solitary dinner, was about the climax of our festivities. But Mrs. Amworth showed us a more gregarious way, and set an example of luncheon-parties and little dinners, which we began to follow. On other nights when no such hospitality was on foot, a lone man like myself found it pleasant to know that a call on the telephone to Mrs. Amworth's house not a hundred yards off, and an inquiry as to whether I might come over after dinner for a game of piquet before bedtime, would probably evoke a response of welcome. There she would be, with a comrade-like eagerness for companionship, and there was a glass of port and a cup of coffee and a cigarette and a game of piquet. She played the piano, too, in a free and exuberant manner, and had a charming voice and sang to her own accompaniment; and as the days grew long and the light lingered late, we played our game in her garden, which in the course of a few months she had turned from being a nursery for slugs and snails into a glowing patch of luxuriant blossoming.

She was always cheery and jolly; she was interested in everything, and in music, in gardening, in games of all sorts was a competent performer. Everybody (with one exception) liked her, everybody felt her to bring with her the tonic of a sunny day. That one exception was Francis Urcombe; he, though he confessed he did not like her, acknowledged that he was vastly interested in her. This always seemed strange to me, for pleasant and jovial as she was, I could see nothing in her that could call forth conjecture or intrigued surmise, so healthy and unmysterious a figure did she present. But of the genuineness of Urcombe's interest there could be no doubt; one could see him watching and scrutinising her. In matter of age, she frankly volunteered the information that she was forty-five; but her briskness, her activity, her unravaged skin, her coal-black hair, made it difficult to believe that she was not adopting an unusual device, and adding ten years on to her age instead of subtracting them.

Often, also, as our quite unsentimental friendship ripened, Mrs. Amworth would ring me up and propose her advent. If I was busy writing, I was to give her, so we definitely bargained, a frank negative, and in answer I could hear her jolly laugh and her wishes for a successful evening of work. Sometimes, before her proposal arrived, Urcombe would already have stepped across from his house opposite for a smoke and a chat, and he, hearing who my intending visitor was, always urged me to beg her to come. She and I should play our piquet, said he, and he would look on, if we did not object, and learn something of the game. But I doubt whether he paid much attention to it, for nothing could be clearer than that, under that penthouse of forehead and thick eyebrows, his attention was fixed not on the cards, but on one of the players. But he seemed to enjoy an hour spent thus, and often, until one particular evening in July, he would watch her with the air of a man who has some deep problem in front of him. She, enthusiastically keen about our game, seemed not to notice his scrutiny. Then came that evening, when, as I see in the light of subsequent events, began the first twitching of the veil that hid the secret horror from my eyes. I did not know it then, though I noticed that thereafter, if she rang up to propose coming round, she always asked not only if I was at leisure, but whether Mr. Urcombe was with me. If so, she said, she would not spoil the chat of two old bachelors, and laughingly wished me goodnight.

Urcombe, on this occasion, had been with me for some half-hour before Mrs. Amworth's appearance, and had been talking to me about the medieval beliefs concerning vampirism, one of those borderland subjects which he declared had not been sufficiently studied before it had been consigned by the medical profession to the dust-heap of exploded superstitions. There he sat, grim and eager, tracing, with that pellucid clearness which had made him in his Cambridge days so admirable a lecturer, the history of those mysterious visitations. In them all there were the same general features: one of those ghoulish spirits took up its abode in a living man or woman, conferring supernatural powers of bat-like flight and glutting itself with nocturnal blood-feasts.

When its host died it continued to dwell in the corpse, which remained undecayed. By day it rested, by night it left the grave and went on its awful errands. No European country in the Middle Ages seemed to have escaped them; earlier yet, parallels were to be found, in Roman and Greek and in Jewish history.

"It's a large order to set all that evidence aside as being moonshine," he said. "Hundreds of totally independent witnesses in many ages have testified to the occurrence of these phenomena, and there's no explanation known to me which covers all the facts. And if you feel inclined to say 'Why, then, if these are facts, do we not come across them now?' there are two answers I can make you. One is that there were diseases known in the Middle Ages, such as the black death; which were certainly existent then and which have become extinct since, but for that reason we do not assert that such diseases never existed. Just as the black death visited England and decimated the population of Norfolk, so here in this very district about three hundred years ago there was certainly an outbreak of vampirism, and Maxley was the centre of it. My second answer is even more convincing, for I tell you that vampirism is by no means extinct now. An outbreak of it certainly occurred in India a year or two ago."

At that moment I heard my knocker plied in the cheerful and peremptory manner in which Mrs. Amworth is accustomed to announce her arrival, and I went to the door to open it.

"Come in at once," I said, "and save me from having my blood curdled. Mr. Urcombe has been trying to alarm me."

Instantly her vital, voluminous presence seemed to fill the room.

"Ah, but how lovely!" she said. "I delight in having my blood curdled. Go on with your ghost story, Mr. Urcombe. I adore ghost stories."

I saw that, as his habit was, he was intently observing her.

"It wasn't a ghost story exactly," said he. "I was only telling our host how vampirism was not extinct yet. I was saying that there was an outbreak of it in India only a few years ago."

There was a more than perceptible pause, and I saw that, if Urcombe was observing her, she on her side was observing him with fixed eye and parted mouth. Then her jolly laugh invaded that rather tense silence.

"Oh, what a shame!" she said. "You're not going to curdle my blood at all. Where did you pick up such a tale, Mr. Urcombe? I have lived for years in India and never heard a rumour of such a thing. Some storyteller in the bazaars must have invented it: they are famous at that."

I could see that Urcombe was on the point of saying something further, but checked himself.

"Ah! Very likely that was it," he said.

But something had disturbed our usual peaceful sociability that night, and something had damped Mrs. Amworth's usual high spirits. She had no gusto for her piquet, and left after a couple of games. Urcombe had been silent too, indeed he hardly spoke again till she departed.

"That was unfortunate," he said, "for the outbreak of – of a very mysterious disease, let us call it, took place at Peshawar, where she and her husband were. And—"

"Well?" I asked.

"He was one of the victims of it," said he. "Naturally I had quite forgotten that when I spoke."

The summer was unreasonably hot and rainless, and Maxley suffered much from drought, and also from a plague of big black night-flying gnats, the bite of which was very irritating and virulent. They came sailing in of an evening, settling on one's skin so quietly that one perceived nothing till the sharp stab announced that one had been bitten. They did not bite the hands or face, but chose always the neck and throat for their feeding ground, and most of us, as the poison spread, assumed a temporary goitre. Then about the middle of August appeared the first of those mysterious cases of illness which our local doctor attributed to the long-continued heat coupled with the bite of these venomous insects. The patient was a boy of sixteen or seventeen, the son of Mrs. Amworth's gardener, and the symptoms were an anemic pallor and a languid prostration, accompanied by great drowsiness and an abnormal appetite. He had, too, on his throat two small punctures where, so Dr. Ross conjectured, one of these great gnats had bitten him. But the odd thing was that there was no swelling or inflammation round the place where he had been bitten.

The heat at this time had begun to abate, but the cooler weather failed to restore him, and the boy, in spite of the quantity of good food which he so ravenously swallowed, wasted away to a skin-clad skeleton.

I met Dr. Ross in the street one afternoon about this time, and in answer to my inquiries about his patient he said that he was afraid the boy was dying. The case, he confessed, completely puzzled him: some obscure form of pernicious anemia was all he could suggest. But he wondered whether Mr. Urcombe would consent to see the boy, on the chance of his being able to throw some new light on the case, and since Urcombe was dining with me that night, I proposed to Dr. Ross to join us. He could not do this, but said he would look in later. When he came, Urcombe at once consented to put his skill at the other's disposal, and together they went off at once. Being thus shorn of my sociable evening, I telephoned to Mrs. Amworth to know if I might inflict myself on her for an hour. Her answer was a welcoming affirmative, and between piquet and music the hour lengthened itself into two. She spoke of the boy who was lying so desperately and mysteriously ill, and told me that she had often been to see him, taking him nourishing and delicate food. But today – and her kind eyes moistened as she spoke – she was afraid she had paid her last visit. Knowing the antipathy between her and Urcombe, I did not tell her that he had been called into consultation; and when I returned home she accompanied me to my door, for the sake of a breath of night air, and in order to borrow a magazine which contained an article on gardening which she wished to read.

"Ah, this delicious night air," she said, luxuriously sniffing in the coolness. "Night air and gardening are the great tonics. There is nothing so stimulating as bare contact with rich mother earth. You are never so fresh as when you have been grubbing in the soil – black hands, black nails, and boots covered with mud." She gave her great jovial laugh. "I'm a glutton for air and earth," she said. "Positively I look forward to death, for then I shall be buried and have the kind earth all round me. No leaden caskets for me – I have given explicit directions. But what shall I do about air? Well, I suppose one can't have everything. The magazine? A thousand thanks, I will faithfully return it. Goodnight: garden and keep your windows open, and you won't have anemia."

"I always sleep with my windows open," said I.

I went straight up to my bedroom, of which one of the windows looks out over the street, and as I undressed I thought I heard voices talking outside not far away. But I paid no particular attention, put out my lights, and falling asleep plunged into the depths of a most horrible dream, distortedly suggested no doubt, by my last words with Mrs. Amworth. I dreamed that I woke, and found that both my bedroom windows were shut. Half-suffocating I dreamed that I sprang out of bed, and went across to open them. The blind over the first was drawn down, and pulling it up I saw, with the indescribable horror of incipient nightmare, Mrs. Amworth's face suspended close to the pane in the darkness outside, nodding and smiling at me. Pulling down the blind again to keep that terror out, I rushed to the second window on the other side of the room, and there again was Mrs. Amworth's face. Then the panic came upon me in full blast; here was I suffocating in the airless room, and whichever window I opened Mrs. Amworth's face would float in, like those noiseless black gnats that bit before one was aware. The nightmare rose to screaming point, and with strangled yells I awoke to find my room cool and quiet with both windows open and blinds up and a half-moon high in its course, casting an oblong of tranquil light on the floor. But even when I was awake the horror persisted, and I lay tossing and turning.

I must have slept long before the nightmare seized me, for now it was nearly day, and soon in the east the drowsy eyelids of morning began to lift.

I was scarcely downstairs next morning – for after the dawn I slept late – when Urcombe rang up to know if he might see me immediately. He came in, grim and preoccupied, and I noticed that he was pulling on a pipe that was not even filled.

"I want your help," he said, "and so I must tell you first of all what happened last night. I went round with the little doctor to see his patient, and found him just alive, but scarcely more. I instantly diagnosed in my own mind what this anemia, unaccountable by any other explanation, meant. The boy is the prey of a vampire."

He put his empty pipe on the breakfast table, by which I had just sat down, and folded his arms, looking at me steadily from under his overhanging brows.

"Now about last night," he said. "I insisted that he should be moved from his father's cottage into my house. As we were carrying him on a stretcher, whom should we meet but Mrs. Amworth? She expressed shocked surprise that we were moving him. Now why do you think she did that?"

With a start of horror, as I remembered my dream that night before, I felt an idea come into my mind so preposterous and unthinkable that I instantly turned it out again.

"I haven't the smallest idea," I said.

"Then listen, while I tell you about what happened later. I put out all light in the room where the boy lay, and watched. One window was a little open, for I had forgotten to close it, and about midnight I heard something outside, trying apparently to push it farther open. I guessed who it was – yes, it was full twenty feet from the ground – and I peeped round the corner of the blind."

"Just outside was the face of Mrs. Amworth and her hand was on the frame of the window. Very softly I crept close, and then banged the window down, and I think I just caught the tip of one of her fingers."

"But it's impossible," I cried. "How could she be floating in the air like that? And what had she come for? Don't tell me such—"

Once more, with closer grip, the remembrance of my nightmare seized me.

"I am telling you what I saw," said he. "And all night long, until it was nearly day, she was fluttering outside, like some terrible bat, trying to gain admittance. Now put together various things I have told you."

He began checking them off on his fingers.

"Number one," he said: "there was an outbreak of disease similar to that which this boy is suffering from at Peshawar, and her husband died of it. Number two: Mrs. Amworth protested against my moving the boy to my house. Number three: she, or the demon that inhabits her body, a creature powerful and deadly, tries to gain admittance. And add this, too: in medieval times there was an epidemic of vampirism here at Maxley. The vampire, so the accounts run, was found to be Elizabeth Chaston...I see you remember Mrs. Amworth's maiden name. Finally, the boy is stronger this morning. He would certainly not have been alive if he had been visited again. And what do you make of it?"

There was a long silence, during which I found this incredible horror assuming the hues of reality.

"I have something to add," I said, "which may or may not bear on it. You say that the – the spectre went away shortly before dawn."

"Yes."

I told him of my dream, and he smiled grimly.

"Yes, you did well to awake," he said. "That warning came from your subconscious self, which never wholly slumbers, and cried out to you of deadly danger. For two reasons, then, you must help me: one to save others, the second to save yourself."

"What do you want me to do?" I asked.

"I want you first of all to help me in watching this boy, and ensuring that she does not come near him. Eventually I want you to help me in tracking the thing down, in exposing and destroying it. It is not human: it is an incarnate fiend. What steps we shall have to take I don't yet know."

It was now eleven of the forenoon, and presently I went across to his house for a twelve-hour vigil while he slept, to come on duty again that night, so that for the next twenty-four hours either Urcombe or myself was always in the room where the boy, now getting stronger every hour, was lying. The day following was Saturday and a morning of brilliant, pellucid weather, and already when I went across to his house to resume my duty the stream of motors down to Brighton had begun. Simultaneously I saw Urcombe with a cheerful face, which boded good news of his patient, coming out of his house, and Mrs. Amworth, with a gesture of salutation to me and a basket in her hand, walking up the broad strip of grass which bordered the road. There we all three met. I noticed (and saw that Urcombe noticed it too) that one finger of her left hand was bandaged.

"Good morning to you both," said she. "And I hear your patient is doing well, Mr. Urcombe. I have come to bring him a bowl of jelly, and to sit with him for an hour. He and I are great friends. I am overjoyed at his recovery."

Urcombe paused a moment, as if making up his mind, and then shot out a pointing finger at her.

"I forbid that," he said. "You shall not sit with him or see him. And you know the reason as well as I do."

I have never seen so horrible a change pass over a human face as that which now blanched hers to the colour of a grey mist. She put up her hand as if to shield herself from that pointing finger, which drew the sign of the cross in the air, and shrank back cowering on to the road.

There was a wild hoot from a horn, a grinding of brakes, a shout – too late – from a passing car, and one long scream suddenly cut short. Her body rebounded from the roadway after the first wheel had gone over it, and the second followed. It lay there, quivering and twitching, and was still.

She was buried three days afterwards in the cemetery outside Maxley, in accordance with the wishes she had told me that she had devised about her interment, and the shock which her sudden and awful death had caused to the little community began by degrees to pass off. To two people only, Urcombe and myself, the horror of it was mitigated from the first by the nature of the relief that her death brought; but, naturally enough, we kept our own counsel, and no hint of what greater horror had been thus averted was ever let slip. But, oddly enough, so it seemed to me, he was still not satisfied about something in connection with her, and would give no answer to my questions on the subject. Then as the days of a tranquil mellow September and the October that followed began to drop away like the leaves of the yellowing trees, his uneasiness relaxed. But before the entry of November the seeming tranquillity broke into hurricane.

I had been dining one night at the far end of the village, and about eleven o'clock was walking home again. The moon was of an unusual brilliance, rendering all that it shone on as distinct as in some etching. I had just come opposite the house which Mrs. Amworth had occupied, where there was a board up telling that it was to let, when I heard the click of her front gate, and next moment I saw, with a sudden chill and quaking of my very spirit, that she stood there. Her profile, vividly illuminated, was turned to me, and I could not be mistaken in my identification of her. She appeared not to see me (indeed the shadow of the yew hedge in front of her garden enveloped me in its blackness) and she went swiftly across the road, and entered the gate of the house directly opposite. There I lost sight of her completely.

My breath was coming in short pants as if I had been running – and now indeed I ran, with fearful backward glances, along the hundred yards that separated me from my house and Urcombe's. It was to his that my flying steps took me, and next minute I was within.

"What have you come to tell me?" he asked. "Or shall I guess?"

"You can't guess," said I.

"No; it's no guess. She has come back and you have seen her. Tell me about it."

I gave him my story.

"That's Major Pearsall's house," he said. "Come back with me there at once."

"But what can we do?" I asked.

"I've no idea. That's what we have got to find out."

A minute later, we were opposite the house. When I had passed it before, it was all dark; now lights gleamed from a couple of windows upstairs. Even as we faced it, the front door opened, and next moment Major Pearsall emerged from the gate. He saw us and stopped.

"I'm on my way to Dr. Ross," he said quickly, "My wife has been taken suddenly ill. She had been in bed an hour when I came upstairs, and I found her white as a ghost and utterly exhausted. She had been to sleep, it seemed – but you will excuse me."

"One moment, Major," said Urcombe. "Was there any mark on her throat?"

"How did you guess that?" said he. "There was: one of those beastly gnats must have bitten her twice there. She was streaming with blood."

"And there's someone with her?" asked Urcombe.

"Yes, I roused her maid."

He went off, and Urcombe turned to me. "I know now what we have to do," he said. "Change your clothes, and I'll join you at your house."

"What is it?" I asked.

"I'll tell you on our way. We're going to the cemetery."

He carried a pick, a shovel, and a screwdriver when he rejoined me, and wore round his shoulders a long coil of rope. As we walked, he gave me the outlines of the ghastly hour that lay before us.

"What I have to tell you," he said, "will seem to you now too fantastic for credence, but before dawn we shall see whether it outstrips reality. By a most fortunate happening, you saw the spectre, the astral body, whatever you choose to call it, of Mrs. Amworth, going on its grisly business, and therefore, beyond doubt, the vampire spirit which abode in her during life animates her again in death. That is not exceptional – indeed, all these weeks since her death I have been expecting it. If I am right, we shall find her body undecayed and untouched by corruption."

"But she has been dead nearly two months," said I.

"If she had been dead two years it would still be so, if the vampire has possession of her. So remember: whatever you see done, it will be done not to her, who in the natural course would now be feeding the grasses above her grave, but to a spirit of untold evil and malignancy, which gives a phantom life to her body."

"But what shall I see done?" said I.

"I will tell you. We know that now, at this moment, the vampire clad in her mortal semblance is out; dining out. But it must get back before dawn, and it will pass into the material form that lies in her grave. We must wait for that, and then with your help I shall dig up her body. If I am right, you will look on her as she was in life, with the full vigour of the dreadful nutriment she has received pulsing in her veins. And then, when dawn has come, and the vampire cannot leave the lair of her body, I shall strike her with this" – and he pointed to his pick – "through the heart, and she, who comes to life again only with the animation the fiend gives her, she and her hellish partner will be dead indeed. Then we must bury her again, delivered at last."

We had come to the cemetery, and in the brightness of the moonshine there was no difficulty in identifying her grave. It lay some twenty yards from the small chapel, in the porch of which, obscured by shadow, we concealed ourselves. From there we had a clear and open sight of the grave, and now we must wait till its infernal visitor returned home. The night was warm and windless, yet even if a freezing wind had been raging I think I should have felt nothing of it, so intense was my preoccupation as to what the night and dawn would bring. There was a bell in the turret of the chapel, that struck the quarters of the hour, and it amazed me to find how swiftly the chimes succeeded one another.

The moon had long set, but a twilight of stars shone in a clear sky, when five o'clock of the morning sounded from the turret. A few minutes more passed, and then I felt Urcombe's hand softly nudging me; and looking out in the direction of his pointing finger, I saw that the form of a woman, tall and large in build, was approaching from the right. Noiselessly, with a motion more of gliding and floating than walking, she moved across the cemetery to the grave which was the centre of our observation. She moved round it as if to be certain of its identity, and for a moment stood directly facing us. In the greyness to which now my eyes had grown accustomed, I could easily see her face, and recognise its features.

She drew her hand across her mouth as if wiping it, and broke into a chuckle of such laughter as made my hair stir on my head. Then she leaped on to the grave, holding her hands high above her head, and inch by inch disappeared into the earth. Urcombe's hand was laid on my arm, in an injunction to keep still, but now he removed it.

"Come," he said.

With pick and shovel and rope we went to the grave. The earth was light and sandy, and soon after six struck, we had delved down to the coffin lid. With his pick he loosened the earth round it, and, adjusting the rope through the handles by which it had been lowered, we tried to raise it.

This was a long and laborious business, and the light had begun to herald day in the east before we had it out, and lying by the side of the grave. With his screwdriver he loosed the fastenings of the lid, and slid it aside, and standing there we looked on the face of Mrs. Amworth. The eyes, once closed in death, were open, the cheeks were flushed with colour, the red, full-lipped mouth seemed to smile.

"One blow and it is all over," he said. "You need not look."

Even as he spoke he took up the pick again, and, laying the point of it on her left breast, measured his distance. And though I knew what was coming I could not look away...

He grasped the pick in both hands, raised it an inch or two for the taking of his aim, and then with full force brought it down on her breast. A fountain of blood, though she had been dead so long, spouted high in the air, falling with the thud of a heavy splash over the shroud, and simultaneously from those red lips came one long, appalling cry, swelling up like some hooting siren, and dying away again. With that, instantaneous as a lightning flash, came the touch of corruption on her face, the colour of it faded to ash, the plump cheeks fell in, the mouth dropped.

"Thank God, that's over," said he, and without pause slipped the coffin lid back into its place.

Day was coming fast now, and, working like men possessed, we lowered the coffin into its place again, and shovelled the earth over it... The birds were busy with their earliest pipings as we went back to Maxley.

The Eyes of the Panther

Ambrose Bierce

Chapter I
One Does Not Always Marry When Insane

A MAN and a woman – nature had done the grouping – sat on a rustic seat, in the late afternoon. The man was middle-aged, slender, swarthy, with the expression of a poet and the complexion of a pirate – a man at whom one would look again. The woman was young, blonde, graceful, with something in her figure and movements suggesting the word 'lithe'. She was habited in a gray gown with odd brown markings in the texture. She may have been beautiful; one could not readily say, for her eyes denied attention to all else. They were gray-green, long and narrow, with an expression defying analysis. One could only know that they were disquieting. Cleopatra may have had such eyes.

The man and the woman talked.

"Yes," said the woman, "I love you, God knows! But marry you, no. I cannot, will not."

"Irene, you have said that many times, yet always have denied me a reason. I've a right to know, to understand, to feel and prove my fortitude if I have it. Give me a reason."

"For loving you?"

The woman was smiling through her tears and her pallor. That did not stir any sense of humor in the man.

"No; there is no reason for that. A reason for not marrying me. I've a right to know. I must know. I will know!"

He had risen and was standing before her with clenched hands, on his face a frown – it might have been called a scowl. He looked as if he might attempt to learn by strangling her. She smiled no more – merely sat looking up into his face with a fixed, set regard that was utterly without emotion or sentiment. Yet it had something in it that tamed his resentment and made him shiver.

"You are determined to have my reason?" she asked in a tone that was entirely mechanical – a tone that might have been her look made audible.

"If you please – if I'm not asking too much."

Apparently this lord of creation was yielding some part of his dominion over his co-creature.

"Very well, you shall know: I am insane."

The man started, then looked incredulous and was conscious that he ought to be amused. But, again, the sense of humor failed him in his need and despite his disbelief he was profoundly disturbed by that which he did not believe. Between our convictions and our feelings there is no good understanding.

"That is what the physicians would say," the woman continued – "if they knew. I might myself prefer to call it a case of 'possession'. Sit down and hear what I have to say."

The man silently resumed his seat beside her on the rustic bench by the wayside. Over-against them on the eastern side of the valley the hills were already sunset-flushed and the stillness all about was of that peculiar quality that foretells the twilight. Something of its mysterious and significant solemnity had imparted itself to the man's mood. In the spiritual, as in the material world, are signs and presages of night. Rarely meeting her look, and whenever he did so conscious of the indefinable dread with which, despite their feline beauty, her eyes always affected him, Jenner Brading listened in silence to the story told by Irene Marlowe. In deference to the reader's possible prejudice against the artless method of an unpractised historian the author ventures to substitute his own version for hers.

Chapter II
A Room May Be Too Narrow for Three, Though One Is Outside

IN A LITTLE log house containing a single room sparely and rudely furnished, crouching on the floor against one of the walls, was a woman, clasping to her breast a child. Outside, a dense unbroken forest extended for many miles in every direction. This was at night and the room was black dark: no human eye could have discerned the woman and the child. Yet they were observed, narrowly, vigilantly, with never even a momentary slackening of attention; and that is the pivotal fact upon which this narrative turns.

Charles Marlowe was of the class, now extinct in this country, of woodmen pioneers – men who found their most acceptable surroundings in sylvan solitudes that stretched along the eastern slope of the Mississippi Valley, from the Great Lakes to the Gulf of Mexico. For more than a hundred years these men pushed ever westward, generation after generation, with rifle and ax, reclaiming from Nature and her savage children here and there an isolated acreage for the plow, no sooner reclaimed than surrendered to their less venturesome but more thrifty successors. At last they burst through the edge of the forest into the open country and vanished as if they had fallen over a cliff. The woodman pioneer is no more; the pioneer of the plains – he whose easy task it was to subdue for occupancy two-thirds of the country in a single generation – is another and inferior creation. With Charles Marlowe in the wilderness, sharing the dangers, hardships and privations of that strange, unprofitable life, were his wife and child, to whom, in the manner of his class, in which the domestic virtues were a religion, he was passionately attached. The woman was still young enough to be comely, new enough to the awful isolation of her lot to be cheerful. By withholding the large capacity for happiness which the simple satisfactions of the forest life could not have filled, Heaven had dealt honorably with her. In her light household tasks, her child, her husband and her few foolish books, she found abundant provision for her needs.

One morning in midsummer Marlowe took down his rifle from the wooden hooks on the wall and signified his intention of getting game.

"We've meat enough," said the wife; "please don't go out today. I dreamed last night, O, such a dreadful thing! I cannot recollect it, but I'm almost sure that it will come to pass if you go out."

It is painful to confess that Marlowe received this solemn statement with less of gravity than was due to the mysterious nature of the calamity foreshadowed. In truth, he laughed.

"Try to remember," he said. "Maybe you dreamed that Baby had lost the power of speech."

The conjecture was obviously suggested by the fact that Baby, clinging to the fringe of his hunting-coat with all her ten pudgy thumbs, was at that moment uttering her sense of the situation in a series of exultant goo-goos inspired by sight of her father's raccoon-skin cap.

The woman yielded: lacking the gift of humor she could not hold out against his kindly badinage. So, with a kiss for the mother and a kiss for the child, he left the house and closed the door upon his happiness forever.

At nightfall he had not returned. The woman prepared supper and waited. Then she put Baby to bed and sang softly to her until she slept. By this time the fire on the hearth, at which she had cooked supper, had burned out and the room was lighted by a single candle. This she afterward placed in the open window as a sign and welcome to the hunter if he should approach from that side. She had thoughtfully closed and barred the door against such wild animals as might prefer it to an open window – of the habits of beasts of prey in entering a house uninvited she was not advised, though with true female prevision she may have considered the possibility of their entrance by way of the chimney. As the night wore on she became not less anxious, but more drowsy, and at last rested her arms upon the bed by the child and her head upon the arms. The candle in the window burned down to the socket, sputtered and flared a moment and went out unobserved; for the woman slept and dreamed.

In her dreams she sat beside the cradle of a second child. The first one was dead. The father was dead. The home in the forest was lost and the dwelling in which she lived was unfamiliar. There were heavy oaken doors, always closed, and outside the windows, fastened into the thick stone walls, were iron bars, obviously (so she thought) a provision against Indians. All this she noted with an infinite self-pity, but without surprise – an emotion unknown in dreams. The child in the cradle was invisible under its coverlet which something impelled her to remove. She did so, disclosing the face of a wild animal! In the shock of this dreadful revelation the dreamer awoke, trembling in the darkness of her cabin in the wood.

As a sense of her actual surroundings came slowly back to her she felt for the child that was not a dream, and assured herself by its breathing that all was well with it; nor could she forbear to pass a hand lightly across its face. Then, moved by some impulse for which she probably could not have accounted, she rose and took the sleeping babe in her arms, holding it close against her breast. The head of the child's cot was against the wall to which the woman now turned her back as she stood. Lifting her eyes she saw two bright objects starring the darkness with a reddish-green glow. She took them to be two coals on the hearth, but with her returning sense of direction came the disquieting consciousness that they were not in that quarter of the room, moreover were too high, being nearly at the level of the eyes – of her own eyes. For these were the eyes of a panther.

The beast was at the open window directly opposite and not five paces away. Nothing but those terrible eyes was visible, but in the dreadful tumult of her feelings as the situation disclosed itself to her understanding she somehow knew that the animal was standing on its hinder feet, supporting itself with its paws on the window-ledge. That signified a malign interest – not the mere gratification of an indolent curiosity. The consciousness of the attitude was an added horror, accentuating the menace of those awful eyes, in whose steadfast fire her strength and courage were alike consumed. Under their silent questioning she shuddered and turned sick. Her knees failed her, and by degrees, instinctively striving to avoid a sudden movement that might bring the beast upon her, she sank to the floor, crouched against the wall and tried to shield the babe with her trembling body without withdrawing her gaze from the luminous orbs that were killing her. No thought of her husband came to her in her agony – no hope nor suggestion of rescue or escape. Her capacity for thought and feeling had narrowed to the dimensions of a single emotion – fear of the animal's spring, of the impact of its body, the buffeting of its great arms, the feel of its teeth in her throat, the mangling of her babe. Motionless now and in absolute silence, she awaited her doom, the moments growing to hours, to years, to ages; and still those devilish eyes maintained their watch.

Returning to his cabin late at night with a deer on his shoulders Charles Marlowe tried the door. It did not yield. He knocked; there was no answer. He laid down his deer and went round to the window. As he turned the angle of the building he fancied he heard a sound as of stealthy footfalls and a rustling in the undergrowth of the forest, but they were too slight for certainty, even to his practised ear. Approaching the window, and to his surprise finding it open, he threw his leg over the sill and entered. All was darkness and silence. He groped his way to the fireplace, struck a match and lit a candle.

Then he looked about. Cowering on the floor against a wall was his wife, clasping his child. As he sprang toward her she rose and broke into laughter, long, loud, and mechanical, devoid of gladness and devoid of sense – the laughter that is not out of keeping with the clanking of a chain. Hardly knowing what he did he extended his arms. She laid the babe in them. It was dead – pressed to death in its mother's embrace.

Chapter III
The Theory of the Defense

THAT IS WHAT occurred during a night in a forest, but not all of it did Irene Marlowe relate to Jenner Brading; not all of it was known to her. When she had concluded the sun was below the horizon and the long summer twilight had begun to deepen in the hollows of the land. For some moments Brading was silent, expecting the narrative to be carried forward to some definite connection with the conversation introducing it; but the narrator was as silent as he, her face averted, her hands clasping and unclasping themselves as they lay in her lap, with a singular suggestion of an activity independent of her will.

"It is a sad, a terrible story," said Brading at last, "but I do not understand. You call Charles Marlowe father; that I know. That he is old before his time, broken by some great sorrow, I have seen, or thought I saw. But, pardon me, you said that you – that you—"

"That I am insane," said the girl, without a movement of head or body.

"But, Irene, you say – please, dear, do not look away from me – you say that the child was dead, not demented."

"Yes, that one – I am the second. I was born three months after that night, my mother being mercifully permitted to lay down her life in giving me mine."

Brading was again silent; he was a trifle dazed and could not at once think of the right thing to say. Her face was still turned away. In his embarrassment he reached impulsively toward the hands that lay closing and unclosing in her lap, but something – he could not have said what – restrained him. He then remembered, vaguely, that he had never altogether cared to take her hand.

"Is it likely," she resumed, "that a person born under such circumstances is like others – is what you call sane?"

Brading did not reply; he was preoccupied with a new thought that was taking shape in his mind – what a scientist would have called a hypothesis; a detective, a theory. It might throw an added light, albeit a lurid one, upon such doubt of her sanity as her own assertion had not dispelled.

The country was still new and, outside the villages, sparsely populated. The professional hunter was still a familiar figure, and among his trophies were heads and pelts of the larger kinds of game. Tales variously credible of nocturnal meetings with savage animals in lonely roads were sometimes current, passed through the customary stages of growth and decay, and were forgotten. A recent addition to these popular apocrypha, originating, apparently, by spontaneous generation in several households, was of a panther which had frightened some of their members by looking in at windows by night. The yarn had caused its little ripple of excitement – had even attained to the distinction of a place in the local newspaper; but Brading had given it no attention. Its likeness to the story to which he had just listened now impressed him as perhaps more than accidental. Was it not possible that the one story had suggested the other – that finding congenial conditions in a morbid mind and a fertile fancy, it had grown to the tragic tale that he had heard?

Brading recalled certain circumstances of the girl's history and disposition, of which, with love's incuriosity, he had hitherto been heedless – such as her solitary life with her father, at whose house no one, apparently, was an acceptable visitor and her strange fear of the night, by which those who knew her best accounted for her never being seen after dark. Surely in such a mind imagination once kindled might burn with a lawless flame, penetrating and enveloping the entire structure. That she was mad, though the conviction gave him the acutest pain, he could no longer doubt; she had only mistaken an effect of her mental disorder for its cause, bringing into imaginary relation with her own personality the vagaries of the local myth-makers. With some vague intention of testing his new 'theory', and no very definite notion of how to set about it he said, gravely, but with hesitation:

"Irene, dear, tell me – I beg you will not take offence, but tell me—"

"I have told you," she interrupted, speaking with a passionate earnestness that he had not known her to show – "I have already told you that we cannot marry; is anything else worth saying?"

Before he could stop her she had sprung from her seat and without another word or look was gliding away among the trees toward her father's house. Brading had risen to detain her; he stood watching her in silence until she had vanished in the gloom. Suddenly he started as if he had been shot; his face took on an expression of amazement and alarm: in one of the black shadows into which she had disappeared he had caught a quick, brief glimpse of shining eyes! For an instant he was dazed and irresolute; then he dashed into the wood after her, shouting: "Irene, Irene, look out! The panther! The panther!"

In a moment he had passed through the fringe of forest into open ground and saw the girl's gray skirt vanishing into her father's door. No panther was visible.

Chapter IV
An Appeal to the Conscience of God

JENNER BRADING, attorney-at-law, lived in a cottage at the edge of the town. Directly behind the dwelling was the forest. Being a bachelor, and therefore, by the Draconian moral code of the time and place denied the services of the only species of domestic servant known thereabout, the 'hired girl', he boarded at the village hotel, where also was his office. The woodside cottage was merely a lodging maintained – at no great cost, to be sure – as an evidence of prosperity and respectability. It would hardly do for one to whom the local newspaper had pointed with pride as 'the foremost jurist of his time' to be 'homeless', albeit he may sometimes have suspected that the words 'home' and 'house' were not strictly synonymous. Indeed, his consciousness of the disparity and his will to harmonize it were matters of logical inference, for it was generally reported that soon after the cottage was built its owner had made a futile venture in the direction of marriage – had, in truth, gone so far as to be rejected by the beautiful but eccentric daughter of Old Man Marlowe, the recluse. This was publicly believed because he had told it himself and she had not – a reversal of the usual order of things which could hardly fail to carry conviction. Brading's bedroom was at the rear of the house, with a single window facing the forest.

One night he was awakened by a noise at that window; he could hardly have said what it was like. With a little thrill of the nerves he sat up in bed and laid hold of the revolver which, with a forethought most commendable in one addicted to the habit of sleeping on the ground floor with an open window, he had put under his pillow. The room was in absolute darkness, but being unterrified he knew where to direct his eyes, and there he held them, awaiting in silence what further might occur. He could now dimly discern the aperture – a square of lighter black. Presently there appeared at its lower edge two gleaming eyes that burned with a malignant lustre inexpressibly terrible! Brading's heart gave a great jump, then seemed to stand still. A chill passed along his spine and through his hair; he felt the blood forsake his cheeks. He could not have cried out – not to save his life; but being a man of courage he would not, to save his life, have done so if he had been able. Some trepidation his coward body might feel, but his spirit was of sterner stuff. Slowly the shining eyes rose with a steady motion that seemed an approach, and slowly rose Brading's right hand, holding the pistol. He fired!

Blinded by the flash and stunned by the report, Brading nevertheless heard, or fancied that he heard, the wild, high scream of the panther, so human in sound, so devilish in suggestion. Leaping from the bed he hastily clothed himself and, pistol in hand, sprang from the door, meeting two or three men who came running up from the road. A brief explanation was followed by a cautious search of the house. The grass was wet with dew; beneath the window it had been trodden and partly leveled for a wide space, from which a devious trail, visible in the light of a lantern, led away into the bushes. One of the men stumbled and fell upon his hands, which as he rose and rubbed them together were slippery. On examination they were seen to be red with blood.

An encounter, unarmed, with a wounded panther was not agreeable to their taste; all but Brading turned back. He, with lantern and pistol, pushed courageously forward into the wood. Passing through a difficult undergrowth he came into a small opening, and there his courage had its reward, for there he found the body of his victim. But it was no panther. What it was is told, even to this day, upon a weather-worn headstone in the village churchyard, and for many years was attested daily at the graveside by the bent figure and sorrow-seamed face of Old Man Marlowe, to whose soul, and to the soul of his strange, unhappy child, peace. Peace and reparation.

The Man with the Nose

Rhoda Broughton

Chapter I

"LET US GET a map and see what places look pleasantest," says she.

"As for that," reply I, "on a map most places look equally pleasant."

"Never mind; get one!"

I obey.

"Do you like the seaside?" asks Elizabeth, lifting her little brown head and her small happy white face from the English sea-coast along which her forefinger is slowly travelling.

"Since you ask me, distinctly *no*," reply I, for once venturing to have a decided opinion of my own, which during the last few weeks of imbecility I can be hardly said to have had. "I broke my last wooden spade five and twenty years ago. I have but a poor opinion of cockles – sandy red-nosed things, are not they? And the air always makes me bilious."

"Then we certainly will not go there," says Elizabeth, laughing. "A bilious bridegroom! Alliterative but horrible! None of our friends show the least eagerness to lend us their country house."

"Oh that God would put it into the hearts of men to take their wives straight home, as their fathers did!" say I with a cross groan.

"It is evident, therefore, that we must go somewhere," returns she, not heeding the aspiration contained in my last speech, making her forefinger resume its employment, and reaching Torquay.

"I suppose so," say I, with a sort of sigh; "for once in our lives we must resign ourselves to having the finger of derision pointed at us by waiters and landlords."

"You shall leave your new portmanteau at home, and I will leave all my best clothes, and nobody will guess that we are bride and bridegroom; they will think that we have been married – oh, ever since the world began" (opening her eyes very wide).

I shake my head. "With an old portmanteau and in rags we shall still have the mark of the beast upon us."

"Do you mind much? Do you hate being ridiculous?" asks Elizabeth, meekly, rather depressed by my view of the case; "because if so, let us go somewhere out of the way, where there will be very few people to laugh at us."

"On the contrary," return I, stoutly, "we will betake ourselves to some spot where such as we do chiefly congregate – where we shall be swallowed up and lost in the multitude of our fellow sinners." A pause devoted to reflection. "What do you say to Killarney?" say I cheerfully.

"There are a great many fleas there, I believe," replies Elizabeth, slowly; "fleabites make large lumps on me; you would not like me if I were covered with large lumps."

At the hideous ideal picture thus presented to me by my little beloved I relapse into inarticulate idiocy; emerging from which by-and-by, I suggest, "The Lakes?" My arm is round her, and I feel her supple body shiver though it is mid-July and the bees are booming about in the still and sleepy noon garden outside.

"Oh – no – no – not *there*!"

"Why such emphasis?" I ask gaily; "more fleas? At this rate, and with this *sine quâ non*, our choice will grow limited."

"Something dreadful happened to me there," she says, with another shudder. "But indeed I did not think there was any harm in it – I never thought anything would come of it."

"What the devil was it?" cry I, in a jealous heat and hurry; "What the mischief *did* you do, and why have not you told me about it before?"

"I did not *do* much," she answers meekly, seeking for my hand, and when found kissing it in timid deprecation of my wrath; "but I was ill – very ill – there; I had a nervous fever. I was in a bed hung with a chintz with a red and green fernleaf pattern on it. I have always hated red and green fernleaf chintzes ever since."

"It would be possible to avoid the obnoxious bed, would it not?" say I, laughing a little. "Where does it lie? Windermere? Ulleswater? Wastwater? Where?"

"We were at Ulleswater," she says, speaking rapidly, while a hot color grows on her small white cheeks – "Papa, mamma, and I; and there came a mesmeriser to Penrith, and we went to see him – everybody did – and he asked leave to mesmerise me – he said I should be such a good medium – and – and – I did not know what it was like. I thought it would be quite good fun – and – and – I let him."

She is trembling exceedingly; even the loving pressure of my arms cannot abate her shivering.

"Well?"

"And after that I do not remember anything – I believe I did all sorts of extraordinary things that he told me – sang and danced, and made a fool of myself – but when I came home I was very ill, very – I lay in bed for five whole weeks, and – and was off my head, and said odd and wicked things that you would not have expected me to say – that dreadful bed! Shall I ever forget it?"

"We will *not* go to the Lakes," I say, decisively, "and we will not talk any more about mesmerism."

"That is right," she says, with a sigh of relief. "I try to think about it as little as possible; but sometimes, in the dead black of the night, when God seems a long way off, and the devil near, it comes back to me so strongly – I feel, do not you know, as if he were *there* somewhere in the room, and I *must* get up and follow him."

"Why should not we go abroad?" suggest I, abruptly turning the conversation.

"Why, indeed?" cries Elizabeth, recovering her gaiety, while her pretty blue eyes begin to dance. "How stupid of us not to have thought of it before; only *abroad* is a big word. *What* abroad?"

"We must be content with something short of Central Africa," I say, gravely, "as I think our one hundred and fifty pounds would hardly take us that far."

"Wherever we go, we must buy a dialogue book," suggests my little bride-elect, "and I will learn some phrases before we start."

"As for that, the Anglo-Saxon tongue takes one pretty well round the world," reply I, with a feeling of complacent British swagger, putting my hands in my breeches pockets.

"Do you fancy the Rhine?" says Elizabeth, with a rather timid suggestion; "I know it is the fashion to run it down nowadays, and call it a cocktail river; but – but – after all it cannot be so *very* contemptible, or Byron could not have said such noble things about it."

"The castled crag of Drachenfels
Frowns o'er the wide and winding Rhine,
Whose breast of waters broadly swells
Between the banks which bear the vine"

say I, spouting. "After all, that proves nothing, for Byron could have made a silk purse out of a sow's ear."

"The Rhine will not do then?" says she resignedly, suppressing a sigh.

"On the contrary, it will do admirably: it *is* a cocktail river, and I do not care who says it is not," reply I, with illiberal positiveness; "but everybody should be able to say so from their own experience, and not from hearsay: the Rhine let it be, by all means."

So the Rhine it is.

Chapter II

I HAVE GOT over it; we have both got over it, tolerably, creditably; but after all, it is a much severer ordeal for a man than a woman, who, with a bouquet to occupy her hands, and a veil to gently shroud her features, need merely be prettily passive. I am alluding, I need hardly say, to the religious ceremony of marriage, which I flatter myself I have gone through with a stiff sheepishness not unworthy of my country. It is a three-days-old event now, and we are getting used to belonging to one another, though Elizabeth still takes off her ring twenty times a day to admire its bright thickness; still laughs when she hears herself called 'Madame'. Three days ago, we kissed all our friends, and left them to make themselves ill on our cake, and criticise our bridal behavior, and now we are at Brussels, she and I feeling oddly, joyfully free from any chaperone. We have been mildly sight-seeing – very mildly most people would say, but we have resolved not to take our pleasure with the railway speed of Americans, or the hasty sadness of our fellow Britons. Slowly and gaily we have been taking ours. Today we have been to visit Wiertz's pictures. Have you ever seen them, oh reader? They are known to comparatively few people, but if you have a taste for the unearthly terrible – if you wish to sup full of horrors, hasten thither. We have been peering through the appointed peep-hole at the horrible cholera picture – the man buried alive by mistake, pushing up the lid of his coffin, and stretching a ghastly face and livid hands out of his winding sheet towards you, while awful grey-blue coffins are piled around, and noisome toads and giant spiders crawl damply about. On first seeing it, I have reproached myself for bringing one of so nervous a temperament as Elizabeth to see so haunting and hideous a spectacle; but she is less impressed than I expected – less impressed than I myself am.

"He is very lucky to be able to get his lid up," she says, with a half-laugh; "we should find it hard work to burst our brass nails, should not we? When you bury me, dear, fasten me down very slightly, in case there may be some mistake."

And now all the long and quiet July evening we have been prowling together about the streets – Brussels is the town of towns for *flâner*-ing – have been flattening our noses against the shop windows, and making each other imaginary presents. Elizabeth has not confined herself to imagination, however; she has made me buy her a little bonnet with feathers – 'in order to look married', as she says, and the result is such a delicious picture of a child playing at being grown up, having practised a theft on its mother's wardrobe, that for the last two hours I have been in a foolish ecstasy of love and laughter over her and it. We are at the Bellevue, and have a fine suite of rooms, *au premier*, evidently specially devoted to the English, to the gratification of whose well-known loyalty the Prince and Princess of Wales are simpering from the walls. Is there anyone in the three kingdoms who knows his own face as well as he knows the faces of Albert Victor and Alexandra? The long evening has at last slidden into night – night far advanced – night melting into earliest day. All Brussels is asleep. One moment ago I also was asleep, soundly as any log. What is it that has made me take this sudden, headlong plunge out of sleep into wakefulness? Who is it that is clutching at and calling upon me? What is it that is making me struggle mistily up into a sitting posture, and try to revive my sleep-numbed senses? A summer night is never wholly dark; by the half light that steals through the closed *persiennes* and open windows I see my wife standing beside my bed; the extremity of terror on her face, and her fingers digging themselves with painful tenacity into my arm.

"Tighter, tighter!" she is crying, wildly. "What are you thinking of? You are letting me go!"

"Good heavens!" say I, rubbing my eyes, while my muddy brain grows a trifle clearer. "What is it? What has happened? Have you had a nightmare?"

"You saw him," she says, with a sort of sobbing breathlessness; "you know you did! You saw him as well as I."

"I!" cry I, incredulously – "not I! Till this second I have been fast asleep. *I* saw nothing."

"You did!" she cries, passionately. "You know you did. Why do you deny it? You were as frightened as I."

"As I live," I answer, solemnly, "I know no more than the dead what you are talking about; till you woke me by calling and catching hold of me, I was as sound asleep as the seven sleepers."

"Is it possible that it can have been a *dream*?" she says, with a long sigh, for a moment loosing my arm, and covering her face with her hands. "But no – in a dream I should have been somewhere else, but I was here – *here* – on that bed, and he stood *there*," pointing with her forefinger, "just *there*, between the foot of it and the window!"

She stops, panting.

"It is all that brute Wiertz," say I, in a fury. "I wish I had been buried alive myself before I had been fool enough to take you to see his beastly daubs."

"Light a candle," she says, in the same breathless way, her teeth chattering with fright. "Let us make sure he is not hidden somewhere in the room."

"How could he be?" say I, striking a match; "the door is locked."

"He might have got in by the balcony," she answers, still trembling violently.

"He would have had to have cut a very large hole in the *persiennes*," say I, half mockingly. "See, they are intact, and well fastened."

She sinks into an arm-chair, and pushes her loose soft hair from her white face.

"It *was* a dream then, I suppose?"

She is silent for a moment or two, while I bring her a glass of water, and throw a dressing gown round her cold and shrinking form.

"Now tell me, my little one," I say coaxingly, sitting down at her feet, "what it was – what you thought you saw?"

"*Thought* I saw!" echoes she, with indignant emphasis, sitting upright, while her eyes sparkle feverishly. "I am as certain that I saw him standing there as I am that I see that candle burning – that I see this chair – that I see you."

"*Him!* But who is *him*?"

She falls forward on my neck, and buries her face in my shoulder.

"That – dreadful – man!" she says, while her whole body trembles.

"*What* dreadful man?" cry I impatiently.

She is silent.

"Who was he?"

"I do not know."

"Did you ever see him before?"

"Oh, no – no, never! I hope to God I may never see him again!"

"What was he like?"

"Come closer to me," she says, laying hold of my hand with her small and chilly fingers; "stay *quite* near me, and I will tell you," – after a pause – "he had a *nose*!"

"My dear soul," cry I, bursting out into a loud laugh in the silence of the night, "do not most people have noses? Would not he have been much more dreadful if he had had *none*?"

"But it was *such* a nose!" she says, with perfect trembling gravity.

"A bottle nose?" suggest I, still cackling.

"For heaven's sake, don't laugh!" she says nervously; "if you had seen his face, you would have been as little disposed to laugh as I."

"But his nose?" return I, suppressing my merriment, "what kind of nose was it? See, I am as grave as a judge."

"It was very prominent," she answers, in a sort of awe-struck half-whisper, "and very sharply chiselled; the nostrils very much cut out." A little pause. "His eyebrows were one straight black line across his face, and under them his eyes burnt like dull coals of fire, that shone and yet did not shine; they looked like dead eyes, sunken, half extinguished, and yet sinister."

"And what did he do?" asked I, impressed, despite myself, by her passionate earnestness; "when did you first see him?"

"I was asleep," she said – "at least, I thought so – and suddenly I opened my eyes, and he was *there* – *there*" – pointing again with trembling finger – "between the window and the bed."

"What was he doing? Was he walking about?"

"He was standing as still as stone – I never saw any live thing so still – *looking* at me; he never called or beckoned, or moved a finger, but his eyes *commanded* me to come to him, as the eyes of the mesmeriser at Penrith did." She stops, breathing heavily. I can hear her heart's loud and rapid beats.

"And you?" I say, pressing her more closely to my side, and smoothing her troubled hair.

"I *hated* it," she cries, excitedly; "I loathed it – abhorred it. I was ice-cold with fear and horror, but – I *felt* myself going to him."

"Yes?"

"And then I shrieked out to you, and you came running, and caught fast hold of me, and held me tight at first – quite tight – but presently I felt your hold slacken – slacken – and though I *longed* to stay with you, though I was *mad* with fright, yet I felt myself pulling strongly away from you – going to him; and he – he stood there always looking – looking – and then I gave one last loud shriek, and I suppose I awoke – and it was a dream!"

"I never heard of a clearer case of nightmare," say I, stoutly; "that vile Wiertz! I should like to see his whole *Musée* burnt."

She shakes her head. "It had nothing to say to Wiertz; what it meant I do not know, but—"

"It meant nothing," I answer, reassuringly, "except that for the future we will go and see none but good and pleasant sights, and steer clear of charnel-house fancies."

Chapter III

ELIZABETH is now in a position to decide whether the Rhine is a cocktail river or no, for she is on it, and so am I. We are sitting, with an awning over our heads, and little wooden stools under our feet. Elizabeth has a small sailor's hat and blue ribbon on her head. The river breeze has blown it rather awry; has tangled her plenteous hair; has made a faint pink stain on her pale cheeks. It is some fête day, and the boat is crowded. Tables, countless camp stools, volumes of black smoke pouring from the funnel, as we steam along. "Nothing to the Caledonian Canal!" cries a burly Scotchman in leggings, speaking with loud authority, and surveying with an air of contempt the eternal vine-clad slopes, that sound so well, and look so *sticky* in reality. "Cannot hold a candle to it!" A rival bride and bridegroom opposite, sitting together like love-birds under an umbrella, look into each other's eyes instead of at the Rhine scenery.

"They might as well have stayed at home, might not they?" says my wife with a little air of superiority. "Come, we are not so bad as that, are we?"

A storm comes on: hailstones beat slantwise and reach us – stone and sting us right under our awning. Everybody rushes down below, and takes the opportunity to feed ravenously. There are few actions more disgusting than eating *can* be made. A handsome girl close to us – her immaturity evidenced by the two long tails of black hair down her back – is thrusting her knife halfway down her throat.

"Come on deck again," says Elizabeth, disgusted and frightened at this last sight. "The hail was much better than this!"

So we return to our camp stools, and sit alone under one mackintosh in the lashing storm, with happy hearts and empty stomachs.

"Is not this better than any luncheon?" asks Elizabeth, triumphantly, while the raindrops hang on her long and curled lashes.

"Infinitely better," reply I, madly struggling with the umbrella to prevent its being blown inside out, and gallantly ignoring a species of gnawing sensation at my entrails.

The squall clears off by-and-by, and we go steaming, steaming on past the unnumbered little villages by the water's edge with church spires and pointed roofs, past the countless rocks with their little pert castles perched on the top of them, past the tall, stiff poplar rows. The church bells are ringing gaily as we go by. A nightingale is singing from a wood. The black eagle of Prussia droops on the stream behind us, swish-swish through the dull green water. A fat woman who is interested in it leans over the back of the boat and, by some happy effect of crinoline, displays to her fellow passengers two yards of thick white cotton legs. She is, fortunately for herself, unconscious of her generosity.

The day steals on; at every stopping place more people come on. There is hardly elbow room; and, what is worse, almost everybody is drunk. Rocks, castles, villages, poplars, slide by, while the paddles churn always the water, and the evening draws greyly on. At Bingen a party of big blue Prussian soldiers, very drunk, 'glorious' as Tam o'Shanter, come and establish themselves close to us. They call for Lager Beer; talk at the tip-top of their strong voices; two of them begin to spar; all seem inclined to sing. Elizabeth is frightened. We are two hours late in arriving at Biebrich. It is half an hour more before we can get ourselves and our luggage into a carriage and set off along the winding road to Wiesbaden. The night is chilly, but not dark. There is only a little shabby bit of a moon, but it shines as hard as it can. Elizabeth is quite worn out, her tired head droops in uneasy sleep on my shoulder. Once she wakes up with a start.

"Are you sure that it meant nothing?" she asks, looking me eagerly in my face; "do people often have such dreams?"

"Often, often," I answer, reassuringly.

"I am always afraid of falling asleep now," she says, trying to sit upright and keep her heavy eyes open, "for fear of seeing him standing there again. Tell me, do you think I shall? Is there any chance, any probability of it?"

"None, none!"

We reach Wiesbaden at last, and drive up to the Hôtel des Quatre Saisons. By this time it is full midnight. Two or three men are standing about the door. Morris, the maid, has got out – so have I, and I am holding out my hand to Elizabeth when I hear her give one piercing scream, and see her with ash-white face and starting eyes point with her forefinger—

"There he is! – there! – there!"

I look in the direction indicated, and just catch a glimpse of a tall figure standing half in the shadow of the night, half in the gas-light from the hotel. I have not time for more than one cursory glance, as I am interrupted by a cry from the bystanders, and turning quickly round, am just in time to catch my wife, who falls in utter insensibility into my arms. We carry her into a room on the ground floor; it is small, noisy, and hot, but it is the nearest at hand. In about an hour she re-opens her eyes. A strong shudder makes her quiver from head to foot.

"Where is he?" she says, in a terrified whisper, as her senses come slowly back. "He is somewhere about – somewhere near. I feel that he is!"

"My dearest child, there is no one here but Morris and me," I answer soothingly. "Look for yourself. See."

I take one of the candles and light up each corner of the room in succession.

"You saw him!" she says, in trembling hurry, sitting up and clenching her hands together. "I know you did – I pointed him out to you – you *cannot* say that it was a dream *this* time."

"I saw two or three ordinary-looking men as we drove up," I answer, in a commonplace, matter-of-fact tone. "I did not notice anything remarkable about any of them; you know, the fact is, darling, that you have had nothing to eat all day, nothing but a biscuit, and you are over-wrought, and fancy things."

"Fancy!" echoes she, with strong irritation. "How you talk! Was I ever one to fancy things? I tell you that as sure as I sit here – as sure as you stand there – I saw him – *him* – the man I saw in my dream, if it was a dream. There was not a hair's breadth of difference between them – and he was looking at me – looking—"

She breaks off into hysterical sobbing.

"My dear child!" say I, thoroughly alarmed, and yet half angry. "For God's sake do not work yourself up into a fever: wait till tomorrow, and we will find out who he is, and all about him; you yourself will laugh when we discover that he is some harmless bagman."

"Why not *now*?" she says, nervously; "why cannot you find out *now – this minute*?"

"Impossible! Everybody is in bed! Wait till tomorrow, and all will be cleared up."

The morrow comes, and I go about the hotel, inquiring. The house is so full, and the data I have to go upon are so small, that for some time I have great difficulty in making it understood to whom I am alluding. At length one waiter seems to comprehend.

"A tall and dark gentleman, with a pronounced and very peculiar nose? Yes; there has been such a one, certainly, in the hotel, but he left at *grand matin* this morning; he remained only one night."

"And his name?"

The *garçon* shakes his head. "That is unknown, monsieur; he did not inscribe it in the visitors' book."

"What countryman was he?"

Another shake of the head. "He spoke German, but with a foreign accent."

"Whither did he go?"

That also is unknown. Nor can I arrive at any more facts about him.

Chapter IV

A FORTNIGHT has passed; we have been hither and thither; now we are at Lucerne. Peopled with better inhabitants, Lucerne might well do for Heaven. It is drawing towards eventide, and Elizabeth and I are sitting hand in hand on a quiet bench, under the shady linden trees, on a high hill up above the lake. There is nobody to see us, so we sit peaceably hand in hand. Up by the still and solemn monastery we came, with its small and narrow windows, calculated to hinder the holy fathers from promenading curious eyes on the world, the flesh, and the devil, tripping past them in blue gauze veils: below us grass and green trees, houses with high-pitched roofs, little dormer-windows, and shutters yet greener than the grass; below us the lake in its rippleless peace, calm, quiet, motionless as Bethesda's pool before the coming of the troubling angel.

"I said it was too good to last," say I, doggedly, "did not I, only yesterday? Perfect peace, perfect sympathy, perfect freedom from nagging worries – when did such a state of things last more than two days?"

Elizabeth's eyes are idly fixed on a little steamer, with a stripe of red along its side, and a tiny puff of smoke from its funnel, gliding along and cutting a narrow white track on Lucerne's sleepy surface.

"This is the fifth false alarm of the gout having gone to his stomach within the last two years," continue I resentfully. "I declare to Heaven, that if it has not really gone there this time, I'll cut the whole concern."

Let no one cast up their eyes in horror, imagining that it is my father to whom I am thus alluding; it is only a great-uncle by marriage, in consideration of whose wealth and vague promises I have dawdled professionless through 28 years of my life.

"You *must* not go," says Elizabeth, giving my hand an imploring squeeze. "The man in the Bible said, 'I have married a wife, and therefore I cannot come'; why should it be a less valid excuse nowadays?"

"If I recollect rightly, it was considered rather a poor one even then," reply I, dryly.

Elizabeth is unable to contradict this; she therefore only lifts two pouted lips (Monsieur Taine objects to the redness of English women's mouths, but I do not) to be kissed, and says, "Stay." I am good enough to comply with her unspoken request, though I remain firm with regard to her spoken one.

"My dearest child," I say, with an air of worldly experience and superior wisdom, "kisses are very good things – in fact, there are few better – but one cannot live upon them."

"Let us try," she says coaxingly.

"I wonder which would get tired first?" I say, laughing. But she only goes on pleading, "Stay, stay."

"How *can* I stay?" I cry impatiently; "you talk as if I *wanted* to go! Do you think it is any pleasanter to me to leave you than to you to be left? But you know his disposition, his rancorous resentment of fancied neglects. For the sake of two days' indulgence, must I throw away what will keep us in ease and plenty to the end of our days?"

"I do not care for plenty," she says, with a little petulant gesture. "I do not see that rich people are any happier than poor ones. Look at the St. Clairs; they have £40,000 a year, and she is a miserable woman, perfectly miserable, because her face gets red after dinner."

"There will be no fear of *our* faces getting red after dinner," say I, grimly, "for we shall have no dinner for them to get red after."

A pause. My eyes stray away to the mountains. Pilatus on the right, with his jagged peak and slender snow-chains about his harsh neck; hill after hill rising silent, eternal, like guardian spirits standing hand in hand around their child, the lake. As I look, suddenly they have all flushed, as at some noblest thought, and over all their sullen faces streams an ineffable rosy joy – a solemn and wonderful effulgence, such as Israel saw reflected from the features of the Eternal in their prophet's transfigured eyes. The unutterable peace and stainless beauty of earth and sky seem to lie softly on my soul. "Would God I could stay! Would God all life could be like this!" I say, devoutly, and the aspiration has the reverent earnestness of a prayer.

"Why do you say, '*Would God!*'" she cries passionately, "when it lies with yourself? Oh my dear love," gently sliding her hand through my arm, and lifting wetly beseeching eyes to my face, "I do not know why I insist upon it so much – I cannot tell you myself – I dare say I seem selfish and unreasonable – but I feel as if your going now would be the end of all things – as if—" She breaks off suddenly.

"My child," say I, thoroughly distressed, but still determined to have my own way, "you talk as if I were going for ever and a day; in a week, at the outside, I shall be back, and then you will thank me for the very thing for which you now think me so hard and disobliging."

"Shall I?" she answers, mournfully. "Well, I hope so."

"You will not be alone, either; you will have Morris."

"Yes."

"And every day you will write me a long letter, telling me every single thing that you do, say, and think."

"Yes."

She answers me gently and obediently; but I can see that she is still utterly unreconciled to the idea of my absence.

"What is it that you are afraid of?" I ask, becoming rather irritated. "What do you suppose will happen to you?"

She does not answer; only a large tear falls on my hand, which she hastily wipes away with her pocket handkerchief, as if afraid of exciting my wrath.

"Can you give me any good reason why I *should* stay?" I ask, dictatorially.

"None – none – only – stay – stay!"

But I am resolved *not* to stay. Early the next morning I set off.

Chapter V

THIS TIME it is not a false alarm; this time it really has gone to his stomach, and, declining to be dislodged thence, kills him. My return is therefore retarded until after the funeral and the reading of the will. The latter is so satisfactory, and my time is so fully occupied with a multiplicity of attendant business, that I have no leisure to regret the delay. I write to Elizabeth, but receive no letters from her. This surprises and makes me rather angry, but does not alarm me. "If she had been ill, if anything had happened, Morris would have written. She never was great at writing, poor little soul. What dear little babyish notes she used to send me during our engagement! Perhaps she wishes to punish me for my disobedience to her wishes. Well, *now* she will see who was in the right." I am drawing near her now; I am walking up from the railway station in Lucerne. I am very joyful as I march along under an umbrella, in the grand broad shining of the summer afternoon. I think with pensive passion of the last glimpse I had of my beloved – her small and wistful face looking out from among the thick fair fleece of her long hair – winking away her tears and blowing kisses to me. It is a new sensation to me to have anyone looking tearfully wistful over my departure. I draw near the great glaring Schweizerhof, with its colonnaded tourist-crowded porch; here are all the pomegranates as I left them, in their green tubs, with their scarlet blossoms, and the dusty oleanders in a row. I look up at our windows; nobody is looking out from them; they are open, and the curtains are alternatively swelled out and drawn in by the softly playful wind. I run quickly upstairs and burst noisily into the sitting room. Empty, perfectly empty! I open the adjoining door into the bedroom, crying, "Elizabeth! Elizabeth!" but I receive no answer. Empty too. A feeling of indignation creeps over me as I think, "Knowing the time of my return, she might have managed to be indoors." I have returned to the silent sitting room, where the only noise is the wind still playing hide-and-seek with the curtains. As I look vacantly round my eye catches sight of a letter lying on the table. I pick it up mechanically and look at the address. Good heavens! What can this mean? It is my own, that I sent her two days ago, unopened, with the seal unbroken. Does she carry her resentment so far as not even to open my letters? I spring at the bell and violently ring it. It is answered by the waiter who has always specially attended us.

"Is madame gone out?"

The man opens his mouth and stares at me.

"Madame! Is monsieur then not aware that madame is no longer at the hotel?"

"*What?*"

"On the same day as monsieur, madame departed."

"*Departed!* Good God! What are you talking about?"

"A few hours after monsieur's departure – I will not be positive as to the exact time, but it must have been between one and two o'clock as the midday *table d'hôte* was in progress – a gentleman came and asked for madame—"

"Yes – be quick."

"I demanded whether I should take up his card, but he said no, that was unnecessary, as he was perfectly well known to madame; and, in fact, a short time afterwards, without saying anything to anyone, she departed with him."

"And did not return in the evening?"

"No, monsieur; madame has not returned since that day."

I clench my hands in an agony of rage and grief. "So this is it! With that pure child-face, with that divine ignorance – only three weeks married – this is the trick she has played me!" I am recalled to myself by a compassionate suggestion from the *garçon*.

"Perhaps it was the brother of madame."

Elizabeth has no brother, but the remark brings back to me the necessity of self-command. "Very probably," I answer, speaking with infinite difficulty. "What sort of looking gentleman was he?"

"He was a very tall and dark gentleman with a most peculiar nose – not quite like any nose that I ever saw before – and most singular eyes. Never have I seen a gentleman who at all resembled him."

I sink into a chair, while a cold shudder creeps over me as I think of my poor child's dream – of her fainting fit at Wiesbaden – of her unconquerable dread of and aversion from my departure. And this happened twelve days ago! I catch up my hat, and prepare to rush like a madman in pursuit.

"How did they go?" I ask incoherently; "by train? – driving? – walking?"

"They went in a carriage."

"What direction did they take? Whither did they go?"

He shakes his head. "It is not known."

"It *must* be known," I cry, driven to frenzy by every second's delay. "Of course the driver could tell; where is he? – where can I find him?"

"He did not belong to Lucerne, neither did the carriage; the gentleman brought them with him."

"But madame's maid," say I, a gleam of hope flashing across my mind; "did she go with her?"

"No, monsieur, she is still here; she was as much surprised as monsieur at madame's departure."

"Send her at once," I cry eagerly; but when she comes I find that she can throw no light on the matter. She weeps noisily and says many irrelevant things, but I can obtain no information from her beyond the fact that she was unaware of her mistress's departure until long after it had taken place, when, surprised at not being rung for at the usual time, she had gone to her room and found it empty, and on inquiring in the hotel, had heard of her sudden departure; that, expecting her to return at night, she had sat up waiting for her till two o'clock in the morning, but that, as I knew, she had not returned, neither had anything since been heard of her.

Not all my inquiries, not all my cross-questionings of the whole staff of the hotel, of the visitors, of the railway officials, of nearly all the inhabitants of Lucerne and its environs, procure me a jot more knowledge. On the next few weeks I look back as on a hellish and insane dream. I can neither eat nor sleep; I am unable to remain one moment quiet; my whole existence, my nights and my days, are spent in seeking, seeking. Everything that human despair and frenzied love can do is done by me. I advertise, I communicate with the police, I employ detectives; but that fatal twelve days' start for ever baffles me. Only on one occasion do I obtain one tittle of information. In a village a few miles from Lucerne the peasants, on the day in question, saw a carriage driving rapidly through their little street. It was closed, but through the windows they could see the occupants – a dark gentleman, with the peculiar physiognomy which has so often been described, and on the opposite seat a lady lying apparently in a state of utter insensibility. But even this leads to nothing.

Oh, reader, these things happened twenty years ago; since then I have searched sea and land, but never have I seen my little Elizabeth again.

The Long Way

Ramsey Campbell

IT MUST have been late autumn. Because everything was bare I saw inside the house.

Dead leaves had been scuttling around me all the way from home. A chill wind kept trying to shrink my face. The sky looked thin with ice, almost as white as the matching houses that made up the estate. Some of the old people who'd been rehoused wouldn't have known where they were on it except for the little wood, where my uncle Philip used to say the council left some trees so they could call it the Greenwood Estate. Nobody was supposed to be living in the three streets around the wood when I used to walk across the estate to help him shop.

So many people in Copse View and Arbour Street and Shady Lane had complained about children climbing trees and swinging from ropes and playing hide and seek that the council put a fence up, but then teenagers used the wood for sex and drink and drugs. Some dealers moved into Shady Lane, and my uncle said it got shadier, and the next road turned into Cops View. He said the other one should be called A Whore Street, though my parents told him not to let me hear. Then the council moved all the tenants out of the triangle, even the old people who'd complained about the children, and boarded up the houses. By the time I was helping my uncle, people had broken in.

They'd left Copse View alone except for one house in the middle of the terrace. Perhaps they'd gone for that one because the boards they'd strewn around the weedy garden looked rotten. They'd uncovered the front door and the downstairs window, but I could never see in for the reflection of sunlight on leaves. Now there weren't many leaves and the sun had a cataract, and the view into the front room was clear. The only furniture was an easy chair with a fractured arm. The chair had a pattern like shadows of ferns and wore a yellowish circular antimacassar. The pinstriped wallpaper was black and white too. A set of shelves was coming loose from the back wall but still displaying a plate printed with a portrait of the queen. Beside the shelves a door was just about open, framing part of a dimmer room.

I wondered why the door was there. In our house you entered the rooms from the hall. My uncle had an extra door made so he could use his wheelchair, and I supposed whoever had lived in this house might have been disabled too. There was a faint hint of a shape beyond the doorway, and I peered over the low garden wall until my eyes ached. Was it a full-length portrait or a life-size dummy? It looked as if it had been on the kind of diet they warned the girls about at school. As I made out its arms I began to think they could reach not just through the doorway but across far too much of the room, and then I saw that they were sticks on which it was leaning slightly forward – sticks not much thinner than its arms. I couldn't distinguish its gender or how it was dressed or even its face. Perhaps it was keeping so still in the hope of going unnoticed, unless it was challenging me to object to its presence. I was happy to leave it alone and head for my uncle's.

He lived on Pasture Boulevard, where he said the only signs of pasture were the lorries that drove past your bedroom all night. The trees along the central reservation were leafy just with litter. My uncle was sitting in the hall of the house where he lived on the ground floor, and wheeled himself out as soon as he saw me. "Sorry I made you wait, Uncle Philip," I said.

"I'll wait for anything that's worth the wait." Having raised a thumb to show this meant me, he said "And what's my name again, Craig?"

"Phil," I had to say, though my parents said I was too young to.

"That's the man. Don't be shy of speaking up. Ready for the go?"

He might have been starting a race at the school where he'd taught physical education – teaching pee, he called it – until he had his first stroke. When I made to push the chair he brought his eyebrows down and thrust his thick lips forward, which might have frightened his pupils but now made his big square face seem to be trying to shrink as the rest of him had. "Never make it easy, Craig," he said. "You don't want my arms going on strike."

I trotted beside him to the Frugo supermarket that had done for most of the shops that were supposed to make the estate feel like a village. Whenever a Frugo lorry thundered past us he would mutter "There's some petrol for your lungs" or "Hold your breath." In the supermarket he flung a week's supply of healthy food from the Frugorganic section into the trolley and bought me a Frugoat bar, joking as usual about how they'd turned the oats into an animal. I pushed the trolley to his flat and helped him unload it and took it back to Frugo. When I passed his window again he opened it, flapping the sports day posters he'd tacked to the wall of the room, to shout "See you in a week if you haven't got yourself a girlfriend."

I had the books I borrowed from the public library instead, but I didn't need him to announce my deficiency. I knew he disapproved of girls for boys my age – they sapped your energy, he said. "I'll always come," I promised and made for Copse View, where the trees looked eager to wave me on. The wind gave up pushing me as I reached them, and I stopped at the house where the boards had been pulled down. As I peered across the front room, resting my fists on the crumbling wall, my eyes began to ache again. However much I stared, the dim figure with the sticks didn't seem to have moved – not in an hour and a half. It had to be a picture; why shouldn't whoever used to live there have put a poster up? I felt worse than stupid for taking so long to realise. My parents and the English teacher at my school said I had imagination, but I could do without that much.

Ten minutes brought me home to Woody Rise. "Well, would he?" my uncle used to say even after my parents gave up laughing or groaning. The houses on this edge of the estate were as big as his but meant for one family each – they looked as if they were trying to pass for part of the suburb that once had the estate for a park. My father was carrying fistfuls of cutlery along the hall. "Here's the boy who cares," he called, and asked me "How's the wheelie kid?"

"Tom," my mother rebuked him from the kitchen.

I thought he deserved more reproof when I wasn't even supposed to shorten my uncle's name, but all I said was "Good."

As my father repeated this several times my mother said "Let's eat in here. Quick as you like, Craig. We've people coming round for a homewatch meeting."

"I thought you were going out."

"Just put your coat on your chair for now. We've rescheduled our pupils for tomorrow. Didn't we say?"

She always seemed resentful if I forgot whichever extra job they were doing when. "I suppose you must have," I tried pretending.

"Had you found some mischief to get up to, Craig?" my father said. "Has she got a name?"

"I hope not," my mother said. "You can welcome the guests if you like, Craig."

"He's already looked after my brother, Rosie."

"And some of us have done more." In the main this was aimed at my father, and she said more gently "All right, Craig. I expect you want to be on your own for a change."

I would rather have been with them by ourselves – not so much at dinner, where I always felt they were waiting for me to drop cutlery or spill food. I managed to conquer the spaghetti bolognese by cutting up the pasta with my fork, though my mother didn't approve much of that either. Once I'd washed up for everyone I was able to take refuge in my bedroom before all the neighbours came to discuss watching out for burglars and car thieves and door-to-door con people and other types to be afraid of. I needed to be alone to write.

Nobody knew I did. My stories tried to be like the kind of film my parents wouldn't let me watch. That night I wrote about a girl whose car broke down miles from anywhere, and the only place she could ask for help was a house full of people who wouldn't come to her. The house was haunted by a maniac who cut off people's feet with a chainsaw so they couldn't escape. I frightened myself with this more than I enjoyed, and when I went to sleep despite the murmur of neighbours downstairs I dreamed that if I opened my eyes I would see a figure standing absolutely still at the end of the bed. I looked once and saw no silhouette against the glow from the next street, but it took me a while to go back to sleep.

For most of Sunday my parents were out of the house. As if they hadn't had enough of teaching at school all week, my mother did her best to coax adults to read and write while my father educated people about computers. They couldn't help reminding me of my school, where I wasn't too unhappy so long as I wasn't noticed. It was in the suburb next to the estate, and some of the boys liked to punch me for stealing their park even though none of us was alive when the estate was built, while a few of the girls seemed to want me to act as uncouth as they thought people from it should be. I tried to keep out of all their ways and not to attract any questions in class. My work proved I wasn't stupid, which was all that mattered to me. I liked English best, except when the teacher made me read out my work. I would mumble and stammer and squirm and blush until the ordeal was done. I hated her and everyone else who could hear my helplessly unmodulated voice, most of all myself.

I wouldn't have dared admit to anyone at school that I quite liked most homework. I could take my own time with it, and there was nobody to distract me, since my parents were at night school several evenings, either teaching or improving their degrees. It must have been hard to pay the mortgage even with two teachers' salaries, but I also thought they were competing with each other for how much they could achieve, and perhaps with my uncle as well. All this left me feeling I should do more for him, but there was no more he would let me do.

Soon it was Saturday again. I was eager to look at the house on Copse View, but once it was in sight I felt oddly nervous. I wasn't going to avoid it by walking around the triangle. That would make me late for my uncle, and I could imagine what he would think of my behaviour if he knew. The sky had turned to chalk, and the sun was a round lump of it caught in the stripped treetops; in the flat pale light the houses looked brittle as shell. The light lay inert in the front room of the abandoned house. The figure with the sticks was there, in exactly the same stance. It wasn't in the same place, though. It had come into the room.

At least, it was leaning through the doorway. It looked poised to jerk the sticks up at me, unless it was about to use them to spring like a huge insect across the room. While the sunlight didn't spare the meagre furniture – the ferny chair and its discoloured antimacassar, the plate with the queen's face on the askew shelf still clinging to the pinstriped wall – it fell short of illuminating the occupier. I could just distinguish that the emaciated shape was dressed in some tattered material – covered with it, at any rate. While the overall impression was greyish, patches were as yellowed as the antimacassar, though I couldn't tell whether these were part of the clothes or showing through. This was also the case with the head. It appeared to be hairless, but I couldn't make out any of the face. When my eyes began to sting with trying I took a thoughtless step towards the garden wall, and then I took several back, enough to trip over the kerb. The instant I regained my balance I dashed out of Copse View.

Perhaps there was a flaw in the window, or the glass was so grimy that it blurred the person in the room, though not the other contents. Perhaps the occupant was wearing some kind of veil. Once I managed to have these thoughts they slowed me down, but not much, and I was breathing hard when I reached my uncle's. He was sitting in the hall again. "All right, Craig, I wasn't going anywhere," he said. "Training for a race?"

Before I could answer he said "Forget I asked. I know the schools won't let you compete any more."

I felt as if he didn't just mean at sports. "I can," I blurted and went red.

"I expect if you think you can that counts."

As we made for Frugo I set out to convince him in a way I thought he would approve of, but he fell behind alongside a lorry not much shorter than a dozen houses. "Don't let me hold you up," he gasped, "if you've got somewhere you'd rather be."

"I thought you liked to go fast. I thought it was how you kept fit."

"That's a lot of past tense. See, you're not the only one that knows his grammar."

I was reminded of a Christmas when my mother told him after some bottles of wine that he was more concerned with muscles than minds. He was still teaching then, and I'd have hoped he would have forgotten by now. He hardly spoke in the supermarket, not even bothering to make his weekly joke as he bought my Frugoat bar. I wondered if I'd exhausted him by forcing him to race, especially when he didn't head for home as fast as I could push the laden trolley. I was dismayed to think he could end up no more mobile than the figure with the sticks.

I helped him unload the shopping and sped the trolley back to Frugo. Did he have a struggle to raise the window as he saw me outside his flat? "Thanks for escorting an old tetch," he called. "Go and make us all proud for a week."

He'd left me feeling ashamed to be timid, which meant not avoiding Copse View. As I marched along the deserted street I thought there was no need to look into the house. I was almost past it when the sense of something eager to be seen dragged my head around. One glimpse was enough to send me fleeing home. The figure was still blurred, though the queen's face on the plate beside the doorway was absolutely clear, but there was no question that the occupant had moved. It was leaning forward on its sticks at least a foot inside the room.

I didn't stop walking very fast until I'd slammed the front door behind me. I wouldn't have been so forceful if I'd realised my parents were home. "That was an entrance," said my father. "Anything amiss we should know about?"

"We certainly should," said my mother.

"I was just seeing if I could run all the way home."

"Don't take your uncle too much to heart," my mother said. "There are better ways for you to impress."

On impulse I showed them my homework books. My father pointed out where the punctuation in my mathematics work was wrong, and my mother wished I'd written about real life and ordinary people instead of ghosts in my essay on the last book I'd read. "Good try," she told me, and my father added "Better next time, eh?"

I was tempted to show them my stories, but I was sure they wouldn't approve. I stayed away from writing any that weekend, because the only ideas I had were about figures that stayed too still or not still enough. I tried not to think about them after dark, and told myself that by the time I went to my uncle's again, whatever was happening on Copse View might have given up for lack of an audience or been sorted out by someone else. But I was there much sooner than next week.

It was Sunday afternoon. While my mother peeled potatoes I was popping peas out of their pods and relishing their clatter in a saucepan. A piece of beef was defrosting in a pool of blood. My father gazed at it for a while and said "That'd do for four of us. We haven't had Phil over for a while."

"We haven't," said my mother.

Although I wouldn't have taken this for enthusiasm, my father said "I'll give him a tinkle."

Surely my uncle could take a taxi – surely nobody would expect me to collect him and help him back to his flat after dark. I squeezed a pod in my fist while I listened to my father on the phone, but there was silence except for the scraping of my mother's knife. My hand was clammy with vegetable juice by the time my father said "He's not answering. That isn't like him."

"Sometimes he isn't much like him these days," said my mother.

"Can you go over and see what's up, Craig?"

As I rubbed my hands together I wondered whether any more of me had turned as green. "Don't you want me to finish these?" I pleaded.

"I'll take over kitchen duty."

My last hope was that my mother would object, but she said "Wash your hands for heaven's sake, Craig. Just don't be long."

While night wouldn't officially fall for an hour, the overcast sky gave me a preview. I was in sight of the woods when I noticed a gap in the railings on Shady Lane. Hadn't I seen another on Arbour Street? Certainly a path had been made through the shrubs from the opening off Shady Lane. It wound between the trees not too far from Copse View.

As I dodged along it bushes and trees kept blocking my view of the boarded-up houses. I couldn't help glancing at the vandalised house; perhaps I thought the distance made me safe. The scrawny figure hadn't changed its posture or its patchwork appearance. It looked as if it was craning forward to watch me or threatening worse. Overnight it had moved as much closer to the street as it had during the whole of the previous week.

I nearly forced my own way through the undergrowth to leave the sight behind. I was afraid I'd encouraged the figure to advance by trying to see it, perhaps even by thinking about it. Had the vandals fled once they'd seen inside the house? No wonder they'd left the rest of the street alone. I fancied the occupant might especially dislike people of my age, even though I hadn't been among those who'd rampaged in the woods. I was almost blind with panic and the early twilight by the time I fought off the last twigs and found the unofficial exit onto Arbour Street.

I was trying to be calmer when I arrived at my uncle's. He seemed to be watching television, which lent its flicker to the front room. I thought he couldn't hear me tapping on the pane for the cheers of the crowd. When I knocked harder he didn't respond, and I was nervous of calling to him. I was remembering a horror film I'd watched on television once until my mother had come home to find me watching. I'd seen enough to know you should be apprehensive if anyone was sitting with his back to you in that kind of film. "Uncle Philip," I said with very little voice.

The wheelchair twisted around, bumping into a sofa scattered with magazines. At first he seemed not to see me, then not to recognise me, and finally not to be pleased that he did. "What are you playing at?" he demanded. "What are you trying to do?"

He waved away my answer as if it were an insect and propelled the chair across the room less expertly than usual. He struggled to shove the lower half of the window up, and his grimace didn't relent once he had. "Speak up for yourself. Weren't you here before?"

"That was yesterday," I mumbled. "Dad sent me. He—"

"Sending an inspector now, is he? You can tell him my mind's as good as ever. I know they don't think that's much."

"He tried to phone you. You didn't answer, so—"

"When did he? Nobody's rung here." My uncle fumbled in his lap and on the chair. "Where is the wretched thing?"

Once he'd finished staring at me as if I'd failed to answer in a class he steered the chair around the room and blundered out of it, muttering more than one word I would never have expected him to use. "Here it is," he said accusingly and reappeared brandishing the cordless phone. "No wonder I couldn't hear it. Can't a man have a nap?"

"I didn't want to wake you. I only did because I was sent."

"Don't put yourself out on my behalf." Before I could deny that he was any trouble he said "So why's Tom checking up on me?"

"They wanted you to come for dinner."

"More like one did if any. I see you're not including yourself."

I don't know why this rather than anything else was too much, but I blurted "Look, I came all this way to find out. Of—"

One reason I was anxious to invite him was the thought of passing the house on Copse View by myself, but he didn't let me finish. "Don't again," he said.

"You'll come, won't you?"

"Tell them no. I'm still up to cooking my own grub."

"Can't you tell them?"

I was hoping that my father would persuade him to change his mind, but he said "I won't be phoning. I'll phone if I want you round."

"I'm sorry," I pleaded. "I didn't mean—"

"I know what you meant," he said and gazed sadly at me. "Never say sorry for telling the truth."

"I wasn't."

I might have tried harder to convince him if I hadn't realised that he'd given me an excuse to stay away from Copse View. "Don't bother," he said and stared at the television. "See, now I've missed a goal."

He dragged the sash down without bothering to glance at me. Even if that hadn't been enough of a dismissal, the night was creeping up on me. I didn't realise how close it was until he switched on the light in the room. That made me feel worse than excluded, and I wasn't slow in heading for home.

Before I reached the woods the streetlamps came on. I began to walk faster until I remembered that most of the lamps around the woods had been smashed. From the corner of the triangle I saw just one was intact – the one outside the house on Copse View. I couldn't help thinking the vandals were scared to go near; they hadn't even broken the window. I couldn't see into the room from the end of the street, but the house looked awakened by the stark light, lent power by the white glare. I wasn't anxious to learn what effect this might have inside the house.

The path would take me too close. I would have detoured through the streets behind Copse View if I hadn't heard the snarl of motorcycles racing up and down them. I didn't want to encounter the riders, who were likely to be my age or younger and protective of their territory. Instead I walked around the woods.

I had my back to the streetlamp all the way down Arbour Street. A few thin shafts of light extended through the trees, but they didn't seem to relieve the growing darkness so much as reach for me on behalf of the house. Now and then I heard wings or litter flapping. When I turned along Shady Lane the light started to jab at my vision, blurring the glimpses the woods let me have of the house. I'd been afraid to see it, but now I was more afraid not to see. I kept having to blink scraps of dazzle out of my eyes, and I waited for my vision to clear when a gap between the trees framed the house.

Was the figure closer to the window? I'd been walking in the road, but I ventured to the pavement alongside the woods. Something besides the stillness of the figure reminded me of the trees on either side of the house. Their cracked bark was grey where it wasn't blackened, and fragments were peeling off, making way for whitish fungus. Far too much of this seemed true of the face beyond the window.

I backed away before I could see anything else and stayed on the far pavement, though the dead houses beside it were no more reassuring than the outstretched shadows of the trees or the secret darkness of the woods, which kept being invaded by glimpses of the house behind the streetlamp. When I reached the corner of the triangle I saw that someone with a spray can had added a letter to the street sign. The first word was no longer just Copse.

Perhaps it was a vandal's idea of a joke, but I ran the rest of the way home, where I had to take time to calm my breath down. As I opened the front door I was nowhere near deciding what to tell my parents. I was sneaking it shut when my mother hurried out of the computer room, waving a pamphlet called Safe Home. "Are you back at last? We were going to phone Philip. Are you by yourself? Where have you been?"

"I had to go a long way. There were boys on bikes."

"Did they do something to you? What did they do?"

"They would have. That's why I went round." I wouldn't have minded some praise for prudence, but apparently I needed to add "They were riding motorbikes. They'd have gone after me."

"We haven't got you thinking there are criminals round every corner, have we?" My father had finished listening none too patiently to the interrogation. "We don't want him afraid to go out, do we, Rosie? It isn't nearly that bad, Craig. What's the problem with my brother?"

"He's already made his dinner."

"He isn't coming." Perhaps my father simply wanted confirmation, but his gaze made me feel responsible. "So why did you have to go over?" he said.

"Because you told me to."

"Sometimes I think you aren't quite with us, Craig," he said, though my mother seemed to feel this was mostly directed at her. "I was asking why he didn't take my call."

"He'd been watching football and—"

I was trying to make sure I didn't give away too much that had happened, but my mother said "He'd rather have his games than us, then."

"He was asleep," I said louder than I was supposed to speak.

"Control yourself, Craig. I won't have a hooligan in my house." Having added a pause, my mother turned her look on my father. "And please don't make it sound as if I've given him a phobia."

"I don't believe anyone said that. Phil's got no reason to call you a sissy, has he, Craig?" When I shook or at least shivered my head my father said "Did he say anything else?"

"Not really."

"Not really or not at all?"

"Not."

"Now who's going on at him?" my mother said in some triumph. "Come and have the dinner there's been so much fuss about."

Throughout the meal I felt as if I were being watched or would be if I even slightly faltered in cutting up my meat and vegetables and inserting forkfuls in my mouth and chewing and chewing and, with an effort that turned my hands clammy, swallowing. I managed to control my intake until dinner was finally done and I'd washed up, and then I was just able not to dash upstairs before flushing the toilet to muffle my sounds. Once I'd disposed of the evidence I lay on my bed for a while and eventually ventured down to watch the end of a programme about gang violence in primary schools. "Why don't you bring whatever you're reading downstairs?" my mother said.

"Maybe it's the kind of thing boys like to read by themselves," said my father.

I went red, not because it was true but on the suspicion that he wanted it to be, and shook my head to placate my mother. She switched off the television in case whatever else it had to offer wasn't suitable for me, and then my parents set about sectioning the Sunday papers, handing me the travel supplements in case those helped with my geography. I would much rather have been helped not to think about the house on Copse View.

Whenever the sight of the ragged discoloured face and the shape crouching over its sticks tried to invade my mind I made myself remember that my uncle didn't want me. I had to remember at night in bed, and in the classroom, and while I struggled not to let my parents see my fear, not to mention any number of situations in between these. I was only wishing to be let off my duty until the occupant of the derelict house somehow went away. My uncle didn't phone during the week, and I was afraid my father might call him and find out the truth, but perhaps he was stubborn as well.

I spent Saturday morning in dread of the phone. It was silent until lunchtime, and while I kept a few mouthfuls of bread and cheese down too. I lingered at the kitchen sink as long as I could, and then my mother said "Better be trotting. You don't want it to be dark."

"I haven't got to go."

"Why not?" my father said before she could.

"Uncle Phil, Uncle Philip said he'd phone when he wanted me."

"Since when has he ever done that?"

"Last week." I was trying to say as little as they would allow. "He really said."

"I think there's more to this than you're telling us," my mother warned me, if she wasn't prompting.

"It doesn't sound like Phil," my father said. "I'm calling him."

My mother watched my father dial and then went upstairs. "Don't say you've nodded off again," my father told the phone, but it didn't bring him an answer. At last he put the phone down. "You'd better go and see what's up this time," he told me.

"I think we should deal with this first," said my mother.

She was at the top of the stairs, an exercise book in her hand. I hoped it was some of my homework until I saw it had a red cover, not the brown one that went with the school uniform. "I knew it couldn't be our work with the community that's been preying on his nerves," she said.

"Feeling he hasn't got any privacy might do that, Rosie. Was there really any need to—"

"I thought he might have unsuitable reading up there, but this shows he's been involved in worse. Heaven knows what he's been watching or where."

"I haven't watched anything like that," I protested. "It's all out of my head."

"If that's true it's worse still," she said and tramped downstairs to thrust the book at my father. "We've done our best to keep you free of such things."

He was leafing through it, stopping every so often to frown, when the phone rang. I tried to take the book, but my mother recaptured it. I watched nervously in case she harmed it while my father said "It is. He is. When? Where? We will. Where? Thanks." He gazed at me before saying "Your uncle's had a stroke on the way home from shopping. He's back in hospital."

I could think of nothing I dared say except "Are we going to see him?"

"We are now."

"Can I have my book?"

My mother raised her eyebrows and grasped it with both hands, but my father took it from her. "I'll handle it, Rosie. You can have it back when we decide you're old enough, Craig."

I wasn't entirely unhappy with this. Once he'd taken it to their room I felt as if some of the ideas the house in Copse View had put in my head were safely stored away. Now I could worry about how I'd harmed my uncle or let him come to harm. As my father drove us to the hospital he and my mother were so silent that I was sure they thought I had.

My uncle was in bed halfway down a rank of patients with barely a movement between them. He looked shrunken, perhaps by his loose robe that tied at the back, and on the way to adopting its pallor. My parents took a hand each, leaving me to shuffle on the spot in front of his blanketed feet. "They'll be reserving you a bed if you carry on like this, Phil," my father joked or tried to joke.

My uncle blinked at me as if he were trying out his eyes and then worked his loose mouth. "Nod, you fool," he more or less said.

I was obeying and doing my best to laugh in case this was expected of me before I grasped what he'd been labouring to pronounce. I hoped my parents also knew he'd said it wasn't my fault, even if I still believed it was. "God, my shopping," he more or less informed them. "Boy writing on the pavement. Went dafter then." I gathered that someone riding on the pavement had got the bags my uncle had been carrying and that he'd gone after them, but what was he saying I should see as he pointed at his limp left arm with the hand my mother had been holding? He'd mentioned her as well. He was resting from his verbal exertions by the time I caught up with them. "Gave me this," he'd meant to say. "Another attack."

My parents seemed to find interpreting his speech almost as much of an effort as it cost him. I didn't mind it or visiting him, even by myself, since the route took me nowhere near Copse View. Over the weeks he regained his ability to speak. I was pleased for him, and I tried to be equally enthusiastic that he was recovering his strength. The trouble was that it would let him go home.

I couldn't wish he would lose it again. The most I could hope, which left me feeling painfully ashamed, was that he might refuse my help with shopping. I was keeping that thought to myself the last time I saw him in hospital. "I wouldn't mind a hand on Saturday," he said, "if you haven't had enough of this old wreck."

I assured him I hadn't, and my expression didn't let me down while he could see it. I managed to finish my dinner that night and even to some extent to sleep. Next day at school I had to blame my inattention and mistakes on worrying about my uncle, who was ill. Before the week was over I was using that excuse at home as well. I was afraid my parents would notice I was apprehensive about something else, and the fears aggravated each other.

While I didn't want my parents to learn how much of a coward I was, on another level I was willing them to rescue me by noticing. They must have been too concerned about the estate – about making it safe for my uncle and people like him. By the time I was due to go to him my parents were at a police forum, where they would be leading a campaign for police to intervene in schools however young the criminals. I loitered in the house, hoping for a call to say my uncle didn't need my help, until I realised that if I didn't go out soon it would be dark.

December was a week old. The sky was a field of snow. My white breaths led me through the streets past abandoned Frugo trolleys and Frugoburger cartons. I was walking too fast to shiver much, even with the chill that had chalked all the veins of the dead leaves near Copse View. The trees were showing every bone, but what else had changed? I couldn't comprehend the sight ahead, unless I was wary of believing in it, until I reached the end of the street that led to the woods. There wasn't a derelict house to be seen. Shady Lane and Arbour Street and, far better, Copse View had been levelled, surrounding the woods with a triangle of waste land.

I remembered hearing sounds like thunder while my uncle was in hospital. The streets the demolition had exposed looked somehow insecure, unconvinced of their own reality, incomplete with just half an alley alongside the back yards. As I hurried along Copse View, where the pavement and the roadway seemed to be waiting for the terrace to reappear, I stared hard at the waste ground where the house with the occupant had been. I could see no trace of the building apart from the occasional chunk of brick, and none at all of the figure with the sticks.

I found my uncle in his chair outside the front door. I wondered if he'd locked himself out until he said "Thought you weren't coming. I'm not as speedy as I was, you know."

As we made for Frugo I saw he could trundle only as fast as his weaker arm was able to propel him. Whenever he lost patience and tried to go faster the chair went into a spin. "Waltzing and can't even see my partner," he complained but refused to let me push. On the way home he was slower still, and I had to unload most of his groceries, though not my Frugoat bar, which he'd forgotten to buy. When I came back from returning the trolley he was at his window, which was open, perhaps because he hadn't wanted me to watch his struggles to raise the sash. "Thanks for the company," he said.

I thought I'd been more than that. At least there was no need for me to wish for any on the walk home. I believed this until the woods came in sight, as much as they could for the dark. Night had arrived with a vengeance, and the houses beyond the triangle of wasteland cut off nearly all the light from the estate. Just a patch at the edge of the woods was lit by the solitary intact streetlamp.

Its glare seemed starkest on the area of rubbly ground where the house with the watchful occupant had been. The illuminated empty stretch reminded me of a stage awaiting a performer. Suppose the last tenant of the house had refused to move? Where would they have gone now that it was demolished? How resentful, even vengeful, might they be? I was heading for the nearest street when I heard the feral snarl of bicycles beyond the houses. Without further thought I made for the woods.

Arbour Street and Shady Lane were far too dark. If the path took me past the site of the house, at least it kept me closer to the streetlamp. I sidled through the gap in the railings and followed the track as fast as the low-lying darkness let me. More than once shadows that turned out to be tendrils of undergrowth almost tripped me up. Trees and bushes kept shutting off the light before letting it display me again, though could anyone be watching? As it blazed in my eyes it turned my breaths the colour of fear, but I didn't need to think that. I was shivering only because much of the chill of the night seemed to have found a home in the woods. The waste ground of Copse View was as deserted as ever. If I glanced at it every time the woods showed it I might collide with something in the dark.

I was concentrating mostly on the path when it brought me alongside the streetlamp. Opposite the ground where the demolished house had been, the glare was so unnaturally pale that it reduced the trees and shrubs and other vegetation to black and white. A stretch of ferns and their shadows beside the path looked more monochrome than alive or real. My shadow ventured past the lamp before I did, and jerked nervously over a discoloured mosaic of dead leaves as I turned my back on the site of the house. Now that the light wasn't in my eyes I could walk faster, even if details of the woods tried to snag my attention: a circular patch of yellowish lichen on a log, lichen so intricate that it resembled embroidery; the vertical pattern on a tree trunk, lines thin and straight as pinstripes; a tangle of branches that put me in mind of collapsed shelves; a fractured branch protruding like a chair arm from a seat in a hollow tree with blanched ferns growing inside the hollow. None of this managed to halt me. It was a glimpse of a face in the darkness that did.

As a shiver held me where I was I saw that the face was peering out of the depths of a bush. It was on the side of the path that was further from Copse View, and some yards away from my route. I was trying to nerve myself to sprint past it when I realised why the face wasn't moving; it was on a piece of litter caught in the bush. I took a step that tried to be casual, and then I faltered again. It wasn't on a piece of paper as I'd thought. It was the queen's portrait on a plate.

At once I felt surrounded by the deserted house or its remains. I swung around to make sure the waste ground was still deserted – that the woods were. Then I stumbled backwards away from the streetlamp and almost sprawled into the undergrowth. No more than half a dozen paces away – perhaps fewer – a figure was leaning on its sticks in the middle of the path.

It was outlined more than illuminated by the light, but I could see how ragged and piebald the scrawny body was. It was crouching forward, as immobile as ever, but I thought it was waiting for me to make the first move, to give it the excuse to hitch itself after me on its sticks. I imagined it coming for me as fast as a spider. I sucked in a breath I might have used to cry for help if any had been remotely likely. Instead I made myself twist around for the fastest sprint of my life, but my legs shuddered to a halt. The figure was ahead of me now, at barely half the distance.

The worst of it was the face, for want of a better word. The eyes and mouth were little more than tattered holes, though just too much more, in a surface that I did my utmost not to see in any detail. Nevertheless they widened, and there was no mistaking their triumph. If I turned away I would find the shape closer to me, but moving forward would bring it closer too. I could only shut my eyes and try to stay absolutely still.

It was too dark inside my eyelids and yet not sufficiently dark. I was terrified to see a silhouette looming on them if I shifted so much as an inch. I didn't dare even open my mouth, but I imagined speaking – imagined it with all the force I could find inside myself. "Go away. Leave me alone. I didn't do anything. Get someone else."

For just an instant I thought of my uncle, to establish that I didn't mean him, and then I concentrated on whoever had robbed him. An icy wind passed through the woods, and a tree creaked like an old door. The wind made me feel alone, and I tried to believe I entirely was. At last I risked looking. There was no sign of the figure ahead or, when I forced myself to turn, behind me or anywhere else.

I no longer felt safe in the woods. I took a few steps along the path before I fought my way through the bushes to the railings. I'd seen a gap left by a single railing, but was it wide enough for me to squeeze through? Once I'd succeeded, scraping my chest and collecting flakes of rust on my prickly skin, I fled home. I slowed and tried to do the same to my breath at the end of my street, and then I made another dash. My mother's car was pulling away from the house.

She halted it beside me, and my father lowered his window. "Where do you think you've been, Craig?"

His grimness and my mother's made me feel more threatened than I understood. "Helping," I said.

"Don't lie to us," said my mother. "Don't start doing that as well."

"I'm not. Why are you saying I am? I was helping Uncle Phil. He's gone slow."

They gazed at me, and my father jerked a hand at the back seat. "Get in."

"Tom, are you sure you want him—"

"Your uncle's been run over."

"He can't have been. I left him in his flat." When this earned no response I demanded "How do you know?"

"They found us in his pocket." Yet more starkly my father added "Next of kin."

I didn't want to enquire any further. When the isolated streetlamp on Copse View came in sight I couldn't tell whether I was more afraid of what else I might see or that my parents should see it as well. I saw nothing to dismay me in the woods or the demolished street, however – nothing all the way to Pasture Boulevard. My mother had to park several hundred yards short of my uncle's flat. The police had put up barriers, beyond which a giant Frugo lorry was skewed across the central strip, uprooting half a dozen trees. In front of and under the cab of the lorry were misshapen pieces of a wheelchair. I tried not to look at the stains on some of them and on the road, but I couldn't avoid noticing the cereal bars strewn across the pavement. "He forgot to buy me one of those and I didn't like to ask," I said. "He must have gone back."

My parents seemed to think I was complaining rather than trying to understand. When I attempted to establish that it hadn't been my fault they acted as if I was making too much of a fuss. Before the funeral the police told them more than one version of the accident. Some witnesses said my uncle had been wheeling his chair so fast that he'd lost control and spun into the road. Some said he'd appeared to be in some kind of panic, others that a gang of cyclists on the pavement had, and he'd swerved out of their way. The cyclists were never identified. As if my parents had achieved one of their aims at last, the streets were free of rogue cyclists for weeks.

I never knew how much my parents blamed me for my uncle's death. When I left school I went into caring for people like him. In due course these included my parents. They're gone now, and while sorting out the contents of our house I found the book with my early teenage stories in it – childish second-hand stuff. I never asked to have it back, and I never wrote stories again. I couldn't shake off the idea that my imagination had somehow caused my uncle's death.

I could easily feel that my imagination has been revived by the exercise book – by the cover embroidered with a cobweb, the paper pinstriped with faded lines, a fern pressed between the yellowed pages and blackened by age. I'm alone with my imagination up here at the top of the stairs leading to the unlit hall. If there's a face at the edge of my vision, it must belong to a picture on the wall, even if I don't remember any there. Night fell while I was leafing through the book, and I have to go over there to switch the light on. Of course I will, although the mere thought of moving seems to make the floorboards creak like sticks. I can certainly move, and there's no reason not to. In a moment – just a moment while I take another breath – I will.

The White Villa

Ralph Adams Cram

WHEN WE LEFT Naples on the 8:10 train for Paestum, Tom and I, we fully intended returning by the 2:46. Not because two hours time seemed enough wherein to exhaust the interests of those deathless ruins of a dead civilization, but simply for the reason that, as our *Indicatore* informed us, there was but one other train, and that at 6:11, which would land us in Naples too late for the dinner at the Turners and the San Carlo afterwards. Not that I cared in the least for the dinner or the theatre; but then, I was not so obviously in Miss Turner's good graces as Tom Rendel was, which made a difference.

However, we had promised, so that was an end of it.

This was in the spring of '88, and at that time the railroad, which was being pushed onward to Reggio, whereby travellers to Sicily might be spared the agonies of a night on the fickle Mediterranean, reached no farther than Agropoli, some twenty miles beyond Paestum; but although the trains were as yet few and slow, we accepted the half-finished road with gratitude, for it penetrated the very centre of Campanian brigandage, and made it possible for us to see the matchless temples in safety, while a few years before it was necessary for intending visitors to obtain a military escort from the Government; and military escorts are not for young architects.

So we set off contentedly, that white May morning, determined to make the best of our few hours, little thinking that before we saw Naples again we were to witness things that perhaps no American had ever seen before.

For a moment, when we left the train at 'Pesto', and started to walk up the flowery lane leading to the temples, we were almost inclined to curse this same railroad. We had thought, in our innocence, that we should be alone, that no one else would think of enduring the long four hours' ride from Naples just to spend two hours in the ruins of these temples; but the event proved our unwisdom. We were *not* alone. It was a compact little party of conventional sight-seers that accompanied us. The inevitable English family with the three daughters, prominent of teeth, flowing of hair, aggressive of scarlet Murrays and Baedekers; the two blond and untidy Germans; a French couple from the pages of *La Vie Parisienne*; and our 'old man of the sea', the white-bearded Presbyterian minister from Pennsylvania who had made our life miserable in Rome at the time of the Pope's Jubilee. Fortunately for us, this terrible old man had fastened himself upon a party of American school-teachers travelling *en Cook*, and for the time we were safe; but our vision of two hours of dreamy solitude faded lamentably away.

Yet how beautiful it was! This golden meadow walled with far, violet mountains, breathless under a May sun; and in the midst, rising from tangles of asphodel and acanthus, vast in the vacant plain, three temples, one silver gray, one golden gray, and one flushed with intangible rose. And all around nothing but velvet meadows stretching from the dim mountains behind, away to the sea, that showed only as a thin line of silver just over the edge of the still grass.

The tide of tourists swept noisily through the Basilica and the temple of Poseidon across the meadow to the distant temple of Ceres, and Tom and I were left alone to drink in all the fine wine of dreams that was possible in the time left us. We gave but little space to examining the temples the tourists had left, but in a few moments found ourselves lying in the grass to the east of Poseidon, looking dimly out towards the sea, heard now, but not seen – a vague and pulsating murmur that blended with the humming of bees all about us.

A small shepherd boy, with a woolly dog, made shy advances of friendship, and in a little time we had set him to gathering flowers for us: asphodels and bee-orchids, anemones, and the little thin green iris so fairylike and frail. The murmur of the tourist crowd had merged itself in the moan of the sea, and it was very still; suddenly I heard the words I had been waiting for – the suggestion I had refrained from making myself, for I knew Thomas.

"I say, old man, shall we let the 2:46 go to thunder?"

I chuckled to myself. "But the Turners?"

"They be blowed, we can tell them we missed the train."

"That is just exactly what we shall do," I said, pulling out my watch, "unless we start for the station right now."

But Tom drew an acanthus leaf across his face and showed no signs of moving; so I filled my pipe again, and we missed the train.

As the sun dropped lower towards the sea, changing its silver line to gold, we pulled ourselves together, and for an hour or more sketched vigorously; but the mood was not on us. It was "too jolly fine to waste time working," as Tom said; so we started off to explore the single street of the squalid town of Pesto that was lost within the walls of dead Poseidonia. It was not a pretty village, – if you can call a rut-riven lane and a dozen houses a village – nor were the inhabitants thereof reassuring in appearance. There was no sign of a church – nothing but dirty huts, and in the midst, one of two stories, rejoicing in the name of *Albergo del Sole*, the first story of which was a black and cavernous smithy, where certain swarthy knaves, looking like banditti out of a job, sat smoking sulkily.

"We might stay here all night," said Tom, grinning askance at this choice company; but his suggestion was not received with enthusiasm.

Down where the lane from the station joined the main road stood the only sign of modern civilization – a great square structure, half villa, half fortress, with round turrets on its four corners, and a ten-foot wall surrounding it. There were no windows in its first story, so far as we could see, and it had evidently been at one time the fortified villa of some Campanian noble. Now, however, whether because brigandage had been stamped out, or because the villa was empty and deserted, it was no longer formidable, the gates of the great wall hung ragging on their hinges, brambles growing all over them, and many of the windows in the upper story were broken and black. It was a strange place, weird and mysterious, and we looked at it curiously. "There is a story about that place," said Tom, with conviction.

It was growing late: the sun was near the edge of the sea as we walked down the ivy-grown walls of the vanished city for the last time, and as we turned back, a red flush poured from the west, and painted the Doric temples in pallid rose against the evanescent purple of the Apennines. Already a thin mist was rising from the meadows, and the temples hung pink in the misty grayness.

It was a sorrow to leave the beautiful things, but we could run no risk of missing this last train, so we walked slowly back towards the temples.

"What is that Johnny waving his arm at us for?" asked Tom, suddenly.

"How should I know? We are not on his land, and the walls don't matter."

We pulled out our watches simultaneously.

"What time are you?" I said.

"Six minutes before six."

"And I am seven minutes. It can't take us all that time to walk to the station."

"Are you sure the train goes at 6:11?"

"Dead sure," I answered; and showed him the *Indicatore*.

By this time a woman and two children were shrieking at us hysterically; but what they said I had no idea, their Italian being of a strange and awful nature.

"Look here," I said, "let's run; perhaps our watches are both slow."

"Or – perhaps the timetable is changed."

Then we ran, and the populace cheered and shouted with enthusiasm; our dignified run became a panic-stricken rout, for as we turned into the lane, smoke was rising from beyond the bank that hid the railroad; a bell rang; we were so near that we could hear the interrogative *Pronte?* the impatient *Partenza!* and the definitive *Andiamo!* But the train was five hundred yards away, steaming towards Naples, when we plunged into the station as the clock struck six, and yelled for the stationmaster.

He came, and we indulged in crimination and recrimination.

When we could regard the situation calmly, it became apparent that the timetable *had* been changed two days before, the 6:11 now leaving at 5:58. A *facchino* came in, and we four sat down and regarded the situation judicially.

"Was there any other train?"

"No."

"Could we stay at the Albergo del Sole?"

A forefinger drawn across the throat by the Capo Stazione with a significant 'cluck' closed that question.

"Then we must stay with you here at the station."

"But, Signori, I am not married. I live here only with the *facchini*. I have only one room to sleep in. It is impossible!"

"But we must sleep somewhere, likewise eat. What can we do?" and we shifted the responsibility deftly on the shoulders of the poor old man, who was growing excited again.

He trotted nervously up and down the station for a minute, then he called the *facchino*. "Giuseppe, go up to the villa and ask if two *forestieri* who have missed the last train can stay there all night!"

Protests were useless. The *facchino* was gone, and we waited anxiously for his return. It seemed as though he would never come. Darkness had fallen, and the moon was rising over the mountains. At last he appeared.

"The Signori may stay all night, and welcome; but they cannot come to dinner, for there is nothing in the house to eat!"

This was not reassuring, and again the old stationmaster lost himself in meditation. The results were admirable, for in a little time the table in the waiting room had been transformed into a dining table, and Tom and I were ravenously devouring a big omelette, and bread and cheese, and drinking a most shocking sour wine as though it were Château Yquem. A *facchino* served us, with clumsy goodwill; and when we had induced our nervous old host to sit down with us and partake of his own hospitality, we succeeded in forming a passably jolly dinner party, forgetting over our sour wine and cigarettes the coming hours from ten until sunrise, which lay before us in a dubious mist.

It was with crowding apprehensions which we strove in vain to joke away that we set out at last to retrace our steps to the mysterious villa, the *facchino* Giuseppe leading the way. By this time the moon was well overhead, and just behind us as we tramped up the dewy lane, white in the moonlight between the ink-black hedgerows on either side. How still it was! Not a breath of air, not a sound of life; only the awful silence that had lain almost unbroken for two thousand years over this vast graveyard of a dead world.

As we passed between the shattered gates and wound our way in the moonlight through the maze of gnarled fruit-trees, decaying farm implements and piles of lumber, towards the small door that formed the only opening in the first story of this deserted fortress, the cold silence was shattered by the harsh baying of dogs somewhere in the distance to the right, beyond the barns that formed one side of the court. From the villa came neither light nor sound. Giuseppe knocked at the weather-worn door, and the sound echoed cavernously within; but there was no other reply. He knocked again and again, and at length we heard the rasping jar of sliding bolts, and the door opened a little, showing an old, old man, bent with age and gaunt with malaria. Over his head he held a big Roman lamp, with three wicks, that cast strange shadows on his face – a face that was harmless in its senility, but intolerably sad. He made no reply to our timid salutations, but motioned tremblingly to us to enter; and with a last "goodnight" to Giuseppe we obeyed, and stood halfway up the stone stairs that led directly from the door, while the old man tediously shot every bolt and adjusted the heavy bar.

Then we followed him in the semi-darkness up the steps into what had been the great hall of the villa. A fire was burning in a great fireplace so beautiful in design that Tom and I looked at each other with interest. By its fitful light we could see that we were in a huge circular room covered by a flat, saucer-shaped dome – a room that must once have been superb and splendid, but that now was a lamentable wreck. The frescoes on the dome were stained and mildewed, and here and there the plaster was gone altogether; the carved doorways that led out on all sides had lost half the gold with which they had once been covered, and the floor was of brick, sunken into treacherous valleys. Rough chests, piles of old newspapers, fragments of harnesses, farm implements, a heap of rusty carbines and cutlasses, nameless litter of every possible kind, made the room into a wilderness which under the firelight seemed even more picturesque than it really was. And on this inexpressible confusion of lumber the pale shapes of the seventeenth-century nymphs, startling in their weather-stained nudity, looked down with vacant smiles.

For a few moments we warmed ourselves before the fire; and then, in the same dejected silence, the old man led the way to one of the many doors, handed us a brass lamp, and with a stiff bow turned his back on us.

Once in our room alone, Tom and I looked at each other with faces that expressed the most complex emotions.

"Well, of all the rum goes," said Tom, "this is the rummiest go I ever experienced!"

"Right, my boy; as you very justly remark, we are in for it. Help me shut this door, and then we will reconnoitre, take account of stock, and size up our chances."

But the door showed no sign of closing; it grated on the brick floor and stuck in the warped casing, and it took our united efforts to jam the two inches of oak into its place, and turn the enormous old key in its rusty lock.

"Better now, much better now," said Tom; "now let us see where we are."

The room was easily twenty-five feet square, and high in proportion; evidently it had been a state apartment, for the walls were covered with carved panelling that had once been white and gold, with mirrors in the panels, the wood now stained every imaginable color, the mirrors cracked and broken, and dull with mildew. A big fire had just been lighted in the fireplace, the shutters were closed, and although the only furniture consisted of two massive bedsteads, and a chair with one leg shorter than the others, the room seemed almost comfortable.

I opened one of the shutters, that closed the great windows that ran from the floor almost to the ceiling, and nearly fell through the cracked glass into the floorless balcony. "Tom, come here, quick," I cried; and for a few minutes neither of us thought about our dubious surroundings, for we were looking at Paestum by moonlight.

A flat, white mist, like water, lay over the entire meadow; from the midst rose against the blue-black sky the three ghostly temples, black and silver in the vivid moonlight, floating, it seemed, in the fog; and behind them, seen in broken glints between the pallid shafts, stretched the line of the silver sea.

Perfect silence – the silence of implacable death.

We watched the white tide of mist rise around the temples, until we were chilled through, and so presently went to bed. There was but one door in the room, and that was securely locked; the great windows were twenty feet from the ground, so we felt reasonably safe from all possible attack.

In a few minutes Tom was asleep and breathing audibly; but my constitution is more nervous than his, and I lay awake for some little time, thinking of our curious adventure and of its possible outcome. Finally, I fell asleep, – for how long I do not know: but I woke with the feeling that someone had tried the handle of the door. The fire had fallen into a heap of coals which cast a red glow in the room, whereby I could see dimly the outline of Tom's bed, the broken-legged chair in front of the fireplace, and the door in its deep casing by the chimney, directly in front of my bed. I sat up, nervous from my sudden awakening under these strange circumstances, and stared at the door. The latch rattled, and the door swung smoothly open. I began to shiver coldly. That door was locked; Tom and I had all we could do to jam it together and lock it. But we *did* lock it; and now it was opening silently. In a minute more it as silently closed.

Then I heard a footstep – I swear I heard a footstep *in the room*, and with it the *frou-frou* of trailing skirts; my breath stopped and my teeth grated against each other as I heard the soft footfalls and the feminine rustle pass along the room towards the fireplace. My eyes saw nothing; yet there was enough light in the room for me to distinguish the pattern on the carved panels of the door. The steps stopped by the fire, and I saw the broken-legged chair lean to the left, with a little jar as its short leg touched the floor.

I sat still, frozen, motionless, staring at the vacancy that was filled with such terror for me; and as I looked, the seat of the chair creaked, and it came back to its upright position again.

And then the footsteps came down the room lightly, towards the window; there was a pause, and then the great shutters swung back, and the white moonlight poured in. Its brilliancy was unbroken by any shadow, by any sign of material substance.

I tried to cry out, to make some sound, to awaken Tom; this sense of utter loneliness in the presence of the Inexplicable was maddening. I don't know whether my lips obeyed my will or no; at all events, Tom lay motionless, with his deaf ear up, and gave no sign.

The shutters closed as silently as they had opened; the moonlight was gone, the firelight also, and in utter darkness I waited. If I could only *see*! If something were visible, I should not mind it so much; but this ghastly hearing of every little sound, every rustle of a gown, every breath, yet seeing nothing, was soul-destroying. I think in my abject terror I prayed that I might see, only see; but the darkness was unbroken.

Then the footsteps began to waver fitfully, and I heard the rustle of garments sliding to the floor, the clatter of little shoes flung down, the rattle of buttons, and of metal against wood.

Rigors shot over me, and my whole body shivered with collapse as I sank back on the pillow, waiting with every nerve tense, listening with all my life.

The coverlid was turned back beside me, and in another moment the great bed sank a little as something slipped between the sheets with an audible sigh.

I called to my aid every atom of remaining strength, and, with a cry that shivered between my clattering teeth, I hurled myself headlong from the bed on to the floor.

I must have lain for some time stunned and unconscious, for when I finally came to myself it was cold in the room, there was no last glow of lingering coals in the fireplace, and I was stiff with chill.

It all flashed over me like the haunting of a heavy dream. I laughed a little at the dim memory, with the thought, "I must try to recollect all the details; they will do to tell Tom," and rose stiffly to return to bed, when – there it was again, and my heart stopped – the hand on the door.

I paused and listened. The door opened with a muffled creak, closed again, and I heard the lock turn rustily. I would have died now before getting into that bed again; but there was terror equally without; so I stood trembling and listened – listened to heavy, stealthy steps creeping along on the other side of the bed. I clutched the coverlid, staring across into the dark.

There was a rush in the air by my face, the sound of a blow, and simultaneously a shriek, so awful, so despairing, so blood-curdling that I felt my senses leaving me again as I sank crouching on the floor by the bed.

And then began the awful duel, the duel of invisible, audible shapes; of things that shrieked and raved, mingling thin, feminine cries with low, stifled curses and indistinguishable words. Round and round the room, footsteps chasing footsteps in the ghastly night, now away by Tom's bed, now rushing swiftly down the great room until I felt the flash of swirling drapery on my hard lips. Round and round, turning and twisting till my brain whirled with the mad cries.

They were coming nearer. I felt the jar of their feet on the floor beside me. Came one long, gurgling moan close over my head, and then, crushing down upon me, the weight of a collapsing body; there was long hair over my face, and in my staring eyes; and as awful silence succeeded the less awful tumult, life went out, and I fell unfathomable miles into nothingness.

The gray dawn was sifting through the chinks in the shutters when I opened my eyes again. I lay stunned and faint, staring up at the mouldy frescoes on the ceiling, struggling to gather together my wandering senses and knit them into something like consciousness. But now as I pulled myself little by little together there was no thought of dreams before me. One after another the awful incidents of that unspeakable night came back, and I lay incapable of movement, of action, trying to piece together the whirling fragments of memory that circled dizzily around me.

Little by little it grew lighter in the room. I could see the pallid lines struggling through the shutters behind me, grow stronger along the broken and dusty floor. The tarnished mirrors reflected dirtily the growing daylight; a door closed, far away, and I heard the crowing of a cock; then by and by the whistle of a passing train.

Years seemed to have passed since I first came into this terrible room. I had lost the use of my tongue, my voice refused to obey my panic-stricken desire to cry out; once or twice I tried in vain to force an articulate sound through my rigid lips; and when at last a broken whisper rewarded my feverish struggles, I felt a strange sense of great victory. How soundly he slept! Ordinarily, rousing him was no easy task, and now he revolted steadily against being awakened at this untimely hour. It seemed to me that I had called him for ages almost, before I heard him grunt sleepily and turn in bed.

"Tom," I cried weakly, "Tom, come and help me!"

"What do you want? What is the matter with you?"

"Don't ask, come and help me!"

"Fallen out of bed I guess"; and he laughed drowsily.

My abject terror lest he should go to sleep again gave me new strength. Was it the actual physical paralysis born of killing fear that held me down? I could not have raised my head from the floor on my life; I could only cry out in deadly fear for Tom to come and help me.

"Why don't you get up and get into bed?" he answered, when I implored him to come to me. "You have got a bad nightmare; wake up!"

But something in my voice roused him at last, and he came chuckling across the room, stopping to throw open two of the great shutters and let a burst of white light into the room. He climbed up on the bed and peered over jeeringly. With the first glance the laugh died, and he leaped the bed and bent over me.

"My God, man, what is the matter with you? You are hurt!"

"I don't know what is the matter; lift me up, get me away from here, and I'll tell you all I know."

"But, old chap, you must be hurt awfully; the floor is covered with blood!"

He lifted my head and held me in his powerful arms. I looked down: a great red stain blotted the floor beside me.

But, apart from the black bruise on my head, there was no sign of a wound on my body, nor stain of blood on my lips. In as few words as possible I told him the whole story.

"Let's get out of this," he said when I had finished; "this is no place for us. Brigands I can stand, but—"

He helped me to dress, and as soon as possible we forced open the heavy door, the door I had seen turn so softly on its hinges only a few hours before, and came out into the great circular hall, no less strange and mysterious now in the half-light of dawn than it had been by firelight. The room was empty, for it must have been very early, although a fire already blazed in the fireplace. We sat by the fire some time, seeing no one. Presently slow footsteps sounded in the stairway, and the old man entered, silent as the night before, nodding to us civilly, but showing by no sign any surprise which he may have felt at our early rising. In absolute silence he moved around, preparing coffee for us; and when at last the frugal breakfast was ready, and we sat around the rough table munching coarse bread and sipping the black coffee, he would reply to our overtures only by monosyllables.

Any attempt at drawing from him some facts as to the history of the villa was received with a grave and frigid repellence that baffled us; and we were forced to say *addio* with our hunger for some explanation of the events of the night still unsatisfied.

But we saw the temples by sunrise, when the mistlike lambent opals bathed the bases of the tall columns salmon in the morning light! It was a rhapsody in the pale and unearthly colors of Puvis de Chavannes vitalized and made glorious with splendid sunlight; the apotheosis of mist; a vision never before seen, never to be forgotten. It was so beautiful that the memory of my ghastly night paled and faded, and it was Tom who assailed the stationmaster with questions while we waited for the train from Agropoli.

Luckily he was more than loquacious, he was voluble under the ameliorating influence of the money we forced upon him; and this, in few words, was the story he told us while we sat on the platform smoking, marvelling at the mists that rose to the east, now veiling, now revealing the lavender Apennines.

"Is there a story of *La Villa Bianca*?"

"Ah, Signori, certainly; and a story very strange and very terrible. It was much time ago, a hundred – two hundred years; I do not know. Well, the Duca di San Damiano married a lady so fair, so most beautiful that she was called *La Luna di Pesto*; but she was of the people – more, she was of the banditti: her father was of Calabria, and a terror of the Campagna. But the Duke was young, and he married her, and for her built the white villa; and it was a wonder throughout Campania – you have seen? It is splendid now, even if a ruin. Well, it was less than a year after they came to the villa before the Duke grew jealous – jealous of the new captain of the banditti who took the place of the father of *La Luna*, himself killed in a great battle up there in the mountains. Was there cause? Who shall know? But there were stories among the people of terrible things in the villa, and how *La Luna* was seen almost never outside the walls. Then the Duke would go for many days to Napoli, coming home only now and then to the villa that was become a fortress, so many men guarded its never-opening gates. And once – it was in the spring – the Duke came silently down from Napoli, and there, by the three poplars you see away towards the north, his carriage was set upon by armed men, and he was almost killed; but he had with him many guards, and after a terrible fight the brigands were beaten off; but before him, wounded, lay the captain – the man whom he feared and hated. He looked at him, lying there under the torchlight, and in his hand saw *his own sword*. Then he became a devil: with the same sword he ran the brigand through, leaped in the carriage, and, entering the villa, crept to the chamber of *La Luna*, and killed her with the sword she had given to her lover.

"This is all the story of the White Villa, except that the Duke came never again to Pesto. He went back to the king at Napoli, and for many years he was the scourge of the banditti of Campania; for the King made him a general, and San Damiano was a name feared by the lawless and loved by the peaceful, until he was killed in a battle down by Mormanno.

"And *La Luna*? Some say she comes back to the villa, once a year, when the moon is full, in the month when she was slain; for the Duke buried her, they say, with his own hands, in the garden that was once under the window of her chamber; and as she died unshriven, so was she buried without the pale of the Church. Therefore she cannot sleep in peace – *non è vero?* I do not know if the story is true, but this is the story, Signori, and there is the train for Napoli. *Ah, grazie! Signori, grazie tanto! A rivederci! Signori, a rivederci!*"

A Night of Horror

Dick Donovan

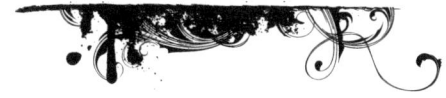

Bleak Hill Castle

My dear old Chum, – Before you leave England for the East I claim the redemption of a promise you made to me some time ago that you would give me the pleasure of a week or two of your company. Besides, as you may have already guessed, I have given up the folly of my bachelor days, and have taken unto myself the sweetest, dearest little woman that ever walked the face of the earth. We have been married just six months, and are as happy as the day is long. And then this place is entirely after your own heart. It will excite all your artistic fancies, and appeal with irresistible force to your romantic nature. To call the building a castle is somewhat pretentious, but I believe it has been known as the Castle ever since it was built, more than two hundred years ago. Hester – need I say that Hester is my better half! – is just delighted with it, and if either of us was in the least degree superstitious, we might see or hear ghosts every hour of the day. Of course, as becomes a castle, we have a haunted room, though my own impression is that it is haunted by nothing more fearsome than rats. Anyway, it is such a picturesque, curious sort of chamber that if it hasn't a ghost it ought to have. But I have no doubt, old chap, that you will make one of us, for, as I remember, you have always had a love for the eerie and creepy, and you cannot forget how angry you used to get with me sometimes for chaffing you about your avowed belief in the occult and supernatural, and what you were pleased to term the 'unexplainable phenomena of psychomancy.' However, it is possible you have got over some of the errors of your youth but whether or not, come down, dear boy, and rest assured that you will meet with the heartiest of welcomes.

Your old pal,
DICK DIRCKMAN.

THE ABOVE LETTER was from my old friend and college chum, who, having inherited a substantial fortune, and being passionately fond of the country and country pursuits, had thus the means of gratifying his tastes to their fullest bent. Although Dick and I were very differently constituted, we had always been greatly attached to each other. In the best sense of the term he was what is generally called a hard-headed, practical man. He was fond of saying he never believed in anything he couldn't see, and even that which he could see he was not prepared to accept as truth without due investigation. In short, Dick was neither romantic, poetical, nor, I am afraid, artistic, in the literal sense. He preferred facts to fancies, and was possessed of what the world generally calls 'an unimpressionable nature'. For nearly four years I had lost sight of my friend, as I had been wandering about Europe as tutor and companion to a delicate young nobleman. His death had set me free; but I had no sooner returned to England than I was offered and accepted a lucrative appointment in the service of his Highness the Nizam of Chundlepore, in Northern India, and there was every probability of my being absent for a number of years.

On returning home I had written to Dick to the chambers he had formerly occupied, telling him of my appointment, and expressing a fear that unless we could snatch a day or two in town I might not be able to see him, as I had so many things to do. It was true I had promised that when opportunity occurred I should do myself the pleasure of accepting his oft-proffered hospitality which I knew to be lavish and generous. I had not heard of his marriage; his letter gave me the first intimation of that fact, and I confess that when I got his missive I experienced some curiosity to know the kind of lady he had succeeded in captivating. I had always had an idea that Dick was cut out for a bachelor, for there was nothing of the ladies' man about him, and he used at one time to speak of the gentler sex with a certain levity and brusqueness of manner that by no means found favour with the majority of his friends. And now Dick was actually married, and living in a remote region, where most town-bred people would die of ennui.

It will be gathered from the foregoing remarks that I did not hesitate about accepting Dick's cordial invitation. I determined to spare a few days at least of my somewhat limited time, and duly noted Dick to that effect, giving him the date of my departure from London, and the hour at which I should arrive at the station nearest to his residence.

Bleak Hill Castle was situated in one of the most picturesque parts of Wales; consequently, on the day appointed I found myself comfortably ensconced in a smoking carriage of a London and North-Western train. And towards the close of the day – the time of the year was May – I was the sole passenger to alight at the wayside station, where Dick awaited me with a smart dog-cart. His greeting was hearty and robust, and when his man had packed in my traps he gave the handsome little mare that drew the cart the reins, and we spanked along the country roads in rare style. Dick always prided himself on his knowledge of horseflesh, and with a sense of keen satisfaction he drew my attention to the points of the skittish little mare which bowled along as if we had been merely featherweights.

A drive of eight miles through the bracing Welsh air so sharpened our appetites that the smell of dinner was peculiarly welcome; and telling me to make a hurried toilet, as his cook would not risk her reputation by keeping a dinner waiting, Dick handed me over to the guidance of a natty chambermaid. As it was dark when we arrived I had no opportunity of observing the external characteristics of Bleak Hill Castle; but there was nothing in the interior that suggested bleakness. Warmth, comfort, light, held forth promise of carnal delights.

Following my guide up a broad flight of stairs, and along a lofty and echoing corridor, I found myself in a large and comfortably furnished bedroom. A bright wood fire burned upon the hearthstone, for although it was May the temperature was still very low on the Welsh hills. Hastily changing my clothes, I made my way to the dining room, where Mrs. Dirckman emphasised the welcome her husband had already given me. She was an exceedingly pretty and rather delicate-looking little woman, in striking contrast to her great, bluff, busy husband. A few neighbours had been gathered together to meet me, and we sat down, a dozen all told, to a dinner that from a gastronomic point of view left nothing to be desired. The viands were appetising, the wines perfect, and all the appointments were in perfect consonance with the good things that were placed before us.

It was perhaps natural, when the coffee and cigar stage had arrived, that conversation should turn upon our host's residence, by way of affording me – a stranger to the district – some information. Of course, the information was conveyed to me in a scrappy way, but I gathered in substance that Bleak Hill Castle had originally belonged to a Welsh family, which was chiefly distinguished by the extravagance and gambling propensities of its male members. It had gone through some exciting times, and numerous strange and startling stories had come to centre round it. There were stories of wrong, and shame, and death, and more than a suggestion of dark crimes. One of these stories turned upon the mysterious disappearance of the wife and daughter of a young scion of the house, whose career had been somewhat shady. His wife was considerably older than he, and it was generally supposed that he had married her for money. His daughter, a girl of about twelve, was an epileptic patient, while the husband and father was a gloomy, disappointed man. Suddenly the wife and daughter disappeared. At first no surprise was felt; but, then some curiosity was expressed to know where they had gone to and curiosity led to wonderment, and wonderment to rumour – for people will gossip, especially in a country district. Of course, Mr. Greeta Jones, the husband, had to submit to much questioning as to where his wife and child were staying. But being sullen and morose of temperament he contented himself by brusquely and tersely saying, "They had gone to London." But as no one had seen them go, and no one had heard of their going, the statement was accepted as a perversion of fact. Nevertheless, incredible as it may seem, no one thought it worth his while to insist upon an investigation, and a few weeks later Greeta Jones himself went away – and to London, as was placed beyond doubt. For a long time Bleak Hill Castle was shut up, and throughout the countryside it began to be whispered that sights and sounds had been seen and heard at the castle which were suggestive of things unnatural, and soon it became a crystallised belief in men's minds that the place was haunted.

On the principle of giving a dog a bad name you have only to couple ghosts with the name of an old country residence like this castle for it to fall into disfavour, and to be generally shunned. As might have been expected in such a region, the castle was shunned; no tenant could be found for it. It was allowed to go to ruin, and for a long time was the haunt of smugglers. They were cleared out in the process of time, and at last hard-headed, practical Dick Dirckman heard of the place through a London agent, went down to see it, took a fancy to it, bought it for an old song, and, having taste and money, he soon converted the half-ruined building into a country gentleman's home, and thither he carried his bride.

Such was the history of Bleak Hill Castle as I gathered it in outline during the postprandial chat on that memorable evening.

On the following day I found the place all that my host had described it in his letter to me. Its situation was beautiful in the extreme; and there wasn't one of its windows that didn't command a magnificent view of landscape and sea. He and I rambled about the house, he evinced a keen delight in showing me every nook and corner, in expatiating on the beauties of the locality generally, and of the advantages of his dwelling-place in particular. Why he reserved taking me to the so-called haunted chamber until the last I never have known; but so it was; and as he threw open the heavy door and ushered me into the apartment he smiled ironically and remarked:

"Well, old man, this is the ghost's den; and as I consider that a country mansion of this kind should, in the interests of all tradition and of fiction writers, who, under the guise of truth, he like Ananias, have its haunted room, I have let this place go untouched, except that I have made it a sort of lumber closet for some antique and mouldering old furniture which I picked up a bargain in Wardour Street, London. But I needn't tell you that I regard the ghost stories as rot."

I did not reply to my friend at once, for the room absorbed my attention. It was unquestionably the largest of the bedrooms in the house, and, while in keeping with the rest of the house, had characteristics of its own. The walls were panelled with dark oak, the floor was oak, polished. There was a deep V-shaped bay, formed by an angle of the castle, and in each side of the bay was a diamond-paned window, and under each window an oak seat, which was also a chest with an ancient iron lock. A large wooden bedstead with massive hangings stood in one corner, and the rest of the furniture was of a very nondescript character, and calls for no special mention. In a word, the room was picturesque, and to me it at once suggested the mise-en-scène for all sorts of dramatic situations of a weird and eerie character. I ought to add that there was a very large fireplace with a most capacious hearthstone, on which stood a pair of ponderous and rusty steel dogs. Finally, the window commanded superb views, and altogether my fancy was pleased, and my artistic susceptibilities appealed to in an irresistible manner, so that I replied to my friend thus:

"I like this room, Dick, awfully. Let me occupy it, will you?"

He laughed.

"Well, upon my word, you are an eccentric fellow to want to give up the comfortable den which I have assigned to you for this mouldy, draughty, dingy old lumber room. However" – here he shrugged his shoulders – "there is no accounting for tastes, and as this is liberty hall, my friends do as they like; so I'll tell the servants to put the bed in order, light a fire, and cart your traps from the other room."

I was glad I had carried my point, for I frankly confess to having romantic tendencies. I was fond of old things, old stories and legends, old furniture, and anything that was removed above the dull level of commonplaceness. This room in a certain sense, was unique, and I was charmed with it.

When pretty little Mrs. Dirckman heard of the arrangements she said, with a laugh that did not conceal a certain nervousness, "I am sorry you are going to sleep in that wretched room. It always makes me shudder, for it seems so uncomfortable. Besides, you know, although Dick laughs at me and calls me a little goose, I am inclined to believe there may be some foundation for the current stories. Anyway, I wouldn't sleep in the room for a crown of gold. I hope you will be comfortable, and not be frightened to death or into insanity by gruesome apparitions."

I hastened to assure my hostess that I should be comfortable enough, while as for apparitions, I was not likely to be frightened by them.

The rest of the day was spent exploring the country round about, and after a recherché dinner Dick and I played billiards until one o'clock, and then having drained a final 'peg', I retired to rest. When I reached the haunted chamber I found that much had been done to give an air of cheerfulness and comfort to the place. Some rugs had been laid about the floor, a modern chair or two introduced, a wood fire blazed on the hearth. On a little 'occasional table' that stood near the fire was a silver jug, filled with hot water, and an antique decanter containing spirits, together with lemon and sugar, in case I wanted a final brew. I could not but feel grateful for my host and hostess's thoughtfulness, and, having donned my dressing gown and slippers, I drew a chair within the radius of the wood fire's glow, and proceeded to fill my pipe for a few whiffs previous to tumbling into bed. This was a habit of mine – a habit of years and years of growth, and, while perhaps an objectionable one in some respects, it afforded me solace and conduced to restful sleep. So I lit my pipe, and fell to pondering and trying to see if I could draw any suggestiveness as to my future from the glowing embers. Suddenly a remarkable thing happened. My pipe was drawn gently from my lips and laid upon the table, and at the same moment I heard what seemed to me to be a sigh. For a moment or two I felt confused, and wondered whether I was awake or dreaming. But there was the pipe on the table, and I could have taken the most solemn oath that to the best of my belief it had been placed there by unseen hands.

My feelings, as may be imagined, were peculiar. It was the first time in my life that I had ever been the subject of a phenomenon which was capable of being attributed to supernatural agency. After a little reflection, and some reasoning with myself, however, I tried to believe that my own senses had made a fool of me, and that in a half-somnolent and dreamy condition I had removed the pipe myself, and placed it on the table. Having come to this conclusion I divested myself of my clothing, extinguished the two tall candles, and jumped into bed. Although usually a good sleeper, I did not go to sleep at once, as was my wont, but lay thinking of many things, and mingling with my changing thoughts was a low, monotonous undertone – nature's symphony – of booming sea on the distant beach, and a bass piping – rising occasionally to a shrill and weird upper note – of the wind. From its situation the house was exposed to every wind that blew, hence its name 'Bleak Hill Castle', and probably a south-east gale would have made itself felt to an uncomfortable degree in this room, which was in the south-east angle of the building. But now the booming sea and wind had a lullaby effect, and my nerves sinking into restful repose I fell asleep. How long I slept I do not know, and never shall know; but I awoke suddenly, and with a start, for it seemed as if a stream of ice-cold water was pouring over my face. With an impulse of indefinable alarm I sprang up in bed, and then a strange, awful, ghastly sight met my view.

I don't know that I could be described as a nervous man in any sense of the word. Indeed, I think I may claim to be freer from nerves than the average man, nor would my worst enemy, if he had a regard for truth, accuse me of lacking courage. And yet I confess here, frankly, that the sight I gazed upon appalled me. Yet was I fascinated with a horrible fascination, that rendered it impossible for me to turn my eyes away. I seemed bound by some strange weird spell. My limbs appeared to have grown rigid; there was a sense of burning in my eyes; my mouth was parched and dry; my tongue swollen, so it seemed. Of course, these were mere sensations, but they were sensations I never wish to experience again. They were sensations that tested my sanity. And the sight that held me in the thrall was truly calculated to test the nerves of the strongest.

There, in mid-air, between floor and ceiling, surrounded or made visible by a trembling nebulous light, that was weird beyond the power of any words to describe, was the head and bust of a woman. The face was paralysed into an unutterably awful expression of stony horror; the long black hair was tangled and dishevelled, and the eyes appeared to be bulging from the head. But this was not all. Two ghostly hands were visible. The fingers of one were twined savagely in the black hair, and the other grasped a long-bladed knife, and with it hacked, and gashed, and tore, and stabbed at the bare white throat of the woman, and the blood gushed forth from the jagged wounds, reddening the spectre hand and flowing in one continuous stream to the oak floor, where I heard it *drip, drip, drip* until my brain seemed as if it would burst, and I felt as if I was going raving mad. Then I saw with my strained eyes the unmistakable sign of death pass over the woman's face; and next, the devilish hands flung the mangled remnants away, and I heard a low chuckle of satisfaction – heard, I say, and swear it, as plainly as I have ever heard anything in this world. The light had faded; the vision of crime and death I had gone, and yet the spell held me. Although the night was cold, I believe I was bathed in perspiration. I think I tried to cry out – nay, I am sure I did – but no sound came from my burning, parched lips; my tongue refused utterance; it clove to the roof of my mouth. Could I have moved so much as a joint of my little finger, I could have broken the spell; at least, such was the idea that occupied my half-stunned brain. It was a nightmare of waking horror, and I shudder now, and shrink within myself as I recall it all. But the revelation – for revelation it was – had not yet reached its final stage. Out of the darkness was once more evolved a faint, phosphorescent glow, and in the midst of it appeared the dead body of a beautiful girl with the throat all gashed and bleeding, the red blood flowing in a crimson blood over her night robe, which only partially concealed her young limbs; and the cruel, spectral hands, dyed with her blood, appeared again, and grasped her, and lifted her, and bore her along. Then that vision faded, and a third appeared. This time I seemed to be looking into a gloomy, damp, arched cave or cellar, and the horror that froze me was intensified as I saw the hands busy preparing a hole in the wall at one end of the cave; and presently they lifted two bodies – the body of the woman, and the body of the young girl – all gory and besmirched; and the hands crushed them into the hole in the wall, and then proceeded to brick them up.

All these things I saw as I have described them, and this I solemnly swear to be the truth as I hope for mercy at the Supreme Judgment.

It was a vision of crime; a vision of merciless, pitiless, damnable murder. How long it all lasted I don't know. Science has told us that dreams which seem to embrace a long series of years, last but seconds; and in the few moments of consciousness that remain to the drowning man his life's scroll is unrolled before his eyes. This vision of mine, therefore, may only have lasted seconds, but it seemed to me hours, years, nay, an eternity. With that final stage in the ghostly drama of blood and death, the spell was broken, and flinging my arms wildly about, I know that I uttered a great cry as I sprang up in bed.

"Have I been in the throes of a ghastly nightmare?" I asked myself.

Every detail of the horrific vision I recalled, and yet somehow it seemed to me that I had been the victim of a hideous nightmare. I felt strangely ill. I was wet and clammy with perspiration, and nervous to a degree that I had never before experienced in my existence. Nevertheless, I noted everything distinctly. On the hearthstone there was still a mass of glowing red embers. I heard the distant booming of the sea, and round the house the wind moaned with a peculiar, eerie, creepy sound.

Suddenly I sprang from the bed, impelled thereto by an impulse I was bound to obey, and by the same impulse was drawn towards the door. I laid my hand on the handle. I turned it, opened the door, and gazed into the long dark corridor. A sigh fell upon my ears. An unmistakable human sigh, in which was expressed all intensity of suffering and sorrow that thrilled me to the heart. I shrank back, and was about to close the door, when out of the darkness was evolved the glowing figure of a woman clad in blood-stained garments and with dishevelled hair. She turned her white corpse-like face towards me, and her eyes pleaded with a pleading that was irresistible, while she pointed the index finger of her left hand downwards, and then beckoned me. Then I followed whither she led. I could no more resist than the unrestrained needle can resist the attracting magnet. Clad only in my night apparel, and with bare feet and legs, I followed the spectre along the corridor, down the broad oak stairs, traversing another passage to the rear of the building until I found myself standing before a heavy barred door. At that moment the spectre vanished, and I retraced my steps like one who walked in a dream. I got back to my bedroom, but how I don't quite know; nor have any recollection of getting into bed. Hours afterwards I awoke. It was broad daylight. The horror of the night came back to me with overwhelming force, and made me faint and ill. I managed, however, to struggle through with my toilet, and hurried from that haunted room. It was a beautifully fine morning. The sun was shining brightly, and the birds carolled blithely in every tree and bush. I strolled out on to the lawn, and paced up and down. I was strangely agitated, and asked myself over and over again if what I had seen or dreamed about had any significance.

Presently my host came out. He visibly started as he saw me.

"Hullo, old chap. What's the matter with you?" he exclaimed. "You look jolly queer; as though you had been having a bad night of it."

"I have had a bad night."

His manner became more serious and grave.

"What – seen anything?"

"Yes."

"The deuce! You don't mean it, really!"

"Indeed I do. I have gone through a night of horror such as I could not live through again. But let us have breakfast first, and then I will try and make you understand what I have suffered, and you shall judge for yourself whether any significance is to be attached to my dream, or whatever you like to call it."

We walked, without speaking, into the breakfast room, where my charming hostess greeted me cordially; but she, like her husband, noticed my changed appearance, and expressed alarm and anxiety. I reassured her by saying I had had a rather restless night, and didn't feel particularly well, but that it was a mere passing ailment. I was unable to partake of much breakfast, and both my good friend and his wife again showed some anxiety, and pressed me to state the cause of my distress. As I could not see any good cause that was to be gained by concealment, and even at the risk of being laughed at by my host, I recounted the experience I had gone through during the night of terror.

So far from my host showing any disposition to ridicule me, as I quite expected he would have done, he became unusually thoughtful, and presently said:

"Either this is a wild fantasy of your own brain, or there is something in it. The door that the ghost of the woman led you to is situated on the top of a flight of stone steps, leading to a vault below the building, which I have never used, and have never even had the curiosity to enter, though I did once go to the bottom of the steps; but the place was so exceedingly suggestive of a tomb that I mentally exclaimed, 'I've no use for this dungeon', and so I shut it up, bolted and barred the door, and have never opened it since."

I answered that the time had come when he must once more descend into that cellar or vault, whatever it was. He asked me if I would accompany him, and, of course, I said I would. So he summoned his head gardener, and after much searching about, the key of the door was found; but even then the door was only opened with difficulty, as lock and key alike were foul with rust.

As we descended the slimy, slippery stone steps, each of us carrying a candle, a rank, mouldy smell greeted us, and a cold noisome atmosphere pervaded the place. The steps led into a huge vault, that apparently extended under the greater part of the building. The roof was arched, and was supported by brick pillars. The floor was the natural earth, and was soft and oozy. The miasma was almost overpowering, notwithstanding that there were ventilating slits in the wall in various places.

We proceeded to explore this vast cellar, and found that there was an air shaft which apparently communicated with the roof of the house; but it was choked with rubbish, old boxes, and the like. The gardener cleared this away, and then looking up, we could see the blue sky overhead.

Continuing our exploration, we noted that in a recess formed by the angle of the walls was a quantity of bricks and mortar. Under other circumstances this would not, perhaps, have aroused our curiosity or suspicions. But in this instance it did; and we examined the wall thereabouts with painful interest, until the conviction was forced upon us that a space of over a yard in width, and extending from door to roof, had recently been filled in. I was drawn towards the new brickwork by some subtle magic, some weird fascination. I examined it with an eager, critical, curious interest, and the thoughts that passed through my brain were reflected in the faces of my companions. We looked at each other, and each knew by some unexplainable instinct what was passing in his fellow's mind.

"It seems to me we are face to face with some mystery," remarked Dick, solemnly. Indeed, throughout all the years I had known him I had never before seen him so serious. Usually his expression was that of good-humoured cynicism, but now he might have been a judge about to pass the doom of death on a red-handed sinner.

"Yes," I answered, "there is a mystery, unless I have been tricked by my own fancy."

"Umph! It is strange," muttered Dick to himself.

"Well, sir," chimed in the gardener, "you know there have been some precious queer stories going about for a long time. And before you come and took the place plenty of folks round about used to say they'd seen some uncanny sights. I never had no faith in them stories myself; but, after all, maybe there's truth in 'em."

Dick picked up half a brick and began to tap the wall with it where the new work was, and the taps gave forth a hollow sound, quite different from the sound produced when the other parts of the wall were struck.

"I say, old chap," exclaimed my host, with a sorry attempt at a smile, "upon my word, I begin to experience a sort of uncanny kind of feeling. I'll be hanged if I am not getting as superstitious as you are."

"You may call me superstitious if you like, but either I have seen what I have seen, or my senses have played the fool with me. Anyway, let us put it to the test."

"How?"

"By breaking away some of that new brickwork."

Dick laughed a laugh that wasn't a laugh, as he asked:

"What do you expect to find?" I hesitated what to say, and he added the answer himself – "Mouldering bones, if our ghostly visitor hasn't deceived you."

"Mouldering bones!" I echoed involuntarily.

"Gardener, have you got a crowbar amongst your tools?" Dick asked.

"Yes, sir."

"Go up and get it."

The man obeyed the command.

"This is a strange sort of business altogether," Dick continued, after glancing round the vast and gloomy cellar. "But, upon my word, to tell you the truth, I'm half ashamed of myself for yielding to anything like superstition. It strikes me that you'll find you are the victim of a trick of the imagination, and that these bogey fancies of yours have placed us in rather a ridiculous position."

In answer to this I could not possibly resist reminding Dick that even scientists admitted that there were certain phenomena – they called them 'natural phenomena' – that could not be accounted for by ordinary laws.

Dick shrugged his shoulders and remarked with assumed indifference:

"Perhaps – perhaps it is so." He proceeded to fill his pipe with tobacco, and having lit it he smoked with a nervous energy quite unusual with him.

The gardener was only away about ten minutes, but it seemed infinitely longer. He brought both a pickaxe and a crowbar with him, and in obedience to his master's orders he commenced to hack at the wall. A brick was soon dislodged. Then the crowbar was inserted in the hole, and a mass prized out. From the opening came forth a sickening odour, so that we all drew back instinctively, and I am sure we all shuddered, and I saw the pipe fall from Dick's lips; but he snatched it up quickly and puffed at it vigorously until a cloud of smoke hung in the fetid and stagnant air. Then picking up a candle from the ground, where it had been placed, he approached the hole, holding the candle in such a position that its rays were thrown into the opening. In a few moments he started back with an exclamation:

"My God! The ghost hasn't lied," he said, and I noticed that his face paled. I peered into the hole and so did the gardener, and we both drew back with a start, for sure enough in that recess were decaying human remains.

"This awful business must be investigated," said Dick. "Come, let us go."

We needed no second bidding. We were only too glad to quit that place of horror, and get into the fresh air and bright sunlight. We verily felt that we had come up out of a tomb, and we knew that once more the adage, 'Murder will out', had proved true.

Half an hour later Dick and I were driving to the nearest town to lay information of the awful discovery we had made, and the subsequent search carried out by the police brought two skeletons to light. Critical medical examination left not the shadow of a doubt that they were the remains of a woman and a girl and each had been brutally murdered. Of course it became necessary to hold an inquest, and the police set to work to collect evidence as to the identity of the bodies hidden in the recess in the wall.

Naturally all the stories which had been current for so many years throughout the country were revived, and the gossips were busy in retelling all they had heard, with many additions of their own, of course. But the chief topic was that of the strange disappearance of the wife and daughter of the once-owner of the castle, Greeta Jones. This story had been touched upon the previous night, during the after-dinner chat in my host's smoking room. Morgan, as was remembered had gambled his fortune away, and married a lady much older than himself, who bore him a daughter who was subject to epileptic fits. When this girl was about twelve she and her mother disappeared from the neighbourhood, and, according to the husband's account, they had gone to London.

Then he left, and people troubled themselves no more about him and his belongings.

A quarter of a century had passed since that period, and Bleak Hill Castle had gone through many vicissitudes until it fell into the hands of my friend Dick Dirckman. The more the history of Greeta Jones was gone into the more it was made clear that the remains which had been bricked up in the cellar were those of his wife and daughter. That the unfortunate girl and woman had been brutally and barbarously murdered there wasn't a doubt. The question was, who murdered them? After leaving Wales Greeta Jones – as was brought to light – led a wild life in London. One night, while in a state of intoxication, he was knocked down by a cab, and so seriously injured that he died while being carried to the hospital; and with him his secret, for could there be any reasonable doubt that, even if he was not the actual murderer, he had connived at the crime. But there was reason to believe that he killed his wife and child with his own hand, and that with the aid of a navvy, whose services he bought, he bricked the bodies up in the cellar. It was remembered that a navvy named Howell Williams had been in the habit of going to the castle frequently, and that suddenly he became possessed of what was, for him, a considerable sum of money. For several weeks he drank hard; then being a single man, he packed up his few belongings and gave out that he was going to California, and all efforts to trace him failed.

So much for this ghastly crime. As to the circumstances that led to its discovery, it was curious that I should have been selected as the medium for bringing it to light. Why it should have been so I cannot and do not pretend to explain. I have recorded facts as they occurred; I leave others to solve the mystery.

A Night on the Borders of the Black Forest

Amelia B. Edwards

MY STORY (if story it can be called, being an episode in my own early life) carries me back to a time when the world and I were better friends than we are likely, perhaps, ever to be again. I was young then. I had good health, good spirits, and tolerably good looks. I had lately come into a snug little patrimony, which I have long since dissipated; and I was in love, or fancied myself in love, with a charming coquette, who afterwards threw me over for a West-country baronet with seven thousand a year.

So much for myself. The subject is not one that I particularly care to dwell upon; but as I happen to be the hero of my own narrative, some sort of self-introduction is, I suppose, necessary.

To begin then – Time: seventeen years ago.

Hour: – three o'clock p.m., on a broiling, cloudless September afternoon.

Scene: – a long, straight, dusty road, bordered with young trees; a far-stretching, undulating plain, yellow for the most part with corn-stubble; singularly barren of wood and water; sprinkled here and there with vineyards, farmsteads, and hamlets; and bounded in the extreme distance by a low chain of purple hills.

Place: – a certain dull, unfrequented district in the little kingdom of Würtemberg, about twelve miles north of Heilbronn, and six south-east of the Neckar.

Dramatis Personae: – myself, tall, sunburnt, dusty; in grey suit, straw hat, knapsack and gaiters. In the distance, a broad-backed pedestrian wielding a long stick like an old English quarter-staff.

Now, not being sure that I took the right turning at the crossroads a mile or two back, and having plodded on alone all day, I resolved to overtake this same pedestrian, and increased my pace accordingly. He, meanwhile, unconscious of the vicinity of another traveller, kept on at an easy 'sling-trot', his head well up, his staff swinging idly in his hand – a practised pedestrian, evidently, and one not easily out-walked through a long day.

I gained upon him, however, at every step, and could have passed him easily; but as I drew near he suddenly came to a halt, disencumbered himself of his wallet, and stretched himself at full length under a tree by the wayside.

I saw now that he was a fine, florid, handsome fellow of about twenty-eight or thirty years of age – a thorough German to look at; frank, smiling, blue-eyed; dressed in a light holland blouse and loose grey trousers, and wearing on his head a little crimson cap with a gold tassel, such as the students wear at Heidelberg university. He lifted it, with the customary "Guten Abend" as I came up, and when I stopped to speak, sprang to his feet with ready politeness, and remained standing.

"Niedersdorf, mein Herr?" said he, in answer to my inquiry. "About four miles farther on. You have but to keep straight forward."

"Many thanks," I said. "You were resting. I am sorry to have disturbed you."

He put up his hand with a deprecating gesture.

"It is nothing," he said. "I have walked far, and the day is warm."

"I have only walked from Heilbronn, and yet I am tired. Pray don't let me keep you standing."

"Will you also sit, mein Herr?" he asked with a pleasant smile. "There is shade for both."

So I sat down, and we fell into conversation. I began by offering him a cigar; but he pulled out his pipe – a great dangling German pipe, with a flexible tube and a painted china bowl like a small coffee-cup.

"A thousand thanks," he said; "but I prefer this old pipe to all the cigars that ever came out of Havannah. It was given to me eight years ago, when I was a student; and my friend who gave it to me is dead."

"You were at Heidelberg?" I said interrogatively.

"Yes; and Fritz (that was my friend) was at Heidelberg also. He was a wonderful fellow; a linguist, a mathematician, a botanist, a geologist. He was only five-and-twenty when the government appointed him naturalist to an African exploring party; and in Africa he died."

"Such a man," said I, "was a loss to the world."

"Ah, yes," he replied simply; "but a greater loss to me."

To this I could answer nothing; and for some minutes we smoked in silence.

"I was not clever like Fritz," he went on presently. "When I left Heidelberg, I went into business, I am a brewer, and I live at Stuttgart. My name is Gustav Bergheim – what is yours?"

"Hamilton," I replied; "Chandos Hamilton."

He repeated the name after me.

"You are an Englishman?" he said.

I nodded.

"Good. I like the English. There was an Englishman at Heidelberg – such a good fellow! His name was Smith. Do you know him?"

I explained that, in these fortunate islands, there were probably some thirty thousand persons named Smith, of whom, however, I did not know one.

"And are you a milord, and a Member of Parliament?"

I laughed, and shook my head.

"No, indeed," I replied; "neither. I read for the bar; but I do not practise. I am an idle man – of very little use to myself, and of none to my country."

"You are travelling for your amusement?"

"I am. I have just been through the Tyrol and as far as the Italian lakes on foot, as you see me. But tell me about yourself. That is far more interesting."

"About myself?" he said smiling. "Ah, mein Herr, there is not much to tell. I have told you that I live at Stuttgart. Well, at this time of the year, I allow myself a few weeks' holiday, and I am now on my way to Frankfort, to see my Mädchen, who lives there with her parents."

"Then I may congratulate you on the certainty of a pleasant time."

"Indeed, yes. We love each other well, my Mädchen and I. Her name is Frederika, and her father is a rich banker and wine merchant. They live in the Neue Mainzer Strasse near the Taunus Gate; but the Herr Hamilton does not, perhaps, know Frankfort?"

I replied that I knew Frankfort very well, and that the Neue Mainzer Strasse was, to my thinking, the pleasantest situation in the city. And then I ventured to ask if the Fräulein Frederika was pretty.

"I think her so," he said with his boyish smile; "but then, you see, my eyes are in love. You shall judge, however, for yourself."

And with this, he disengaged a locket from his watch-chain, opened it, and showed me the portrait of a golden-haired girl, who, without being actually handsome, had a face as pleasant to look upon as his own.

"Well?" he said anxiously. "What do you say?"

"I say that she has a charming expression," I replied.

"But you do not think her pretty?"

"Nay, she is better than pretty. She has the beauty of real goodness."

His face glowed with pleasure.

"It is true," he said, kissing the portrait, and replacing it upon his chain. "She is an angel! We are to be married in the Spring."

Just at this moment, a sturdy peasant came trudging up from the direction of Niedersdorf, under the shade of a huge red cotton umbrella. He had taken his coat off, probably for coolness, or it might be for economy, and was carrying it, neatly folded up, in a large, new wooden bucket. He saluted us with the usual "Guten Abend" as he approached.

To which Bergheim laughingly replied by asking if the bucket was a love-token from his sweetheart.

"Nein, nein," he answered stolidly; "I bought it at the Kermess up yonder."

"So! There is a Kermess at Niedersdorf?"

"Ach, Himmel! – a famous Kermess. All the world is there today."

And with a nod, he passed on his way.

My new friend indulged in a long and dismal whistle.

"Der Teufel!" he said, "this is awkward. I'll be bound, now, there won't be a vacant room at any inn in the town. And I had intended to sleep at Niedersdorf tonight. Had you?"

"Well, I should have been guided by circumstances. I should perhaps have put up at Niedersdorf, if I had found myself tired and the place comfortable; or I might have dined there, and after dinner taken some kind of light vehicle as far as Rotheskirche."

"Rotheskirche!" he repeated. "Where is that?"

"It is a village on the Neckar. My guidebook mentions it as a good starting-point for pedestrians, and I am going to walk from there to Heidelberg."

"But have you not been coming out of your way?"

"No; I have only taken a shortcut inland, and avoided the dull part of the river. You know the Neckar, of course?"

"Only as far as Neckargemünd; but I have heard that higher up it is almost as fine as the Rhine."

"Hadn't you better join me?" I said, as we adjusted our knapsacks and prepared to resume our journey.

He shook his head, smiling.

"Nay," he replied, "my route leads me by Buchen and Darmstadt. I have no business to go round by Heidelberg."

"It would be worth the détour."

"Ah, yes; but it would throw me two days later."

"Not if you made up for lost time by taking the train from Heidelberg."

He hesitated.

"I should like it," he said.

"Then why not do it?"

"Well – yes – I will do it. I will go with you. There! Let us shake hands on it, and be friends."

So we shook hands, and it was settled.

The shadows were now beginning to lengthen; but the sun still blazed in the heavens with unabated intensity. Bergheim, however, strode on as lightly, and chatted as gaily, as if his day's work was only just beginning. Never was there so simple, so open-hearted a fellow. He wore his heart literally upon his sleeve, and, as we went along, told me all his little history; how, for instance, his elder sister, having been betrothed to his friend Fritz, had kept single ever since for his sake; how he was himself an only son, and the idol of his mother, now a widow; how he had resolved never to leave either her or his maiden sister; but intended when he married to take a larger house, and bring his wife into their common home; how Frederika's father had at first opposed their engagement for that reason; how Frederika (being, as he had already said, an angel) had won the father's consent last New Year's Day; and how happy he was now; and how happy they should be in the good time coming; together with much more to the same effect.

To all this I listened, and smiled, and assented, putting in a word here and there, as occasion offered, and encouraging him to talk on to his heart's content.

And now with every mile that brought us nearer to Niedersdorf, the signs of fair-time increased and multiplied. First came straggling groups of homeward-bound peasants – old men and women tottering under the burden of newly purchased household goods; little children laden with gingerbread and toys; young men and women in their holiday-best – the latter with garlands of oak-leaves bound about their hats. Then came an open cart full of laughing girls; then more pedestrians; then an old man driving a particularly unwilling pig; then a roystering party of foot-soldiers; and so on, till not only the road, but the fields on either side and every path in sight, swarmed with a double stream of wayfarers – the one coming from the fair – the other setting towards it.

Presently, through the clouds of dust and tobacco-smoke that fouled the air, a steeple and cottages became visible; and then, quite suddenly, we found ourselves in the midst of the fair.

Here a compact, noisy, smoking, staring, laughing, steaming crowd circulated among the booths; some pushing one way, some another – some intent on buying – some on eating and drinking – some on love-making and dancing. In one place we came upon rows of little open stalls for the sale of every commodity under heaven. In another, we peeped into a great restaurant-booth full of country folks demolishing pyramids of German sausage and seas of Bairisch beer. Yonder, on a raised stage in front of a temporary theatre, strutted a party of strolling players in their gaudy tinsels and ballet-dresses. The noise, the smells, the elbowing, the braying of brass bands, the insufferable heat and clamour, made us glad to push our way through as fast as possible, and take refuge in the village inn. But even here we could scarcely get a moment's attention. There were parties dining and drinking in every room in the house – even in the bedrooms; while the passages, the bar, and the little gardens, front and back, were all full of soldiers, freeshooters, and farmers.

Having with difficulty succeeded in capturing a couple of platters of bread and meat and a measure of beer, we went round to the stable-yard, which was crowded with charrettes, einspänner, and country carts of all kinds. The drivers of some of these were asleep in their vehicles; others were gambling for kreutzers on the ground; none were willing to put their horses to for the purpose of driving us to Rotheskirche-on-the-Neckar.

"Ach, Herr Gott!" said one, "I brought my folks from Frühlingsfeld – near upon ten stunden – and shall have to take them back by and by. That's as much as my beasts can do in one day, and they shouldn't do more for the king!"

"I've just refused five florins to go less than half that distance," said another.

At length one fellow, being somewhat less impracticable than the rest, consented to drive us as far as a certain point where four roads met, on condition that we shared his vehicle with two other travellers, and that the two other travellers consented to let us do so.

"And even so," he added, "I shall have to take them two miles out of their way – but, perhaps, being fair-time, they won't mind that."

As it happened, they were not in a condition to mind that or anything very much, being a couple of freeshooters from the Black Forest, wild with fun and frolic, and somewhat the worse for many potations of Lager-bier. One of them, it seemed, had won a prize at some shooting match that same morning, and they had been celebrating this triumph all day. Having kept us waiting, with the horses in, for at least three-quarters of an hour, they came, escorted by a troop of their comrades, all laughing, talking, and wound up to the highest pitch of excitement. Then followed a scene of last health-drinkings, last hand-shakings, last embracements. Finally, we drove off just as it was getting dusk, followed by many huzzahs, and much waving of grey and green caps.

For the first quarter of an hour they were both very noisy, exchanging boisterous greetings with every passer-by, singing snatches of songs, and laughing incessantly. Then, as the dusk deepened and we left the last stragglers behind, they sank into a tipsy stupor, and ended by falling fast asleep.

Meanwhile, the driver lit his pipe and let his tired horses choose their own pace; the stars came out one by one overhead; and the road, leaving the dead level of the plain, wound upwards through a district that became more hilly with every mile.

Then I also fell asleep – I cannot tell for how long – to be waked by-and-by by the stopping of the charrette, and the voice of the driver, saying:

"This is the nearest point to which I can take these Herren. Will they be pleased to alight?"

I sat up and rubbed my eyes. It was bright starlight. Bergheim was already leaning out, and opening the door. Our fellow-travellers were still sound asleep. We were in the midst of a wild, hilly country, black with bristling pine woods; and had drawn up at an elevated point where four roads meet.

"Which of these are we to take?" asked Bergheim, as he pulled out his purse and counted the stipulated number of florins into the palm of the driver.

The man pointed with his whip in a direction at right angles to the road by which he was himself driving.

"And how far shall we have to walk?"

"To Rotheskirche?"

"Yes – to Rotheskirche."

He grunted doubtfully. "Ugh!" he said, "I can't be certain to a mile or so. It may be twelve or fourteen."

"A good road?"

"Yes – a good road; but hilly. These Herren have only to keep straight forward. They cannot miss the way."

And so he drives off, and leaves us standing in the road. The moon is now rising behind a slope of dark trees – the air is chill – an owl close by utters its tremulous, melancholy cry. Place and hour considered, the prospect of twelve or fourteen miles of a strange road, in a strange country, is anything but exhilarating. We push on, however, briskly; and Bergheim, whose good spirits are invincible, whistles and chatters, and laughs away as gaily as if we were just starting on a brilliant May morning.

"I wonder if you were ever tired in your life!" I exclaim by and by, half peevishly.

"Tired!" he echoes. "Why, I am as tired at this moment as a dog; and would gladly lie down by the roadside, curl myself up under a tree, and sleep till morning. I wonder, by the way, what o'clock it is."

I pulled out my fusee-box, struck a light, and looked at my watch. It was only ten o'clock.

"We have been walking," said Bergheim, "about half an hour, and I don't believe we have done two miles in the time. Well, it can't go on uphill like this all the way!"

"Impossible," I replied. "Rotheskirche is on the level of the river. We must sooner or later begin descending towards the valley of the Neckar."

"I wish it might be sooner, then," laughed my companion, "for I had done a good twenty miles today before you overtook me."

"Well, perhaps we may come upon some place halfway. If so, I vote that we put up for the night, and leave Rotheskirche till the morning."

"Ay, that would be capital!" said he. "If it wasn't that I am as hungry as a wolf, I wouldn't say no to the hut of a charcoal-burner tonight."

And now, plodding on more and more silently as our fatigue increased, we found the pine forests gradually drawing nearer, till by and by they enclosed us on every side, and our road lay through the midst of them. Here in the wood, all was dark – all was silent – not a breath stirred. The moon was rising fast; but the shadows of the pines lay long and dense upon the road, with only a sharp silvery patch breaking through here and there. By and by we came upon a broad space of clearing, dotted over with stacks of brushwood and great symmetrical piles of barked trunks. Then followed another tract of close forest. Then our road suddenly emerged into the full moonlight, and sometimes descending abruptly, sometimes keeping at a dead level for half a mile together, continued to skirt the forest on the left.

"I see a group of buildings down yonder," said Bergheim, pointing to a spot deep in the shadow of the hillside.

I could see nothing resembling buildings, but he stuck to his opinion.

"That they are buildings," he said, "I am positive. More I cannot tell by this uncertain light. It may be a mere cluster of cottages, or it may be a farmhouse, with stacks and sheds close by. I think it is the latter."

Animated by this hope, we now pushed on more rapidly. For some minutes our road carried us out of sight of the spot; but when we next saw it, a long, low, white-fronted house and some other smaller buildings were distinctly visible.

"A mountain farmstead, by all the gods of Olympus!" exclaimed Bergheim, joyously. "This is good fortune! And they are not gone to bed yet, either."

"How do you know that?" I asked.

"Because I saw a light."

"But suppose they do not wish to take us in?" I suggested.

"Suppose an impossibility! Whoever heard of inhospitality among our Black Forest folk?"

"Black Forest!" I repeated. "Do you call this the Black Forest?"

"Undoubtedly. All these wooded hills south of Heidelberg and the Odenwald are outlying spurs and patches of the old legendary Schwarzwald – now dwindling year by year. Hark! The dogs have found us out already!"

As he spoke, a dog barked loudly in the direction of the farm; and then another, and another. Bergheim answered them with a shout. Suddenly a bright light flashed across the darkness – flitted vaguely for a moment to and fro, and then came steadily towards us; resolving itself presently into a lanthorn carried by a man.

We hurried eagerly to meet him – at all, square-built, heavy-browed peasant, about forty years of age.

"Who goes there?" he said, holding the lanthorn high above his head, and shading his eyes with his hand.

"Travellers," replied my companion. "Travellers wanting food and shelter for the night."

The man looked at us for a moment in silence.

"You travel late," he said, at length.

"Ay – and we must have gone on still later, if we had not come upon your house. We were bound for Rotheskirche. Can you take us in."

"Yes," he said sullenly. "I suppose so. This way."

And, swinging the lanthorn as he went, he turned on his heel abruptly, and led the way back to the house.

"A boorish fellow enough!" said I, as we followed.

"Nay – a mere peasant!" replied Bergheim. "A mere peasant – rough, but kindly."

As we drew near the house, two large mastiff pups came rushing out from a yard somewhere at the back, and a huge, tawny dog chained up in an open shed close by, strained at his collar and yelled savagely.

"Down, Caspar! Down, Schwartz!" growled our conductor, with an oath.

And immediately the pups slunk back into the yard, and the dog in the shed dropped into a low snarl, eyeing us fiercely as we passed.

The house-door opened straight upon a large, low, raftered kitchen, with a cavernous fireplace at the further end, flanked on each side by a high-backed settle. The settles, the long table in the middle of the room, the stools and chairs ranged round the walls, the heavy beams overhead, from which hung strings of dried herbs, ropes of onions, hams, and the like, were all of old, dark oak. The ceiling was black with the smoke of at least a century. An oak dresser laden with rough blue and grey ware and rows of metal-lidded drinking mugs; an old blunderbuss and a horn-handled riding-whip over the chimney-piece; a couple of hatchets, a spade, and a fishing rod behind the door; and a Swiss clock in the corner, completed the furniture of the room. A couple of half-charred logs smouldered on the hearth. An oil-lamp flared upon the middle of the table, at one corner of which sat two men with a stone jug and a couple of beer-mugs between them, playing at cards, and a third man looking on. The third man rose as we entered, and came forward. He was so like the one who had come out to meet us, that I saw at once they must be brothers.

"Two travellers," said our conductor, setting down his lanthorn, and shutting the door behind us.

The players laid down their greasy cards to stare at us. The second brother, a trifle more civil than the first, asked if we wished for anything before going to bed.

Bergheim unslung his wallet, flung himself wearily into a corner of the settle, and said:

"Heavens and earth! Yes. We are almost starving. We have been on the road all day, and have had no regular dinner. Is this a farmhouse or an inn?"

"Both."

"What have you in the house?"

"Ham – eggs – voorst – cheese – wine – beer – coffee."

"Then bring us the best you have, and plenty of it, and as fast as you can. We'll begin on the voorst and a bottle of your best wine, while the ham and eggs are frying; and we'll have the coffee to finish."

The man nodded; went to a door at the other end of the room – repeated the order to someone out of sight; and came back again, his hands in his pockets. The first brother, meanwhile, was lounging against the table, looking on at the players.

"It's a long game," he said.

"Ay – but it's just ended," replied one of the men, putting down his card with an air of triumph. His adversary pondered, threw down his hand, and, with a round oath, owned himself beaten. Then they divided the remaining contents of the stone jug, drained their mugs, and rose to go. The loser pulled out a handful of small coin, and paid the reckoning for both.

"We've sat late," said he, with a glance at the clock. "Goodnight, Karl – goodnight, Friedrich."

The first brother, whom I judged to be Karl, nodded sulkily. The second muttered a gruff sort of goodnight. The countrymen lit their pipes, took another long stare at Bergheim and myself, touched their hats, and went away.

The first brother, Karl, who was evidently the master, went out with them, shutting the door with a tremendous bang. The younger, Friedrich, cleared the board, opened a cupboard under the dresser, brought out a loaf of black bread, a lump of voorst, and part of a goat's milk cheese, and then went to fetch the wine. Meanwhile we each drew a chair to the table, and fell to vigorously. When Friedrich returned with the wine, a pleasant smell of broiling ham came in with him through the door.

"You are hungry," he said, looking down at us from under his black brows.

"Ay, and thirsty," replied Gustav, reaching out his hand for the bottle. "Is your wine good?"

The man shrugged his shoulders.

"Drink and judge for yourself," he answered. "It's the best we have."

"Then drink with us," said my companion, good-humouredly, filling a glass and pushing it towards him across the table.

But he shook his head with an ungracious "Nein, nein," and again left the room. The next moment we heard his heavy footfall going to and fro overhead.

"He is preparing our beds," I said. "Are there no women, I wonder, about the place?"

"Well, yes – this looks like one," laughed Bergheim, as the door leading to the inner kitchen again opened, and a big stolid-looking peasant girl came in with a smoking dish of ham and eggs, which she set down before us on the table. "Stop! Stop!" he exclaimed, as she turned away. "Don't be in such a hurry, my girl. What is your name?"

She stopped with a bewildered look, but said nothing. Bergheim repeated the question.

"My – my name?" she stammered. "Annchen."

"Good. Then, Annchen" (filling a bumper and draining it at a draught), "I drink to thy health. Wilt thou drink to mine?" And he pointed to the glass poured out for the landlord's brother.

But she only looked at him in the same scared, stupid way, and kept edging away towards the door.

"Let her go," I said. "She is evidently half an idiot."

"She's no idiot to refuse that wine," replied Bergheim, as the door closed after her. "It's the most abominable mixture I ever put inside my lips. Have you tasted it?"

I had not tasted it as yet, and now I would not; so, the elder brother coming back just at that moment, we called for beer.

"Don't you like the wine?" he said, scowling.

"No," replied Bergheim. "Do you? If so you're welcome to the rest of it."

The landlord took up the bottle and held it between his eyes and the lamp.

"Bad as it is," he said, "you've drunk half of it."

"Not I – only one glass, thanks be to Bacchus! There stands the other. Let us have a Schoppen of your best beer – and I hope it will be better than your best wine."

The landlord looked from Bergheim to the glass – from the glass to the bottle. He seemed to be measuring with his eye how much had really been drunk. Then he went to the inner door;

called to Friedrich to bring a Schoppen of the Bairisch, and went away, shutting the door after him. From the sound of his footsteps, it seemed to us as if he also was gone upstairs, but into some more distant part of the house. Presently the younger brother reappeared with the beer, placed it before us in silence, and went away as before.

"The most forbidding, disagreeable, uncivil pair I ever saw in my life!" said I.

"They're not fascinating, I admit," said Bergheim, leaning back in his chair with the air of a man whose appetite is somewhat appeased. "I don't know which is the worst – their wine or their manners."

And then he yawned tremendously, and pushed out his plate, which I heaped afresh with ham and eggs. When he had swallowed a few mouthfuls, he leaned his head upon his hand, and declared he was too tired to eat more.

"And yet," he added, "I am still hungry."

"Nonsense!" I said; "eat enough now you are about it. How is the beer?"

He took a pull at the Schoppen.

"Capital," he said. "Now I can go on again."

The next instant he was nodding over his plate.

"I am ashamed to be so stupid," he said, rousing himself presently; "but I am overpowered with fatigue. Let us have the coffee; it will wake me up a bit."

But he had no sooner said this than his chin dropped on his breast, and he was sound asleep.

I did not call for the coffee immediately. I let him sleep, and went on quietly with my supper. Just as I had done, however, the brothers came back together, Friedrich bringing the coffee – two large cups on a tray. The elder, standing by the table, looked down at Bergheim with his unfriendly frown.

"Your friend is tired," he said.

"Yes, he has walked far today – much farther than I have."

"Humph! You will be glad to go to bed."

"Indeed we shall. Are our rooms ready?"

"Yes."

I took one of the cups, and put the other beside Bergheim's plate.

"Here, Bergheim," I said, "wake up; the coffee is waiting."

But he slept on, and never heard me.

I then lifted my own cup to my lips – paused – set it down untasted. It had an odd, pungent smell that I did not like.

"What is the matter with it?" I said, "it does not smell like pure coffee."

The brothers exchanged a rapid glance.

"It is the Kirschenwasser," said Karl. "We always put it in our black coffee."

I tasted it, but the flavour of the coffee was quite drowned in that of the coarse, fiery spirit.

"Do you not like it?" asked the younger brother.

"It is very strong," I said.

"But it is very good," replied he; "real Black Forest Kirsch – the best thing in the world, if one is tired after a journey. Drink it off, mein Herr; it is of no use to sip it. It will make you sleep."

This was the longest speech either of them had yet made.

"Thanks," I said, pulling out my cigar case, "but this stuff is too powerful to be drunk at a draught. I shall make it last out a cigar or two."

"And your friend?"

"He is better without the Kirsch, and may sleep till I am ready to go to bed."

Again they looked at each other.

"You need not sit up," I said impatiently; for it annoyed me, somehow, to have them standing there, one at each side of the table, alternately looking at me and at each other. "I will call the Mädchen to show us to our rooms when we are ready."

"Good," said the elder brother, after a moment's hesitation. "Come, Friedrich."

Friedrich turned at once to follow him, and they both left the room.

I listened. I heard them for a while moving to and fro in the inner kitchen; then the sound of their double footsteps going up the stairs; then the murmur of their voices somewhere above, yet not exactly overhead; then silence.

I felt more comfortable, now that they were fairly gone, and not likely to return. I breathed more freely. I had disliked the brothers from the first. I had felt uneasy from the moment I crossed their threshold. Nothing, I told myself, should induce me at any time, or under any circumstances, to put up under their roof again.

Pondering thus, I smoked on, and took another sip of the coffee. It was not so hot now, and some of the strength of the spirit had gone off; but under the flavour of the Kirschenwasser I could (or fancied I could) detect another flavour, pungent and bitter – a flavour, in short, just corresponding to the smell that I had at first noticed.

This startled me. I scarcely knew why, but it did startle me, and somewhat unpleasantly. At the same instant I observed that Bergheim, in the heaviness and helplessness of sleep, had swayed over on one side, and was hanging very uncomfortably across one arm of his chair.

"Come, come," I said, "wake up, Herr fellow-traveller. This sort of dozing will do you no good. Wake up, and come to bed."

And with this I took him by the arm, and tried to rouse him. Then for the first time I observed that his face was deadly white – that his teeth were fast clenched – that his breathing was unnatural and laboured.

I sprang to my feet. I dragged him into an upright posture; I tore open his neckcloth; I was on the point of rushing to the door to call for help, when a suspicion – one of those terrible suspicions which are suspicion and conviction in one – flashed suddenly upon me.

The rejected glass of wine was still standing on the table. I smelt it – tasted it. My dread was confirmed. It had the same pungent odour, the same bitter flavour as the coffee.

In a moment I measured all the horror of my position; alone – unarmed – my unconscious fellow-traveller drugged and helpless on my hands – the murderers overhead, biding their time – the silence and darkness of night – the unfrequented road – the solitary house – the improbability of help from without – the imminence of the danger from within... I saw it all! What could I do? Was there any way, any chance, any hope?

I turned cold and dizzy. I leaned against the table for support. Was I also drugged, and was my turn coming? I looked round for water, but there was none upon the table. I did not dare to touch the beer, lest it also should be doctored.

At that instant I heard a faint sound outside, like the creaking of a stair. My presence of mind had not as yet for a moment deserted me, and now my strength came back at the approach of danger. I cast a rapid glance round the room. There was the blunderbuss over the chimney-piece – there were the two hatchets in the corner. I moved a chair loudly, and hummed some snatches of songs.

They should know that I was awake – this might at least keep them off a little longer. The scraps of songs covered the sound of my footsteps as I stole across the room and secured the hatchets. One of these I laid before me on the table; the other I hid among the wood in the wood-basket beside the hearth – singing, as it were to myself, all the time.

Then I listened breathlessly.

All was silent.

Then I clinked my tea-spoon in my cup – feigned a long yawn – under cover of the yawn took down the blunderbuss from its hook – and listened again.

Still all was silent – silent as death – save only the loud ticking of the clock in the corner, and the heavy beating of my heart.

Then, after a few seconds that dragged past like hours, I distinctly heard a muffled tread stealing softly across the floor overhead, and another very faint retreating creak or two upon the stairs.

To examine the blunderbuss, find it loaded with a heavy charge of slugs, test the dryness of the powder, cock it, and place it ready for use beside the hatchet on the table, was but the work of a moment.

And now my course was taken. My spirits rose with the possession of a certain means of defence, and I prepared to sell my own life, and the life of the poor fellow beside me, as dearly as might be.

I must turn the kitchen into a fortress, and defend my fortress as long as defence was possible. If I could hold it till daylight came to my aid, bringing with it the chances of traffic, of passers-by, of farm-labourers coming to their daily work – then I felt we should be comparatively safe. If, however, I could not keep the enemy out so long, then I had another resource… But of this there was no time to think at present. First of all, I must barricade my fortress.

The windows were already shuttered-up and barred on the inside. The key of the house-door was in the lock, and only needed turning. The heavy iron bolt, in like manner, had only to be shot into its place. To do this, however, would make too much noise just now. First and most important was the door communicating with the inner kitchen and the stairs. This, above all, I must secure; and this, as I found to my dismay, had no bolts or locks whatever on the inside – nothing but a clumsy wooden latch!

To pile against it every moveable in the room was my obvious course; but then it was one that, by the mere noise it must make, would at once alarm the enemy. No! I must secure that door but secure it silently – at all events for the next few minutes.

Inspired by dread necessity, I became fertile in expedients. With a couple of iron forks snatched from the table, I pinned the latch down, forcing the prongs by sheer strength of hand deep into the woodwork of the door. This done, I tore down one of the old rusty bits from its nail above the mantel-shelf, and, linking it firmly over the thump-piece of the latch on one side, and over the clumsy catch on the other, I improvised a door-chain that would at least act as a momentary check in case the door was forced from without. Lastly, by means of some half-charred splinters from the hearth, I contrived to wedge up the bottom of the door in such a manner that, the more it was pushed inwards, the more firmly fixed it must become.

So far my work had been noiseless, but now the time was come when it could be so no longer. The house-door must be secured at all costs; and I knew beforehand that I could not move those heavy fastenings unheard. Nor did I. The key, despite all my efforts, grated loudly in the lock, and the bolt resisted the rusty staples. I got it in, however, and the next moment heard rapid footsteps overhead.

I knew now that the crisis was coming, and from this moment prepared for open resistance.

Regardless of noise, I dragged out first one heavy oaken settle, and then the other – placed them against the inner door – piled them with chairs, stools, firewood, every heavy thing I could lay hands upon – raked the slumbering embers, and threw more wood upon the hearth, so as to bar that avenue, if any attempt was made by way of the chimney – and hastily ransacked every drawer in the dresser, in the hope of finding something in the shape of ammunition.

Meanwhile, the brothers had taken alarm, and having tried the inner door, had now gone round to the front, where I heard them try first the house-door and then the windows.

"Open! Open, I say!" shouted the elder – (I knew him by his voice). "What is the matter within?"

"The matter is that I choose to spend the night in this room," I shouted in reply.

"It is a public room – you have no right to shut the doors!" he said, with a thundering blow upon the lock.

"Right or no right," I answered, "I shoot dead the first man who forces his way in!"

There was a momentary silence, and I heard them muttering together outside.

I had by this time found, at the back of one of the drawers, a handful of small shot screwed up in a bit of newspaper, and a battered old powder-flask containing about three charges of powder. Little as it was, it helped to give me confidence.

Then the parleying began afresh.

"Once more, accursed Englishman will you open the door?"

"No."

A torrent of savage oaths – then a pause.

"Force us to break it open, and it will be the worse for you!"

"Try."

All this time I had been wrenching out the hooks from the dresser, and the nails, wherever I could find any, from the walls. Already I had enough to reload the blunderbuss three times, with my three charges of powder. If only Bergheim were himself now…!

I still heard the murmuring of the brothers' voices outside – then the sound of their retreating footsteps – then an outburst of barking and yelping at the back, which showed they had let loose the dogs. Then all was silent.

Where were they gone? How would they begin the attack? In what way would it all end? I glanced at my watch. It was just twenty minutes past one. In two hours and at half, or three hours, it would be dawn. Three hours! Great Heavens! What an eternity!

I looked round to see if there was anything I could still do for defence; but it seemed to me that I had already done what little it was possible to do with the material at hand. I could only wait.

All at once I heard their footsteps in the house again. They were going rapidly to and fro overhead; then up and down the stairs; then overhead again; and presently I heard a couple of bolts shot, and apparently a heavy wooden bar put up, on the other side of the inner kitchen-door which I had just been at so much pains to barricade. This done, they seemed to go away. A distant door banged heavily; and again there was silence.

Five minutes, ten minutes, went by. Bergheim still slept heavily; but his breathing, I fancied, was less stertorous, and his countenance less rigid, than when I first discovered his condition. I had no water with which to bathe his head; but I rubbed his forehead and the palms of his hands with beer, and did what I could to keep his body upright.

Then I heard the enemy coming back to the front, slowly, and with heavy footfalls. They paused for a moment at the front door, seemed to set something down, and then retreated quickly. After an interval of about three minutes, they returned in the same way; stopped at the same place; and hurried off as before. This they did several times in succession. Listening with suspended breath and my ear against the keyhole, I distinctly heard them deposit some kind of burden each time – evidently a weighty burden, from the way in which they carried it; and yet, strange to say, one that, despite its weight, made scarcely any noise in the setting down.

Just at this moment, when all my senses were concentrated in the one act of listening, Bergheim stirred for the first time, and began muttering.

"The man!" he said, in a low, suppressed tone. "The man under the hearth!"

I flew to him at the first sound of his voice. He was recovering. Heaven be thanked, he was recovering! In a few minutes we should be two – two against two – right and might on our side – both ready for the defence of our lives!

"One man under the hearth," he went on, in the same unnatural tone. "Four men at the bottom of the pond – all murdered – foully murdered!"

I had scarcely heeded his first words; but now, as their sense broke upon me, that great rush of exultation and thankfulness was suddenly arrested. My heart stood still; I trembled; I turned cold with horror.

Then the veins swelled on his forehead; his face became purple; and he struck out blindly, as one oppressed with some horrible nightmare.

"Blood!" he gasped. "Everywhere blood – don't touch it. God's vengeance – help!"

And so, struggling violently in my arms, he opened his eyes, stared wildly round, and made an effort to get upon his feet.

"What is the matter?" he said, sinking back again, and trembling from head to foot. "Was I asleep?"

I rubbed his hands and forehead again with beer. I tasted it, and finding no ill flavour upon it, put a tiny drop to his lips.

"You are all right now," I said. "You were very tired, and you fell asleep after supper. Don't you remember?"

He put his hand to his head. "Ah, yes," he said, "I remember. I have been dreaming…"

He looked round the room in a bewildered way; then, struck all at once by the strange disorder of the furniture, asked what was the matter.

I told him in the least alarming way, and with the fewest words I could muster, but before I could get to the end of my explanation he was up, ready for resistance, and apparently himself again.

"Where are they?" he said. "What are they doing now? Outside, do you say? Why, good heavens! Man, they're blocking us in. Listen! – don't you hear? – it is the rustling of straw. Bring the blunderbuss! Quick! – to the window… God grant we may not be too late!"

We both rushed to the window; Bergheim to undo the shutter, and I to shoot down the first man in sight.

"Look there!" he said, and pointed to the door.

A thin stream of smoke was oozing under the threshold and stealing upward in a filmy cloud that already dimmed the atmosphere of the room.

"They are going to burn us out!" I exclaimed.

"No, they are going to burn us alive," replied Bergheim, between his clenched teeth. "We know too much, and they are determined to silence us at all costs, though they burn the house down over our heads. Now hold your breath, for I am going to open the window, and the smoke will rush in like a torrent."

He opened it, but very little came in – for this reason, that the outside was densely blocked with straw, which had not yet ignited.

In a moment we had dragged the table under the window – put our weapons aside ready for use – and set to work to cut our way out.

Bergheim, standing on the table, wrenched away the straw in great armfuls. I caught it, and hurled it into the middle of the room. We laboured at the work like giants. In a few moments the pile had mounted to the height of the table. Then Bergheim cried out that the straw under his hands was taking fire, and that he dared throw it back into the room no longer!

I sprang to his aid with the two hatchets. I gave him one – I fell to work with the other. The smoke and flame rushed in our faces, as we hewed down the burning straw.

Meanwhile, the room behind us was full of smoke, and above the noise of our own frantic labour we heard a mighty crackling and hissing, as of a great conflagration.

"Take the blunderbuss – quick!" cried Bergheim, hoarsely. "There is nothing but smoke outside now, and burning straw below. Follow me! Jump as far out as you can, and shoot the first you see!"

And with this, he leaped out into the smoke, and was gone!

I only waited to grope out the blunderbuss; then, holding it high above my head, I shut my eyes and sprang after him, clearing the worst of the fire, and falling on my hands and knees among a heap of smouldering straw and ashes beyond. At the same instant that I touched the ground, I heard the sharp crack of a rifle, and saw two figures rush past me.

To dash out in pursuit without casting one backward glance at the burning house behind me – to see a tall figure vanishing among the trees, and two others in full chase – to cover the foremost of these two and bring him down as one would bring down a wolf in the open, was for me but the work of a second.

I saw him fall. I saw the other hesitate, look back, throw up his hands with a wild gesture, and fly towards the hills.

* * *

The rest of my story is soon told. The one I had shot was Friedrich, the younger brother. He died in about half an hour, and never spoke again. The elder escaped into the forest, and there succeeded in hiding himself for several weeks among the charcoal-burners. Being hunted down, however, at last, he was tried at Heilbronn, and there executed.

The pair, it seemed, were practised murderers. The pond, when dragged, was found to contain four of their victims; and when the crumbling ruins of the homestead were cleared for the purpose, the mortal remains of a fifth were discovered under the hearth, in that kitchen which had so nearly proved our grave. A store of money, clothes, and two or three watches, was also found secreted in a granary near the house; and these things served to identify three out of the five corpses thus providentially brought to light.

My friend, Gustav Bergheim (now the friend of seventeen years) is well and prosperous; married to his 'Mädchen'; and the happy father of a numerous family. He often tells the tale of our terrible night on the borders of the Black Forest, and avers that in that awful dream in which his senses came back to him, he distinctly saw, as in a vision, the mouldering form beneath the hearth, and the others under the sluggish waters of the pond.

The Familiar

Joseph Sheridan Le Fanu

Prologue

OUT OF ABOUT two hundred and thirty cases, more or less nearly akin to that I have entitled 'Green Tea', I select the following, which I call 'The Familiar'.

To this MS. Doctor Hesselius, has, after his wont, attached some sheets of letter-paper, on which are written, in his hand nearly as compact as print, his own remarks upon the case. He says:

> *In point of conscience, no more unexceptionable narrator, than the venerable Irish Clergyman who has given me this paper, on Mr. Barton's case, could have been chosen. The statement is, however, medically imperfect. The report of an intelligent physician, who had marked its progress, and attended the patient, from its earlier stages to its close, would have supplied what is wanting to enable me to pronounce with confidence. I should have been acquainted with Mr. Barton's probable hereditary pre-dispositions; I should have known, possibly, by very early indications, something of a remoter origin of the disease than can now be ascertained.*

> *In a rough way, we may reduce all similar cases to three distinct classes. They are founded on the primary distinction between the subjective and the objective. Of those whose senses are alleged to be subject to supernatural impressions – some are simply visionaries, and propagate the illusions of which they complain, from diseased brain or nerves. Others are, unquestionably, infested by, as we term them, spiritual agencies, exterior to themselves. Others, again, owe their sufferings to a mixed condition. The interior sense, it is true, is opened; but it has been and continues open by the action of disease. This form of disease may, in one sense, be compared to the loss of the scarf-skin, and a consequent exposure of surfaces for whose excessive sensitiveness, nature has provided a muffling. The loss of this covering is attended by an habitual impassability, by influences against which we were intended to be guarded. But in the case of the brain, and the nerves immediately connected with its functions and its sensuous impressions, the cerebral circulation undergoes periodically that vibratory disturbance, which, I believe, I have satisfactorily examined and demonstrated, in my MS. Essay, A. 17. This vibratory disturbance differs, as I there prove, essentially from the congestive disturbance, the phenomena of which are examined in A. 19. It is, when excessive, invariably accompanied by illusions.*

> *Had I seen Mr. Barton, and examined him upon the points, in his case, which need elucidation, I should have without difficulty referred those phenomena to their proper disease. My diagnosis is now, necessarily, conjectural.*

Thus writes Doctor Hesselius; and adds a great deal which is of interest only to a scientific physician.

The Narrative of the Rev. Thomas Herbert, which furnishes all that is known of the case, will be found in the chapters that follow.

Chapter I
Footsteps

I WAS a young man at the time, and intimately acquainted with some of the actors in this strange tale; the impression which its incidents made on me, therefore, were deep, and lasting. I shall now endeavour, with precision, to relate them all, combining, of course, in the narrative, whatever I have learned from various sources, tending, however imperfectly, to illuminate the darkness which involves its progress and termination.

Somewhere about the year 1794, the younger brother of a certain baronet, whom I shall call Sir James Barton, returned to Dublin. He had served in the navy with some distinction, having commanded one of His Majesty's frigates during the greater part of the American war. Captain Barton was apparently some two- or three-and-forty years of age. He was an intelligent and agreeable companion when he pleased it, though generally reserved, and occasionally even moody.

In society, however, he deported himself as a man of the world, and a gentleman. He had not contracted any of the noisy brusqueness sometimes acquired at sea; on the contrary, his manners were remarkably easy, quiet, and even polished. He was in person about the middle size, and somewhat strongly formed – his countenance was marked with the lines of thought, and on the whole wore an expression of gravity and melancholy; being, however, as I have said, a man of perfect breeding, as well as of good family, and in affluent circumstances, he had, of course, ready access to the best society of Dublin, without the necessity of any other credentials.

In his personal habits Mr. Barton was unexpensive. He occupied lodgings in one of the then fashionable streets in the south side of the town – kept but one horse and one servant – and though a reputed free-thinker, yet lived an orderly and moral life – indulging neither in gaming, drinking, nor any other vicious pursuit – living very much to himself, without forming intimacies, or choosing any companions, and appearing to mix in gay society rather for the sake of its bustle and distraction, than for any opportunities it offered of interchanging thought or feeling with its votaries.

Barton was therefore pronounced a saving, prudent, unsocial sort of fellow, who bid fair to maintain his celibacy alike against stratagem and assault, and was likely to live to a good old age, die rich, and leave his money to a hospital.

It was now apparent, however, that the nature of Mr. Barton's plans had been totally misconceived. A young lady, whom I shall call Miss Montague, was at this time introduced into the gay world, by her aunt, the Dowager Lady L—. Miss Montague was decidedly pretty and accomplished, and having some natural cleverness, and a great deal of gaiety, became for a while a reigning toast.

Her popularity, however, gained her, for a time, nothing more than that unsubstantial admiration which, however, pleasant as an incense to vanity, is by no means necessarily antecedent to matrimony – for, unhappily for the young lady in question, it was an understood thing, that beyond her personal attractions, she had no kind of earthly provision. Such being the state of affairs, it will readily be believed that no little surprise was consequent upon the appearance of Captain Barton as the avowed lover of the penniless Miss Montague.

His suit prospered, as might have been expected, and in a short time it was communicated by old Lady L— to each of her hundred-and-fifty particular friends in succession, that Captain Barton had actually tendered proposals of marriage, with her approbation, to her niece, Miss Montague, who had, moreover, accepted the offer of his hand, conditionally upon the consent of her father, who was then upon his homeward voyage from India, and expected in two or three weeks at the furthest.

About this consent there could be no doubt – the delay, therefore, was one merely of form – they were looked upon as absolutely engaged, and Lady L—, with a rigour of old-fashioned decorum with which her niece would, no doubt, gladly have dispensed, withdrew her thenceforward from all further participation in the gaieties of the town.

Captain Barton was a constant visitor, as well as a frequent guest at the house, and was permitted all the privileges of intimacy which a betrothed suitor is usually accorded. Such was the relation of parties, when the mysterious circumstances which darken this narrative first began to unfold themselves.

Lady L— resided in a handsome mansion at the north side of Dublin, and Captain Barton's lodgings, as we have already said, were situated at the south. The distance intervening was considerable, and it was Captain Barton's habit generally to walk home without an attendant, as often as he passed the evening with the old lady and her fair charge.

His shortest way in such nocturnal walks, lay, for a considerable space, through a line of street which had as yet merely been laid out, and little more than the foundations of the houses constructed.

One night, shortly after his engagement with Miss Montague had commenced, he happened to remain unusually late, in company with her and Lady L—. The conversation had turned upon the evidences of revelation, which he had disputed with the callous scepticism of a confirmed infidel. What were called 'French principles', had in those days found their way a good deal into fashionable society, especially that portion of it which professed allegiance to Whiggism, and neither the old lady nor her charge was so perfectly free from the taint, as to look upon Mr. Barton's views as any serious objection to the proposed union.

The discussion had degenerated into one upon the supernatural and the marvellous, in which he had pursued precisely the same line of argument and ridicule. In all this, it is but truth to state, Captain Barton was guilty of no affectation – the doctrines upon which he insisted, were, in reality, but too truly the basis of his own fixed belief, if so it might be called; and perhaps not the least strange of the many strange circumstances connected with my narrative, was the fact that the subject of the fearful influences I am about to describe was himself, from the deliberate conviction of years, an utter disbeliever in what are usually termed preternatural agencies.

It was considerably past midnight when Mr. Barton took his leave, and set out upon his solitary walk homeward. He had now reached the lonely road, with its unfinished dwarf walls tracing the foundations of the projected row of houses on either side – the moon was shining mistily, and its imperfect light made the road he trod but additionally dreary – that utter silence which has in it something indefinably exciting, reigned there, and made the sound of his steps, which alone broke it, unnaturally loud and distinct.

He had proceeded thus some way, when he, on a sudden, heard other footfalls, pattering at a measured pace, and, as it seemed, about two score steps behind him.

The suspicion of being dogged is at all times unpleasant; it is, however, especially so in a spot so lonely; and this suspicion became so strong in the mind of Captain Barton, that he abruptly turned about to confront his pursuer; but, though there was quite sufficient moonlight to disclose any object upon the road he had traversed, no form of any kind was visible there.

The steps he had heard could not have been the reverberation of his own, for he stamped his foot upon the ground, and walked briskly up and down, in the vain attempt to awake an echo; though by no means a fanciful person, therefore he was at last fain to charge the sounds upon his imagination, and treat them as an illusion. Thus satisfying himself, he resumed his walk, and before he had proceeded a dozen paces, the mysterious footfall was again audible from behind, and this time, as if with the special design of showing that the sounds were not the responses of an echo – the steps sometimes slackened nearly to a halt, and sometimes hurried for six or eight strides to a run, and again abated to a walk.

Captain Barton, as before, turned suddenly round, and with the same result – no object was visible above the deserted level of the road. He walked back over the same ground, determined that, whatever might have been the cause of the sounds which had so disconcerted him, it should not escape his search – the endeavour, however, was unrewarded.

In spite of all his scepticism, he felt something like a superstitious fear stealing fast upon him, and with these unwonted and uncomfortable sensations, he once more turned and pursued his way. There was no repetition of these haunting sounds, until he had reached the point where he had last stopped to retrace his steps – here they were resumed – and with sudden starts of running, which threatened to bring the unseen pursuer up to the alarmed pedestrian.

Captain Barton arrested his course as formerly – the unaccountable nature of the occurrence filled him with vague and disagreeable sensations – and yielding to the excitement that was gaining upon him, he shouted sternly, "Who goes there?" The sound of one's own voice, thus exerted, in utter solitude, and followed by total silence, has in it something unpleasantly dismaying, and he felt a degree of nervousness which, perhaps, from no cause had he ever known before.

To the very end of this solitary street the steps pursued him – and it required a strong effort of stubborn pride on his part, to resist the impulse that prompted him every moment to run for safety at the top of his speed. It was not until he had reached his lodging, and sat by his own fireside, that he felt sufficiently reassured to rearrange and reconsider in his own mind the occurrences which had so discomposed him. So little a matter, after all, is sufficient to upset the pride of scepticism and vindicate the old simple laws of nature within us.

Chapter II
The Watcher

MR. BARTON was next morning sitting at a late breakfast, reflecting upon the incidents of the previous night, with more of inquisitiveness than awe, so speedily do gloomy impressions upon the fancy disappear under the cheerful influence of day, when a letter just delivered by the postman was placed upon the table before him.

There was nothing remarkable in the address of this missive, except that it was written in a hand which he did not know – perhaps it was disguised – for the tall narrow characters were sloped backward; and with the self-inflicted suspense which we often see practised in such cases, he puzzled over the inscription for a full minute before he broke the seal. When he did so, he read the following words, written in the same hand:

"Mr. Barton, late captain of the Dolphin, is warned of DANGER. He will do wisely to avoid —— street – [here the locality of his last night's adventure was named] – if he walks there as usual he will meet with something unlucky – let him take warning, once for all, for he has reason to dread THE WATCHER."

Captain Barton read and re-read this strange effusion; in every light and in every direction he turned it over and over; he examined the paper on which it was written, and scrutinized the handwriting once more. Defeated here, he turned to the seal; it was nothing but a patch of wax, upon which the accidental impression of a thumb was imperfectly visible.

There was not the slightest mark, or clue of any kind, to lead him to even a guess as to its possible origin. The writer's object seemed a friendly one, and yet he subscribed himself as one whom he had 'reason to dread'. Altogether the letter, its author, and its real purpose were to him an inexplicable puzzle, and one, moreover, unpleasantly suggestive, in his mind, of other associations connected with his last night's adventure.

In obedience to some feeling – perhaps of pride – Mr. Barton did not communicate, even to his intended bride, the occurrences which I have just detailed. Trifling as they might appear, they had in reality most disagreeably affected his imagination, and he cared not to disclose, even to the young lady in question, what she might possibly look upon as evidences of weakness. The letter might very well be but a hoax, and the mysterious footfall but a delusion or a trick. But although he affected to treat the whole affair as unworthy of a thought it yet haunted him pertinaciously, tormenting him with perplexing doubts, and depressing him with undefined apprehensions. Certain it is, that for a considerable time afterwards he carefully avoided the street indicated in the letter as the scene of danger.

It was not until about a week after the receipt of the letter which I have transcribed, that anything further occurred to remind Captain Barton of its contents, or to counteract the gradual disappearance from his mind of the disagreeable impressions then received.

He was returning one night, after the interval I have stated, from the theatre, which was then situated in Crow Street, and having there seen Miss Montague and Lady L— into their carriage, he loitered for some time with two or three acquaintances.

With these, however, he parted close to the college, and pursued his way alone. It was now fully one o'clock, and the streets were quite deserted. During the whole of his walk with the companions from whom he had just parted, he had been at times painfully aware of the sound of steps, as it seemed, dogging them on their way.

Once or twice he had looked back, in the uneasy anticipation that he was again about to experience the same mysterious annoyances which had so disconcerted him a week before, and earnestly hoping that he might see some form to account naturally for the sounds. But the street was deserted – no one was visible.

Proceeding now quite alone upon his homeward way, he grew really nervous and uncomfortable, as he became sensible, with increased distinctness, of the well-known and now absolutely dreaded sounds.

By the side of the dead wall which bounded the college park, the sounds followed, recommencing almost simultaneously with his own steps. The same unequal pace – sometimes slow, sometimes for a score yards or so, quickened almost to a run – was audible from behind him. Again and again he turned; quickly and stealthily he glanced over his shoulder – almost at every half-dozen steps; but no one was visible.

The irritation of this intangible and unseen pursuit became gradually all but intolerable; and when at last he reached his home, his nerves were strung to such a pitch of excitement that he could not rest, and did not attempt even to lie down until after the daylight had broken.

He was awakened by a knock at his chamber-door, and his servant entering, handed him several letters which had just been received by the penny post. One among them instantly arrested his attention – a single glance at the direction aroused him thoroughly. He at once recognised its character, and read as follows:

"You may as well think, Captain Barton, to escape from your own shadow as from me; do what you may, I will see you as often as I please, and you shall see me, for I do not want to hide myself, as you fancy. Do not let it trouble your rest, Captain Barton; for, with a good conscience, what need you fear from the eye of THE WATCHER."

It is scarcely necessary to dwell upon the feelings that accompanied a perusal of this strange communication. Captain Barton was observed to be unusually absent and out of spirits for several days afterwards, but no one divined the cause.

Whatever he might think as to the phantom steps which followed him, there could be no possible illusion about the letters he had received; and, to say the least, their immediate sequence upon the mysterious sounds which had haunted him, was an odd coincidence.

The whole circumstance was, in his own mind, vaguely and instinctively connected with certain passages in his past life, which, of all others, he hated to remember.

It happened, however, that in addition to his own approaching nuptials, Captain Barton had just then – fortunately, perhaps, for himself – some business of an engrossing kind connected with the adjustment of a large and long-litigated claim upon certain properties.

The hurry and excitement of business had its natural effect in gradually dispelling the gloom which had for a time occasionally oppressed him, and in a little while his spirits had entirely recovered their accustomed tone.

During all this time, however, he was, now and then, dismayed by indistinct and half-hearted repetitions of the same annoyance, and that in lonely places, in the daytime as well as after nightfall. These renewals of the strange impressions from which he had suffered so much, were, however, desultory and faint, insomuch that often he really could not, to his own satisfaction, distinguish between them and the mere suggestions of an excited imagination.

One evening he walked down to the House of Commons with a Member, an acquaintance of his and mine. This was one of the few occasions upon which I have been in company with Captain Barton. As we walked down together, I observed that he became absent and silent, and to a degree that seemed to argue the pressure of some urgent and absorbing anxiety.

I afterwards learned that during the whole of our walk, he had heard the well-known footsteps tracking him as we proceeded.

This, however, was the last time he suffered from this phase of the persecution, of which he was already the anxious victim. A new and a very different one was about to be presented.

Chapter III
An Advertisement

OF THE NEW SERIES of impressions which were afterwards gradually to work out his destiny, I that evening witnessed the first; and but for its relation to the train of events which followed, the incident would scarcely have been now remembered by me.

As we were walking in at the passage from College Green, a man, of whom I remember only that he was short in stature, looked like a foreigner, and wore a kind of fur travelling-cap, walked very rapidly, and as if under fierce excitement, directly towards us, muttering to himself, fast and vehemently the while.

This odd-looking person walked straight towards Barton, who was foremost of the three, and halted, regarding him for a moment or two with a look of maniacal menace and fury; and then turning about as abruptly, he walked before us at the same agitated pace, and disappeared at a side passage. I do distinctly remember being a good deal shocked at the countenance and bearing of this man, which indeed irresistibly impressed me with an undefined sense of danger, such as I have never felt before or since from the presence of anything human; but these sensations were, on my part, far from amounting to anything so disconcerting as to flurry or excite me – I had seen only a singularly evil countenance, agitated, as it seemed, with the excitement of madness.

I was absolutely astonished, however, at the effect of this apparition upon Captain Barton. I knew him to be a man of proud courage and coolness in real danger – a circumstance which made his conduct upon this occasion the more conspicuously odd. He recoiled a step or two as the stranger advanced, and clutched my arm in silence, with what seemed to be a spasm of agony or terror! And then, as the figure disappeared, shoving me roughly back, he followed it for a few paces, stopped in great disorder, and sat down upon a form. I never beheld a countenance more ghastly and haggard.

"For God's sake, Barton, what is the matter?" said ——, our companion, really alarmed at his appearance. "You're not hurt, are you? – or unwell? What is it?

"What did he say? – I did not hear it – what was it?" asked Barton, wholly disregarding the question.

"Nonsense," said ——, greatly surprised; "who cares what the fellow said. You are unwell, Barton – decidedly unwell; let me call a coach."

"Unwell! No – not unwell," he said, evidently making an effort to recover his self-possession; "but, to say the truth, I am fatigued – a little over-worked – and perhaps over anxious. You know I have been in chancery, and the winding up of a suit is always a nervous affair. I have felt uncomfortable all this evening; but I am better now. Come, come – shall we go on?"

"No, no. Take my advice, Barton, and go home; you really do need rest! You are looking quite ill. I really do insist on your allowing me to see you home," replied his friend.

I seconded ——'s advice, the more readily as it was obvious that Barton was not himself disinclined to be persuaded. He left us, declining our offered escort. I was not sufficiently intimate with —— to discuss the scene we had both just witnessed. I was, however, convinced from his manner in the few common-place comments and regrets we exchanged, that he was just as little satisfied as I with the extempore plea of illness with which he had accounted for the strange exhibition, and that we were both agreed in suspecting some lurking mystery in the matter.

I called next day at Barton's lodgings, to enquire for him, and learned from the servant that he had not left his room since his return the night before; but that he was not seriously indisposed, and hoped to be out in a few days. That evening he sent for Dr. R—, then in large and fashionable practice in Dublin, and their interview was, it is said, an odd one.

He entered into a detail of his own symptoms in an abstracted and desultory way, which seemed to argue a strange want of interest in his own cure, and, at all events, made it manifest that there was some topic engaging his mind of more engrossing importance than his present ailment. He complained of occasional palpitations and headache.

Doctor R— asked him among other questions whether there was any irritating circumstance or anxiety then occupying his thoughts. This he denied quickly and almost peevishly; and the physician thereupon declared his opinion, that there was nothing amiss except some slight derangement of the digestion, for which he accordingly wrote a prescription, and was about to withdraw, when Mr. Barton, with the air of a man who recollects a topic which had nearly escaped him, recalled him.

"I beg your pardon, Doctor, but I really almost forgot; will you permit me to ask you two or three medical questions – rather odd ones, perhaps, but as a wager depends upon their solutions you will, I hope, excuse my unreasonableness."

The physician readily undertook to satisfy the inquirer.

Barton seemed to have some difficulty about opening the proposed interrogatories, for he was silent for a minute, then walked to his book-case, and returned as he had gone; at last he sat down, and said:

"You'll think them very childish questions, but I can't recover my wager without a decision; so I must put them. I want to know first about lock-jaw. If a man actually has had that complaint, and appears to have died of it – so much so, that a physician of average skill pronounces him actually dead – may he, after all, recover?"

The physician smiled, and shook his head.

"But – but a blunder may be made," resumed Barton. "Suppose an ignorant pretender to medical skill; may he be so deceived by any stage of the complaint, as to mistake what is only a part of the progress of the disease, for death itself?"

"No one who had ever seen death," answered he, "could mistake it in a case of lock-jaw."

Barton mused for a few minutes. "I am going to ask you a question, perhaps, still more childish; but first, tell me, are the regulations of foreign hospitals, such as that of, let us say, Naples, very lax and bungling. May not all kinds of blunders and slips occur in their entries of names, and so forth?"

Doctor R— professed his incompetence to answer that query.

"Well, then, Doctor, here is the last of my questions. You will, probably, laugh at it; but it must out, nevertheless. Is there any disease, in all the range of human maladies, which would have the effect of perceptibly contracting the stature, and the whole frame – causing the man to shrink in all his proportions, and yet to preserve his exact resemblance to himself in every particular – with the one exception, his height and bulk; any disease, mark – no matter how rare – how little believed in, generally – which could possibly result in producing such an effect?"

The physician replied with a smile, and a very decided negative.

"Tell me, then," said Barton, abruptly, "if a man be in reasonable fear of assault from a lunatic who is at large, can he not procure a warrant for his arrest and detention?"

"Really that is more a lawyer's question than one in my way," replied Dr. R—, "but I believe, on applying to a magistrate, such a course would be directed."

The physician then took his leave; but, just as he reached the hall door, remembered that he had left his cane upstairs, and returned. His reappearance was awkward, for a piece of paper, which he recognised as his own prescription, was slowly burning upon the fire, and Barton sitting close by with an expression of settled gloom and dismay.

Doctor R— had too much tact to observe what presented itself; but he had seen quite enough to assure him that the mind, and not the body, of Captain Barton was in reality the seat of suffering.

A few days afterwards, the following advertisement appeared in the Dublin newspapers.

If Sylvester Yelland, formerly a foremastman on board His Majesty's frigate Dolphin, or his nearest of kin, will apply to Mr. Hubert Smith, attorney, at his office, Dame Street, he or they may hear of something greatly to his or their advantage. Admission may be had at any hour up to twelve o'clock at night, should parties desire to avoid observation; and the strictest secrecy, as to all communications intended to be confidential, shall be honourably observed.

The Dolphin, as I have mentioned, was the vessel which Captain Barton had commanded; and this circumstance, connected with the extraordinary exertions made by the circulation of handbills, &c., as well as by repeated advertisements, to secure for this strange notice the utmost possible publicity, suggested to Dr. R— the idea that Captain Barton's extreme uneasiness was somehow connected with the individual to whom the advertisement was addressed, and he himself the author of it.

This, however, it is needless to add, was no more than a conjecture. No information whatsoever, as to the real purpose of the advertisement was divulged by the agent, nor yet any hint as to who his employer might be.

Chapter IV
He Talks with a Clergyman

MR. BARTON, although he had latterly begun to earn for himself the character of a hypochondriac, was yet very far from deserving it. Though by no means lively, he had yet, naturally, what are termed 'even spirits', and was not subject to undue depressions.

He soon, therefore, began to return to his former habits; and one of the earliest symptoms of this healthier tone of spirits was, his appearing at a grand dinner of the Freemasons, of which worthy fraternity he was himself a brother. Barton, who had been at first gloomy and abstracted, drank much more freely than was his wont – possibly with the purpose of dispelling his own secret anxieties – and under the influence of good wine, and pleasant company, became gradually (unlike himself) talkative, and even noisy.

It was under this unwonted excitement that he left his company at about half past ten o'clock; and, as conviviality is a strong incentive to gallantry, it occurred to him to proceed forthwith to Lady L—'s and pass the remainder of the evening with her and his destined bride.

Accordingly, he was soon at —— street, and chatting gaily with the ladies. It is not to be supposed that Captain Barton had exceeded the limits which propriety prescribes to good fellowship – he had merely taken enough wine to raise his spirits, without, however, in the least degree unsteadying his mind, or affecting his manners.

With this undue elevation of spirits had supervened an entire oblivion or contempt of those undefined apprehensions which had for so long weighed upon his mind, and to a certain extent estranged him from society; but as the night wore away, and his artificial gaiety began to flag, these painful feelings gradually intruded themselves again, and he grew abstracted and anxious as heretofore.

He took his leave at length, with an unpleasant foreboding of some coming mischief, and with a mind haunted with a thousand mysterious apprehensions, such as, even while he acutely felt their pressure, he, nevertheless, inwardly strove, or affected to contemn.

It was this proud defiance of what he regarded as his own weakness, which prompted him upon the present occasion to that course which brought about the adventure I am now about to relate.

Mr. Barton might have easily called a coach, but he was conscious that his strong inclination to do so proceeded from no cause other than what he desperately persisted in representing to himself to be his own superstitious tremors.

He might also have returned home by a route different from that against which he had been warned by his mysterious correspondent; but for the same reason he dismissed this idea also, and with a dogged and half desperate resolution to force matters to a crisis of some kind, if there were any reality in the causes of his former suffering, and if not, satisfactorily to bring their delusiveness to the proof, he determined to follow precisely the course which he had trodden upon the night so painfully memorable in his own mind as that on which his strange persecution commenced. Though, sooth to say, the pilot who for the first time steers his vessel under the muzzles of a hostile battery, never felt his resolution more severely tasked than did Captain Barton as he breathlessly pursued this solitary path – a path which, spite of every effort of scepticism and reason, he felt to be infested by some (as respected him) malignant being.

He pursued his way steadily and rapidly, scarcely breathing from intensity of suspense; he, however, was troubled by no renewal of the dreaded footsteps, and was beginning to feel a return of confidence, as more than three-fourths of the way being accomplished with impunity, he approached the long line of twinkling oil lamps which indicated the frequented streets.

This feeling of self-congratulation was, however, but momentary. The report of a musket at some hundred yards behind him, and the whistle of a bullet close to his head, disagreeably and startlingly dispelled it. His first impulse was to retrace his steps in pursuit of the assassin; but the road on either side was, as we have said, embarrassed by the foundations of a street, beyond which extended waste fields, full of rubbish and neglected lime and brick-kilns, and all now as utterly silent as though no sound had ever disturbed their dark and unsightly solitude. The futility of, single-handed, attempting, under such circumstances, a search for the murderer, was apparent, especially as no sound, either of retreating steps or any other kind, was audible to direct his pursuit.

With the tumultuous sensations of one whose life has just been exposed to a murderous attempt, and whose escape has been the narrowest possible, Captain Barton turned again; and without, however, quickening his pace actually to a run, hurriedly pursued his way.

He had turned, as I have said, after a pause of a few seconds, and had just commenced his rapid retreat, when on a sudden he met the well-remembered little man in the fur cap. The encounter was but momentary. The figure was walking at the same exaggerated pace, and with the same strange air of menace as before; and as it passed him, he thought he heard it say, in a furious whisper, "Still alive – still alive!"

The state of Mr. Barton's spirits began now to work a corresponding alteration in his health and looks, and to such a degree that it was impossible that the change should escape general remark.

For some reasons, known but to himself, he took no step whatsoever to bring the attempt upon his life, which he had so narrowly escaped, under the notice of the authorities; on the contrary, he kept it jealously to himself; and it was not for many weeks after the occurrence that he mentioned it, and then in strict confidence, to a gentleman, whom the torments of his mind at last compelled him to consult.

Spite of his blue devils, however, poor Barton, having no satisfactory reason to render to the public for any undue remissness in the attentions exacted by the relation subsisting between him and Miss Montague was obliged to exert himself, and present to the world a confident and cheerful bearing.

The true source of his sufferings, and every circumstance connected with them, he guarded with a reserve so jealous, that it seemed dictated by at least a suspicion that the origin of his strange persecution was known to himself, and that it was of a nature which, upon his own account, he could not or dared not disclose.

The mind thus turned in upon itself, and constantly occupied with a haunting anxiety which it dared not reveal or confide to any human breast, became daily more excited, and, of course, more vividly impressible, by a system of attack which operated through the nervous system; and in this state he was destined to sustain, with increasing frequency, the stealthy visitations of that apparition which from the first had seemed to possess so terrible a hold upon his imagination.

* * *

It was about this time that Captain Barton called upon the then celebrated preacher, Dr. ——, with whom he had a slight acquaintance, and an extraordinary conversation ensued.

The divine was seated in his chambers in college, surrounded with works upon his favourite pursuit, and deep in theology, when Barton was announced.

There was something at once embarrassed and excited in his manner, which, along with his wan and haggard countenance, impressed the student with the unpleasant consciousness that his visitor must have recently suffered terribly indeed, to account for an alteration so striking – almost shocking.

After the usual interchange of polite greeting, and a few commonplace remarks, Captain Barton, who obviously perceived the surprise which his visit had excited, and which Doctor —— was unable wholly to conceal, interrupted a brief pause by remarking:

"This is a strange call, Doctor ——, perhaps scarcely warranted by an acquaintance so slight as mine with you. I should not under ordinary circumstances have ventured to disturb you; but my visit is neither an idle nor impertinent intrusion. I am sure you will not so account it, when I tell you how afflicted I am."

Doctor —— interrupted him with assurances such as good breeding suggested, and Barton resumed:

"I am come to task your patience by asking your advice. When I say your patience, I might, indeed, say more; I might have said your humanity – your compassion; for I have been and am a great sufferer."

"My dear sir," replied the churchman, "it will, indeed, afford me infinite gratification if I can give you comfort in any distress of mind; but – you know—"

"I know what you would say," resumed Barton, quickly; "I am an unbeliever, and, therefore, incapable of deriving help from religion; but don't take that for granted. At least you must not assume that, however unsettled my convictions may be, I do not feel a deep – a very deep – interest in the subject. Circumstances have lately forced it upon my attention, in such a way as to compel me to review the whole question in a more candid and teachable spirit, I believe, than I ever studied it in before."

"Your difficulties, I take it for granted, refer to the evidences of revelation," suggested the clergyman.

"Why – no – not altogether; in fact I am ashamed to say I have not considered even my objections sufficiently to state them connectedly; but – but there is one subject on which I feel a peculiar interest."

He paused again, and Doctor —— pressed him to proceed.

"The fact is," said Barton, "whatever may be my uncertainty as to the authenticity of what we are taught to call revelation, of one fact I am deeply and horribly convinced, that there does exist beyond this a spiritual world – a system whose workings are generally in mercy hidden from us – a system which may be, and which is sometimes, partially and terribly revealed. I am sure – I know," continued Barton, with increasing excitement, "that there is a God – a dreadful God – and that retribution follows guilt, in ways the most mysterious and stupendous – by agencies the most inexplicable and terrific; there is a spiritual system – great God, how I have been convinced! – a system malignant, and implacable, and omnipotent, under whose persecutions I am, and have been, suffering the torments of the damned! – yes, sir – yes – the fires and frenzy of hell!"

As Barton spoke, his agitation became so vehement that the Divine was shocked, and even alarmed. The wild and excited rapidity with which he spoke, and, above all, the indefinable horror, that stamped his features, afforded a contrast to his ordinary cool and unimpassioned self-possession striking and painful in the last degree.

Chapter V
Mr. Barton States His Case

"MY DEAR SIR," said Doctor ——, after a brief pause, "I fear you have been very unhappy, indeed; but I venture to predict that the depression under which you labour will be found to originate in purely physical causes, and that with a change of air, and the aid of a few tonics, your spirits will return, and the tone of your mind be once more cheerful and tranquil as heretofore. There was, after all, more truth than we are quite willing to admit in the classic theories which assigned the undue predominance of any one affection of the mind, to the undue action or torpidity of one or other of our bodily organs. Believe me, that a little attention to diet, exercise, and the other essentials of health, under competent direction, will make you as much yourself as you can wish."

"Doctor ——," said Barton, with something like a shudder, "I cannot delude myself with such a hope. I have no hope to cling to but one, and that is, that by some other spiritual agency more potent than that which tortures me, it may be combated, and I delivered. If this may not be, I am lost – now and forever lost."

"But, Mr. Barton, you must remember," urged his companion, "that others have suffered as you have done, and—"

"No, no, no," interrupted he, with irritability – "no, sir, I am not a credulous – far from a superstitious man. I have been, perhaps, too much the reverse – too sceptical, too slow of belief; but unless I were one whom no amount of evidence could convince, unless I were to contemn the repeated, the perpetual evidence of my own senses, I am now – now at last constrained to believe – I have no escape from the conviction – the overwhelming certainty – that I am haunted and dogged, go where I may, by – by a DEMON!"

There was a preternatural energy of horror in Barton's face, as, with its damp and death-like lineaments turned towards his companion, he thus delivered himself.

"God help you, my poor friend," said Dr. ——, much shocked, "God help you; for, indeed, you are a sufferer, however your sufferings may have been caused."

"Ay, ay, God help me," echoed Barton, sternly; "but will he help me – will he help me?"

"Pray to him – pray in a humble and trusting spirit," said he.

"Pray, pray," echoed he again; "I can't pray – I could as easily move a mountain by an effort of my will. I have not belief enough to pray; there is something within me that will not pray. You prescribe impossibilities – literal impossibilities."

"You will not find it so, if you will but try," said Doctor ——.

"Try! I have tried, and the attempt only fills me with confusion; and, sometimes, terror; I have tried in vain, and more than in vain. The awful, unutterable idea of eternity and infinity oppresses and maddens my brain whenever my mind approaches the contemplation of the Creator; I recoil from the effort scared. I tell you, Doctor ——, if I am to be saved, it must be by other means. The idea of an eternal Creator is to me intolerable – my mind cannot support it."

"Say, then, my dear sir," urged he, "say how you would have me serve you – what you would learn of me – what I can do or say to relieve you?"

"Listen to me first," replied Captain Barton, with a subdued air, and an effort to suppress his excitement, "listen to me while I detail the circumstances of the persecution under which my life has become all but intolerable – a persecution which has made me fear death and the world beyond the grave as much as I have grown to hate existence."

Barton then proceeded to relate the circumstances which I have already detailed, and then continued:

"This has now become habitual – an accustomed thing. I do not mean the actual seeing him in the flesh – thank God, that at least is not permitted daily. Thank God, from the ineffable horrors of that visitation I have been mercifully allowed intervals of repose, though none of security; but from the consciousness that a malignant spirit is following and watching me wherever I go, I have never, for a single instant, a temporary respite. I am pursued with blasphemies, cries of despair and appalling hatred. I hear those dreadful sounds called after me as I turn the corners of the streets; they come in the night-time, while I sit in my chamber alone; they haunt me everywhere, charging me with hideous crimes, and – great God! – threatening me with coming vengeance and eternal misery. Hush! Do you hear that?" he cried with a horrible smile of triumph; "there – there, will that convince you?"

The clergyman felt a chill of horror steal over him, while, during the wail of a sudden gust of wind, he heard, or fancied he heard, the half articulate sounds of rage and derision mingling in the sough.

"Well, what do you think of that?" at length Barton cried, drawing a long breath through his teeth.

"I heard the wind," said Doctor ——. "What should I think of it – what is there remarkable about it?"

"The prince of the powers of the air," muttered Barton, with a shudder.

"Tut, tut! My dear sir," said the student, with an effort to reassure himself; for though it was broad daylight, there was nevertheless something disagreeably contagious in the nervous excitement under which his visitor so miserably suffered. "You must not give way to those wild fancies; you must resist these impulses of the imagination."

"Ay, ay; 'resist the devil and he will flee from thee'," said Barton, in the same tone; "but how resist him? Ay, there it is – there is the rub. What – what am I to do? What can I do?"

"My dear sir, this is fancy," said the man of folios; "you are your own tormentor."

"No, no, sir – fancy has no part in it," answered Barton, somewhat sternly. "Fancy! Was it that made you, as well as me, hear, but this moment, those accents of hell? Fancy, indeed! No, no."

"But you have seen this person frequently," said the ecclesiastic; "why have you not accosted or secured him? Is it not a little precipitate, to say no more, to assume, as you have done, the existence of preternatural agency, when, after all, everything may be easily accountable, if only proper means were taken to sift the matter."

"There are circumstances connected with this – this appearance," said Barton, "which it is needless to disclose, but which to me are proof of its horrible nature. I know that the being that follows me is not human – I say I know this; I could prove it to your own conviction." He paused for a minute, and then added, "And as to accosting it, I dare not, I could not; when

I see it I am powerless; I stand in the gaze of death, in the triumphant presence of infernal power and malignity. My strength, and faculties, and memory, all forsake me. O God, I fear, sir, you know not what you speak of. Mercy, mercy; heaven have pity on me!"

He leaned his elbow on the table, and passed his hand across his eyes, as if to exclude some image of horror, muttering the last words of the sentence he had just concluded, again and again.

"Doctor," he said, abruptly raising himself, and looking full upon the clergyman with an imploring eye, "I know you will do for me whatever may be done. You know now fully the circumstances and the nature of my affliction. I tell you I cannot help myself; I cannot hope to escape; I am utterly passive. I conjure you, then, to weigh my case well, and if anything may be done for me by vicarious supplication – by the intercession of the good – or by any aid or influence whatsoever, I implore of you, I adjure you in the name of the Most High, give me the benefit of that influence – deliver me from the body of this death. Strive for me, pity me; I know you will; you cannot refuse this; it is the purpose and object of my visit. Send me away with some hope, however little, some faint hope of ultimate deliverance, and I will nerve myself to endure, from hour to hour, the hideous dream into which my existence has been transformed."

Doctor —— assured him that all he could do was to pray earnestly for him, and that so much he would not fail to do. They parted with a hurried and melancholy valediction. Barton hastened to the carriage that awaited him at the door, drew down the blinds, and drove away, while Doctor —— returned to his chamber, to ruminate at leisure upon the strange interview which had just interrupted his studies.

Chapter VI
Seen Again

IT WAS NOT to be expected that Captain Barton's changed and eccentric habits should long escape remark and discussion. Various were the theories suggested to account for it. Some attributed the alteration to the pressure of secret pecuniary embarrassments; others to a repugnance to fulfil an engagement into which he was presumed to have too precipitately entered; and others, again, to the supposed incipiency of mental disease, which latter, indeed, was the most plausible as well as the most generally received of the hypotheses circulated in the gossip of the day.

From the very commencement of this change, at first so gradual in its advances, Miss Montague had of course been aware of it. The intimacy involved in their peculiar relation, as well as the near interest which it inspired afforded, in her case, a like opportunity and motive for the successful exercise of that keen and penetrating observation peculiar to her sex.

His visits became, at length, so interrupted, and his manner, while they lasted, so abstracted, strange, and agitated, that Lady L—, after hinting her anxiety and her suspicions more than once, at length distinctly stated her anxiety, and pressed for an explanation.

The explanation was given, and although its nature at first relieved the worst solicitudes of the old lady and her niece, yet the circumstances which attended it, and the really dreadful consequences which it obviously indicated, as regarded the spirits, and indeed the reason of the now wretched man, who made the strange declaration, were enough, upon little reflection, to fill their minds with perturbation and alarm.

General Montague, the young lady's father, at length arrived. He had himself slightly known Barton, some ten or twelve years previously, and being aware of his fortune and connections, was disposed to regard him as an unexceptionable and indeed a most desirable match for his daughter. He laughed at the story of Barton's supernatural visitations, and lost no time in calling upon his intended son-in-law.

"My dear Barton," he continued, gaily, "after a little conversation, my sister tells me that you are a victim to blue devils, in quite a new and original shape."

Barton changed countenance, and sighed profoundly.

"Come, come; I protest this will never do," continued the General; "you are more like a man on his way to the gallows than to the altar. These devils have made quite a saint of you." Barton made an effort to change the conversation.

"No, no, it won't do," said his visitor laughing; "I am resolved to say what I have to say upon this magnificent mock mystery of yours. You must not be angry, but really it is too bad to see you at your time of life, absolutely frightened into good behaviour, like a naughty child by a bugaboo, and as far as I can learn, a very contemptible one. Seriously, I have been a good deal annoyed at what they tell me; but at the same time thoroughly convinced that there is nothing in the matter that may not be cleared up, with a little attention and management, within a week at furthest."

"Ah, General, you do not know—" he began.

"Yes, but I do know quite enough to warrant my confidence," interrupted the soldier; "don't I know that all your annoyance proceeds from the occasional appearance of a certain little man in a cap and great-coat, with a red vest and a bad face, who follows you about, and pops upon you at corners of lanes, and throws you into ague fits. Now, my dear fellow, I'll make it my business to catch this mischievous little mountebank, and either beat him to a jelly with my own hands, or have him whipped through the town, at the cart's-tail, before a month passes."

"If you knew what I knew," said Barton, with gloomy agitation, "you would speak very differently. Don't imagine that I am so weak as to assume, without proof the most overwhelming, the conclusion to which I have been forced – the proofs are here, locked up here." As he spoke he tapped upon his breast, and with an anxious sigh continued to walk up and down the room.

"Well, well, Barton," said his visitor, "I'll wager a rump and a dozen I collar the ghost, and convince even you before many days are over."

He was running on in the same strain when he was suddenly arrested, and not a little shocked, by observing Barton, who had approached the window, stagger slowly back, like one who had received a stunning blow; his arm extended toward the street – his face and his very lips white as ashes – while he muttered, "There – by heaven! – there – there!"

General Montague started mechanically to his feet, and from the window of the drawing room, saw a figure corresponding as well as his hurry would permit him to discern, with the description of the person, whose appearance so persistently disturbed the repose of his friend.

The figure was just turning from the rails of the area upon which it had been leaning, and, without waiting to see more, the old gentleman snatched his cane and hat, and rushed down the stairs and into the street, in the furious hope of securing the person, and punishing the audacity of the mysterious stranger. He looked round him, but in vain, for any trace of the person he had himself distinctly seen. He ran breathlessly to the nearest corner, expecting to see from thence the retiring figure, but no such form was visible. Back and forward, from crossing to crossing, he ran, at fault, and it was not until the curious gaze and laughing countenances of the passers-by reminded him of the absurdity of his pursuit, that he checked his hurried pace, lowered his walking cane from the menacing altitude which he had mechanically given it, adjusted his hat, and walked composedly back again, inwardly vexed and flurried. He found Barton pale and trembling in every joint; they both remained silent, though under emotions very different. At last Barton whispered, "You saw it?"

"It! – him – someone – you mean – to be sure I did," replied Montague, testily. "But where is the good or the harm of seeing him? The fellow runs like a lamp-lighter. I wanted to catch him, but he had stolen away before I could reach the hall-door. However, it is no great matter; next time, I dare say, I'll do better; and egad, if I once come within reach of him, I'll introduce his shoulders to the weight of my cane."

Notwithstanding General Montague's undertakings and exhortations, however, Barton continued to suffer from the self-same unexplained cause; go how, when, or where he would, he was still constantly dogged or confronted by the being who had established over him so horrible an influence.

Nowhere and at no time was he secure against the odious appearance which haunted him with such diabolic perseverance.

His depression, misery, and excitement became more settled and alarming every day, and the mental agonies that ceaselessly preyed upon him, began at last so sensibly to affect his health, that Lady L— and General Montague succeeded, without, indeed, much difficulty, in persuading him to try a short tour on the Continent, in the hope that an entire change of scene would, at all events, have the effect of breaking through the influences of local association, which the more sceptical of his friends assumed to be by no means inoperative in suggesting and perpetuating what they conceived to be a mere form of nervous illusion.

General Montague indeed was persuaded that the figure which haunted his intended son-in-law was by no means the creation of his imagination, but, on the contrary, a substantial form of flesh and blood, animated by a resolution, perhaps with some murderous object in perspective, to watch and follow the unfortunate gentleman.

Even this hypothesis was not a very pleasant one; yet it was plain that if Barton could ever be convinced that there was nothing preternatural in the phenomenon which he had hitherto regarded in that light, the affair would lose all its terrors in his eyes, and wholly cease to exercise upon his health and spirits the baleful influence which it had hitherto done. He therefore reasoned, that if the annoyance were actually escaped by mere locomotion and change of scene, it obviously could not have originated in any supernatural agency.

Chapter VII
Flight

YIELDING to their persuasions, Barton left Dublin for England, accompanied by General Montague. They posted rapidly to London, and thence to Dover, whence they took the packet with a fair wind for Calais. The General's confidence in the result of the expedition on Barton's spirits had risen day by day, since their departure from the shores of Ireland; for to the inexpressible relief and delight of the latter, he had not since then, so much as even once fancied a repetition of those impressions which had, when at home, drawn him gradually down to the very depths of despair.

This exemption from what he had begun to regard as the inevitable condition of his existence, and the sense of security which began to pervade his mind, were inexpressibly delightful; and in the exultation of what he considered his deliverance, he indulged in a thousand happy anticipations for a future into which so lately he had hardly dared to look; and in short, both he and his companion secretly congratulated themselves upon the termination of that persecution which had been to its immediate victim a source of such unspeakable agony.

It was a beautiful day, and a crowd of idlers stood upon the jetty to receive the packet, and enjoy the bustle of the new arrivals. Montague walked a few paces in advance of his friend, and as he made his way through the crowd, a little man touched his arm, and said to him, in a broad provincial patois:

"Monsieur is walking too fast; he will lose his sick comrade in the throng, for, by my faith, the poor gentleman seems to be fainting."

Montague turned quickly, and observed that Barton did indeed look deadly pale. He hastened to his side.

"My dear fellow, are you ill?" he asked anxiously.

The question was unheeded and twice repeated, ere Barton stammered:

"I saw him – by ——, I saw him!"

"Him! – the wretch – who – where now? – where is he?" cried Montague, looking around him. "I saw him – but he is gone," repeated Barton, faintly.

"But where – where? For God's sake speak," urged Montague, vehemently.

"It is but this moment here," said he.

"But what did he look like – what had he on – what did he wear – quick, quick," urged his excited companion, ready to dart among the crowd and collar the delinquent on the spot.

"He touched your arm – he spoke to you – he pointed to me. God be merciful to me, there is no escape," said Barton, in the low, subdued tones of despair.

Montague had already bustled away in all the flurry of mingled hope and rage; but though the singular personnel of the stranger who had accosted him was vividly impressed upon his recollection, he failed to discover among the crowd even the slightest resemblance to him.

After a fruitless search, in which he enlisted the services of several of the bystanders, who aided all the more zealously, as they believed he had been robbed, he at length, out of breath and baffled, gave over the attempt.

"Ah, my friend, it won't do," said Barton, with the faint voice and bewildered, ghastly look of one who had been stunned by some mortal shock; "there is no use in contending; whatever it is, the dreadful association between me and it, is now established – I shall never escape – never!"

"Nonsense, nonsense, my dear Barton; don't talk so," said Montague with something at once of irritation and dismay; "you must not, I say; we'll jockey the scoundrel yet; never mind, I say – never mind."

It was, however, but labour lost to endeavour henceforward to inspire Barton with one ray of hope; he became desponding.

This intangible, and, as it seemed, utterly inadequate influence was fast destroying his energies of intellect, character, and health. His first object was now to return to Ireland, there, as he believed, and now almost hoped, speedily to die.

To Ireland accordingly he came and one of the first faces he saw upon the shore, was again that of his implacable and dreaded attendant. Barton seemed at last to have lost not only all enjoyment and every hope in existence, but all independence of will besides. He now submitted himself passively to the management of the friends most nearly interested in his welfare.

With the apathy of entire despair, he implicitly assented to whatever measures they suggested and advised; and as a last resource, it was determined to remove him to a house of Lady L—'s, in the neighbourhood of Clontarf, where, with the advice of his medical attendant, who persisted in his opinion that the whole train of consequences resulted merely from some nervous derangement, it was resolved that he was to confine himself, strictly to the house, and to make use only of those apartments which commanded a view of an enclosed yard, the gates of which were to be kept jealously locked.

Those precautions would certainly secure him against the casual appearance of any living form, that his excited imagination might possibly confound with the spectre which, as it was contended, his fancy recognised in every figure that bore even a distant or general resemblance to the peculiarities with which his fancy had at first invested it.

A month or six weeks' absolute seclusion under these conditions, it was hoped might, by interrupting the series of these terrible impressions, gradually dispel the predisposing apprehensions, and the associations which had confirmed the supposed disease, and rendered recovery hopeless.

Cheerful society and that of his friends was to be constantly supplied, and on the whole, very sanguine expectations were indulged in, that under the treatment thus detailed, the obstinate hypochondria of the patient might at length give way.

Accompanied, therefore, by Lady L—, General Montague and his daughter – his own affianced bride – poor Barton – himself never daring to cherish a hope of his ultimate emancipation from the horrors under which his life was literally wasting away – took possession of the apartments, whose situation protected him against the intrusions, from which he shrank with such unutterable terror.

After a little time, a steady persistence in this system began to manifest its results, in a very marked though gradual improvement, alike in the health and spirits of the invalid. Not, indeed, that anything at all approaching complete recovery was yet discernible. On the contrary, to those who had not seen him since the commencement of his strange sufferings, such an alteration would have been apparent as might well have shocked them.

The improvement, however, such as it was, was welcomed with gratitude and delight, especially by the young lady, whom her attachment to him, as well as her now singularly painful position, consequent on his protracted illness, rendered an object scarcely one degree less to be commiserated than himself.

A week passed – a fortnight – a month – and yet there had been no recurrence of the hated visitation. The treatment had, so far forth, been followed by complete success. The chain of associations was broken. The constant pressure upon the overtasked spirits had been removed, and, under these comparatively favourable circumstances, the sense of social community with the world about him, and something of human interest, if not of enjoyment, began to reanimate him.

It was about this time that Lady L— who, like most old ladies of the day, was deep in family receipts, and a great pretender to medical science, dispatched her own maid to the kitchen garden, with a list of herbs, which were there to be carefully culled, and brought back to her housekeeper for the purpose stated. The handmaiden, however, returned with her task scarce half completed, and a good deal flurried and alarmed. Her mode of accounting for her precipitate retreat and evident agitation was odd, and, to the old lady, startling.

Chapter VIII
Softened

IT APPEARED THAT she had repaired to the kitchen garden, pursuant to her mistress's directions, and had there begun to make the specified election among the rank and neglected herbs which crowded one corner of the enclosure, and while engaged in this pleasant labour, she carelessly sang a fragment of an old song, as she said, 'to keep herself company'. She was, however, interrupted by an ill-natured laugh; and, looking up, she saw through the old thorn hedge, which surrounded the garden, a singularly ill-looking little man, whose countenance wore the stamp of menace and malignity, standing close to her, at the other side of the hawthorn screen.

She described herself as utterly unable to move or speak, while he charged her with a message for Captain Barton; the substance of which she distinctly remembered to have been to the effect, that he, Captain Barton, must come abroad as usual, and show himself to his friends, out of doors, or else prepare for a visit in his own chamber.

On concluding this brief message, the stranger had, with a threatening air, got down into the outer ditch, and, seizing the hawthorn stems in his hands, seemed on the point of climbing through the fence – a feat which might have been accomplished without much difficulty.

Without, of course, awaiting this result, the girl – throwing down her treasures of thyme and rosemary – had turned and run, with the swiftness of terror, to the house. Lady L— commanded her, on pain of instant dismissal, to observe an absolute silence respecting all that passed of the incident which related to Captain Barton; and, at the same time, directed instant search to be made by her men, in the garden and the fields adjacent. This measure, however, was as usual, unsuccessful, and, filled with undefinable misgivings, Lady L— communicated the incident to her brother. The story, however, until long afterwards, went no further, and, of course, it was jealously guarded from Barton, who continued to amend, though slowly.

Barton now began to walk occasionally in the courtyard which I have mentioned, and which being enclosed by a high wall, commanded no view beyond its own extent. Here he, therefore, considered himself perfectly secure: and, but for a careless violation of orders by one of the grooms, he might have enjoyed, at least for some time longer, his much-prized immunity. Opening upon the public road, this yard was entered by a wooden gate, with a wicket in it, and was further defended by an iron gate upon the outside. Strict orders had been given to keep both carefully locked; but, spite of these, it had happened that one day, as Barton was slowly pacing this narrow enclosure, in his accustomed walk, and reaching the further extremity, was turning to retrace his steps, he saw the boarded wicket ajar, and the face of his tormentor immovably looking at him through the iron bars. For a few seconds he stood riveted to the earth – breathless and bloodless – in the fascination of that dreaded gaze, and then fell helplessly insensible, upon the pavement.

There he was found a few minutes afterwards, and conveyed to his room – the apartment which he was never afterwards to leave alive. Henceforward a marked and unaccountable change was observable in the tone of his mind. Captain Barton was now no longer the excited and despairing man he had been before; a strange alteration had passed upon him – an unearthly tranquillity reigned in his mind – it was the anticipated stillness of the grave.

"Montague, my friend, this struggle is nearly ended now," he said, tranquilly, but with a look of fixed and fearful awe. "I have, at last, some comfort from that world of spirits, from which my punishment has come. I now know that my sufferings will soon be over."

Montague pressed him to speak on.

"Yes," said he, in a softened voice, "my punishment is nearly ended. From sorrow, perhaps I shall never, in time or eternity, escape; but my agony is almost over. Comfort has been revealed to me, and what remains of my allotted struggle I will bear with submission – even with hope."

"I am glad to hear you speak so tranquilly, my dear Barton," said Montague; "peace and cheer of mind are all you need to make you what you were."

"No, no – I never can be that," said he mournfully. "I am no longer fit for life. I am soon to die. I am to see him but once again, and then all is ended."

"He said so, then?" suggested Montague.

"He? – No, no: good tidings could scarcely come through him; and these were good and welcome; and they came so solemnly and sweetly – with unutterable love and melancholy, such as I could not – without saying more than is needful, or fitting, of other long-past scenes and persons – fully explain to you." As Barton said this he shed tears.

"Come, come," said Montague, mistaking the source of his emotions, "you must not give way. What is it, after all, but a pack of dreams and nonsense; or, at worst, the practices of a scheming rascal that enjoys his power of playing upon your nerves, and loves to exert it – a sneaking vagabond that owes you a grudge, and pays it off this way, not daring to try a more manly one."

"A grudge, indeed, he owes me – you say rightly," said Barton, with a sudden shudder; "a grudge as you call it. Oh, my God! When the justice of Heaven permits the Evil one to carry out a scheme of vengeance – when its execution is committed to the lost and terrible victim of sin, who owes his own ruin to the man, the very man, whom he is commissioned to pursue – then, indeed, the torments and terrors of hell are anticipated on earth. But heaven has dealt mercifully with me – hope has opened to me at last; and if death could come without the dreadful sight I am doomed to see, I would gladly close my eyes this moment upon the world. But though death is welcome, I shrink with an agony you cannot understand – an actual frenzy of terror – from the last encounter with that – that *demon*, who has drawn me thus to the verge of the chasm, and who is himself to plunge me down. I am to see him again – once more – but under circumstances unutterably more terrific than ever."

As Barton thus spoke, he trembled so violently that Montague was really alarmed at the extremity of his sudden agitation, and hastened to lead him back to the topic which had before seemed to exert so tranquillizing an effect upon his mind.

"It was not a dream," he said, after a time; "I was in a different state – I felt differently and strangely; and yet it was all as real, as clear, and vivid, as what I now see and hear – it was a reality."

"And what did you see and hear?" urged his companion.

"When I wakened from the swoon I fell into on seeing him," said Barton, continuing as if he had not heard the question, "it was slowly, very slowly – I was lying by the margin of a broad lake, with misty hills all round, and a soft, melancholy, rose-coloured light illuminated it all. It was unusually sad and lonely, and yet more beautiful than any earthly scene. My head was leaning on the lap of a girl, and she was singing a song, that told, I know not how – whether by words or harmonies – of all my life – all that is past, and all that is still to come; and with the song the old feelings that I thought had perished within me came back, and tears flowed from my eyes – partly for the song and its mysterious beauty, and partly for the unearthly sweetness of her voice; and yet I knew the voice – oh! how well; and I was spellbound as I listened and looked at the solitary scene, without stirring, almost without breathing – and, alas! alas! without turning my eyes towards the face that I knew was near me, so sweetly powerful was the enchantment that held me. And so, slowly, the song and scene grew fainter, and fainter, to my senses, till all was dark and still again. And then I awoke to this world, as you saw, comforted, for I knew that I was forgiven much."

Barton wept again long and bitterly.

From this time, as we have said, the prevailing tone of his mind was one of profound and tranquil melancholy. This, however, was not without its interruptions. He was thoroughly impressed with the conviction that he was to experience another and a final visitation, transcending in horror all he had before experienced. From this anticipated and unknown agony, he often shrank in such paroxysms of abject terror and distraction, as filled the whole household with dismay and superstitious panic. Even those among them who affected to discredit the theory of preternatural agency, were often in their secret souls visited during the silence of night with qualms and apprehensions, which they would not have readily confessed; and none of them attempted to dissuade Barton from the resolution on which he now systematically acted, of shutting himself up in his own apartment. The window-blinds of this room were kept jealously down; and his own man was seldom out of his presence, day or night, his bed being placed in the same chamber.

This man was an attached and respectable servant; and his duties, in addition to those ordinarily imposed upon valets, but which Barton's independent habits generally dispensed with, were to attend carefully to the simple precautions by means of which his master hoped to exclude the dreaded intrusion of the 'Watcher'. And, in addition to attending to those arrangements, which amounted merely to guarding against the possibility of his master's being, through any unscreened window or open door, exposed to the dreaded influence, the valet was never to suffer him to be alone – total solitude, even for a minute, had become to him now almost as intolerable as the idea of going abroad into the public ways – it was an instinctive anticipation of what was coming.

Chapter IX
Requiescat

IT IS NEEDLESS to say, that under these circumstances, no steps were taken towards the fulfilment of that engagement into which he had entered. There was quite disparity enough in point of years, and indeed of habits, between the young lady and Captain Barton, to have precluded anything like very vehement or romantic attachment on her part. Though grieved and anxious, therefore, she was very far from being heartbroken.

Miss Montague, however, devoted much of her time to the patient but fruitless attempt to cheer the unhappy invalid. She read for him, and conversed with him; but it was apparent that whatever exertions he made, the endeavour to escape from the one ever waking fear that preyed upon him, was utterly and miserably unavailing.

Young ladies are much given to the cultivation of pets; and among those who shared the favour of Miss Montague was a fine old owl, which the gardener, who caught him napping among the ivy of a ruined stable, had dutifully presented to that young lady.

The caprice which regulates such preferences was manifested in the extravagant favour with which this grim and ill-favoured bird was at once distinguished by his mistress; and, trifling as this whimsical circumstance may seem, I am forced to mention it, inasmuch as it is connected, oddly enough, with the concluding scene of the story.

Barton, so far sharing in this liking for the new favourite, regarded it from the first with an antipathy as violent as it was utterly unaccountable. Its very vicinity was unsupportable to him. He seemed to hate and dread it with a vehemence absolutely laughable, and which, to those who have never witnessed the exhibition of antipathies of this kind, would seem all but incredible.

With these few words of preliminary explanation, I shall proceed to state the particulars of the last scene in this strange series of incidents. It was almost two o'clock one winter's night, and Barton was, as usual at that hour, in his bed; the servant we have mentioned occupied a smaller bed in the same room, and a light was burning. The man was on a sudden aroused by his master, who said – "I can't get it out of my head that that accursed bird has got out somehow, and is lurking in some corner of the room. I have been dreaming about him. Get up, Smith, and look about; search for him. Such hateful dreams!"

The servant rose, and examined the chamber, and while engaged in so doing, he heard the well-known sound, more like a long-drawn gasp than a hiss, with which these birds from their secret haunts affright the quiet of the night.

This ghostly indication of its proximity – for the sound proceeded from the passage upon which Barton's chamber-door opened – determined the search of the servant, who, opening the door, proceeded a step or two forward for the purpose of driving the bird away. He had however, hardly entered the lobby, when the door behind him slowly swung to under the impulse, as it seemed, of some gentle current of air; but as immediately over the door there was a kind of window, intended in the daytime to aid in lighting the passage, and through which at present the rays of the candle were issuing, the valet could see quite enough for his purpose.

As he advanced he heard his master – who, lying in a well-curtained bed, had not, as it seemed, perceived his exit from the room – call him by name, and direct him to place the candle on the table by his bed. The servant, who was now some way in the long passage, and not liking to raise his voice for the purpose of replying, lest he should startle the sleeping inmates of the house, began to walk hurriedly and softly back again, when, to his amazement, he heard a voice in the interior of the chamber answering calmly, and actually saw, through the window which overtopped the door, that the light was slowly shifting, as if carried across the room in answer to his master's call. Palsied by a feeling akin to terror, yet not unmingled with curiosity, he stood breathless and listening at the threshold, unable to summon resolution to push open the door and enter. Then came a rustling of the curtains, and a sound like that of one who in a low voice hushes a child to rest, in the midst of which he heard Barton say, in a tone of stifled horror – "Oh, God – oh, my God!" and repeat the same exclamation several times. Then ensued a silence, which again was broken by the same strange soothing sound; and at last there burst forth, in one swelling peal, a yell of agony so appalling and hideous, that, under some impulse of ungovernable horror, the man rushed to the door, and with his whole strength strove to force it open. Whether it was that, in his agitation, he had himself but imperfectly turned the handle, or that the door was really secured upon the inside, he failed to effect an entrance; and as he tugged and pushed, yell after yell rang louder and wilder through the chamber, accompanied all the while by the same hushed sounds. Actually freezing with terror, and scarce knowing what he did, the man turned and ran down the passage, wringing his hands in the extremity of horror and irresolution. At the stair-head he was encountered by General Montague, scared and eager, and just as they met the fearful sounds had ceased.

"What is it? Who – where is your master?" said Montague with the incoherence of extreme agitation. "Has anything – for God's sake is anything wrong?"

"Lord have mercy on us, it's all over," said the man staring wildly towards his master's chamber. "He's dead, sir, I'm sure he's dead."

Without waiting for inquiry or explanation, Montague, closely followed by the servant, hurried to the chamber-door, turned the handle, and pushed it open. As the door yielded to his pressure, the ill-omened bird of which the servant had been in search, uttering its spectral warning, started suddenly from the far side of the bed, and flying through the doorway close over their heads, and extinguishing, in his passage, the candle which Montague carried, crashed through the skylight that overlooked the lobby, and sailed away into the darkness of the outer space.

"There it is, God bless us," whispered the man, after a breathless pause.

"Curse that bird," muttered the General, startled by the suddenness of the apparition, and unable to conceal his discomposure.

"The candle is moved," said the man, after another breathless pause, pointing to the candle that still burned in the room; "see, they put it by the bed."

"Draw the curtains, fellow, and don't stand gaping there," whispered Montague, sternly. The man hesitated.

"Hold this, then," said Montague, impatiently thrusting the candlestick into the servant's hand, and himself advancing to the bedside, he drew the curtains apart. The light of the candle, which was still burning at the bedside, fell upon a figure huddled together, and half upright, at the head of the bed. It seemed as though it had slunk back as far as the solid panelling would allow, and the hands were still clutched in the bedclothes.

"Barton, Barton, Barton!" cried the General, with a strange mixture of awe and vehemence. He took the candle, and held it so that it shone full upon the face. The features were fixed, stern, and white; the jaw was fallen; and the sightless eyes, still open, gazed vacantly forward towards the front of the bed. "God Almighty! He's dead," muttered the General, as he looked upon this fearful spectacle. They both continued to gaze upon it in silence for a minute or more. "And cold, too," whispered Montague, withdrawing his hand from that of the dead man.

"And see, see – may I never have life, sir," added the man, after another pause, with a shudder, "but there was something else on the bed with him. Look there – look there – see that, sir."

As the man thus spoke, he pointed to a deep indenture, as if caused by a heavy pressure, near the foot of the bed.

Montague was silent.

"Come, sir, come away, for God's sake," whispered the man, drawing close up to him, and holding fast by his arm, while he glanced fearfully round; "what good can be done here now – come away, for God's sake!"

At this moment they heard the steps of more than one approaching, and Montague, hastily desiring the servant to arrest their progress, endeavoured to loose the rigid grip with which the fingers of the dead man were clutched in the bedclothes, and drew, as well as he was able, the awful figure into a reclining posture; then closing the curtains carefully upon it, he hastened himself to meet those persons that were approaching.

* * *

It is needless to follow the personages so slightly connected with this narrative, into the events of their afterlife; it is enough to say that no clue to the solution of these mysterious occurrences was ever after discovered; and so long an interval having now passed since the event which I have just described concluded this strange history, it is scarcely to be expected that time can throw any new lights upon its dark and inexplicable outline. Until the secrets of the earth shall be no longer hidden, therefore, these transactions must remain shrouded in their original obscurity.

The only occurrence in Captain Barton's former life to which reference was ever made, as having any possible connection with the sufferings with which his existence closed, and which he himself seemed to regard as working out a retribution for some grievous sin of his past life, was a circumstance which not for several years after his death was brought to light. The nature of this disclosure was painful to his relatives, and discreditable to his memory.

It appeared that some six years before Captain Barton's final return to Dublin, he had formed, in the town of Plymouth, a guilty attachment, the object of which was the daughter of one of the ship's crew under his command. The father had visited the frailty of his unhappy child with extreme harshness, and even brutality, and it was said that she had died heartbroken. Presuming upon Barton's implication in her guilt, this man had conducted himself towards him with marked insolence, and Barton retaliated this, and what he resented with still more exasperated bitterness – his treatment of the unfortunate girl – by a systematic exercise of those terrible and arbitrary severities which the regulations of the navy placed at the command of those who are responsible for its discipline. The man had at length made his escape, while the vessel was in port at Naples, but died, as it was said, in a hospital in that town, of the wounds inflicted in one of his recent and sanguinary punishments.

Whether these circumstances in reality bear, or not, upon the occurrences of Barton's afterlife, it is, of course, impossible to say. It seems, however, more than probable that they were at least, in his own mind, closely associated with them. But however the truth may be, as to the origin and motives of this mysterious persecution, there can be no doubt that, with respect to the agencies by which it was accomplished, absolute and impenetrable mystery is like to prevail until the day of doom.

* * *

POSTSCRIPT BY THE EDITOR

The preceding narrative is given in the *ipsissima verba* of the good old clergyman, under whose hand it was delivered to Doctor Hesselius. Notwithstanding the occasional stiffness and redundancy of his sentences, I thought it better to reserve to myself the power of assuring the reader, that in handing to the printer, the MS. of a statement so marvellous, the Editor has not altered one letter of the original text. – [*Ed. Papers of Dr. Hesselius.*]

Knock, Knock, Wolf

P.G. Galalis

IT WAS TIME to kill the sparrows.

Every autumn, after the last leaves fell and the bare trees rattled their bone song to an empty sky, the widow Clarabel started baking. Five parts flour, three parts water, a pinch of salt and emptins for leavening, plus a handful of the devil's blend, finely ground. She would let the loaf go stale for a day, then scatter it about the field between her cottage and the forest.

A knock on the door was the worst sound in the world if you asked Clarabel, when beggars and travelers and all kinds of wretched, needy folk would flee winter in the high peaks. Fortunately, Clarabel had discovered that a lone cottage in a field of dead sparrows seldom received any visitors.

Late one afternoon, though, in that season of travelers, after she'd been walking in the woods all day to gather her ingredients, there was a knock.

It was the boy from over the hill with a moustache of dirt and snot.

"I don't know where your kitten is," Clarabel said.

The boy's eyes widened. "No, Miss Clarabel, it's not – wait, is she missing?"

"Isn't that why you usually bother me? I only killed the one, and that was two years back."

The boy wiped his nose. "No, Miss Clarabel. Papa sent me over. Something for you to see out our way."

Clarabel sighed, tied her kerchief around her head, and closed the door behind her.

At the Trundlin farm, the boy's lumbering father, ragged mother, and five grimy sisters were all inspecting the mud at the bottom of the sloping turnip field, along with a smattering of neighbors. The children leaned closer to their parents as Clarabel swept by, and the parents shifted nervously too as she shoved her way through to see what was on the ground.

Four-toed paw prints, the size of a man's foot, and two-legged, not four.

In the shade of the tall fir that marked the boundary between Trundlin's field and Firny's, the prints turned human. Five toes, instep and heel. Plain bare footprints. And then a wolf's again on the other side of the tree.

"Pack your things and your children," Clarabel said. "Leave before sundown. Go down the valley to the village. Further if you can. Don't come back till I send for you."

Clarabel had no use for neighbors, but it didn't mean she wanted them dead. Likely that would just rouse suspicions again.

She made to leave, then stopped when no one else budged. "Or stay," she said. "It makes no matter to me."

They scattered.

Good. It would be easier without them around.

* * *

When Clarabel was a little girl, home with her grandmother while her father was away, a stranger had arrived late one afternoon. Her grandmother grew stiff as she invited him in for a bit of supper and a place by the hearth. Then she quietly sent Clarabel out to gather thistledown. "Don't come back till you fill the pouch," she told her.

Clarabel was halfway over the second hill, the pouch still empty, by the time she realized that the season for thistledown was already over. She raced through the gloaming back to the cottage. Though she did not know exactly what, she knew there were horrible things a strange man could do to a poor old woman.

When she opened the door, she found Grandmother cleaning her long knife, while a wolf the size of a man hung upside down from the rafter, blood running into the feed pail like rain through a leaky roof.

When Grandmother saw how pale Clarabel was, she tut-tutted. "Death is for the weak," she said.

Grandmother taught Clarabel how to skin the wolf and tan its hide, and when Clarabel's father returned, Grandmother sent him to gather a hunting party, and she sent Clarabel to fetch the silversmith.

The morning the men set off for the mountains was the last Clarabel ever saw of her father. They never came back. But neither did the wolves.

The memory made old Clarabel wonder now if she ought to be fleeing to the village herself. But no – she couldn't stomach it. The people. The filth.

She'd do her best to keep the wolf away, and if not, she'd be ready for him. Death was for the weak.

* * *

On the way back to her cottage, she checked her protections.

The invisible, wayward trails she'd lain over the forest paths last spring had mostly decayed beneath a blackened carpet of leaves. No time to fix those now.

In the field, beneath the slate sky, she visited her scarecrow and whispered him a spell, but he was already drowsy with winter.

At the rickety wooden gate that clicked and clacked with every gust, she bound the latch with a simple ward. Good against prying children, but not much more.

At her doorstep, she inspected the sentinel jack-o-lantern, carved in the proper and ancient way her grandmother had taught her. It had started caving in days ago, rotting from the inside out in a mélange of pinks, blacks, and grays, and now it stank like the dead. No good.

When she opened the door to her dark cottage, she felt near to frozen, body and soul. So the widow Clarabel did what she always did when the chill gnawed inside: she put on a pot of soup. It was the only thing to do. The simple magics.

No time to waste. Into the pot went the last of the vegetables she'd saved from the first hard frost, along with the carcass of the chicken she'd slaughtered and plucked, gutted and divined, and then cooked and eaten last Sunday. There wasn't enough water left to both fill the pot and have enough for her bedtime tea, and she didn't want to go out in the dark later to draw more, so she filled the pot halfway and topped off the rest with her own crabapple cider, pressed the way her grandmother had taught her, and which she did not like to share.

She had barely put the lid on the pot when there came a sharp *knock-knock-knock*.

"Who is it?" she cried.

A pause. Then a muffled reply that her old ears couldn't make out through the oak. She cracked the door.

A large man stood there, brown and bushy, his cheeks covered in whiskers that stopped above a clean-shaven chin. He smiled awkwardly, and he smelled like the forest.

"Forgive me, ma'am, didn't mean to startle you," he said. "There's wild things about and, uh, twilight's gettin' on… I was wonderin' if you might have some room on your floor, maybe even out back in your woodshed, for a poor stranger to bed down for the night?"

His voice was deep and gruff. *Wild things, indeed.*

She opened the door the rest of the way. There was nothing to do but let him in. The worst bad luck not to. Old magic, that.

He stooped under the lintel and stomped his boots on the mat, then after considering her clean swept floor, he bent to unlace the boots and entered barefoot instead.

She eyed his feet, measured them against the footprints in the field.

When they skinned the wolf so long ago, Grandmother had told little Clarabel all about the bootless travelers who came begging at your door late on a cold autumn day. Turn them away, and they'd return for you under the moon, in their true form. No, you must invite them in, Grandmother had said, make them comfortable, tame the beast. Only after feeding and entertaining them and offering a bed for the night would they leave you be and vanish by morning.

The gruff and bushy traveler noticed Clarabel staring. "Sorry," he said. "Wouldn't want to be stampin' the mud in. Besides, my feet is kind of sore, if you don't mind."

Barefoot travelers. Wolves under the moon.

He looked at the pot on the stove and sniffed.

"The soup's not quite ready yet," Clarabel said. "But please, come sit by the stove and warm yourself."

Make them comfortable. Tame the beast.

They were touchy guests, her grandmother had warned. A bit wild, naturally. Easy to offend. Tales were told of unlucky hosts who would commit some unintended slight, let slip some bit of carelessness. Sometimes they just disappeared; sometimes a well-gnawed bone or a few stray fingers would be found come morning.

Clarabel flexed her achy hands, knuckles like knobs of pain under wrinkled skin, tired old bones gnawed by the season's labors.

Her visitor sat and took in the meager furnishings, the cast-iron stove, the small cot in the dark corner across the room.

"Don't often find an old woman all by her lonesome so close by the mountains."

Clarabel picked up the wooden spoon and shrugged. "My son checks in now and then." She stirred and tasted the soup. "He lives down in the village."

"Well, he best be careful next time he comes up. Like I said, there's wild things about."

"Oh?" she said.

"Early cold in the peaks is what's brought 'em down. Bad winter on the way. Haven't been this far in years."

"I know," Clarabel said.

He considered her in silence. The soup bubbled. "You lived here long?"

"Since I married my husband a lifetime ago, and ever since," she said.

She watched him look for a man's boots, a man's coat on the peg, a gun by the front or back door.

"He's dead now," she said.

"Hmph. Gone long?"

"A year after we married. He died suddenly of a cough."

He nodded once. "Tough woman."

The silence fell awkwardly. No good, those eyes. Something savage in them.

"I don't know you," she said. "I know everyone from around here."

"I'm from a ways up in the mountains."

"On your way to the village?"

He stared at her, and a smile curled one corner of his mouth. "Depends what I find here. I'm a hunter, of sorts."

She humphed. "And there are wild things about?"

He splayed his hands and inclined his head as if to say, *Exactly.* Or maybe, *Here I am.*

"Well, I've put my protections up," she said.

"Your jack-o-lantern is rotting," he said. "It's wore out."

"Even so," Clarabel said. "The scarecrow's in the garden."

"Sleepin' scarecrow won't do any good against what's come down from the mountains."

"Well is the moon out yet?"

He shook his head. "Still cloudy."

"Well then."

She turned and checked the soup. The knife still lay on the cutting board beside the stove. She appraised it. It could kill a chicken well enough, gut a squirrel or rabbit in one easy slice. But it was no good, him looking right at her. Soon as she grabbed it and turned, he'd be on her.

"What was that?" she said.

"What?"

"The noise outside."

"I didn't hear nothing."

"Please, will you check?" She let her voice waver.

He furrowed his brow and pushed himself out of the chair.

"Oh, thank you," she said.

He put his boots back on and reached for the door handle. She reached for the knife, and just as she wrapped her fingers around its well-worn handle, and just as the door creaked open, a howl pierced the twilight without.

He put his head out the door, and she heard him sniff the air long and slow. He turned back in with a toothy grin that remained even when he saw her hand over the knife on the cutting board. "That won't do you much good," he said. He closed the door and bent to take off his boots again.

"What if you need to go out?" she said.

"Danger's a ways off yet," he said.

"I'd feel better."

He paused to study her, then he shrugged, retied his boots, and sat down with them on. Her hand was still on the knife.

He stared at her. "I'm hungry," he growled.

She released the knife. She felt distant, aware only of her heartbeat in her ears as she pulled two bowls from the shelf, two spoons, the ladle from its hook.

It was the pouch of devil's blend on the shelf beside the ladle that snapped her back to her senses. That would do. Yes, that would do nicely in his soup. And if the howl meant there was another one about? Fine. Let them all come. She'd made plenty of soup.

With her back to him, she took the pouch, poked her gnarled fingers in for a pinch of the potpourri of deadly herbs and mushrooms that Grandmother had taught her, and dropped it into one of the bowls as she ladled the piping-hot soup. She set the one with the extra bits down in front of him and then took hers and joined him at the table.

They ate. She sipped at her spoon delicately, blowing a little on each spoonful. He set to, ravenously. Wolfishly, even. *Yes, yes, eat up.* She watched and slurped softly from her spoon, and felt herself begin to warm up again at last.

When he was done, he sighed and pushed the bowl away. "That was good," he said. "Thank you."

"Where's your gun?" she said. "If you're a hunter."

He blinked. "Out by the gate. Didn't think it proper to bring in."

She sipped at her spoon. Convenient. She'd give him her left arm for his pudding if he really had a gun outside.

"Besides," he said. "It's a good warning." He cleared his throat.

"Oh?" she said.

"Yes," he croaked. He tried to clear his throat again. "It's a mighty famous gun. Those I hunt know it well." He tried to smile, but he coughed instead, and tried to clear his throat once more.

Now she smiled.

"What?" he managed before a violent coughing fit seized him. It reminded her of her husband.

"Nothing," she said once he stopped. "Just that you're trying awfully hard to put me at ease." She peered out the window through the gap in the curtains. Almost full night, but still cloudy. "Waiting for moonlight, I suppose."

He began choking, wheezing, gasping for breath. He shoved his chair from the table and stood, hacking desperately.

"My grandmother taught me all about you," she said. "You thought you could come under her granddaughter's roof, share her granddaughter's supper? Trick me and trap me and eat me up?" She laughed. "Not as sly you thought, you naughty little wolf."

His eyes looked confused, then went wide. The coughing stopped. He struggled like a rabbit against the snare, frothing, his throat closing tighter and tighter. He clawed at it—

He fell.

She waited.

His pulse throbbed in his neck. She watched it slow. She watched it stop.

She rose, drew the knife off the cutting board and stood over him, blade poised, watching.

A minute passed.

He remained perfectly still.

She sat back down and waited more, the knife on the table beside her, just in case, but he remained as he was, and the tiniest doubt began to whisper like a moth on the lantern.

The moon, that was it. It would take the moonlight for him to turn, even in death. She stood and parted the curtains. It was overcast, but the dark clouds were scudding by on a swift, high wind.

She filled her kettle, set it on the stove, and waited. In another minute the pale light flooded through the window and fell across the body.

And nothing happened.

It occurred to Clarabel to check outside. She opened the front door and peered down the walk through the vegetable patch to the gate. Propped against the gatepost was a long, sleek rifle, gleaming in the moonlight. She fetched it inside.

It was a beautiful weapon, with a silver barrel and a stock inlaid with thin silver, some arcane script that seemed distantly familiar. Her hands shook as she set it down.

Clarabel, you old witch, what have you done?

The night carried on and the clouds fled the sky. The widow Clarabel knelt by the body for some time, and wept, and touched his face, and scrabbled to find some excuse, some remorse, but there was nothing inside her except the rattle of dead branches and dried leaves over cold hard stone.

What did he think would happen, coming around, a stranger, on a night like this? What did he expect?

She could hardly be blamed, an old woman all by herself.

Yet she couldn't help but curse her haste. She might have used him well. Instead, the wolf was still out there.

She considered the knife. A resurrection spell? She'd never tried one on anything so large. And it would be hard to do, this time of year. Dead autumn. Winter poised on the air. Very hard.

Grandmother had taught her that spring was easiest for such things. She'd given Clarabel the secret just before dying, so many springs ago, before Clarabel had decided not to bring her back. She'd gone out picking flowers, instead, to put on the fresh grave.

This time of year, it would take more blood, probably more than she had to give. Besides, was there even time? A difficult spell in the best conditions. What if the wolf should come while she was in the middle of it? What then? A guest, slain on the floor? She'd probably be gobbled up on the spot.

Unless she could persuade him. Plead that it was for him, the wolf, an offering to the wild wanderers going about their dark and righteous work. Might she? She had persuaded people of more difficult things before.

Of course, none of them had been inclined to eat her. No, it was too dangerous. And death was for the weak – Grandmother, the hunter – not for Clarabel.

Only one thing left to do, then. The wood shed was just out the back.

She was breathing heavily in the cold and had him only halfway out the back door when another *knock-knock-knock* rapped at the front.

She dropped the hunter's heavy arms with a thud. "Who's there?" she called through the house.

No response. Just another sharp *knock-knock-knock*.

"Just a minute!" She stepped over the body into the warm cottage, fought his massive legs as high as she could and leaned into them with both her small shoulders until she had the tree-trunk limbs bent all the way up from his waist. She pushed them past the jamb and then shoved them to the side. One boot heel rested against the outer wall of the cottage, but the other started sliding back through the doorway, so she shoved it back out and slammed the door shut quick.

She waited. Nothing but the sound of her heavy breathing.

The kettle began to murmur softly on the stove.

Maybe whoever it was had gone.

She crept across the cottage, trying not to creak the floorboards, and listened at the door. Nothing. She was just about to open up when a gleam caught her eye.

The gun was still on the table.

She grabbed it and shoved it under her bed across the room, just as another *knock-knock-knock* started. "All right!" she cried.

The moon had risen high enough that the eaves covered the doorway in shadow. There stood a hooded man, slight of build, who looked at her with sharp bright eyes and a large smile full of gleaming teeth. He was handsome.

She heard herself say, "Won't you come in?"

He said nothing, and he stepped over the threshold with bare, dirt-browned feet. He was careful not to remove his hood until she had closed the door on the moonlit night behind him. An animal stink followed him in.

He was young and gray-haired, sleek, with dark eyes flecked with gold. He eyed the room and he eyed her.

Clarabel, now you've gone and done it.

"Come in by the stove, you must be cold," she said. "You'll want a drink, I suppose."

He sat in the same chair the hunter had occupied, and considered her. "Don't trouble yourself," he said. His voice was low, with a fine grit like dirt on a floorboard.

She poured him half a mug of cider anyway. No way she'd be taken in that easily. She thought about the devil's blend, but no, how would that look, bits of flotsam in his cider?

When she turned to set it down, he was staring at the knife and the empty pair of dirty bowls still on the table.

Clarabel, you fool.

"I suppose you've come down from the mountains too," she said.

The young man looked up. "Yes."

Clarabel cleared the bowls away and returned the knife to the cutting board. "It figures. You're my second visitor tonight."

The young man narrowed his eyes.

"He was a hunter, I think. Said something about early winter up the mountains and some nonsense about wild things coming down."

"He's not wrong," the young man said.

"Well, we may be rustic out here, but the wild things know to stay out."

"Oh?" he said.

"You saw my scarecrow, didn't you? And my jack-o-lantern?"

He smiled. "Yes, I saw them."

A chill skittered down her spine like the last dead leaf of autumn.

"You must be hungry," she said. "Let me get you some soup."

"I am hungry," he said. He drained his cider mug, licked his lips, and propped his filthy feet on her table. "But I don't care for soup."

She glanced at her knife.

"What was that sound?" she gasped.

He stared at her. "Nothing. There wasn't any sound."

Her pulse quickened. She searched for something else, anything, that might do the trick.

A steady jet of steam was pouring from the kettle. "Tea!" she said.

He tilted his head quizzically.

"The hunter. I promised him some tea when he came back."

"He's coming back?" He sat up, put his feet on the floor.

Like a cornered dog, the way he growled.

"I think so," Clarabel said.

She pulled the kettle from the stove and crumbled the tea leaves into it. The pouch of devil's blend was still beside the cutting board. She hesitated, then dumped the rest of it into the kettle as well. "At least he said he'd come back for tea, after he checked around outside."

The young man started to get up.

"No, stay!" she almost yelled. "Won't you wait with me and have a cup?"

He eased back down, eyeing her. There, there, now. He couldn't resist a lonely widow's hospitality. The bedrock magics.

She set three cups beside the cutting board. "I really do appreciate the company. He was a frightening man."

"Yes, he is."

She took her time. She covered all three cups with a piece of cheesecloth. As she poured, the devil's blend hid among the sodden tea leaves that gathered and sagged over each cup. She folded up the cheesecloth and put it aside.

"Don't worry," she said. She placed one cup in front of the young man, sat down with one for herself, and set the third down on the table as well. "This is my own blend. It ought to do you nicely."

She brought her cup to her lips, blew on it, and feigned a sip – carefully, carefully, not letting the tea touch her lips. Close enough to feel the steam like devil's breath. She flinched and said "Hot!" and set her cup down.

He blew on his own, tested it, then slurped.

They sat with their tea in the deepening night, she feigning one or two more delicate sips, he draining his cup in a few grimaces, watching the front door, the back door, the windows, sniffing the air. She drank his unease.

He finished and set the empty cup down. Looked at it.

"Was it nice?" she said.

He glanced up to speak, but his words caught on the phlegm in his throat.

He coughed once.

He swallowed.

He smiled.

"Quite," he said.

Clarabel put her tea down to hide her shaking hand. Her cup was still full. He looked at it, looked at her.

"The hunter. How far was he going?" he asked.

"Oh, not far. Be back in a minute I expect."

He rose. "I'll have a look."

She watched him leave.

As soon as the front door shut, she grabbed her knife and started for the back door, throwing off the lies she'd told herself before. There was still time. She knew the Words, knew how to make them work, even if it was nigh winter. After all, it hadn't been spring yet, all those years ago, when she brought her son back, the babe gray and lifeless in the cradle. Slash herself long and deep, let it pour over him, and the hunter would spring up like a colt new-fallen from the foal. And if she put his gun in his hands first, she wagered he'd know what to do, even as she dropped dead in her own blood.

Dead. She, Clarabel?

She paused with her fingers on the back door's handle. Removed them and touched a finger to the knife. *So sharp.*

No, he was dead. Not her. Not yet.

Death was for the weak.

She put the knife on the table and felt under her bed for the gun. She dragged it out, rehearsed what she remembered her father teaching her. Slide open the chamber. Check for a round.

Empty.

Of course he wouldn't leave his gun loaded outside.

She set the gun on the floor, glanced at the back door, glanced at the front. She'd have to be quick about it.

She'd forgotten about the heel of the dead man's right boot, propped against the door, and it caught her above the eye. Blood trickled along her brow. She tried to ignore it.

She threw both legs aside and straddled the corpse, her breath steaming out in the cold air as if to spite the dead. She patted down his pockets: his coat, his shirt, his trousers. There, on his belt, stuck through a line of small loops, was a row of silver bullets. She poked one out, thought about it, then poked out a handful more.

A howl sounded over the roof, from in front of the cottage, wild and thrilling, running through her like the first winter wind, and then a dead silence covered the night.

The front gate creaked.

She leapt back inside and wrestled the dead man's legs. She tried to throw them out and slam the door closed but she wasn't fast enough. A heavy boot caught between the door and the jamb. The blood was dripping into her eye now.

She heard him padding toward the house, his steps loud on the gravel walk in the cold night.

She gave the lifeless foot a shove and slammed the door shut, spun, and dove for the rifle on the floor. The silver bullets scattered. She scrabbled for one and raced to load it with her shaking hands when the front door burst open.

She jammed the bullet in, slammed the bolt shut, lifted the gun and fumbled for the trigger. He leapt across the room and slapped the muzzle aside. Thunder exploded in the cottage and the bullet smacked the wall and whizzed away, and then she was on her back and the gun was across the room and the hooded figure loomed over her.

"Mercy!" she cried, and something skidded loudly against the back door, exactly like a pair of heavy boots scraping across the wood, and caught the jamb with a thud.

The young man snarled and leapt across the wash of moonlight to the door. Her heart emptied like the November sky to see the sleek gray fur on his forearm, the taut sinew and muscle of ankle and paw, the wolf. A man again in the shadows, he paused, then snatched the door open and jumped back as the dead man's legs tumbled in. He turned to Clarabel, grinned wider than a man could, and stepped back into the moonlight.

She fled – out the front door, through her vegetable patch, out the gate where she should have left the gun and, her mind a wild bramble of animal fear, out into the cold and misty night. A howl sang after her.

Thoughtless as a rabbit in the open she ran, across the field, over the hill, faster than she'd run in years. A memory of youthful speed stirred briefly in her old bones before it ebbed and stumbled into agony.

On hands and knees she cried for help, but the surrounding farmsteads stood dark and silent. The night was an empty grave.

Her breath calmed, her heart calmed, her own voice spoke to her in the cold, dark silence.

What a fool she'd been. Death was a fine end. All her life she'd courted and tamed and wielded it, darling Death, and now it was time to let it in, and it would welcome her to a lonely grave, quiet and lovely.

She sat up and faced away over the open countryside, the dark woods distant, and braced for his sharp claws in her back. They could not be sharper than the pains of her years. She awaited the fangs in her wrinkled flesh, the hot wash of her own hot blood against her cold skin. They could not pierce any deeper than life's wounds ever had.

She heard him, a skitter through the leaves, then a panting mass of fur and muscle pressed her frail body to the hard ground. She felt the beast's hot breath and writhed to meet her death, gasped as his maw engulfed her shoulder and neck.

The bite was gentle. A lover beneath the moon. A mother with her cub by the nape. The blood trickled its warmth over her collar bone. Her breath was the rattle of leaves in the wind.

He released her and loped away. A long howl sounded in the night.

She waited, relished her thrumming heart, her wheezing breath. Gingerly, she pushed herself up and blessed whatever grace had saved her. She, Clarabel. She, the murderer! She had life in her yet. How silly she'd been! Death was for the weak.

She managed only a step before she collapsed. She felt herself falling, past the cold ground, down into a bottomless hunger where ancient winter devoured her soul and death was a spring that would never come.

Oh, Clarabel! What have you done?

She cried out a wild cry, keening with agony, soaring to the clear, cold sky. Another howl answered over the hills.

* * *

After several days without word from old Clarabel, some of the neighbors ventured back. Trundlin and Firny tracked two sets of large wolf prints through the forest but did not follow them into the mountains. They puzzled over the widow's empty cottage, and they marveled at the silver rifle inside. The remains of the devoured corpse they found beside it would live long in their nightmares.

They said little as they dug a grave for what was left of the man, and they worried about what could have happened to Clarabel. They took some comfort, though, in the swarms of happy sparrows chittering across the fields.

Mrs. Courcy's Folly

Kevin J.J. Gallivan

"DO YOU INTEND, Madam, to forsake your religion and prance about in goatskins, offering all manner of unholy sacrifice to such pagan and blasphemous gods as the Greeks worshipped?"

"I most certainly do not, sir!" Mrs. Courcy responded in a tone intended to cut him dead. The very idea of Mrs. Courcy prancing, let alone prancing in a goatskin, appalled her by its temerity as much as it seemed to divert the other members of her party. It was in the early years of the reign of the young Queen Victoria, when such a suggestion was especially outrageous, and Mrs. Courcy was most certainly the least likely of Her Majesty's subjects to so disport herself.

Captain Beatty, who told the most notorious stories to scandalize the other guests at dinner, now, it seemed to Mrs. Courcy, presumed to criticize her plans for beautifying the Park. In fact, he now ridiculed the jewel of Mrs. Courcy's crowning glory, her Grecian Folly.

"Then ma'am, if I may make so bold as to ask, why would you, in this day and age, want to build a temple to some long ago Greek god?"

Mrs. Courcy had thought to entertain her guests with a tour of Ollinway Park in order that they might have the opportunity to view its natural attractions and comment upon her many improvements. The party had travelled to the various points from which to regard the grounds and house to best effect. Each point elicited the appropriate responses concerning both the natural and artificial appointments. It was duly appreciated how artful the natural scenes appeared and how natural the artificial settings seemed.

Captain Beatty, much to the general interest and Mrs. Courcy's displeasure, always seemed to be reminded of something bigger or better that he had encountered in some unchristian place in the Pacific Ocean or China Sea or other equally uncivilized body of water. At one particularly inspiring spot, he had made *sotto voce*, some reference to the gentlemen in the party concerning Brighton, which elicited stifled laughter and winks and which Mrs. Courcy could only take as some veiled insult.

Oak Hill, which dominated the view of the Park, was certainly the estate's most impressive feature. A massive oak tree, six or seven centuries old, perhaps more, stood apart and above a copse of beech and elm. The immense tree, Promethean in its dimensions, seemed to dominate not only the smaller trees about it, but also, from its station atop the hill, every other thing in the Park. Even the three-storied hall below seemed to occupy its space at the sufferance of the great oak.

It was not until the culmination of the tour that Mrs. Courcy took her guests to the very top of Oak Hill. The size of the tree was even more impressive when viewed at close quarters, and the view it commanded over the county was very nearly overwhelming. It overwhelmed all Mrs. Courcy's guests save Captain Beatty, who, admitting that there was nothing so majestic and inspiring as a good old English oak, commented that he had once seen a baobab tree two, perhaps three times its size in Madagascar. The Captain could not compare the views, since he was standing below the oak, whereas he had climbed the baobab and, before he could enjoy the vista, had been attacked by vulture of spectacular proportions which nested there.

It was then that an exasperated Mrs. Courcy guided her party around the oak to reveal the temple. Dwarfed by the oak, it nonetheless drew the eye and dominated the scene, reducing the stately tree to a mere appurtenance. It was a small, circular structure about fifteen feet in diameter. Three steps led up to a stone altar surround by a circle of thirteen Doric columns, only four of which retained their full height of eight feet. The altar was a simple rectangle of stone with a cracked and weathered face carved on it in bas-relief. Little could be made of the features other than that they were those of a smiling man; although his smile seemed to have weathered into a leer.

This sight met with very appreciative responses from the assembled guests. All, that is, except Captain Beatty, who pursed his lips and furrowed his brow and made his unfortunate remark about dancing in goatskins.

"It is a folly, sir," Mrs. Courcy told the Captain, fixing him with her eyes. "As…as in the fashion of Lord Elgin. Many great houses have *faux* Grecian temples. The idea of a genuine, ancient temple taken stone by stone from its native country and brought to our shores is one which is very much in vogue." And one, Mrs. Courcy might have added, she had paid an architect very handsomely to think of and import.

The old sailor seemed to regard his hostess with the same curiosity he might have given one of the cannibal chieftains in his tales. "Vogue it may be, ma'am. Folly it is for certain. It is not a good thing to build temples to gods you do not intend to worship."

"Surely, my dear Captain," interjected the vicar of Castringham on behalf of his stepsister, "There can be no harm in constructing such a diversion. A folly as it were. And most certainly you, as a Christian gentleman, would not propose that everyone with a Grecian temple in his grounds should worship, say, Zeus or Diana."

"Sir," replied the Captain, "we all came here this week in answer to this lady and her husband's gracious invitation. I'll be bound that we'd be greatly put out if, when we arrived, there'd been no dinner for us, no rooms, nothing. If we'd've been left standing before a closed door with our invitations in our hands we'd be put out, I'll be bound. With this 'folly', as you'd have it, you invite some pagan hobgoblin with no intention of entertaining him."

Mrs. Courcy certainly wished that the Captain had been left standing outside a closed door. All she could bring herself to say, without forgetting her station, was, "It is a folly, sir. That is all. It is expected to be very dramatic. It is all the vogue."

"Vogue it may be, ma'am, but mind me: it would be better that you dance about in goatskins by the full moon than have it stand idle. It is not a good thing to build a temple to a god you do not intend to worship. That is my last word upon the subject. I shall await you all in the carriage. I am anxious for my luncheon."

It was simply too good, Mrs. Courcy told her husband, the Colonel, later that afternoon; it was simply too good how Captain Beatty had ruined her day and now risked ruining her house party. Mrs. Courcy spoke with knit brow and clenched fists, and Colonel Courcy knew that it was not simply *too* good at all.

The Colonel, a kindly man, who in his salad days had withstood French cavalry charges in Spain and pursued Pathan bandits across the snowbound wastes of the Hindu Kush, now in his autumn years found himself flinching before the assaults of gout and his wife. In truth, his foot had for some weeks spared him discomfort; however, he would gladly have suffered that crippling misery instead of Mrs. Courcy's displeasure at his old friend. He could have his foot wrapped in a warm compress and placed upon pillows and find surcease with a good book and a toddy; but there was no abating the formidable Mrs. Courcy's ire unless his friend, Captain Beatty, should leave before the midsummer festivities, and that was quite impossible.

"M'dear," said the Colonel, "I am quite sure that the Captain in no way meant offense. It was not criticism, m'dear. If anything, it was advice. Yes, that is it precisely. Beatty was giving advice."

The Colonel seemed both satisfied and surprised at this seemingly felicitous interpretation of events. Mrs. Courcy, realizing she had found no ally and that the Captain would remain the week, regarded her husband through narrowed eyes and said, "It was an opinion. Most decidedly an opinion. Unsought and uncalled for and altogether too good!"

Mrs. Courcy was a handsome woman and in her youth had been a beauty. Like so many beauties she could have been a silly thing beneath a pretty bonnet, laid out as bait to flirt for a husband, but she was a young woman with a sizable income and therefore had the luxury of choice. The choice, of course, was made for her by her guardian, and it was a good choice. A woman with an income, she was married to a man with a greater income. Colonel Courcy was a younger son whose family had been able to buy him his place in the army; moreover, he was a younger son who had an elder brother who died with no lineal heir. After an eventful career, the Colonel was able to retire to substantial estates made even more substantial by a good match.

Colonel Courcy was a man who had suffered in war and wanted little more than to live quietly in peace. However, being a man of wealth and influence, he had benefices within his gift. Confident and secure in his position in society, and of an unambitious nature, the Colonel, therefore, consented to be ruled by his wife.

Mrs. Courcy, a woman of Amazonian temperament, was even more suited to battle than her husband had been. With such an easy conquest at home, Mrs. Courcy set out for other worlds to subdue. Had she had children, she could have occupied herself making good matches, campaigning each season in London for suitable husbands and wives for them. But she had no children. Her stepbrother, an unmarried vicar, had not even provided her with a niece to oversee. Mrs. Courcy was, therefore, spared the arduous rituals of society. However, without these rituals, there were no challenges; and challenge was what Mrs. Courcy craved most.

Mrs. Courcy could have been a general or a great statesman had she not been a woman. But she was a woman and this point was not lost on her. Nature and society had dictated that if she were to fight battles, her weapons were to be calling cards, invitations and the latest fashions. The women of the gentry were her natural enemies and her allies, and proscriptions of society her rules of war. The years had made her an accomplished general but, even in the midst of her greatest victories, her spirit was more akin to Napoleon on Elba than Wellington at Waterloo. Every social triumph was one more bar for the cage that held her spirit.

It was midsummer and the hub of the world – or at least that part of the world that mattered – was London. While the peers and members of Parliament sat, their wives, daughters, mothers, and maiden aunts orbited about them in a series of calls, teas, dinners, and balls. It was the season when young ladies came out into society and matches were made. This was to be Mrs. Courcy's challenge. Not content with simply taking on society upon its own ground, she would drag society on to hers. It was unheard of; but that was the appeal.

That spring, Colonel and Mrs. Courcy had presided over the opening of a railway station in the nearby town of Cernchester. The Age of Industry and Commerce had laid open a road from London to Ollinway Park and an uncomfortable journey of two days by coach was now reduced to a matter of four hours by first class railway carriage in only moderate discomfort.

And with that event the seed was planted; the challenge laid. Mrs. Courcy had, through sheer force of will and spirit (augmented by the new railway timetable), shifted the very axis of the globe and, during one glorious long weekend in summer, the world revolved around Ollinway Park.

Mrs. Courcy had planned a gala midsummer house party that would last five days. There would be balls and entertainments and fireworks. She had accomplished a positive coup by assuring the presence of the Duchess of Aberline, as well as her eligible nephew, the Viscount Maurney. The Earl of Quince, a celebrated poet, promised to attend and recite his latest poem on the death of Byron. Mrs. Courcy also garnered an earl with a brood of eligible daughters and an assortment of baronets and back benchers. The local gentry would, of course, dance attendance as their fealty to Mrs. Courcy dictated.

The height of the week was to be the performance of *A Midsummer Night's Dream* by a professional touring company. Mr. Lorenzo Candy, the impresario and featured player, was to play both Theseus and Oberon, king of the fairies. As a delicious touch, the play was to be performed at the folly. What better setting, Mrs. Courcy thought and Mr. Candy agreed, for a tale of ancient romance and magic spirits of the night.

After a splendid dinner, which almost rivaled one presided over by some fabulous sultan of Captain Beatty's acquaintance, the guests were transported in open chaises to Oak Hill. There, they were led up a torchlit path through the grove to the folly by sprites brandishing flickering lights like jack o'lanterns. The effect was accentuated by similar sprites running some distance off among the trees and by hidden pipers trilling on their instruments unseen.

The mysterious elfin folk flickering and piping magically about the hill had been provided by a local workhouse and were under strict orders from the beadle to be of extremely good and sober character. This sobriety of character was further strengthened by the promise of cake and cider and sixpence apiece at the end of the play.

The evening promised to be an absolute sensation. Mrs. Courcy positively tingled at the prospect of her triumph. In fact, in spite of the warm evening air, Mrs. Courcy's arms were absolute gooseflesh. The depth of her excitement took even Mrs. Courcy herself by surprise.

A heady aroma filled the night air. Mr. Candy must have given orders for the burning of incense. It was a distinct touch that Mrs. Courcy appreciated. Although, she thought a moment later, he could have used a less heady perfume. The scent, pleasant at first, seemed cloying after a time; yet Mrs. Courcy found herself inhaling deeply. There was something delicious about it. Intoxicating. Yes, positively intoxicating.

Mr. Candy had once been Claudius to Mr. Kean's Hamlet and it was said – usually by Mr. Candy himself – that the audience's sympathy would lie with the usurping Danish king rather than the mercurial prince by the end of the performance. Such success with the public, coupled with Mr. Kean's professional insecurity, provided Mr. Candy with the impetus to form his own provincial company.

Whatever Mr. Candy might say for himself, his Oberon was superlative. He truly captured the regal menace of the ethereal tyrant of the night, thought Mrs. Courcy. This result was enhanced to great effect by the supernumeraries of the cast. Every gesture seemed to bestir the air with magic life as the fairy king ordered his minion, Puck, to serve him in his machinations.

"I know a bank where the wild thyme blows," intoned Mr. Candy; yet it seemed to Mrs. Courcy that Oberon himself was truly speaking. "There sleeps Titania sometime of the night / Lull'd in these flowers with dances and delight."

Mrs. Courcy was utterly entranced by the glamor of his performance. She could smell the wild thyme. The lights suspended among the limbs of the oak became glittering eyes. Wild creatures seemed to form around Oberon: strange, feline beasts possessed of an almost liquid grace of movement. Mrs. Courcy found herself paying less attention to Mr. Candy's Oberon and more to these creatures that seemed to materialize into women; wild, half naked women with glowing, animal eyes. Their lithe, sinuous, undulating bodies coiled about the pillars of the folly and seemed to insinuate themselves unnoticed between Oberon and Puck. Their searing eyes held Mrs. Courcy's gaze and seemed to burn deep into her.

"And with the juice of this I'll streak her eyes / and make her full of hateful fantasies."

Suddenly, they disappeared. Oberon and Puck stood in stunned silence before the altar. All the party turned, equally stunned. All eyes were on Mrs. Courcy, who had stood up, shrieked, and swooned back into her chair.

After she had been revived, Mrs. Courcy, her evening – her weekend – in ruins, set upon Mr. Candy. It was scandalous! What on earth had possessed him to dress the women in his company in such a scandalous fashion and have them caper about before their betters so scandalously?

Mr. Candy, who had grown up in the theatre and was used to all manner of dramatic outbursts – was, in fact, well known in his circle for his own – was completely nonplussed by Mrs. Courcy's onslaught and, with great difficulty, assured her that there was no one in his company so attired. Much to Mrs. Courcy's consternation, Mr. Candy very much insisted that he and Puck had been alone in the scene which had been interrupted by her outburst. This was nervously corroborated by Mrs. Courcy's stepbrother, the vicar. Colonel Courcy claimed neutrality, as he had been resting his eyes during much of the performance.

Mrs. Courcy then turned upon the beadle of the workhouse in her effort to discover the culprit responsible for ruining everything. She berated the poor official for so allowing the unfortunate women in his charge to present themselves is such a scandalous state of *déshabillé*. The beadle, much overwrought, assembled his company in a desperate effort to prove that there had been no women among them.

Mrs. Courcy sought some support from her guests, who were rather taken aback. Not a one of the ladies, nor any of the gentlemen who had been awake, admitted to seeing such a display. One gentleman made the aside that if he had known there was to have been such a scene he would have made every effort to stay alert. This prompted a tittering that Mrs. Courcy did not appreciate.

Mrs. Courcy rounded again on Mr. Candy for his use of such an intoxicating incense. Her head was still spinning from its influence. Here, again, Mr. Candy demurred. He had ordered no incense burnt. And, again, here Mrs. Courcy's assemblage failed her. None recalled such Oriental odors, although a young baronet sheepishly confessed to smoking a trichonopoly cigar at the back of the audience.

Pulling up one of the torchieres that lit the way to the folly, Mrs. Courcy set off down the hill alone. Colonel Courcy made apologies to all and sundry and the guests followed her down at a distance.

The next morning, Mrs. Courcy received Mr. Candy in the library in order to settle his account. The transaction passed in virtual silence until Mr. Candy bowed at the doorway to take his leave. After a moment's hesitation he came back into the room and stood before Mrs. Courcy, fumbling with his hat in his hand. He cleared his throat.

"Madam, I did not think to mention it last night, as you were so greatly distressed… but let me say this now: I know that there were only myself and Jefferson in that scene, and throughout the play there were no such women as you…"

"You have your remuneration, Mr. Candy. Take it and your opinion of me and begone."

"Pray, madam, let me continue. What I mean to say is that I do not doubt what you saw."

Mrs. Courcy, who, up until that moment, had been affecting the reading of a book, turned to look Mr. Candy full in the face. "What do you mean, Mr. Candy? Either what I saw was there or there was nothing. It is the charitable opinion that the week's events have strained my nerves and that I imagined the scene."

"Madam, up at that place, yesternight, I very definitely felt that there was something present besides ourselves. Something not of nature as we know it. We of the theatre give our lives to illusion. All that we do is create illusion. For that reason, many believe that we can no longer tell the real from the illusory. I believe that – perhaps – it gives us a greater sense of what is real. I say now as I said then that I saw no one but Jefferson with me in that scene; but I swear before all that I hold sacred that I felt in my bones – nay, madam, in my very soul – that we were not alone. There were other beings, other sprites there besides Oberon and Puck. Madam, as my confreres so abjure the Scottish Play, so will I now abjure this ill-begotten comedy. I swear before you that Lorenzo Candy's Oberon shall ne'er more tread the boards, nor my company perform A Midsummer Night's Dream. Enough now, I have had my say. I leave you, good lady, with one final word. Tear down that heathen temple. Let not one stone stand upon another. Tear it down and sow the ground with salt. Adieu, dear lady."

And so, with an appropriate flourish, Mr. Lorenzo Candy left Mrs. Courcy to contemplate her folly.

The weekend concluded with a ball and fireworks. It was, of course, acclaimed a success: unparalleled, unprecedented, and, surely, unrepeatable. Mrs. Courcy's outburst on the evening of the play was generously ascribed to the strain of producing so fantastic a spectacle. A physician in the party commented, well out of earshot of Mrs. Courcy, that women at her time of life quite often went insane.

On the eve of her guests' departure, the Earl of Quince amazed the company with his latest poetic endeavor, inspired by his train trip to Ollinway Park. It was a minor epic commemorating the inauguration of the first railway in England, the Liverpool and Manchester Line, a few years previous. That event had been marred by a former Cabinet minister, William Huskisson, being run over by the locomotive Rocket as he was standing in front of the Duke of Wellington. The earl's work was rife with dramatic irony and pathos. Huskisson and the Iron Duke had just that moment reconciled after a political estrangement when the hapless minister was felled and mangled by the oncoming train.

"His helpless limb wrent from its bloodied socket / 'Neath th' uncaring wheel of the mighty Rocket," intoned the young Earl of Quince, his handkerchief brandished melodramatically, "Mashed to a pulp with indifferent rage / A screaming sacrifice to a modern age."

Needless to say, Mrs. Courcy's unfortunate excitement on Oak Hill was even further removed from the minds of her company the next day as they quitted Ollinway for their journey by rail back to London. The earl's stirring evocation of someone being ground to a jelly beneath a railway carriage was contemplated by one and all as they awaited their departure upon the station platform at Cernchester.

The accolades heaped upon Mrs. Courcy by her departing guests rang hollow in her ears.

After the last visitor was seen off, Colonel and Mrs. Courcy were left to themselves in the great house of Ollinway Park. Instead of gala dinners and picnics, Colonel and Mrs. Courcy dined alone, often in silence, with servants moving quietly like ghosts. At night, as the lights of the great house were extinguished one by one, the Colonel and his lady would retire to their separate rooms alone.

The Colonel, who left the running of his estate to his agent much as he had left the running of his regiment to the regimental sergeant major in his army days, preoccupied himself with preparing notes for his memoirs. It was not a project which truly interested him, but it was, he felt, something that a man of his station and experience should do. For her part, Mrs. Courcy was left to oversee the running of the great house, which was competently managed by a butler and housekeeper, often in spite of Mrs. Courcy's supervision.

However, Mrs. Courcy showed little enthusiasm for her duties. She would walk the halls of Ollinway to no purpose and would often seem surprised at where she found herself, as if she had got there in a dream. She seemed to have no desire to walk abroad in daylight; but when night fell she grew restless and could often be seen traversing the garden like a sentry in crinoline.

One day, in early August, she complained to her husband about the gypsies.

"Gypsies, m'dear? What gypsies?" was the Colonel's reply.

"Surely you must have heard them? I hear them laughing and singing at night. I suppose it carries with the wind but it seems as if they are singing under my very window."

"Laughing and singing? Under your window?"

"As I said, the sound may be carried by the night wind. I do think it comes from Oak Hill. I find it most disturbing. And I am not altogether certain they have not been closer to the house. I do believe I heard voices as I walked in the garden the other night."

"This is extraordinary!" The Colonel reached for the bell and rang it savagely, "I shall send for Pyke and get to the bottom of this. Why am I keeping the man as groundskeeper if I'm to have all manner of vagabonds prowling about m'house at all hours of the night?"

Pyke, the groundskeeper, was duly sent for. He was an imposing figure and it was well known throughout the neighborhood that those who trespassed on Ollinway Park did so at peril of life and limb. Pyke vouchsafed that there were no gypsies in the Park, as none would dare set foot on the Colonel's land. Nevertheless, as Mrs. Courcy had heard them, Pyke and the lads would scour the Park from Oak Hill to the mere.

Days past and Pyke reported no progress in locating the miscreant gypsies. The Colonel, recalling the episode of the play, said nothing and hoped the matter would rest. Mrs. Courcy also said nothing as she had come to look forward to the nightly music from the hill.

It was a night in mid-August. The day had been oppressively hot and the setting of the sun seemed to have brought little surcease. Mrs. Courcy lay upon her bed staring vacantly at the ceiling. The windows were open wide in a futile effort to entice some wayward breeze. All was quiet. Mrs. Courcy's hands clutched the bedclothes, her knuckles white. She lay there expectant and afraid. She knew not what to expect nor what it was she feared. Soon the music would begin. She feared its beginning, yet she yearned for it as well. She both feared and yearned for the voices that accompanied it.

Slowly, Mrs. Courcy moved her eyes from the blank ceiling to the window that opened on Oak Hill. There, in the distance, she could make out the ancient, white marble of the Grecian folly shimmering in the moonlight. She did not notice that there was no moon. Mrs. Courcy's lips moved in silent prayer and then went still when the words forming on her lips seemed alien to her.

Young George Hawkins, the stable lad, had been pulled from a fitful sleep by a hand shaking his shoulder. He thought he was still dreaming when he saw the mistress of Ollinway Park in her nightclothes standing over him holding a lantern. He obeyed her sharp commands and, pulling on his clothes, harnessed a horse to the trap. Then, with Mrs. Courcy sitting beside him, Hawkins found himself riding towards Oak Hill.

"It is a warm night, is it not?" These were Mrs. Courcy's first words since they had left the stable.

"Uncommon warm, ma'am," the nervous youth replied. He glanced sidelong at his mistress. Her hair flowed down her back and she held her robe loose about her shoulders. He'd often heard tales about the doings of the gentry. He knew of their demands and their foibles, but this was his first experience of something genuinely strange. The boy was frightened of the woman beside him as they rode the rest of the way in silence.

She ordered Hawkins to stop the trap when it reached the foot of Oak Hill. Taking the lantern, she bid him wait and walked up the hill. In spite of the warm night air, Hawkins felt a chill tingle through him as he watched the light flicker and disappear among the trees.

Mrs. Courcy walked faster and faster up the hillside until she was almost running towards the altar. It was as if she were afraid of being late. She did not know what it was she could be late for. Breathless, she fell against the stone of the altar. It was warm to the touch; warm and yielding, like flesh. She pulled herself away at the thought.

Why was she here? She did not know. She held up the lantern and her eyes strained into the darkness. What was she looking for? She did not know. Her heart beat wildly. Was it from her run up the hill or was it fear? Of what had she to be afraid? She was frightened to know.

"Uncommon warm, ma'am."

"Hawkins. I told you to wait." She was suddenly relieved that the boy had disobeyed and followed her. The very thought of his presence seemed to break the spell, to bring her back to herself. She turned to the sound of the voice – but there was no one there.

"I have been waiting." The voice was not that of her servant. There was a rich, deep tone to it like strange, beautiful music. It seemed to be carried on the air all around her.

"Who are you? Where are you?" She spun about wildly, looking for whomever was speaking. The light from her lantern made the shadows beneath the oak dance madly.

The air seemed still and warm, yet the leaves of the oak rustled as if a breeze was passing through them. A strange, heavy fragrance seemed carried on the breeze. It grew stronger and stronger, and Mrs. Courcy breathed deeply. The aroma was strangely sweet, exotic yet familiar. It grew stifling and she feared she might choke. Then, suddenly, it seemed to flow through her and she breathed deeper and deeper, drinking it in until she felt filled with it. Until she felt she could breathe nothing else ever again.

Mrs. Courcy sensed a warm stirring all about her. It opened her robe and moved among the folds of her nightdress. She felt the warmth against her skin – every inch of her skin, as if she were naked. Her long hair was lifted from her shoulders as if by some unseen hand and she felt the pressure of unseen lips upon the nape of her neck. The lantern fell from her hand and the flame was extinguished, yet the shadows beneath the oak still danced wildly. Her nightclothes fell from her swaying body and she joined the shadows in their dance.

Far below, Hawkins was wakened in the trap by the sound of what he thought was women's laughter. Then there was a stillness so complete that he ached to hear a sound. Soon, he drifted off to sleep again. He was next awakened in the fading gray of early morning by the jostling of the cart. Mrs. Courcy sat next to him driving the trap.

"I did not wish to wake you." She said, "I'm sorry to have kept you out all night."

"No trouble, ma'am. I'm sorry to have fallen asleep."

Hawkins had always thought Mrs. Courcy a handsome woman but, as he watched her, he thought she looked absolutely beautiful. Perhaps it was the morning light or, perhaps the effects of the night air.

Mrs. Courcy said nothing further until they reached the house; then she simply told Hawkins to care for the horse and instruct the cook to fix him breakfast.

Colonel Courcy had been having a dream in which he was playing cards with the Duchess of Aberline, a woman who always reminded him of a bandit chief he had known in the Kashmir. They were playing Beggar My Neighbor and talking about pineapples. It did not make much sense but the Colonel knew it was a dream, so it didn't matter. The room in which they were playing had been indistinct to begin with but it gradually began to darken. The Colonel noticed for the first time that the Duchess's eyes glowed in the dark. Slowly, the Duchess began to transform into a rather voluptuous animal. Something like a wolf but also like a cat. She reached across the card table, grasped the Colonel by the shoulders and pulled him to her.

The Duchess had now disappeared and the Colonel knew only that he was being devoured by some magnificent beast. He found himself absolutely unwilling to resist until, with considerable surprise, he realized that it was no longer simply a dream.

The Colonel forced himself awake and was shocked at seeing his wife completely naked and sitting astride him. His bedclothes were in wild disarray and his nightshirt had been completely torn off.

"Mrs. Courcy!" The Colonel gasped, "Madam, you forget yourself!"

Mrs. Courcy clamped her lips over his open mouth and her tongue uncoiled into it.

* * *

There were no more galas at Ollinway Park. No one came to shoot partridge in September or pheasant in October, even though the Colonel's woods were reputedly the finest in the county. No one came for Christmas or New Year because no one was invited. After that August night, the Colonel kept the door to his room locked. He also ordered the Grecian folly pulled down. At the suggestion of Mrs. Courcy's stepbrother, the vicar, a stone cross was erected on the folly's site. A windstorm blew up one night and a limb was torn from the oak and sent crashing down on the cross, which was destroyed. Not long after, the Colonel ordered the oak cut down.

As for Mrs. Courcy, the Colonel yielded to her a considerable portion of her fortune and she chartered a yacht, which, the following midsummer, set off for a tour of the Greek Isles. Although the Colonel subsequently put it out that his wife died of cholera in Athens, there is no record of her death with the British consulate. There were, however, rumors of an Englishwoman having established a lady's seminary on a small, isolated island somewhere in the Aegean. Sailing parties passing that island have observed goatskin-clad women on the shoreline performing dances of a distinctly artistic character.

Clarimonde

Théophile Gautier, translated by Lafcadio Hearn

BROTHER, you ask me if I have ever loved. Yes. My story is a strange and terrible one; and though I am sixty-six years of age, I scarcely dare even now to disturb the ashes of that memory. To you I can refuse nothing; but I should not relate such a tale to any less experienced mind. So strange were the circumstances of my story, that I can scarcely believe myself to have ever actually been a party to them. For more than three years I remained the victim of a most singular and diabolical illusion. Poor country priest though I was, I led every night in a dream – would to God it had been all a dream! – a most worldly life, a damning life, a life of Sardanapalus. One single look too freely cast upon a woman well-nigh caused me to lose my soul; but finally by the grace of God and the assistance of my patron saint, I succeeded in casting out the evil spirit that possessed me. My daily life was long interwoven with a nocturnal life of a totally different character. By day I was a priest of the Lord, occupied with prayer and sacred things; by night, from the instant that I closed my eyes I became a young nobleman, a fine connoisseur in women, dogs, and horses; gambling, drinking, and blaspheming; and when I awoke at early daybreak, it seemed to me, on the other hand, that I had been sleeping, and had only dreamed that I was a priest. Of this somnambulistic life there now remains to me only the recollection of certain scenes and words which I cannot banish from my memory; but although I never actually left the walls of my presbytery, one would think to hear me speak that I were a man who, weary of all worldly pleasures, had become a religious, seeking to end a tempestuous life in the service of God, rather than a humble seminarist who has grown old in this obscure curacy, situated in the depths of the woods and even isolated from the life of the century.

Yes, I have loved as none in the world ever loved – with an insensate and furious passion – so violent that I am astonished it did not cause my heart to burst asunder. Ah, what nights – what nights!

From my earliest childhood I had felt a vocation to the priesthood, so that all my studies were directed with that idea in view. Up to the age of twenty-four my life had been only a prolonged novitiate. Having completed my course of theology I successively received all the minor orders, and my superiors judged me worthy, despite my youth, to pass the last awful degree. My ordination was fixed for Easter week.

I had never gone into the world. My world was confined by the walls of the college and the seminary. I knew in a vague sort of a way that there was something called Woman, but I never permitted my thoughts to dwell on such a subject, and I lived in a state of perfect innocence. Twice a year only I saw my infirm and aged mother, and in those visits were comprised my sole relations with the outer world.

I regretted nothing; I felt not the least hesitation at taking the last irrevocable step; I was filled with joy and impatience. Never did a betrothed lover count the slow hours with more feverish ardour; I slept only to dream that I was saying mass; I believed there could be nothing in the world more delightful than to be a priest; I would have refused to be a king or a poet in preference. My ambition could conceive of no loftier aim.

I tell you this in order to show you that what happened to me could not have happened in the natural order of things, and to enable you to understand that I was the victim of an inexplicable fascination.

At last the great day came. I walked to the church with a step so light that I fancied myself sustained in air, or that I had wings upon my shoulders. I believed myself an angel, and wondered at the sombre and thoughtful faces of my companions, for there were several of us. I had passed all the night in prayer, and was in a condition well-nigh bordering on ecstasy. The bishop, a venerable old man, seemed to me God the Father leaning over His Eternity, and I beheld Heaven through the vault of the temple.

You well know the details of that ceremony – the benediction, the communion under both forms, the anointing of the palms of the hands with the Oil of Catechumens, and then the holy sacrifice offered in concert with the bishop.

Ah, truly spake Job when he declared that the imprudent man is one who hath not made a covenant with his eyes! I accidentally lifted my head, which until then I had kept down, and beheld before me, so close that it seemed that I could have touched her – although she was actually a considerable distance from me and on the further side of the sanctuary railing – a young woman of extraordinary beauty, and attired with royal magnificence. It seemed as though scales had suddenly fallen from my eyes. I felt like a blind man who unexpectedly recovers his sight. The bishop, so radiantly glorious but an instant before, suddenly vanished away, the tapers paled upon their golden candlesticks like stars in the dawn, and a vast darkness seemed to fill the whole church. The charming creature appeared in bright relief against the background of that darkness, like some angelic revelation. She seemed herself radiant, and radiating light rather than receiving it.

I lowered my eyelids, firmly resolved not to again open them, that I might not be influenced by external objects, for distraction had gradually taken possession of me until I hardly knew what I was doing.

In another minute, nevertheless, I reopened my eyes, for through my eyelashes I still beheld her, all sparkling with prismatic colours, and surrounded with such a penumbra as one beholds in gazing at the sun.

Oh, how beautiful she was! The greatest painters, who followed ideal beauty into heaven itself, and thence brought back to earth the true portrait of the Madonna, never in their delineations even approached that wildly beautiful reality which I saw before me. Neither the verses of the poet nor the palette of the artist could convey any conception of her. She was rather tall, with a form and bearing of a goddess. Her hair, of a soft blonde hue, was parted in the midst and flowed back over her temples in two rivers of rippling gold; she seemed a diademed queen. Her forehead, bluish-white in its transparency, extended its calm breadth above the arches of her eyebrows, which by a strange singularity were almost black, and admirably relieved the effect of sea-green eyes of unsustainable vivacity and brilliancy. What eyes! With a single flash they could have decided a man's destiny. They had a life, a limpidity, an ardour, a humid light which I have never seen in human eyes; they shot forth rays like arrows, which I could distinctly *see* enter my heart. I know not if the fire which illumined them came from heaven or from hell, but assuredly it came from one or the other. That woman was either an angel or a demon, perhaps both. Assuredly she never sprang from the flank of Eve, our common mother. Teeth of the most lustrous pearl gleamed in her ruddy smile, and at every inflection of her lips little dimples appeared in the satiny rose of her adorable cheeks. There was a delicacy and pride in the regal outline of her nostrils bespeaking noble blood. Agate gleams played over the smooth lustrous skin of her half-bare shoulders, and strings of great blonde pearls – almost equal to her neck in beauty of colour – descended upon her bosom. From time to time she elevated her head with the undulating grace of a startled serpent or peacock, thereby imparting a quivering motion to the high lace ruff which surrounded it like a silver trellis-work.

She wore a robe of orange-red velvet, and from her wide ermine-lined sleeves there peeped forth patrician hands of infinite delicacy, and so ideally transparent that, like the fingers of Aurora, they permitted the light to shine through them.

All these details I can recollect at this moment as plainly as though they were of yesterday, for notwithstanding I was greatly troubled at the time, nothing escaped me; the faintest touch of shading, the little dark speck at the point of the chin, the imperceptible down at the corners of the lips, the velvety floss upon the brow, the quivering shadows of the eyelashes upon the cheeks – I could notice everything with astonishing lucidity of perception.

And gazing I felt opening within me gates that had until then remained closed; vents long obstructed became all clear, permitting glimpses of unfamiliar perspectives within; life suddenly made itself visible to me under a totally novel aspect. I felt as though I had just been born into a new world and a new order of things. A frightful anguish commenced to torture my heart as with red-hot pincers. Every successive minute seemed to me at once but a second and yet a century. Meanwhile the ceremony was proceeding, and I shortly found myself transported far from that world of which my newly born desires were furiously besieging the entrance. Nevertheless I answered 'Yes' when I wished to say 'No', though all within me protested against the violence done to my soul by my tongue. Some occult power seemed to force the words from my throat against my will. Thus it is, perhaps, that so many young girls walk to the altar firmly resolved to refuse in a startling manner the husband imposed upon them, and that yet not one ever fulfils her intention. Thus it is, doubtless, that so many poor novices take the veil, though they have resolved to tear it into shreds at the moment when called upon to utter the vows. One dares not thus cause so great a scandal to all present, nor deceive the expectation of so many people. All those eyes, all those wills seem to weigh down upon you like a cope of lead, and, moreover, measures have been so well taken, everything has been so thoroughly arranged beforehand and after a fashion so evidently irrevocable, that the will yields to the weight of circumstances and utterly breaks down.

As the ceremony proceeded the features of the fair unknown changed their expression. Her look had at first been one of caressing tenderness; it changed to an air of disdain and of mortification, as though at not having been able to make itself understood.

With an effort of will sufficient to have uprooted a mountain, I strove to cry out that I would not be a priest, but I could not speak; my tongue seemed nailed to my palate, and I found it impossible to express my will by the least syllable of negation. Though fully awake, I felt like one under the influence of a nightmare, who vainly strives to shriek out the one word upon which life depends.

She seemed conscious of the martyrdom I was undergoing, and, as though to encourage me, she gave me a look replete with divinest promise. Her eyes were a poem; their every glance was a song.

She said to me:

"If thou wilt be mine, I shall make thee happier than God Himself in His paradise. The angels themselves will be jealous of thee. Tear off that funeral shroud in which thou art about to wrap thyself. I am Beauty, I am Youth, I am Life. Come to me! Together we shall be Love. Can Jehovah offer thee aught in exchange? Our lives will flow on like a dream, in one eternal kiss.

"Fling forth the wine of that chalice, and thou art free. I will conduct thee to the Unknown Isles. Thou shalt sleep in my bosom upon a bed of massy gold under a silver pavilion, for I love thee and would take thee away from thy God, before whom so many noble hearts pour forth floods of love which never reach even the steps of His throne!"

These words seemed to float to my ears in a rhythm of infinite sweetness, for her look was actually sonorous, and the utterances of her eyes were re-echoed in the depths of my heart as though living lips had breathed them into my life. I felt myself willing to renounce God, and yet my tongue mechanically fulfilled all the formalities of the ceremony. The fair one gave me another look, so beseeching, so despairing that keen blades seemed to pierce my heart, and I felt my bosom transfixed by more swords than those of Our Lady of Sorrows.

All was consummated; I had become a priest.

Never was deeper anguish painted on human face than upon hers. The maiden who beholds her affianced lover suddenly fall dead at her side, the mother bending over the empty cradle of her child, Eve seated at the threshold of the gate of Paradise, the miser who finds a stone substituted for his stolen treasure, the poet who accidentally permits the only manuscript of his finest work to fall into the fire, could not wear a look so despairing, so inconsolable. All the blood had abandoned her charming face, leaving it whiter than marble; her beautiful arms hung lifelessly on either side of her body as though their muscles had suddenly relaxed, and she sought the support of a pillar, for her yielding limbs almost betrayed her. As for myself, I staggered toward the door of the church, livid as death, my forehead bathed with a sweat bloodier than that of Calvary; I felt as though I were being strangled; the vault seemed to have flattened down upon my shoulders, and it seemed to me that my head alone sustained the whole weight of the dome.

As I was about to cross the threshold a hand suddenly caught mine – a woman's hand! I had never till then touched the hand of any woman. It was cold as a serpent's skin, and yet its impress remained upon my wrist, burnt there as though branded by a glowing iron. It was she. "Unhappy man! Unhappy man! What hast thou done?" she exclaimed in a low voice, and immediately disappeared in the crowd.

The aged bishop passed by. He cast a severe and scrutinising look upon me. My face presented the wildest aspect imaginable: I blushed and turned pale alternately; dazzling lights flashed before my eyes. A companion took pity on me. He seized my arm and led me out. I could not possibly have found my way back to the seminary unassisted. At the corner of a street, while the young priest's attention was momentarily turned in another direction, a negro page, fantastically garbed, approached me, and without pausing on his way slipped into my hand a little pocket-book with gold-embroidered corners, at the same time giving me a sign to hide it. I concealed it in my sleeve, and there kept it until I found myself alone in my cell. Then I opened the clasp. There were only two leaves within, bearing the words, *Clarimonde. At the Concini Palace.* So little acquainted was I at that time with the things of this world that I had never heard of Clarimonde, celebrated as she was, and I had no idea as to where the Concini Palace was situated. I hazarded a thousand conjectures, each more extravagant than the last; but, in truth, I cared little whether she were a great lady or a courtesan, so that I could but see her once more.

My love, although the growth of a single hour, had taken imperishable root. I did not even dream of attempting to tear it up, so fully was I convinced such a thing would be impossible. That woman had completely taken possession of me. One look from her had sufficed to change my very nature. She had breathed her will into my life, and I no longer lived in myself, but In her and for her. I gave myself up to a thousand extravagancies. I kissed the place upon my hand which she had touched, and I repeated her name over and over again for hours in succession. I only needed to close my eyes in order to see her distinctly as though she were actually present; and I reiterated to myself the words she had uttered in my ear at the church porch: "Unhappy man! Unhappy man! What hast thou done?" I comprehended at last the full horror of my situation, and the funereal and awful restraints of the state into which I had just entered became clearly revealed to me. To be a priest! – that is, to be chaste, to never love, to observe no distinction of sex or age, to turn from the sight of all beauty, to put out one's own eyes, to hide forever crouching in the chill shadows of some church or cloister, to visit none but the dying, to watch by unknown corpses, and ever bear about with one the black soutane as a garb of mourning for oneself, so that your very dress might serve as a pall for your coffin.

And I felt life rising within me like a subterranean lake, expanding and overflowing; my blood leaped fiercely through my arteries; my long-restrained youth suddenly burst into active being, like the aloe which blooms but once in a hundred years, and then bursts into blossom with a clap of thunder.

What could I do in order to see Clarimonde once more? I had no pretext to offer for desiring to leave the seminary, not knowing any person in the city. I would not even be able to remain there but a short time, and was only waiting my assignment to the curacy which I must thereafter occupy. I tried to remove the bars of the window; but it was at a fearful height from the ground, and I found that as I had no ladder it would be useless to think of escaping thus. And, furthermore, I could descend thence only by night in any event, and afterward how should I be able to find my way through the inextricable labyrinth of streets? All these difficulties, which to many would have appeared altogether insignificant, were gigantic to me, a poor seminarist who had fallen in love only the day before for the first time, without experience, without money, without attire.

"Ah!" cried I to myself in my blindness, "were I not a priest I could have seen her every day; I might have been her lover, her spouse. Instead of being wrapped in this dismal shroud of mine I would have had garments of silk and velvet, golden chains, a sword, and fair plumes like other handsome young cavaliers. My hair, instead of being dishonoured by the tonsure, would flow down upon my neck in waving curls; I would have a fine waxed moustache; I would be a gallant." But one hour passed before an altar, a few hastily articulated words, had forever cut me off from the number of the living, and I had myself sealed down the stone of my own tomb; I had with my own hand bolted the gate of my prison! I went to the window. The sky was beautifully blue; the trees had donned their spring robes; nature seemed to be making parade of an ironical joy. The *Place* was filled with people, some going, others coming; young beaux and young beauties were sauntering in couples toward the groves and gardens; merry youths passed by, cheerily trolling refrains of drinking songs   it was all a picture of vivacity, life, animation, gaiety, which formed a bitter contrast with my mourning and my solitude. On the steps of the gate sat a young mother playing with her child. She kissed its little rosy mouth still impearled with drops of milk, and performed, in order to amuse it, a thousand divine little puerilities such as only mothers know how to invent. The father standing at a little distance smiled gently upon the charming group, and with folded arms seemed to hug his joy to his heart. I could not endure that spectacle. I closed the window with violence, and flung myself on my bed, my heart filled with frightful hate and jealousy, and gnawed my fingers and my bedcovers like a tiger that has passed ten days without food.

I know not how long I remained in this condition, but at last, while writhing on the bed in a fit of spasmodic fury, I suddenly perceived the Abbé Sérapion, who was standing erect in the centre of the room, watching me attentively. Filled with shame of myself, I let my head fall upon my breast and covered my face with my hands.

"Romuald, my friend, something very extraordinary is transpiring within you," observed Sérapion, after a few moments' silence; "your conduct is altogether inexplicable. You – always so quiet, so pious, so gentle – you to rage in your cell like a wild beast! Take heed, brother – do not listen to the suggestions of the devil The Evil Spirit, furious that you have consecrated yourself forever to the Lord, is prowling around you like a ravening wolf and making a last effort to obtain possession of you. Instead of allowing yourself to be conquered, my dear Romuald, make to yourself a cuirass of prayers, a buckler of mortifications, and combat the enemy like a valiant man; you will then assuredly overcome him. Virtue must be proved by temptation, and gold comes forth purer from the hands of the assayer. Fear not. Never allow yourself to become discouraged. The most watchful and steadfast souls are at moments liable to such temptation. Pray, fast, meditate, and the Evil Spirit will depart from you."

The words of the Abbé Sérapion restored me to myself, and I became a little more calm. "I came," he continued, "to tell you that you have been appointed to the curacy of C—. The priest who had charge of it has just died, and Monseigneur the Bishop has ordered me to have you installed there at once. Be ready, therefore, to start tomorrow.' I responded with an inclination of the head, and the Abbé retired. I opened my missal and commenced reading some prayers, but the letters became confused and blurred under my eyes, the thread of the ideas entangled itself hopelessly in my brain, and the volume at last fell from my hands without my being aware of it.

To leave tomorrow without having been able to see her again, to add yet another barrier to the many already interposed between us, to lose forever all hope of being able to meet her, except, indeed, through a miracle! Even to write to her, alas! would be impossible, for by whom could I dispatch my letter? With my sacred character of priest, to whom could I dare unbosom myself, in whom could I confide? I became a prey to the bitterest anxiety.

Then suddenly recurred to me the words of the Abbé Sérapion regarding the artifices of the devil; and the strange character of the adventure, the supernatural beauty of Clarimonde, the phosphoric light of her eyes, the burning imprint of her hand, the agony into which she had thrown me, the sudden change wrought within me when all my piety vanished in a single instant – these and other things clearly testified to the work of the Evil One, and perhaps that satiny hand was but the glove which concealed his claws. Filled with terror at these fancies, I again picked up the missal which had slipped from my knees and fallen upon the floor, and once more gave myself up to prayer.

Next morning Sérapion came to take me away. Two mules freighted with our miserable valises awaited us at the gate. He mounted one, and I the other as well as I knew how.

As we passed along the streets of the city, I gazed attentively at all the windows and balconies in the hope of seeing Clarimonde, but it was yet early in the morning, and the city had hardly opened its eyes. Mine sought to penetrate the blinds and window-curtains of all the palaces before which we were passing. Sérapion doubtless attributed this curiosity to my admiration of the architecture, for he slackened the pace of his animal in order to give me time to look around me. At last we passed the city gates and commenced to mount the hill beyond. When we arrived at its summit I turned to take a last look at the place where Clarimonde dwelt. The shadow of a great cloud hung over all the city; the contrasting colours of its blue and red roofs were lost in the uniform half-tint, through which here and there floated upward, like white flakes of foam, the smoke of freshly kindled fires. By a singular optical effect one edifice, which surpassed in height all the neighbouring buildings that were still dimly veiled by the vapours, towered up, fair and lustrous with the gilding of a solitary beam of sunlight – although actually more than a league away it seemed quite near. The smallest details of its architecture were plainly distinguishable – the turrets, the platforms, the window-casements, and even the swallow-tailed weather-vanes.

"What is that palace I see over there, all lighted up by the sun?" I asked Sérapion. He shaded his eyes with his hand, and having looked in the direction indicated, replied: "It is the ancient palace which the Prince Concini has given to the courtesan Clarimonde. Awful things are done there!"

At that instant, I know not yet whether it was a reality or an illusion, I fancied I saw gliding along the terrace a shapely white figure, which gleamed for a moment in passing and as quickly vanished. It was Clarimonde.

Oh, did she know that at that very hour, all feverish and restless – from the height of the rugged road which separated me from her, and which, alas! I could never more descend – I was directing my eyes upon the palace where she dwelt, and which a mocking beam of sunlight seemed to bring nigh to me, as though inviting me to enter therein as its lord? Undoubtedly she must have known it, for her soul was too sympathetically united with mine not to have felt its least emotional thrill, and that subtle sympathy it must have been which prompted her to climb – although clad only in her nightdress – to the summit of the terrace, amid the icy dews of the morning.

The shadow gained the palace, and the scene became to the eye only a motionless ocean of roofs and gables, amid which one mountainous undulation was distinctly visible. Sérapion urged his mule forward, my own at once followed at the same gait, and a sharp angle in the road at last hid the city of S— forever from my eyes, as I was destined never to return thither. At the close of a weary three-days' journey through dismal country fields, we caught sight of the cock upon the steeple of the church which I was to take charge of, peeping above the trees, and after having followed some winding roads fringed with thatched cottages and little gardens, we found ourselves in front of the façade, which certainly possessed few features of magnificence. A porch ornamented with some mouldings, and two or three pillars rudely hewn from sandstone; a tiled roof with counterforts of the same sandstone as the pillars – that was all. To the left lay the cemetery, overgrown with high weeds, and having a great iron cross rising up in its centre; to the right stood the presbytery under the shadow of the church. It was a house of the most extreme simplicity and frigid cleanliness. We entered the enclosure. A few chickens were picking up some oats scattered upon the ground; accustomed, seemingly, to the black habit of ecclesiastics, they showed no fear of our presence and scarcely troubled themselves to get out of our way. A hoarse, wheezy barking fell upon our ears, and we saw an aged dog running toward us.

It was my predecessor's dog. He had dull bleared eyes, grizzled hair, and every mark of the greatest age to which a dog can possibly attain. I patted him gently, and he proceeded at once to march along beside me with an air of satisfaction unspeakable. A very old woman, who had been the housekeeper of the former curé, also came to meet us, and after having invited me into a little back parlour, asked whether I intended to retain her. I replied that I would take care of her, and the dog, and the chickens, and all the furniture her master had bequeathed her at his death. At this she became fairly transported with joy, and the Abbé Sérapion at once paid her the price which she asked for her little property.

As soon as my installation was over, the Abbé Sérapion returned to the seminary. I was, therefore, left alone, with no one but myself to look to for aid or counsel. The thought of Clarimonde again began to haunt me, and in spite of all my endeavours to banish it, I always found it present in my meditations. One evening, while promenading in my little garden along the walks bordered with box-plants, I fancied that I saw through the elm-trees the figure of a woman, who followed my every movement, and that I beheld two sea-green eyes gleaming through the foliage; but it was only an illusion, and on going round to the other side of the garden, I could find nothing except a footprint on the sanded walk – a footprint so small that it seemed to have been made by the foot of a child. The garden was enclosed by very high walls. I searched every nook and corner of it, but could discover no one there. I have never succeeded in fully accounting for this circumstance, which, after all, was nothing compared with the strange things which happened to me afterward.

For a whole year I lived thus, filling all the duties of my calling with the most scrupulous exactitude, praying and fasting, exhorting and lending ghostly aid to the sick, and bestowing alms even to the extent of frequently depriving myself of the very necessaries of life. But I felt a great aridness within me, and the sources of grace seemed closed against me. I never found that happiness which should spring from the fulfilment of a holy mission; my thoughts were far away, and the words of Clarimonde were ever upon my lips like an involuntary refrain. Oh, brother, meditate well on this! Through having but once lifted my eyes to look upon a woman, through one fault apparently so venial, I have for years remained a victim to the most miserable agonies, and the happiness of my life has been destroyed forever.

I will not longer dwell upon those defeats, or on those inward victories invariably followed by yet more terrible falls, but will at once proceed to the facts of my story. One night my doorbell was long and violently rung. The aged housekeeper arose and opened to the stranger, and the figure of a man, whose complexion was deeply bronzed, and who was richly clad in a foreign costume, with a poniard at his girdle, appeared under the rays of Barbara's lantern. Her first impulse was one of terror, but the stranger reassured her, and stated that he desired to see me at once on matters relating to my holy calling. Barbara invited him upstairs, where I was on the point of retiring. The stranger told me that his mistress, a very noble lady, was lying at the point of death, and desired to see a priest. I replied that I was prepared to follow him, took with me the sacred articles necessary for extreme unction, and descended in all haste. Two horses black as the night itself stood without the gate, pawing the ground with impatience, and veiling their chests with long streams of smoky vapour exhaled from their nostrils. He held the stirrup and aided me to mount upon one; then, merely laying his hand upon the pommel of the saddle, he vaulted on the other, pressed the animal's sides with his knees, and loosened rein. The horse bounded forward with the velocity of an arrow. Mine, of which the stranger held the bridle, also started off at a swift gallop, keeping up with his companion. We devoured the road. The ground flowed backward beneath us in a long streaked line of pale gray, and the black silhouettes of the trees seemed fleeing by us on either side like an army in rout. We passed through a forest so profoundly gloomy that I felt my flesh creep in the chill darkness with superstitious fear. The showers of bright sparks which flew from the stony road under the ironshod feet of our horses remained glowing in our wake like a fiery trail; and had anyone at that hour of the night beheld us both – my guide and myself – he must have taken us for two spectres riding upon nightmares. Witch-fires ever and anon flitted across the road before us, and the night birds shrieked fearsomely in the depth of the woods beyond, where we beheld at intervals glow the phosphorescent eyes of wild cats. The manes of the horses became more and more dishevelled, the sweat streamed over their flanks, and their breath came through their nostrils hard and fast. But when he found them slacking pace, the guide reanimated them by uttering a strange, gutteral, unearthly cry, and the gallop recommenced with fury. At last the whirlwind race ceased; a huge black mass pierced through with many bright points of light suddenly rose before us, the hoofs of our horses echoed louder upon a strong wooden drawbridge, and we rode under a great vaulted archway which darkly yawned between two enormous towers. Some great excitement evidently reigned in the castle. Servants with torches were crossing the courtyard in every direction, and above lights were ascending and descending from landing to landing. I obtained a confused glimpse of vast masses of architecture – columns, arcades, flights of steps, stairways – a royal voluptuousness and elfin magnificence of construction worthy of fairyland. A negro page – the same who had before brought me the tablet from Clarimonde, and whom I instantly recognised – approached to aid me in dismounting, and the major-domo, attired in black velvet with a gold chain about his neck, advanced to meet me, supporting himself upon an ivory cane. Large tears were falling from his eyes and streaming over his cheeks and white beard. "Too late!" he cried, sorrowfully shaking his venerable head. "Too late, sir priest! But if you have not been able to save the soul, come at least to watch by the poor body."

He took my arm and conducted me to the death-chamber. I wept not less bitterly than he, for I had learned that the dead one was none other than that Clarimonde whom I had so deeply and so wildly loved. A *prie-dieu* stood at the foot of the bed; a bluish flame flickering in a bronze patern filled all the room with a wan, deceptive light, here and there bringing out in the darkness at intervals some projection of furniture or cornice. In a chiselled urn upon the table there was a faded white rose, whose leaves – excepting one that still held – had all fallen, like odorous tears, to the foot of the vase. A broken black mask, a fan, and disguises of every variety, which were lying on the armchairs, bore witness that death had entered suddenly and unannounced into that sumptuous dwelling. Without daring to cast my eyes upon the bed, I knelt down and commenced to repeat the Psalms for the Dead, with exceeding fervour, thanking God that He had placed the tomb between me and the memory of this woman, so that I might thereafter be able to utter her name in my prayers as a name forever sanctified by death. But my fervour gradually weakened, and I fell insensibly into a reverie. That chamber bore no semblance to a chamber of death. In lieu of the fetid and cadaverous odours which I had been accustomed to breathe during such funereal vigils, a languorous vapour of Oriental perfume – I know not what amorous odour of woman – softly floated through the tepid air. That pale light seemed rather a twilight gloom contrived for voluptuous pleasure, than a substitute for the yellow-flickering watch-tapers which shine by the side of corpses. I thought upon the strange destiny which enabled me to meet Clarimonde again at the very moment when she was lost to me forever, and a sigh of regretful anguish escaped from my breast. Then it seemed to me that someone behind me had also sighed, and I turned round to look. It was only an echo. But in that moment my eyes fell upon the bed of death which they had till then avoided. The red damask curtains, decorated with large flowers worked in embroidery and looped up with gold bullion, permitted me to behold the fair dead, lying at full length, with hands joined upon her bosom. She was covered with a linen wrapping of dazzling whiteness, which formed a strong contrast with the gloomy purple of the hangings, and was of so fine a texture that it concealed nothing of her body's charming form, and allowed the eye to follow those beautiful outlines – undulating like the neck of a swan – which even death had not robbed of their supple grace. She seemed an alabaster statue executed by some skilful sculptor to place upon the tomb of a queen, or rather, perhaps, like a slumbering maiden over whom the silent snow had woven a spotless veil.

I could no longer maintain my constrained attitude of prayer. The air of the alcove intoxicated me, that febrile perfume of half-faded roses penetrated my very brain, and I commenced to pace restlessly up and down the chamber, pausing at each turn before the bier to contemplate the graceful corpse lying beneath the transparency of its shroud. Wild fancies came thronging to my brain. I thought to myself that she might not, perhaps, be really dead; that she might only have feigned death for the purpose of bringing me to her castle, and then declaring her love. At one time I even thought I saw her foot move under the whiteness of the coverings, and slightly disarrange the long straight folds of the winding-sheet.

And then I asked myself: "Is this indeed Clarimonde? What proof have I that it is she? Might not that black page have passed into the service of some other lady? Surely, I must be going mad to torture and afflict myself thus!" But my heart answered with a fierce throbbing: "It is she; it is she indeed!" I approached the bed again, and fixed my eyes with redoubled attention upon the object of my incertitude. Ah, must I confess it? That exquisite perfection of bodily form, although purified and made sacred by the shadow of death, affected me more voluptuously than it should have done; and that repose so closely resembled slumber that one might well have mistaken it for such. I forgot that I had come there to perform a funeral ceremony; I fancied myself a young bridegroom entering the chamber of the bride, who all modestly hides her fair face, and through coyness seeks to keep herself wholly veiled. Heartbroken with grief, yet wild with hope, shuddering at once with fear and pleasure, I bent over her and grasped the corner of the sheet. I lifted it back, holding my breath all the while through fear of waking her. My arteries throbbed with such violence that I felt them hiss through my temples, and the sweat poured from my forehead in streams, as though I had lifted a mighty slab of marble. There, indeed, lay Clarimonde, even as I had seen her at the church on the day of my ordination. She was not less charming than then. With her, death seemed but a last coquetry. The pallor of her cheeks, the less brilliant carnation of her lips, her long eyelashes lowered and relieving their dark fringe against that white skin, lent her an unspeakably seductive aspect of melancholy chastity and mental suffering; her long loose hair, still intertwined with some little blue flowers, made a shining pillow for her head, and veiled the nudity of her shoulders with its thick ringlets; her beautiful hands, purer, more diaphanous, than the Host, were crossed on her bosom in an attitude of pious rest and silent prayer, which served to counteract all that might have proven otherwise too alluring – even after death – in the exquisite roundness and ivory polish of her bare arms from which the pearl bracelets had not yet been removed. I remained long in mute contemplation, and the more I gazed, the less could I persuade myself that life had really abandoned that beautiful body forever. I do not know whether it was an illusion or a reflection of the lamplight, but it seemed to me that the blood was again commencing to circulate under that lifeless pallor, although she remained all motionless. I laid my hand lightly on her arm; it was cold, but not colder than her hand on the day when it touched mine at the portals of the church. I resumed my position, bending my face above her, and bathing her cheek with the warm dew of my tears. Ah, what bitter feelings of despair and helplessness, what agonies unutterable did I endure in that long watch! Vainly did I wish that I could have gathered all my life into one mass that I might give it all to her, and breathe into her chill remains the flame which devoured me. The night advanced, and feeling the moment of eternal separation approach, I could not deny myself the last sad sweet pleasure of imprinting a kiss upon the dead lips of her who had been my only love... Oh, miracle! A faint breath mingled itself with my breath, and the mouth of Clarimonde responded to the passionate pressure of mine. Her eyes unclosed, and lighted up with something of their former brilliancy; she uttered a long sigh, and uncrossing her arms, passed them around my neck with a look of ineffable delight. "Ah, it is thou, Romuald!" she murmured in a voice languishingly sweet as the last vibrations of a harp. "What ailed thee, dearest? I waited so long for thee that I am dead; but we are now betrothed: I can see thee and visit thee. Adieu, Romuald, adieu! I love thee. That is all I wished to tell thee, and I give thee back the life which thy kiss for a moment recalled. We shall soon meet again."

Her head fell back, but her arms yet encircled me, as though to retain me still. A furious whirlwind suddenly burst in the window, and entered the chamber. The last remaining leaf of the white rose for a moment palpitated at the extremity of the stalk like a butterfly's wing, then it detached itself and flew forth through the open casement, bearing with it the soul of Clarimonde. The lamp was extinguished, and I fell insensible upon the bosom of the beautiful dead.

When I came to myself again I was lying on the bed in my little room at the presbytery, and the old dog of the former curé was licking my hand, which had been hanging down outside of the covers. Barbara, all trembling with age and anxiety, was busying herself about the room, opening and shutting drawers, and emptying powders into glasses. On seeing me open my eyes, the old woman uttered a cry of joy, the dog yelped and wagged his tail, but I was still so weak that I could not speak a single word or make the slightest motion. Afterward I learned that I had lain thus for three days, giving no evidence of life beyond the faintest respiration. Those three days do not reckon in my life, nor could I ever imagine whither my spirit had departed during those three days; I have no recollection of aught relating to them. Barbara told me that the same coppery-complexioned man who came to seek me on the night of my departure from the presbytery had brought me back the next morning in a close litter, and departed immediately afterward. When I became able to collect my scattered thoughts, I reviewed within my mind all the circumstances of that fateful night. At first I thought I had been the victim of some magical illusion, but ere long the recollection of other circumstances, real and palpable in themselves, came to forbid that supposition. I could not believe that I had been dreaming, since Barbara as well as myself had seen the strange man with his two black horses, and described with exactness every detail of his figure and apparel. Nevertheless it appeared that none knew of any castle in the neighbourhood answering to the description of that in which I had again found Clarimonde.

One morning I found the Abbé Sérapion in my room. Barbara had advised him that I was ill, and he had come with all speed to see me. Although this haste on his part testified to an affectionate interest in me, yet his visit did not cause me the pleasure which it should have done. The Abbé Sérapion had something penetrating and inquisitorial in his gaze which made me feel very ill at ease. His presence filled me with embarrassment and a sense of guilt. At the first glance he divined my interior trouble, and I hated him for his clairvoyance.

While he inquired after my health in hypocritically honeyed accents, he constantly kept his two great yellow lion-eyes fixed upon me, and plunged his look into my soul like a sounding-lead. Then he asked me how I directed my parish, if I was happy in it, how I passed the leisure hours allowed me in the intervals of pastoral duty, whether I had become acquainted with many of the inhabitants of the place, what was my favourite reading, and a thousand other such questions. I answered these inquiries as briefly as possible, and he, without ever waiting for my answers, passed rapidly from one subject of query to another. That conversation had evidently no connection with what he actually wished to say. At last, without any premonition, but as though repeating a piece of news which he had recalled on the instant, and feared might otherwise be forgotten subsequently, he suddenly said, in a clear vibrant voice, which rang in my ears like the trumpets of the Last Judgment:

"The great courtesan Clarimonde died a few days ago, at the close of an orgie which lasted eight days and eight nights. It was something infernally splendid. The abominations of the banquets of Belshazzar and Cleopatra were re-enacted there. Good God, what age are we living in? The guests were served by swarthy slaves who spoke an unknown tongue, and who seemed to me to be veritable demons. The livery of the very least among them would have served for the gala-dress of an emperor. There have always been very strange stories told of this Clarimonde, and all her lovers came to a violent or miserable end. They used to say that she was a ghoul, a female vampire; but I believe she was none other than Beelzebub himself."

He ceased to speak, and commenced to regard me more attentively than ever, as though to observe the effect of his words on me. I could not refrain from starting when I heard him utter the name of Clarimonde, and this news of her death, in addition to the pain it caused me by reason of its coincidence with the nocturnal scenes I had witnessed, filled me with an agony and terror which my face betrayed, despite my utmost endeavours to appear composed. Sérapion fixed an anxious and severe look upon me, and then observed: "My son, I must warn you that you are standing with foot raised upon the brink of an abyss; take heed lest you fall therein. Satan's claws are long, and tombs are not always true to their trust. The tombstone of Clarimonde should be sealed down with a triple seal, for, if report be true, it is not the first time she has died. May God watch over you, Romuald!"

And with these words the Abbé walked slowly to the door. I did not see him again at that time, for he left for S — almost immediately.

I became completely restored to health and resumed my accustomed duties. The memory of Clarimonde and the words of the old Abbé were constantly in my mind; nevertheless no extraordinary event had occurred to verify the funereal predictions of Sérapion, and I had commenced to believe that his fears and my own terrors were over-exaggerated, when one night I had a strange dream. I had hardly fallen asleep when I heard my bed-curtains drawn apart, as their rings slided back upon the curtain rod with a sharp sound. I rose up quickly upon my elbow, and beheld the shadow of a woman standing erect before me. I recognised Clarimonde immediately. She bore in her hand a little lamp, shaped like those which are placed in tombs, and its light lent her fingers a rosy transparency, which extended itself by lessening degrees even to the opaque and milky whiteness of her bare arm. Her only garment was the linen winding-sheet which had shrouded her when lying upon the bed of death. She sought to gather its folds over her bosom as though ashamed of being so scantily clad, but her little hand was not equal to the task. She was so white that the colour of the drapery blended with that of her flesh under the pallid rays of the lamp. Enveloped with this subtle tissue which betrayed all the contour of her body, she seemed the marble statue of some fair antique rather than a woman endowed with life. But dead or living, statue or woman, shadow or body, her beauty was still the same, only that the green light of her eyes was less brilliant, and her mouth, once so warmly crimson, was only tinted with a faint tender rosiness, like that of her cheeks. The little blue flowers which I had noticed entwined in her hair were withered and dry, and had lost nearly all their leaves, but this did not prevent her from being charming – so charming that, notwithstanding the strange character of the adventure, and the unexplainable manner in which she had entered my room, I felt not even for a moment the least fear.

She placed the lamp on the table and seated herself at the foot of my bed; then bending toward me, she said, in that voice at once silvery clear and yet velvety in its sweet softness, such as I never heard from any lips save hers:

"I have kept thee long in waiting, dear Romuald, and it must have seemed to thee that I had forgotten thee. But I come from afar off, very far off, and from a land whence no other has ever yet returned. There is neither sun nor moon in that land whence I come: all is but space and shadow; there is neither road nor pathway: no earth for the foot, no air for the wing; and nevertheless behold me here, for Love is stronger than Death and must conquer him in the end. Oh what sad faces and fearful things I have seen on my way hither! What difficulty my soul, returned to earth through the power of will alone, has had in finding its body and reinstating itself therein! What terrible efforts I had to make ere I could lift the ponderous slab with which they had covered me! See, the palms of my poor hands are all bruised! Kiss them, sweet love, that they may be healed!" She laid the cold palms of her hands upon my mouth, one after the other. I kissed them, indeed, many times, and she the while watched me with a smile of ineffable affection.

I confess to my shame that I had entirely forgotten the advice of the Abbé Sérapion and the sacred office wherewith I had been invested. I had fallen without resistance, and at the first assault. I had not even made the least effort to repel the tempter. The fresh coolness of Clarimonde's skin penetrated my own, and I felt voluptuous tremors pass over my whole body. Poor child! In spite of all I saw afterward, I can hardly yet believe she was a demon; at least she had no appearance of being such, and never did Satan so skilfully conceal his claws and horns. She had drawn her feet up beneath her, and squatted down on the edge of the couch in an attitude full of negligent coquetry. From time to time she passed her little hand through my hair and twisted it into curls, as though trying how a new style of wearing it would become my face. I abandoned myself to her hands with the most guilty pleasure, while she accompanied her gentle play with the prettiest prattle. The most remarkable fact was that I felt no astonishment whatever at so extraordinary an adventure, and as in dreams one finds no difficulty in accepting the most fantastic events as simple facts, so all these circumstances seemed to me perfectly natural in themselves.

"I loved thee long ere I saw thee, dear Romuald, and sought thee everywhere. Thou wast my dream, and I first saw thee in the church at the fatal moment. I said at once, 'It is he!' I gave thee a look into which I threw all the love I ever had, all the love I now have, all the love I shall ever have for thee – a look that would have damned a cardinal or brought a king to his knees at my feet in view of all his court. Thou remainedst unmoved, preferring thy God to me!

"Ah, how jealous I am of that God whom thou didst love and still lovest more than me!

"Woe is me, unhappy one that I am! I can never have thy heart all to myself, I whom thou didst recall to life with a kiss – dead Clarimonde, who for thy sake bursts asunder the gates of the tomb, and comes to consecrate to thee a life which she has resumed only to make thee happy!"

All her words were accompanied with the most impassioned caresses, which bewildered my sense and my reason to such an extent, that I did not fear to utter a frightful blasphemy for the sake of consoling her, and to declare that I loved her as much as God.

Her eyes rekindled and shone like chrysoprases. "In truth? – in very truth? – as much as God!" she cried, flinging her beautiful arms around me. "Since it is so, thou wilt come with me; thou wilt follow me whithersoever I desire. Thou wilt cast away thy ugly black habit. Thou shalt be the proudest and most envied of cavaliers; thou shalt be my lover! To be the acknowledged lover of Clarimonde, who has refused even a Pope! That will be something to feel proud of. Ah, the fair, unspeakably happy existence, the beautiful golden life we shall live together! And when shall we depart, my fair sir?"

"Tomorrow! Tomorrow!" I cried in my delirium.

"Tomorrow, then, so let it be!" she answered. "In the meanwhile I shall have opportunity to change my toilet, for this is a little too light and in nowise suited for a voyage. I must also forthwith notify all my friends who believe me dead, and mourn for me as deeply as they are capable of doing. The money, the dresses, the carriages – all will be ready. I shall call for thee at this same hour. Adieu, dear heart!" And she lightly touched my forehead with her lips. The lamp went out, the curtains closed again, and all became dark; a leaden, dreamless sleep fell on me and held me unconscious until the morning following.

I awoke later than usual, and the recollection of this singular adventure troubled me during the whole day. I finally persuaded myself that it was a mere vapour of my heated imagination. Nevertheless its sensations had been so vivid that it was difficult to persuade myself that they were not real, and it was not without some presentiment of what was going to happen that I got into bed at last, after having prayed God to drive far from me all thoughts of evil, and to protect the chastity of my slumber.

I soon fell into a deep sleep, and my dream was continued. The curtains again parted, and I beheld Clarimonde, not as on the former occasion, pale in her pale winding-sheet, with the violets of death upon her cheeks, but gay, sprightly, jaunty, in a superb travelling-dress of green velvet, trimmed with gold lace, and looped up on either side to allow a glimpse of satin petticoat. Her blonde hair escaped in thick ringlets from beneath a broad black felt hat, decorated with white feathers whimsically twisted into various shapes. In one hand she held a little riding-whip terminated by a golden whistle. She tapped me lightly with it, and exclaimed: "Well, my fine sleeper, is this the way you make your preparations? I thought I would find you up and dressed. Arise quickly, we have no time to lose."

I leaped out of bed at once.

"Come, dress yourself, and let us go," she continued, pointing to a little package she had brought with her. "The horses are becoming impatient of delay and champing their bits at the door. We ought to have been by this time at least ten leagues distant from here."

I dressed myself hurriedly, and she handed me the articles of apparel herself one by one, bursting into laughter from time to time at my awkwardness, as she explained to me the use of a garment when I had made a mistake. She hurriedly arranged my hair, and this done, held up before me a little pocket-mirror of Venetian crystal, rimmed with silver filigree-work, and playfully asked: "How dost find thyself now? Wilt engage me for thy valet de chambre?"

I was no longer the same person, and I could not even recognise myself. I resembled my former self no more than a finished statue resembles a block of stone. My old face seemed but a coarse daub of the one reflected in the mirror. I was handsome, and my vanity was sensibly tickled by the metamorphosis.

That elegant apparel, that richly embroidered vest had made of me a totally different personage, and I marvelled at the power of transformation owned by a few yards of cloth cut after a certain pattern. The spirit of my costume penetrated my very skin and within ten minutes more I had become something of a coxcomb.

In order to feel more at ease in my new attire, I took several turns up and down the room. Clarimonde watched me with an air of maternal pleasure, and appeared well satisfied with her work. "Come, enough of this child's play! Let us start, Romuald, dear. We have far to go, and we may not get there in time." She took my hand and led me forth. All the doors opened before her at a touch, and we passed by the dog without awaking him.

At the gate we found Margheritone waiting, the same swarthy groom who had once before been my escort. He held the bridles of three horses, all black like those which bore us to the castle – one for me, one for him, one for Clarimonde. Those horses must have been Spanish genets born of mares fecundated by a zephyr, for they were fleet as the wind itself, and the moon, which had just risen at our departure to light us on the way, rolled over the sky like a wheel detached from her own chariot. We beheld her on the right leaping from tree to tree, and putting herself out of breath in the effort to keep up with us. Soon we came upon a level plain where, hard by a clump of trees, a carriage with four vigorous horses awaited us. We entered it, and the postillions urged their animals into a mad gallop. I had one arm around Clarimonde's waist, and one of her hands clasped in mine; her head leaned upon my shoulder, and I felt her bosom, half bare, lightly pressing against my arm. I had never known such intense happiness. In that hour I had forgotten everything, and I no more remembered having ever been a priest than I remembered what

I had been doing in my mother's womb, so great was the fascination which the evil spirit exerted upon me. From that night my nature seemed in some sort to have become halved, and there were two men within me, neither of whom knew the other. At one moment I believed myself a priest who dreamed nightly that he was a gentleman, at another that I was a gentleman who dreamed he was a priest. I could no longer distinguish the dream from the reality, nor could I discover where the reality began or where ended the dream. The exquisite young lord and libertine railed at the priest, the priest loathed the dissolute habits of the young lord. Two spirals entangled and confounded the one with the other, yet never touching, would afford a fair representation of this bicephalic life which I lived. Despite the strange character of my condition, I do not believe that I ever inclined, even for a moment, to madness. I always retained with extreme vividness all the perceptions of my two lives. Only there was one absurd fact which I could not explain to myself – namely, that the consciousness of the same individuality existed in two men so opposite in character. It was an anomaly for which I could not account – whether I believed myself to be the curé of the little village of C—, or *Il Signor Romualdo*, the titled lover of Clarimonde.

Be that as it may, I lived, at least I believed that I lived, in Venice. I have never been able to discover rightly how much of illusion and how much of reality there was in this fantastic adventure. We dwelt in a great palace on the Canaleio, filled with frescoes and statues, and containing two Titians in the noblest style of the great master, which were hung in Clarimonde's chamber. It was a palace well worthy of a king. We had each our gondola, our *barcarolli* in family livery, our music hall, and our special poet. Clarimonde always lived upon a magnificent scale; there was something of Cleopatra in her nature. As for me, I had the retinue of a prince's son, and I was regarded with as much reverential respect as though I had been of the family of one of the twelve Apostles or the four Evangelists of the Most Serene Republic. I would not have turned aside to allow even the Doge to pass, and I do not believe that since Satan fell from heaven, any creature was ever prouder or more insolent than I. I went to the Ridotto, and played with a luck which seemed absolutely infernal. I received the best of all society – the sons of ruined families, women of the theatre, shrewd knaves, parasites, hectoring swashbucklers. But notwithstanding the dissipation of such a life, I always remained faithful to Clarimonde. I loved her wildly. She would have excited satiety itself, and chained inconstancy. To have Clarimonde was to have twenty mistresses; ay, to possess all women: so mobile, so varied of aspect, so fresh in new charms was she all in herself a very chameleon of a woman, in sooth. She made you commit with her the infidelity you would have committed with another, by donning to perfection the character, the attraction, the style of beauty of the woman who appeared to please you. She returned my love a hundred-fold, and it was in vain that the young patricians and even the Ancients of the Council of Ten made her the most magnificent proposals. A Foscari even went so far as to offer to espouse her. She rejected all his overtures. Of gold she had enough. She wished no longer for anything but love – a love youthful, pure, evoked by herself, and which should be a first and last passion. I would have been perfectly happy but for a cursed nightmare which recurred every night, and in which I believed myself to be a poor village curé, practising mortification and penance for my excesses during the day. Reassured by my constant association with her, I never thought further of the strange manner in which I had become acquainted with Clarimonde. But the words of the Abbé Sérapion concerning her recurred often to my memory, and never ceased to cause me uneasiness.

For some time the health of Clarimonde had not been so good as usual; her complexion grew paler day by day. The physicians who were summoned could not comprehend the nature of her malady and knew not how to treat it. They all prescribed some insignificant remedies, and never called a second time. Her paleness, nevertheless, visibly increased, and she became colder and colder, until she seemed almost as white and dead as upon that memorable night in the unknown castle. I grieved with anguish unspeakable to behold her thus slowly perishing; and she, touched by my agony, smiled upon me sweetly and sadly with the fateful smile of those who feel that they must die.

One morning I was seated at her bedside, and breakfasting from a little table placed close at hand, so that I might not be obliged to leave her for a single instant. In the act of cutting some fruit I accidentally inflicted rather a deep gash on my finger. The blood immediately gushed forth in a little purple jet, and a few drops spurted upon Clarimonde. Her eyes flashed, her face suddenly assumed an expression of savage and ferocious joy such as I had never before observed in her. She leaped out of her bed with animal agility – the agility, as it were, of an ape or a cat – and sprang upon my wound, which she commenced to suck with an air of unutterable pleasure. She swallowed the blood in little mouthfuls, slowly and carefully, like a connoisseur tasting a wine from Xeres or Syracuse. Gradually her eyelids half closed, and the pupils of her green eyes became oblong instead of round. From time to time she paused in order to kiss my hand, then she would recommence to press her lips to the lips of the wound in order to coax forth a few more ruddy drops. When she found that the blood would no longer come, she arose with eyes liquid and brilliant, rosier than a May dawn; her face full and fresh, her hand warm and moist – in fine, more beautiful than ever, and in the most perfect health.

"I shall not die! I shall not die!" she cried, clinging to my neck, half mad with joy. "I can love thee yet for a long time. My life is thine, and all that is of me comes from thee. A few drops of thy rich and noble blood, more precious and more potent than all the elixirs of the earth, have given me back life."

This scene long haunted my memory, and inspired me with strange doubts in regard to Clarimonde; and the same evening, when slumber had transported me to my presbytery, I beheld the Abbé Sérapion, graver and more anxious of aspect than ever. He gazed attentively at me, and sorrowfully exclaimed: "Not content with losing your soul, you now desire also to lose your body. Wretched young man, into how terrible a plight have you fallen!" The tone in which he uttered these words powerfully affected me, but in spite of its vividness even that impression was soon dissipated, and a thousand other cares erased it from my mind. At last one evening, while looking into a mirror whose traitorous position she had not taken into account, I saw Clarimonde in the act of emptying a powder into the cup of spiced wine which she had long been in the habit of preparing after our repasts. I took the cup, feigned to carry it to my lips, and then placed it on the nearest article of furniture as though intending to finish it at my leisure. Taking advantage of a moment when the fair one's back was turned, I threw the contents under the table, after which I retired to my chamber and went to bed, fully resolved not to sleep, but to watch and discover what should come of all this mystery. I did not have to wait long, Clarimonde entered in her nightdress, and having removed her apparel, crept into bed and lay down beside me. When she felt assured that I was asleep, she bared my arm, and drawing a gold pin from her hair, commenced to murmur in a low voice:

"One drop, only one drop! One ruby at the end of my needle… Since thou lovest me yet, I must not die! … Ah, poor love! His beautiful blood, so brightly purple, I must drink it. Sleep, my only treasure! Sleep, my god, my child! I will do thee no harm; I will only take of thy life what I must to keep my own from being forever extinguished. But that I love thee so much, I could well resolve to have other lovers whose veins I could drain; but since I have known thee all other men have become hateful to me... Ah, the beautiful arm! How round it is! How white it is! How shall I ever dare to prick this pretty blue vein!" And while thus murmuring to herself she wept, and I felt her tears raining on my arm as she clasped it with her hands. At last she took the resolve, slightly punctured me with her pin, and commenced to suck up the blood which oozed from the place. Although she swallowed only a few drops, the fear of weakening me soon seized her, and she carefully tied a little band around my arm, afterward rubbing the wound with an unguent which immediately cicatrised it. Further doubts were impossible. The Abbé Sérapion was right. Notwithstanding this positive knowledge, however, I could not cease to love Clarimonde, and I would gladly of my own accord have given her all the blood she required to sustain her factitious life. Moreover, I felt but little fear of her. The woman seemed to plead with me for the vampire, and what I had already heard and seen sufficed to reassure me completely. In those days I had plenteous veins, which would not have been so easily exhausted as at present; and I would not have thought of bargaining for my blood, drop by drop. I would rather have opened myself the veins of my arm and said to her: "Drink, and may my love infiltrate itself throughout thy body together with my blood!" I carefully avoided ever making the least reference to the narcotic drink she had prepared for me, or to the incident of the pin, and we lived in the most perfect harmony.

Yet my priestly scruples commenced to torment me more than ever, and I was at a loss to imagine what new penance I could invent in order to mortify and subdue my flesh. Although these visions were involuntary, and though I did not actually participate in anything relating to them, I could not dare to touch the body of Christ with hands so impure and a mind defiled by such debauches whether real or imaginary. In the effort to avoid falling under the influence of these wearisome hallucinations, I strove to prevent myself from being overcome by sleep. I held my eyelids open with my fingers, and stood for hours together leaning upright against the wall, fighting sleep with all my might; but the dust of drowsiness invariably gathered upon my eyes at last, and finding all resistance useless, I would have to let my arms fall in the extremity of despairing weariness, and the current of slumber would again bear me away to the perfidious shores. Sérapion addressed me with the most vehement exhortations, severely reproaching me for my softness and want of fervour. Finally, one day when I was more wretched than usual, he said to me: "There is but one way by which you can obtain relief from this continual torment, and though it is an extreme measure it must be made use of; violent diseases require violent remedies. I know where Clarimonde is buried. It is necessary that we shall disinter her remains, and that you shall behold in how pitiable a state the object of your love is. Then you will no longer be tempted to lose your soul for the sake of an unclean corpse devoured by worms, and ready to crumble into dust. That will assuredly restore you to yourself." For my part, I was so tired of this double life that I at once consented, desiring to ascertain beyond a doubt whether a priest or a gentleman had been the victim of delusion. I had become fully resolved either to kill one of the two men within me for the benefit of the other, or else to kill both, for so terrible an existence could not last long and be endured. The Abbé Sérapion provided himself with a mattock, a lever, and a lantern, and at midnight we wended our way to the cemetery of ——, the location and place of which were perfectly familiar to him. After having directed the rays of the dark lantern upon the inscriptions of several tombs, we came at last upon a great slab, half concealed by huge weeds and devoured by mosses and parasitic plants, whereupon we deciphered the opening lines of the epitaph:

Here lies Clarimonde
Who was famed in her lifetime
As the fairest of women.[1]

"It is here without a doubt," muttered Sérapion, and placing his lantern on the ground, he forced the point of the lever under the edge of the stone and commenced to raise it. The stone yielded, and he proceeded to work with the mattock. Darker and more silent than the night itself, I stood by and watched him do it, while he, bending over his dismal toil, streamed with sweat, panted, and his hard-coming breath seemed to have the harsh tone of a death rattle. It was a weird scene, and had any persons from without beheld us, they would assuredly have taken us rather for profane wretches and shroud-stealers than for priests of God. There was something grim and fierce in Sérapion's zeal which lent him the air of a demon rather than of an apostle or an angel, and his great aquiline face, with all its stern features, brought out in strong relief by the lantern-light, had something fearsome in it which enhanced the unpleasant fancy. I felt an icy sweat come out upon my forehead in huge beads, and my hair stood up with a hideous fear. Within the depths of my own heart I felt that the act of the austere Sérapion was an abominable sacrilege; and I could have prayed that a triangle of fire would issue from the entrails of the dark clouds, heavily rolling above us, to reduce him to cinders. The owls which had been nestling in the cypress trees, startled by the gleam of the lantern, flew against it from time to time, striking their dusty wings against its panes, and uttering plaintive cries of lamentation; wild foxes yelped in the far darkness, and a thousand sinister noises detached themselves from the silence. At last Sérapion's mattock struck the coffin itself, making its planks re-echo with a deep sonorous sound, with that terrible sound nothingness utters when stricken. He wrenched apart and tore up the lid, and I beheld Clarimonde, pallid as a figure of marble, with hands joined; her white winding-sheet made but one fold from her head to her feet. A little crimson drop sparkled like a speck of dew at one corner of her colourless mouth. Sérapion, at this spectacle, burst into fury: "Ah, thou art here, demon! Impure courtesan! Drinker of blood and gold!" And he flung holy water upon the corpse and the coffin, over which he traced the sign of the cross with his sprinkler. Poor Clarimonde had no sooner been touched by the blessed spray than her beautiful body crumbled into dust, and became only a shapeless and frightful mass of cinders and half-calcined bones.

"Behold your mistress, my Lord Romuald!" cried the inexorable priest, as he pointed to these sad remains. "Will you be easily tempted after this to promenade on the Lido or at Fusina with your beauty?" I covered my face with my hands, a vast ruin had taken place within me. I returned to my presbytery, and the noble Lord Romuald, the lover of Clarimonde, separated himself from the poor priest with whom he had kept such strange company so long. But once only, the following night, I saw Clarimonde. She said to me, as she had said the first time at the portals of the church: "Unhappy man! Unhappy man! What hast thou done? Wherefore have hearkened to that imbecile priest? Wert thou not happy? And what harm had I ever done thee that thou shouldst violate my poor tomb, and lay bare the miseries of my nothingness? All communication between our souls and our bodies is henceforth forever broken. Adieu! Thou wilt yet regret me!" She vanished in air as smoke, and I never saw her more.

Alas! she spoke truly indeed. I have regretted her more than once, and I regret her still. My soul's peace has been very dearly bought. The love of God was not too much to replace such a love as hers. And this, brother, is the story of my youth. Never gaze upon a woman, and walk abroad only with eyes ever fixed upon the ground; for however chaste and watchful one may be, the error of a single moment is enough to make one lose eternity.

Footnotes for 'Clarimonde'

1. The broken beauty of the lines is unavoidably lost in the translation.

Ici gît Clarimonde
Qui fut de son vivant
La plus belle du monde.

The Viy

Nikolai Gogol, translated by Claud Field

The 'Viy' is a monstrous creation of popular fancy. It is the name which the inhabitants of Little Russia give to the king of the gnomes, whose eyelashes reach to the ground. The following story is a specimen of such folk-lore. I have made no alterations, but reproduce it in the same simple form in which I heard it.

— Author's Note.

Chapter I

AS SOON AS the clear seminary bell began sounding in Kieff in the morning, the pupils would come flocking from all parts of the town. The students of grammar, rhetoric, philosophy, and theology hastened with their books under their arms over the streets.

The 'grammarians' were still mere boys. On the way they pushed against each other and quarrelled with shrill voices. Nearly all of them wore torn or dirty clothes, and their pockets were always crammed with all kinds of things – push-bones, pipes made out of pens, remains of confectionery, and sometimes even young sparrows. The latter would sometimes begin to chirp in the midst of deep silence in the school, and bring down on their possessors severe canings and thrashings.

The 'rhetoricians' walked in a more orderly way. Their clothes were generally untorn, but on the other hand their faces were often strangely decorated; one had a black eye, and the lips of another resembled a single blister, etc. These spoke to each other in tenor voices.

The 'philosophers' talked in a tone an octave lower; in their pockets they only had fragments of tobacco, never whole cakes of it; for what they could get hold of, they used at once. They smelt so strongly of tobacco and brandy, that a workman passing by them would often remain standing and sniffing with his nose in the air, like a hound.

About this time of day the market-place was generally full of bustle, and the market women, selling rolls, cakes, and honey-tarts, plucked the sleeves of those who wore coats of fine cloth or cotton.

"Young sir! Young sir! Here! Here!" they cried from all sides. "Rolls and cakes and tasty tarts, very delicious! I have baked them myself!"

Another drew something long and crooked out of her basket and cried, "Here is a sausage, young sir! Buy a sausage!"

"Don't buy anything from her!" cried a rival. "See how greasy she is, and what a dirty nose and hands she has!"

But the market women carefully avoided appealing to the philosophers and theologians, for these only took handfuls of eatables merely to taste them.

Arrived at the seminary, the whole crowd of students dispersed into the low, large classrooms with small windows, broad doors, and blackened benches. Suddenly they were filled with a many-toned murmur. The teachers heard the pupils' lessons repeated, some in shrill and others in deep voices which sounded like a distant booming. While the lessons were being said, the teachers kept a sharp eye open to see whether pieces of cake or other dainties were protruding from their pupils' pockets; if so, they were promptly confiscated.

When this learned crowd arrived somewhat earlier than usual, or when it was known that the teachers would come somewhat late, a battle would ensue, as though planned by general agreement. In this battle all had to take part, even the monitors who were appointed to look after the order and morality of the whole school. Two theologians generally arranged the conditions of the battle: whether each class should split into two sides, or whether all the pupils should divide themselves into two halves.

In each case the grammarians began the battle, and after the rhetoricians had joined in, the former retired and stood on the benches, in order to watch the fortunes of the fray. Then came the philosophers with long black moustaches, and finally the thick-necked theologians. The battle generally ended in a victory for the latter, and the philosophers retired to the different classrooms rubbing their aching limbs, and throwing themselves on the benches to take breath.

When the teacher, who in his own time had taken part in such contests, entered the classroom he saw by the heated faces of his pupils that the battle had been very severe, and while he caned the hands of the rhetoricians, in another room another teacher did the same for the philosophers.

On Sundays and Festival Days the seminarists took puppet-theatres to the citizens' houses. Sometimes they acted a comedy, and in that case it was always a theologian who took the part of the hero or heroine – Potiphar or Herodias, etc. As a reward for their exertions, they received a piece of linen, a sack of maize, half a roast goose, or something similar. All the students, lay and clerical, were very poorly provided with means for procuring themselves necessary subsistence, but at the same time very fond of eating; so that, however much food was given to them, they were never satisfied, and the gifts bestowed by rich landowners were never adequate for their needs.

Therefore the Commissariat Committee, consisting of philosophers and theologians, sometimes dispatched the grammarians and rhetoricians under the leadership of a philosopher – themselves sometimes joining in the expedition – with sacks on their shoulders, into the town, in order to levy a contribution on the fleshpots of the citizens, and then there was a feast in the seminary.

The most important event in the seminary year was the arrival of the holidays; these began in July, and then generally all the students went home. At that time all the roads were thronged with grammarians, rhetoricians, philosophers, and theologians. He who had no home of his own would take up his quarters with some fellow student's family; the philosophers and theologians looked out for tutors' posts, taught the children of rich farmers, and received for doing so a pair of new boots and sometimes also a new coat.

A whole troop of them would go off in close ranks like a regiment; they cooked their porridge in common, and encamped under the open sky. Each had a bag with him containing a shirt and a pair of socks. The theologians were especially economical; in order not to wear out their boots too quickly, they took them off and carried them on a stick over their shoulders, especially when the road was very muddy. Then they tucked up their breeches over their knees and waded bravely through the pools and puddles. Whenever they spied a village near the highway, they at once left it, approached the house which seemed the most considerable, and began with loud voices to sing a psalm. The master of the house, an old Cossack engaged in agriculture, would listen for a long time with his head propped in his hands, then with tears on his cheeks say to his wife, "What the students are singing sounds very devout; bring out some lard and anything else of the kind we have in the house."

After thus replenishing their stores, the students would continue their way. The farther they went, the smaller grew their numbers, as they dispersed to their various houses, and left those whose homes were still farther on.

On one occasion, during such a march, three students left the main road in order to get provisions in some village, since their stock had long been exhausted. This party consisted of the theologian Khalava, the philosopher Thomas Brutus, and the rhetorician Tiberius Gorobetz.

The first was a tall youth with broad shoulders and of a peculiar character; everything which came within reach of his fingers he felt obliged to appropriate. Moreover, he was of a very melancholy disposition, and when he had got intoxicated he hid himself in the most tangled thickets so that the seminary officials had the greatest trouble in finding him.

The philosopher Thomas Brutus was a more cheerful character. He liked to lie for a long time on the same spot and smoke his pipe; and when he was merry with wine, he hired a fiddler and danced the 'tropak'. Often he got a whole quantity of 'beans', *i.e.* thrashings; but these he endured with complete philosophic calm, saying that a man cannot escape his destiny.

The rhetorician Tiberius Gorobetz had not yet the right to wear a moustache, to drink brandy, or to smoke tobacco. He only wore a small crop of hair, as though his character was at present too little developed. To judge by the great bumps on his forehead, with which he often appeared in the classroom, it might be expected that some day he would be a valiant fighter. Khalava and Thomas often pulled his hair as a mark of their special favour, and sent him on their errands.

Evening had already come when they left the high-road; the sun had just gone down, and the air was still heavy with the heat of the day. The theologian and the philosopher strolled along, smoking in silence, while the rhetorician struck off the heads of the thistles by the wayside with his stick. The way wound on through thick woods of oak and walnut; green hills alternated here and there with meadows. Twice already they had seen cornfields, from which they concluded that they were near some village; but an hour had already passed, and no human habitation appeared. The sky was already quite dark, and only a red gleam lingered on the western horizon.

"The deuce!" said the philosopher Thomas Brutus. "I was almost certain we would soon reach a village."

The theologian still remained silent, looked round him, then put his pipe again between his teeth, and all three continued their way.

"Good heavens!" exclaimed the philosopher, and stood still. "Now the road itself is disappearing."

"Perhaps we shall find a farm farther on," answered the theologian, without taking his pipe out of his mouth.

Meanwhile the night had descended; clouds increased the darkness, and according to all appearance there was no chance of moon or stars appearing. The seminarists found that they had lost the way altogether.

After the philosopher had vainly sought for a footpath, he exclaimed, "Where have we got to?"

The theologian thought for a while, and said, "Yes, it is really dark."

The rhetorician went on one side, lay on the ground, and groped for a path; but his hands encountered only fox-holes. All around lay a huge steppe over which no one seemed to have passed. The wanderers made several efforts to get forward, but the landscape grew wilder and more inhospitable.

The philosopher tried to shout, but his voice was lost in vacancy, no one answered; only, some moments later, they heard a faint groaning sound, like the whimpering of a wolf.

"Curse it all! What shall we do?" said the philosopher.

"Why, just stop here, and spend the night in the open air," answered the theologian. So saying, he felt in his pocket, brought out his timber and steel, and lit his pipe.

But the philosopher could not agree with this proposal; he was not accustomed to sleep till he had first eaten five pounds of bread and five of dripping, and so he now felt an intolerable emptiness in his stomach. Besides, in spite of his cheerful temperament, he was a little afraid of the wolves.

"No, Khalava," he said, "that won't do. To lie down like a dog and without any supper! Let us try once more; perhaps we shall find a house, and the consolation of having a glass of brandy to drink before going to sleep."

At the word 'brandy', the theologian spat on one side and said, "Yes, of course, we cannot remain all night in the open air."

The students went on and on, and to their great joy they heard the barking of dogs in the distance. After listening a while to see from which direction the barking came, they went on their way with new courage, and soon espied a light.

"A village, by heavens, a village!" exclaimed the philosopher.

His supposition proved correct; they soon saw two or three houses built round a courtyard. Lights glimmered in the windows, and before the fence stood a number of trees. The students looked through the crevices of the gates and saw a courtyard in which stood a large number of roving tradesmen's carts. In the sky there were now fewer clouds, and here and there a star was visible.

"See, brother!" one of them said, "we must now cry 'halt!' Cost what it may, we must find entrance and a night's lodging."

The three students knocked together at the gate, and cried "Open!"

The door of one of the houses creaked on its hinges, and an old woman wrapped in a sheepskin appeared. "Who is there?" she exclaimed, coughing loudly.

"Let us spend the night here, mother; we have lost our way, our stomachs are empty, and we do not want to spend the night out of doors."

"But what sort of people are you?"

"Quite harmless people; the theologian Khalava, the philosopher Brutus, and the rhetorician Gorobetz."

"It is impossible," answered the old woman. "The whole house is full of people, and every corner occupied. Where can I put you up? You are big and heavy enough to break the house down. I know these philosophers and theologians; when once one takes them in, they eat one out of house and home. Go farther on! There is no room here for you!"

"Have pity on us, mother! How can you be so heartless? Don't let Christians perish. Put us up where you like, and if we eat up your provisions, or do any other damage, may our hands wither up, and all the punishment of heaven light on us!"

The old woman seemed a little touched. "Well," she said after a few moments' consideration, "I will let you in; but I must put you in different rooms, for I should have no quiet if you were all together at night."

"Do just as you like; we won't say any more about it," answered the students.

The gates moved heavily on their hinges, and they entered the courtyard.

"Well now, mother," said the philosopher, following the old woman, "if you had a little scrap of something! By heavens! My stomach is as empty as a drum. I have not had a bit of bread in my mouth since early this morning!"

"Didn't I say so?" replied the old woman. "There you go begging at once. But I have no food in the house, nor any fire."

"But we will pay for everything," continued the philosopher.

"We will pay early tomorrow in cash."

"Go on and be content with what you get. You are fine fellows whom the devil has brought here!"

Her reply greatly depressed the philosopher Thomas; but suddenly his nose caught the odour of dried fish; he looked at the breeches of the theologian, who walked by his side, and saw a huge fish's tail sticking out of his pocket. The latter had already seized the opportunity to steal a whole fish from one of the carts standing in the courtyard. He had not done this from hunger so much as from the force of habit. He had quite forgotten the fish, and was looking about to see whether he could not find something else to appropriate. Then the philosopher put his hand in the theologian's pocket as though it were his own, and laid hold of his prize.

The old woman found a special resting-place for each student; the rhetorician she put in a shed, the theologian in an empty store-room, and the philosopher in a sheep's stall.

As soon as the philosopher was alone, he devoured the fish in a twinkling, examined the fence which enclosed the stall, kicked away a pig from a neighbouring stall, which had inquiringly inserted its nose through a crevice, and lay down on his right side to sleep like a corpse.

Then the low door opened, and the old woman came crouching into the stall.

"Well, mother, what do you want here?" asked the philosopher.

She made no answer, but came with outstretched arms towards him.

The philosopher shrank back; but she still approached, as though she wished to lay hold of him. A terrible fright seized him, for he saw the old hag's eyes sparkle in an extraordinary way. "Away with you, old witch, away with you!" he shouted. But she still stretched her hands after him.

He jumped up in order to rush out, but she placed herself before the door, fixed her glowing eyes upon him, and again approached him. The philosopher tried to push her away with his hands, but to his astonishment he found that he could neither lift his hands nor move his legs, nor utter an audible word. He only heard his heart beating, and saw the old woman approach him, place his hands crosswise on his breast, and bend his head down. Then with the agility of a cat she sprang on his shoulders, struck him on the side with a broom, and he began to run like a race-horse, carrying her on his shoulders.

All this happened with such swiftness, that the philosopher could scarcely collect his thoughts. He laid hold of his knees with both hands in order to stop his legs from running; but to his great astonishment they kept moving forward against his will, making rapid springs like a Caucasian horse.

Not till the house had been left behind them and a wide plain stretched before them, bordered on one side by a black gloomy wood, did he say to himself, "Ah! It is a witch!"

The half-moon shone pale and high in the sky. Its mild light, still more subdued by intervening clouds, fell like a transparent veil on the earth. Woods, meadows, hills, and valleys – all seemed to be sleeping with open eyes; nowhere was a breath of air stirring. The atmosphere was moist and warm; the shadows of the trees and bushes fell sharply defined on the sloping plain. Such was the night through which the philosopher Thomas Brutus sped with his strange rider.

A strange, oppressive, and yet sweet sensation took possession of his heart. He looked down and saw how the grass beneath his feet seemed to be quite deep and far away; over it there flowed a flood of crystal-clear water, and the grassy plain looked like the bottom of a transparent sea. He saw his own image, and that of the old woman whom he carried on his back, clearly reflected in it. Then he beheld how, instead of the moon, a strange sun shone there; he heard the deep tones of bells, and saw them swinging. He saw a water-nixie rise from a bed of tall reeds; she turned to him, and her face was clearly visible, and she sang a song which penetrated his soul; then she approached him and nearly reached the surface of the water, on which she burst into laughter and again disappeared.

Did he see it or did he not see it? Was he dreaming or was he awake? But what was that below – wind or music? It sounded and drew nearer, and penetrated his soul like a song that rose and fell. "What is it?" he thought as he gazed into the depths, and still sped rapidly along.

The perspiration flowed from him in streams; he experienced simultaneously a strange feeling of oppression and delight in all his being. Often he felt as though he had no longer a heart, and pressed his hand on his breast with alarm.

Weary to death, he began to repeat all the prayers which he knew, and all the formulas of exorcism against evil spirits. Suddenly he experienced a certain relief. He felt that his pace was slackening; the witch weighed less heavily on his shoulders, and the thick herbage of the plain was again beneath his feet, with nothing especial to remark about it.

"Splendid!" thought the philosopher Thomas, and began to repeat his exorcisms in a still louder voice.

Then suddenly he wrenched himself away from under the witch, and sprang on her back in his turn. She began to run, with short, trembling steps indeed, but so rapidly that he could hardly breathe. So swiftly did she run that she hardly seemed to touch the ground. They were still on the plain, but owing to the rapidity of their flight everything seemed indistinct and confused before his eyes. He seized a stick that was lying on the ground, and began to belabour the hag with all his might. She uttered a wild cry, which at first sounded raging and threatening; then it became gradually weaker and more gentle, till at last it sounded quite low like the pleasant tones of a silver bell, so that it penetrated his innermost soul. Involuntarily the thought passed through his mind:

"Is she really an old woman?"

"Ah! I can go no farther," she said in a faint voice, and sank to the earth.

He knelt beside her, and looked in her eyes. The dawn was red in the sky, and in the distance glimmered the gilt domes of the churches of Kieff. Before him lay a beautiful maiden with thick, dishevelled hair and long eyelashes. Unconsciously she had stretched out her white, bare arms, and her tear-filled eyes gazed at the sky.

Thomas trembled like an aspen-leaf. Sympathy, and a strange feeling of excitement, and a hitherto unknown fear overpowered him. He began to run with all his might. His heart beat violently, and he could not explain to himself what a strange, new feeling had seized him. He did not wish to return to the village, but hastened towards Kieff, thinking all the way as he went of his weird, unaccountable adventure.

There were hardly any students left in the town; they were all scattered about the country, and had either taken tutors' posts or simply lived without occupation; for at the farms in Little Russia one can live comfortably and at ease without paying a farthing. The great half-decayed building in which the seminary was established was completely empty; and however much the philosopher searched in all its corners for a piece of lard and bread, he could not find even one of the hard biscuits which the seminarists were in the habit of hiding.

But the philosopher found a means of extricating himself from his difficulties by making friends with a certain young widow in the market-place who sold ribbons, etc. The same evening he found himself being stuffed with cakes and fowl; in fact it is impossible to say how many things were placed before him on a little table in an arbour shaded by cherry-trees.

Later on the same evening the philosopher was to be seen in an ale-house. He lay on a bench, smoked his pipe in his usual way, and threw the Jewish publican a gold piece. He had a jug of ale standing before him, looked on all who went in and out in a cold-blooded, self-satisfied way, and thought no more of his strange adventure.

* * *

About this time a report spread about that the daughter of a rich colonel, whose estate lay about fifty versts distant from Kieff, had returned home one day from a walk in a quite broken-down condition. She had scarcely enough strength to reach her father's house; now she lay dying, and had expressed a wish that for three days after her death the prayers for the dead should be recited by a Kieff seminarist named Thomas Brutus.

This fact was communicated to the philosopher by the rector of the seminary himself, who sent for him to his room and told him that he must start at once, as a rich colonel had sent his servants and a kibitka for him. The philosopher trembled, and was seized by an uncomfortable feeling which he could not define. He had a gloomy foreboding that some evil was to befall him. Without knowing why, he declared that he did not wish to go.

"Listen, Thomas," said the rector, who under certain circumstances spoke very politely to his pupils; "I have no idea of asking you whether you wish to go or not. I only tell you that if you think of disobeying, I will have you so soundly flogged on the back with young birch-rods, that you need not think of having a bath for a long time."

The philosopher scratched the back of his head, and went out silently, intending to make himself scarce at the first opportunity. Lost in thought, he descended the steep flight of steps which led to the courtyard, thickly planted with poplars; there he remained standing for a moment, and heard quite distinctly the rector giving orders in a loud voice to his steward, and to another person, probably one of the messengers sent by the colonel.

"Thank your master for the peeled barley and the eggs," said the rector; "and tell him that as soon as the books which he mentions in his note are ready, I will send them. I have already given them to a clerk to be copied. And don't forget to remind your master that he has some excellent fish, especially prime sturgeon, in his ponds; he might send me some when he has the opportunity, as here in the market the fish are bad and dear. And you, Jantukh, give the colonel's man a glass of brandy. And mind you tie up the philosopher, or he will show you a clean pair of heels."

"Listen to the scoundrel!" thought the philosopher. "He has smelt a rat, the long-legged stork!"

He descended into the courtyard and beheld there a kibitka, which he at first took for a barn on wheels. It was, in fact, as roomy as a kiln, so that bricks might have been made inside it. It was one of those remarkable Cracow vehicles in which Jews travelled from town to town in scores, wherever they thought they would find a market. Six stout, strong, though somewhat elderly Cossacks were standing by it. Their gold-braided coats of fine cloth showed that their master was rich and of some importance; and certain little scars testified to their valour on the battlefield.

"What can I do?" thought the philosopher. "There is no escaping one's destiny." So he stepped up to the Cossacks and said "Good day, comrades."

"Welcome, Mr. Philosopher!" some of them answered.

"Well, I am to travel with you! It is a magnificent vehicle," he continued as he got into it. "If there were only musicians present, one might dance in it."

"Yes, it is a roomy carriage," said one of the Cossacks, taking his seat by the coachman. The latter had tied a cloth round his head, as he had already found an opportunity of pawning his cap in the ale-house. The other five, with the philosopher, got into the capacious kibitka, and sat upon sacks which were filled with all sorts of articles purchased in the city.

"I should like to know," said the philosopher, "if this equipage were laden with salt or iron, how many horses would be required to draw it?"

"Yes," said the Cossack who sat by the coachman, after thinking a short time, "it would require a good many horses."

After giving this satisfactory answer, the Cossack considered himself entitled to remain silent for the whole of the rest of the journey.

The philosopher would gladly have found out who the colonel was, and what sort of a character he had. He was also curious to know about his daughter, who had returned home in such a strange way and now lay dying, and whose destiny seemed to be mingled with his own; and wanted to know the sort of life that was lived in the colonel's house. But the Cossacks were probably philosophers like himself, for in answer to his inquiries they only blew clouds of tobacco and settled themselves more comfortably on their sacks.

Meanwhile, one of them addressed to the coachman on the box a brief command: "Keep your eyes open, Overko, you old sleepy-head, and when you come to the ale-house on the road to Tchukrailoff, don't forget to pull up and wake me and the other fellows if we are asleep." Then he began to snore pretty loud. But in any case his admonition was quite superfluous; for scarcely had the enormous equipage begun to approach the aforesaid ale-house, than they all cried with one mouth "Halt! Halt!" Besides this, Overko's horse was accustomed to stop outside every inn of its own accord.

In spite of the intense July heat, they all got out and entered a low, dirty room where a Jewish innkeeper received them in a friendly way as old acquaintances. He brought in the skirt of his long coat some sausages, and laid them on the table, where, though forbidden by the Talmud, they looked very seductive. All sat down at table, and it was not long before each of the guests had an earthenware jug standing in front of him. The philosopher Thomas had to take part in the feast, and as the Little Russians when they are intoxicated always begin to kiss each other or to weep, the whole room soon began to echo with demonstrations of affection.

"Come here, come here, Spirid, let me embrace thee!"

"Come here, Dorosch, let me press you to my heart!"

One Cossack, with a grey moustache, the eldest of them all, leant his head on his hand and began to weep bitterly because he was an orphan and alone in God's wide world. Another tall, loquacious man did his best to comfort him, saying, "Don't weep, for God's sake, don't weep! For over there – God knows best."

The Cossack who had been addressed as Dorosch was full of curiosity, and addressed many questions to the philosopher Thomas. "I should like to know," he said, "what you learn in your seminary; do you learn the same things as the deacon reads to us in church, or something else?"

"Don't ask," said the consoler; "let them learn what they like. God knows what is to happen; God knows everything."

"No, I will know," answered Dorosch, "I will know what is written in their books; perhaps it is something quite different from that in the deacon's book."

"O good heavens!" said the other, "why all this talk? It is God's will, and one cannot change God's arrangements."

"But I will know everything that is written; I will enter the seminary too, by heaven I will! Do you think perhaps I could not learn? I will learn everything, everything."

"Oh, heavens!" exclaimed the consoler, and let his head sink on the table, for he could no longer hold it upright.

The other Cossacks talked about the nobility, and why there was a moon in the sky.

When the philosopher Thomas saw the state they were in, he determined to profit by it, and to make his escape. In the first place he turned to the grey-headed Cossack, who was lamenting the loss of his parents. "But, little uncle," he said to him, "why do you weep so? I too am an orphan! Let me go, children; why do you want me?"

"Let him go!" said some of them, "he is an orphan, let him go where he likes."

They were about to take him outside themselves, when the one who had displayed a special thirst for knowledge, stopped them, saying, "No, I want to talk with him about the seminary; I am going to the seminary myself."

Moreover, it was not yet certain whether the philosopher could have executed his project of flight, for when he tried to rise from his chair, he felt as though his feet were made of wood, and he began to see such a number of doors leading out of the room that it would have been difficult for him to have found the right one.

It was not till evening that the company remembered that they must continue their journey. They crowded into the kibitka, whipped up the horses, and struck up a song, the words and sense of which were hard to understand. During a great part of the night, they wandered about, having lost the road which they ought to have been able to find blindfolded. At last they drove down a steep descent into a valley, and the philosopher noticed, by the sides of the road, hedges, behind which he caught glimpses of small trees and house-roofs. All these belonged to the colonel's estate.

It was already long past midnight. The sky was dark, though little stars glimmered here and there; no light was to be seen in any of the houses. They drove into a large courtyard, while the dogs barked. On all sides were barns and cottages with thatched roofs. Just opposite the gateway was a house, which was larger than the others, and seemed to be the colonel's dwelling. The kibitka stopped before a small barn, and the travellers hastened into it and laid themselves down to sleep. The philosopher however attempted to look at the exterior of the house, but, rub his eyes as he might, he could distinguish nothing; the house seemed to turn into a bear, and the chimney into the rector of the seminary. Then he gave it up and lay down to sleep.

When he woke up the next morning, the whole house was in commotion; the young lady had died during the night. The servants ran hither and thither in a distracted state; the old women wept and lamented; and a number of curious people gazed through the enclosure into the courtyard, as though there were something special to be seen. The philosopher began now to inspect the locality and the buildings, which he had not been able to do during the night.

The colonel's house was one of those low, small buildings, such as used formerly to be constructed in Russia. It was thatched with straw; a small, high-peaked gable, with a window shaped like an eye, was painted all over with blue and yellow flowers and red crescent-moons; it rested on little oaken pillars, which were round above the middle, hexagonal below, and whose capitals were adorned with quaint carvings. Under this gable was a small staircase with seats at the foot of it on either side.

The walls of the house were supported by similar pillars. Before the house stood a large pear tree of pyramidal shape, whose leaves incessantly trembled. A double row of buildings formed a broad street leading up to the colonel's house. Behind the barns near the entrance-gate stood two three-cornered wine-houses, also thatched with straw; each of the stone walls had a door in it, and was covered with all kinds of paintings. On one was represented a Cossack sitting on a barrel and swinging a large pitcher over his head; it bore the inscription 'I will drink all that!' Elsewhere were painted large and small bottles, a beautiful girl, a running horse, a pipe, and a drum bearing the words 'Wine is the Cossack's joy.'

In the loft of one of the barns one saw through a huge round window a drum and some trumpets. At the gate there stood two cannons. All this showed that the colonel loved a cheerful life, and the whole place often rang with sounds of merriment. Before the gate were two windmills, and behind the house gardens sloped away; through the tree-tops the dark chimneys of the peasants' houses were visible. The whole village lay on a broad, even plateau, in the middle of a mountain-slope which culminated in a steep summit on the north side. When seen from below, it looked still steeper. Here and there on the top the irregular stems of the thick steppe-brooms showed in dark relief against the blue sky. The bare clay soil made a melancholy impression, worn as it was into deep furrows by rain-water. On the same slope there stood two cottages, and over one of them a huge apple-tree spread its branches; the roots were supported by small props, whose interstices were filled with mould. The apples, which were blown off by the wind, rolled down to the courtyard below. A road wound round the mountain to the village.

When the philosopher looked at this steep slope, and remembered his journey of the night before, he came to the conclusion that either the colonel's horses were very sagacious, or that the Cossacks must have very strong heads, as they ventured, even when the worse for drink, on such a road with the huge kibitka.

When the philosopher turned and looked in the opposite direction, he saw quite another picture. The village reached down to the plain; meadows stretched away to an immense distance, their bright green growing gradually dark; far away, about twenty versts off, many other villages were visible. To the right of these meadows were chains of hills, and in the remote distance one saw the Dnieper shimmer and sparkle like a mirror of steel.

"What a splendid country!" said the philosopher to himself. "It must be fine to live here! One could catch fish in the Dnieper, and in the ponds, and shoot and snare partridges and bustards; there must be quantities here. Much fruit might be dried here and sold in the town, or, better still, brandy might be distilled from it, for fruit-brandy is the best of all. But what prevents me thinking of my escape after all?"

Behind the hedge he saw a little path which was almost entirely concealed by the high grass of the steppe. The philosopher approached it mechanically, meaning at first to walk a little along it unobserved, and then quite quietly to gain the open country behind the peasants' houses. Suddenly he felt the pressure of a fairly heavy hand on his shoulder.

Behind him stood the same old Cossack who yesterday had so bitterly lamented the death of his father and mother, and his own loneliness. "You are giving yourself useless trouble, Mr. Philosopher, if you think you can escape from us," he said. "One cannot run away here; and besides, the roads are too bad for walkers. Come to the colonel; he has been waiting for you for some time in his room."

"Yes, of course! What are you talking about? I will come with the greatest pleasure," said the philosopher, and followed the Cossack.

The colonel was an elderly man; his moustache was grey, and his face wore the signs of deep sadness. He sat in his room by a table, with his head propped on both hands. He seemed about five-and-fifty, but his attitude of utter despair, and the pallor on his face, showed that his heart had been suddenly broken, and that all his former cheerfulness had forever disappeared.

When Thomas entered with the Cossack, he answered their deep bows with a slight inclination of the head.

"Who are you, whence do you come, and what is your profession, my good man?" asked the colonel in an even voice, neither friendly nor austere.

"I am a student of philosophy; my name is Thomas Brutus."

"And who was your father?"

"I don't know, sir."

"And your mother?"

"I don't know either; I know that I must have had a mother, but who she was, and where she lived, by heavens, I do not know."

The colonel was silent, and seemed for a moment lost in thought. "Where did you come to know my daughter?"

"I do not know her, gracious sir; I declare I do not know her."

"Why then has she chosen you, and no one else, to offer up prayers for her?"

The philosopher shrugged his shoulders. "God only knows. It is a well-known fact that grand people often demand things which the most learned man cannot comprehend; and does not the proverb say, 'Dance, devil, as the Lord commands!'"

"Aren't you talking nonsense, Mr. Philosopher?"

"May the lightning strike me on the spot if I lie."

"If she had only lived a moment longer," said the colonel sadly, "then I had certainly found out everything. She said, 'Let no one offer up prayers for me, but send, father, at once to the seminary in Kieff for the student Thomas Brutus; he shall pray three nights running for my sinful soul – he knows.' But what he really knows she never said. The poor dove could speak no more, and died. Good man, you are probably well known for your sanctity and devout life, and she has perhaps heard of you."

"What? Of me?" said the philosopher, and took a step backward in amazement. "I and sanctity!" he exclaimed, and stared at the colonel. "God help us, gracious sir! What are you saying? It was only last Holy Thursday that I paid a visit to the tart-shop."

"Well, she must at any rate have had some reason for making the arrangement, and you must begin your duties today."

"I should like to remark to your honour – naturally everyone who knows the Holy Scripture at all can in his measure – but I believe it would be better on this occasion to send for a deacon or subdeacon. They are learned people, and they know exactly what is to be done. I have not got a good voice, nor any official standing."

"You may say what you like, but I shall carry out all my dove's wishes. If you read the prayers for her three nights through in the proper way, I will reward you; and if not – I advise the devil himself not to oppose me!"

The colonel spoke the last words in such an emphatic way that the philosopher quite understood them.

"Follow me!" said the colonel.

They went into the hall. The colonel opened a door which was opposite his own. The philosopher remained for a few minutes in the hall in order to look about him; then he stepped over the threshold with a certain nervousness.

The whole floor of the room was covered with red cloth. In a corner under the icons of the saints, on a table covered with a gold-bordered, velvet cloth, lay the body of the girl. Tall candles, round which were wound branches of the 'calina', stood at her head and feet, and burned dimly in the broad daylight. The face of the dead was not to be seen, as the inconsolable father sat before his daughter, with his back turned to the philosopher. The words which the latter overheard filled him with a certain fear:

"I do not mourn, my daughter, that in the flower of your age you have prematurely left the earth, to my grief; but I mourn, my dove, that I do not know my deadly enemy who caused your death. Had I only known that anyone could even conceive the idea of insulting you, or of speaking a disrespectful word to you, I swear by heaven he would never have seen his children again, if he had been as old as myself; nor his father and mother, if he had been young. And I would have thrown his corpse to the birds of the air, and the wild beasts of the steppe. But woe is me, my flower, my dove, my light! I will spend the remainder of my life without joy, and wipe the bitter tears which flow out of my old eyes, while my enemy will rejoice and laugh in secret over the helpless old man!"

He paused, overpowered by grief, and streams of tears flowed down his cheeks.

The philosopher was deeply affected by the sight of such inconsolable sorrow. He coughed gently in order to clear his throat. The colonel turned and signed to him to take his place at the head of the dead girl, before a little prayer-desk on which some books lay.

"I can manage to hold out for three nights," thought the philosopher; "and then the colonel will fill both my pockets with ducats."

He approached the dead girl, and after coughing once more, began to read, without paying attention to anything else, and firmly resolved not to look at her face.

Soon there was deep silence, and he saw that the colonel had left the room. Slowly he turned his head in order to look at the corpse. A violent shudder thrilled through him; before him lay a form of such beauty as is seldom seen upon earth. It seemed to him that never in a single face had so much intensity of expression and harmony of feature been united. Her brow, soft as snow and pure as silver, seemed to be thinking; the fine, regular eyebrows shadowed proudly the closed eyes, whose lashes gently rested on her cheeks, which seemed to glow with secret longing; her lips still appeared to smile. But at the same time he saw something in these features which appalled him; a terrible depression seized his heart, as when in the midst of dance and song someone begins to chant a dirge. He felt as though those ruby lips were coloured with his own heart's blood. Moreover, her face seemed dreadfully familiar.

"The witch!" he cried out in a voice which sounded strange to himself; then he turned away and began to read the prayers with white cheeks. It was the witch whom he had killed.

Chapter II

WHEN THE SUN had sunk below the horizon, the corpse was carried into the church. The philosopher supported one corner of the black-draped coffin upon his shoulder, and felt an ice-cold shiver run through his body. The colonel walked in front of him, with his right hand resting on the edge of the coffin.

The wooden church, black with age and overgrown with green lichen, stood quite at the end of the village in gloomy solitude; it was adorned with three round cupolas. One saw at the first glance that it had not been used for divine worship for a long time.

Lighted candles were standing before almost every icon. The coffin was set down before the altar. The old colonel kissed his dead daughter once more, and then left the church, together with the bearers of the bier, after he had ordered his servants to look after the philosopher and to take him back to the church after supper.

The coffin-bearers, when they returned to the house, all laid their hands on the stove. This custom is always observed in Little Russia by those who have seen a corpse.

The hunger which the philosopher now began to feel caused him for a while to forget the dead girl altogether. Gradually all the domestics of the house assembled in the kitchen; it was really a kind of club, where they were accustomed to gather. Even the dogs came to the door, wagging their tails in order to have bones and offal thrown to them.

If a servant was sent on an errand, he always found his way into the kitchen to rest there for a while, and to smoke a pipe. All the Cossacks of the establishment lay here during the whole day on and under the benches – in fact, wherever a place could be found to lie down in. Moreover, everyone was always leaving something behind in the kitchen – his cap, or his whip, or something of the sort. But the numbers of the club were not complete till the evening, when the groom came in after tying up his horses in the stable, the cowherd had shut up his cows in their stalls, and others collected there who were not usually seen in the daytime. During suppertime even the tongues of the laziest were set in motion. They talked of all and everything – of the new pair of breeches which someone had ordered for himself, of what might be in the centre of the earth, and of the wolf which someone had seen. There were a number of wits in the company – a class which is always represented in Little Russia.

The philosopher took his place with the rest in the great circle which sat round the kitchen door in the open air. Soon an old woman with a red cap issued from it, bearing with both hands a large vessel full of hot 'galuchkis', which she distributed among them. Each drew out of his pocket a wooden spoon, or a one-pronged wooden fork. As soon as their jaws began to move a little more slowly, and their wolfish hunger was somewhat appeased, they began to talk. The conversation, as might be expected, turned on the dead girl.

"Is it true," said a young shepherd, "is it true – though I cannot understand it – that our young mistress had traffic with evil spirits?"

"Who, the young lady?" answered Dorosch, whose acquaintance the philosopher had already made in the kibitka. "Yes, she was a regular witch! I can swear that she was a witch!"

"Hold your tongue, Dorosch!" exclaimed another – the one who, during the journey, had played the part of a consoler. "We have nothing to do with that. May God be merciful to her! One ought not to talk of such things."

But Dorosch was not at all inclined to be silent; he had just visited the wine-cellar with the steward on important business, and having stooped two or three times over one or two casks, he had returned in a very cheerful and loquacious mood.

"Why do you ask me to be silent?" he answered. "She has ridden on my own shoulders, I swear she has."

"Say, uncle," asked the young shepherd, "are there signs by which to recognise a sorceress?"

"No, there are not," answered Dorosch; "even if you knew the Psalter by heart, you could not recognise one."

"Yes, Dorosch, it is possible; don't talk such nonsense," retorted the former consoler. "It is not for nothing that God has given each some special peculiarity; the learned maintain that every witch has a little tail."

"Every old woman is a witch," said a grey-headed Cossack quite seriously.

"Yes, you are a fine lot," retorted the old woman who entered at that moment with a vessel full of fresh 'galuchkis'. "You are great fat pigs!"

A self-satisfied smile played round the lips of the old Cossack whose name was Javtuch, when he found that his remark had touched the old woman on a tender point. The shepherd burst into such a deep and loud explosion of laughter as if two oxen were lowing together.

This conversation excited in the philosopher a great curiosity, and a wish to obtain more exact information regarding the colonel's daughter. In order to lead the talk back to the subject, he turned to his next neighbour and said, "I should like to know why all the people here think that the young lady was a witch. Has she done harm to anyone, or killed them by witchcraft?"

"Yes, there are reports of that kind," answered a man, whose face was as flat as a shovel. "Who does not remember the huntsman Mikita, or the—"

"What has the huntsman Mikita got to do with it?" asked the philosopher.

"Stop; I will tell you the story of Mikita," interrupted Dorosch.

"No, I will tell it," said the groom, "for he was my godfather."

"I will tell the story of Mikita," said Spirid.

"Yes, yes, Spirid shall tell it," exclaimed the whole company; and Spirid began.

"You, Mr. Philosopher Thomas, did not know Mikita. Ah! He was an extraordinary man. He knew every dog as though he were his own father. The present huntsman, Mikola, who sits three places away from me, is not fit to hold a candle to him, though good enough in his way; but compared to Mikita, he is a mere milksop."

"You tell the tale splendidly," exclaimed Dorosch, and nodded as a sign of approval.

Spirid continued.

"He saw a hare in the field quicker than you can take a pinch of snuff. He only needed to whistle 'Come here, Rasboy! Come here, Bosdraja!' and flew away on his horse like the wind, so that you could not say whether he went quicker than the dog or the dog than he. He could empty a quart pot of brandy in the twinkling of an eye. Ah! He was a splendid huntsman, only for some time he always had his eyes fixed on the young lady. Either he had fallen in love with her or she had bewitched him – in short, he went to the dogs. He became a regular old woman; yes, he became the devil knows what – it is not fitting to relate it."

"Very good," remarked Dorosch.

"If the young lady only looked at him, he let the reins slip out of his hands, called Bravko instead of Rasboy, stumbled, and made all kinds of mistakes. One day when he was currycombing a horse, the young lady came to him in the stable. 'Listen, Mikita,' she said. 'I should like for once to set my foot on you.' And he, the booby, was quite delighted, and answered, 'Don't only set your foot there, but sit on me altogether.' The young lady lifted her white little foot, and as soon as he saw it, his delight robbed him of his senses. He bowed his neck, the idiot, took her feet in both hands, and began to trot about like a horse all over the place. Whither they went he could not say; he returned more dead than alive, and from that time he wasted away and became as dry as a chip of wood. At last someone coming into the stable one day found instead of him only a handful of ashes and an empty jug; he had burned completely out. But it must be said he was a huntsman such as the world cannot match."

When Spirid had ended his tale, they all began to vie with one another in praising the deceased huntsman.

"And have you heard the story of Cheptchicha?" asked Dorosch, turning to Thomas.

"No."

"Ha! Ha! One sees they don't teach you much in your seminary. Well, listen. We have here in our village a Cossack called Cheptoun, a fine fellow. Sometimes indeed he amuses himself by stealing and lying without any reason; but he is a fine fellow for all that. His house is not far away from here. One evening, just about this time, Cheptoun and his wife went to bed after they had finished their day's work. Since it was fine weather, Cheptchicha went to sleep in the courtyard, and Cheptoun in the house – no! I mean Cheptchicha went to sleep in the house on a bench and Cheptoun outside—"

"No, Cheptchicha didn't go to sleep on a bench, but on the ground," interrupted the old woman who stood at the door.

Dorosch looked at her, then at the ground, then again at her, and said after a pause, "If I tore your dress off your back before all these people, it wouldn't look pretty."

The rebuke was effectual. The old woman was silent, and did not interrupt again.

Dorosch continued.

"In the cradle which hung in the middle of the room lay a one-year-old child. I do not know whether it was a boy or a girl. Cheptchicha had lain down, and heard on the other side of the door a dog scratching and howling loud enough to frighten anyone. She was afraid, for women are such simple folk that if one puts out one's tongue at them behind the door in the dark, their hearts sink into their boots. 'But,' she thought to herself, 'I must give this cursed dog one on the snout to stop his howling!' So she seized the poker and opened the door. But hardly had she done so than the dog rushed between her legs straight to the cradle. Then Cheptchicha saw that it was not a dog but the young lady; and if it had only been the young lady as she knew her it wouldn't have mattered, but she looked quite blue, and her eyes sparkled like fiery coals. She seized the child, bit its throat, and began to suck its blood. Cheptchicha shrieked, 'Ah! My darling child!' and rushed out of the room. Then she saw that the house-door was shut and rushed up to the attic and sat there, the stupid woman, trembling all over. Then the young lady came after her and bit her too, poor fool! The next morning Cheptoun carried his wife, all bitten and wounded, down from the attic, and the next day she died. Such strange things happen in the world. One may wear fine clothes, but that does not matter; a witch is and remains a witch."

After telling his story, Dorosch looked around him with a complacent air, and cleaned out his pipe with his little finger in order to fill it again. The story of the witch had made a deep impression on all, and each of them had something to say about her. One had seen her come to the door of his house in the form of a hayrick; from others she had stolen their caps or their pipes; she had cut off the hair-plaits of many girls in the village, and drunk whole pints of the blood of others.

At last the whole company observed that they had gossiped over their time, for it was already night. All looked for a sleeping place – some in the kitchen and others in the barn or the courtyard.

"Now, Mr. Thomas, it is time that we go to the dead," said the grey-headed Cossack, turning to the philosopher. All four – Spirid, Dorosch, the old Cossack, and the philosopher – betook themselves to the church, keeping off with their whips the wild dogs who roamed about the roads in great numbers and bit the sticks of passers-by in sheer malice.

Although the philosopher had seized the opportunity of fortifying himself beforehand with a stiff glass of brandy, yet he felt a certain secret fear which increased as he approached the church, which was lit up within. The strange tales he had heard had made a deep impression on his imagination. They had passed the thick hedges and trees, and the country became more open. At last they reached the small enclosure round the church; behind it there were no more trees, but a huge, empty plain dimly visible in the darkness. The three Cossacks ascended the steep steps with Thomas, and entered the church. Here they left the philosopher, expressing their hope that he would successfully accomplish his duties, and locked him in as their master had ordered.

He was left alone. At first he yawned, then he stretched himself, blew on both hands, and finally looked round him. In the middle of the church stood the black bier; before the dark pictures of saints burned the candles, whose light only illuminated the icons, and cast a faint glimmer into the body of the church; all the corners were in complete darkness. The lofty icons seemed to be of considerable age; only a little of the original gilt remained on their broken traceries; the faces of the saints had become quite black and looked uncanny.

Once more the philosopher cast a glance around him. "Bother it!" said he to himself. "What is there to be afraid about? No living creature can get in, and as for the dead and those who come from the 'other side', I can protect myself with such effectual prayers that they cannot touch me with the tips of their fingers. There is nothing to fear," he repeated, swinging his arms. "Let us begin the prayers!"

As he approached one of the side-aisles, he noticed two packets of candles which had been placed there.

"That is fine," he thought. "I must illuminate the whole church, till it is as bright as day. What a pity that one cannot smoke in it."

He began to light the candles on all the wall-brackets and all the candelabra, as well as those already burning before the holy pictures; soon the whole church was brilliantly lit up. Only the darkness in the roof above seemed still denser by contrast, and the faces of the saints peering out of the frames looked as unearthly as before. He approached the bier, looked nervously at the face of the dead girl, could not help shuddering slightly, and involuntarily closed his eyes. What terrible and extraordinary beauty!

He turned away and tried to go to one side, but the strange curiosity and peculiar fascination which men feel in moments of fear, compelled him to look again and again, though with a similar shudder. And in truth there was something terrible about the beauty of the dead girl. Perhaps she would not have inspired so much fear had she been less beautiful; but there was nothing ghastly or deathlike in the face, which wore rather an expression of life, and it seemed to the philosopher as though she were watching him from under her closed eyelids. He even thought he saw a tear roll from under the eyelash of her right eye, but when it was halfway down her cheek, he saw that it was a drop of blood.

He quickly went into one of the stalls, opened his book, and began to read the prayers in a very loud voice in order to keep up his courage. His deep voice sounded strange to himself in the grave-like silence; it aroused no echo in the silent and desolate wooden walls of the church.

"What is there to be afraid of?" he thought to himself. "She will not rise from her bier, since she fears God's word. She will remain quietly resting. Yes, and what sort of a Cossack should I be, if I were afraid? The fact is, I have drunk a little too much – that is why I feel so queer. Let me take a pinch of snuff. It is really excellent – first-rate!"

At the same time he cast a furtive glance over the pages of the prayer-book towards the bier, and involuntarily he said to himself, "There! See! She is getting up! Her head is already above the edge of the coffin!"

But a death-like silence prevailed; the coffin was motionless, and all the candles shone steadily. It was an awe-inspiring sight, this church lit up at midnight, with the corpse in the midst, and no living soul near but one. The philosopher began to sing in various keys in order to stifle his fears, but every moment he glanced across at the coffin, and involuntarily the question came to his lips, "Suppose she rose up after all?"

But the coffin did not move. Nowhere was there the slightest sound nor stir. Not even did a cricket chirp in any corner. There was nothing audible but the slight sputtering of some distant candle, or the faint fall of a drop of wax.

"Suppose she rose up after all?"

He raised his head. Then he looked round him wildly and rubbed his eyes. Yes, she was no longer lying in the coffin, but sitting upright. He turned away his eyes, but at once looked again, terrified, at the coffin. She stood up; then she walked with closed eyes through the church, stretching out her arms as though she wanted to seize someone.

She now came straight towards him. Full of alarm, he traced with his finger a circle round himself; then in a loud voice he began to recite the prayers and formulas of exorcism which he had learnt from a monk who had often seen witches and evil spirits.

She had almost reached the edge of the circle which he had traced; but it was evident that she had not the power to enter it. Her face wore a bluish tint like that of one who has been several days dead.

Thomas had not the courage to look at her, so terrible was her appearance; her teeth chattered and she opened her dead eyes, but as in her rage she saw nothing, she turned in another direction and felt with outstretched arms among the pillars and corners of the church in the hope of seizing him.

At last she stood still, made a threatening gesture, and then lay down again in the coffin.

The philosopher could not recover his self-possession, and kept on gazing anxiously at it. Suddenly it rose from its place and began hurtling about the church with a whizzing sound. At one time it was almost directly over his head; but the philosopher observed that it could not pass over the area of his charmed circle, so he kept on repeating his formulas of exorcism. The coffin now fell with a crash in the middle of the church, and remained lying there motionless. The corpse rose again; it had now a greenish-blue colour, but at the same moment the distant crowing of a cock was audible, and it lay down again.

The philosopher's heart beat violently, and the perspiration poured in streams from his face; but heartened by the crowing of the cock, he rapidly repeated the prayers.

As the first light of dawn looked through the windows, there came a deacon and the grey-haired Javtuk, who acted as sacristan, in order to release him. When he had reached the house, he could not sleep for a long time; but at last weariness overpowered him, and he slept till noon. When he awoke, his experiences of the night appeared to him like a dream. He was given a quart of brandy to strengthen him.

At table he was again talkative and ate a fairly large sucking pig almost without assistance. But none the less he resolved to say nothing of what he had seen, and to all curious questions only returned the answer, "Yes, some wonderful things happened."

The philosopher was one of those men who, when they have had a good meal, are uncommonly amiable. He lay down on a bench, with his pipe in his mouth, looked blandly at all, and expectorated every minute.

But as the evening approached, he became more and more pensive. About suppertime nearly the whole company had assembled in order to play 'krapli'. This is a kind of game of skittles, in which, instead of bowls, long staves are used, and the winner has the right to ride on the back of his opponent. It provided the spectators with much amusement; sometimes the groom, a huge man, would clamber on the back of the swineherd, who was slim and short and shrunken; another time the groom would present his own back, while

Dorosch sprang on it shouting, "What a regular ox!" Those of the company who were more staid sat by the threshold of the kitchen. They looked uncommonly serious, smoked their pipes, and did not even smile when the younger ones went into fits of laughter over some joke of the groom or Spirid.

Thomas vainly attempted to take part in the game; a gloomy thought was firmly fixed like a nail in his head. In spite of his desperate efforts to appear cheerful after supper, fear had overmastered his whole being, and it increased with the growing darkness.

"Now it is time for us to go, Mr. Student!" said the grey-haired Cossack, and stood up with Dorosch. "Let us betake ourselves to our work."

Thomas was conducted to the church in the same way as on the previous evening; again he was left alone, and the door was bolted behind him.

As soon as he found himself alone, he began to feel in the grip of his fears. He again saw the dark pictures of the saints in their gilt frames, and the black coffin, which stood menacing and silent in the middle of the church.

"Nevermind!" he said to himself. "I am over the first shock. The first time I was frightened, but I am not so at all now – no, not at all!"

He quickly went into a stall, drew a circle round him with his finger, uttered some prayers and formulas for exorcism, and then began to read the prayers for the dead in a loud voice and with the fixed resolution not to look up from the book nor take notice of anything.

He did so for an hour, and began to grow a little tired; he cleared his throat and drew his snuff-box out of his pocket, but before he had taken a pinch he looked nervously towards the coffin.

A sudden chill shot through him. The witch was already standing before him on the edge of the circle, and had fastened her green eyes upon him. He shuddered, looked down at the book, and began to read his prayers and exorcisms aloud. Yet all the while he was aware how her teeth chattered, and how she stretched out her arms to seize him. But when he cast a hasty glance towards her, he saw that she was not looking in his direction, and it was clear that she could not see him.

Then she began to murmur in an undertone, and terrible words escaped her lips – words that sounded like the bubbling of boiling pitch. The philosopher did not know their meaning, but he knew that they signified something terrible, and were intended to counteract his exorcisms.

After she had spoken, a stormy wind arose in the church, and there was a noise like the rushing of many birds. He heard the noise of their wings and claws as they flapped against and scratched at the iron bars of the church windows. There were also violent blows on the church door, as if someone were trying to break it in pieces.

The philosopher's heart beat violently; he did not dare to look up, but continued to read the prayers without a pause. At last there was heard in the distance the shrill sound of a cock's crow. The exhausted philosopher stopped and gave a great sigh of relief.

Those who came to release him found him more dead than alive; he had leant his back against the wall, and stood motionless, regarding them without any expression in his eyes. They were obliged almost to carry him to the house; he then shook himself, asked for and drank a quart of brandy. He passed his hand through his hair and said, "There are all sorts of horrors in the world, and such dreadful things happen that—" Here he made a gesture as though to ward off something. All who heard him bent their heads forward in curiosity. Even a small boy, who ran on everyone's errands, stood by with his mouth wide open.

Just then a young woman in a close-fitting dress passed by. She was the old cook's assistant, and very coquettish; she always stuck something in her bodice by way of ornament, a ribbon or a flower, or even a piece of paper if she could find nothing else.

"Good day, Thomas," she said, as she saw the philosopher. "Dear me! What has happened to you?" she exclaimed, striking her hands together.

"Well, what is it, you silly creature?"

"Good heavens! You have grown quite grey!"

"Yes, so he has!" said Spirid, regarding him more closely. "You have grown as grey as our old Javtuk."

When the philosopher heard that, he hastened into the kitchen, where he had noticed on the wall a dirty, three-cornered piece of looking-glass. In front of it hung some forget-me-nots, evergreens, and a small garland – a proof that it was the toilette-glass of the young coquette. With alarm he saw that it actually was as they had said – his hair was quite grizzled.

He sank into a reverie; at last he said to himself, "I will go to the colonel, tell him all, and declare that I will read no more prayers. He must send me back at once to Kieff." With this intention he turned towards the doorsteps of the colonel's house.

The colonel was sitting motionless in his room; his face displayed the same hopeless grief which Thomas had observed on it on his first arrival, only the hollows in his cheeks had deepened. It was obvious that he took very little or no food. A strange paleness made him look almost as though made of marble.

"Good day," he said as he observed Thomas standing, cap in hand, at the door. "Well, how are you getting on? All right?"

"Yes, sir, all right! Such hellish things are going on, that one would like to rush away as far as one's feet can carry one."

"How so?"

"Your daughter, sir… When one considers the matter, she is, of course, of noble descent – no one can dispute that; but don't be angry, and may God grant her eternal rest!"

"Very well! What about her?"

"She is in league with the devil. She inspires one with such dread that all prayers are useless."

"Pray! Pray! It was not for nothing that she sent for you. My dove was troubled about her salvation, and wished to expel all evil influences by means of prayer."

"I swear, gracious sir, it is beyond my power."

"Pray! Pray!" continued the colonel in the same persuasive tone. "There is only one night more; you are doing a Christian work, and I will reward you richly."

"However great your rewards may be, I will not read the prayers anymore, sir," said Thomas in a tone of decision.

"Listen, philosopher!" said the colonel with a menacing air. "I will not allow any objections. In your seminary you may act as you like, but here it won't do. If I have you knouted, it will be somewhat different to the rector's canings. Do you know what a strong 'kantchuk' is?"

"Of course I do," said the philosopher in a low voice; "a number of them together are insupportable."

"Yes, I think so too. But you don't know yet how hot my fellows can make it," replied the colonel threateningly. He sprang up, and his face assumed a fierce, despotic expression, betraying the savagery of his nature, which had been only temporarily modified by grief. "After the first flogging they pour on brandy and then repeat it. Go away and finish your work. If you don't obey, you won't be able to stand again, and if you do, you will get a thousand ducats."

"That is a devil of a fellow," thought the philosopher to himself, and went out. "One can't trifle with him. But wait a little, my friend; I will escape you so cleverly, that even your hounds can't find me!"

He determined, under any circumstances, to run away, and only waited till the hour after dinner arrived, when all the servants were accustomed to take a nap on the hay in the barn, and to snore and puff so loudly that it sounded as if machinery had been set up there. At last the time came. Even Javtuch stretched himself out in the sun and closed his eyes. Tremblingly, and on tiptoe, the philosopher stole softly into the garden, whence he thought he could escape more easily into the open country. This garden was generally so choked up with weeds that it seemed admirably adapted for such an attempt. With the exception of a single path used by the people of the house, the whole of it was covered with cherry trees, elder bushes, and tall heath-thistles with fibrous red buds. All these trees and bushes had been thickly overgrown with ivy, which formed a kind of roof. Its tendrils reached to the hedge and fell down on the other side in snake-like curves among the small, wild field-flowers. Behind the hedge which bordered the garden was a dense mass of wild heather, in which it did not seem probable that anyone would care to venture himself, and the strong, stubborn stems of which seemed likely to baffle any attempt to cut them.

As the philosopher was about to climb over the hedge, his teeth chattered, and his heart beat so violently that he felt frightened at it. The skirts of his long cloak seemed to cling to the ground as though they had been fastened to it by pegs. When he had actually got over the hedge he seemed to hear a shrill voice crying behind him "Whither? Whither?"

He jumped into the heather and began to run, stumbling over old roots and treading on unfortunate moles. When he had emerged from the heather he saw that he still had a wide field to cross, behind which was a thick, thorny underwood. This, according to his calculation, must stretch as far as the road leading to Kieff, and if he reached it he would be safe. Accordingly he ran over the field and plunged into the thorny copse. Every sharp thorn he encountered tore a fragment from his coat. Then he reached a small open space; in the centre of it stood a willow, whose branches hung down to the earth, and close by flowed a clear spring bright as silver. The first thing the philosopher did was to lie down and drink eagerly, for he was intolerably thirsty.

"Splendid water!" he said, wiping his mouth. "This is a good place to rest in."

"No, better run farther; perhaps we are being followed," said a voice immediately behind him.

Thomas started and turned; before him stood Javtuch.

"This devil of a Javtuch!" he thought. "I should like to seize him by the feet and smash his hang-dog face against the trunk of a tree."

"Why did you go round such a long way?" continued Javtuch. "You had much better have chosen the path by which I came; it leads directly by the stable. Besides, it is a pity about your coat. Such splendid cloth! How much did it cost an ell? Well, we have had a long enough walk; it is time to go home."

The philosopher followed Javtuch in a very depressed state.

"Now the accursed witch will attack me in earnest," he thought. "But what have I really to fear? Am I not a Cossack? I have read the prayers for two nights already; with God's help I will get through the third night also. It is plain that the witch must have a terrible load of guilt upon her, else the evil one would not help her so much."

Feeling somewhat encouraged by these reflections, he returned to the courtyard and asked Dorosch, who sometimes, by the steward's permission, had access to the wine-cellar, to fetch him a small bottle of brandy. The two friends sat down before a barn and drank a pretty large one. Suddenly the philosopher jumped up and said, "I want musicians! Bring some musicians!"

But without waiting for them he began to dance the 'tropak' in the courtyard. He danced till tea-time, and the servants, who, as is usual in such cases, had formed a small circle round him, grew at last tired of watching him, and went away saying, "By heavens, the man can dance!"

Finally the philosopher lay down in the place where he had been dancing, and fell asleep. It was necessary to pour a bucket of cold water on his head to wake him up for supper. At the meal he enlarged on the topic of what a Cossack ought to be, and how he should not be afraid of anything in the world.

"It is time," said Javtuch; "let us go."

"I wish I could put a lighted match to your tongue," thought the philosopher; then he stood up and said, "Let us go."

On their way to the church, the philosopher kept looking round him on all sides, and tried to start a conversation with his companions; but both Javtuch and Dorosch remained silent. It was a weird night. In the distance wolves howled continually, and even the barking of the dogs had something unearthly about it.

"That doesn't sound like wolves howling, but something else," remarked Dorosch.

Javtuch still kept silence, and the philosopher did not know what answer to make.

They reached the church and walked over the old wooden planks, whose rotten condition showed how little the lord of the manor cared about God and his soul. Javtuch and Dorosch left the philosopher alone, as on the previous evenings.

There was still the same atmosphere of menacing silence in the church, in the centre of which stood the coffin with the terrible witch inside it.

"I am not afraid, by heavens, I am not afraid!" he said; and after drawing a circle round himself as before, he began to read the prayers and exorcisms.

An oppressive silence prevailed; the flickering candles filled the church with their clear light. The philosopher turned one page after another, and noticed that he was not reading what was in the book. Full of alarm, he crossed himself and began to sing a hymn. This calmed him somewhat, and he resumed his reading, turning the pages rapidly as he did so.

Suddenly in the midst of the sepulchral silence the iron lid of the coffin sprang open with a jarring noise, and the dead witch stood up. She was this time still more terrible in aspect than at first. Her teeth chattered loudly and her lips, through which poured a stream of dreadful curses, moved convulsively. A whirlwind arose in the church; the icons of the saints fell on the ground, together with the broken windowpanes. The door was wrenched from its hinges, and a huge mass of monstrous creatures rushed into the church, which became filled with the noise of beating wings and scratching claws. All these creatures flew and crept about, seeking for the philosopher, from whose brain the last fumes of intoxication had vanished. He crossed himself ceaselessly and uttered prayer after prayer, hearing all the time the whole unclean swarm rustling about him, and brushing him with the tips of their wings. He had not the courage to look at them; he only saw one uncouth monster standing by the wall, with long, shaggy hair and two flaming eyes. Over him something hung in the air which looked like a gigantic bladder covered with countless crabs' claws and scorpions' stings, and with black clods of earth hanging from it. All these monsters stared about seeking him, but they could not find him, since he was protected by his sacred circle.

"Bring the Viy! Bring the Viy!" cried the witch.

A sudden silence followed; the howling of wolves was heard in the distance, and soon heavy footsteps resounded through the church. Thomas looked up furtively and saw that an ungainly human figure with crooked legs was being led into the church. He was quite covered with black soil, and his hands and feet resembled knotted roots. He trod heavily and stumbled at every step. His eyelids were of enormous length. With terror, Thomas saw that his face was of iron. They led him in by the arms and placed him near Thomas's circle.

"Raise my eyelids! I can't see anything!" said the Viy in a dull, hollow voice, and they all hastened to help in doing so.

"Don't look!" an inner voice warned the philosopher; but he could not restrain from looking.

"There he is!" exclaimed the Viy, pointing an iron finger at him; and all the monsters rushed on him at once.

Struck dumb with terror, he sank to the ground and died.

At that moment there sounded a cock's crow for the second time; the earth-spirits had not heard the first one. In alarm they hurried to the windows and the door to get out as quickly as possible. But it was too late; they all remained hanging as though fastened to the door and the windows.

When the priest came he stood amazed at such a desecration of God's house, and did not venture to read prayers there. The church remained standing as it was, with the monsters hanging on the windows and the door. Gradually it became overgrown with creepers, bushes, and wild heather, and no one can discover it now.

* * *

When the report of this event reached Kieff, and the theologian Khalava heard what a fate had overtaken the philosopher Thomas, he sank for a whole hour into deep reflection. He had greatly altered of late; after finishing his studies he had become bell-ringer of one of the chief churches in the city, and he always appeared with a bruised nose, because the belfry staircase was in a ruinous condition.

"Have you heard what has happened to Thomas?" said Tiberius Gorobetz, who had become a philosopher and now wore a moustache.

"Yes; God had appointed it so," answered the bell-ringer. "Let us go to the ale house; we will drink a glass to his memory."

The young philosopher, who, with the enthusiasm of a novice, had made such full use of his privileges as a student that his breeches and coat and even his cap reeked of brandy and tobacco, agreed readily to the proposal.

"He was a fine fellow, Thomas," said the bell-ringer as the limping innkeeper set the third jug of beer before him. "A splendid fellow! And lost his life for nothing!"

"I know why he perished," said Gorobetz; "because he was afraid. If he had not feared her, the witch could have done nothing to him. One ought to cross oneself incessantly and spit exactly on her tail, and then not the least harm can happen. I know all about it, for here, in Kieff, all the old women in the market-place are witches."

The bell-ringer nodded assent. But being aware that he could not say any more, he got up cautiously and went out, swaying to the right and left in order to find a hiding-place in the thick steppe grass outside the town. At the same time, in accordance with his old habits, he did not forget to steal an old boot-sole which lay on the ale-house bench.

The Blackdamp

Ali Habashi

"WHAT'S *your name, stranger?"*

Julia was thinking of him again. But then, she always was, whether she wanted to or not. The flash of her camera shocked away the shadows for a heartbeat before the dark drew in around the twin beams of her flashlight and headlamp once again. The bright burst had completely illuminated the long throat of the mine, partially blocked by rubble. It may have been a cave-in, but more likely the dirt had been placed there expressly to stop people like her from exploring it.

Rather like the Keep Out sign.

She had become desensitized to the glaring red warnings and the half-hearted fencing, more often than not vandalized by the explorers who had come before her. A solid wall of grey brick had blocked the opening to this particular mine. It very well may have ended Julia's progress before it began, but luckily for her, some kind anarchist had already taken the liberty of smashing through the barrier. Clambering through the opening had been easy enough, and she had silently thanked the thrill seekers or copper hunters that had thought to bring along a sledge hammer.

The rubber soles of her Wellingtons slid loudly over the pile of rock choking the mine. She brushed off her jeans and aimed her camera down the new stretch on the other side of the obstruction. Another flash seared through the mine, revealing the aging columns of timber supports framing the path ahead.

This would be a good place to film.

She quashed the thought. Filming their explorations had been Anthony's thing. He brought the quick commentary, editing skills, and the night vision camera. Julia was the photographer with the coal-mining grandfather, and therefore just enough expertise to identify some of the abandoned equipment. They were perfect together, for each other and for their bizarre shared hobby of mine exploration.

A year after the break-up Julia still wasn't sure what she'd done wrong. She remembered their last day in sharp detail. When he had told her calmly that they both knew that it wouldn't last. When mild panic had stolen over his features when she had wailed that *no*, she had no idea that they weren't meant to be together. The way that the panic had morphed into confusion when she explained that he had been her *everything*, everything she had ever wanted and needed.

It hurt. It physically *hurt*. And God help her, it hurt still, like there was a raw bloody hollow in her chest.

This was her first mine since the break-up.

A crown of sweat was beginning to form underneath the lining of her helmet. As far as abandoned coal mines went, this was actually one of the more interesting ones she had explored. In pursuit of her dangerous hobby she had dealt with cramped passages, rusty hazards, and enough orange slime to permanently singe her olfactory nerve. The sudden appearance of water was her least favorite. It was cold and toxic at best, foreshadowing for an unwanted visit by the Blackdamp at worst.

When Julia's grandfather was still alive, he delighted in spinning horror stories inspired by his long days working in the mine. Endlessly creative, he would tell his tales right up until her grandmother appeared and swatted at him with a dish towel for scaring her.

"There is a monster that lives down in the mine," he'd say, cigarette smoke clinging to his breath. "It doesn't look like a monster though. Looks like a person, like a nice person. A person you'd trust. Well that person lives down in that mine, and it doesn't like visitors. Not at all. That's *its* mine, and it don't share."

"What's its name?" Julia would ask.

"*Blackdamp*." He'd lean forward, and the rough scratch of his voice around that word always made her shiver.

"Now, you can never tell when the Blackdamp will show up. Sometimes it creeps on out of the walls, skin all sooty with coal dust. Sometimes it just floats in the air, waiting for you to stray too close. But its favorite place to hide is in the water, deep down where there isn't any air at all, and if your boot splashes a bit too close, then it *GRABS YA!*"

He would rock forward, snatching at her as she squealed and slid back out of his reach.

"If Blackdamp ever catches you, it'll hang on real tight so you can't get away, and then it'll steal the air right out of your lungs."

This was usually the part of the story where Julia's grandmother would come to rescue her, but on the days that she didn't, Julia would get to hear the ending.

"I met the Blackdamp once. Back when I was a young man."

"How did you get away?"

"Well you see I'd brought the Blackdamp a snack that day. The Blackdamp likes to steal air, but it also likes to eat these little yellow birds called canaries. I was working down in the coal mine listening to the canary sing its song, until suddenly I couldn't hear the song anymore. I turned around and I saw the Blackdamp, standing there, looking me dead in the face.

"It had the canary in its hand, and slowly it brought it up to its mouth and GULP! Ate the whole thing down. I turned tail and ran after that, running from the Blackdamp before it could steal my air away and gulp it down like it did with that canary."

No horror movie had ever been able to scare her the way that story had when she was young. Even while exploring the mines with Anthony, seeing a passage suddenly dip down and vanish into a deceptively clear stretch of water had never failed to make her nervous. Anthony would tease her; shove her towards the glassy surface until she squealed and clung to him, the dancing shadows making it impossible to tell if there was something crawling out of the depths.

Julia would feign anger after that, until Anthony managed to make her smile or sneak a quick kiss on her cheek. The mine would inevitably fill with her laughter as he scrambled ahead and over the rocks, just so that he could pop his head back up and make faces at her.

"What's your name, stranger?" he'd ask flirtatiously. "Come here often?"

After he left her, months seemed to pass by with nothing but the tangle of unwashed sheets around her legs and the glare of the computer screen to keep her company. Anthony's online profiles were overactive, and Julia hungrily followed his latest posts, no matter how mundane. She watched the videos of their old mine explorations on a loop, analyzing everything that was said, as though she might find out why her heart had been broken from the old dialogue.

Anthony stopped texting her back after the fifth month of their post-break-up friendship, that inevitable lie that every couple agrees to if the relationship doesn't end in violence or betrayal. A softer killing blow. When Julia noticed the new woman in all of Anthony's photos, she understood his silence. All of her carefully worded texts, the thread-thin lifeline connecting her to him – to hope – cut in an instant.

The desperate rebounds that followed were endlessly unsatisfying. The men that she dated all seemed to be the same person. The shows they binged, the music they listened to, even their craft beer preference were cut and pasted over and over, a faux personality gift-wrapped in flannel. Dating apps were a repetitive horror gallery – Man with Fish, Man with Dog, Man on Hike, Man with Fish…

The pictures blurred together, and the ache in her chest yawned wider.

Julia stumbled when the toe of her boot caught on a raised ridge. She quickly aimed the flashlight beam at her feet to check the path.

Worn tracks shot through the center of the tunnel, orange with age and partially obscured by the uneven stones. The camera snapped awake as Julia began to document her find. She'd never seen tracks like this before. Only rock, water and slime, with the occasional calling card from an old miner or an earlier explorer. Up until then, her expeditions had been more akin to spelunking than mine exploration, at least in her own mind.

This was something new, something interesting. The flare of excitement dimmed quickly in the absence of company, and all at once that familiar loneliness poured into the hollow where her heart used to be.

She missed Anthony. Without him this hobby was just another depressing reminder of his absence, perhaps the most obvious one. She was alone in a forgotten place with nothing but her camera and these tracks that had no purpose and no destination.

He was everything she needed, and he was gone.

The sadness was so sudden that Julia felt faint with it. She didn't want to be here anymore, but still she trudged onwards, trying and failing to find even a whisper of the happiness she used to feel when exploring abandoned mines. Her boots dragged and her breath came in short bursts as she turned a corner.

She froze.

There at the end of the short stretch of tunnel, was a man.

Instinctual fear overpowered her misery from before. Her own body betrayed her as all of her muscles went rigid at once. Falling, asphyxiating, or simply getting lost in the dark were all common causes of death in these old mines. But a man standing at the end of an empty tunnel was something altogether more sinister.

The flashlight beam was a spotlight in the dark, and while her limbs were locked in place, she scanned his features. She recognized them. Of course, *of course*. Before they had become a couple, he used to come into these places by himself to look around. Her mouth opened and her tears blurred the lines of his face.

"Anthony?"

He smiled at her, the laugh lines around his mouth and eyes crinkling just the way she remembered. Julia laughed breathlessly as he held a hand out to her. She stumbled towards him wondering how this was possible, how they had found each other here, of all places.

It was a daydream that she often indulged in: running into him, reconnecting as though they had never been apart, righting her tilted world and stitching together her halved heart. She still went to all of the places that they had gone together – the grocery store, the restaurants, the bars – just for a chance to see him again. The reason she still lived in Pennsylvania at all was because he lived there as well.

And now here he was at the dead end of a mine, standing knee-deep in water.

Julia hesitated just outside of his reach. She was still breathless, dizzy with the reappearance of the one person she most wanted to see. Her eyes traced over his frame and shivers ran under her skin.

No backpack, no jacket, no flashlight. He was standing in the dark, smiling, waiting for her. The hand that extended towards her was stained a dusty black. As the light slid over his features, it failed to reflect in the deep dark of his eyes, as if they too were tunnels.

She glanced nervously at the water around his legs. No ripples.

"What's your name, stranger?" she breathed.

Anthony opened his mouth, and behind his teeth, something struggled. The yellow bird was a drop of sunlight in the gloom. The bright pop of its bloody plumage and sharp gleam of the white bone protruding from its half-digested body a macabre calling card of the Blackdamp.

A person you'd trust.

The bird shrieked, and in a wave of flittering horror, a flock of canaries poured forth from the Blackdamp's throat.

The air was thin and Julia was screaming with the last of her breath, boots flying over the tracks and back towards the entrance of the mine. Rocks rolled beneath her rubber soles as the canaries clouded her vision in red and gold, the sharp points of their beaks and bones razing the exposed skin on her hands and face.

She wanted to look back, to see if the Blackdamp itself was pursuing her. The tease of grasping fingers through her hair and down her spine was enough to force her eyes forward. Her grandfather's voice echoed through her memories as she scrambled over the collapsed rubble.

If Blackdamp ever catches you, it'll hang on real tight so you can't get away, and then it'll steal the air right out of your lungs.

The ragged entrance of the mine appeared and Julia struggled to judge its distance with her impaired depth perception. Slowing slightly when a pair of small talons attempted to rip at her right eye, Julia gasped weakly as she felt fingers curl around her throat.

She imagined Anthony behind her – the freckles on his nose, the tattoos on his arms, the curl of his hair. And although she knew that this apparition was not really Anthony, for the first time since the break-up, she hated him.

Yanking the Blackdamp's grip away from her neck before it became a noose, Julia's adrenaline surged and she flew forward faster than the birds that pursued her. She shoved through the broken brick and into the fresh air.

Julia only stopped running when she reached the Keep Out sign. She leaned against it, acutely aware of each precious breath that flowed in and out of her lungs. She stayed there, whole body heaving with air, for some time. She was not afraid of the Blackdamp, not out here where the sky was powder blue and cotton white. When Julia did walk away from the abandoned site, she was accompanied only by her own relieved laughter.

She did not look back.

It's Easy to Shoot a Dog

Maria Haskins

IT'S EASY to shoot a dog. Susanna watched Papa do it one bitter morning, winter before last, when old Karo couldn't get up off his blankets, so she knows how it's done.

You tie the dog to a fence post, put a soup-bone on the ground, load the musket with the right measure of powder and a lead bullet, aim it at the dog's head, and light the charge with the match-cord. Long as your hands don't shake, and the dog doesn't move, you'll blow its head clean off.

"It is an act of kindness and of mercy," Papa told her when he saw her watching from the porch, "to spare him the suffering otherwise to come."

Then he lit the powder, rough hands steady as the discharge scattered a flock of crows into the clouds.

Restless now on her cot beneath the rafters, listening to the quiet breaths of her own dog asleep beside her on the floor, Susanna hears that musket blast again, feels the shudder of the recoil through her bones, the sting of powder in her nostrils sharp enough to make her wince.

Judging by the moonlight, it's long past midnight and she knows it's time to go, yet she lingers beneath the covers.

She thinks of how she brought this dog home as a pup one October day ten years ago when she was seven, same year as Mama raised a stone with her brother's name in the boneyard; thinks of how old Karo took to that pup right away, watching it with kindly hang-dog eyes as it blundered wobbly-legged through the yard and garden.

That pup grew up with her; became this rangy, flop-eared mutt that curls up beneath the table when she eats, sniffs out hares and grouse in the woods for her, twines its body 'round her knees to greet her when she comes in from the barn. For ten years, she's cared for it with gentle patience, the way no one's ever cared for her, and for ten years it's followed her wherever, sharing her bed, her paths, her warmth; its soul and shadow mingling with hers beneath this tarred roof, beneath this well-worn patch of sky and heaven.

It's easy to shoot a dog. Easier still if you don't think about it too long; if you can heft that musket clean of doubt or guilt.

Cold floorboards bend and creak beneath her stockinged feet as she gets up, reaching for her clothes in the darkness. There's the gleam of frost outside, even though it's only early fall, but then, it's been a hard year already. A year of bad omens; a harsh winter followed by a slow spring, wolves ravaging sheep, church-silver stolen off the altar. They even burned a witch in town, just after Easter. She went to look, but though the woman's hair was shorn and she was already burning, Susanna could tell it wasn't anyone she knew. After, when the bones still smouldered, the priest in his stiff black cassock puffed himself up before the crowd, assuring them the witch's spells and crafts would all unravel now that she was dead. Susanna stood there until dusk, waiting to see if anything would change, but the world remained the same as far as she could tell.

Beneath the shearling coat and felted woolen breeches on the chair beside the bed, Susanna's fingertips brush the embossed cover of Nana's ancient hymnal, but tonight she has no prayers to tuck between its yellowed pages. Instead, she reaches down, finding the warmth of fur and breath that has always been more dependable than faith and supplication.

The dog yawns as it stretches, gazing up at her with brown and faithful eyes, jaunty tail already wagging. It's eager to go with her, watching as she gathers up Papa's musket, tucks the tinderbox into her pocket, slings the supple leather pouch that holds the powder and the bullet across her chest.

"Come," she whispers so as not to wake Mama or Papa, and heads downstairs, slipping into the dark with the dog trotting keen on white-toed paws, following.

* * *

Far back as Susanna can remember, she always wanted a dog of her own, but Mama and Papa would not allow it. No matter how she begged or pleaded, they did not relent. Mama even struck her at the end of one long day when she got tired of her cheek. Old Karo was enough, they thought, keeping the yard and barn safe with his growl and bark; but much as she loved that jowly hound, she knew he was not wholly hers, knew he loved her Papa and her waddling, weak-chinned brother more than her. She craved a creature that would be bound to her, to love and roam with as she saw fit.

For months she prayed for a puppy, hands clasped around Nana's hymnal every Sunday as she sat in church beneath that soaring vault crowded with angels and apostles. Peering up at the Mother and the Son, at the vines and doves; staring at the polished silver cross studded with sardonyx and amber above the altar.

But God did not relent either, and one chill October morning she wandered off into the forest to find a pup herself. She was seven years old, hemmed in on all sides by chores and rules and commandments, her brother scampering in her wake. As always, she was supposed to watch him, the louse, same as every day since he'd been born.

"Stay here," she ordered, telling him of the ravenous wolves stalking the glades and paths, of their howls threading through mist and moonlight; of the witch weaving blood and bone into magic spells, changing children into pigs and sheep before she took their skins; of the trolls lurking 'neath the bridges and the rocks; of the Vittra roaming the dells and hollows, snaring the unwary.

But he would not leave her alone no matter what she said or did, toddling along behind her undaunted.

At first she followed the trails she knew, to the places she'd gone to gather firewood and berries, to harvest birch bark for baskets, to forage for sticky-capped mushrooms in early fall and bright-green spruce-shoots in spring. Then she wandered farther, across the bridge, across the river, to where she'd sometimes let the goats graze, meadows hazy with tall timothy grass and yarrow in summer, yet no dog could she find in that frosty wilted pasture, nor anywhere else her feet would take her.

"There *is* a pup," she told her brother, when he wept and said that he was hungry. There were countless places in the woods where a pup might hide, waiting to be found, waiting to be saved. "We just have to find him. Just a little farther."

She kept saying it, clinging to the words as if speaking them out loud would make it so.

Her brother cried most of the way. Because his ankle twisted. Because he was four years old. Because the wolves howled. Because he was cold and she'd forgotten to bring his mittens.

Because he was too far away from Mama, no matter how hard and unforgiving her calloused hands were most days.

When darkness fell, they trudged on, her brother sucking his fingers and holding on to her coat. He followed her wherever, because that was the way it had always been, since the first day Mama placed him in her care.

* * *

Ten years ago, when she walked home through the woods with that new pup whimpering in her arms, when she snuggled it close and felt the warmth of its soft, pink belly, she did not regret the choice she'd made. She did not regret it even when Mama and Papa shrieked and cried, asking where she'd been, asking about her brother. She told them he'd run off; that she'd followed but could not find him, no matter how she looked.

Even at the age of seven, the lies felt smooth and true upon her tongue.

And Mama wailing, like she'd ever cared for him, and Papa's face gone hard as rocks and iron, as if he'd even once held him close.

"You were supposed to watch him," Mama said, her voice so rough with anger it raked Susanna's skin.

"I did. I tried."

Papa saw the pup then, cowering between her legs.

"I found it in the woods when I was searching," she said and picked it up, felt their two hearts pounding, close like breath and blood. "It's mine to keep."

Papa raised his hand. Mama raised her voice. But what could they do? They placed a stone with the boy's name in the boneyard once they'd combed the woods in vain. After that, Papa went back to the fields and forest and Mama went back to washing laundry for the burghers.

* * *

Ten years ago Susanna had spent three days and nights wandering the woods with her brother, scrounging for frost-bitten berries off the rowans, chewing bark and pine-sap to fend off the hunger. In the dark, she whispered lullabies to hush her brother up, trying not to shout or strike him, even when he would not stop wailing.

By the time the old woman found them, they were chilled through bone and marrow; her brother sniveling snot and tears. Susanna was crying too, at least when no one saw. The old woman looked them over long and thoughtful, her gnarled hand resting on the curved blade tucked into her belt, though Susanna did not think she'd need that steel to end them. Once they'd been weighed and measured beneath that gaze, the woman took them to a sod-roofed cottage, evergreen ivy and withered bougainvillea snaking up the timbered logs and eaves, skulls and bones dangling in the trees outside, fresh hides stretched tight in wooden frames for tanning in the yard.

The woman fed them mutton soup and fresh-baked bread. She combed the pine needles and mud out of their hair. She put a fatwood pine-root on the fire to warm them. She wrapped the boy in a sheepskin and laid him down on a cot by the hearth.

Susanna sat at the table, sipping soup and watching. She saw the way the old woman used her mortar and her pestle, the way she hung the bunches of gathered herbs from the rafters, the way she mixed the potions and the salves on the counter below the deep-set window, the way she opened that heavy black book of hers, inked letters twined about with gold and scarlet. She listened to her sing, chanting words over her brother to mend his broken foot.

She knew what that woman was, and the woman knew she knew it, but neither of them spoke the word.

"All I wanted was a dog," Susanna said, though no one had asked for any explanation. "I'd give anything for a pup of my own."

The woman shook her head, her small bird-bone earrings clicking beneath her waist-long, gray-streaked hair. "Silly girl. Pups come along all the time. Wait till spring. They'll be rolling out of every barn and cottage."

"I've waited years already. I want a dog to care for now, before winter comes."

The woman laughed at that, at Susanna. Yet she looked at her with something akin to understanding.

"No patience in you, is there? Don't go looking for things to love, girl. Life's easier if you're not shackled to another." She nodded at the sleeping boy, gave a knife's edge of a grin. "One such chain of care has been slipped on you already, and as you grow there will be others, and they will be tighter still."

Susanna looked at her little brother. He was quiet then, but well did she remember his whining and his weeping, how he slowed her down and clung to her at every step.

"You're a clever girl, I can tell. Once I, too, was a clever girl who wanted things that would not be given to me. There are ways to get the things you want, but the getting's rarely free or easy." She gazed at Susanna, then turned away. "No. I do not think you want the dog that I could give you. Go home. Obey your parents. Become what they want you to be."

Susanna looked at her, thinking of the black book the woman had closed when she saw Susanna peeking, of the words she'd sung to change and heal the boy's bones and flesh; she thought of whispered winter-tales of children gone astray and of the raging hellfire awaiting those who used charms and curses to get what God and prayer would not supply.

"I'd give anything for a puppy."

The old woman turned from the cauldron, a gleam of embers in her sharp blue eyes as she peered through the murk of smoke and steam, seeing true and through. "Not many are willing to give *anything*. What would you give to get what you want?"

Susanna swallowed another mouthful of that soup, listening to her brother snuffling beneath the sheepskin; looking at that gnarled-root of a hand stirring the cauldron, and she thought she knew what the question and the answer meant.

"Anything."

* * *

Ten years on, Susanna is walking through the woods with the dog scampering in her wake. Might be his gait is stiffer now, might be his maw is grizzled, but he still follows her wherever; his soul and shadow still mingled with her own.

"There's a price for everything," the old woman told her that night beside the fire, "but you are only seven, and clever as you are, I'll still give you ten years until payment's due for what I'll give you. By then, the shackles of your life will be chafing both your skin and soul. Then you must bring yourself to me, to learn and listen, to stay beneath my roof as long as I see fit. And you must bring back what I gave you, for me to keep."

Ten years ago, as Susanna gazed at the fatwood smouldering low, as she listened to her own fiery heart burning hot and greedy beneath her ribs, the deal she struck seemed a well-considered bargain. She never thought ten years would pass by so quick – and if she thought of the deal at all those first few years after the old woman showed her the way home, she mostly thought of the snug bed in that small cottage, of the smell of herbs and mutton, of days without chores or errands, of the inked and illuminated pages of that heavy book, of the liberty to roam beneath the trees rather than feel the burn of lye as she helped Mama launder sheets by the creek.

But lately, as the years have run down through the glass, she's turned and twisted all the words the old woman spoke; she's run her fingers over them, the smooth and the rough, pondering their full meaning as she's laid awake at night with the dog warm and heavy by her side.

Bring back what I gave you, for me to keep.

She's thought of the scraped-clean skulls hanging from the branches, of bones boiled white, of hides stretched and drying beneath the trees. She's thought of the wicked knife in the old woman's belt, of the claws and teeth dangling from the charms. She's felt the dog's soft ears between her fingers, felt the curve and sleekness of his skull and jaw beneath the silken fur. And the fear that only tickled 'neath her skin ten years ago has turned into a constant itch and ache.

She's tried to find a way out. She prayed for salvation in church, with the wine and bread burning on her tongue, hands clasped around Nana's hymnal, even though she knows neither the Mother nor the Son nor the angels and apostles will help a girl like her.

It's easy to shoot a dog. As a kindness, as a mercy, to spare it the pains and suffering otherwise to come (beneath that wicked knife and chanted words). Susanna has held the musket more than once; felt the weight of it, heavy like her own heart in her hands.

Ten years. It is a decent length of life for any dog; yet even so, the old woman's words no longer seem like a fair trade or trusty promise. They seem a threat and portent, a shadow creeping ever closer through the pines and spruce. Susanna knows the payment's overdue. She knows the old woman will claim it, one way or another, whether Susanna goes to her or whether Susanna waits for her to come knocking on the door.

She knows the price; knows what she would lose and gain if she were to pay it.

So she's learned the things that might confound an old woman such as that: sardonyx and amber, salt and silver, mistletoe and iron, scattered pebbles on the path, a hag stone on the fencepost by the road, hazel planted near the house.

Even so, her fear runs deep. How many times has she stayed awake listening for the old woman's steps coming up the pebble-strewn path, crossing the line of salt she laid at the threshold, climbing up the creaking stairs? How many nights has she waited for her barred door to shiver, for the latch and hook to bend and warp and snap, for the hinges to break, the wood to crack beneath the old woman's power?

It's easy to shoot a dog.

It's harder to shoot a witch.

* * *

The bright frost shatters beneath Susanna's boots as she heads deeper in between the boles, searching out the way she came and went ten years ago.

She's never cried, not in ten years; not once. Not so as anyone could see or hear it, anyway. And even if she tasted those tears, even then, she knows she'd make the same bargain again.

Anything, is what she said. But whatever promise she made when she was seven, she knows now that she cannot give up this dog, cannot let him suffer beneath the knife, cannot let his skin be taken, cannot aim the muzzle at his head even to spare him the pain otherwise to come.

Susanna walks with one hand on the musket, treading through dawn and day and dusk, into the shiver-dark of another night with the dog beside her. She walks until she finds the sod-roofed cottage, one candle lit in its northern window. In the rippled moonlight slipping through the chasing clouds, she sees the pale skulls hanging from the trees, hears their hollow song of wind and bone, and she sees an empty frame set up to tan a new hide behind the house, wooden pegs and sinew-thread ready for the stretching.

The old woman knows they're coming, her heavy feet already treading the warped wooden boards within the timbered walls. When the door glints open, there's a breath of utter silence when Susanna thinks she might turn back or falter. But no. There the old woman is, in the doorway, gray hair tangled 'round her brow, blue eyes peering through the shadows. Just a thin line of darkness between them now.

"Come inside," the old woman coos. "I thought you might not come. Thought you'd changed your mind. Thought they'd find a way to hinder you, perhaps. I should not have worried. At seventeen, you are still a clever girl."

The wood and metal of Papa's musket is smooth and heavy in Susanna's hands. She can smell the powder, smell the slow-burning match-cord – woven hemp cooked with saltpeter. In the darkness, she puts one hand on Brother's head – to calm him, to calm herself. And yet they both tremble.

"I told you I would teach you, and I will," the old woman whispers, soft words snaking 'round Susanna's pounding heart. "I'll teach you all the things you'll never learn at home, not from the preacher, not from that good book of yours, nor from any husband they might choose for you. I'll teach you all the craft a clever girl might want to know."

Susanna knows it is the truth. She knows she could reach for all that power, pay the price, watch Brother's hide scraped and stretched in that yard and be done with it. She knows the old woman could teach her how to grasp the forces of earth and sky and fire, of wind and water, and bend them to her will. She knows the old woman would open that heavy book and let her read its pages, learn the chants and verses written there; stranger songs than any printed in Nana's hymnal.

It would be easy to keep the bargain, to pay the debt she owes, leave everything behind. Easier than trying to take it all with naught but a loaded musket in her hand and Brother by her side.

Behind her, Brother stirs, his growl no more than ragged breath.

"You've brought him, as agreed. Good. A fair trade for both of us. Let me take him off your hands before you step inside, because I allow no shackles of love nor duty here. It's best to put away such childish things, and you'll soon learn that freedom's ever so much sweeter than the fetters you have known."

In the wan light, Brother's eyes are fixed on Susanna's, brown and faithful even now. Even now he hearkens to her. Even now he trusts her.

It is right that he should trust her. After all, what would he have been without the deal she made? Nothing but another useless crofter's runt, working his fingers to the bone, staggering beneath some richer man's yoke, bending his knees and back beneath the priest's commandments.

She does not want Papa's musket or the witch's knife to end Brother's life. She does not want her own life to come undone, either, and to see her sin turn into human flesh again.

She wants it all, just as she always did – the dog by her side, the magic between the illuminated pages hers to wield, this cottage their new home.

Standing on the threshold, Susanna knows there is a price for everything: for love, for knowledge, for life. For betrayal, too.

The musket's loaded, just like she's learned from watching Papa, even though he never would teach her. Here's the match-cord lit and smoldering, threaded through the prongs atop the lock. A bit of priming powder in the pan. The right measure of powder down the barrel, too, and a bullet, as smooth and warm and heavy as her guilty heart, as her tarnished soul.

She's already dropped that bullet down the muzzle, tamping down ball and powder with the scouring stick. And now she stands here, the lit end of the match-cord glowing hot and red like a demon's eye in the murk.

She thinks of all the things she'd give right now, rather than Brother's skull and hide. Even Mama's and Papa's lives she'd trade without regret. But not him. Not this dog. Not Brother.

The old woman sees the musket, sees Susanna raising it, aiming it at her head, but she's not worried. She thinks it's loaded with naught but a ball of lead, easily averted. She does not know how patiently Brother waited at the church door while Susanna snatched that hallowed cross off the altar – the Mother gazing down upon her sacrilege. She does not know about the silver Susanna snipped off that cross with Papa's tongs to melt and put into the bullet mould. She does not know about the sardonyx and amber Susanna pried off it and dropped into the ladle as the molten lead and silver swirled there, glossy-hot and gray. She does not know about the three long gray hairs Susanna plucked off the old woman's cloak ten years ago while she lay sleeping, while the fatwood burned low, while a seven-year-old girl pondered the deal she'd made. She does not know how safe Susanna has kept those gray strands, tucked between the pages of Nana's hymnal.

There is no going back. Not to who she was ten years ago, before her hot and greedy heart burned away all chances of salvation. Not to Mama and Papa, telling her each day to marry and be gone. Not to church, with the priest leaning close in the confessional, asking about those dog tracks in the snow beside the church gate, about the errant boot-prints by the altar.

But if the bullet finds its mark, if the witch's craft should come undone, if her skein unravels here, what then for her, what then for Brother, what then for both of them? For him, the slow death of a stunted life. For herself, the stocks, the pyre, a shallow grave in unhallowed ground.

Susanna grips the musket firmly, Brother quivering at her side. He won't leave her, no matter how this ends, no matter what she does or where she goes, because that's how it is, how it's always been between them: no matter where the path leads, or what words the witch spoke ten years ago to change him, or what Susanna did to get what she wanted. Through it all, Brother's eyes stayed steadfast and true and always will. This dog will follow her to the ends of this world and into the next.

She knows the truth of it now, standing here at the end and the beginning. It isn't easy to shoot a dog, not even as a mercy and a kindness, not even to spare him the pain and suffering otherwise to come. Not when your souls and shadows have mingled since the day he was wrenched from Mama's womb. Because the real bargain she made, before any other, though the words were never spoken and Susanna did not understand the weight and depth of it before tonight, was to take care of him, of this dog, her Brother, till the end of his days, till the end of hers.

It's hard to shoot a witch.

Harder still when Brother starts barking at the old woman's feet, snapping at her hem and sleeves, but still she must take aim.

Hands shaking, she touches the match-cord to the powder.

The crack and smoke of Papa's musket fills the night.

As the tangled bodies of witch and dog collapse in the doorway, Susanna stumbles forward, breathing one word into the silence – a plea and question, both. Kneeling, she blinks away the sudden sting of tears and reaches through the bitter smoke, praying for the warmth of fur and breath, praying for the power of sardonyx and amber, praying that the spell won't break.

The Mines of Falun

E.T.A. Hoffmann, translated by Major Alex. Ewing

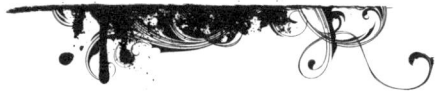

"**ONE BRIGHT,** sunny day in July the whole population of Goethaborg was assembled at the harbour. A fine East-Indiaman, happily returned from her long voyage, was lying at anchor, with her long, homeward-bound pennant, and the Swedish flag fluttering gaily in the azure sky. Hundreds of boats, skiffs, and other small craft, thronged with rejoicing seafolk, were going to and fro on the mirroring waters of the Goethaelf, and the cannon of Masthuggetorg thundered their far-echoing greeting out to sea. The gentlemen of the East-India Company were walking up and down on the quay, reckoning up, with smiling faces, the plentiful profits they had netted, and rejoicing their hearts at the yearly increasing success of their hazardous enterprise, and at the growing commercial importance of their good town of Goethaborg. For the same reasons everybody looked at these brave adventurers with pleasure and pride, and shared their rejoicing; for their success brought sap and vigour into the whole life of the place.

"The crew of the East-Indiaman, about a hundred strong, landed in a number of boats (gaily dressed with flags for the occasion) and prepared to hold their 'Hoensning'. That is the name of the feast which the sailors hold on such occasions; it often goes on for several days. Musicians went before them, in strange, gay dresses, playing lustily on violins, oboes, fifes and drums, whilst others sung merry songs; after them came the crew, walking two and two; some, with gay ribbons on their hats and jackets, waved fluttering streamers; others danced and skipped; and all of them shouted and cheered at the tops of their voices, till the sounds of merriment rang far and wide.

"Thus the gay procession passed through the streets, and on to the Haga suburb, where a feast of eating and drinking was ready for them in a tavern.

"Here the best of 'Oel' flowed in rivers and bumper after bumper was quaffed. Numbers of women joined them, as is always the case when sailors come home from a long voyage; dancing began, and wilder and wilder grew the revel, and louder and louder the din.

"One sailor only – a slender, handsome lad of about twenty, or scarcely so much – had slipped away from the revel, and was sitting alone outside, on the bench at the door of the tavern.

"Two or three of his shipmates came out to him, and cried, laughing loudly:

"'Now then, Elis Froebom! Are you going to be a donkey, as usual, and sit out here in the sulks, instead of joining the sport like a man? Why, you might as well part company from the old ship altogether, and set sail on your own hook, as fight shy of the "Hoensning". One would think you were a regular long-shore land-lubber, and had never been afloat on blue water. All the same, you've got as good pluck as any sailor that walks a deck – ay, and as cool and steady a head in a gale of wind as ever I came athwart; but, you see, you can't take your liquor! You'd sooner keep the ducats in your pocket than serve them out to the land-sharks ashore here. There, lad! take a drink of that; or Naecken, the sea-devil, and all the Troll will be foul of your hawse before you know where you are!'

"Elis Froebom jumped up quickly from the bench; glared angrily at his shipmates; took the tumbler – which was filled to the brim with brandy – and emptied it at a draught; then he said:

"'You see I can take my glass with any man of you, Ivens; and you can ask the captain if I'm a good sailor-man, or not; so stow away that long tongue of yours, and sheer off! I don't care about all this drink and row here; and what I'm doing out here by myself is no business of yours; you have nothing to do with it.'

"'All right, my hearty!' answered Ivens. 'I know all about it. You're one of these Nerica men – and a moony lot the whole cargo of them are too. They're the sort of chaps that would rather sit and pipe their eye about nothing particular, than take a good glass, and see what the pretty lasses at home are made of, after a twelve-month's cruise! But just you belay there a bit. Steer full and bye, and stand off and on, and I'll send somebody out to you that'll cut you adrift, in a pig's whisper, from that old bench where you've cast your anchor.'

"They went; and presently a very pretty, rather refined-looking girl came out of the tavern, and sat down beside the melancholy Elis, who was still sitting, silent and thoughtful, on the bench. From her dress and general appearance there could be no doubt as to her terrible calling. But the life she was leading had not yet quite marred the delicacy of the wonderfully tender features of her beautiful face; there was no trace of repulsive boldness about the expression of her dark eyes – rather a quiet, melancholy longing.

"'Aren't you coming to join your shipmates, Elis?' she said. 'Now that you're back safe and sound, after all you've gone through on your long voyage, aren't you glad to be home in the old country again?'

"The girl spoke in a soft, gentle voice, putting her arms about him. Elis Froebom looked into her eyes, as if roused from a dream. He took her hand; he pressed her to his breast. It was evident that what she had said had made its way to his heart.

"'Ah!' he said, as if collecting his thoughts, 'it's no use talking about my enjoying myself. I can't join in all that riot and uproar; there's no pleasure in it, for me. You go away, my dear child! Sing and shout like the rest of them, if you can, and let the gloomy, melancholy Elis stay out here by himself; he would only spoil your pleasure. Wait a minute, though! I like you, and I should wish you to think of me sometimes, when I'm away on the sea again.'

"With that he took two shining ducats out of his pocket, and a beautiful Indian handkerchief from his breast, and gave them to the girl. But her eyes streamed with tears; she rose, laid the money on the bench, and said:

"'Oh, keep your ducats; they only make me miserable; but I'll wear the handkerchief in dear remembrance of you. You're not likely to find me next year when you hold your Hoensning in the Haga.'

"And she crept slowly away down the street, with her hands pressed to her face.

"Elis fell back into his gloomy reveries. At length, as the uproar in the tavern grew loud and wild, he cried:

"'Oh, that I were lying deep, deep beneath the sea! For there's nobody left in the wide, wide world that I can be happy with now!'

"A deep, harsh voice spoke, close behind him: 'You must have been most unfortunate, youngster, to wish to die, just when life should be opening before you.'

"Elis looked round, and saw an old miner standing leaning against the boarded wall of the tavern, with folded arms, looking down at him with a grave, penetrating glance.

"As Elis looked at him, a feeling came to him as if some familiar figure had suddenly come into the deep, wild solitude in which he had thought himself lost. He pulled himself together, and told the old miner that his father had been a stout sailor, but had perished in the storm from which he himself had been saved as by a miracle; that his two soldier brothers had died in battle, and he had supported his mother with the liberal pay he drew for sailing to the East

Indies. He said he had been obliged to follow the life of a sailor, having been brought up to it from childhood, and it had been a great piece of good fortune that he got into the service of the East-India Company. This voyage, the profits had been greater than usual, and each of the crew had been given a sum of money over and above his pay; so that he had hastened, in the highest spirits, with his pockets full of ducats, to the little cottage where his mother lived. But strange faces looked at him from the windows, and a young woman who opened the door to him at last told him, in a cold, harsh tone, that his mother had died three months before, and that he would find the few bits of things that were left, after paying the funeral expenses, waiting for him at the Town Hall. The death of his mother broke his heart. He felt alone in the world – as much so as if he had been wrecked on some lonely reef, helpless and miserable. All his life at sea seemed to him to have been a mistaken, purposeless driving. And when he thought of his mother, perhaps badly looked after by strangers, he thought it a wrong and horrible thing that he should have gone to sea at all, instead of staying at home and taking proper care of her. His comrades had dragged him to the Hoensning in spite of himself, and he had thought, too, that the uproar, and even the drink, might have deadened his pain; but instead of that, all the veins in his breast seemed to be bursting, and he felt as if he must bleed to death.

"'Well,' said the old miner, 'you'll soon be off to sea again, Elis, and then your sorrow will soon be over. Old folks must die; there's no help for that: she has only gone from this miserable world to a better.'

"Ah!' said Elis, 'it is just because nobody believes in my sorrow, and that they all think me a fool to feel it – I say it's that which is driving me out of the world! I shan't go to sea anymore; I'm sick of existence altogether. When the ship used to go flying along through the water, with all sail set, spreading like glorious wings, the waves playing and dashing in exquisite music, and the wind singing in the rigging, my heart used to bound. Then I could hurrah and shout on deck like the best of them. And when I was on look-out duty of dark, quiet nights, I used to think about getting home, and how glad my dear old mother would be to have me back. I could enjoy a Hoensning like the rest of them, then. And when I had shaken the ducats into mother's lap, and given her the handkerchiefs and all the other pretty things I had brought home, her eyes would sparkle with pleasure, and she would clap her hands for joy, and run out and in, and fetch me the "Aehl" which she had kept for my homecoming. And when I sat with her of an evening, I would tell her of all the strange folks I had seen, and their ways and customs, and about the wonderful things I had come across in my long voyages. This delighted her; and she would tell me of my father's wonderful cruises in the far North, and serve me up lots of strange, sailor's yarns, which I had heard a hundred times, but never could hear too often. Ah! Who will give me that happiness back again? No, no! Never more on land! – never more at sea! What should I do among my shipmates? They would only laugh at me. Where should I find any heart for my work? It would be nothing but an objectless striving.'

"It gives me real satisfaction to listen to you, youngster,' said the old miner. 'I have been observing you, without your knowledge, for the last hour or two, and have had my own enjoyment in so doing. All that you have said and done has shown me that you possess a profoundly thoughtful mind, and a character and nature pious, simple, and sincere. Heaven could have given you no more precious gifts; but you were never in all your born days in the least cut out for a sailor. How should the wild, unsettled sailor's life suit a meditative, melancholy Neriker like you? – for I can see that you come from Nerica by your features, and whole appearance. You are right to say goodbye to that life for ever. But you're not going to walk about idle, with your hands in your pockets? Take my advice, Elis Froebom. Go to Falun, and be a miner. You are young and strong. You'll soon be a first-class pick-hand; then a hewer; presently a surveyor, and so get higher and higher. You have a lot of ducats in your pocket. Take care of them; invest them; add more to them. Very likely you'll soon get a "Hemmans" of your own, and then a share in the works. Take my advice, Elis Froebom; be a miner.'

"The old man's words caused him a sort of fear.

"'What?' he cried. 'Would you have me leave the bright, sunny sky that revives and refreshes me, and go down into that dreadful, hell-like abyss, and dig and tunnel like a mole for metals and ores, merely to gain a few wretched ducats? Oh, never!'

"'The usual thing,' said the old man. 'People despise what they have had no chance of knowing anything about! As if all the constant wearing, petty anxieties inseparable from business up here on the surface, were nobler than the miner's work. To his skill, knowledge, and untiring industry Nature lays bare her most secret treasures. You speak of gain with contempt, Elis Froebom. Well, there's something infinitely higher in question here, perhaps: the mole tunnels the ground from blind instinct; but, it may be, in the deepest depths, by the pale glimmer of the mine candle, men's eyes get to see clearer, and at length, growing stronger and stronger, acquire the power of reading in the stones, the gems, and the minerals, the mirroring of secrets which are hidden above the clouds. You know nothing about mining, Elis. Let me tell you a little.'

"He sat down on the bench beside Elis, and began to describe the various processes minutely, placing all the details before him in the clearest and brightest colours. He talked of the Mines of Falun, in which he said he had worked since he was a boy; he described the great main-shaft, with its dark brown sides; he told how incalculably rich the mine was in gems of the finest water. More and more vivid grew his words, more and more glowing his face. He went, in his description, through the different shafts as if they had been the alleys of some enchanted garden. The jewels came to life, the fossils began to move; the wondrous Pyrosmalite and the Almandine flashed in the light of the miner's candles; the Rock-Crystals glittered, and darted their rays.

"Elis listened intently. The old man's strange way of speaking of all these subterranean marvels as if he were standing in the midst of them, impressed him deeply. His breast felt stifled; it seemed to him as if he were already down in these depths with the old man, and would never more look upon the friendly light of day. And yet it seemed as though the old man were opening to him a new and unknown world, to which he really properly belonged, and that he had somehow felt all the magic of that world, in mystic forebodings, since his boyhood.

"Elis Froebom,' said the old man at length, 'I have laid before you all the glories of a calling for which Nature really destined you. Think the subject well over with yourself, and then act as your better judgment counsels you.'

"He rose quickly from the bench, and strode away without any goodbye to Elis, without looking at him even. Soon he disappeared from his sight.

"Meanwhile quietness had set in in the tavern. The strong 'Aehl' and brandy had got the upper hand. Many of the sailors had gone away with the girls; others were lying snoring in corners. Elis – who could go no more to his old home – asked for, and was given, a little room to sleep in.

"Scarcely had he thrown himself, worn and weary as he was, upon his bed, when dreams began to wave their pinions over him. He thought he was sailing in a beautiful vessel on a sea calm and clear as a mirror, with a dark, cloudy sky vaulted overhead. But when he looked down into the sea he presently saw that what he had thought was water was a firm, transparent, sparkling substance, in the shimmer of which the ship, in a wonderful manner, melted away, so that he found himself standing upon this floor of crystal, with a vault of black rock above him, for that was rock which he had taken at first for clouds. Impelled by some power unknown to him he stepped onwards, but, at that moment, everything around him began to move, and wonderful plants and flowers, of glittering metal, came shooting up out of the crystal mass he was standing on, and entwined their leaves and blossoms in the loveliest manner. The crystal floor was so transparent that Elis could distinctly see the roots of these plants. But soon, as his glance penetrated deeper and deeper, he saw, far, far down in the depths, innumerable beautiful maidens, holding each other embraced with white, gleaming arms; and it was from their hearts that the roots, plants, and flowers were growing. And when these maidens smiled, a sweet sound rang all through the vault above, and the wonderful metal flowers shot up higher, and waved their leaves and branches in joy. An indescribable sense of rapture came upon the lad; a world of love and passionate longing awoke in his heart.

"'Down, down to you!' he cried, and threw himself with outstretched arras down upon the crystal ground. But it gave way under him, and he seemed to be floating in shimmering æther.

"'Ha! Elis Froebom; what think you of this world of glory?' a strong voice cried. It was the old miner. But as Elis looked at him, he seemed to expand into gigantic size, and to be made of glowing metal. Elis was beginning to be terrified; but a brilliant light came darting, like a sudden lightning-flash, out of the depths of the abyss, and the earnest face of a grand, majestic woman appeared. Elis felt the rapture of his heart swelling and swelling into destroying pain. The old man had hold of him, and cried:

"'Take care, Elis Froebom! That is the queen. You may look up now.'

"He turned his head involuntarily, and saw the stars of the night sky shining through a cleft in the vault overhead. A gentle voice called his name as if in inconsolable sorrow. It was his mother's. He thought he saw her form up at the cleft. But it was a young and beautiful woman who was calling him, and stretching her hands down into the vault.

"'Take me up!' he cried to the old man. I tell you I belong to the upper world, and its familiar, friendly sky.'

"'Take care, Froebom,' said the old man solemnly; 'be faithful to the queen, whom you have devoted yourself to.'

"But now, when he looked down again into the immobile face of the majestic woman, he felt that his personality dissolved away into glowing molten stone. He screamed aloud, in nameless fear, and awoke from this dream of wonder, whose rapture and terror echoed deep within his being.

"'I suppose I could scarcely help dreaming all this extraordinary stuff,' he said to himself, as he collected his senses with difficulty; 'the old miner told me so much about the glories of the subterranean world that of course my head's quite full of it. But I never in my life felt as I do now. Perhaps I'm dreaming still. No, no; I suppose I must be a little out of sorts. Let's get into the open air. The fresh sea breeze'll soon set me all right.'

"He pulled himself together, and ran to the Klippa Haven, where the uproar of the Hoensning was breaking out again. But he soon found that all enjoyment passed him by, that he couldn't hold any thought fast in his mind, that presages and wishes, to which he could give no name, went crossing each other in his mind. He thought of his dead mother with the bitterest sorrow; but then, again, it seemed to him that what he most longed for was to see that girl again – the one whom he gave the handkerchief to – who had spoken so nicely to him the evening before. And yet he was afraid that if she were to come meeting him out of some street she would turn out to be the old miner in the end. And he was afraid of *him*; though, at the same time, he would have liked to hear more from him of the wonders of the mine.

"Driven hither and thither by all these fancies, he looked down into the water, and then he thought he saw the silver ripples hardening into the sparkling glimmer in which the grand ships melted away, while the dark clouds, which were beginning to gather and obscure the blue sky, seemed to sink down and thicken into a vault of rock. He was in his dream again, gazing into the immobile face of the majestic woman, and the devouring pain of passionate longing took possession of him as before.

"His shipmates roused him from his reverie to go and join one of their processions, but an unknown voice seemed to whisper in his ear:

"'What are you doing here? Away, away! Your home is in the Mines of Falun. There all the glories which you saw in your dream are waiting for you. Away, away to Falun!'

"For three days Elis hung and loitered about the streets of Goethaborg, constantly haunted by the wonderful imagery of his dream, continually urged by the unknown voice. On the fourth day he was standing at the gate through which the road to Gefle goes, when a tall man walked through it, passing him. Elis fancied he recognised in this man the old miner, and he hastened on after him, but could not overtake him.

"He followed him on and on, without stopping.

"He knew he was on the road to Falun, and this circumstance quieted him in a curious way; for he felt certain that the voice of destiny had spoken to him through the old miner, and that it was he who was now leading him on to his appointed place and fate.

"And, in fact, he many times – particularly if there was any uncertainty about the road – saw the old man suddenly appear out of some ravine, or from thick bushes, or gloomy rocks, stalk away before him, without looking round, and then disappear again.

"At last, after journeying for many weary days, Elis saw, in the distance, two great lakes, with a thick vapour rising between them. As he mounted the hill to westward, he saw some towers and black roofs rising through the smoke. The old man appeared before him, grown to gigantic size, pointed with outstretched hand towards the vapour, and disappeared again amongst the rocks.

"'There lies Falun,' said Elis, 'the end of my journey.'

"He was right; for people, coming up from behind him, said the town of Falun lay between the lakes Runn and Warpann, and that the hill he was ascending was the Guffrisberg, where the main-shaft of the mine was.

"He went bravely on. But when he came to the enormous gulf, like the jaws of hell itself, the blood curdled in his veins, and he stood as if turned to stone at the sight of this colossal work of destruction.

"The main-shaft of the Falun mines is some twelve hundred feet long, six hundred feet broad, and a hundred and eighty feet deep. Its dark brown sides go, at first for the most part, perpendicularly down, till about halfway they are sloped inwards towards the centre by enormous accumulations of stones and refuse. In these, and on the sides, there peeped out here and there timberings of old shafts, formed of strong shores set close together and strongly rabbeted at the ends, in the way that blockhouses are built. Not a tree, not a blade of grass to be seen in all the bare, blank, crumbling congeries of stony chasms; the pointed, jagged, indented masses of rock tower aloft all round in wonderful forms, often like monstrous animals turned to stone, often like colossal human beings. In the abyss itself lie, in wild confusion – pell-mell stones, slag, and scoria, and an eternal, stupefying sulphury vapour rises from the depths, as if the hell-broth, whose reek poisons and kills all the green gladsomeness of nature, were being brewed down below. One would think this was where Dante went down and saw the Inferno, with all its horror and immitigable pain.

"As Elis looked down into this monstrous abyss, he remembered what an old sailor, one of his shipmates, had told him once. This shipmate of his, at a time when he was down with fever, thought the sea had suddenly all gone dry, and the boundless depths of the abyss had opened under him, so that he saw all the horrible creatures of the deep twining and writhing about amongst thousands of extraordinary shells, and groves of coral, in dreadful contortions, till they died, and lay dead, with their mouths all gaping. The old sailor said that to see such a vision meant death, ere long, in the waves; and in fact he did very soon after fall overboard, no one knew exactly how, and was drowned without possibility of rescue. Elis thought of that: for indeed the abyss seemed to him to be a good deal like the bottom of the sea run dry; and the black rocks, and the blue and red slag and scoria, were like horrible monsters shooting out polype-arms at him. Two or three miners happened, just then, to be coming up from work in the mine, and in their dark mining clothes, with their black, grimy faces, they were much like ugly, diabolical creatures of some sort, slowly and painfully crawling, and forcing their way up to the surface.

"Elis felt a shudder of dread go through him, and – what he had never experienced in all his career as a sailor – his head got giddy. Unseen hands seemed to be dragging him down into the abyss.

"He closed his eyes and ran a few steps away from it; and it was not till he began climbing up the Guffrisberg again, far from the shaft, and could look up at the bright, sunny sky, that he quite lost the feeling of terror which had taken possession of him. He breathed freely once more, and cried, from the depths of his heart:

"'Lord of my Life! What are the dangers of the sea compared with the horror which dwells in that awful abyss of rock? The storm may rage, the black clouds may come whirling down upon the breaking billows, but the beautiful, glorious sun soon gets the mastery again, and the storm is past. But never does the sun penetrate into these black, gloomy caverns; never a freshening breeze of spring can revive the heart down there. No! I shall not join you, black earthworms that you are! Never could I bring myself to lead that terrible life.'

"He resolved to spend that night in Falun, and set off back to Goethaborg the first thing in the morning.

"When he got to the market-place, he found a crowd of people there. A train of miners with their mine-candles in their hands, and musicians before them, was halted before a handsome house. A tall, slightly-built man, of middle age, came out, looking round him with kindly smiles. It was easy to see, by his frank manner, his open brow, and his bright, dark-blue eyes, that he was a genuine Dalkarl. The miners formed a circle round him, and he shook them each cordially by the hand, saying kindly words to them all.

"Elis learned that this was Pehrson Dahlsjoe, Alderman, and owner of a fine 'Fraelse' at Stora-Kopparberg. 'Fraelse' is the name given in Sweden to landed property leased out for the working of the lodes of copper and silver contained in it. The owners of these lands have shares in the mines and are responsible for their management.

"Elis was told, further, that the Assizes were just over that day, and that then the miners went round in procession to the houses of the aldermen, the chief engineers and the minemasters, and were hospitably entertained.

"When he looked at these fine, handsome fellows, with their kindly, frank faces, he forgot all about the earthworms he had seen coming up the shaft. The healthy gladsomeness which broke out afresh in the whole circle, as if new-fanned by a spring breeze, when Pehrson Dahlsjoe came out, was of a different kidney to the senseless noise and uproar of the sailors' Hoensning. The manner in which these miners enjoyed themselves went straight to the serious Elis's heart. He felt indescribably happy; but he could scarce restrain his tears when some of the young pickmen sang an ancient ditty in praise of the miner's calling, and of the happiness of his lot, to a simple melody which touched his heart and soul.

"When this song was ended, Pehrson Dahlsjoe opened his door, and the miners all went into his house one after another. Elis followed involuntarily, and stood at the threshold, so that he overlooked the spacious floor, where the miners took their places on benches. Then the doors at the side opposite to him opened, and a beautiful young lady, in evening dress, came in. She was in the full glory of the freshest bloom of youth, tall and slight, with dark hair in many curls, and a bodice fastened with rich clasps. The miners all stood up, and a low murmur of pleasure ran through their ranks. "Ulla Dahlsjoe!" they said. "What a blessing Heaven has bestowed on our hearty alderman in her!" Even the oldest miners' eyes sparkled when she gave them her hand in kindly greeting, as she did to them all. Then she brought beautiful silver tankards, filled them with splendid Aehl (such as Falun is famous for), and handed them to the guests with a face beaming with kindness and hospitality.

"When Elis saw her a lightning flash seemed to go through his heart, kindling all the heavenly bliss, the love-longings, the passionate ardour lying hidden and imprisoned there. For it was Ulla Dahlsjoe who had held out the hand of rescue to him in his mysterious dream. He thought he understood, now, the deep significance of that dream, and, forgetting the old miner, praised the stroke of fortune which had brought him to Falun.

"Alas! He felt he was but an unknown, unnoticed stranger, standing there on the doorstep miserable, comfortless, alone – and he wished he had died before he saw Ulla, as he now must perish for love and longing. He could not move his eyes from the beautiful creature, and, as she passed close to him, he pronounced her name in a low, trembling voice. She turned, and saw him standing there with a face as red as fire, unable to utter a syllable. So she went up to him, and said, with a sweet smile:

"'I suppose you are a stranger, friend, as you are dressed as a sailor. Well! Why are you standing at the door? Come in and join us."

"Elis felt as if in the blissful paradise of some happy dream, from which he would presently waken to inexpressible wretchedness. He emptied the tankard which she had given him; and Pehrson Dahlsjoe came up, and, after kindly shaking hands with him, asked him where he came from, and what had brought him to Falun.

"Elis felt the warming power of the noble liquor in his veins, and, looking the hearty Dahlsjoe in the eyes, he felt happy and courageous. He told him he was a sailor's son and had been at sea since his childhood, had just come home from the East Indies and found his mother dead; that he was now alone in the world; that the wild sea life had become altogether distasteful to him; that his keenest inclination led him to a miner's calling, and that he wished to get employment as a miner here in Falun. The latter statement, quite the reverse of his recent determination, escaped him involuntarily; it was as if he could not have said anything else to the alderman, nay as if it were the most ardent desire of his soul, although he had not known it till now, himself.

"Pehrson Dahlsjoe looked at him long and carefully, as if he would read his heart; then he said:

"'I cannot suppose, Elis Froebom, that it is mere thoughtless fickleness and the love of change that lead you to give up the calling you have followed hitherto, nor that you have omitted to maturely weigh and consider all the difficulties and hardships of the miner's life before making up your mind to take to it. It is an old belief with us that the mighty elements with which the miner has to deal, and which he controls so bravely, destroy him unless he strains all his being to keep command of them – if he gives place to other thoughts which weaken that vigour which he has to reserve wholly for his constant conflict with Earth and Fire. But if you have properly tested the sincerity of your inward call, and it has withstood the trial, you are come in a good hour. Workmen are wanted in my part of the mine. If you like, you can stay here with me, from now, and tomorrow the Captain will take you down with him, and show you what to set about.'

"Elis's heart swelled with gladness at this. He thought no more of the terror of the awful, hell-like abyss into which he had looked. The thought that he was going to see Ulla every day, and live under the same roof with her, filled him with rapture and delight. He gave way to the sweetest hopes.

"Pehrson Dahlsjoe told the miners that a young hand had applied for employment, and presented him to them then and there. They all looked approvingly at the well-knit lad, and thought he was quite cut out for a miner, as regarded his light, powerful figure, having no doubt that he would not fail in industry and straightforwardness, either.

"One of the men, well advanced in years, came and shook hands with him cordially, saying he was Head-Captain in Pehrson Dahlsjoe's part of the mine, and would be very glad to give him any help and instruction in his power. Elis had to sit down beside this man, who at once began, over his tankard of Aehl, to describe with much minuteness the sort of work which Elis would have to commence with.

"Elis remembered the old miner whom he had seen at Goethaborg, and, strangely enough, found he was able to repeat nearly all that he had told him.

"'Ay,' cried the Head-Captain. 'Where can you have learned all that? It's most surprising! There can't be a doubt that you will be the finest pickman in the mine in a very short time.'

"Ulla – going backwards and forwards amongst the guests and attending to them – often nodded kindly to Elis, and told him to be sure and enjoy himself. 'You're not a stranger now, you know,' she said, 'but one of the household. You have nothing more to do with the treacherous sea – the rich mines of Falun are your home.'

"A heaven of bliss and rapture dawned upon Elis at these words of Ulla's. It was evident that she liked to be near him; and Pehrson Dahlsjoe watched his quiet earnestness of character with manifest approval.

"But Elis's heart beat violently when he stood again by the reeking hell-mouth, and went down the mine with the Captain, in his miner's clothes, with the heavy, iron-shod Dalkarl shoes on his feet. Hot vapours soon threatened to suffocate him; and then, presently, the candles flickered in the cutting draughts of cold air that blew in the lower levels. They went down deeper and deeper, on iron ladders at last scarcely a foot wide; and Elis found that his sailor's adroitness at climbing was not of the slightest service to him there.

"They got to the lowest depths of the mine at last, and the Captain showed him what work he was to set about.

"Elis thought of Ulla. Like some bright angel he saw her hovering over him, and he forgot all the terror of the abyss, and the hardness of the toilsome labour.

"It was clear in all his thoughts that it was only if he devoted himself with all the power of his mind, and with all the exertion which his body would endure, to mining work here with Pehrson Dahlsjoe, that there was any possibility of his fondest hopes being some day realised. Wherefore it came about that he was as good at his work as the most practised hand, in an incredibly short space of time.

"Staunch Pehrson Dahlsjoe got to like this good, industrious lad better and better every day, and often told him plainly that he had found in him one whom he regarded as a dear son, as well as a first-class mine-hand. Also Ulla's regard for him became more and more unmistakeable. Often, when he was going to his work, and there was any prospect of danger, she would enjoin him to be sure to take care of himself, with tears in her eyes. And she would come running to meet him when he came back, and always had the finest of Aehl, or some other refreshment, ready for him. His heart danced for joy one day when Pehrson said to him that as he had brought a good sum of money with him, there could be no doubt that – with his habits of economy and industry – he would soon have a 'Hemmans', or perhaps even a 'Fraelse'; and then not a mineowner in all Falun would say him nay if he asked for his daughter. Fain would Elis have told him at once how unspeakably he loved Ulla, and how all his hopes of happiness were based upon her. But unconquerable shyness, and the doubt whether Ulla really liked him – though he often thought she did – sealed his lips.

"One day it chanced that Elis was at work in the lowest depths of the mine, shrouded in thick, sulphurous vapour, so that his candle only shed a feeble glimmer, and he could scarcely distinguish the run of the lode. Suddenly he heard – as if coming from some still deeper cutting – a knocking resounding, as if somebody was at work with a pick-hammer. As that sort of work was scarcely possible at such a depth, and as he knew nobody was down there that day but himself – because the Captain had got all the men employed in another part of the mine – this knocking and hammering struck him as strange and uncanny. He stopped working, and listened to the hollow sounds, which seemed to come nearer and nearer. All at once he saw, close by him, a black shadow and – as a keen draught of air blew away the sulphur vapour – the old miner whom he had seen in Goethaborg.

"'Good luck,' he cried, 'good luck to Elis Froebom, down here among the stones! What think you of the life, comrade?'

"Elis would fain have asked in what wonderful way the old man had got into the mine; but he kept striking his hammer on the rocks with such force that the fire-sparks went whirling all round, and the mine rang as if with distant thunder. Then he cried, in a terrible voice:

"'There's a grand run of trap just here; but a scurvy, ignorant scoundrel like you sees nothing in it but a narrow streak of 'Trumm' not worth a beanstalk. Down here you're a sightless mole, and you'll always be a mere abomination to the Metal Prince. You're of no use up above either – trying to get hold of the pure Regulus; which you never will – hey! You want to marry Pehrson Dahlsjoe's daughter; that's what you've taken to mine work for, not from any love of your own for the thing. Mind what you're after, double-face; take care that the Metal Prince, whom you are trying to deceive, doesn't take you and dash you down so that the sharp rocks tear you limb from limb. And Ulla will never be your wife; that much I tell you.'

"Elis's anger was kindled at the old man's insulting words.

"'What are you about,' he cried, 'here in my master, Herr Pehrson Dahlsjoe's shaft, where I am doing my duty, and working as hard at it as I can? Be off out of this the way you came, or we'll see which of us two will dash the other's brains out down here.'

"With which he placed himself in a threatening attitude, and swung his hammer about the old man's ears; who only gave a sneering laugh, and Elis saw with terror how he swarmed up the narrow ladder rungs like a squirrel, and disappeared amongst the black labyrinths of the chasms.

"The young man felt paralysed in all his limbs; he could not go on with his work, but went up. When the old Head-Captain – who had been busy in another part of the mine – saw him, he cried:

"'For God's sake, Elis, what has happened to you? You're as pale as death. I suppose it's the sulphur gas; you're not accustomed to it yet. Here, take a drink, my lad; that'll do you good.'

"Elis took a good mouthful of brandy out of the flask which the Head-Captain handed to him; and then, feeling better, told him what had happened down in the mine, as also how he had made the uncanny old miner's acquaintance in Goethaborg.

"The Head-Captain listened silently; then dubiously shook his head and said:

"'That must have been old Torbern that you met with, Elis; and I see, now, that there really is something in the tales that people tell about him. More than one hundred years ago, there was a miner here of the name of Torbern. He seems to have been one of the first to bring mining into a flourishing condition at Falun here, and in his time the profits far exceeded anything that we know of now. Nobody at that time knew so much about mining as Torbern, who had great scientific skill, and thoroughly understood all the ins and outs of the business. The richest lodes seemed to disclose themselves to him, as if he had been endowed with higher powers peculiar to himself; and as he was a gloomy, meditative man, without wife or child – with no regular home, indeed – and very seldom came up to the surface, it couldn't fail that a story soon went about that he was in compact with the mysterious power which dwells in the bowels of the earth, and fuses the metals. Disregarding Torbern's solemn warnings – for he always prophesied that some calamity would happen as soon as the miners' impulse to work ceased to be sincere love for the marvellous metals and ores – people went on enlarging the excavations more and more for the sake of mere profit, till, on St. John's Day of the year 1678, came the terrible landslip and subsidence which formed our present enormous main-shaft, laying waste the whole of the works, as they were then, in the process. It was only after many months' labour that several of the shafts were, with much difficulty, got into workable order again. Nothing was seen or heard of Torbern. There seemed to be no doubt that he had been at work down below at the time of the catastrophe, so that there could be no question what his fate had been. But not long after, and particularly when the work was beginning to go on better again, the miners said they had seen old Torbern in the mine, and that he had given them valuable advice, and pointed out rich lodes to them. Others had come across him at the top of the main-shaft, walking round it, sometimes lamenting, sometimes shouting in wild anger. Other young fellows have come here in the way you yourself did, saying that an old miner had advised them to take to mining, and shewn them the way to Falun. This always happened when there was a scarcity of hands; very likely it was Torbern's way of helping on the cause. But if it really was he whom you had those words with in the mine, and if he spoke of a fine run of trap, there isn't a doubt that there must be a grand vein of ore thereabouts, and we must see, tomorrow, if we can come across it. Of course you remember that we call rich veins of the kind "trap-runs", and that a "Trumm" is a vein which goes sub-dividing into several smaller ones, and probably gets lost altogether.'

"When Elis, tossed hither and thither by various thoughts, went into Pehrson Dahlsjoe's, Ulla did not come meeting him as usual. She was sitting with downcast looks, and – as he thought – eyes which had been weeping; and beside her was a handsome young fellow, holding her hand, and trying to say all sorts of kind and amusing things, to which she seemed to pay little attention. Pehrson Dahlsjoe took Elis – who, seized by gloomy presentiments, was keeping a darksome glance riveted on the pair – into another room, and said:

"'Well, Elis, you will soon have it in your power to give me a proof of your regard and sincerity. I have always looked upon you as a son, but you will soon take the place of one altogether. The man whom you see in there is a well-to-do merchant, Eric Olavsen by name, from Goethaborg. I am giving him my daughter for his wife, at his desire. He will take her to Goethaborg, and then you will be left alone with me, my only support in my declining years. Well, you say nothing? You turn pale? I trust this step doesn't displease you, and that now that I'm going to lose my daughter you are not going to leave me too? But I hear Olavsen mentioning my name; I must go in.'

"With which he went back to the room.

"Elis felt a thousand red-hot irons tearing at his heart. He could find no words, no tears. In wild despair he ran out, out of the house, away to the great mine-shrift.

"That monstrous chasm had a terrible appearance by day; but now, when night had fallen, and the moon was just peeping down into it, the desolate crags looked like a numberless horde of horrible monsters, the direful brood of hell, rolling and writhing, in wildest confusion, all about its reeking sides and clefts, and flashing up fiery eyes, and shooting forth glowing claws to clutch the race of mortals.

"'Torbern, Torbern,' Elis cried, in a terrible voice, which made the rocks re-echo. 'Torbern, I am here; you were not wrong – I was a wretched fool to fix my hopes on any earthly love, up on the surface here. My treasure, and my life, my all-in-all, are down below. Torbern! Take me down with you! Show me the richest veins, the lodes of ore, the glowing metal! I will dig and bore, and toil and labour. Never, never more will I come back to see the light of day. Torbern! Torbern! Take me down to you!'

"He took his flint and steel from his pocket, lighted his candle, and went quickly down the shaft, into the deep cutting where he had been on the previous day, without seeing anything of the old man. But what was his amazement when, at the deepest point, he saw the vein of metal with the utmost clearness and distinctness, so that he could trace every one of its ramifications, and its risings and fallings. But as he kept his gaze fixed more and more firmly on this wonderful vein, a dazzling light seemed to come shining through the shaft, and the walls of rock grew transparent as crystal. That mysterious dream which he had had in Goethaborg came back upon him. He was looking upon those Elysian Fields of glorious metallic trees and plants, on which, by way of fruits, buds, and blossoms, hung jewels streaming with fire. He saw the maidens, and he looked upon the face of the mighty queen. She put out her arms, drew him to her, and pressed him to her breast. Then a burning ray darted through his heart, and all his consciousness was merged in a feeling of floating in waves of some blue, transparent, glittering mist.

"'Elis Froebom! Elis Froebom!' a powerful voice from above cried out, and the reflection of torches began shining in the shaft. It was Pehrson Dahlsjoe come down with the Captain to search for the lad, who had been seen running in the direction of the main-shaft like a mad creature.

"They found him standing as if turned to stone, with his face pressed against the cold, hard rock.

"'What are you doing down here in the night-time, you foolish fellow?' cried Pehrson. 'Pull yourself together, and come up with us. Who knows what good news you may hear.'

"Elis went up in profound silence after Dahlsjoe, who did not cease to rate him soundly for exposing himself to such danger. It was broad daylight in the morning when they got to the house.

"Ulla threw herself into Elis's arms with a great cry, and called him by the fondest names, and Pehrson said to him:

"'You foolish fellow! How could I help seeing, long ago, that you were in love with Ulla, and that it was on her account, in all probability, that you were working so hard in the mine? Neither could I help seeing that she was just as fond of you. Could I wish for a better son-in-law than a fine, hearty, hard-working, honest miner – than just yourself, Elis? What vexed me was that you never would speak.'

"'We scarcely knew ourselves,' said Ulla, 'how fond we were of each other.'

"'However that may be,' said Pehrson, 'I was annoyed that Elis didn't tell me openly and candidly of his love for you, and that was why I made up the story about Eric Olavsen, which was so nearly being the death of you, you silly fellow. Not but what I wished to try you, Ulla, into the bargain. Eric Olavsen has been married for many a day, and I give my daughter to you, Elis Froebom, for, I say it again, I couldn't wish for a better son-in-law.'

"Tears of joy and happiness ran down Elis's cheeks. The highest bliss which his imagination had pictured had come to pass so suddenly and unexpectedly that he could scarce believe it was anything but another blissful dream. The workpeople came to dinner, by Dahlsjoe's invitation, in honour of the event. Ulla had dressed in her prettiest attire, and looked more charming than ever, so that they all cried, over and over again, 'Ey! What a sweet and charming creature Elis has got for a betrothed! May God bless them and make them happy!'

"Yet the terror of the past night still lay upon Elis's pale face, and he often stared about him as if he were far away from all that was going on round him. 'Elis, darling, what is the matter?' Ulla asked anxiously. He pressed her to his heart and said, 'Yes, yes, you are my own, and all is well.' But in the midst of all his happiness he often felt as though an icy hand clutched at his heart, and a dismal voice asked him:

"Is it your highest ideal, then, to be betrothed to Ulla? Wretched fool! Have you not looked upon the face of the queen?'

"He felt himself overpowered by an indescribable, anxious alarm. He was haunted and tortured by the thought that one of the workmen would suddenly assume gigantic proportions, and to his horror he would recognise in him Torbern, come to remind him, in a terrible manner, of the subterranean realm of gems and metals to which he had devoted himself.

"And yet he could see no reason why the spectral old man should be hostile to him, or what connection there was between his mining work and his love.

"Pehrson, seeing Elis's disordered condition, attributed it to the trouble he had gone through, and his nocturnal visit to the mine. Not so, Ulla, who, seized by a secret presentiment, implored her lover to tell her what terrible thing had happened to him to tear him away from her so entirely. This almost broke his heart. It was in vain that he tried to tell her of the wonderful face which had revealed itself to him in the depths of the mine. Some unknown power seemed to seal his lips forcibly; he felt as though the terrible face of the queen were looking out from his heart, so that if he mentioned her everything about him would turn to stone, to dark, black rock, as at the sight of the Medusa's frightful head. All the glory and magnificence which had filled him with rapture in the abyss appeared to him now as a pandemonium of immitigable torture, deceptively decked out to allure him to his ruin.

"Dahlsjoe told him he must stay at home for a few days, so as to shake off the sickness which he seemed to have fallen into. And during this time Ulla's affection, which now streamed bright and clear from her candid, child-like heart, drove away the memory of his fateful adventure in the mine-depths. Joy and happiness brought him back to life, and to belief in his good fortune, and in the impossibility of its being ever interfered with by any evil power.

"When he went down the pit again, everything appeared quite different to what it used to be. The most glorious veins lay clear and distinct before his eyes. He worked twice as zealously as before; he forgot everything else. When he got to the surface again, it cost him an effort of thought to remember about Pehrson Dahlsjoe, about his Ulla, even. He felt as if divided into two halves, as if his better self, his real personality, went down to the central point of the earth, and there rested in bliss in the queen's arms, whilst *he* went to his darksome dwelling in Falun. When Ulla spoke of their love, and the happiness of their future life together, he would begin to talk of the splendours of the depths, and the inestimably precious treasures that lay hidden there, and in so doing would get entangled in such wonderful, incomprehensible sayings, that alarm and terrible anxiety took possession of the poor child, who could not divine why Elis should be so completely altered from his former self. He kept telling the Captain, and Dahlsjoe himself, with the greatest delight, that he had discovered the richest veins and the most magnificent trap-runs, and when these turned out to be nothing but unproductive rock, he would laugh contemptuously and say that none but he understood the secret signs, the significant writing, fraught with hidden meaning, which the queen's own hand had inscribed on the rocks, and that it was sufficient to understand those signs without bringing to light what they indicated.

"The old Captain looked sorrowfully at Elis, who spoke, with wild gleaming eyes, of the glorious paradise which glowed down in the depths of the earth. 'That terrible old Torbern has been at him,' he whispered in Dahlsjoe's ear.

"'Pshaw! Don't believe these miners' yarns,' cried Dahlsjoe. 'He's a deep-thinking serious fellow, and love has turned his head, that's all. Wait till the marriage is over, then we'll hear no more of the trap-runs, the treasures, and the subterranean paradise.'

"The wedding day, fixed by Dahlsjoe, came at last. For a few days previously Elis had been more tranquil, more serious, more sunk in deep reflection than ever. But, on the other hand, never had he shown such affection for Ulla as at this time. He could not leave her for a moment, and never went down the mine at all. He seemed to have forgotten his restless excitement about mining work, and never a word of the subterranean kingdom crossed his lips. Ulla was all rapture. Her fear lest the dangerous powers of the subterranean world, of which she had heard old miners speak, had been luring him to his destruction, had left her; and Dahlsjoe, too, said, laughing to the Captain, 'You see, Elis was only a little light-headed for love of my Ulla.'

"Early on the morning of the wedding day, which was St. John's Day as it chanced, Elis knocked at the door of Ulla's room. She opened it, and started back terrified at the sight of Elis, dressed in his wedding clothes already, deadly pale, with dark gloomy fire sparkling in his eyes.

"'I only want to tell you, my beloved Ulla,' he said, in a faint, trembling voice, 'that we are just arrived at the summit of the highest good fortune which it is possible for mortals to attain. Everything has been revealed to me in the night which is just over. Down in the depths below, hidden in chlorite and mica, lies the cherry-coloured sparkling almandine, on which the tablet of our lives is graven. I have to give it to you as a wedding present. It is more splendid than the most glorious blood-red carbuncle, and when, united in truest affection, we look into its streaming splendour together, we shall see and understand the peculiar manner in which our hearts and souls have grown together into the wonderful branch which shoots from the queen's heart, at the central point of the globe. All that is necessary is that I go and bring this stone to the surface, and that I will do now, as fast as I can. Take care of yourself meanwhile, beloved darling. I will be back to you directly.'

"Ulla implored him, with bitter tears, to give up all idea of such a dream-like undertaking, for she felt a strong presentiment of disaster; but Elis declared that without this stone he should never know a moment's peace or happiness, and that there was not the slightest danger of any kind. He pressed her fondly to his heart, and was gone.

"The guests were all assembled to accompany the bridal pair to the church of Copparberg, where they were to be married, and a crowd of girls, who were to be the bridesmaids and walk in procession before the bride (as is the custom of the place), were laughing and playing round Ulla. The musicians were tuning their instruments to begin a wedding march. It was almost noon, but Elis had not made his appearance. Suddenly some miners came running up, horror in their pale faces, with the news that there had been a terrible catastrophe, a subsidence of the earth, which had destroyed the whole of Pehrson Dahlsjoe's part of the mine.

"'Elis! oh, Elis! You are gone!' screamed Ulla, wildly, and fell as if dead. Then only, for the first time, Dahlsjoe learned from the Captain that Elis had gone down the main-shaft in the morning. Nobody else had been in the mine, the rest of the men having been invited to the wedding. Dahlsjoe and all the others hurried off to search, at the imminent danger of their own lives. In vain! Elis Froebom was not to be found. There could be no question that the earth-fall had buried him in the rock. And thus came desolation and mourning upon the house of brave Pehrson Dahlsjoe, at the moment when he thought he was assured of peace and happiness for the remainder of his days.

* * *

"Long had stout Pehrson Dahlsjoe been dead, his daughter Ulla long lost sight of and forgotten. Nobody in Falun remembered them. More than fifty years had gone by since Froebom's luckless wedding day, when it chanced that some miners who were making a connection-passage between two shafts, found, at a depth of three hundred yards, buried in vitriolated water, the body of a young miner, which seemed, when they brought it to the daylight, to be turned to stone.

"The young man looked as if he were lying in a deep sleep, so perfectly preserved were the features of his face, so wholly without trace of decay his new suit of miner's clothes, and even the flowers in his breast. The people of the neighbourhood all collected round the young man, but no one recognised him or could say who he had been, and none of the workmen missed any comrade.

"The body was going to be taken to Falun, when out of the distance an old, old woman came creeping slowly and painfully up on crutches.

"Here's the old St. John's Day grandmother!' the miners said. They had given her this name because they had noticed that she came always every year on St. John's Day up to the main-shaft, and looked down into its depths, weeping, lamenting, and wringing her hands as she crept round it, then going away again.

"The moment she saw the body she threw away her crutches, lifted her arms to Heaven, and cried, in the most heartrending accents of the deepest lamentation:

"'Oh! Elis Froebom! Oh, my sweet, sweet bridegroom!'

"And she cowered down beside the body, took the stony hands and pressed them to her heart, chilled with age, but throbbing still with the fondest love, like some naphtha flame under the surface ice.

"'Ah!' she said, looking round at the spectators, 'nobody, nobody among you all, remembers poor Ulla Dahlsjoe, this poor boy's happy bride fifty long years ago. When I went away, in my terrible sorrow and despair, to Ornaes, old Torbern comforted me, and told me I should see my poor Elis, who was buried in the rock upon our wedding day, yet once more here upon earth. And I have come every year and looked for him, all longing and faithful love. And now this blessed meeting has been granted me this day. Oh, Elis! Elis! My beloved husband!'

"She wound her arms about him as if she would never part from him more, and the people all stood round in the deepest emotion.

"Fainter and fainter grew her sobs and sighs, till they ceased to be audible.

"The miners closed round. They would have raised poor Ulla, but she had breathed out her life upon her bridegroom's body. The spectators noticed now that it was beginning to crumble into dust. The appearance of petrifaction had been deceptive.

"In the church of Copparberg, where they were to have been married fifty years before, they laid in the earth the ashes of Elis Froebom, and with them the body of her who had been thus 'Faithful unto death'."

The Three Sisters

W.W. Jacobs

THIRTY YEARS AGO on a wet autumn evening the household of Mallett's Lodge was gathered round the deathbed of Ursula Mallow, the eldest of the three sisters who inhabited it. The dingy moth-eaten curtains of the old wooden bedstead were drawn apart, the light of a smoking oil-lamp falling upon the hopeless countenance of the dying woman as she turned her dull eyes upon her sisters. The room was in silence except for an occasional sob from the youngest sister, Eunice. Outside the rain fell steadily over the steaming marshes.

"Nothing is to be changed, Tabitha," gasped Ursula to the other sister, who bore a striking likeness to her although her expression was harder and colder; "this room is to be locked up and never opened."

"Very well," said Tabitha brusquely, "though I don't see how it can matter to you then."

"It does matter," said her sister with startling energy. "How do you know, how do I know that I may not sometimes visit it? I have lived in this house so long I am certain that I shall see it again. I will come back. Come back to watch over you both and see that no harm befalls you."

"You are talking wildly," said Tabitha, by no means moved at her sister's solicitude for her welfare. "Your mind is wandering; you know that I have no faith in such things."

Ursula sighed, and beckoning to Eunice, who was weeping silently at the bedside, placed her feeble arms around her neck and kissed her.

"Do not weep, dear," she said feebly. "Perhaps it is best so. A lonely woman's life is scarce worth living. We have no hopes, no aspirations; other women have had happy husbands and children, but we in this forgotten place have grown old together. I go first, but you must soon follow."

Tabitha, comfortably conscious of only forty years and an iron frame, shrugged her shoulders and smiled grimly.

"I go first," repeated Ursula in a new and strange voice as her heavy eyes slowly closed, "but I will come for each of you in turn, when your lease of life runs out. At that moment I will be with you to lead your steps whither I now go."

As she spoke the flickering lamp went out suddenly as though extinguished by a rapid hand, and the room was left in utter darkness. A strange suffocating noise issued from the bed, and when the trembling women had relighted the lamp, all that was left of Ursula Mallow was ready for the grave.

That night the survivors passed together. The dead woman had been a firm believer in the existence of that shadowy borderland which is said to form an unhallowed link between the living and the dead, and even the stolid Tabitha, slightly unnerved by the events of the night, was not free from certain apprehensions that she might have been right.

With the bright morning their fears disappeared. The sun stole in at the window, and seeing the poor earth-worn face on the pillow so touched it and glorified it that only its goodness and weakness were seen, and the beholders came to wonder how they could ever have felt any dread of aught so calm and peaceful. A day or two passed, and the body was transferred to a massive coffin long regarded as the finest piece of work of its kind ever turned out of the village carpenter's workshop. Then a slow and melancholy cortege headed by four bearers wound its solemn way across the marshes to the family vault in the grey old church, and all that was left of Ursula was placed by the father and mother who had taken that self-same journey some thirty years before.

To Eunice as they toiled slowly home the day seemed strange and Sabbath-like, the flat prospect of marsh wilder and more forlorn than usual, the roar of the sea more depressing. Tabitha had no such fancies. The bulk of the dead woman's property had been left to Eunice, and her avaricious soul was sorely troubled and her proper sisterly feelings of regret for the deceased sadly interfered with in consequence.

"What are you going to do with all that money, Eunice?" she asked as they sat at their quiet tea.

"I shall leave it as it stands," said Eunice slowly. "We have both got sufficient to live upon, and I shall devote the income from it to supporting some beds in a children's hospital."

"If Ursula had wished it to go to a hospital," said Tabitha in her deep tones, "she would have left the money to it herself. I wonder you do not respect her wishes more."

"What else can I do with it then?" inquired Eunice.

"Save it," said the other with gleaming eyes, "save it."

Eunice shook her head.

"No," said she, "it shall go to the sick children, but the principal I will not touch, and if I die before you it shall become yours and you can do what you like with it."

"Very well," said Tabitha, smothering her anger by a strong effort; "I don't believe that was what Ursula meant you to do with it, and I don't believe she will rest quietly in the grave while you squander the money she stored so carefully."

"What do you mean?" asked Eunice with pale lips. "You are trying to frighten me; I thought that you did not believe in such things."

Tabitha made no answer, and to avoid the anxious inquiring gaze of her sister, drew her chair to the fire, and folding her gaunt arms, composed herself for a nap.

For some time life went on quietly in the old house. The room of the dead woman, in accordance with her last desire, was kept firmly locked, its dirty windows forming a strange contrast to the prim cleanliness of the others. Tabitha, never very talkative, became more taciturn than ever, and stalked about the house and the neglected garden like an unquiet spirit, her brow roughened into the deep wrinkles suggestive of much thought. As the winter came on, bringing with it the long dark evenings, the old house became more lonely than ever, and an air of mystery and dread seemed to hang over it and brood in its empty rooms and dark corridors. The deep silence of night was broken by strange noises for which neither the wind nor the rats could be held accountable. Old Martha, seated in her distant kitchen, heard strange sounds upon the stairs, and once, upon hurrying to them, fancied that she saw a dark figure squatting upon the landing, though a subsequent search with candle and spectacles failed to discover anything. Eunice was disturbed by several vague incidents, and, as she suffered from a complaint of the heart, rendered very ill by them. Even Tabitha admitted a strangeness about the house, but, confident in her piety and virtue, took no heed of it, her mind being fully employed in another direction.

Since the death of her sister all restraint upon her was removed, and she yielded herself up entirely to the stern and hard rules enforced by avarice upon its devotees. Her housekeeping expenses were kept rigidly separate from those of Eunice and her food limited to the coarsest dishes, while in the matter of clothes, the old servant was by far the better dressed. Seated alone in her bedroom this uncouth, hard-featured creature revelled in her possessions, grudging even the expense of the candle-end which enabled her to behold them. So completely did this passion change her that both Eunice and Martha became afraid of her, and lay awake in their beds night after night trembling at the chinking of the coins at her unholy vigils.

One day Eunice ventured to remonstrate. "Why don't you bank your money, Tabitha?" she said; "it is surely not safe to keep such large sums in such a lonely house."

"Large sums!" repeated the exasperated Tabitha, "large sums! What nonsense is this? You know well that I have barely sufficient to keep me."

"It's a great temptation to housebreakers," said her sister, not pressing the point. "I made sure last night that I heard somebody in the house."

"Did you?" said Tabitha, grasping her arm, a horrible look on her face. "So did I. I thought they went to Ursula's room, and I got out of bed and went on the stairs to listen."

"Well?" said Eunice faintly, fascinated by the look on her sister's face.

"There was something there," said Tabitha slowly. "I'll swear it, for I stood on the landing by her door and listened; something scuffling on the floor round and round the room. At first I thought it was the cat, but when I went up there this morning the door was still locked, and the cat was in the kitchen."

"Oh, let us leave this dreadful house," moaned Eunice.

"What!" said her sister grimly; "afraid of poor Ursula? Why should you be? Your own sister who nursed you when you were a babe, and who perhaps even now comes and watches over your slumbers."

"Oh!" said Eunice, pressing her hand to her side, "if I saw her I should die. I should think that she had come for me as she said she would. O God! Have mercy on me, I am dying."

She reeled as she spoke, and before Tabitha could save her, sank senseless to the floor.

"Get some water," cried Tabitha, as old Martha came hurrying up the stairs, "Eunice has fainted."

The old woman, with a timid glance at her, retired, reappearing shortly afterwards with the water, with which she proceeded to restore her much-loved mistress to her senses. Tabitha, as soon as this was accomplished, stalked off to her room, leaving her sister and Martha sitting drearily enough in the small parlour, watching the fire and conversing in whispers.

It was clear to the old servant that this state of things could not last much longer, and she repeatedly urged her mistress to leave a house so lonely and so mysterious. To her great delight Eunice at length consented, despite the fierce opposition of her sister, and at the mere idea of leaving gained greatly in health and spirits. A small but comfortable house was hired in Morville, and arrangements made for a speedy change.

It was the last night in the old house, and all the wild spirits of the marshes, the wind and the sea seemed to have joined forces for one supreme effort. When the wind dropped, as it did at brief intervals, the sea was heard moaning on the distant beach, strangely mingled with the desolate warning of the bell-buoy as it rocked to the waves. Then the wind rose again, and the noise of the sea was lost in the fierce gusts which, finding no obstacle on the open marshes, swept with their full fury upon the house by the creek. The strange voices of the air shrieked in its chimneys windows rattled, doors slammed, and even, the very curtains seemed to live and move.

Eunice was in bed, awake. A small night light in a saucer of oil shed a sickly glare upon the worm-eaten old furniture, distorting the most innocent articles into ghastly shapes. A wilder gust than usual almost deprived her of the protection afforded by that poor light, and she lay listening fearfully to the creakings and other noises on the stairs, bitterly regretting that she had not asked Martha to sleep with her. But it was not too late even now. She slipped hastily to the floor, crossed to the huge wardrobe, and was in the very act of taking her dressing gown from its peg when an unmistakable footfall was heard on the stairs. The robe dropped from her shaking fingers, and with a quickly beating heart she regained her bed.

The sounds ceased and a deep silence followed, which she herself was unable to break although she strove hard to do so. A wild gust of wind shook the windows and nearly extinguished the light, and when its flame had regained its accustomed steadiness she saw that the door was slowly opening, while the huge shadow of a hand blotted the papered wall. Still her tongue refused its office. The door flew open with a crash, a cloaked figure entered and, throwing aside its coverings, she saw with a horror past all expression the napkin-bound face of the dead Ursula smiling terribly at her. In her last extremity she raised her faded eyes above for succour, and then as the figure noiselessly advanced and laid its cold hand upon her brow, the soul of Eunice Mallow left its body with a wild shriek and made its way to the Eternal.

Martha, roused by the cry, and shivering with dread, rushed to the door and gazed in terror at the figure which stood leaning over the bedside. As she watched, it slowly removed the cowl and the napkin and exposed the fell face of Tabitha, so strangely contorted between fear and triumph that she hardly recognised it.

"Who's there?" cried Tabitha in a terrible voice as she saw the old woman's shadow on the wall.

"I thought I heard a cry," said Martha, entering. "Did anybody call?"

"Yes, Eunice," said the other, regarding her closely. "I, too, heard the cry, and hurried to her. What makes her so strange? Is she in a trance?"

"Ay," said the old woman, falling on her knees by the bed and sobbing bitterly, "the trance of death. Ah, my dear, my poor lonely girl, that this should be the end of it! She has died of fright," said the old woman, pointing to the eyes, which even yet retained their horror. "She has seen something devilish."

Tabitha's gaze fell. "She has always suffered with her heart," she muttered; "the night has frightened her; it frightened me."

She stood upright by the foot of the bed as Martha drew the sheet over the face of the dead woman.

"First Ursula, then Eunice," said Tabitha, drawing a deep breath. "I can't stay here. I'll dress and wait for the morning."

She left the room as she spoke, and with bent head proceeded to her own. Martha remained by the bedside, and gently closing the staring eyes, fell on her knees, and prayed long and earnestly for the departed soul. Overcome with grief and fear she remained with bowed head until a sudden sharp cry from Tabitha brought her to her feet.

"Well," said the old woman, going to the door.

"Where are you?" cried Tabitha, somewhat reassured by her voice.

"In Miss Eunice's bedroom. Do you want anything?"

"Come down at once. Quick! I am unwell."

Her voice rose suddenly to a scream. "Quick! For God's sake! Quick, or I shall go mad. There is some strange woman in the house."

The old woman stumbled hastily down the dark stairs. "What is the matter?" she cried, entering the room. "Who is it? What do you mean?"

"I saw it," said Tabitha, grasping her convulsively by the shoulder. "I was coming to you when I saw the figure of a woman in front of me going up the stairs. Is it – can it be Ursula come for the soul of Eunice, as she said she would?"

"Or for yours?" said Martha, the words coming from her in some odd fashion, despite herself.

Tabitha, with a ghastly look, fell cowering by her side, clutching tremulously at her clothes. "Light the lamps," she cried hysterically. "Light a fire, make a noise; oh, this dreadful darkness! Will it never be day!"

"Soon, soon," said Martha, overcoming her repugnance and trying to pacify her. "When the day comes you will laugh at these fears."

"I murdered her," screamed the miserable woman, "I killed her with fright. Why did she not give me the money? 'Twas no use to her. Ah! Look there!"

Martha, with a horrible fear, followed her glance to the door, but saw nothing.

"It's Ursula," said Tabitha from between her teeth. "Keep her off! Keep her off!"

The old woman, who by some unknown sense seemed to feel the presence of a third person in the room, moved a step forward and stood before her. As she did so Tabitha waved her arms as though to free herself from the touch of a detaining hand, half rose to her feet, and without a word fell dead before her.

At this the old woman's courage forsook her, and with a great cry she rushed from the room, eager to escape from this house of death and mystery. The bolts of the great door were stiff with age, and strange voices seemed to ring in her ears as she strove wildly to unfasten them. Her brain whirled. She thought that the dead in their distant rooms called to her, and that a devil stood on the step outside laughing and holding the door against her. Then with a supreme effort she flung it open, and heedless of her nightclothes passed into the bitter night. The path across the marshes was lost in the darkness, but she found it; the planks over the ditches slippery and narrow, but she crossed them in safety, until at last, her feet bleeding and her breath coming in great gasps, she entered the village and sank down more dead than alive on a cottage doorstep.

Canon Alberic's Scrap-book

M.R. James

ST. BERTRAND DE COMMINGES is a decayed town on the spurs of the Pyrenees, not very far from Toulouse, and still nearer to Bagnères-de-Luchon. It was the site of a bishopric until the Revolution, and has a cathedral which is visited by a certain number of tourists. In the spring of 1883 an Englishman arrived at this old-world place – I can hardly dignify it with the name of city, for there are not a thousand inhabitants. He was a Cambridge man, who had come specially from Toulouse to see St. Bertrand's Church, and had left two friends, who were less keen archaeologists than himself, in their hotel at Toulouse, under promise to join him on the following morning. Half an hour at the church would satisfy *them*, and all three could then pursue their journey in the direction of Auch. But our Englishman had come early on the day in question, and proposed to himself to fill a notebook and to use several dozens of plates in the process of describing and photographing every corner of the wonderful church that dominates the little hill of Comminges. In order to carry out this design satisfactorily, it was necessary to monopolise the verger of the church for the day. The verger or sacristan (I prefer the latter appellation, inaccurate as it may be) was accordingly sent for by the somewhat brusque lady who keeps the inn of the Chapeau Rouge; and when he came, the Englishman found him an unexpectedly interesting object of study. It was not in the personal appearance of the little, dry, wizened old man that the interest lay, for he was precisely like dozens of other church-guardians in France, but in a curious furtive or rather hunted and oppressed air which he had. He was perpetually half glancing behind him; the muscles of his back and shoulders seemed to be hunched in a continual nervous contraction, as if he were expecting every moment to find himself in the clutch of an enemy. The Englishman hardly knew whether to put him down as a man haunted by a fixed delusion, or as one oppressed by a guilty conscience, or as an unbearably henpecked husband. The probabilities, when reckoned up, certainly pointed to the last idea; but, still, the impression conveyed was that of a more formidable persecutor even than a termagant wife.

However, the Englishman (let us call him Dennistoun) was soon too deep in his notebook and too busy with his camera to give more than an occasional glance to the sacristan. Whenever he did look at him, he found him at no great distance, either huddling himself back against the wall or crouching in one of the gorgeous stalls. Dennistoun became rather fidgety after a time. Mingled suspicions that he was keeping the old man from his *déjeuner*, that he was regarded as likely to make away with St. Bertrand's ivory crozier, or with the dusty stuffed crocodile that hangs over the font, began to torment him.

"Won't you go home?" he said at last; "I'm quite well able to finish my notes alone; you can lock me in if you like. I shall want at least two hours more here, and it must be cold for you, isn't it?"

"Good heavens!" said the little man, whom the suggestion seemed to throw into a state of unaccountable terror, "such a thing cannot be thought of for a moment. Leave monsieur alone in the church? No, no; two hours, three hours, all will be the same to me. I have breakfasted, I am not at all cold, with many thanks to monsieur."

"Very well, my little man," quoth Dennistoun to himself: "you have been warned, and you must take the consequences."

Before the expiration of the two hours, the stalls, the enormous dilapidated organ, the choir-screen of Bishop John de Mauléon, the remnants of glass and tapestry, and the objects in the treasure-chamber had been well and truly examined; the sacristan still keeping at Dennistoun's heels, and every now and then whipping round as if he had been stung, when one or other of the strange noises that trouble a large empty building fell on his ear. Curious noises they were, sometimes.

"Once," Dennistoun said to me, "I could have sworn I heard a thin metallic voice laughing high up in the tower. I darted an inquiring glance at my sacristan. He was white to the lips. 'It is he – that is – it is no one; the door is locked,' was all he said, and we looked at each other for a full minute."

Another little incident puzzled Dennistoun a good deal. He was examining a large dark picture that hangs behind the altar, one of a series illustrating the miracles of St. Bertrand. The composition of the picture is well-nigh indecipherable, but there is a Latin legend below, which runs thus:

Qualiter S. Bertrandus liberavit hominem quem diabolus diu volebat strangulare.
(How St. Bertrand delivered a man whom the Devil long sought to strangle.)

Dennistoun was turning to the sacristan with a smile and a jocular remark of some sort on his lips, but he was confounded to see the old man on his knees, gazing at the picture with the eye of a suppliant in agony, his hands tightly clasped, and a rain of tears on his cheeks. Dennistoun naturally pretended to have noticed nothing, but the question would not go away from him, "Why should a daub of this kind affect anyone so strongly?" He seemed to himself to be getting some sort of clue to the reason of the strange look that had been puzzling him all the day: the man must be a monomaniac; but what was his monomania?

It was nearly five o'clock; the short day was drawing in, and the church began to fill with shadows, while the curious noises – the muffled footfalls and distant talking voices that had been perceptible all day – seemed, no doubt because of the fading light and the consequently quickened sense of hearing, to become more frequent and insistent.

The sacristan began for the first time to show signs of hurry and impatience. He heaved a sigh of relief when camera and notebook were finally packed up and stowed away, and hurriedly beckoned Dennistoun to the western door of the church, under the tower. It was time to ring the Angelus. A few pulls at the reluctant rope, and the great bell Bertrande, high in the tower, began to speak, and swung her voice up among the pines and down to the valleys, loud with mountain-streams, calling the dwellers on those lonely hills to remember and repeat the salutation of the angel to her whom he called Blessed among women. With that a profound quiet seemed to fall for the first time that day upon the little town, and Dennistoun and the sacristan went out of the church.

On the doorstep they fell into conversation.

"Monsieur seemed to interest himself in the old choir-books in the sacristy."

"Undoubtedly. I was going to ask you if there were a library in the town."

"No, monsieur; perhaps there used to be one belonging to the Chapter, but it is now such a small place—" Here came a strange pause of irresolution, as it seemed; then, with a sort of plunge, he went on: "But if monsieur is *amateur des vieux livres*, I have at home something that might interest him. It is not a hundred yards."

At once all Dennistoun's cherished dreams of finding priceless manuscripts in untrodden corners of France flashed up, to die down again the next moment. It was probably a stupid missal of Plantin's printing, about 1580. Where was the likelihood that a place so near Toulouse would not have been ransacked long ago by collectors? However, it would be foolish not to go; he would reproach himself forever after if he refused. So they set off. On the way the curious irresolution and sudden determination of the sacristan recurred to Dennistoun, and he wondered in a shamefaced way whether he was being decoyed into some purlieu to be made away with as a supposed rich Englishman. He contrived, therefore, to begin talking with his guide, and to drag in, in a rather clumsy fashion, the fact that he expected two friends to join him early the next morning. To his surprise, the announcement seemed to relieve the sacristan at once of some of the anxiety that oppressed him.

"That is well," he said quite brightly – "that is very well. Monsieur will travel in company with his friends: they will be always near him. It is a good thing to travel thus in company – sometimes."

The last word appeared to be added as an afterthought and to bring with it a relapse into gloom for the poor little man.

They were soon at the house, which was one rather larger than its neighbours, stone-built, with a shield carved over the door, the shield of Alberic de Mauléon, a collateral descendant, Dennistoun tells me, of Bishop John de Mauléon. This Alberic was a Canon of Comminges from 1680 to 1701. The upper windows of the mansion were boarded up, and the whole place bore, as does the rest of Comminges, the aspect of decaying age.

Arrived on his doorstep, the sacristan paused a moment.

"Perhaps," he said, "perhaps, after all, monsieur has not the time?"

"Not at all – lots of time – nothing to do till tomorrow. Let us see what it is you have got."

The door was opened at this point, and a face looked out, a face far younger than the sacristan's, but bearing something of the same distressing look: only here it seemed to be the mark, not so much of fear for personal safety as of acute anxiety on behalf of another. Plainly the owner of the face was the sacristan's daughter; and, but for the expression I have described, she was a handsome girl enough. She brightened up considerably on seeing her father accompanied by an able-bodied stranger. A few remarks passed between father and daughter of which Dennistoun only caught these words, said by the sacristan: "He was laughing in the church," words which were answered only by a look of terror from the girl.

But in another minute they were in the sitting room of the house, a small, high chamber with a stone floor, full of moving shadows cast by a wood-fire that flickered on a great hearth. Something of the character of an oratory was imparted to it by a tall crucifix, which reached almost to the ceiling on one side; the figure was painted of the natural colours, the cross was black. Under this stood a chest of some age and solidity, and when a lamp had been brought, and chairs set, the sacristan went to this chest, and produced therefrom, with growing excitement and nervousness, as Dennistoun thought, a large book, wrapped in a white cloth, on which cloth a cross was rudely embroidered in red thread. Even before the wrapping had been removed, Dennistoun began to be interested by the size and shape of the volume. "Too large for a missal," he thought, "and not the shape of an antiphoner; perhaps it may be something good, after all." The next moment the book was open, and Dennistoun felt that he had at last lit upon something better than good. Before him lay a large folio, bound, perhaps, late in the seventeenth century, with the arms of Canon Alberic de Mauléon stamped in gold on the sides.

There may have been a hundred and fifty leaves of paper in the book, and on almost every one of them was fastened a leaf from an illuminated manuscript. Such a collection Dennistoun had hardly dreamed of in his wildest moments. Here were ten leaves from a copy of Genesis, illustrated with pictures, which could not be later than A.D. 700. Further on was a complete set of pictures from a Psalter, of English execution, of the very finest kind that the thirteenth century could produce; and, perhaps best of all, there were twenty leaves of uncial writing in Latin, which, as a few words seen here and there told him at once, must belong to some very early unknown patristic treatise. Could it possibly be a fragment of the copy of Papias 'On the Words of Our Lord', which was known to have existed as late as the twelfth century at Nimes?[1] In any case, his mind was made up; that book must return to Cambridge with him, even if he had to draw the whole of his balance from the bank and stay at St. Bertrand till the money came. He glanced up at the sacristan to see if his face yielded any hint that the book was for sale. The sacristan was pale, and his lips were working.

"If monsieur will turn on to the end," he said.

So monsieur turned on, meeting new treasures at every rise of a leaf; and at the end of the book he came upon two sheets of paper, of much more recent date than anything he had seen yet, which puzzled him considerably. They must be contemporary, he decided, with the unprincipled Canon Alberic, who had doubtless plundered the Chapter library of St. Bertrand to form this priceless scrap-book. On the first of the paper sheets was a plan, carefully drawn and instantly recognisable by a person who knew the ground, of the south aisle and cloisters of St. Bertrand's. There were curious signs looking like planetary symbols, and a few Hebrew words in the corners; and in the north-west angle of the cloister was a cross drawn in gold paint. Below the plan were some lines of writing in Latin, which ran thus:

Responsa 12(mi) Dec. 1694. Interrogatum est: Inveniamne? Responsum est: Invenies. Fiamne dives? Fies. Vivamne invidendus? Vives. Moriarne in lecto meo? Ita. (Answers of the 12th of December, 1694. It was asked: Shall I find it? Answer: Thou shalt. Shall I become rich? Thou wilt. Shall I live an object of envy? Thou wilt. Shall I die in my bed? Thou wilt.)

"A good specimen of the treasure-hunter's record – quite reminds one of Mr. Minor-Canon Quatremain in *Old St. Paul's*," was Dennistoun's comment, and he turned the leaf.

What he then saw impressed him, as he has often told me, more than he could have conceived any drawing or picture capable of impressing him. And, though the drawing he saw is no longer in existence, there is a photograph of it (which I possess) which fully bears out that statement. The picture in question was a sepia drawing at the end of the seventeenth century, representing, one would say at first sight, a Biblical scene; for the architecture (the picture represented an interior) and the figures had that semi-classical flavour about them which the artists of two hundred years ago thought appropriate to illustrations of the Bible. On the right was a king on his throne, the throne elevated on twelve steps, a canopy overhead, soldiers on either side – evidently King Solomon. He was bending forward with outstretched sceptre, in attitude of command; his face expressed horror and disgust, yet there was in it also the mark of imperious command and confident power. The left half of the picture was the strangest, however. The interest plainly centred there.

On the pavement before the throne were grouped four soldiers, surrounding a crouching figure which must be described in a moment. A fifth soldier lay dead on the pavement, his neck distorted, and his eyeballs starting from his head. The four surrounding guards were looking at the King. In their faces, the sentiment of horror was intensified; they seemed, in fact, only restrained from flight by their implicit trust in their master. All this terror was plainly excited by the being that crouched in their midst.

I entirely despair of conveying by any words the impression which this figure makes upon anyone who looks at it. I recollect once showing the photograph of the drawing to a lecturer on morphology – a person of, I was going to say, abnormally sane and unimaginative habits of mind. He absolutely refused to be alone for the rest of that evening, and he told me afterwards that for many nights he had not dared to put out his light before going to sleep. However, the main traits of the figure I can at least indicate.

At first you saw only a mass of coarse, matted black hair; presently it was seen that this covered a body of fearful thinness, almost a skeleton, but with the muscles standing out like wires. The hands were of a dusky pallor, covered, like the body, with long, coarse hairs, and hideously taloned. The eyes, touched in with a burning yellow, had intensely black pupils, and were fixed upon the throned King with a look of beast-like hate. Imagine one of the awful bird-catching spiders of South America translated into human form, and endowed with intelligence just less than human, and you will have some faint conception of the terror inspired by the appalling effigy. One remark is universally made by those to whom I have shown the picture: "It was drawn from the life."

As soon as the first shock of his irresistible fright had subsided, Dennistoun stole a look at his hosts. The sacristan's hands were pressed upon his eyes; his daughter, looking up at the cross on the wall, was telling her beads feverishly.

At last the question was asked: "Is this book for sale?"

There was the same hesitation, the same plunge of determination that he had noticed before, and then came the welcome answer: "If monsieur pleases."

"How much do you ask for it?"

"I will take two hundred and fifty francs."

This was confounding. Even a collector's conscience is sometimes stirred, and Dennistoun's conscience was tenderer than a collector's.

"My good man!" he said again and again, "your book is worth far more than two hundred and fifty francs. I assure you – far more."

But the answer did not vary: "I will take two hundred and fifty francs – not more."

There was really no possibility of refusing such a chance. The money was paid, the receipt signed, a glass of wine drunk over the transaction, and then the sacristan seemed to become a new man. He stood upright, he ceased to throw those suspicious glances behind him, he actually laughed or tried to laugh. Dennistoun rose to go.

"I shall have the honour of accompanying monsieur to his hotel?" said the sacristan.

"Oh, no, thanks! It isn't a hundred yards. I know the way perfectly, and there is a moon."

The offer was pressed three or four times and refused as often.

"Then, monsieur will summon me if – if he finds occasion; he will keep the middle of the road, the sides are so rough."

"Certainly, certainly," said Dennistoun, who was impatient to examine his prize by himself; and he stepped out into the passage with his book under his arm.

Here he was met by the daughter; she, it appeared, was anxious to do a little business on her own account; perhaps, like Gehazi, to 'take somewhat' from the foreigner whom her father had spared.

"A silver crucifix and chain for the neck; monsieur would perhaps be good enough to accept it?"

Well, really, Dennistoun hadn't much use for these things. What did mademoiselle want for it?

"Nothing – nothing in the world. Monsieur is more than welcome to it."

The tone in which this and much more was said was unmistakably genuine, so that Dennistoun was reduced to profuse thanks, and submitted to have the chain put round his neck. It really seemed as if he had rendered the father and daughter some service which they hardly knew how to repay. As he set off with his book they stood at the door looking after him, and they were still looking when he waved them a last goodnight from the steps of the Chapeau Rouge.

Dinner was over, and Dennistoun was in his bedroom, shut up alone with his acquisition. The landlady had manifested a particular interest in him since he had told her that he had paid a visit to the sacristan and bought an old book from him. He thought, too, that he had heard a hurried dialogue between her and the said sacristan in the passage outside the *salle à manger*; some words to the effect that "Pierre and Bertrand would be sleeping in the house" had closed the conversation.

All this time a growing feeling of discomfort had been creeping over him – nervous reaction, perhaps, after the delight of his discovery. Whatever it was, it resulted in a conviction that there was someone behind him, and that he was far more comfortable with his back to the wall. All this, of course, weighed light in the balance as against the obvious value of the collection he had acquired. And now, as I said, he was alone in his bedroom, taking stock of Canon Alberic's treasures, in which every moment revealed something more charming.

"Bless Canon Alberic!" said Dennistoun, who had an inveterate habit of talking to himself. "I wonder where he is now? Dear me! I wish that landlady would learn to laugh in a more cheering manner; it makes one feel as if there was someone dead in the house. Half a pipe more, did you say? I think perhaps you are right. I wonder what that crucifix is that the young woman insisted on giving me? Last century, I suppose. Yes, probably. It is rather a nuisance of a thing to have round one's neck – just too heavy. Most likely her father has been wearing it for years. I think I might give it a clean up before I put it away."

He had taken the crucifix off, and laid it on the table, when his attention was caught by an object lying on the red cloth just by his left elbow. Two or three ideas of what it might be flitted through his brain with their own incalculable quickness.

A penwiper? No, no such thing in the house. A rat? No, too black. A large spider? I trust to goodness not – no. Good God! A hand like the hand in that picture!

In another infinitesimal flash he had taken it in. Pale, dusky skin, covering nothing but bones and tendons of appalling strength; coarse black hairs, longer than ever grew on a human hand; nails rising from the ends of the fingers and curving sharply down and forward, grey, horny, and wrinkled.

He flew out of his chair with deadly, inconceivable terror clutching at his heart. The shape, whose left hand rested on the table, was rising to a standing posture behind his seat, its right hand crooked above his scalp. There was black and tattered drapery about it; the coarse hair covered it as in the drawing. The lower jaw was thin – what can I call it? – shallow, like a beast's; teeth showed behind the black lips; there was no nose; the eyes, of a fiery yellow, against which the pupils showed black and intense, and the exulting hate and thirst to destroy life which shone there, were the most horrifying features in the whole vision. There was intelligence of a kind in them – intelligence beyond that of a beast, below that of a man.

The feelings which this horror stirred in Dennistoun were the intensest physical fear and the most profound mental loathing. What did he do? What could he do? He has never been quite certain what words he said, but he knows that he spoke, that he grasped blindly at the silver crucifix, that he was conscious of a movement towards him on the part of the demon, and that he screamed with the voice of an animal in hideous pain.

Pierre and Bertrand, the two sturdy little serving-men, who rushed in, saw nothing, but felt themselves thrust aside by something that passed out between them, and found Dennistoun in a swoon. They sat up with him that night, and his two friends were at St. Bertrand by nine o'clock next morning. He himself, though still shaken and nervous, was almost himself by that time, and his story found credence with them, though not until they had seen the drawing and talked with the sacristan.

Almost at dawn the little man had come to the inn on some pretence, and had listened with the deepest interest to the story retailed by the landlady. He showed no surprise.

"It is he – it is he! I have seen him myself," was his only comment; and to all questionings but one reply was vouchsafed: *"Deux fois je l'ai vu: mille fois je l'ai senti."* He would tell them nothing of the provenance of the book, nor any details of his experiences. "I shall soon sleep, and my rest will be sweet. Why should you trouble me?" he said.[2]

We shall never know what he or Canon Alberic de Mauléon suffered. At the back of that fateful drawing were some lines of writing which may be supposed to throw light on the situation:

> *Contradictio Salomonis cum demonio nocturno.*
> *Albericus de Mauléone delineavit.*
> *V. Deus in adiutorium. Ps. Qui habitat.*
> *Sancte Bertrande, demoniorum effugator, intercede pro me miserrimo.*
> *Primum uidi nocte 12(mi) Dec. 1694:*
> *uidebo mox ultimum. Peccaui et passus*
> *sum, plura adhuc passurus.*
> *Dec. 29, 1701.*[3]

I have never quite understood what was Dennistoun's view of the events I have narrated. He quoted to me once a text from Ecclesiasticus: "Some spirits there be that are created for vengeance, and in their fury lay on sore strokes." On another occasion he said: "Isaiah was a very sensible man; doesn't he say something about night monsters living in the ruins of Babylon? These things are rather beyond us at present."

Another confidence of his impressed me rather, and I sympathised with it. We had been, last year, to Comminges, to see Canon Alberic's tomb. It is a great marble erection with an effigy of the Canon in a large wig and soutane, and an elaborate eulogy of his learning below. I saw Dennistoun talking for some time with the Vicar of St. Bertrand's, and as we drove away he said to me: "I hope it isn't wrong: you know I am a Presbyterian – but I – I believe there will be 'saying of Mass and singing of dirges' for Alberic de Mauléon's rest." Then he added, with a touch of the Northern British in his tone, "I had no notion they came so dear."

* * *

The book is in the Wentworth Collection at Cambridge. The drawing was photographed and then burnt by Dennistoun on the day when he left Comminges on the occasion of his first visit.

Footnotes for 'Canon Alberic's Scrap-book'

1. We now know that these leaves did contain a considerable fragment of that work, if not of that actual copy of it.
2. He died that summer; his daughter married, and settled at St. Papoul. She never understood the circumstances of her father's 'obsession'.
3. *i.e.*, The Dispute of Solomon with a demon of the night. Drawn by Alberic de Mauléon. Versicle. O Lord, make haste to help me. Psalm. Whoso dwelleth xci.
   Saint Bertrand, who puttest devils to flight, pray for me most unhappy. I saw it first on the night of Dec. 12, 1694: soon I shall see it for the last time. I have sinned and suffered, and have more to suffer yet.
   Dec. 29, 1701.

The 'Gallia Christiana' gives the date of the Canon's death as December 31, 1701, 'in bed, of a sudden seizure' Details of this kind are not common in the great work of the Sammarthani.

Amour Dure

Vernon Lee

PASSAGES *from the Diary of Spiridion Trepka:*

Part I

Urbania, August 20th, 1885.—

I had longed, these years and years, to be in Italy, to come face to face with the Past; and was this Italy, was this the Past? I could have cried, yes cried, for disappointment when I first wandered about Rome, with an invitation to dine at the German Embassy in my pocket, and three or four Berlin and Munich Vandals at my heels, telling me where the best beer and sauerkraut could be had, and what the last article by Grimm or Mommsen was about.

Is this folly? Is it falsehood? Am I not myself a product of modern, northern civilisation; is not my coming to Italy due to this very modern scientific vandalism, which has given me a travelling scholarship because I have written a book like all those other atrocious books of erudition and art-criticism? Nay, am I not here at Urbania on the express understanding that, in a certain number of months, I shall produce just another such book? Dost thou imagine, thou miserable Spiridion, thou Pole grown into the semblance of a German pedant, doctor of philosophy, professor even, author of a prize essay on the despots of the fifteenth century, dost thou imagine that thou, with thy ministerial letters and proof-sheets in thy black professorial coat-pocket, canst ever come in spirit into the presence of the Past?

Too true, alas! But let me forget it, at least, every now and then; as I forgot it this afternoon, while the white bullocks dragged my gig slowly winding along interminable valleys, crawling along interminable hillsides, with the invisible droning torrent far below, and only the bare grey and reddish peaks all around, up to this town of Urbania, forgotten of mankind, towered and battlemented on the high Apennine ridge. Sigillo, Penna, Fossombrone, Mercatello, Montemurlo – each single village name, as the driver pointed it out, brought to my mind the recollection of some battle or some great act of treachery of former days. And as the huge mountains shut out the setting sun, and the valleys filled with bluish shadow and mist, only a band of threatening smoke-red remaining behind the towers and cupolas of the city on its mountain-top, and the sound of church bells floated across the precipice from Urbania, I almost expected, at every turning of the road, that a troop of horsemen, with beaked helmets and clawed shoes, would emerge, with armour glittering and pennons waving in the sunset. And then, not two hours ago, entering the town at dusk, passing along the deserted streets, with only a smoky light here and there under a shrine or in front of a fruit-stall, or a fire reddening the blackness of a smithy;

passing beneath the battlements and turrets of the palace... Ah, that was Italy, it was the Past!

* * *

August 21st.—

And this is the Present! Four letters of introduction to deliver, and an hour's polite conversation to endure with the Vice-Prefect, the Syndic, the Director of the Archives, and the good man to whom my friend Max had sent me for lodgings...

* * *

August 22nd–27th.—

Spent the greater part of the day in the Archives, and the greater part of my time there in being bored to extinction by the Director thereof, who today spouted Aeneas Sylvius' *Commentaries* for three-quarters of an hour without taking breath. From this sort of martyrdom (what are the sensations of a former racehorse being driven in a cab? If you can conceive them, they are those of a Pole turned Prussian professor) I take refuge in long rambles through the town. This town is a handful of tall black houses huddled on to the top of an Alp, long narrow lanes trickling down its sides, like the slides we made on hillocks in our boyhood, and in the middle the superb red brick structure, turreted and battlemented, of Duke Ottobuono's palace, from whose windows you look down upon a sea, a kind of whirlpool, of melancholy grey mountains. Then there are the people, dark, bushy-bearded men, riding about like brigands, wrapped in green-lined cloaks upon their shaggy pack-mules; or loitering about, great, brawny, low-headed youngsters, like the parti-colored bravos in Signorelli's frescoes; the beautiful boys, like so many young Raphaels, with eyes like the eyes of bullocks, and the huge women, Madonnas or St. Elizabeths, as the case may be, with their clogs firmly poised on their toes and their brass pitchers on their heads, as they go up and down the steep black alleys. I do not talk much to these people; I fear my illusions being dispelled. At the corner of a street, opposite Francesco di Giorgio's beautiful little portico, is a great blue and red advertisement, representing an angel descending to crown Elias Howe, on account of his sewing-machines; and the clerks of the Vice-Prefecture, who dine at the place where I get my dinner, yell politics, Minghetti, Cairoli, Tunis, ironclads, &c., at each other, and sing snatches of *La Fille de Mme. Angot*, which I imagine they have been performing here recently.

No; talking to the natives is evidently a dangerous experiment. Except indeed, perhaps, to my good landlord, Signor Notaro Porri, who is just as learned, and takes considerably less snuff (or rather brushes it off his coat more often) than the Director of the Archives. I forgot to jot down (and I feel I must jot down, in the vain belief that some day these scraps will help, like a withered twig of olive or a three-wicked Tuscan lamp on my table, to bring to my mind, in that hateful Babylon of Berlin, these happy Italian days) – I forgot to record that I am lodging in the house of a dealer in antiquities. My window looks up the principal street to where the little column with Mercury on the top rises in the midst of the awnings and porticoes of the market-place. Bending over the chipped ewers and tubs full of sweet basil, clove pinks, and marigolds, I can just see a corner of the palace turret, and the vague ultramarine of the hills beyond. The house, whose back goes sharp down into the ravine, is a queer up-and-down black place, white-washed rooms, hung with the Raphaels and Francias and Peruginos, whom mine host regularly carries to the chief inn whenever a stranger is expected; and surrounded by old carved chairs, sofas of the Empire, embossed and gilded wedding-chests, and the cupboards which contain bits of old damask and embroidered altar-cloths scenting the place with the smell of old incense and mustiness; all of which are presided over by Signor Porri's three maiden sisters – Sora Serafina, Sora Lodovica, and Sora Adalgisa – the three Fates in person, even to the distaffs and their black cats.

Sor Asdrubale, as they call my landlord, is also a notary. He regrets the Pontifical Government, having had a cousin who was a Cardinal's train-bearer, and believes that if only you lay a table for two, light four candles made of dead men's fat, and perform certain rites about which he is not very precise, you can, on Christmas Eve and similar nights, summon up San Pasquale Baylon, who will write you the winning numbers of the lottery upon the smoked back of a plate, if you have previously slapped him on both cheeks and repeated three Ave Marias. The difficulty consists in obtaining the dead men's fat for the candles, and also in slapping the saint before he has time to vanish.

"If it were not for that," says Sor Asdrubale, "the Government would have had to suppress the lottery ages ago – eh!"

* * *

Sept. 9th.—

This history of Urbania is not without its romance, although that romance (as usual) has been overlooked by our Dryasdusts. Even before coming here I felt attracted by the strange figure of a woman, which appeared from out of the dry pages of Gualterio's and Padre de Sanctis' histories of this place. This woman is Medea, daughter of Galeazzo IV. Malatesta, Lord of Carpi, wife first of Pierluigi Orsini, Duke of Stimigliano, and subsequently of Guidalfonso II., Duke of Urbania, predecessor of the great Duke Robert II.

This woman's history and character remind one of that of Bianca Cappello, and at the same time of Lucrezia Borgia. Born in 1556, she was affianced at the age of twelve to a cousin, a Malatesta of the Rimini family. This family having greatly gone down in the world, her engagement was broken, and she was betrothed a year later to a member of the Pico family, and married to him by proxy at the age of fourteen. But this match not satisfying her own or her father's ambition, the marriage by proxy was, upon some pretext, declared null, and the suit encouraged of the Duke of Stimigliano, a great Umbrian feudatory of the Orsini family. But the bridegroom, Giovanfrancesco Pico, refused to submit, pleaded his case before the Pope, and tried to carry off by force his bride, with whom he was madly in love, as the lady was most lovely and of most cheerful and amiable manner, says an old anonymous chronicle. Pico waylaid her litter as she was going to a villa of her father's, and carried her to his castle near Mirandola, where he respectfully pressed his suit; insisting that he had a right to consider her as his wife. But the lady escaped by letting herself into the moat by a rope of sheets, and Giovanfrancesco Pico was discovered stabbed in the chest, by the hand of Madonna Medea da Carpi. He was a handsome youth only eighteen years old.

The Pico having been settled, and the marriage with him declared null by the Pope, Medea da Carpi was solemnly married to the Duke of Stimigliano, and went to live upon his domains near Rome.

Two years later, Pierluigi Orsini was stabbed by one of his grooms at his castle of Stimigliano, near Orvieto; and suspicion fell upon his widow, more especially as, immediately after the event, she caused the murderer to be cut down by two servants in her own chamber; but not before he had declared that she had induced him to assassinate his master by a promise of her love. Things became so hot for Medea da Carpi that she fled to Urbania and threw herself at the feet of Duke Guidalfonso II., declaring that she had caused the groom to be killed merely to avenge her good fame, which he had slandered, and that she was absolutely guiltless of the death of her husband. The marvelous beauty of the widowed Duchess of Stimigliano, who was only nineteen, entirely turned the head of the Duke of Urbania. He affected implicit belief in her innocence, refused to give her up to the Orsinis, kinsmen of her late husband, and assigned to her magnificent apartments in the left wing of the palace, among which the room containing the famous fireplace ornamented with marble Cupids on a blue ground. Guidalfonso fell madly in love with his beautiful guest. Hitherto timid and domestic in character, he began publicly to neglect his wife, Maddalena Varano of Camerino, with whom, although childless, he had hitherto lived on excellent terms; he not only treated with contempt the admonitions of his advisers and of his suzerain the Pope, but went so far as to take measures to repudiate his wife, on the score of quite imaginary ill-conduct. The Duchess Maddalena, unable to bear this treatment, fled to the convent of the bare-footed sisters at Pesaro, where she pined away, while Medea da Carpi reigned in her place at Urbania, embroiling Duke Guidalfonso in quarrels both with the powerful Orsinis, who continued to accuse her of Stimigliano's murder, and with the Varanos, kinsmen of the injured Duchess Maddalena; until at length, in the year 1576, the Duke of Urbania, having become suddenly, and not without suspicious circumstances, a widower, publicly married Medea da Carpi two days after the decease of his unhappy wife. No child was born of this marriage; but such was the infatuation of Duke Guidalfonso, that the new Duchess induced him to settle the inheritance of the Duchy (having, with great difficulty, obtained the consent of the Pope) on the boy Bartolommeo, her son by Stimigliano, but whom the Orsinis refused to acknowledge as such, declaring him to be the child of that Giovanfrancesco Pico to whom Medea had been married by proxy, and whom, in defense, as she had said, of her honour, she had assassinated; and this investiture of the Duchy of Urbania on to a stranger and a bastard was at the expense of the obvious rights of the Cardinal Robert, Guidalfonso's younger brother.

In May 1579 Duke Guidalfonso died suddenly and mysteriously, Medea having forbidden all access to his chamber, lest, on his deathbed, he might repent and reinstate his brother in his rights. The Duchess immediately caused her son, Bartolommeo Orsini, to be proclaimed Duke of Urbania, and herself regent; and, with the help of two or three unscrupulous young men, particularly a certain Captain Oliverotto da Narni, who was rumoured to be her lover, seized the reins of government with extraordinary and terrible vigour, marching an army against the Varanos and Orsinis, who were defeated at Sigillo, and ruthlessly exterminating every person who dared question the lawfulness of the succession; while, all the time, Cardinal Robert, who had flung aside his priest's garb and vows, went about in Rome, Tuscany, Venice – nay, even to the Emperor and the King of Spain, imploring help against the usurper. In a few months he had turned the tide of sympathy against the Duchess-Regent; the Pope solemnly declared the investiture of Bartolommeo Orsini worthless, and published the accession of Robert II., Duke of Urbania and Count of Montemurlo; the Grand Duke of Tuscany and the Venetians secretly promised assistance, but only if Robert were able to assert his rights by main force. Little by little, one town after the other of the Duchy went over to Robert, and Medea da Carpi found herself surrounded in the mountain citadel of Urbania like a scorpion surrounded by flames. (This simile is not mine, but belongs to Raffaello Gualterio, historiographer to Robert II.) But, unlike the scorpion, Medea refused to commit suicide. It is perfectly marvelous how, without money or allies, she could so long keep her enemies at bay; and Gualterio attributes this to those fatal fascinations which had brought Pico and Stimigliano to their deaths, which had turned the once honest Guidalfonso into a villain, and which were such that, of all her lovers, not one but preferred dying for her, even after he had been treated with ingratitude and ousted by a rival; a faculty which Messer Raffaello Gualterio clearly attributed to hellish connivance.

At last the ex-Cardinal Robert succeeded, and triumphantly entered Urbania in November 1579. His accession was marked by moderation and clemency. Not a man was put to death, save Oliverotto da Narni, who threw himself on the new Duke, tried to stab him as he alighted at the palace, and who was cut down by the Duke's men, crying, "Orsini, Orsini! Medea, Medea! Long live Duke Bartolommeo!" with his dying breath, although it is said that the Duchess had treated him with ignominy. The little Bartolommeo was sent to Rome to the Orsinis; the Duchess, respectfully confined in the left wing of the palace.

It is said that she haughtily requested to see the new Duke, but that he shook his head, and, in his priest's fashion, quoted a verse about Ulysses and the Sirens; and it is remarkable that he persistently refused to see her, abruptly leaving his chamber one day that she had entered it by stealth. After a few months a conspiracy was discovered to murder Duke Robert, which had obviously been set on foot by Medea. But the young man, one Marcantonio Frangipani of Rome, denied, even under the severest torture, any complicity of hers; so that Duke Robert, who wished to do nothing violent, merely transferred the Duchess from his villa at Sant' Elmo to the convent of the Clarisse in town, where she was guarded and watched in the closest manner. It seemed impossible that Medea should intrigue any further, for she certainly saw and could be seen by no one. Yet she contrived to send a letter and her portrait to one Prinzivalle degli Ordelaffi, a youth, only nineteen years old, of noble Romagnole family, and who was betrothed to one of the most beautiful girls of Urbania. He immediately broke off his engagement, and, shortly afterwards, attempted to shoot Duke Robert with a holster-pistol as he knelt at mass on the festival of Easter Day. This time Duke Robert was determined to obtain proofs against Medea. Prinzivalle degli Ordelaffi was kept some days without food, then submitted to the most violent tortures, and finally condemned. When he was going to be flayed with red-hot pincers and quartered by horses, he was told that he might obtain the grace of immediate death by confessing the complicity of the Duchess; and the confessor and nuns of the convent, which stood in the place of execution outside Porta San Romano, pressed

Medea to save the wretch, whose screams reached her, by confessing her own guilt. Medea asked permission to go to a balcony, where she could see Prinzivalle and be seen by him. She looked on coldly, then threw down her embroidered kerchief to the poor mangled creature. He asked the executioner to wipe his mouth with it, kissed it, and cried out that Medea was innocent. Then, after several hours of torments, he died. This was too much for the patience even of Duke Robert. Seeing that as long as Medea lived his life would be in perpetual danger, but unwilling to cause a scandal (somewhat of the priest-nature remaining), he had Medea strangled in the convent, and, what is remarkable, insisted that only women – two infanticides to whom he remitted their sentence – should be employed for the deed.

"This clement prince," writes Don Arcangelo Zappi in his life of him, published in 1725, "can be blamed only for one act of cruelty, the more odious as he had himself, until released from his vows by the Pope, been in holy orders. It is said that when he caused the death of the infamous Medea da Carpi, his fear lest her extraordinary charms should seduce any man was such, that he not only employed women as executioners, but refused to permit her a priest or monk, thus forcing her to die unshriven, and refusing her the benefit of any penitence that may have lurked in her adamantine heart."

Such is the story of Medea da Carpi, Duchess of Stimigliano Orsini, and then wife of Duke Guidalfonso II. of Urbania. She was put to death just two hundred and ninety-seven years ago, December 1582, at the age of barely seven-and twenty, and having, in the course of her short life, brought to a violent end five of her lovers, from Giovanfrancesco Pico to Prinzivalle degli Ordelaffi.

* * *

Sept. 20th.—

A grand illumination of the town in honour of the taking of Rome fifteen years ago. Except Sor Asdrubale, my landlord, who shakes his head at the Piedmontese, as he calls them, the people here are all Italianissimi. The Popes kept them very much down since Urbania lapsed to the Holy See in 1645.

* * *

Sept. 28th.—

I have for some time been hunting for portraits of the Duchess Medea. Most of them, I imagine, must have been destroyed, perhaps by Duke Robert II.'s fear lest even after her death this terrible beauty should play him a trick. Three or four I have, however, been able to find – one a miniature in the Archives, said to be that which she sent to poor Prinzivalle degli Ordelaffi in order to turn his head; one a marble bust in the palace lumber-room; one in a large composition, possibly by Baroccio, representing Cleopatra at the feet of Augustus. Augustus is the idealised portrait of Robert II., round cropped head, nose a little awry, clipped beard and scar as usual, but in Roman dress. Cleopatra seems to me, for all her Oriental dress, and although she wears a black wig, to be meant for Medea da Carpi; she is kneeling, baring her breast for the victor to strike, but in reality to captivate him, and he turns away with an awkward gesture of loathing. None of these portraits seem very good, save the miniature, but that is an exquisite work, and with it, and the suggestions of the bust, it is easy to reconstruct the beauty of this terrible being. The type is that most admired by the late Renaissance, and, in some measure, immortalised by Jean Goujon and the French. The face is a perfect oval, the forehead somewhat over-round, with minute curls, like a fleece, of bright auburn hair; the nose a trifle over-aquiline, and the cheek-bones a trifle too low; the eyes grey, large, prominent, beneath exquisitely curved brows and lids just a little too tight at the corners; the mouth also, brilliantly red and most delicately designed, is a little too tight, the lips strained a trifle over the teeth. Tight eyelids and tight lips give a strange refinement, and, at the same time, an air of mystery, a somewhat sinister seductiveness; they seem to take, but not to give. The mouth with a kind of childish pout, looks as if it could bite or suck like a leech. The complexion is dazzlingly fair, the perfect transparent rosette lily of a red-haired beauty; the head, with hair elaborately curled and plaited close to it, and adorned with pearls, sits like that of the antique Arethusa on a long, supple, swan-like neck. A curious, at first rather conventional, artificial-looking sort of beauty, voluptuous yet cold, which, the more it is contemplated, the more it troubles and haunts the mind. Round the lady's neck is a gold chain with little gold lozenges at intervals, on which is engraved the posy or pun (the fashion of French devices is common in those days), 'Amour Dure – Dure Amour.' The same posy is inscribed in the hollow of the bust, and, thanks to it, I have been able to identify the latter as Medea's portrait. I often examine these tragic portraits, wondering what this face, which led so many men to their death, may have been like when it spoke or smiled, what at the moment when Medea da Carpi fascinated her victims into love unto death – 'Amour Dure – Dure Amour', as runs her device – love that lasts, cruel love – yes indeed, when one thinks of the fidelity and fate of her lovers.

* * *

Oct. 13th.—
I have literally not had time to write a line of my diary all these days. My whole mornings have gone in those Archives, my afternoons taking long walks in this lovely autumn weather (the highest hills are just tipped with snow). My evenings go in writing that confounded account of the Palace of Urbania which Government requires, merely to keep me at work at something useless. Of my history I have not yet been able to write a word... By the way, I must note down a curious circumstance mentioned in an anonymous MS. life of Duke Robert, which I fell upon today. When this prince had the equestrian statue of himself by Antonio Tassi, Gianbologna's pupil, erected in the square of the Corte, he secretly caused to be made, says my anonymous MS., a silver statuette of his familiar genius or angel – '*familiaris ejus angelus seu genius, quod a vulgo dicitur idolino*' – which statuette or idol, after having been consecrated by the astrologers – '*ab astrologis quibusdam ritibus sacrato*' – was placed in the cavity of the chest of the effigy by Tassi, in order, says the MS., that his soul might rest until the general Resurrection. This passage is curious, and to me somewhat puzzling; how could the soul of Duke Robert await the general Resurrection, when, as a Catholic, he ought to have believed that it must, as soon as separated from his body, go to Purgatory? Or is there some semi-pagan superstition of the Renaissance (most strange, certainly, in a man who had been a Cardinal) connecting the soul with a

guardian genius, who could be compelled, by magic rites ('*ab astrologis sacrato*', the MS. says of the little idol), to remain fixed to earth, so that the soul should sleep in the body until the Day of Judgment? I confess this story baffles me. I wonder whether such an idol ever existed, or exists nowadays, in the body of Tassi's bronze effigy?

* * *

Oct. 20th.—

I have been seeing a good deal of late of the Vice-Prefect's son: an amiable young man with a love-sick face and a languid interest in Urbanian history and archaeology, of which he is profoundly ignorant. This young man, who has lived at Siena and Lucca before his father was promoted here, wears extremely long and tight trousers, which almost preclude his bending his knees, a stick-up collar and an eyeglass, and a pair of fresh kid gloves stuck in the breast of his coat, speaks of Urbania as Ovid might have spoken of Pontus, and complains (as well he may) of the barbarism of the young men, the officials who dine at my inn and howl and sing like madmen, and the nobles who drive gigs, showing almost as much throat as a lady at a ball. This person frequently entertains me with his amori, past, present, and future; he evidently thinks me very odd for having none to entertain him with in return; he points out to me the pretty (or ugly) servant-girls and dressmakers as we walk in the street, sighs deeply or sings in falsetto behind every tolerably young-looking woman, and has finally taken me to the house of the lady of his heart, a great black-mustachioed countess, with a voice like a fish-crier; here, he says, I shall meet all the best company in Urbania and some beautiful women – ah, too beautiful, alas! I find three huge half-furnished rooms, with bare brick floors, petroleum lamps, and horribly bad pictures on bright washball-blue and gamboge walls, and in the midst of it all, every evening, a dozen ladies and gentlemen seated in a circle, vociferating at each other the same news a year old; the younger ladies in bright yellows and greens, fanning themselves while my teeth chatter, and having sweet things whispered behind their fans by officers with hair brushed up like a hedgehog. And these are the women my friend expects me to fall in love with! I vainly wait for tea or supper which does not come, and rush home, determined to leave alone the Urbanian beau monde.

It is quite true that I have no amori, although my friend does not believe it. When I came to Italy first, I looked out for romance; I sighed, like Goethe in Rome, for a window to open and a wondrous creature to appear, '*welch mich versengend erquickt*'. Perhaps it is because Goethe was a German, accustomed to German Fraus, and I am, after all, a Pole, accustomed to something very different from Fraus; but anyhow, for all my efforts, in Rome, Florence, and Siena, I never could find a woman to go mad about, either among the ladies, chattering bad French, or among the lower classes, as cute and cold as money-lenders; so I steer clear of Italian womankind, its shrill voice and gaudy toilettes. I am wedded to history, to the Past, to women like Lucrezia Borgia, Vittoria Accoramboni, or that Medea da Carpi, for the present; some day I shall perhaps find a grand passion, a woman to play the Don Quixote about, like the Pole that I am; a woman out of whose slipper to drink, and for whose pleasure to die; but not here! Few things strike me so much as the degeneracy of Italian women. What has become of the race of Faustinas, Marozias, Bianca Cappellos? Where discover nowadays (I confess she haunts me) another Medea da Carpi? Were it only possible to meet a woman of that extreme distinction of beauty, of that terribleness of nature, even if only potential, I do believe I could love her, even to the Day of Judgment, like any Oliverotto da Narni, or Frangipani or Prinzivalle.

* * *

Oct. 27th.—

Fine sentiments the above are for a professor, a learned man! I thought the young artists of Rome childish because they played practical jokes and yelled at night in the streets, returning from the Caffè Greco or the cellar in the Via Palombella; but am I not as childish to the full – I, melancholy wretch, whom they called Hamlet and the Knight of the Doleful Countenance?

* * *

Nov. 5th.—

I can't free myself from the thought of this Medea da Carpi. In my walks, my mornings in the Archives, my solitary evenings, I catch myself thinking over the woman. Am I turning novelist instead of historian? And still it seems to me that I understand her so well; so much better than my facts warrant. First, we must put aside all pedantic modern ideas of right and wrong. Right and wrong in a century of violence and treachery does not exist, least of all for creatures like Medea. Go preach right and wrong to a tigress, my dear sir! Yet is there in the world anything nobler than the huge creature, steel when she springs, velvet when she treads, as she stretches her supple body, or smooths her beautiful skin, or fastens her strong claws into her victim?

Yes; I can understand Medea. Fancy a woman of superlative beauty, of the highest courage and calmness, a woman of many resources, of genius, brought up by a petty princelet of a father, upon Tacitus and Sallust, and the tales of the great Malatestas, of Caesar Borgia and such-like! – a woman whose one passion is conquest and empire – fancy her, on the eve of being wedded to a man of the power of the Duke of Stimigliano, claimed, carried off by a small fry of a Pico, locked up in his hereditary brigand's castle, and having to receive the young fool's red-hot love as an honour and a necessity! The mere thought of any violence to such a nature is an abominable outrage; and if Pico chooses to embrace such a woman at the risk of meeting a sharp piece of steel in her arms, why, it is a fair bargain. Young hound – or, if you prefer, young hero – to think to treat a woman like this as if she were any village wench! Medea marries her Orsini. A marriage, let it be noted, between an old soldier of fifty and a girl of sixteen. Reflect what that means: it means that this imperious woman is soon treated like a chattel, made roughly to understand that her business is to give the Duke an heir, not advice; that she must never ask "wherefore this or that?" that she must courtesy before the Duke's counselors, his captains, his mistresses; that, at the least suspicion of rebelliousness, she is subject to his foul words and blows; at the least suspicion of infidelity, to be strangled or starved to death, or thrown down an oubliette. Suppose that she knew that her husband has taken it into his head that she has looked too hard at this man or that, that one of his lieutenants or one of his women have whispered that, after all, the boy Bartolommeo might as soon be a Pico as an Orsini. Suppose she knew that she must strike or be struck? Why, she strikes, or gets someone to strike for her. At what price? A promise of love, of love to a groom, the son of a serf! Why, the dog must be mad or drunk to believe such a thing possible; his very belief in anything so monstrous makes him worthy of death. And then he dares to blab! This is much worse than Pico. Medea is bound to defend her honour a second time; if she could stab Pico, she can certainly stab this fellow, or have him stabbed.

Hounded by her husband's kinsmen, she takes refuge at Urbania. The Duke, like every other man, falls wildly in love with Medea, and neglects his wife; let us even go so far as to say, breaks his wife's heart. Is this Medea's fault? Is it her fault that every stone that comes beneath her chariot-wheels is crushed? Certainly not. Do you suppose that a woman like Medea feels the smallest ill-will against a poor, craven Duchess Maddalena? Why, she ignores her very existence. To suppose Medea a cruel woman is as grotesque as to call her an immoral woman. Her fate is, sooner or later, to triumph over her enemies, at all events to make their victory almost a defeat; her magic faculty is to enslave all the men who come across her path; all those who see her, love her, become her slaves; and it is the destiny of all her slaves to perish. Her lovers, with the exception of Duke Guidalfonso, all come to an untimely end; and in this there is nothing unjust. The possession of a woman like Medea is a happiness too great for a mortal man; it would turn his head, make him forget even what he owed her; no man must survive long who conceives himself to have a right over her; it is a kind of sacrilege. And only death, the willingness to pay for such happiness by death, can at all make a man worthy of being her lover; he must be willing to love and suffer and die. This is the meaning of her device – 'Amour Dure – Dure Amour'. The love of Medea da Carpi cannot fade, but the lover can die; it is a constant and a cruel love.

* * *

Nov. 11th.—

I was right, quite right in my idea. I have found – Oh, joy! I treated the Vice-Prefect's son to a dinner of five courses at the Trattoria La Stella d'Italia out of sheer jubilation – I have found in the Archives, unknown, of course, to the Director, a heap of letters – letters of Duke Robert about Medea da Carpi, letters of Medea herself! Yes, Medea's own handwriting – a round, scholarly character, full of abbreviations, with a Greek look about it, as befits a learned princess who could read Plato as well as Petrarch. The letters are of little importance, mere drafts of business letters for her secretary to copy, during the time that she governed the poor weak Guidalfonso. But they are her letters, and I can imagine almost that there hangs about these mouldering pieces of paper a scent as of a woman's hair.

The few letters of Duke Robert show him in a new light. A cunning, cold, but craven priest. He trembles at the bare thought of Medea – 'la pessima Medea' – worse than her namesake of Colchis, as he calls her. His long clemency is a result of mere fear of laying violent hands upon her. He fears her as something almost supernatural; he would have enjoyed having had her burnt as a witch. After letter on letter, telling his crony, Cardinal Sanseverino, at Rome his various precautions during her lifetime – how he wears a jacket of mail under his coat; how he drinks only milk from a cow which he has milked in his presence; how he tries his dog with morsels of his food, lest it be poisoned; how he suspects the wax-candles because of their peculiar smell; how he fears riding out lest some one should frighten his horse and cause him to break his neck – after all this, and when Medea has been in her grave two years, he tells his correspondent of his fear of meeting the soul of Medea after his own death, and chuckles over the ingenious device (concocted by his astrologer and a certain Fra Gaudenzio, a Capuchin) by which he shall secure the absolute peace of his soul until that of the wicked Medea be finally 'chained up in hell among the lakes of boiling pitch and the ice of Caina described by the immortal bard' – old pedant! Here, then, is the explanation of that silver image – *quod vulgo dicitur idolino* – which he caused to be soldered into his effigy by Tassi. As long as the image of his soul was attached to the image of his body, he should sleep awaiting the Day of Judgment, fully convinced that Medea's soul will then be properly tarred and feathered, while his – honest man! – will fly straight to Paradise. And to think that, two weeks ago, I believed this man to be a hero! Aha! My good Duke Robert, you shall be shown up in my history; and no amount of silver idolinos shall save you from being heartily laughed at!

* * *

Nov. 15th.—

Strange! That idiot of a Prefect's son, who has heard me talk a hundred times of Medea da Carpi, suddenly recollects that, when he was a child at Urbania, his nurse used to threaten him with a visit from Madonna Medea, who rode in the sky on a black he-goat. My Duchess Medea turned into a bogey for naughty little boys!

* * *

Nov. 20th.—

I have been going about with a Bavarian Professor of mediaeval history, showing him all over the country. Among other places we went to Rocca Sant'Elmo, to see the former villa of the Dukes of Urbania, the villa where Medea was confined between the accession of Duke Robert and the conspiracy of Marcantonio Frangipani, which caused her removal to the nunnery immediately outside the town. A long ride up the desolate Apennine valleys, bleak beyond words just now with their thin fringe of oak scrub turned russet, thin patches of grass seared by the frost, the last few yellow leaves of the poplars by the torrents shaking and fluttering about in the chill Tramontana; the mountain-tops are wrapped in thick grey cloud; tomorrow, if the wind continues, we shall see them round masses of snow against the cold blue sky. Sant' Elmo is a wretched hamlet high on the Apennine ridge, where the Italian vegetation is already replaced by that of the North. You ride for miles through leafless chestnut woods, the scent of the soaking brown leaves filling the air, the roar of the torrent, turbid with autumn rains, rising from the precipice below; then suddenly the leafless chestnut woods are replaced, as at Vallombrosa, by a belt of black, dense fir plantations. Emerging from these, you come to an open space, frozen blasted meadows, the rocks of snow clad peak, the newly fallen snow, close above you; and in the midst, on a knoll, with a gnarled larch on either side, the ducal villa of Sant' Elmo, a big black stone box with a stone escutcheon, grated windows, and a double flight of steps in front. It is now let out to the proprietor of the neighbouring woods, who uses it for the storage of chestnuts, faggots, and charcoal from the neighbouring ovens. We tied our horses to the iron rings and entered: an old woman, with disheveled hair, was alone in the house. The villa is a mere hunting-lodge, built by Ottobuono IV., the father of Dukes Guidalfonso and Robert, about 1530. Some of the rooms have at one time been frescoed and paneled with oak carvings, but all this has disappeared. Only, in one of the big rooms, there remains a large marble fireplace, similar to those in the palace at Urbania, beautifully carved with Cupids on a blue ground; a charming naked boy sustains a jar on either side, one containing clove pinks, the other roses. The room was filled with stacks of faggots.

We returned home late, my companion in excessively bad humour at the fruitlessness of the expedition. We were caught in the skirt of a snowstorm as we got into the chestnut woods. The sight of the snow falling gently, of the earth and bushes whitened all round, made me feel back at Posen, once more a child. I sang and shouted, to my companion's horror. This will be a bad point against me if reported at Berlin. A historian of twenty-four who shouts and sings, and that when another historian is cursing at the snow and the bad roads! All night I lay awake watching the embers of my wood fire, and thinking of Medea da Carpi mewed up, in winter, in that solitude of Sant' Elmo, the firs groaning, the torrent roaring, the snow falling all round; miles and miles away from human creatures. I fancied I saw it all, and that I, somehow, was Marcantonio Frangipani come to liberate her – or was it Prinzivalle degli Ordelaffi? I suppose it was because of the long ride, the unaccustomed pricking feeling of the snow in the air; or perhaps the punch which my professor insisted on drinking after dinner.

* * *

Nov. 23rd.—

Thank goodness, that Bavarian professor has finally departed! Those days he spent here drove me nearly crazy. Talking over my work, I told him one day my views on Medea da Carpi; whereupon he condescended to answer that those were the usual tales due to the mythopoeic (old idiot!) tendency of the Renaissance; that research would disprove the greater part of them, as it had disproved the stories current about the Borgias, &c.; that, moreover, such a woman as I made out was psychologically and physiologically impossible. Would that one could say as much of such professors as he and his fellows!

* * *

Nov. 24th.—

I cannot get over my pleasure in being rid of that imbecile; I felt as if I could have throttled him every time he spoke of the Lady of my thoughts – for such she has become – Metea, as the animal called her!

* * *

Nov. 30th.—

I feel quite shaken at what has just happened; I am beginning to fear that that old pedant was right in saying that it was bad for me to live all alone in a strange country, that it would make me morbid. It is ridiculous that I should be put into such a state of excitement merely by the chance discovery of a portrait of a woman dead these three hundred years. With the case of my uncle Ladislas, and other suspicions of insanity in my family, I ought really to guard against such foolish excitement.

Yet the incident was really dramatic, uncanny. I could have sworn that I knew every picture in the palace here; and particularly every picture of Her. Anyhow, this morning, as I was leaving the Archives, I passed through one of the many small rooms – irregular-shaped closets – which fill up the ins and outs of this curious palace, turreted like a French château. I must have passed through that closet before, for the view was so familiar out of its window; just the particular bit of round tower in front, the cypress on the other side of the ravine, the belfry beyond, and the piece of the line of Monte Sant' Agata and the Leonessa, covered with snow, against the sky. I suppose there must be twin rooms, and that I had got into the wrong one; or rather, perhaps some shutter had been opened or curtain withdrawn. As I was passing, my eye was caught by a very beautiful old mirror-frame let into the brown and yellow inlaid wall. I approached, and looking at the frame, looked also, mechanically, into the glass. I gave a great start, and almost shrieked, I do believe – (it's lucky the Munich professor is safe out of Urbania!). Behind my own image stood another, a figure close to my shoulder, a face close to mine; and that figure, that face, hers! Medea da Carpi's! I turned sharp round, as white, I think, as the ghost I expected to see. On the wall opposite the mirror, just a pace or two behind where I had been standing, hung a portrait. And such a portrait! – Bronzino never painted a grander one. Against a background of harsh, dark blue, there stands out the figure of the Duchess (for it is Medea, the real Medea, a thousand times more real, individual, and powerful than in the other portraits), seated stiffly in a high-backed chair, sustained, as it were, almost rigid, by the stiff brocade of skirts and stomacher, stiffer for plaques of embroidered silver flowers and rows of seed pearl. The dress is, with its mixture of silver and pearl, of a strange dull red, a wicked poppy-juice colour, against which the flesh of the long, narrow hands with fringe-like fingers; of the long slender neck, and the face with bared forehead, looks white and hard, like alabaster. The face is the same as in the other portraits: the same rounded forehead, with the short fleece-like, yellowish-red curls; the same beautifully curved eyebrows, just barely marked; the same eyelids, a little tight across the eyes; the same lips, a little tight across the mouth; but with a purity of line, a dazzling splendour of skin, and intensity of look immeasurably superior to all the other portraits.

She looks out of the frame with a cold, level glance; yet the lips smile. One hand holds a dull-red rose; the other, long, narrow, tapering, plays with a thick rope of silk and gold and jewels hanging from the waist; round the throat, white as marble, partially confined in the tight dull-red bodice, hangs a gold collar, with the device on alternate enameled medallions, 'AMOUR DURE – DURE AMOUR'.

On reflection, I see that I simply could never have been in that room or closet before; I must have mistaken the door. But, although the explanation is so simple, I still, after several hours, feel terribly shaken in all my being. If I grow so excitable I shall have to go to Rome at Christmas for a holiday. I feel as if some danger pursued me here (can it be fever?); and yet, and yet, I don't see how I shall ever tear myself away.

* * *

Dec. 10th.—

I have made an effort, and accepted the Vice-Prefect's son's invitation to see the oil-making at a villa of theirs near the coast. The villa, or farm, is an old fortified, towered place, standing on a hillside among olive-trees and little osier-bushes, which look like a bright orange flame. The olives are squeezed in a tremendous black cellar, like a prison: you see, by the faint white daylight, and the smoky yellow flare of resin burning in pans, great white bullocks moving round a huge millstone; vague figures working at pulleys and handles: it looks, to my fancy, like some scene of the Inquisition. The Cavaliere regaled me with his best wine and rusks. I took some long walks by the seaside; I had left Urbania wrapped in snow-clouds; down on the coast there was a bright sun; the sunshine, the sea, the bustle of the little port on the Adriatic seemed to do me good. I came back to Urbania another man. Sor Asdrubale, my landlord, poking about in slippers among the gilded chests, the Empire sofas, the old cups and saucers and pictures which no one will buy, congratulated me upon the improvement in my looks. "You work too much," he says; "youth requires amusement, theatres, promenades, amori – it is time enough to be serious when one is bald" – and he took off his greasy red cap. Yes, I am better! And, as a result, I take to my work with delight again. I will cut them out still, those wiseacres at Berlin!

* * *

Dec. 14th.—

I don't think I have ever felt so happy about my work. I see it all so well – that crafty, cowardly Duke Robert; that melancholy Duchess Maddalena; that weak, showy, would-be chivalrous Duke Guidalfonso; and above all, the splendid figure of Medea. I feel as if I were the greatest historian of the age; and, at the same time, as if I were a boy of twelve. It snowed yesterday for the first time in the city, for two good hours. When it had done, I actually went into the square and taught the ragamuffins to make a snowman; no, a snow-woman; and I had the fancy to call her Medea. "La pessima Medea!" cried one of the boys – "the one who used to ride through the air on a goat?" "No, no," I said; "she was a beautiful lady, the Duchess of Urbania, the most beautiful woman that ever lived." I made her a crown of tinsel, and taught the boys to cry "Evviva, Medea!" But one of them said, "She is a witch! She must be burnt!" At which they all rushed to fetch burning faggots and tow; in a minute the yelling demons had melted her down.

* * *

Dec. 15th.—

What a goose I am, and to think I am twenty-four, and known in literature! In my long walks I have composed to a tune (I don't know what it is) which all the people are singing and whistling in the street at present, a poem in frightful Italian, beginning "Medea, mia dea", calling on her in the name of her various lovers. I go about humming between my teeth, "Why am I not Marcantonio? or Prinzivalle? or he of Narni? or the good Duke Alfonso? that I might be beloved by thee, Medea, mia dea," &c. &c. Awful rubbish! My landlord, I think, suspects that Medea must be some lady I met while I was staying by the seaside. I am sure Sora Serafina, Sora Lodovica, and Sora Adalgisa – the three Parcae or Norns, as I call them – have some such notion. This afternoon, at dusk, while tidying my room, Sora Lodovica said to me, "How beautifully the Signorino has taken to singing!" I was scarcely aware that I had been vociferating, "Vieni, Medea, mia dea," while the old lady bobbed about making up my fire. I stopped; a nice reputation I shall get! I thought, and all this will somehow get to Rome, and thence to Berlin. Sora Lodovica was leaning out of the window, pulling in the iron hook of the shrine-lamp which marks Sor Asdrubale's house. As she was trimming the lamp previous to swinging it out again, she said in her odd, prudish little way, "You are wrong to stop singing, my son" (she varies between calling me Signor Professore and such terms of affection as "Nino", "Viscere mie," &c.); "you are wrong to stop singing, for there is a young lady there in the street who has actually stopped to listen to you."

I ran to the window. A woman, wrapped in a black shawl, was standing in an archway, looking up to the window.

"Eh, eh! The Signor Professore has admirers," said Sora Lodovica.

"Medea, mia dea!" I burst out as loud as I could, with a boy's pleasure in disconcerting the inquisitive passer-by. She turned suddenly round to go away, waving her hand at me; at that moment Sora Lodovica swung the shrine-lamp back into its place. A stream of light fell across the street. I felt myself grow quite cold; the face of the woman outside was that of Medea da Carpi!

What a fool I am, to be sure!

Part II

Dec. 17th.—

I fear that my craze about Medea da Carpi has become well known, thanks to my silly talk and idiotic songs. That Vice-Prefect's son – or the assistant at the Archives, or perhaps some of the company at the Contessa's, is trying to play me a trick! But take care, my good ladies and gentlemen, I shall pay you out in your own coin! Imagine my feelings when, this morning, I found on my desk a folded letter addressed to me in a curious handwriting which seemed strangely familiar to me, and which, after a moment, I recognised as that of the letters of Medea da Carpi at the Archives. It gave me a horrible shock. My next idea was that it must be a present from some one who knew my interest in Medea – a genuine letter of hers on which some idiot had written my address instead of putting it into an envelope. But it was addressed to me, written to me, no old letter; merely four lines, which ran as follows:—

> *To Spiridion.—*
> *A person who knows the interest you bear her will be at the Church of San Giovanni Decollato this evening at nine. Look out, in the left aisle, for a lady wearing a black mantle, and holding a rose.*

By this time I understood that I was the object of a conspiracy, the victim of a hoax. I turned the letter round and round. It was written on paper such as was made in the sixteenth century, and in an extraordinarily precise imitation of Medea da Carpi's characters. Who had written it? I thought over all the possible people. On the whole, it must be the Vice-Prefect's son, perhaps in combination with his lady-love, the Countess. They must have torn a blank page off some old letter; but that either of them should have had the ingenuity of inventing such a hoax, or the power of committing such a forgery, astounds me beyond measure. There is more in these people than I should have guessed. How pay them off? By taking no notice of the letter? Dignified, but dull. No, I will go; perhaps someone will be there, and I will mystify them in their turn. Or, if no one is there, how I shall crow over them for their imperfectly carried out plot! Perhaps this is some folly of the Cavalier Muzio's to bring me into the presence of some lady whom he destines to be the flame of my future amori. That is likely enough. And it would be too idiotic and professorial to refuse such an invitation; the lady must be worth knowing who can forge sixteenth-century letters like this, for I am sure that languid swell Muzio never could. I will go! By Heaven! I'll pay them back in their own coin! It is now five – how long these days are!

Dec. 18th.—

Am I mad? Or are there really ghosts? That adventure of last night has shaken me to the very depth of my soul.

I went at nine, as the mysterious letter had bid me. It was bitterly cold, and the air full of fog and sleet; not a shop open, not a window unshuttered, not a creature visible; the narrow black streets, precipitous between their high walls and under their lofty archways, were only the blacker for the dull light of an oil-lamp here and there, with its flickering yellow reflection on the wet flags. San Giovanni Decollato is a little church, or rather oratory, which I have always hitherto seen shut up (as so many churches here are shut up except on great festivals); and situate behind the ducal palace, on a sharp ascent, and forming the bifurcation of two steep paved lanes. I have passed by the place a hundred times, and scarcely noticed the little church, except for the marble high relief over the door, showing the grizzly head of the Baptist in the charger, and for the iron cage close by, in which were formerly exposed the heads of criminals; the decapitated, or, as they call him here, decollated, John the Baptist, being apparently the patron of axe and block.

A few strides took me from my lodgings to San Giovanni Decollato. I confess I was excited; one is not twenty-four and a Pole for nothing. On getting to the kind of little platform at the bifurcation of the two precipitous streets, I found, to my surprise, that the windows of the church or oratory were not lighted, and that the door was locked! So this was the precious joke that had been played upon me; to send me on a bitter cold, sleety night, to a church which was shut up and had perhaps been shut up for years! I don't know what I couldn't have done in that moment of rage; I felt inclined to break open the church door, or to go and pull the Vice-Prefect's son out of bed (for I felt sure that the joke was his). I determined upon the latter course; and was walking towards his door, along the black alley to the left of the church, when I was suddenly stopped by the sound as of an organ close by, an organ, yes, quite plainly, and the voice of choristers and the drone of a litany. So the church was not shut, after all! I retraced my steps to the top of the lane. All was dark and in complete silence. Suddenly there came again a faint gust of organ and voices. I listened; it clearly came from the other lane, the one on the right-hand side. Was there, perhaps, another door there? I passed beneath the archway, and descended a little way in the direction whence the sounds seemed to come. But no door, no light, only the black walls, the black wet flags, with their faint yellow reflections of flickering oil-lamps; moreover, complete silence. I stopped a minute, and then the chant rose again; this time it seemed to me most certainly from the lane I had just left. I went back – nothing. Thus backwards and forwards, the sounds always beckoning, as it were, one way, only to beckon me back, vainly, to the other.

At last I lost patience; and I felt a sort of creeping terror, which only a violent action could dispel. If the mysterious sounds came neither from the street to the right, nor from the street to the left, they could come only from the church. Half-maddened, I rushed up the two or three steps, and prepared to wrench the door open with a tremendous effort. To my amazement, it opened with the greatest ease. I entered, and the sounds of the litany met me louder than before, as I paused a moment between the outer door and the heavy leathern curtain. I raised the latter and crept in. The altar was brilliantly illuminated with tapers and garlands of chandeliers; this was evidently some evening service connected with Christmas. The nave and aisles were comparatively dark, and about half full. I elbowed my way along the right aisle towards the altar. When my eyes had got accustomed to the unexpected light, I began to look round me, and with a beating heart. The idea that all this was a hoax, that I should meet merely some acquaintance of my friend the Cavaliere's, had somehow departed: I looked about. The people were all wrapped up, the men in big cloaks, the women in woollen veils and mantles. The body of the church was comparatively dark, and I could not make out anything very clearly, but it seemed to me, somehow, as if, under the cloaks and veils, these people were dressed in a rather extraordinary fashion. The man in front of me, I remarked, showed yellow stockings beneath his cloak; a woman, hard by, a red bodice, laced behind with gold tags. Could these be peasants from some remote part come for the Christmas festivities, or did the inhabitants of Urbania don some old-fashioned garb in honour of Christmas?

As I was wondering, my eye suddenly caught that of a woman standing in the opposite aisle, close to the altar, and in the full blaze of its lights. She was wrapped in black, but held, in a very conspicuous way, a red rose, an unknown luxury at this time of the year in a place like Urbania. She evidently saw me, and turning even more fully into the light, she loosened her heavy black cloak, displaying a dress of deep red, with gleams of silver and gold embroideries; she turned her face towards me; the full blaze of the chandeliers and tapers fell upon it. It was the face of Medea da Carpi! I dashed across the nave, pushing people roughly aside, or rather, it seemed to me, passing through impalpable bodies. But the lady turned and walked rapidly down the aisle towards the door. I followed close upon her, but somehow I could not get up with her. Once, at the curtain, she turned round again. She was within a few paces of me. Yes, it was Medea. Medea herself, no mistake, no delusion, no sham; the oval face, the lips tightened over the mouth, the eyelids tight over the corner of the eyes, the exquisite alabaster complexion! She raised the curtain and glided out. I followed; the curtain alone separated me from her. I saw the wooden door swing to behind her. One step ahead of me! I tore open the door; she must be on the steps, within reach of my arm!

I stood outside the church. All was empty, merely the wet pavement and the yellow reflections in the pools: a sudden cold seized me; I could not go on. I tried to re-enter the church; it was shut. I rushed home, my hair standing on end, and trembling in all my limbs, and remained for an hour like a maniac. Is it a delusion? Am I too going mad? O God, God! Am I going mad?

* * *

Dec. 19th.—

A brilliant, sunny day; all the black snow-slush has disappeared out of the town, off the bushes and trees. The snow-clad mountains sparkle against the bright blue sky. A Sunday, and Sunday weather; all the bells are ringing for the approach of Christmas. They are preparing for a kind of fair in the square with the colonnade, putting up booths filled with coloured cotton and woollen ware, bright shawls and kerchiefs, mirrors, ribbons, brilliant pewter lamps; the whole turn-out of the peddler in *Winter's Tale*. The pork-shops are all garlanded with green and with paper flowers, the hams and cheeses stuck full of little flags and green twigs. I strolled out to see the cattle-fair outside the gate; a forest of interlacing horns, an ocean of lowing and stamping: hundreds of immense white bullocks, with horns a yard long and red tassels, packed close together on the little piazza d'armi under the city walls. Bah! Why do I write this trash? What's the use of it all? While I am forcing myself to write about bells, and Christmas festivities, and cattle-fairs, one idea goes on like a bell within me: Medea, Medea! Have I really seen her, or am I mad?

* * *

Two hours later.—

That Church of San Giovanni Decollato — so my landlord informs me — has not been made use of within the memory of man. Could it have been all a hallucination or a dream — perhaps a dream dreamed that night? I have been out again to look at that church. There it is, at the bifurcation of the two steep lanes, with its bas-relief of the Baptist's head over the door. The door does look as if it had not been opened for years. I can see the cobwebs in the windowpanes; it does look as if, as Sor Asdrubale says, only rats and spiders congregated within it. And yet – and yet; I have so clear a remembrance, so distinct a consciousness of it all. There was a picture of the daughter of Herodias dancing, upon the altar; I remember her white turban with a scarlet tuft of feathers, and Herod's blue caftan; I remember the shape of the central chandelier; it swung round slowly, and one of the wax lights had got bent almost in two by the heat and draught.

Things, all these, which I may have seen elsewhere, stored unawares in my brain, and which may have come out, somehow, in a dream; I have heard physiologists allude to such things. I will go again: if the church be shut, why then it must have been a dream, a vision, the result of over-excitement. I must leave at once for Rome and see doctors, for I am afraid of going mad. If, on the other hand – pshaw! there is no other hand in such a case. Yet if there were – why then, I should really have seen Medea; I might see her again; speak to her. The mere thought sets my blood in a whirl, not with horror, but with... I know not what to call it. The feeling terrifies me, but it is delicious. Idiot! There is some little coil of my brain, the twentieth of a hair's-breadth out of order – that's all!

* * *

Dec. 20th.—

I have been again; I have heard the music; I have been inside the church; I have seen Her! I can no longer doubt my senses. Why should I? Those pedants say that the dead are dead, the past is past. For them, yes; but why for me? – why for a man who loves, who is consumed with the love of a woman? – a woman who, indeed – yes, let me finish the sentence. Why should there not be ghosts to such as can see them? Why should she not return to the earth, if she knows that it contains a man who thinks of, desires, only her?

A hallucination? Why, I saw her, as I see this paper that I write upon; standing there, in the full blaze of the altar. Why, I heard the rustle of her skirts, I smelt the scent of her hair, I raised the curtain which was shaking from her touch. Again I missed her. But this time, as I rushed out into the empty moonlit street, I found upon the church steps a rose – the rose which I had seen in her hand the moment before – I felt it, smelt it; a rose, a real, living rose, dark red and only just plucked. I put it into water when I returned, after having kissed it, who knows how many times? I placed it on the top of the cupboard; I determined not to look at it for twenty-four hours lest it should be a delusion. But I must see it again; I must... Good Heavens! This is horrible, horrible; if I had found a skeleton it could not have been worse! The rose, which last night seemed freshly plucked, full of colour and perfume, is brown, dry – a thing kept for centuries between the leaves of a book – it has crumbled into dust between my fingers. Horrible, horrible! But why so, pray? Did I not know that I was in love with a woman dead three hundred years? If I wanted fresh roses which bloomed yesterday, the Countess Fiammetta or any little sempstress in Urbania might have given them me. What if the rose has fallen to dust? If only I could hold Medea in my arms as I held it in my fingers, kiss her lips as I kissed its petals, should I not be satisfied if she too were to fall to dust the next moment, if I were to fall to dust myself?

* * *

Dec. 22nd, Eleven at night.—

I have seen her once more! – almost spoken to her. I have been promised her love! Ah, Spiridion! You were right when you felt that you were not made for any earthly amori. At the usual hour I betook myself this evening to San Giovanni Decollato. A bright winter night; the high houses and belfries standing out against a deep blue heaven luminous, shimmering like steel with myriads of stars; the moon has not yet risen. There was no light in the windows; but, after a little effort, the door opened and I entered the church, the altar, as usual, brilliantly illuminated. It struck me suddenly that all this crowd of men and women standing all round, these priests chanting and moving about the altar, were dead – that they did not exist for any man save me. I touched, as if by accident, the hand of my neighbour; it was cold, like wet clay. He turned round, but did not seem to see me: his face was ashy, and his eyes staring, fixed, like those of a blind man or a corpse. I felt as if I must rush out. But at that moment my eye fell upon Her, standing as usual by the altar steps, wrapped in a black mantle, in the full blaze of the lights. She turned round; the light fell straight upon her face, the face with the delicate features, the eyelids and lips a little tight, the alabaster skin faintly tinged with pale pink. Our eyes met.

I pushed my way across the nave towards where she stood by the altar steps; she turned quickly down the aisle, and I after her. Once or twice she lingered, and I thought I should overtake her; but again, when, not a second after the door had closed upon her, I stepped out into the street, she had vanished. On the church step lay something white. It was not a flower this time, but a letter. I rushed back to the church to read it; but the church was fast shut, as if it had not been opened for years. I could not see by the flickering shrine-lamps – I rushed home, lit my lamp, pulled the letter from my breast. I have it before me. The handwriting is hers; the same as in the Archives, the same as in that first letter:—

> *To Spiridion.—*
>
> *Let thy courage be equal to thy love, and thy love shall be rewarded. On the night preceding Christmas, take a hatchet and saw; cut boldly into the body of the bronze rider who stands in the Corte, on the left side, near the waist. Saw open the body, and within it thou wilt find the silver effigy of a winged genius. Take it out, hack it into a hundred pieces, and fling them in all directions, so that the winds may sweep them away. That night she whom thou lovest will come to reward thy fidelity.*
>
> *On the brownish wax is the device – 'AMOUR DURE – DURE AMOUR'.*

* * *

Dec. 23rd.—

So it is true! I was reserved for something wonderful in this world. I have at last found that after which my soul has been straining. Ambition, love of art, love of Italy, these things which have occupied my spirit, and have yet left me continually unsatisfied, these were none of them my real destiny. I have sought for life, thirsting for it as a man in the desert thirsts for a well; but the life of the senses of other youths, the life of the intellect of other men, have never slaked that thirst. Shall life for me mean the love of a dead woman? We smile at what we choose to call the superstition of the past, forgetting that all our vaunted science of today may seem just such another superstition to the men of the future; but why should the present be right and the past wrong? The men who painted the pictures and built the palaces of three hundred years ago were certainly of as delicate fiber, of as keen reason, as ourselves, who merely print calico and build locomotives. What makes me think this, is that I have been calculating my nativity by help of an old book belonging to Sor Asdrubale – and see, my horoscope tallies almost exactly with that of Medea da Carpi, as given by a chronicler. May this explain? No, no; all is explained by the fact that the first time I read of this woman's career, the first time I saw her portrait, I loved her, though I hid my love to myself in the garb of historical interest. Historical interest indeed!

I have got the hatchet and the saw. I bought the saw of a poor joiner, in a village some miles off; he did not understand at first what I meant, and I think he thought me mad; perhaps I am. But if madness means the happiness of one's life, what of it? The hatchet I saw lying in a timber-yard, where they prepare the great trunks of the fir trees which grow high on the Apennines of Sant' Elmo. There was no one in the yard, and I could not resist the temptation; I handled the thing, tried its edge, and stole it. This is the first time in my life that I have been a thief; why did I not go into a shop and buy a hatchet? I don't know; I seemed unable to resist the sight of the shining blade. What I am going to do is, I suppose, an act of vandalism; and certainly I have no right to spoil the property of this city of Urbania. But I wish no harm either to the statue or the city, if I could plaster up the bronze, I would do so willingly. But I must obey Her; I must avenge Her; I must get at that silver image which Robert of Montemurlo had made and consecrated in order that his cowardly soul might sleep in peace, and not encounter that of the being whom he dreaded most in the world. Aha! Duke Robert, you forced her to die unshriven, and you stuck the image of your soul into the image of your body, thinking thereby that, while she suffered the tortures of Hell, you would rest in peace, until your well-scoured little soul might fly straight up to Paradise; – you were afraid of Her when both of you should be dead, and thought yourself very clever to have prepared for all emergencies! Not so, Serene Highness. You too shall taste what it is to wander after death, and to meet the dead whom one has injured.

What an interminable day! But I shall see her again tonight.

* * *

Eleven o'clock.—

No; the church was fast closed; the spell had ceased. Until tomorrow I shall not see her. But tomorrow! Ah, Medea! Did any of thy lovers love thee as I do?

Twenty-four hours more till the moment of happiness – the moment for which I seem to have been waiting all my life. And after that, what next? Yes, I see it plainer every minute; after that, nothing more. All those who loved Medea da Carpi, who loved and who served her, died: Giovanfrancesco Pico, her first husband, whom she left stabbed in the castle from which she fled; Stimigliano, who died of poison; the groom who gave him the poison, cut down by her orders; Oliverotto da Narni, Marcantonio Frangipani, and that poor boy of the Ordelaffi, who had never even looked upon her face, and whose only reward was that handkerchief with which the hangman wiped the sweat off his face, when he was one mass of broken limbs and torn flesh: all had to die, and I shall die also.

The love of such a woman is enough, and is fatal – 'Amour Dure', as her device says. I shall die also. But why not? Would it be possible to live in order to love another woman? Nay, would it be possible to drag on a life like this one after the happiness of tomorrow? Impossible; the others died, and I must die. I always felt that I should not live long; a gipsy in Poland told me once that I had in my hand the cut-line which signifies a violent death. I might have ended in a duel with some brother-student, or in a railway accident. No, no; my death will not be of that sort! Death – and is not she also dead? What strange vistas does such a thought not open! Then the others – Pico, the Groom, Stimigliano, Oliverotto, Frangipani, Prinzivalle degli Ordelaffi – will they all be there? But she shall love me best – me by whom she has been loved after she has been three hundred years in the grave!

* * *

Dec. 24th.—

I have made all my arrangements. Tonight at eleven I slip out; Sor Asdrubale and his sisters will be sound asleep. I have questioned them; their fear of rheumatism prevents their attending midnight mass. Luckily there are no churches between this and the Corte; whatever movement Christmas night may entail will be a good way off. The Vice-Prefect's rooms are on the other side of the palace; the rest of the square is taken up with state-rooms, archives, and empty stables and coach-houses of the palace. Besides, I shall be quick at my work.

I have tried my saw on a stout bronze vase I bought of Sor Asdrubale; and the bronze of the statue, hollow and worn away by rust (I have even noticed holes), cannot resist very much, especially after a blow with the sharp hatchet. I have put my papers in order, for the benefit of the Government which has sent me hither. I am sorry to have defrauded them of their 'History of Urbania'. To pass the endless day and calm the fever of impatience, I have just taken a long walk. This is the coldest day we have had. The bright sun does not warm in the least, but seems only to increase the impression of cold, to make the snow on the mountains glitter, the blue air to sparkle like steel. The few people who are out are muffled to the nose, and carry earthenware braziers beneath their cloaks; long icicles hang from the fountain with the figure of Mercury upon it; one can imagine the wolves trooping down through the dry scrub and beleaguering this town. Somehow this cold makes me feel wonderfully calm – it seems to bring back to me my boyhood.

As I walked up the rough, steep, paved alleys, slippery with frost, and with their vista of snow mountains against the sky, and passed by the church steps strewn with box and laurel, with the faint smell of incense coming out, there returned to me – I know not why – the recollection, almost the sensation, of those Christmas Eves long ago at Posen and Breslau, when I walked as a child along the wide streets, peeping into the windows where they were beginning to light the tapers of the Christmas trees, and wondering whether I too, on returning home, should be let into a wonderful room all blazing with lights and gilded nuts and glass beads. They are hanging the last strings of those blue and red metallic beads, fastening on the last gilded and silvered walnuts on the trees out there at home in the North; they are lighting the blue and red tapers; the wax is beginning to run on to the beautiful spruce green branches; the children are waiting with beating hearts behind the door, to be told that the Christ-Child has been. And I, for what am I waiting? I don't know; all seems a dream; everything vague and unsubstantial about me, as if time had ceased, nothing could happen, my own desires and hopes were all dead, myself absorbed into I know not what passive dreamland. Do I long for tonight? Do I dread it? Will tonight ever come? Do I feel anything, does anything exist all round me?

I sit and seem to see that street at Posen, the wide street with the windows illuminated by the Christmas lights, the green fir-branches grazing the windowpanes.

* * *

Christmas Eve, Midnight.—

I have done it. I slipped out noiselessly. Sor Asdrubale and his sisters were fast asleep. I feared I had waked them, for my hatchet fell as I was passing through the principal room where my landlord keeps his curiosities for sale; it struck against some old armour which he has been piecing. I heard him exclaim, half in his sleep; and blew out my light and hid in the stairs. He came out in his dressing gown, but finding no one, went back to bed again. "Some cat, no doubt!" he said. I closed the house door softly behind me. The sky had become stormy since the afternoon, luminous with the full moon, but strewn with grey and buff-coloured vapours; every now and then the moon disappeared entirely. Not a creature abroad; the tall gaunt houses staring in the moonlight.

I know not why, I took a roundabout way to the Corte, past one or two church doors, whence issued the faint flicker of midnight mass. For a moment I felt a temptation to enter one of them; but something seemed to restrain me. I caught snatches of the Christmas hymn. I felt myself beginning to be unnerved, and hastened towards the Corte. As I passed under the portico at San Francesco I heard steps behind me; it seemed to me that I was followed. I stopped to let the other pass. As he approached his pace flagged; he passed close by me and murmured, "Do not go: I am Giovanfrancesco Pico." I turned round; he was gone. A coldness numbed me; but I hastened on.

Behind the cathedral apse, in a narrow lane, I saw a man leaning against a wall. The moonlight was full upon him; it seemed to me that his face, with a thin pointed beard, was streaming with blood. I quickened my pace; but as I grazed by him he whispered, "Do not obey her; return home: I am Marcantonio Frangipani." My teeth chattered, but I hurried along the narrow lane, with the moonlight blue upon the white walls. At last I saw the Corte before me: the square was flooded with moonlight, the windows of the palace seemed brightly illuminated, and the statue of Duke Robert, shimmering green, seemed advancing towards me on its horse. I came into the shadow. I had to pass beneath an archway. There started a figure as if out of the wall, and barred my passage with his outstretched cloaked arm. I tried to pass. He seized me by the arm, and his grasp was like a weight of ice. "You shall not pass!" he cried, and, as the moon came out once more, I saw his face, ghastly white and bound with an embroidered kerchief; he seemed almost a child. "You shall not pass!" he cried; "you shall not have her! She is mine, and mine alone! I am Prinzivalle degli Ordelaffi." I felt his ice-cold clutch, but with my other arm I laid about me wildly with the hatchet which I carried beneath my cloak. The hatchet struck the wall and rang upon the stone. He had vanished.

I hurried on. I did it. I cut open the bronze; I sawed it into a wider gash. I tore out the silver image, and hacked it into innumerable pieces. As I scattered the last fragments about, the moon was suddenly veiled; a great wind arose, howling down the square; it seemed to me that the earth shook. I threw down the hatchet and the saw, and fled home. I felt pursued, as if by the tramp of hundreds of invisible horsemen.

Now I am calm. It is midnight; another moment and she will be here! Patience, my heart! I hear it beating loud. I trust that no one will accuse poor Sor Asdrubale. I will write a letter to the authorities to declare his innocence should anything happen.... One! the clock in the palace tower has just struck... 'I hereby certify that, should anything happen this night to me, Spiridion Trepka, no one but myself is to be held...' A step on the staircase! It is she! It is she! At last, Medea, Medea! Ah! AMOUR DURE – DURE AMOUR!

* * *

NOTE. – Here ends the diary of the late Spiridion Trepka. The chief newspapers of the province of Umbria informed the public that, on Christmas morning of the year 1885, the bronze equestrian statue of Robert II had been found grievously mutilated; and that Professor Spiridion Trepka of Posen, in the German Empire, had been discovered dead of a stab in the region of the heart, given by an unknown hand.

The Beast in the Cave

H.P. Lovecraft

THE HORRIBLE CONCLUSION which had been gradually intruding itself upon my confused and reluctant mind was now an awful certainty. I was lost, completely, hopelessly lost in the vast and labyrinthine recess of the Mammoth Cave. Turn as I might, in no direction could my straining vision seize on any object capable of serving as a guidepost to set me on the outward path. That nevermore should I behold the blessed light of day, or scan the pleasant hills and dales of the beautiful world outside, my reason could no longer entertain the slightest unbelief. Hope had departed. Yet, indoctrinated as I was by a life of philosophical study, I derived no small measure of satisfaction from my unimpassioned demeanour; for although I had frequently read of the wild frenzies into which were thrown the victims of similar situations, I experienced none of these, but stood quiet as soon as I clearly realised the loss of my bearings.

Nor did the thought that I had probably wandered beyond the utmost limits of an ordinary search cause me to abandon my composure even for a moment. If I must die, I reflected, then was this terrible yet majestic cavern as welcome a sepulchre as that which any churchyard might afford, a conception which carried with it more of tranquillity than of despair.

Starving would prove my ultimate fate; of this I was certain. Some, I knew, had gone mad under circumstances such as these, but I felt that this end would not be mine. My disaster was the result of no fault save my own, since unknown to the guide I had separated myself from the regular party of sightseers; and, wandering for over an hour in forbidden avenues of the cave, had found myself unable to retrace the devious windings which I had pursued since forsaking my companions.

Already my torch had begun to expire; soon I would be enveloped by the total and almost palpable blackness of the bowels of the earth. As I stood in the waning, unsteady light, I idly wondered over the exact circumstances of my coming end. I remembered the accounts which I had heard of the colony of consumptives, who, taking their residence in this gigantic grotto to find health from the apparently salubrious air of the underground world, with its steady, uniform temperature, pure air, and peaceful quiet, had found, instead, death in strange and ghastly form. I had seen the sad remains of their ill-made cottages as I passed them by with the party, and had wondered what unnatural influence a long sojourn in this immense and silent cavern would exert upon one as healthy and vigorous as I. Now, I grimly told myself, my opportunity for settling this point had arrived, provided that want of food should not bring me too speedy a departure from this life.

As the last fitful rays of my torch faded into obscurity, I resolved to leave no stone unturned, no possible means of escape neglected; so, summoning all the powers possessed by my lungs, I set up a series of loud shoutings, in the vain hope of attracting the attention of the guide by my clamour. Yet, as I called, I believed in my heart that my cries were to no purpose, and that my voice, magnified and reflected by the numberless ramparts of the black maze about me, fell upon no ears save my own.

All at once, however, my attention was fixed with a start as I fancied that I heard the sound of soft approaching steps on the rocky floor of the cavern.

Was my deliverance about to be accomplished so soon? Had, then, all my horrible apprehensions been for naught, and was the guide, having marked my unwarranted absence from the party, following my course and seeking me out in this limestone labyrinth? Whilst these joyful queries arose in my brain, I was on the point of renewing my cries, in order that my discovery might come the sooner, when in an instant my delight was turned to horror as I listened; for my ever acute ear, now sharpened in even greater degree by the complete silence of the cave, bore to my benumbed understanding the unexpected and dreadful knowledge that these footfalls were not like those of any mortal man. In the unearthly stillness of this subterranean region, the tread of the booted guide would have sounded like a series of sharp and incisive blows. These impacts were soft, and stealthy, as of the paws of some feline. Besides, when I listened carefully, I seemed to trace the falls of four instead of two feet.

I was now convinced that I had by my own cries aroused and attracted some wild beast, perhaps a mountain lion which had accidentally strayed within the cave. Perhaps, I considered, the Almighty had chosen for me a swifter and more merciful death than that of hunger; yet the instinct of self-preservation, never wholly dormant, was stirred in my breast, and though escape from the oncoming peril might but spare me for a sterner and more lingering end, I determined nevertheless to part with my life at as high a price as I could command. Strange as it may seem, my mind conceived of no intent on the part of the visitor save that of hostility. Accordingly, I became very quiet, in the hope that the unknown beast would, in the absence of a guiding sound, lose its direction as had I, and thus pass me by. But this hope was not destined for realisation, for the strange footfalls steadily advanced, the animal evidently having obtained my scent, which in an atmosphere so absolutely free from all distracting influences as is that of the cave, could doubtless be followed at great distance.

Seeing therefore that I must be armed for defense against an uncanny and unseen attack in the dark, I groped about me the largest of the fragments of rock which were strewn upon all parts of the floor of the cavern in the vicinity, and grasping one in each hand for immediate use, awaited with resignation the inevitable result. Meanwhile the hideous pattering of the paws drew near. Certainly, the conduct of the creature was exceedingly strange. Most of the time, the tread seemed to be that of a quadruped, walking with a singular lack of unison betwixt hind and fore feet, yet at brief and infrequent intervals I fancied that but two feet were engaged in the process of locomotion. I wondered what species of animal was to confront me; it must, I thought, be some unfortunate beast who had paid for its curiosity to investigate one of the entrances of the fearful grotto with a life-long confinement in its interminable recesses. It doubtless obtained as food the eyeless fish, bats and rats of the cave, as well as some of the ordinary fish that are wafted in at every freshet of Green River, which communicates in some occult manner with the waters of the cave. I occupied my terrible vigil with grotesque conjectures of what alteration cave life might have wrought in the physical structure of the beast, remembering the awful appearances ascribed by local tradition to the consumptives who had died after long residence in the cave. Then I remembered with a start that, even should I succeed in felling my antagonist, I should never behold its form, as my torch had long since been extinct, and I was entirely unprovided with matches. The tension on my brain now became frightful. My disordered fancy conjured up hideous and fearsome shapes from the sinister darkness that surrounded me, and that actually seemed to press upon my body. Nearer, nearer, the dreadful footfalls approached. It seemed that I must give vent to a piercing scream, yet had I been sufficiently irresolute to attempt such a thing, my voice could scarce have responded. I was petrified, rooted to the spot. I doubted if my right arm would allow me to hurl its missile at the oncoming thing when the crucial moment should arrive. Now the steady *pat, pat,* of the steps was close at hand; now very close. I could hear the laboured breathing of the animal, and terror-struck as I was, I realised that it must have come from a considerable distance, and was correspondingly fatigued. Suddenly the spell broke. My right hand, guided by my ever trustworthy sense of hearing, threw with full force the sharp-angled bit of limestone which it contained, toward that point in the darkness from which emanated the breathing and pattering, and, wonderful to relate, it nearly reached its goal, for I heard the thing jump, landing at a distance away, where it seemed to pause.

Having readjusted my aim, I discharged my second missile, this time most effectively, for with a flood of joy I listened as the creature fell in what sounded like a complete collapse and evidently remained prone and unmoving. Almost overpowered by the great relief which rushed over me, I reeled back against the wall. The breathing continued, in heavy, gasping inhalations and expirations, whence I realised that I had no more than wounded the creature. And now all desire to examine the thing ceased. At last something allied to groundless, superstitious fear had entered my brain, and I did not approach the body, nor did I continue to cast stones at it in order to complete the extinction of its life. Instead, I ran at full speed in what was, as nearly as I could estimate in my frenzied condition, the direction from which I had come. Suddenly I heard a sound or rather, a regular succession of sounds. In another instant they had resolved themselves into a series of sharp, metallic clicks. This time there was no doubt. It was the guide. And then I shouted, yelled, screamed, even shrieked with joy as I beheld in the vaulted arches above the faint and glimmering effulgence which I knew to be the reflected light of an approaching torch. I ran to meet the flare, and before I could completely understand what had occurred, was lying upon the ground at the feet of the guide, embracing his boots and gibbering, despite my boasted reserve, in a most meaningless and idiotic manner, pouring out my terrible story, and at the same time overwhelming my auditor with protestations of gratitude. At length, I awoke to something like my normal consciousness. The guide had noted my absence upon the arrival of the party at the entrance of the cave, and had, from his own intuitive sense of direction, proceeded to make a thorough canvass of by-passages just ahead of where he had last spoken to me, locating my whereabouts after a quest of about four hours.

By the time he had related this to me, I, emboldened by his torch and his company, began to reflect upon the strange beast which I had wounded but a short distance back in the darkness, and suggested that we ascertain, by the flashlight's aid, what manner of creature was my victim. Accordingly I retraced my steps, this time with a courage born of companionship, to the scene of my terrible experience. Soon we descried a white object upon the floor, an object whiter even than the gleaming limestone itself. Cautiously advancing, we gave vent to a simultaneous ejaculation of wonderment, for of all the unnatural monsters either of us had in our lifetimes beheld, this was in surpassing degree the strangest. It appeared to be an anthropoid ape of large proportions, escaped, perhaps, from some itinerant menagerie. Its hair was snow-white, a thing due no doubt to the bleaching action of a long existence within the inky confines of the cave, but it was also surprisingly thin, being indeed largely absent save on the head, where it was of such length and abundance that it fell over the shoulders in considerable profusion. The face was turned away from us, as the creature lay almost directly upon it. The inclination of the limbs was very singular, explaining, however, the alternation in their use which I had before noted, whereby the beast used sometimes all four, and on other occasions but two for its progress. From the tips of the fingers or toes, long rat-like claws extended. The hands or feet were not prehensile, a fact that I ascribed to that long residence in the cave which, as I before mentioned, seemed evident from the all-pervading and almost unearthly whiteness so characteristic of the whole anatomy. No tail seemed to be present.

The respiration had now grown very feeble, and the guide had drawn his pistol with the evident intent of despatching the creature, when a sudden sound emitted by the latter caused the weapon to fall unused. The sound was of a nature difficult to describe. It was not like the normal note of any known species of simian, and I wonder if this unnatural quality were not the result of a long continued and complete silence, broken by the sensations produced by the advent of the light, a thing which the beast could not have seen since its first entrance into the cave. The sound, which I might feebly attempt to classify as a kind of deep-tone chattering, was faintly continued.

All at once a fleeting spasm of energy seemed to pass through the frame of the beast. The paws went through a convulsive motion, and the limbs contracted. With a jerk, the white body rolled over so that its face was turned in our direction. For a moment I was so struck with horror at the eyes thus revealed that I noted nothing else. They were black, those eyes, deep jetty black, in hideous contrast to the snow-white hair and flesh. Like those of other cave denizens, they were deeply sunken in their orbits, and were entirely destitute of iris. As I looked more closely, I saw that they were set in a face less prognathous than that of the average ape, and infinitely less hairy. The nose was quite distinct. As we gazed upon the uncanny sight presented to our vision, the thick lips opened, and several sounds issued from them, after which the thing relaxed in death.

The guide clutched my coat sleeve and trembled so violently that the light shook fitfully, casting weird moving shadows on the walls.

I made no motion, but stood rigidly still, my horrified eyes fixed upon the floor ahead.

The fear left, and wonder, awe, compassion, and reverence succeeded in its place, for the sounds uttered by the stricken figure that lay stretched out on the limestone had told us the awesome truth. The creature I had killed, the strange beast of the unfathomed cave, was, or had at one time been a MAN!

The White Wolf of the Hartz Mountains

Frederick Marryat

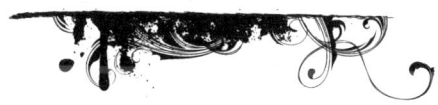

SCARCELY had the soldiers performed their task, and thrown down their shovels, when they commenced an altercation. It appeared that this money was to be again the cause of slaughter and bloodshed. Philip and Krantz determined to sail immediately in one of the peroquas, and leave them to settle their disputes as they pleased. He asked permission of the soldiers to take from the provisions and water, of which there was ample supply, a larger proportion than was their share; stating, that he and Krantz had a long voyage and would require it, and pointing out to them that there were plenty of cocoa-nuts for their support. The soldiers, who thought of nothing but their newly acquired wealth, allowed him to do as he pleased; and, having hastily collected as many cocoa-nuts as they could, to add to their stock of provisions, before noon, Philip and Krantz had embarked and made sail in the peroqua, leaving the soldiers with their knives again drawn, and so busy in their angry altercation as to be heedless of their departure.

"There will be the same scene over again, I expect," observed Krantz, as the vessel parted swiftly from the shore.

"I have little doubt of it; observe, even now they are at blows and stabs."

"If I were to name that spot, it should be the 'Accursed Isle'."

"Would not any other be the same, with so much to inflame the passions of men?"

"Assuredly: what a curse is gold!"

"And what a blessing!" replied Krantz. "I am sorry Pedro is left with them."

"It is their destiny," replied Philip; "so let's think no more of them. Now what do you propose? With this vessel, small as she is, we may sail over these seas in safety, and we have, I imagine, provisions sufficient for more than a month."

"My idea is, to run into the track of the vessels going to the westward, and obtain a passage to Goa."

"And if we do not meet with any, we can, at all events, proceed up the Straits, as far as Pulo Penang without risk. There we may safely remain until a vessel passes."

"I agree with you; it is our best, nay our only, place; unless, indeed, we were to proceed to Cochin, where junks are always leaving for Goa."

"But that would be out of our way, and the junks cannot well pass us in the Straits, without their being seen by us."

They had no difficulty in steering their course; the islands by day, and the clear stars by night, were their compass. It is true that they did not follow the more direct track, but they followed the more secure, working up the smooth waters, and gaining to the northward more than to the west. Many times they were chased by the Malay proas which infested the islands, but the swiftness of their little peroqua was their security; indeed, the chase was, generally speaking, abandoned as soon as the smallness of the vessel was made out by the pirates, who expected that little or no booty was to be gained.

That Amine and Philip's mission was the constant theme of their discourse, may easily be imagined. One morning, as they were sailing between the isles, with less wind than usual, Philip observed:

"Krantz, you said that there were events in your own life, or connected with it, which would corroborate the mysterious tale I confided to you. Will you now tell me to what you referred?"

"Certainly," replied Krantz; "I've often thought of doing so, but one circumstance or another has hitherto prevented me; this is, however, a fitting opportunity. Prepare, therefore, to listen to a strange story, quite as strange, perhaps, as your own—"

"I take it for granted, that you have heard people speak of the Hartz Mountains," observed Krantz.

"I have never heard people speak of them, that I can recollect," replied Philip; "but I have read of them in some book, and of the strange things which have occurred there."

"It is indeed a wild region," rejoined Krantz, "and many strange tales are told of it; but strange as they are, I have good reason for believing them to be true. I have told you, Philip, that I fully believe in your communion with the other world – that I credit the history of your father, and the lawfulness of your mission; for that we are surrounded, impelled, and worked upon by beings different in their nature from ourselves, I have had full evidence, as you will acknowledge, when I state what has occurred in my own family. Why such malevolent beings as I am about to speak of, should be permitted to interfere with us, and punish, I may say, comparatively unoffending mortals, is beyond my comprehension; but that they are so permitted is most certain."

"The great principle of all evil fulfils his work of evil; why, then, not the other minor spirits of the same class?" inquired Philip. "What matters it to us, whether we are tried by, and have to suffer from, the enmity of our fellow mortals, or whether we are persecuted by beings more powerful and more malevolent than ourselves? We know that we have to work out our salvation, and that we shall be judged according to our strength; if then there be evil spirits who delight to oppress man, there surely must be, as Amine asserts, good spirits, whose delight is to do him service. Whether, then, we have to struggle against our passions only, or whether we have to struggle not only against our passions, but also the dire influence of unseen enemies, we ever struggle with the same odds in our favour, as the good are stronger than the evil which we combat. In either case we are on the vantage ground, whether, as in the first, we fight the good cause single-handed, or as in the second, although opposed, we have the host of Heaven ranged on our side. Thus are the scales of Divine justice evenly balanced, and man is still a free agent, as his own virtuous or vicious propensities must ever decide whether he shall gain or lose the victory."

"Most true," replied Krantz, "and now to my history:"

* * *

"My father was not born, or originally a resident, in the Hartz Mountains; he was the serf of a Hungarian nobleman, of great possessions, in Transylvania; but, although a serf, he was not by any means a poor or illiterate man. In fact, he was rich and his intelligence and respectability were such, that he had been raised by his lord to the stewardship; but, whoever may happen to be born a serf, a serf must he remain, even though he become a wealthy man: and such was the condition of my father. My father had been married for about five years; and by his marriage had three children – my eldest brother Caesar, myself (Hermann), and a sister named Marcella. You know, Philip, that Latin is still the language spoken in that country; and that will account for our high-sounding names. My mother was a very beautiful woman unfortunately more beautiful than virtuous: she was seen and admired by the lord of the soil; my father was sent away upon some mission; and, during his absence, my mother, flattered by the attentions, and won by the assiduities, of this nobleman, yielded to his wishes. It so happened that my father returned very unexpectedly, and discovered the intrigue. The evidence of my mother's shame was positive; he surprised her in the company of her seducer! Carried away by the impetuosity of his feelings, he watched the opportunity of a meeting taking place between them, and murdered both his wife and her seducer. Conscious that, as a serf, not even the provocation which he had received would be allowed as a justification of his conduct, he hastily collected together what money he could lay his hands upon, and, as we were then in the depth of winter, he put his horses to the sleigh, and taking his children with him, he set off in the middle of the night, and was far away before the tragical circumstance had transpired. Aware that he would be pursued, and that he had no chance of escape if he remained in any portion of his native country (in which the authorities could lay hold of him), he continued his flight without intermission until he had buried himself in the intricacies and seclusion of the Hartz Mountains. Of course, all that I have now told you I learned afterwards. My oldest recollections are knit to a rude, yet comfortable cottage, in which I lived with my father, brother, and sister. It was on the confines of one of those vast forests which cover the northern part of Germany; around it were a few acres of ground, which, during the summer months, my father cultivated, and which, though they yielded a doubtful harvest, were sufficient for our support. In the winter we remained much indoors, for, as my father followed the chase, we were left alone, and the wolves, during that season, incessantly prowled about. My father had purchased the cottage, and land about it, of one of the rude foresters, who gain their livelihood partly by hunting, and partly by burning charcoal, for the purpose of smelting the ore from the neighbouring mines; it was distant about two miles from any other habitation. I can call to mind the whole landscape now: the tall pines which rose up on the mountain above us, and the wide expanse of forest beneath, on the topmost boughs and heads of whose trees we looked down from our cottage, as the mountain below us rapidly descended into the distant valley. In summer-time the prospect was beautiful: but during the severe winter, a more desolate scene could not well be imagined.

"I said that, in the winter, my father occupied himself with the chase; every day he left us, and often would he lock the door, that we might not leave the cottage. He had no one to assist him, or to take care of us – indeed, it was not easy to find a female servant who would live in such a solitude; but could he have found one, my father would not have received her, for he had imbibed a horror of the sex, as the difference of his conduct towards us, his two boys, and my poor little sister, Marcella evidently proved. You may suppose we were sadly neglected; indeed, we suffered much, for my father, fearful that we might come to some harm, would not allow us fuel, when he left the cottage; and we were obliged, therefore, to creep under the heaps of bears' skins, and there to keep ourselves as warm as we could until he returned in the evening, when a blazing fire was our delight. That my father chose this restless sort of life may appear strange, but the fact was, that he could not remain quiet; whether from the remorse for having committed murder, or from the misery consequent on his change of situation, or from both combined, he was never happy unless he was in a state of activity. Children, however, when left much to themselves, acquire a thoughtfulness not common to their age. So it was with us; and during the short cold days of winter, we would sit silent, longing for the happy hours when the snow would melt and the leaves would burst out, and the birds begin their songs, and when we should again be set at liberty.

"Such was our peculiar and savage sort of life until my brother Caesar was nine, myself seven, and my sister five years old, when the circumstances occurred on which is based the extraordinary narrative which I am about to relate.

"One evening my father returned home rather later than usual; he had been unsuccessful, and, as the weather was very severe, and many feet of snow were upon the ground, he was not only very cold, but in a very bad humour. He had brought in wood, and we were all three gladly assisting each other in blowing on the embers to create the blaze, when he caught poor little Marcella by the arm and threw her aside; the child fell, struck her mouth, and bled very much. My brother ran to raise her up. Accustomed to ill-usage and afraid of my father, she did not dare to cry, but looked up in his face very piteously. My father drew his stool nearer to the hearth, muttered something in abuse of women, and busied himself with the fire, which both my brother and I had deserted when our sister was so unkindly treated. A cheerful blaze was soon the result of his exertions; but we did not, as usual, crowd round it. Marcella, still bleeding, retired to a corner, and my brother and I took our seats beside her, while my father hung over the fire gloomily and alone. Such had been our position for about half an hour, when the howl of a wolf, close under the window of the cottage, fell on our ears. My father started up, and seized his gun: the howl was repeated, he examined the priming, and then hastily left the cottage, shutting the door after him. We all waited (anxiously listening), for we thought that if he succeeded in shooting the wolf, he would return in a better humour; and, although he was harsh to all of us, and particularly so to our little sister, still we loved our father, and loved to see him cheerful and happy, for what else had we to look up to? And I may here observe, that perhaps there never were three children who were fonder of each other; we did not, like other children, fight and dispute together; and if, by chance, any disagreement did arise between my elder brother and me, little Marcella would run to us, and kissing us both, seal, through her entreaties, the peace between us. Marcella was a lovely, amiable child; I can recall her beautiful features even now – Alas! Poor little Marcella."

"She is dead, then?" observed Philip.

"Dead! Yes, dead! – but how did she die? – But I must not anticipate, Philip; let me tell my story.

"We waited for some time, but the report of the gun did not reach us, and my elder brother then said, 'Our father has followed the wolf, and will not be back for some time. Marcella, let us wash the blood from your mouth, and then we will leave this corner, and go to the fire and warm ourselves.'

"We did so, and remained there until near midnight, every minute wondering, as it grew later, why our father did not return. We had no idea that he was in any danger, but we thought that he must have chased the wolf for a very long time. 'I will look out and see if father is coming,' said my brother Caesar, going to the door. 'Take care,' said Marcella, 'the wolves must be about now, and we cannot kill them, brother.' My brother opened the door very cautiously, and but a few inches: he peeped out. – 'I see nothing,' said he, after a time, and once more he joined us at the fire. 'We have had no supper,' said I, for my father usually cooked the meat as soon as he came home; and during his absence we had nothing but the fragments of the preceding day.

"'And if our father comes home after his hunt, Caesar,' said Marcella, 'he will be pleased to have some supper; let us cook it for him and for ourselves.' Caesar climbed upon the stool, and reached down some meat – I forget now whether it was venison or bear's meat; but we cut off the usual quantity, and proceeded to dress it, as we used to do under our father's superintendence. We were all busy putting it into the platters before the fire, to await his coming, when we heard the sound of a horn. We listened – there was a noise outside, and a minute afterwards my father entered, ushering in a young female, and a large dark man in a hunter's dress,

"Perhaps I had better now relate what was only known to me many years afterwards. When my father had left the cottage, he perceived a large white wolf about thirty yards from him; as soon as the animal saw my father, it retreated slowly, growling and snarling. My father followed; the animal did not run, but always kept at some distance; and my father did not like to fire until he was pretty certain that his ball would take effect; thus they went on for some time, the wolf now leaving my father far behind, and then stopping and snarling defiance at him, and then, again, on his approach, setting off at speed.

"Anxious to shoot the animal (for the white wolf is very rare) my father continued the pursuit for several hours, during which he continually ascended the mountain.

"You must know, Philip, that there are peculiar spots on those mountains which are supposed, and, as my story will prove, truly supposed, to be inhabited by the evil influences: they are well known to the huntsmen, who invariably avoid them. Now, one of these spots, an open space in the pine forests above us, had been pointed out to my father as dangerous on that account. But, whether he disbelieved these wild stories, or whether, in his eager pursuit of the chase, he disregarded them, I know not; certain, however, it is, that he was decoyed by the white wolf to this open space, when the animal appeared to slacken her speed. My father approached, came close up to her, raised his gun to his shoulder, and was about to fire, when the wolf suddenly disappeared. He thought that the snow on the ground must have dazzled his sight, and he let down his gun to look for the beast – but she was gone; how she could have escaped over the clearance, without his seeing her, was beyond his comprehension. Mortified at the ill success of his chase, he was about to retrace his steps, when he heard the distant sound of a horn. Astonishment at such a sound – at such an hour – in such a wilderness, made him forget for the moment his disappointment, and he remained riveted to the spot. In a minute the horn was blown a second time, and at no great distance; my father stood still, and listened: a third time it was blown. I forget the term used to express it, but it was the signal which, my father well knew, implied that the party was lost in the woods. In a few minutes more my father beheld a man on horseback, with a female seated on the crupper, enter the cleared space, and ride up to him. At first, my father called to mind the strange stories which he had heard of the supernatural beings who were said to frequent these mountains; but the nearer approach of the parties satisfied him that they were mortals like himself. As soon as they came up to him, the man who guided the horse accosted him. 'Friend Hunter, you are out late, the better fortune for us; we have ridden far, and are in fear of our lives which are eagerly sought after. These mountains have enabled us to elude our pursuers; but if we find not shelter and refreshment, that will avail us little, as we must perish from hunger and the inclemency of the night. My daughter, who rides behind me, is now more dead than alive – say, can you assist us in our difficulty?'

"'My cottage is some few miles distant,' replied my father, 'but I have little to offer you besides a shelter from the weather; to the little I have you are welcome. May I ask whence you come?'

"'Yes, friend, it is no secret now; we have escaped from Transylvania, where my daughter's honour and my life were equally in jeopardy!'

"This information was quite enough to raise an interest in my father's heart, he remembered his own escape; he remembered the loss of his wife's honour, and the tragedy by which it was wound up. He immediately, and warmly, offered all the assistance which he could afford them.

"'There is no time to be lost then, good sir,' observed the horseman; 'my daughter is chilled with the frost, and cannot hold out much longer against the severity of the weather.'

"'Follow me,' replied my father, leading the way towards his home.

"'I was lured away in pursuit of a large white wolf,' observed my father; 'it came to the very window of my hut, or I should not have been out at this time of night.'

"'The creature passed by us just as we came out of the wood,' said the female, in a silvery tone.

"'I was nearly discharging my piece at it,' observed the hunter; 'but since it did us such good service, I am glad I allowed it to escape.'

"In about an hour and a half, during which my father walked at a rapid pace, the party arrived at the cottage, and, as I said before, came in.

"'We are in good time, apparently,' observed the dark hunter, catching the smell of the roasted meat, as he walked to the fire and surveyed my brother and sister, and myself. 'You have young cooks here, Meinheer.' 'I am glad that we shall not have to wait,' replied my father. 'Come, mistress, seat yourself by the fire; you require warmth after your cold ride.' 'And where can I put up my horse, Meinheer?' observed the huntsman. 'I will take care of him,' replied my father, going out of the cottage door.

"The female must, however, be particularly described. She was young, and apparently twenty years of age. She was dressed in a travelling dress, deeply bordered with white fur, and wore a cap of white ermine on her head. Her features were very beautiful, at least I thought so, and so my father has since declared. Her hair was flaxen, glossy, and shining, and bright as a mirror; and her mouth, although somewhat large when it was open, showed the most brilliant teeth I have ever beheld. But there was something about her eyes, bright as they were, which made us children afraid; they were so restless, so furtive; I could not at that time tell why, but I felt as if there was cruelty in her eye; and when she beckoned us to come to her, we approached her with fear and trembling. Still she was beautiful, very beautiful. She spoke kindly to my brother and myself, patted our heads and caressed us; but Marcella would not come near her; on the contrary, she slunk away, and hid herself in the bed, and would not wait for the supper, which half an hour before she had been so anxious for.

"My father, having put the horse into a close shed, soon returned, and supper was placed upon the table. When it was over, my father requested that the young lady would take possession of his bed, and he would remain at the fire, and sit up with her father. After some hesitation on her part, this arrangement was agreed to, and I and my brother crept into the other bed with Marcella, for we had as yet always slept together.

"But we could not sleep; there was something so unusual, not only in seeing strange people, but in having those people sleep at the cottage, that we were bewildered. As for poor little Marcella, she was quiet, but I perceived that she trembled during the whole night, and sometimes I thought that she was checking a sob. My father had brought out some spirits, which he rarely used, and he and the strange hunter remained drinking and talking before the fire. Our ears were ready to catch the slightest whisper – so much was our curiosity excited.

"'You said you came from Transylvania?' observed my father.

"'Even so, Meinheer,' replied the hunter. 'I was a serf to the noble house of ——; my master would insist upon my surrendering up my fair girl to his wishes: it ended in my giving him a few inches of my hunting-knife.'

"'We are countrymen, and brothers in misfortune,' replied my father, taking the huntsman's hand, and pressing it warmly.

"'Indeed! Are you then from that country?'

"'Yes; and I too have fled for my life. But mine is a melancholy tale.'

"'Your name?' inquired the hunter.

"'Krantz.'

"'What! Krantz of ——? I have heard your tale; you need not renew your grief by repeating it now. Welcome, most welcome, Meinheer, and, I may say, my worthy kinsman. I am your second cousin, Wilfred of Barnsdorf,' cried the hunter, rising up and embracing my father.

"They filled their horn-mugs to the brim, and drank to one another after the German fashion. The conversation was then carried on in a low tone; all that we could collect from it was that our new relative and his daughter were to take up their abode in our cottage, at least for the present. In about an hour they both fell back in their chairs and appeared to sleep.

"'Marcella, dear, did you hear?' said my brother, in a low tone.

"'Yes,' replied Marcella in a whisper, 'I heard all. Oh! brother, I cannot bear to look upon that woman – I feel so frightened.'

"My brother made no reply, and shortly afterwards we were all three fast asleep.

"When we awoke the next morning, we found that the hunter's daughter had risen before us. I thought she looked more beautiful than ever. She came up to little Marcella and caressed her: the child burst into tears, and sobbed as if her heart would break.

"But, not to detain you with too long a story, the huntsman and his daughter were accommodated in the cottage. My father and he went out hunting daily, leaving Christina with us. She performed all the household duties; was very kind to us children; and, gradually, the dislike even of little Marcella wore away. But a great change took place in my father; he appeared to have conquered his aversion to the sex, and was most attentive to Christina. Often, after her father and we were in bed would he sit up with her, conversing in a low tone by the fire. I ought to have mentioned that my father and the huntsman Wilfred slept in another portion of the cottage, and that the bed which he formerly occupied, and which was in the same room as ours, had been given up to the use of Christina. These visitors had been about three weeks at the cottage, when, one night, after we children had been sent to bed, a consultation was held. My father had asked Christina in marriage, and had obtained both her own consent and that of Wilfred; after this, a conversation took place, which was, as nearly as I can recollect, as follows.

"'You may take my child, Meinheer Krantz, and my blessing with her, and I shall then leave you and seek some other habitation – it matters little where.'

"'Why not remain here, Wilfred?'

"'No, no, I am called elsewhere; let that suffice, and ask no more questions. You have my child.'

"'I thank you for her, and will duly value her; but there is one difficulty.'

"'I know what you would say; there is no priest here in this wild country: true; neither is there any law to bind; still must some ceremony pass between you, to satisfy a father. Will you consent to marry her after my fashion? If so, I will marry you directly.'

"'I will,' replied my father.

"'Then take her by the hand. Now, Meinheer, swear.'

"'I swear,' repeated my father.

"'By all the spirits of the Hartz mountains—'

"'Nay, why not by Heaven?' interrupted my father.

"'Because it is not my humour,' rejoined Wilfred; 'if I prefer that oath, less binding perhaps, than another, surely you will not thwart me.'

"'Well be it so then; have your humour. Will you make me swear by that in which I do not believe?'

"'Yet many do so, who in outward appearance are Christians,' rejoined Wilfred; 'say, will you be married, or shall I take my daughter away with me?'

"'Proceed,' replied my father, impatiently.

"'I swear by all the spirits of the Hartz mountains, by all their power for good or for evil, that I take Christina for my wedded wife; that I will ever protect her, cherish her, and love her; that my hand shall never be raised against her to harm her.'

"My father repeated the words after Wilfred.

"'And if I fail in this my vow, may all the vengeance of the spirits fall upon me and upon my children; may they perish by the vulture, by the wolf, or other beasts of the forest; may their flesh be torn from their limbs, and their bones blanch in the wilderness: all this I swear.'

"My father hesitated, as he repeated the last words; little Marcella could not restrain herself, and as my father repeated the last sentence, she burst into tears. This sudden interruption appeared to discompose the party, particularly my father; he spoke harshly to the child, who controlled her sobs, burying her face under the bedclothes.

"Such was the second marriage of my father. The next morning, the hunter Wilfred mounted his horse, and rode away.

"My father resumed his bed, which was in the same room as ours; and things went on much as before the marriage, except that our new mother-in-law did not show any kindness towards us; indeed during my father's absence, she would often beat us, particularly little Marcella, and her eyes would flash fire, as she looked eagerly upon the fair and lovely child.

"One night, my sister awoke me and my brother.

"'What is the matter?' said Caesar.

"'She has gone out,' whispered Marcella.

"'Gone out!'

"'Yes, gone out at the door, in her nightclothes,' replied the child; 'I saw her get out of bed, look at my father to see if he slept, and then she went out at the door.'

"What could induce her to leave her bed, and all undressed to go out, in such bitter wintry weather, with the snow deep on the ground was to us incomprehensible; we lay awake, and in about an hour we heard the growl of a wolf, close under the window.

"'There is a wolf,' said Caesar. 'She will be torn to pieces.'

"'Oh no!' cried Marcella.

"In a few minutes afterwards our mother-in-law appeared; she was in her nightdress, as Marcella had stated. She let down the latch of the door, so as to make no noise, went to a pail of water, and washed her face and hands, and then slipped into the bed where my father lay.

"We all three trembled – we hardly knew why; but we resolved to watch the next night: we did so; and not only on the ensuing night, but on many others, and always at about the same hour, would our mother-in-law rise from her bed and leave the cottage; and after she was gone we invariably heard the growl of a wolf under our window, and always saw her, on her return, wash herself before she retired to bed. We observed also that she seldom sat down to meals, and that when she did she appeared to eat with dislike; but when the meat was taken down to be prepared for dinner, she would often furtively put a raw piece into her mouth.

"My brother Caesar was a courageous boy; he did not like to speak to my father until he knew more. He resolved that he would follow her out, and ascertain what she did. Marcella and I endeavoured to dissuade him from this project; but he would not be controlled; and the very next night he lay down in his clothes, and as soon as our mother-in-law had left the cottage he jumped up, took down my father's gun, and followed her.

"You may imagine in what a state of suspense Marcella and I remained during his absence. After a few minutes we heard the report of a gun. It did not awaken my father; and we lay trembling with anxiety. In a minute afterwards we saw our mother-in-law enter the cottage – her dress was bloody. I put my hand to Marcella's mouth to prevent her crying out, although I was myself in great alarm. Our mother-in-law approached my father's bed, looked to see if he was asleep, and then went to the chimney and blew up the embers into a blaze.

"'Who is there?' said my father, waking up

"'Lie still, dearest,' replied my mother-in-law; 'it is only me; I have lighted the fire to warm some water; I am not quite well.'

"My father turned round, and was soon asleep; but we watched our mother-in-law. She changed her linen, and threw the garments she had worn into the fire; and we then perceived that her right leg was bleeding profusely, as if from a gun-shot wound. She bandaged it up, and then dressing herself, remained before the fire until the break of day.

"Poor little Marcella, her heart beat quick as she pressed me to her side – so indeed did mine. Where was our brother Caesar? How did my mother-in-law receive the wound unless from his gun? At last my father rose, and then for the first time I spoke, saying, 'Father, where is my brother Caesar?'

"'Your brother!' exclaimed he; 'why, where can he be?'

"'Merciful Heaven! I thought, as lay very restless last night,' observed our mother-in-law, 'that I heard somebody open the latch of the door; and, dear me, husband, what has become of your gun?'

"My father cast his eyes up above the chimney, and perceived that his gun was missing. For a moment he looked perplexed; then, seizing a broad axe, he went out of the cottage without saying another word.

"He did not remain away from us long; in a few minutes he returned, bearing in his arms the mangled body of my poor brother; he laid it down, and covered up his face.

"My mother-in-law rose up, and looked at the body, while Marcella and I threw ourselves by its side, wailing and sobbing bitterly.

"'Go to bed again, children,' said she, sharply. 'Husband,' continued she, 'your boy must have taken the gun down, to shoot a wolf, and the animal has been too powerful for him. Poor boy! He has paid dearly for his rashness.'

"My father made no reply. I wished to speak – to tell all – but Marcella who perceived my intention, held me by the arm, and looked at me so imploringly, that I desisted.

"My father, therefore, was left in his error; but Marcella and I, although we could not comprehend it, were conscious that our mother-in-law was in some way connected with my brother's death.

"That day my father went out and dug a grave; and when he hid the body in the earth, he piled up stones over it so that the wolves should not be able to dig it up. The shock of this catastrophe was to my poor father very severe; for several days he never went to the chase, although at times he would utter bitter anathemas and vengeance against the wolves.

"But during this time of mourning on his part, my mother-in-law's nocturnal wanderings continued with the same regularity as before.

"At last my father took down his gun to repair to the forest; but he soon returned, and appeared much annoyed.

"'Would you believe it, Christina, that the wolves – perdition to the whole race – have actually contrived to dig up the body of my poor boy, and now there is nothing left of him but his bones?'

"'Indeed!' replied my mother-in-law. Marcella looked at me; and I saw in her intelligent eye all she would have uttered.

"'A wolf growls under our window every night, father,' said I.

"'Ay, indeed! Why did you not tell me, boy? Wake me the next time you hear it.'

"I saw my mother-in-law turn away; her eyes flashed fire, and she gnashed her teeth.

"My father went out again, and covered up with a larger pile of stones the little remnants of my poor brother which the wolves had spared. Such was the first act of the tragedy.

"The spring now came on; the snow disappeared, and we were permitted to leave the cottage; but never would I quit for one moment my dear little sister, to whom since the death of my brother, I was more ardently attached than ever; indeed, I was afraid to leave her alone with my mother-in-law, who appeared to have a particular pleasure in ill-treating the child. My father was now employed upon his little farm, and I was able to render him some assistance.

"Marcella used to sit by us while we were at work, leaving my mother-in-law alone in the cottage. I ought to observe that, as the spring advanced, so did my mother-in-law decrease her nocturnal rambles, and that we never heard the growl of the wolf under the window after I had spoken of it to my father.

"One day, when my father and I were in the field, Marcella being with us, my mother-in-law came out, saying that she was going into the forest to collect some herbs my father wanted, and that Marcella must go to the cottage and watch the dinner. Marcella went; and my mother-in-law soon disappeared in the forest, taking a direction quite contrary to that in which the cottage stood, and leaving my father and I, as it were, between her and Marcella.

"About an hour afterwards we were startled by shrieks from the cottage – evidently the shrieks of little Marcella. 'Marcella has burnt herself, father,' said I, throwing down my spade. My father threw down his, and we both hastened to the cottage. Before we could gain the door, out darted a large white wolf, which fled with the utmost celerity. My father had no weapon; he rushed into the cottage, and there saw poor little Marcella expiring. Her body was dreadfully mangled, and the blood pouring from it had formed a large pool on the cottage floor. My father's first intention had been to seize his gun and pursue; but he was checked by this horrid spectacle; he knelt down by his dying child, and burst into tears. Marcella could just look kindly on us for a few seconds, and then her eyes were closed in death.

"My father and I were still hanging over my poor sister's body, when my mother-in-law came in. At the dreadful sight she expressed much concern; but she did not appear to recoil from the sight of blood, as most women do.

"'Poor child!' said she, 'it must have been that great white wolf which passed me just now, and frightened me so. She's quite dead, Krantz.'

"'I know it – I know it!' cried my father, in agony.

"I thought my father would never recover from the effects of this second tragedy; he mourned bitterly over the body of his sweet child, and for several days would not consign it to its grave, although frequently requested by my mother-in-law to do so. At last he yielded, and dug a grave for her close by that of my poor brother, and took every precaution that the wolves should not violate her remains.

"I was now really miserable, as I lay alone in the bed which I had formerly shared with my brother and sister. I could not help thinking that my mother-in-law was implicated in both their deaths, although I could not account for the manner; but I no longer felt afraid of her; my little heart was full of hatred and revenge.

"The night after my sister had been buried, as I lay awake, I perceived my mother-in-law get up and go out of the cottage. I waited some time, then dressed myself, and looked out through the door, which I half opened. The moon shone bright and I could see the spot where my brother and my sister had been buried; and what was my horror when I perceived my mother-in-law busily removing the stones from Marcella's grave!

"She was in her white nightdress and the moon shone full upon her. She was digging with her hands, and throwing away the stones behind her with all the ferocity of a wild beast.

It was some time before I could collect my senses, and decide what I should do. At last I perceived that she had arrived at the body, and raised it up to the side of the grave. I could bear it no longer, I ran to my father and awoke him.

"'Father, father!' cried I, 'dress yourself, and get your gun.'

"'What!' cried my father, 'the wolves are there, are they?'

"He jumped out of bed, threw on his clothes, and, in his anxiety, did not appear to perceive the absence of his wife. As soon as he was ready I opened the door; he went out, and I followed him.

"Imagine his horror, when (unprepared as he was for such a sight) he beheld, as he advanced towards the grave not a wolf, but his wife, in her nightdress, on her hands and knees, crouching by the body of my sister, and tearing off large pieces of the flesh, and devouring them with all the avidity of a wolf. She was too busy to be aware of our approach. My father dropped his gun; his hair stood on end, so did mine; he breathed heavily, and then his breath for a time stopped. I picked up the gun and put it into his hand. Suddenly he appeared as if concentrated rage had restored him to double vigour; he levelled his piece, fired, and with a loud shriek down fell the wretch whom he had fostered in his bosom.

"'God of Heaven!' cried my father, sinking down upon the earth in a swoon, as soon as he had discharged his gun.

"I remained some time by his side before he recovered. 'Where am I?' said he, 'what has happened? Oh! – yes, yes! I recollect now. Heaven forgive me!'

"He rose and we walked up to the grave; what again was our astonishment and horror to find that, instead of the dead body of my mother-in-law, as we expected, there was lying over the remains of my poor sister, a large white she-wolf.

"'The white wolf!' exclaimed my father, 'the white wolf which decoyed me into the forest – I see it all now – I have dealt with the spirits of the Hartz Mountains.'

"For some time my father remained in silence and deep thought. He then carefully lifted up the body of my sister, replaced it in the grave, an covered it over as before, having struck the head of the dead animal with the heel of his boot, and raving like a madman. He walked back to the cottage, shut the door, and threw himself on the bed; I did the same, for I was in a stupor of amazement.

"Early in the morning we were both roused by a loud knocking at the door, and in rushed the hunter Wilfred.

"'My daughter — man — my daughter! where is my daughter?' cried he in a rage.

"'Where the wretch, the fiend, should be, I trust,' replied my father, starting up, and displaying equal choler; 'where she should be – in hell! Leave this cottage, or you may fare worse.'

"'Ha – ha!' replied the hunter, 'would you harm a potent spirit of the Hartz Mountains. Poor mortal, who must needs wed a werewolf.'

"'Out, demon! I defy thee and thy power.'

"'Yet shall you feel it; remember your oath – your solemn oath – never to raise your hand against her to harm her.'

"'I made no compact with evil spirits.'

"'You did, and if you failed in your vow, you were to meet the vengeance of the spirits. Your children were to perish by the vulture, the wolf—'

"'Out, out, demon!'

"'And their bones blanch in the wilderness. Ha! – ha!'

"My father, frantic with rage, seized his axe, and raised it over Wilfred's head to strike.

"'All this I swear,' continued the huntsman, mockingly.

"The axe descended; but it passed through the form of the hunter, and my father lost his balance, and fell heavily on the floor.

"'Mortal!' said the hunter, striding over my father's body, 'we have power over those only who have committed murder. You have been guilty of a double murder: you shall pay the penalty attached to your marriage vow. Two of your children are gone, the third is yet to follow – and follow them he will, for your oath is registered. Go – it were kindness to kill thee – your punishment is, that you live!'

"With these words the spirit disappeared. My father rose from the floor, embraced me tenderly, and knelt down in prayer.

"The next morning he quitted the cottage forever. He took me with him, and bent his steps to Holland, where we safely arrived. He had some little money with him; but he had not been many days in Amsterdam before he was seized with a brain fever, and died raving mad. I was put into the asylum, and afterwards was sent to sea before the mast. You now know all my history. The question is, whether I am to pay the penalty of my father's oath? I am myself perfectly convinced that, in some way or another, I shall."

* * *

On the twenty-second day the high land of the south of Sumatra was in view: as there were no vessels in sight, they resolved to keep their course through the Straits, and run for Pulo Penang, which they expected, as their vessel lay so close to the wind, to reach in seven or eight days. By constant exposure Philip and Krantz were now so bronzed that with their long beards and Mussulman dresses, they might easily have passed off for natives. They had steered the whole of the days exposed to a burning sun; they had lain down and slept in the dew of the night; but their health had not suffered. But for several days, since he had confided the history of his family to Philip, Krantz had become silent and melancholy: his usual flow of spirits had vanished and Philip had often questioned him as to the cause. As they entered the Straits, Philip talked of what they should do upon their arrival at Goa; when Krantz gravely replied, "For some days, Philip, I have had a presentiment that I shall never see that city."

"You are out of health, Krantz," replied Philip.

"No, I am in sound health, body and mind. I have endeavoured to shake off the presentiment, but in vain; there is a warning voice that continually tells me that I shall not be long with you. Philip, will you oblige me by making me content on one point? I have gold about my person which may be useful to you; oblige me by taking it, and securing it on your own."

"What nonsense, Krantz."

"It is no nonsense, Philip. Have you not had your warnings? Why should I not have mine? You know that I have little fear in my composition, and that I care not about death; but I feel the presentiment which I speak of more strongly every hour. It is some kind spirit who would warn me to prepare for another world. Be it so. I have lived long enough in this world to leave it without regret; although to part with you and Amine, the only two now dear to me, is painful, I acknowledge."

"May not this arise from over-exertion and fatigue, Krantz? Consider how much excitement you have laboured under within these last four months. Is not that enough to create a corresponding depression? Depend upon it, my dear friend, such is the fact."

"I wish it were; but I feel otherwise, and there is a feeling of gladness connected with the idea that I am to leave this world, arising from another presentiment, which equally occupies my mind."

"I hardly can tell you – but Amine and you are connected with it. In my dreams I have seen you meet again; but it has appeared to me as if a portion of your trial was purposely shut from my sight in dark clouds; and I have asked, 'May not I see what is there concealed?' – and an invisible has answered, 'No! 'twould make you wretched. Before these trials take place, you will be summoned away': and then I have thanked Heaven, and felt resigned."

"These are the imaginings of a disturbed brain, Krantz; that I am destined to suffering may be true; but why Amine should suffer, or why you, young, in full health and vigour should not pass your days in peace, and live to a good old age, there is no cause for believing. You will be better tomorrow."

"Perhaps so," replied Krantz; "but still you must yield to my whim, and take the gold. If I am wrong, and we do arrive safe, you know, Philip, you can let me have it back," observed Krantz, with a faint smile – "but you forget, our water is nearly out, and we must look out for a rill on the coast to obtain a fresh supply."

"I was thinking of that when you commenced this unwelcome topic. We had better look out for the water before dark, and as soon as we have replenished our jars, we will make sail again."

At the time that this conversation took place, they were on the eastern side of the strait, about forty miles to the northward. The interior of the coast was rocky and mountainous; but it slowly descended to low land of alternate forest and jungles, which continued to the beach: the country appeared to be uninhabited. Keeping close in to the shore, they discovered, after two hours' run, a fresh stream which burst in a cascade from the mountains, and swept its devious course through the jungle, until it poured its tribute into the waters of the strait.

They ran close in to the mouth of the stream, lowered the sails, and pulled the peroqua against the current, until they had advanced far enough to assure them that the water was quite fresh. The jars were soon filled, and they were again thinking of pushing off; when, enticed by the beauty of the spot, the coolness of the fresh water, and wearied with their long confinement on board of the peroqua, they proposed to bathe – a luxury hardly to be appreciated by those who have not been in a similar situation. They threw off their Mussulman dresses, and plunged into the stream, where they remained for some time. Krantz was the first to get out: he complained of feeling chilled, and he walked on to the banks where their clothes had been laid. Philip also approached nearer to the beach, intending to follow him.

"And now, Philip," said Krantz, "this will be a good opportunity for me to give you the money. I will open my sash and pour it out, and you can put it into your own before you put it on."

Philip was standing in the water, which was about level with his waist.

"Well, Krantz," said he, "I suppose if it must be so, it must – but it appears to me an idea so ridiculous – however, you shall have your own way."

Philip quitted the run, and sat down by Krantz, who was already busy in shaking the doubloons out of the folds of his sash – at last he said:

"I believe, Philip, you have got them all now? – I feel satisfied."

"What danger there can be to you, which I am not equally exposed to, I cannot conceive," replied Philip; "however—"

Hardly had he said these words, when there was a tremendous roar – a rush like a mighty wind through the air – a blow which threw him on his back – a loud cry – and a contention. Philip recovered himself, and perceived the naked form of Krantz carried off with the speed of an arrow by an enormous tiger through the jungle. He watched with distended eyeballs; in a few seconds the animal and Krantz had disappeared!

"God of Heaven! Would that thou hadst spared me this," cried Philip, throwing himself down in agony on his face. "Oh! Krantz, my friend – my brother – too sure was your presentiment. Merciful God! Have pity – but thy will be done"; and Philip burst into a flood of tears.

For more than an hour did he remain fixed upon the spot, careless and indifferent to the danger by which he was surrounded. At last, somewhat recovered, he rose, dressed himself, and then again sat down – his eyes fixed upon the clothes of Krantz, and the gold which still lay on the sand.

"He would give me that gold. He foretold his doom. Yes! Yes! It was his destiny, and it has been fulfilled. His bones will bleach in the wilderness, and the spirit-hunter and his wolfish daughter are avenged."

The shades of evening now set in, and the low growling of the beasts of the forest recalled Philip to a sense of his own danger. He thought of Amine; and hastily making the clothes of Krantz and the doubloons into a package, he stepped into the peroqua, with difficulty shoved it off, and with a melancholy heart, and in silence, hoisted the sail, and pursued his course.

"Yes, Amine," thought Philip, as he watched the stars twinkling and coruscating; "yes, you are right, when you assert that the destinies of men are foreknown, and may by some be read. My destiny is, alas! that I should be severed from all I value upon earth, and die friendless and alone. Then welcome death, if such is to be the case; welcome – a thousand welcomes! What a relief wilt thou be to me! What joy to find myself summoned to where the weary are at rest! I have my task to fulfil. God grant that it may soon be accomplished, and let not my life be embittered by any more trials such as this."

Again did Philip weep, for Krantz had been his long-tried, valued friend, his partner in all his dangers and privations, from the period that they had met when the Dutch fleet attempted the passage round Cape Horn.

After seven days of painful watching and brooding over bitter thoughts, Philip arrived at Pulo Penang, where he found a vessel about to sail for the city to which he was destined. He ran his peroqua alongside of her, and found that she was a brig under the Portuguese flag, having, however, but two Portuguese on board, the rest of the crew being natives. Representing himself as an Englishman in the Portuguese service, who had been wrecked, and offering to pay for his passage, he was willingly received, and in a few days the vessel sailed.

Their voyage was prosperous; in six weeks they anchored in the roads of Goa; the next day they went up the river. The Portuguese captain informed Philip where he might obtain lodging; and passing him off as one of his crew, there was no difficulty raised as to his landing. Having located himself at his new lodging, Philip commenced some inquiries of his host relative to Amine, designating her merely as a young woman who had arrived there in a vessel some weeks before, but he could obtain no information concerning her. "Signor," said the host, "tomorrow is the grand auto-da-fé; we can do nothing until that is over; afterwards, I will put you in the way to find out what you wish. In the meantime, you can walk about the town; tomorrow I will take you to where you can behold the grand procession, and then we will try what we can do to assist you in your search."

Philip went out, procured a suit of clothes, removed his beard, and then walked about the town, looking up at every window to see if he could perceive Amine. At a corner of one of the streets, he thought he recognised Father Mathias, and ran up to him; but the monk had drawn his cowl over his head, and when addressed by that name, made no reply.

"I was deceived," thought Philip; "but I really thought it was him." And Philip was right; it was Father Mathias, who thus screened himself from Philip's recognition.

Tired, at last he returned to his hotel, just before it was dark. The company there were numerous; everybody for miles distant had come to Goa to witness the auto-da-fé – and everybody was discussing the ceremony.

"I will see this grand procession," said Philip to himself, as he threw himself on his bed. "It will drive thought from me for a time; and God knows how painful my thoughts have now become. Amine, dear Amine, may angels guard thee!"

The Cure for Boredom

S.R. Masters

WHAT YOU FIRST *have to know is that our generation, those of us who came of age in the 80s and 90s: we cured boredom.*

Sometimes my boys ask me what I used to do with my time, when they take a break from the endless stream of YouTube videos or computer games or films or social media or instant conversations with friends at their fingertips. And, of course we had computer games then, yes. But while they looked less realistic, they were lifelike in so many other ways. How frustrating they were, how repetitive. And when you died back then, you died. Game over. That meant you didn't always want to be playing them, you eventually wanted to be outside, out in the world, doing real things, exploring things. Causing things.

Don't get me wrong though, I'm not one of those people who thinks everything was better then. Who thinks that time was some golden age for kids between the horrors of being stuck up a chimney and being imprisoned in their homes by overprotective parents and handheld devices. It really wasn't. I know it wasn't.

I'm not one of those people who looks back on things and thinks we all need to shut down our computers, go outside and smell the sweet, sweet air.

No. Keep kids inside. Lock them up. Childhood is dangerous. It's brutal and serrated, to be navigated like the Argo through the clashing rocks. How many times did I nearly die as a kid? Fall from a tree. Electrocute myself. Almost get run over. And did I get through it by judgement, or luck?

All that time we had. All that empty time.

* * *

Adam stopped at mine on the way to school looking pained, and when we got to the end of my drive I saw why. There was a dead cat in the road. It hadn't been there last night.

"I reckon it's just happened," Adam said. "Looks fresh."

The chunky longhair lay intact at the foot of the far curb, its fluffy back end stuck out into the road. Rush hour cars hurtled along Magnolia Street East, moving into the other lane to avoid squashing it.

"We should make sure Emily doesn't see," Adam said, school tie flapping in a lorry's wake.

I nodded, wishing I'd said it first.

Emily lived next door to me. As always she was out of the front door before we were halfway down her drive.

"Did you see the dead cat?" she said, throwing her bag over her shoulder and barging past us to get a closer look.

The passing cars sent waves through its hot-chocolate-coloured fur.

"Should we move it?" I said.

"It's Mrs. Boyle's," Emily said. "She'll be in her garden soon. She'll sort it." But she sounded uncertain.

We turned away and started the trek to school, but the first car that passed us on the opposite side didn't move over.

All of us stopped, knowing. Hearing.

Adam was the one that looked back. "Oh, shit," he said. "Nooo." There was a little laddish laughter accompanying his delivery, but it only hid his horror.

Emily and I shared a glance. We didn't look back.

* * *

It was the last day before the summer holidays and lessons finished at lunchtime. The three of us said goodbye to our school-hours friends and ambled home in the sun. Passing the well-spaced detached homes that lined our road at the edge of the village, we talked about how boring last summer had been – that we couldn't let this one be as bad.

The cat, half of it now a pulpy red ruin, was still outside my house. We sat at the top of where my front garden sloped down to the pavement, paying our respects.

We debated going to tell Mrs. Boyle, but she came out then. We didn't mean to sit like crows watching her scrape it up into a carrier bag. It was just it might look suspicious, us walking away once she arrived. Like we'd had something to do with it. So we just sat there. She only looked our way once, and did so with a single head shake.

We were feeling pretty sorry for her. Only then, instead of taking the cat to the garden to bury it, she walked over to the black dustbin in front of her garage, lifted the lid, and dropped the bag inside.

The three of us shook *our* heads.

* * *

Adam, Emily and I agreed the cat deserved a proper send off.

Adam was particularly insistent, perhaps because he'd lost his the year before, and now his parents only let him have rabbits – charmless idiots called Ozzy and Geezer. The trouble was getting it out from the bin, which could only be done safely at night.

At that age I struggled to sleep, and I'd often stare out of my bedroom window once the lights were out, finding the people rushing past in their cars and the night routines of the neighbours opposite comforting. From this I knew that the traffic thinned out at about 11:30pm, and that by then Mrs. Boyle was asleep. Being cautious, we agreed to meet at midnight in the entrance to the alley next to Adam's house, a few doors down Magnolia Street East to the right of mine.

I read *The Secret Seven* under the covers until I could hear both my parents snoring. Then I crept out the back door.

I didn't really believe Emily would come. But there she was in the shadows, Adam absent. She was even prettier in her own clothes, free of her school uniform.

"Well done," she said, touching my arm.

Adam arrived, and Emily stepped away.

"Everyone's here," he said. "I can't believe we all came." He touched my arm and Emily's, and Emily touched my arm again, completing our excited circle.

When it was quiet, we ran across Magnolia Street East and into the moon shadow of Mrs. Boyle's perimeter laurel. We edged towards the bin, bringing our feet down carefully on the stony drive to avoid making a sound. With just a few metres to go, the security light came on. Panicked, Emily and I ran back to the safety of the alley.

Adam wasn't with us.

"What happens if she catches him?" Emily said.

A car shot past and we both jumped. Instinctively we stepped deeper into the darkness.

Adam burst into the alley a moment later. He crashed into us, out of breath, laughing, the plastic bag in his hand.

"I got it, I got it," he said.

"Our hero," Emily said and now touched his arm.

My enthusiasm shrivelled up like a crisp packet to a flame. She probably fancied him. It was to be expected. Adam had gone out with Lauren Moore, one of the prettiest girls in the year – although it had only been for two weeks right at the start when nobody quite knew their place.

"Come on," Adam said, leading us into the alley.

"You're so brilliant for going back," Emily said, and skipped after him.

Then she looked back and made a gesture with her head that I should come too. Instantly it was okay again.

I should have gone back for the cat though. I should have been the hero.

* * *

The alley ran in parallel with the houses on either side. Once beyond the long back gardens, it opened out into a dark, wooded area before continuing on to a modern suburb. We stopped at the woods. It was scary in the daytime; now only Emily kept me from going back home.

"Is it safe here?" I said.

"We're just behind my house," Adam said, disappearing into the trees.

We followed him, branches poking at us, until we reached a steep slope down to another clearing behind the fences of the back gardens.

"No one ever comes here," Adam said. "It's a good place for a grave."

We dug a hole about three feet deep with a spade he'd left there earlier that day. After we'd patted down the soil and covered it over with twigs and old leaves, Adam bowed his head. Emily and I copied him.

"God," he said. "Jesus. The others. Please accept this... cat—" He looked at the two of us. "—into heaven?" He shrugged; we nodded.

"Amen," said Emily.

"Amen," said Adam and I.

At the entrance to the alley again, Emily hugged Adam goodbye. When we parted ways outside my house, she only waved.

* * *

Next morning we went back to finish the grave. We marked it with a little cross we made from wooden dental spatulas Emily had stolen from her mom, a dentist. On the footpath we'd also found a dead shrew, so we buried it next to the cat. Only seemed fair.

Adam had a biro. RIP Fluffy, he wrote on the cat's spatula. Emily named the shrew, and Adam wrote RIP Stu.

"This is like that film Pet Sematary, isn't it?" Adam said. "Have you not seen Pet Sematary?"

Emily and I shook our heads. We hadn't seen a lot of the films Adam had seen. They were 18s, and we didn't have an older sibling.

"It's amazing," he said. "These people all live on a main road, like us, and their pets keep getting flattened by big trucks. So there is this big burial ground where they put them, the pet cemetery, and it brings them back to life. Only they start coming back wrong. And in the end they all sort of join together under the soil and come back as this giant zombie monster to get everyone in America. My brother says, anyway."

"Really?" I said.

"Sounds silly," she said.

It *was* silly, though Adam didn't seem bothered by Emily's criticism. He didn't even hear when she said what we were doing was more like Walker Hamilton.

* * *

A week later, the three of us sat in the park on the new estate behind the alley. Fat flies attacked our heads and we tried not to swallow them when we yawned.

"When I'm older," Adam said. "I'm going to cure boredom. I'll make a computer game we can just live inside."

All three of our houses were friend-free zones during the daytime. My parents were house-proud after their renovation, and Adam's dad was a pest controller with chemicals in the house he was scared we'd drink. Emily's mom was off work depressed so was just in all the time.

"Can we go somewhere else?" Emily said, pointing to the nearby dead squirrel at the foot of the park's only tree.

Adam's eyes grew wide. "Or we could bury it in the pet cemetery," he said.

As simply as that we found the summer's purpose.

* * *

We managed to find something dead to put into a plastic bag and take back to the cemetery almost every day of the next week. Mostly we found birds. A pigeon, a magpie, even a baby owl. We came across a badger on Cherry Lane, a winding back road with one or two farms, the only noticeable occupants of which were some angry guard dogs. The badger we went back for after dark, partly for the thrill. It was the first time we had to deal with any sort of smell. After that Emily always brought latex gloves, again stolen from her mom.

Cherry Lane was good for frogs too, often flattened and baked into the tarmac and particularly easy to transport. Sadly, they ended up in mass graves, so often would there be a massacre following a sudden summer storm.

One afternoon Adam cried after we'd buried half a field mouse. Emily held him so that his face pressed to her neck. I saw her expression over his shoulder. How perfect all her little features were: the bow of her lips, the freckles on her nose.

Later Emily told me Adam had been thinking of his grandad, who used to put him to bed and sing *Three Blind Mice*. I hadn't cried about anything real since infant school. I only cried over books.

* * *

Adam's grandad's funeral was last October. Those two days Emily and I had walked to school together without him. Adam usually talked a lot, so it was the first time we realised we liked all the same books. *Roald Dahl, Point Horror, Secret Seven.* Even *Anne of Green Gables.* Emily talked about Anne and Gilbert, then asked if I fancied anyone at school. I said not really, and she'd frowned. Then when I asked if she did, she said she thought she might. She wouldn't say who it was, but when I asked if it was someone I knew she said, yes, then added: "very well".

I assumed she meant Adam, and tried not to think about Emily that way again. In December she asked if I wanted to go with her to a book fair at the NEC. I didn't like big crowds and new experiences, and nervous, I said no. I don't know if she ever asked Adam to go.

* * *

"We might need to go further out," Emily said when we'd reached twenty graves and the pickings were slim, no animals found at all after whole days trawling.

Adam agreed.

I suggested the motorway. If you followed Cherry Lane right to the end, you could cross a field over to the embankment of the M42. We scoured that embankment but after finding nothing, gave up. The next day we went back and walked down the hard shoulder. Cars *beeped* at us although no one slowed down or pulled over. About a mile down we found a baby deer in the central reservation. It no longer had a recognisable head and looked heavy, but if we could get it over to our side we could take it as far as Cherry Lane and retrieve it at night.

We sat watching the traffic's patterns from behind a collision barrier, eventually getting what we thought was the pace of all three lanes. We waited a long time for a gap, and eventually Adam grew bored and ran out into the road, only just getting to the deer before a sports car flew past blaring its complaint. It was so close to catching his heels I yelped. Adam ignored the symphony of horns accompanying his struggle to unstick the carcass from the ground, and once free he dragged the thing as quickly as he could back to where we were waiting for him. Only he'd misjudged it, and when he entered the slow lane a blue Toyota would certainly have hit him had it not swung quickly into the middle lane, where it avoided another collision with a white van only thanks to the van man's quick reactions.

More horns. The squeal of tyres.

"We should probably come back for this," Adam said.

"You're such an idiot," Emily said. Again, she hugged him.

* * *

The motorway scared us. Only Adam wanted to go back for the deer, but gave up mentioning it after a few days; he never saw how close the car came to clipping him.

We stopped seeing each other for a while. Time slowed.

Emily's parents bought her two kittens, maybe to keep her from playing with us, or maybe because she was sick of dead animals. Sometimes, if I went to my parents' bedroom window, I'd see Emily and her mom playing with them in their manicured back garden.

After Brains my parents wouldn't let me have another dog. They said the road was too dangerous.

Sometimes I'd see Emily looking up at my house, and I'd wonder if she was thinking about me.

I played on my Master System and I read three books. I toyed with coming up with some plan to impress Emily, to make myself seem brave like Adam.

* * *

"Come and see this," Emily said. She was standing at my door, frowning.

She took me over to her bins at the side of her house. A dead rat lay between them. It was huge, almost the length of my arm and much thicker. Its mouth was open slightly.

The three of us buried it that afternoon, and reinvigorated, we went to Cherry Lane to see what else we could find. We collected an intact squirrel and brought it back to the alley. Some of the graves looked recently disturbed. Adam said some animal, probably a fox, had tried digging out one of the plots, so he'd come back with the spade to clean it up.

"I feel good about that," Emily said following prayers for the squirrel.

"Doing good's addictive, isn't it?" Adam said.

From our position at the slope's top all forty grave markers were visible. It looked like a lot. The aftermath of a big battle. It looked weird, too. For the first real time I saw it through someone else's eyes having been away a while. What would they think of this? Of us?

Adam's gaze was on me, awaiting my contribution. "Yeah," I said. "I wonder what we'll do if space runs out?"

* * *

Early the next morning Emily knocked at my door again. I was pleased to see her until she took me out and showed me a rat at the entrance of our drive.

"Do you think there's an infestation?" I said.

"Maybe," Emily said.

"What's killing them?" I said. "It's not your kittens is it?"

"No," she said. "They're tiny."

She didn't sound that impressed with them, so I asked, "Don't you like them?"

"Oh, they're fine," Emily said. "But mom only got them so I'll stop talking to her all the time. She thinks I'm lonely."

"Are you?" I said.

"Hey," she said, eyes alight with understanding. "Maybe it's poison. Maybe Mrs. Boyle's using poison to kill rats."

"We can ask Adam," I said, "he'll probably know."

* * *

Adam said he'd ask his dad, but had no idea himself what might've killed the rats.

"I wonder if I'll get a rat on my drive tomorrow," he said once the new rat was in the ground. "That'd be weird. Like an animal serial killer leaving us a message."

Emily sniggered. Increasingly I was noticing her feelings for Adam. When it was just the two of us, she talked non-stop, easily and without weirdness. Around Adam she was so quiet and almost shy. Like I was around her.

"I have a thing Dad wants me to do," I said, wanting to leave them to it.

"You don't want some Cherry Lane times?" Adam said.

Emily raised her eyebrows at me by way of encouragement. "May as well," she said.

That was when we found our best animal yet: a skinny black and white sheepdog not far from where we'd found the badger. It would have to be collected at night, and we all agreed that it might belong to one of the farms, and that we should leave it for them to try and find first. There wasn't a collar, although there was a ring of cleaner fur around its neck.

"We should just tell someone," I said.

"What if they think we had something to do with it?" Adam said.

"And then what if they discovered the cemetery?" Emily said.

"We can't risk it," Adam said.

Adam pulled the dog off the road and into the long grass there. He claimed it was to stop it getting damaged in the road. When we walked away it was barely noticeable anymore, which I said, but the other two ignored. It wasn't surprising that two days later it was still there. We took it to the cemetery after dark, Adam convinced it was a stray.

* * *

Things went quiet for a few days, and I didn't mind that. I was bored of the pet cemetery, scared we'd get caught now there were so many graves.

I worked up the courage to walk over to Emily's one hot afternoon. She heard me crunching up her drive and came down.

"I was thinking of going to the park to read," I said. "Do you want to come?"

I didn't know if it was because she heard the wobble in my voice or if it was because she thought it was a horrible idea, but a little smile appeared on her face.

"I mean, we could go get Adam, too," I said.

"He doesn't read," she said. "I'll go and get a book."

We cut through the alley without mentioning the pet cemetery. In the park we sat under an oak. She kept complaining how uncomfortable she was. She asked if she could lie with her head on my lap. I said yes, but once she was there I got nervous that maybe my clothes might smell that close up or something. Was this just her being friendly, or did she expect me to do something? Stroke her hair maybe.

"*We* should spend more time together at school," she said.

"Yeah. We should."

Not long after we went home.

"There's a party tomorrow," she said at my drive. "Some Year 9 kid in Blythe invited my friend, who said yes, but only if I was allowed to come. You could pretend to be my boyfriend, stop any other boys bothering me." She laughed and looked away.

"I'll think about it," I said, smiling to make her happy, smiling so I didn't have to say no. All I pictured was drunk kids throwing up or older boys starting a fight on me.

I didn't go. I made up something about doing a job for my dad.

* * *

"Ozzy died," Adam said on the way over to Emily's the next day. "His head got caught in the chicken wire cage. It's horrible. His head was poking out, and I think a fox ate his ear while it was stuck there. Ear was gone. Don't know if he choked or died of fright."

"Poor Ozzy."

The three of us went to dig it up from Adam's garden and bury it in the pet cemetery. I didn't know why Adam wanted to do that. He said it was important we did. That it made sense of the summer.

"All these dead animals mean something," he said.

And he was right, because they were what brought us together. Every time we drifted apart the pet cemetery brought us back again. Even though I wish it could have been something better that united us, around the village this was as good as it got.

Although I should have gone to the party. And the book fair. I should have been brave, like Adam, and gone.

* * *

I started reading the book of *Pet Sematary*, which didn't help me sleep. It was nothing like Adam said. Year 9 of school was coming up soon too, playing on my mind.

That's why I was staring out the window.

A shadow moved on Emily's drive, a person. The shape was right for Emily, only it was nearly one in the morning, too late for her to be up. The figure walked towards the road hunched over, carrying something maybe. A car drove past, and the figure hid on the inside of the laurels at the drive entrance. A moment later the shadow ran out into the road, placed something down by the far curb, then crossed back to the pavement.

In the streetlight I could see two things clearly: the figure was Emily, and the object she'd placed in the road was a kitten. It was still for a moment. Then it ran back to Emily. She picked it up, and took it back into the road, shaking her head.

She lifted the kitten above her head with both hands and threw it down with so much force that she lost her balance and stumbled backwards. I felt the same sort of impact deep in my gut.

The kitten didn't move again.

When she ran back across to her house she looked up at my window. She saw me, must have realised I'd seen her too because she stopped.

I held up my hand and waved. She gestured for me to come down. I didn't want to, but I nodded.

She was behind me when I closed the back door. She made me jump. Tear tracks marked her face.

"What's wrong?" I said, afraid to ask her anything else. Afraid of what she would say.

"You saw me," she said. She stepped forward and wrapped her arms around me, burying her head into my shoulder. We were about the same height. Her hair smelled of strawberry shampoo. Her body shook. I should have stepped away.

"I only did it for you," she said, her voice choked. "Do you even like me?"

"I like you," I said.

"They didn't suffer," she said into my pyjama top. "Adam told me how to. But he didn't know. He just thought I was asking."

"What did you do?" I said.

"The animals."

"How many?" I said.

She hesitated before saying: "For the cemetery," like it was a number. "I didn't know how else to spend time with you."

"For the cemetery."

She pulled her head away to look at me. "*Do* you like me?" she said.

I stepped back. Even in the dim starlight, what I saw on her face was more awful than any of the dead things buried in our cemetery. Some other Emily, that came up once the sun went down, had possessed and contorted all her delicate features.

Though she never stopped being pretty. Even then, and I retreated no further.

"Yes," I said.

"Good," she said. She was scowling. "Because I miss you all the time." She crossed her wrists over her heart.

Her eyes were wet. She kissed me. My first kiss.

I tried to do it like I'd read about, and I ignored some fox's distant scream.

The Wolf

Guy de Maupassant

THIS IS WHAT the old Marquis d'Arville told us after St. Hubert's dinner at the house of the Baron des Ravels.

We had killed a stag that day. The marquis was the only one of the guests who had not taken part in this chase. He never hunted.

During that long repast we had talked about hardly anything but the slaughter of animals. The ladies themselves were interested in bloody and exaggerated tales, and the orators imitated the attacks and the combats of men against beasts, raised their arms, romanced in a thundering voice.

M. d'Arville talked well, in a certain flowery, high-sounding, but effective style. He must have told this story frequently, for he told it fluently, never hesitating for words, choosing them with skill to make his description vivid.

* * *

Gentlemen, I have never hunted, neither did my father, nor my grandfather, nor my great-grandfather. This last was the son of a man who hunted more than all of you put together. He died in 1764. I will tell you the story of his death.

His name was Jean. He was married, father of that child who became my great-grandfather, and he lived with his younger brother, Francois d'Arville, in our castle in Lorraine, in the midst of the forest.

Francois d'Arville had remained a bachelor for love of the chase.

They both hunted from one end of the year to the other, without stopping and seemingly without fatigue. They loved only hunting, understood nothing else, talked only of that, lived only for that.

They had at heart that one passion, which was terrible and inexorable. It consumed them, had completely absorbed them, leaving room for no other thought.

They had given orders that they should not be interrupted in the chase for any reason whatever. My great-grandfather was born while his father was following a fox, and Jean d'Arville did not stop the chase, but exclaimed: "The deuce! The rascal might have waited till after the view – halloo!"

His brother Francois was still more infatuated. On rising he went to see the dogs, then the horses, then he shot little birds about the castle until the time came to hunt some large game.

In the countryside they were called M. le Marquis and M. le Cadet, the nobles then not being at all like the chance nobility of our time, which wishes to establish a hereditary hierarchy in titles; for the son of a marquis is no more a count, nor the son of a viscount a baron, than a son of a general is a colonel by birth. But the contemptible vanity of today finds profit in that arrangement.

My ancestors were unusually tall, bony, hairy, violent and vigorous. The younger, still taller than the older, had a voice so strong that, according to a legend of which he was proud, all the leaves of the forest shook when he shouted.

When they were both mounted to set out hunting, it must have been a superb sight to see those two giants straddling their huge horses.

Now, toward the midwinter of that year, 1764, the frosts were excessive, and the wolves became ferocious.

They even attacked belated peasants, roamed at night outside the houses, howled from sunset to sunrise, and robbed the stables.

And soon a rumour began to circulate. People talked of a colossal wolf with grey fur, almost white, who had eaten two children, gnawed off a woman's arm, strangled all the watch dogs in the district, and even come without fear into the farmyards. The people in the houses affirmed that they had felt his breath, and that it made the flame of the lights flicker. And soon a panic ran through all the province. No one dared go out any more after nightfall. The darkness seemed haunted by the image of the beast.

The brothers d'Arville determined to find and kill him, and several times they brought together all the gentlemen of the country to a great hunt.

They beat the forests and searched the coverts in vain; they never met him. They killed wolves, but not that one. And every night after a battue the beast, as if to avenge himself, attacked some traveller or killed someone's cattle, always far from the place where they had looked for him.

Finally, one night he stole into the pigpen of the Chateau d'Arville and ate the two fattest pigs.

The brothers were roused to anger, considering this attack as a direct insult and a defiance. They took their strong bloodhounds, used to pursue dangerous animals, and they set off to hunt, their hearts filled with rage.

From dawn until the hour when the empurpled sun descended behind the great naked trees, they beat the woods without finding anything.

At last, furious and disgusted, both were returning, walking their horses along a lane bordered with hedges, and they marvelled that their skill as huntsmen should be baffled by this wolf, and they were suddenly seized with a mysterious fear.

The elder said:

"That beast is not an ordinary one. You would say it had a mind like a man."

The younger answered:

"Perhaps we should have a bullet blessed by our cousin, the bishop, or pray some priest to pronounce the words which are needed."

Then they were silent.

Jean continued:

"Look how red the sun is. The great wolf will do some harm tonight."

He had hardly finished speaking when his horse reared; that of Franqois began to kick. A large thicket covered with dead leaves opened before them, and a mammoth beast, entirely grey, jumped up and ran off through the wood.

Both uttered a kind of grunt of joy, and bending over the necks of their heavy horses, they threw them forward with an impulse from all their body, hurling them on at such a pace, urging them, hurrying them away, exciting them so with voice and with gesture and with spur that the experienced riders seemed to be carrying the heavy beasts between their thighs and to bear them off as if they were flying.

Thus they went, plunging through the thickets, dashing across the beds of streams, climbing the hillsides, descending the gorges, and blowing the horn as loud as they could to attract their people and the dogs.

And now, suddenly, in that mad race, my ancestor struck his forehead against an enormous branch which split his skull; and he fell dead on the ground, while his frightened horse took himself off, disappearing in the gloom which enveloped the woods.

The younger d'Arville stopped quick, leaped to the earth, seized his brother in his arms, and saw that the brains were escaping from the wound with the blood.

Then he sat down beside the body, rested the head, disfigured and red, on his knees, and waited, regarding the immobile face of his elder brother. Little by little a fear possessed him, a strange fear which he had never felt before, the fear of the dark, the fear of loneliness, the fear of the deserted wood, and the fear also of the weird wolf who had just killed his brother to avenge himself upon them both.

The gloom thickened; the acute cold made the trees crack. Francois got up, shivering, unable to remain there longer, feeling himself growing faint. Nothing was to be heard, neither the voice of the dogs nor the sound of the horns – all was silent along the invisible horizon; and this mournful silence of the frozen night had something about it terrific and strange.

He seized in his immense hands the great body of Jean, straightened it, and laid it across the saddle to carry it back to the chateau; then he went on his way softly, his mind troubled as if he were in a stupor, pursued by horrible and fear-giving images.

And all at once, in the growing darkness a great shape crossed his path. It was the beast. A shock of terror shook the hunter; something cold, like a drop of water, seemed to glide down his back, and, like a monk haunted of the devil, he made a great sign of the cross, dismayed at this abrupt return of the horrible prowler. But his eyes fell again on the inert body before him, and passing abruptly from fear to anger, he shook with an indescribable rage.

Then he spurred his horse and rushed after the wolf.

He followed it through the copses, the ravines, and the tall trees, traversing woods which he no longer recognised, his eyes fixed on the white speck which fled before him through the night.

His horse also seemed animated by a force and strength hitherto unknown. It galloped straight ahead with outstretched neck, striking against trees, and rocks, the head and the feet of the dead man thrown across the saddle. The limbs tore out his hair; the brow, beating the huge trunks, spattered them with blood; the spurs tore their ragged coats of bark. Suddenly the beast and the horseman issued from the forest and rushed into a valley, just as the moon appeared above the mountains. The valley here was stony, inclosed by enormous rocks.

Francois then uttered a yell of joy which the echoes repeated like a peal of thunder, and he leaped from his horse, his cutlass in his hand.

The beast, with bristling hair, the back arched, awaited him, its eyes gleaming like two stars. But, before beginning battle, the strong hunter, seizing his brother, seated him on a rock, and, placing stones under his head, which was no more than a mass of blood, he shouted in the ears as if he was talking to a deaf man: "Look, Jean; look at this!"

Then he attacked the monster. He felt himself strong enough to overturn a mountain, to bruise stones in his hands. The beast tried to bite him, aiming for his stomach; but he had seized the fierce animal by the neck, without even using his weapon, and he strangled it gently, listening to the cessation of breathing in its throat and the beatings of its heart. He laughed, wild with joy, pressing closer and closer his formidable embrace, crying in a delirium of joy, "Look, Jean, look!" All resistance ceased; the body of the wolf became limp. He was dead.

Francois took him up in his arms and carried him to the feet of the elder brother, where he laid him, repeating, in a tender voice: "There, there, there, my little Jean, see him!"

Then he replaced on the saddle the two bodies, one upon the other, and rode away.

He returned to the chateau, laughing and crying, like Gargantua at the birth of Pantagruel, uttering shouts of triumph, and boisterous with joy as he related the death of the beast, and grieving and tearing his beard in telling of that of his brother.

And often, later, when he talked again of that day, he would say, with tears in his eyes: "If only poor Jean could have seen me strangle the beast, he would have died content, that I am sure!"

The widow of my ancestor inspired her orphan son with that horror of the chase which has transmitted itself from father to son as far down as myself.

* * *

The Marquis d'Arville was silent. Someone asked:

"That story is a legend, isn't it?"

And the storyteller answered:

"I swear to you that it is true from beginning to end."

Then a lady declared, in a little, soft voice:

"All the same, it is fine to have passions like that."

Under Barrow Downs

Damien Mckeating

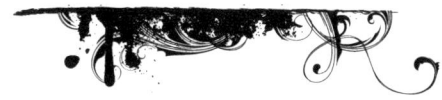

SOPHIE knew all about Grandma Annabelle's fear of the dark. There was always an electric night light next to her bed, and a candle in case the power went out. Granny Anna, as she was known, had been a little girl during the Blitz. When the bombers had flown overhead, she hadn't been allowed a light. Ever since then, for nearly seventy years, she'd slept with a light on. Darkness meant bad things were coming.

Anna's house was at the end of a row of cottages. It backed onto Barrow Downs; wild grassy hills and woods that stretched for miles. It was an untamed wilderness ripe for exploring and adventure, but filled with dangers. Sophie remembered visiting with her brother and cousins and being constantly warned to stay off the Downs.

Returning to the house was bittersweet for Sophie. It looked older and, as Anna's health had failed, she had not been able to maintain it. Sophie's memories of summer days and warm nights were filtered through a new reality of overgrown weeds, peeling paint, a cracked window and a faulty boiler.

There was also the reason for her return. Anna had never married; her betrothed had died weeks before their wedding. What she did have was a small army of nieces and nephews. But she had asked for Sophie specifically, to come and see her during her final days. Members of the family had suggested, with some bitterness, that Anna was going to leave everything to Sophie and that this 'death watch' was the price she had to pay.

Sophie struggled to understand how she felt. The sadness of Anna's illness, the responsibility of caring for her, the financial relief the inheritance would bring, the guilt over thinking that at all, the disruption of her memories: it all weighed on her and left her stomach churning.

She arrived at the house a little after lunch and spent the afternoon tidying as best she could. Aside from Helen, a local nurse, and Margery, an old bingo friend, there were few visitors to the house, but Sophie wanted the house to look as it once had done.

Often she stopped to check on Anna, who was mostly bedridden. She took her cups of tea and snacks, but Anna had no appetite. She was faded and grey, the illness stealing her away a piece at a time.

A sideboard in the hallway was covered in family photos. There was an old one of Anna. Sophie looked in the mirror and compared the photo to herself. It was shocking how similar they were. They both had black hair and green eyes, and they were both short and petite. There had always been an intensity to Granny Anna, like she could look through you, and people had told Sophie she had the same look about her.

She imagined herself stepping into Anna's place and taking on the cottage. It didn't seem like such a bad life.

She immediately felt guilty. She was here to care for her grandmother's passing, not to think about the inheritance.

At night the house was peaceful. The open fireplace created a warm, soft glow in the lounge. Open beams, alcoves and nooks made for a house of shadow and depth. It felt like a cocoon.

"Here," Anna said, as Sophie prepared her for bed. "This is for you." She handed Sophie a plug-in night light. "You must use it."

"I will," Sophie said. She tried to move away but Anna held her tight.

"Promise me," the old woman begged in a paper-thin voice.

"I promise," Sophie said. "It's okay, Granny."

"It's best not to let the night in," Anna said, and then collapsed back on to her pillows. Her eyes closed and after a few moments her chest rose and fell with long, steady breaths.

Sophie crept from the room and pulled the door closed behind her.

Lying in bed, she realised, for all their visits as children, it would be her first time staying in the house overnight. She lay snuggled in the thick duvet and listened to the rhythms of the house; creaking floorboards, trees branches rustling in the garden, the call of night birds, the clanking of the boiler.

She lay in the darkness and enjoyed the sensation of being somewhere new. The night light lay on the bedside table, unused. Sophie had never been afraid of the dark. Outside she heard a fox yowl and she smiled at the sensation of life all around them.

She woke to total darkness and her first thought echoed Anna's words: she had let the night in. Clouds covered the moon and there were no streetlights nearby; the darkness now was thick and heavy.

Goosebumps prickled up her legs and she reached for the duvet that had fallen to the floor, shivering in her vest top and shorts. The boiler must have given out. She should go downstairs and check it.

A floorboard creaked on the landing.

The sound had weight to it; someone was standing at the top of the stairs. Sophie held her breath.

It must be Granny, she thought.

A smell of earth reached her. It was thick with wet soil, leaves and animal fur. It was the smell of underground, of deep forests, of places far removed from human towns and cities.

Sophie drew in a shaky breath. She clutched the duvet to her, her hands clenched at her chest, feeling her heart beating too fast.

The floorboard creaked again and this time she heard the step. A gentle thud, like a great weight stepping lightly.

Thud.

Thud.

They were at her door.

Something rapped at the door, a series of tip-tap sounds, like someone drumming their fingers once across the wood.

They're going to come in, Sophie thought. What about Granny? She had to do something. She needed to call the police. She needed a weapon.

Sophie lunged from the bed and flicked on the light switch. A clatter of thuds sounded in the hall. By the hazy glow of the bulb, Sophie rushed towards the small, bedroom fireplace and snatched up a poker.

She turned to the door, brandishing the weapon.

The thuds hammered down the stairs. She heard them under her feet, crashing through the house, thumping across the tiles in the kitchen. She heard the back door slam and a sound like a horse trotting down the garden path.

Silence.

Sophie gulped down breaths.

Clutching the poker, she stepped into the hallway and over to Granny's room. Light spilled from under the door. She pushed it open and looked inside.

Anna sat up in bed, awake, and looking at Sophie.

"I told you," Anna said. "It's best not to let the night in."

Dawn came slowly. Sophie dozed fitfully, sitting on the bed next to Anna, who refused to talk until the morning.

"Some things should not be spoken of at night; they listen for their names."

In the morning Sophie found herself twitching at every sound. A neighbor slammed a car door and she flinched, scattering a spoonful of coffee across the countertop. A black cat sidled into the garden and its insinuating darkness made her startle and fumble against the wall. She clenched and unclenched her hands, willing them to stop shaking.

"What was it?" she asked Granny, sitting on the edge of Anna's bed.

"Long Jack."

Sophie knew the folklore; it had been a common enough story. Long Jack was a sort of local fertility symbol. He was a wild man, a spirit of the deep forest, and young women were often told not to go out alone in case Long Jack spirited them away with his devilish charms. Older women made pointed comments to each other, saying "Long Jack, indeed," and sharing secret smiles. It had been some years before Sophie had understood their humor.

"It's real," Sophie said. She did not doubt her own senses. Looking at the polished floorboards this morning, she had seen scuff marks, and there were muddy clumps on the kitchen floor that had not been there before. "Could it be a trick?" She asked, trying to persuade herself as much as Anna. "One of the locals?"

"For seventy-two years?" Anna smiled grimly.

All that time? Every story about Granny sleeping with the light on: had she been haunted in the night for seventy-two years?

"But why? And why the light?" Sophie asked.

"Because I never could refuse a dare," Anna said, with something of the old twinkle in her eyes. "Spend the night under Barrow Downs, in Long Jack's cave. No one dared, of course. There were all sorts of stories about what he did in there. But I wasn't afraid."

"And he was there."

"Oh, he was."

"What happened?"

"I lost my nerve. I ran. I ran like the rabbit runs from the fox. He must have had quite the shock when he saw me move. I doubt he's ever had a chase like it." There was a touch of pride in her voice.

"And then, all this time…"

Anna nodded. Her voice turned hard, "Going to his cave is as good as an invitation for Long Jack and, for his kind, once an invitation is given it cannot be taken back. So, every night he comes for me, and every night he sees the light and goes back."

"He doesn't like the light."

"What he does, what he's supposed to do, it's best in the dark," Anna chuckled. "Most people do it in the dark."

Sophie went cold. It was hideous. The harassment, what it intended to do, it was… She shivered at the thought of what Granny Anna had endured, and what might have happened to her. What could still happen to her…

The sun that day felt warmer and brighter than any autumn day Sophie had known. Like a cat, she relished the feel of it on her skin, and found herself stretching and enjoying its warmth seeping into her bones. She followed the daylight around the house as she tidied and repaired the place, and felt a creeping dread as twilight grew and the sun sank towards the ground.

She thought of Long Jack. How old was he? Fertility rituals dated as far back as people. Was he something from ancient, dark days when survival depended on children being born?

That evening she said goodnight to Granny.

"Keep the light on," Anna said. "Don't let the night in."

Sophie sat in her room fully clothed, the poker resting on the bed next to her. Alongside it was a flashlight and a pack of spare batteries. She also had her phone. It was difficult to get a signal in the cottage, but she wasn't thinking of making a call.

She kept the light off and sat on the bed so she could see out of the window. The curtains were open wide, and she could see the length of the garden to Barrow Downs.

She waited.

The moon set close to midnight.

The night became darker.

And a shadow came from the Downs.

It was difficult to see, just another shade of darkness in the night. It looked as tall as a man, but it moved with bounding leaps, as if it might be dancing. It was big, broad, and it moved deceptively fast. No sooner had Sophie seen it than she heard the back door, the one she had bolted and locked, creak open.

She sat herself at the bedroom door and waited. She listened to Long Jack approaching in the night.

Thud.

Creak.

Up the stairs.

Now she was expecting it, the smell caught her senses sooner; that animal musk that carried a promise of sex and violence in equal measure.

Thud.

Creak.

It was at Granny's door.

Sophie shifted her weight. The floorboards beneath her gave the tiniest squeak of protest. She thought she heard Long Jack's breath catch.

Thud.

Creak.

At her door.

Sophie opened up the torch app on her phone. It had a dimmer setting, and she had adjusted it to give out the faintest light.

There was a scratch at the door and Sophie flinched.

But Long Jack stayed outside.

Sophie inched forward.

She pressed her face to the door.

Tip-tap came the sound, like fingernails on wood.

She heard a deep sigh, one filled with terrible lust and longing.

Her own breath came in shaking gasps, caught between fear and excitement.

Long Jack gave a low, pining moan.

Sophie's fingers felt numb. She struggled to hold her phone. She fumbled at the screen, until she finally adjusted the slider and turned up the dimmer. Light blazed out, shining under the door.

Long Jack hissed.

The thudding steps retreated back down the stairs. With them came a grinding, scratching sound and the silence when it stopped was heavy and threatening.

She had caught its attention, which she had wanted to do, wanted to distract it from Granny. But she had also annoyed it. She had teased it. And she did not know what that would mean.

She turned the lights on and slept as much as she could. In the morning she saw scratch marks on the woodwork and plaster. She placed her own hands over them, and saw how the four gouges might match the nails of a hand; but a hand much larger than hers.

"How do we make him stop?" she asked Anna.

"There is no stopping him. He's a force of nature. Might as well ask the sheep not to make lambs. Or try to stop young women sneaking off with young men."

"There must be something." Sophie stood in Anna's room. She was holding the poker and the weight of iron in her hands made her think of folklore and legends. Iron was supposed to be good against magic. And salt. Would they do anything against Long Jack? Could she lock the house against him?

She went into the town for some supplies and chatted to Emma at the post office, a lovely local lady who asked after Anna's health. Sophie spent the rest of the day preparing as best she could, aware of the approaching night. She thought she could feel the world turning beneath her, bringing the horizon to the sun, bringing the night.

At every window and door Sophie poured a thick line of salt. She placed horseshoes over every entryway. A painfully slow internet search using Anna's intermittent connection revealed that hawthorn was used in folklore as protection. Sophie cut pieces from hawthorn branches and laid them at the doorways and windows.

Night came quickly. The shadows did not creep, they raced with gleeful abandon. The world was in autumn, turning to winter, and the darkness seized on its opportunity. The last sliver of red sunlight dipped below the horizon and was gone.

Sophie paced the house, poker in her hands, and checked on Granny.

"He won't stop," Anna said.

"We'll try," Sophie replied.

Clouds covered the night sky, obscuring the moon and what light she brought with her. The night was deep and dark, the kind of dark you can only find in the country. No glimmer of a streetlight. No headlights from passing cars. Not even the glow or hum of electrical devices.

Sophie stood in the cottage, determined to face her fear.

Let the night come, she thought.

And Long Jack came.

She heard him creep down the garden path. He paused at the back door. He snuffled. Scratched at the wood.

The door swung open.

Sophie grit her teeth and fought back tears. Her plan had not worked.

She backed up the stairs and into her room.

Long Jack followed her.

Thud.

Creak.

Sophie backed up until her legs bumped against her bed. The bedroom door stayed open, and it looked sideways onto the stairs. Long Jack needed to be confronted. He needed to be stopped. What he was doing was monstrous. But, her hands shook, her throat tightened, her tongue stuck in her dry mouth.

What could she do?

Long Jack climbed the stairs and his head came into view. He was a shadow, but he moved slowly, and Sophie saw the shape of him clearly. His hair was tangled and matted. Long, curved horns protruded from the front of his head. Powerful arms reached out to grasp the bannister rail, and his fingers ended in long nails that tip-tapped against the wood.

Sophie trembled.

Long Jack turned to look at her.

For a moment his eyes flashed in the night, like a cat's.

Thud.

Creak.

He continued to climb. She lost sight of him as he reached the landing. He passed Granny Anna's door and came to Sophie's room.

He stood in the doorway, filling it with his massive bulk. His legs were covered in fur and ended in hooves that clomped and scraped at the floorboards. The knees bent backwards, making him crouched and ready to pounce. His chest was broad and muscular, turning him into a slab of darkness. The smell of night air, earth and sex, rolled from him.

His head tilted as he looked at Sophie and a long, low rumble sounded deep in his throat. It put Sophie in mind of a cat purring. As he moved, the shadows changed, and Sophie caught a fleeting glimpse of a sharp face, a bearded chin and a tongue that reached out and flexed, as if tasting the air.

The eyes flashed again and she felt him looking her up and down, appraising her, lusting for her. His hands moved towards the deep shadow that obscured his groin and he presented himself to her.

Sophie lost all sense of herself. Her body did not feel like her own. She was removed from it. Her actions were beyond her control.

She picked up the poker and stood, feeling weightless.

"Get out," she said. She raised the poker and Long Jack stepped back. "Get out of this house. You're not welcome here. You are not wanted." She hissed the last word, stressing it in terms she hoped he understood. He was not desired.

Long Jack hesitated by the stairs. He looked towards Anna's room, to Sophie, back to Anna's room. He seemed caught by indecision.

Sophie whacked the poker against the bannister rail, leaving a deep indent in the wood. "Get out!"

Long Jack scurried backwards, half falling and half scrambling down the stairs. Sophie stood outside Anna's bedroom door, poker gripped in two hands, and listened to Long Jack scamper out of the house.

That was the last time, she promised.

She relocked the doors and, for the first time since she had arrived, she slept soundly.

"It's about consent," she said to Anna the next morning.

"Oh, he understands that," Anna replied. She sat up in bed, a breakfast tray resting on her lap. She had sipped some tea and nibbled some toast, but that was all. Her health was failing. Sophie was determined her last days would be peaceful.

"No, he doesn't. Just because you went to his cave once, that doesn't give him permission to harass you every night since."

"He's a wilful creature. Born of nature. His intent is pure, what drives him is base and powerful. Unyielding."

"He'll yield to me," Sophie said. She knew it was true. She had not been to his cave, she had not invited him. During any of his previous visits she was certain he could have broken down the door or overpowered her. He could take what he wanted by force, but he hadn't. So, yes, he understood consent. Now she'd make him understand that consent could be revoked as well as given.

"What are you going to do?" Anna asked.

"Where's his cave?" she asked.

"Under Barrow Downs."

"Where?" Sophie insisted.

She went into town for supplies and spent the morning resting and mentally preparing herself. Tonight she would face Long Jack on the Barrow Downs.

She made sure Anna was comfortable and set out early for Long Jack's cave.

It took several hours, and even with Anna's directions, Long Jack's resting place was not easy to find. Barrow Downs was a wilderness of steep hills, long grass, and stretches of thick forest. There were dangers on the Downs; mud, caves, collapsed tunnels, bogs. There were no paths: it was no place for day-trippers or dog walkers.

Sophie pushed on and followed a narrow stream between the hills until she came to the forest. She fought through bracken and briar, working her way deeper and deeper through the trees.

Twilight fell into night as she travelled. The forest became dark. The air cooled and Sophie's breath started to mist. The night-time world came alive: birds, beasts and bugs. Sophie felt herself slip from one world into another. She was part of the night now.

Finally, she came to a clearing and saw the last of the markers Anna had described: a tall oak, its trunk split so that it looked like two trees growing from one base. Beyond it a tree-covered hill rose steeply, and in the side of the hill was an ancient opening, wreathed in ivy and holly.

Sophie approached the cave and stopped at its threshold. It was taller than her. The sides were a mixture of stone and soil. Tree roots poked out from its roof and from somewhere inside she heard the drip of water. A familiar smell seeped out of the ground; the musky smell of an animal in heat.

She realised that she couldn't go inside.

She backed away and set down the two electric lanterns she had brought, pointed them at the cave entrance, and flicked them on. She stood back in the shadows and stared into the dark opening, rendered flat and shadowless by the twin beams of light. In one hand she held the poker.

Long Jack didn't like the light; he liked to stay hidden, like every kind of bully and abuser. She would show him what he was. He didn't like the poker, he didn't like to fight. She would stand up to him.

In the cave there was a shift of shadow. Long Jack sniffed at the night air. He pined like a dog, whimpering from the safety of the darkness.

"You'll face me now," Sophie said.

The snap of a twig behind her made Sophie turn, so the blow glanced across the side of her face rather than the back of her skull. She reeled, stumbled through the leaves, and crashed into the ground. She tasted mud, tried to rise, twisted with the spinning world and fell back down.

She heard the lanterns smash. The light vanished. Night returned.

Long Jack growled.

Sophie rolled onto her side.

A figure walked towards her. It was a woman, dressed in a long, white night dress, and with a short wooden club in one hand.

"Granny?" Sophie said and heard the single word slur into something too long. Her head ached and the urge to vomit clenched her stomach.

"Sophie," Anna shook her head. Long Jack loped from his lair and stood behind her. He wrapped his arms around her and nuzzled into her neck. Anna craned her head against him. She reached up with a hand to stroke his hair.

Sophie's vision blurred as she started to cry. "You were lying."

"So prudish. So naïve. Every generation thinks they invented sex, but they didn't, of course. You'd be shocked at what your grandparents got up to in the night."

Sophie rolled onto her back. Through a gap in the trees she saw the stars. It was a beautiful night. The stars spun and she wondered why the galaxies were moving so quickly. Maybe time was running away from her. Running out.

"All this time?" Sophie asked.

"Ever since that first Blitz. I got scared and ran into the woods, just a slip of a girl. Long Jack found me. We've been friendly ever since. He even saved me from what would have been an exceptionally dull marriage. Poor girl; you were wrong about so much, and so nearly right in so many ways."

"What do you mean?" Sophie rolled her head back and forth, trying to make her vision clear.

"The consent was key; Long Jack cannot take what is not freely given. He is the animal drive given form, but he's not a monster. The salt and iron were a clever idea, but you misunderstood. The old scholars were talking in code: salt and iron is the blood, dear. Only by blood can Long Jack be bound."

Sophie tasted a bitterness in her throat. She wondered if she was going to choke to death on her own blood and thought she should feel more afraid. But, like before, she felt distant and weightless.

"You were never ill," she managed to say.

"Oh, I'm very ill," Anna said as she slipped out of Long Jack's embrace and knelt down by Sophie. "I'm dying. That was rather the point you see; what it's all been about. I want your body. But for that you had to come here, freely, and so you have."

Sophie tried to sink into the ground. She clawed at the soil and felt the cold metal of the poker under her fingers.

"Youth is wasted on the young," Anna said. "It's best to give it to me."

"Okay," Sophie said. She grit her teeth, ignored the pain and the spiralling world, gripped the poker, and swung.

It was an awkward swing, with little strength behind it, but Anna was ill, old and frail. The poker hit her across the face and she crumpled with a scream.

Sophie rolled onto her hands and knees and spit blood onto the damp leaves. She set the poker into the ground and levered herself up.

Anna lay in the dirt, shaking, blood dripping down her face. She raised her hands to the wound and stared at the blood on her fingers.

Long Jack growled and backed away.

"A lover, not a fighter," Sophie sneered at him. She staggered towards Anna, weaving with every wave of nausea that swept over her. "Here's your blood," she said.

She raised the poker.

It flashed red in the moonlight.

Sophie brought it down.

It connected with a wet thump.

Long Jack scampered back towards his cave. Sophie watched him go. She flung the poker onto the ground, next to the white and red corpse of her grandmother.

Footsteps sounded around her. Sophie looked up to see figures in dark robes stepping out of the forest, towards the clearing around the cave. They reached up and pulled down their hoods and she saw that they were all women. She recognised Helen, the nurse, Emma from the post office, and Margery, from bingo.

"Welcome, sister," Margery said.

Sophie faced them. Behind her, at the cave mouth, she heard Long Jack sigh and felt him stand at her back.

"Bound by blood," another woman said.

"Now, would you like to see?" asked another voice.

"See what?" Sophie replied.

"What it is that we do in the night…"

Cold, Wet Hands

John Moralee

THE SUMMERHOUSE was so far away. Maddy could barely see it on the horizon, where the silver-blue lake met the dark-green hills. She felt as though she had been swimming for days because her limbs were aching and the water's coldness had sapped her strength. As she increased the speed of her crawl, Maddy stared at the distant shore and wished she had never started her morning with a swim. She was no longer a fit teenager, like she had been the last time she stayed at the summerhouse.

Ten years of adulthood – working in a law firm in Chicago, where her life consisted of sitting at a desk writing reports – had reduced her fitness and stamina to a dangerous level. After only swimming to the middle – an easy feat when she was sixteen – Maddy was too breathless to continue to the far shore. She had decided to turn back. But it was the same frightening distance to the summerhouse. For the first time in her life, Maddy was afraid of drowning. Her faster strokes didn't seem to be shortening the distance. They were tiring her at her quicker rate. Ahead was a vast ocean and below her was a deep, dark hell.

Heart pounding, lungs burning, Maddy stopped swimming as a sharp pain in her side brought tears to her eyes. Not a stitch – not now! Chilling water poured into her mouth, making her cough and splutter. It tasted brackish. She started choking. The pain of her stitch and the shock of the water in her lungs made her panic. Forgetting how to swim, she started to thrash and lose control, drawing more water into her lungs.

Before she understood what was happening, her head was under the water and she was sinking to the murky lake bottom, a trail of air bubbles coming out of her mouth and noise.

The surface was a long, long way above, but she could do nothing to slow her spiralling descent. Her peripheral vision was shrinking as oxygen failed to reach her brain – darkness creeping up on her from all sides.

As the last air bubbles left her mouth, Maddy knew she was dying. Her conscious mind was shutting down. She stopped struggling, stopped fighting. She closed her eyes.

Death was coming.

She could feel its warm embrace.

Maddy was at least twenty feet down when her survival instinct returned. Her rational mind told her to do something, anything, if she wanted to live. By then she was in semi-darkness, not sure which way was up.

Something slimy touched her bare legs, feeling like oily hands trying to grab her and pull her down. Down! Yes! Her sense of direction was working again. Got to go up. Got to escape. Swim UP! Maddy kicked out and thrashed her legs, aiming herself upwards, until she burst out of the water into the hot sunlight, gasping for air.

She retched violently. After sucking in several long breaths, she trod water until her heart slowed and the chest pain subsided.

Really scared by her near-drowning, Maddy switched to a slow and steady breaststroke, keeping the summerhouse as her focus, her way home. When she finally reached the rocky shore, she climbed out, shivering and sobbing, relieved to be alive.

She staggered to a safe distance before flopping down on the grassy embankment, taking in deep, painful breaths. She wept like a little girl. After a couple of minutes, she had the energy to sit up and look back at the tranquil lake, feeling as though she had been betrayed by a lover.

Lake Kachika looked beautiful with the sunlight flashing on the water like glittering diamonds, but she would never trust the water again.

Maddy grabbed the towel left on a rock and wrapped it around her wet torso, hurrying onto the wooden deck leading to the summerhouse, where she saw her nineteen-year-old sister lounging in the sun, wearing a skimpy red bikini and heart-shaped sunglasses. Izzy was reading Proust's *Remembrance of Things Past* in the original French. She was also smoking a cigarette – a bad habit she'd started in college.

"You look like crap," Izzy said.

"Thanks. I almost drowned."

"Ah – that'd explain the pale vampire look. I thought you were auditioning for a new *Twilight* movie."

"Not funny. I was really scared. I thought I was going to die."

"Seriously?"

Maddy nodded. Tears stung her eyes.

Izzy looked concerned, abandoning her book and cigarette. "Hey – I'm sorry. I thought you were exaggerating. What happened?"

"It's so stupid. I went under and nearly drowned because I forgot I'm not as fit as I used to be. It's a long swim when you're out of practice, believe me. I'm never going in that water again."

"Are you all right now?"

Maddy wanted to say yes, but nothing came out of her mouth except a miserable whimper.

Seeing her distress, Izzy jumped up and hugged her. "You're freezing. You might be in shock. Come on – take a nice hot shower. I'll make you a warm coffee."

"S-screw coffee," Maddy sniffled. "Give me that cigarette."

* * *

An hour later, Maddy was in her bathroom, vomiting into the toilet bowl, her head pounding with every pulse of her heart. She'd never felt as sick in her life. She moaned, heaving and heaving, a cold sweat coating her body. Eventually the nausea subsided, but only after her throat was sore and her head ached like her worst-ever hangover.

She flushed away the vomit, then brushed her teeth, then showered. To fight the headache, she opened the medicine cabinet and found some long-expired paracetamol pills. Swallowing four pills with cold water, she looked at herself in the bathroom mirror. Her left eye was bloodshot, probably as a result of her close call with the Grim Reaper. It looked horrific, like someone had punched her. To hide it, she tried brushing her dark-brown hair over that side of her face, but it made her look like the creepy girl in *The Ring*. There was a pair of sunglasses on her dresser – so she went to get them. The bright sun through the windows gave her stabbing pain behind her eyes. As soon as she slipped the sunglasses on, she felt an instant relief, though her head still pounded. Feeling sorry for herself, she sat on her bed checking her phone for messages. Nothing interesting on Facebook, Twitter or Instagram.

Sighing, she lay down and closed her eyes. She wanted to sleep. But she remembered the feeling of drowning and felt her heart racing. Sleep was impossible.

Maddy listened to the silence. The summerhouse used to be filled with sounds of talking and laughter, but it was quiet. During the summers when she was a kid, the summerhouse had always been full of friends and relatives visiting from all across the country, invited to stay by her wealthy parents. It sounded deathly quiet without them. Their parents had divorced seven years ago. Maddy remembered the good times they'd had as a family at the summerhouse before everything went wrong, before her dad left them for his PA and her mom married a Russian oligarch called Ivan. Deep down, Maddy wanted her parents to be there – happy together – instead of living on different continents.

Half dozing, Maddy heard her sister's feet on the hardwood floor as she came into her room without knocking. Izzy's footsteps sounded wet as she lightly padded across the floor. Maddy heard Izzy stop next to the bed, breathing slowly. Izzy didn't speak – so Maddy assumed it was because her sister wasn't sure if she was awake or not. Maddy opened her eyes, ready to say something about respecting her privacy. Nobody was there – but she had heard Izzy in her room just moments earlier. There were wet footprints on the hardwood floor, leading from the closed door to the bed. Maddy frowned.

"Izzy, where are you?"

There was no reply.

"IZZY, WHERE ARE YOU?"

"Outside!" her sister called.

"Outside?" Maddy rushed to her window and looked down at her sister sunbathing on the deck. "Izzy, have you just been up here?"

"What? No. Why?"

"Have you been in my room when I was dozing?"

"No! Why?"

"I thought—" She sighed. "Sorry. Never mind. I must've been dreaming." But that didn't make sense because she'd seen the wet footprints. She was sure her own feet had been dry when she came up to her room. Maddy turned around and stared at the floor where she'd seen the trail.

The wet footprints had gone.

* * *

"What are you looking for?" Izzy said, wandering into the kitchen, where Maddy was staring into the refrigerator with no memory of having come downstairs. Maddy had been standing there long enough to feel the chill on her bare legs. Since there were only bottles of water and expired orange juice on the shelves, she didn't know why she had been staring. She closed the door and faced her sister. "We need to go shopping. I'm starving."

"Good idea. Hey – what's up with your legs?"

Frowning, Maddy looked down at herself, noticing a nasty red rash on both of her lower legs, roughly in the shape of five long fingers. It looked like she had been slapped hard and the redness had not faded. "Urgh. That's weird. I must be allergic to whatever weeds are at the bottom of the lake. I remember it felt like slimy hands."

"They look like bruises. Your eye's burst, too. I didn't notice that before. Maybe you need to see a doctor, sis. You look terrible."

"No. I'm okay. I'll be fine once I put on some hydrocortisone cream."

There wasn't any in the summerhouse – so they decided to take their dad's Jeep into the local town to buy supplies for their vacation. They drove to Drury – a little coastal town a few miles north, near the border of Maine. Maddy bought everything she needed in the small mall, plus a whole load of candy and chips that was an impulse buy, then she joined her sister in The Blue Lobster, the best and only seafood restaurant.

Maddy loved the rustic charm. The restaurant's owner had given the interior a nautical theme – fishing nets, plastic crabs and starfish hung on the walls among photographs of sailing boats and brave fishermen in raging storms. The owner normally greeted them like old friends as they went in, but she was not there that day. Instead, a James Franco lookalike working as a waiter shamelessly flirted with her sister. He offered them the best booth by the windows, looking out on the harbour. Izzy flirted back, while Maddy wondered why the ridiculously handsome waiter had not even looked at her. Not long ago she had been the centre of male attention on her visits to Drury. She hoped it was her bloodshot eye making her repulsive and not her general appearance. Being in her younger sister's shadow made her feel old and ugly. After the waiter had gone to help some other customers, Maddy sighed.

"That guy certainly likes you," she said. "But I think he thought I was Swamp Thing."

"Here, wear my shades," Izzy said, passing her sunglasses across the table. "I can't stand looking at that funky eye. Dude, check out the size of the menus. They're huge. It's just like I remember when Mom and Dad used to bring us here. Hmm. I don't know what to pick."

"I'm having the surf'n'turf."

Izzy raised an eyebrow. "You're having meat?"

Maddy was puzzled. "Yeah, so?"

"You're vegan."

"I am? Oh. Yeah. I forgot." She'd been a vegan since she was sixteen. A Greenpeace documentary on slaughterhouses had convinced her eating meat was wrong. But for a moment she had really craved a juicy steak.

"You forgot? Dude, you're acting weird. Seriously, you need to see a doctor."

"I'm fine. I just need to eat something." She spoke to James Franco's lookalike. "For starters, I'll have the chilli fries and the vegetarian pizza with a Coca-Cola. Regular – not diet, please."

"And what can I get you?" he said to her sister.

"What do you recommend?"

"The Special is good."

"I'll have that," Izzy said, looking at his name tag. "Thanks, Evan."

"My pleasure," Evan said. "What's your name?"

"Izzy."

"Cool name. I'll bring your meal in ten minutes. Have a good day, Izzy."

As he walked away, Izzy licked her lips. "He's hot."

"Yeah," Maddy admitted. "I wouldn't mind a slice of that myself. Yum-yum!"

They started laughing loudly. Five locals at a table turned and stared. Maddy found their hostile looks intimidating. What was their problem? Didn't they like laughing? They were wearing dirty blue uniforms marked with the logo of Greystone Fisheries. Most of the men were in their fifties or sixties. One had short salt-and-pepper hair and a long beard. His hairy arms were covered in tattoos of bare-breasted women entwined with snakes.

Maddy didn't like the way he looked at her.

I know him!

She felt a sudden, intense pain in the middle of her forehead, as though she had been jabbed with a hot needle. The pain stunned. She screamed something that made no sense.

"Gremlin!" she yelled, then she felt a hot liquid running down her face, into her eyes, stinging, blinding her.

Somewhere nearby Maddy heard her sister calling her name over and over, but Maddy could not see her.

Everything was dark.

And cold.

And wet.

She was drowning again.

* * *

Maddy woke in a hospital bed, confused but pain-free. Her sister was there, along with a doctor with a nice smile. He said some kind and reassuring words, then left them alone.

"What happened to me? How'd I get here?"

"You passed out in The Blue Lobster and I couldn't wake you up. Evan – the waiter – called for an ambulance. You were conscious when it arrived, but you were talking nonsense."

"Like what?"

"Oh, all kinds of crazy stuff. You called me Angela and insisted your name was Maureen."

"Maureen?" She didn't know anyone with that name. Or Angela. "That's weird."

"Yeah. It was creepy. The paramedics brought you here, where the doctors did a bunch of tests. They found nothing wrong with you physically, except for the rash and a mild fever. They gave you some antibiotics and fluids. The doctors told me you'd recover if you have plenty of rest." Izzy grabbed her hand and squeezed it. "Don't scare me like that!"

"I'll try not to," she said. "I don't remember any of that. Maureen and Angela? Why would I say those names?"

Izzy shrugged. "Who knows? The good news is you're going to be fine. The better news is Evan gave me his phone number. He's not just a waiter, you know. His mother owns the restaurant, so he was helping her out because they're short on staff. He's studying music in Portland. He's in a local band called Picklehead. They're doing a gig at the Rusty Nail on Friday night and he's invited me."

"I'm glad my illness got you a date. Can I get out of here, now?"

"No. They want to keep you under observation until the morning, but I'll stay and keep you company. I'll find the clicker so we can watch some TV."

"I'm not in the mood for TV. You don't need to stay all night. You need to get a proper night's sleep, too. Can you do me a favour before you go?"

"Anything."

"I need you to ask your boyfriend if he knows who the guy was at the restaurant with the sexist tattoos of naked women."

"That's a strange request."

"Yeah, but will you do it?"

"Uh – sure. I'll ask text him." She pulled out her phone. "I don't see the point of this, but whatever. Uh. Evan says he knows the guy. He's a regular. His name is Tad Peters."

"Tad Peters?" The name meant nothing, but it sounded familiar. "Izzy, any idea why I said the word 'gremlin' earlier?"

"No idea."

* * *

That night Maddy had a strange dream. She imagined herself naked and wandering around the moonlit town like she was lost, her long hair dripping with icy water. She was looking for something, but she didn't know where to go.

She stopped at a dark house with a small garden, where she slipped inside through an unlocked door without making a sound. Her bare feet left wet marks on the carpet.

She found Tad Peters snoring on a couch, passed out from drinking too much beer.

Without waking him, she leant over him and locked her mouth onto his as though kissing him passionately, though there was no passion in the act. Her tongue forced his mouth open.

Suddenly, brackish water was pouring from her mouth into Tad's throat, making him choke in his sleep. Tad opened his eyes and struggled, but she held him down with incredible, unnatural strength.

More and more water filled Tad's throat – until Maddy jerked awake in her hospital bed, vividly recalling the dream, her entire body soaked in cold sweat.

* * *

The next morning Maddy was feeling stronger when Izzy picked her up in the Jeep. The hospital food had been terrible, so they stopped at The Blue Lobster for breakfast. Evan served them.

"Have you seen Tad Peters today?"

"No – but his friends were here. One told me they saw an ambulance at his house last night. He's been taken to hospital with pneumonia."

"Is he okay?"

"I don't know."

I did that, Maddy thought. I tried to kill him.

"Something wrong?" her sister said.

"Yes. I had a dream about drowning him. Something's happening. It's like I'm not me anymore."

"What do you mean?"

"Tad Peters did something very bad. I'm sure of it, but I don't remember what. I need to see him. He has to tell me what happened. I'm going back to the hospital."

"Maddy, you can't."

"I have to see him!"

"Okay, okay. I'll come with you. Just don't do anything crazy."

Maddy and Izzy returned to the hospital. It wasn't hard to find out which room Tad Peters was in. Drury General didn't have the tight security of a city hospital. It was easy to enter his room without anyone noticing. Tad Peters was connected to beeping monitoring equipment. He was awake, but his eye were unfocused. He stiffened when he saw Maddy.

"No!" he said. "Please don't kill me, Maureen. I didn't mean to hurt you. It was a mistake. I'm sorry. I'm sorry."

"How do you know me?" Maddy asked, but he didn't answer. His heart rate and blood pressure rocketed, triggering alarms. It looked like he was having a heart attack.

Izzy grabbed Maddy's hand, dragging her out of the room. "Let's get out of here, Maddy. We can't be caught in here."

Maddy hurried into the corridor before the doctors and nurses arrived. Luckily, the staff were too busy to notice Maddy and Izzy making a hasty exit.

"What the hell is going on, Maddy?"

"I don't know. Why did he think I was someone called Maureen?"

"She must be someone he knows," Izzy said. "We can Google her."

"We can't Google a first name. There are millions of Maureens. We need a surname."

"If Maureen is a local person, she'll probably be in an old yearbook. I'll ask Evan for help."

Evan visited that afternoon, bringing a stack of yearbooks. "Why do you need these?"

"Just research," Izzy told him.

'Maureen' was a dated name – so they started looking in the yearbooks from the 1960s and 1970s. They found several. Only one was interesting. A girl called Maureen Nielsen. She had been a chunky girl with lank brown hair and bad acne. There was a deep sadness in her eyes, like she'd never had a day of happiness in her life. She had been in the same class as Tad Peters. A Google search revealed she had gone missing in 1972, aged fifteen.

"Izzy, this will sound mad, but I think she drowned in the lake. That's why nobody found her. Her body's down there in the dark, but her spirit made contact with me. She's trying to tell me what happened. Tad Peters must have killed her and she wants revenge. She's possessed me."

"Maddy, you don't really believe that, do you?"

"Yes! No! I don't know. Look – she had a sister called Angela. She's still alive. I need to see her. Will you come?"

"Yes, but I'm worried about you."

"So am I," Maddy said. "But I need to do it."

* * *

Angela Nielsen's home was a little cottage in Drury.

"Hi!" Maddy said to the grey-haired woman who answered the door. "Are you Angela Nielson?"

"Yes?" the woman said suspiciously. "How can I help you?"

Maddy and Izzy had formulated a plan before arriving. They pretended to be journalists writing a story about Angela's missing sister for a crime blog. Maddy hated lying, but it was easier than explaining the truth, that she thought Maureen had possessed her after a near-death experience. Angela seemed pleased to have two strangers visiting her to talk about her missing sister.

"Come in, please. I'll make some coffee, then you can ask me anything."

The coffee was too strong, but Maddy sipped it with a smile. "What can you tell us about your sister?"

"Maureen was lovely, sweet girl – but she was bullied a lot in high school because she was overweight. I remember her being so unhappy because the popular girls called her Miss Piggy. No boys liked her. There was only one boy who did and that was only after she started swimming to lose weight. She was dating him when she disappeared. His name was Tad Peters."

"Was he a suspect?"

"The police questioned him, but he claimed he'd been driving around in his Gremlin with his friends. They said they didn't see Maureen."

"What do you believe?"

"I never liked Tad. He was using her."

"Using her for what?"

"What do you think?"

"Oh. That."

"Yes."

"So, what do you think happened?"

"Tad killed her. Unfortunately, I have no proof."

* * *

That night Maddy had a dream of a hot summer day in 1972. Maureen was in a car with Tad and his teenage friends. They were all drinking beers and smoking weed. They stopped on the south side of Lake Kachika.

For hours they drank beers and got high, laughing and having a good time. Next, Tad persuaded her to strip for his friends. She didn't like revealing her naked body, but she did it to please him. Tad's mood changed then. He starting calling her nasty names and making piggy noises. His friends joined in. Maureen cried.

As a final humiliation, Tad and his friends grabbed her clothes and drove off in his Gremlin, leaving her naked and alone.

She waited hours for them to come back, but they never did.

It was too far to walk home – but she could take a shortcut across the lake. There was a summerhouse on the other side, where some hippies lived. They would give her clothes and drive her home. She set off swimming.

Ahead, some little boys were on the shore, skipping stones. They saw her coming. She hoped they'd help. They didn't. For laughs, they started throwing stones at her. One stone smacked her in the forehead, drawing blood, and the kids ran off, leaving her to drown.

* * *

When Maddy opened her eyes, she understood everything. For decades Maureen's soul had been tormented and lost. After fifty years, only her skeleton would remain, but at least Maureen could find some peace if Maddy hired a diver to search and recover her bones. That was all Maureen wanted now. Not revenge. Burial and final rest.

Feeling lighter, Maddy walked outside and stopped at the water's edge, saying goodbye to the girl in the lake.

The House of Silence

Edith Nesbit

THE THIEF stood close under the high wall, and looked to right and left. To the right the road wound white and sinuous, lying like a twisted ribbon over the broad grey shoulder of the hill; to the left the road turned sharply down towards the river; beyond the ford the road went away slowly in a curve, prolonged for miles through the green marshes.

No least black fly of a figure stirred on it. There were no travellers at such an hour on such a road.

The thief looked across the valley, at the top of the mountain flushed with sunset, and at the grey-green of the olives about its base. The terraces of olives were already dusk with twilight, but his keen eyes could not have missed the smallest variance or shifting of their lights and shadows. Nothing stirred there. He was alone.

Then, turning, he looked again at the wall behind him. The face of it was grey and sombre, but all along the top of it, in the crannies of the coping stones, orange wallflowers and sulphur-coloured snapdragons shone among the haze of feathery-flowered grasses. He looked again at the place where some of the stones had fallen from the coping – had fallen within the wall, for none lay in the road without. The bough of a mighty tree covered the gap with its green mantle from the eyes of any chance wayfarer; but the thief was no chance wayfarer, and he had surprised the only infidelity of the great wall to its trust.

To the chance wayfarer, too, the wall's denial had seemed absolute, unanswerable. Its solid stone, close-knit by mortar hardly less solid, showed not only a defence, it offered a defiance – a menace. But the thief had learnt his trade; he saw that the mortar might be loosened a little here, broken a little there, and now the crumbs of it fell rustling onto the dry, dusty grass of the roadside. He drew back, took two quick steps forward, and, with a spring, sudden and agile as a cat's, grasped the wall where the gap showed, and drew himself up. Then he rubbed his hands on his knees, because his hands were bloody from the sudden grasping of the rough stones, and sat astride on the wall.

He parted the leafy boughs and looked down; below him lay the stones that had fallen from the wall – already grass was growing upon the mound they made. As he ventured his head beyond the green leafage, the level light of the sinking sun struck him in the eyes. It was like a blow. He dropped softly from the wall and stood in the shadow of the tree – looking, listening.

Before him stretched the park – wide and still; dotted here and there with trees, and overlaid with gold poured from the west. He held his breath and listened. There was no wind to stir the leaves to those rustlings which may deceive and disconcert the keenest and the boldest; only the sleepy twitter of birds, and the little sudden soft movements of them in the dusky privacy of the thick-leaved branches. There was in all the broad park no sign of any other living thing.

The thief trod softly along under the wall where the trees were thickest, and at every step he paused to look and listen.

It was quite suddenly that he came upon the little lodge near the great gates of wrought iron with the marble gate-posts bearing upon them the two gaunt griffins, the cognisance of the noble house whose lands these were. The thief drew back into the shadow and stood still, only his heart beat thickly. He stood still as the tree trunk beside him, looking, listening. He told himself that he heard nothing – saw nothing – yet he became aware of things. That the door of the lodge was not closed, that some of its windows were broken, and that into its little garden straw and litter had drifted from the open door: and that between the stone step and the threshold grass was growing inches high. When he was aware of this he stepped forward and entered the lodge. All the sordid sadness of a little deserted home met him here – broken crocks and bent pans, straw, old rags, and a brooding, dusty stillness.

"There has been no one here since the old keeper died. They told the truth," said the thief; and he made haste to leave the lodge, for there was nothing in it now that any man need covet – only desolation and the memory of death.

So he went slowly among the trees, and by devious ways drew a little nearer to the great house that stood in its walled garden in the middle of the park. From very far off, above the green wave of trees that broke round it, he could see the towers of it rising black against the sunset; and between the trees came glimpses of its marble white where the faint grey light touched it from the east.

Moving slowly – vigilant, alert, with eyes turning always to right and to left, with ears which felt the intense silence more acutely than they could have felt any tumult – the thief reached the low wall of the garden, at the western side. The last redness of the sunset's reflection had lighted all the many windows, and the vast place blazed at him for an instant before the light dipped behind the black bar of the trees, and left him face to face with a pale house, whose windows now were black and hollow, and seemed like eyes that watched him. Every window was closed; the lower ones were guarded by jalousies; through the glass of the ones above he could see the set painted faces of the shutters.

From far off he had heard, and known, the plash-plash of fountains, and now he saw their white changing columns rise and fall against the background of the terrace. The garden was full of rose bushes trailing and unpruned; and the heavy, happy scent of the roses, still warm from the sun, breathed through the place, exaggerating the sadness of its tangled desolation. Strange figures gleamed in the deepening dusk, but they were too white to be feared. He crept into a corner where Psyche drooped in marble, and, behind her pedestal, crouched. He took food from his pockets and ate and drank. And between the mouthfuls he listened and watched.

The moon rose, and struck a pale fire from the face of the house and from the marble limbs of the statues, and the gleaming water of the fountains drew the moonbeams into the unchanging change of its rise and fall.

Something rustled and stirred among the roses. The thief grew rigid: his heart seemed suddenly hollow; he held his breath. Through the deepening shadows something gleamed white; and not marble, for it moved, it came towards him. Then the silence of the night was shattered by a scream, as the white shape glided into the moonlight. The thief resumed his munching, and another shape glimmered after the first. "Curse the beasts!" he said, and took another draught from his bottle, as the white peacocks were blotted out by the shadows of the trees, and the stillness of the night grew more intense.

In the moonlight the thief went round and about the house, pushing through the trailing briers that clung to him – and now grown bolder he looked closely at doors and windows. But all were fast barred as the doors of a tomb. And the silence deepened as the moonlight waxed.

There was one little window, high up, that showed no shutter. He looked at it; measured its distance from the ground and from the nearest of the great chestnut trees. Then he walked along under the avenue of chestnuts with head thrown back and eyes fixed on the mystery of their interlacing branches.

At the fifth tree he stopped; leaped to the lowest bough, missed it; leaped again, caught it, and drew up his body. Then climbing, creeping, swinging, while the leaves, agitated by his progress, rustled to the bending of the boughs, he passed to that tree, to the next – swift, assured, unhesitating. And so from tree to tree, till he was at the last tree – and on the bough that stretched to touch the little window with its leaves.

He swung from this. The bough bent and cracked, and would have broken, but that at the only possible instant the thief swung forward, felt the edge of the window with his feet, loosed the bough, sprang, and stood, flattened against the mouldings, clutching the carved drip-stone with his hands. He thrust his knee through the window, waiting for the tinkle of the falling glass to settle into quietness, opened the window, and crept in. He found himself in a corridor: he could see the long line of its white windows, and the bars of moonlight falling across the inlaid wood of its floor.

He took out his thief's lantern – high and slender like a tall cup – lighted it, and crept softly along the corridor, listening between his steps till the silence grew to be like a humming in his ears.

And slowly, stealthily, he opened door after door; the rooms were spacious and empty – his lantern's yellow light flashing into their corners told him this. Some poor, plain furniture he discerned, a curtain or a bench here and there, but not what he sought. So large was the house, that presently it seemed to the thief that for many hours he had been wandering along its galleries, creeping down its wide stairs, opening the grudging doors of the dark, empty rooms, whose silence spoke ever more insistently in his ears.

"But it is as he told me," he said inwardly: "no living soul in all the place. The old man – a servant of this great house – he told me; he knew, and I have found all even as he said."

Then the thief turned away from the arched emptiness of the grand staircase, and in a far corner of the hall he found himself speaking in a whisper because now it seemed to him that nothing would serve but that this clamorous silence should be stilled by a human voice.

"The old man said it would be thus – all emptiness, and not profit to a man; and he died, and I tended him. Dear Jesus! How our good deeds come home to us! And he told me how the last of the great family had gone away none knew whither. And the tales I heard in the town – how the great man had not gone, but lived here in hiding – it is not possible. There is the silence of death in this house."

He moistened his lips with his tongue. The stillness of the place seemed to press upon him like a solid thing. "It is like a dead man on one's shoulders," thought the thief, and he straightened himself up and whispered again: "The old man said, 'The door with the carved griffin, and the roses enwreathed, and the seventh rose holds the secret in its heart.'"

With that the thief set forth again, creeping softly across the bars of moonlight down the corridor.

And after much seeking he found at last, under the angle of the great stone staircase behind a mouldering tapestry wrought with peacocks and pines, a door, and on it carved a griffin, wreathed about with roses. He pressed his finger into the deep heart of each carven rose, and when he pressed the rose that was seventh in number from the griffin, he felt the inmost part of it move beneath his finger as though it sought to escape. So he pressed more strongly, leaning against the door till it swung open, and he passed through it, looking behind him to see that nothing followed. The door he closed as he entered.

And now he was, as it seemed, in some other house. The chambers were large and lofty as those whose hushed emptiness he had explored – but these rooms seemed warm with life, yet held no threat, no terror. To the dim yellow flicker from the lantern came out of the darkness hints of a crowded magnificence, a lavish profusion of beautiful objects such as he had never in his life dreamed of, though all that life had been one dream of the lovely treasures which rich men hoard, and which, by the thief's skill and craft, may come to be his.

He passed through the rooms, turning the light of his lantern this way and that, and ever the darkness withheld more than the light revealed. He knew that thick tapestries hung from the walls, velvet curtains masked the windows; his hand, exploring eagerly, felt the rich carving of chairs and presses; the great beds were hung with silken cloth wrought in gold thread with glimmering strange starry devices. Broad sideboards flashed back to his lantern's questionings the faint white laugh of silver; the tall cabinets could not, with all their reserve, suppress the confession of wrought gold, and, from the caskets into whose depths he flashed the light, came the trembling avowal of rich jewels. And now, at last, that carved door closed between him and the poignant silence of the deserted corridors, the thief felt a sudden gaiety of heart, a sense of escape, of security. He was alone, yet warmed and companioned. The silence here was no longer a horror, but a consoler, a friend.

And, indeed, now he was not alone. The ample splendours about him, the spoils which long centuries had yielded to the grasp of a noble family – these were companions after his own heart.

He flung open the shade of his lantern and held it high above his head. The room still kept half its secrets. The discretion of the darkness should be broken down. He must see more of this splendour – not in unsatisfying dim detail, but in the lit gorgeous mass of it. The narrow bar of the lantern's light chafed him. He sprang on to the dining table, and began to light the half-burnt chandelier. There were a hundred candles, and he lighted all, so that the chandelier swung like a vast living jewel in the centre of the hall. Then, as he turned, all the colour in the room leapt out at him. The purple of the couches, the green gleam of the delicate glass, the blue of the tapestries, and the vivid scarlet of the velvet hangings, and with the colour sprang the gleams of white from the silver, of yellow from the gold, of many-coloured fire from strange inlaid work and jewelled caskets, till the thief stood aghast with rapture in the strange, sudden revelation of this concentrated splendour.

He went along the walls with a lighted candle in his hand – the wax dripped warm over his fingers as he went – lighting one after another, the tapers in the sconces of the silver-framed glasses. In the state bedchamber he drew back suddenly, face to face with a death-white countenance in which black eyes blazed at him with triumph and delight. Then he laughed aloud. He had not known his own face in the strange depths of this mirror. It had no sconces like the others, or he would have known it for what it was. It was framed in Venice glass – wonderful, gleaming, iridescent.

The thief dropped the candle and threw his arms wide with a gesture of supreme longing.

"If I could carry it all away! All, all! Every beautiful thing! To sell some – the less beautiful, and to live with the others all my days!"

And now a madness came over the thief. So little a part of all these things could he bear away with him; yet all were his – his for the taking – even the huge carved presses and the enormous vases of solid silver, too heavy for him to lift – even these were his: had he not found them – he, by his own skill and cunning? He went about in the rooms, touching one after the other the beautiful, rare things. He caressed the gold and the jewels. He threw his arms round the great silver vases; he wound round himself the heavy red velvet of the curtain where the griffins gleamed in embossed gold, and shivered with pleasure at the soft clinging of its embrace. He found, in a tall cupboard, curiously-shaped flasks of wine, such wine as he had never tasted, and he drank of it slowly – in little sips – from a silver goblet and from a green Venice glass, and from a cup of rare pink china, knowing that any one of his drinking vessels was worth enough to keep him in idleness for a long year. For the thief had learnt his trade, and it is a part of a thief's trade to know the value of things.

He threw himself on the rich couches, sat in the stately carved chairs, leaned his elbows on the ebony tables. He buried his hot face in the chill, smooth linen of the great bed, and wondered to find it still scented delicately as though some sweet woman had lain there but last night. He went hither and thither laughing with pure pleasure, and making to himself an unbridled carnival of the joys of possession.

In this wise the night wore on, and with the night his madness wore away. So presently he went about among the treasures – no more with the eyes of a lover, but with the eyes of a Jew – and he chose those precious stones which he knew for the most precious, and put them in the bag he had brought, and with them some fine-wrought goldsmith's work and the goblet out of which he had drunk the wine. Though it was but of silver, he would not leave it. The green Venice glass he broke and the cup, for he said: "No man less fortunate than I, tonight, shall ever again drink from them." But he harmed nothing else of all the beautiful things, because he loved them.

Then, leaving the low, uneven ends of the candles still alight, he turned to the door by which he had come in. There were two doors, side by side, carved with straight lilies, and between them a panel wrought with the griffin and the seven roses enwreathed. He pressed his finger in the heart of the seventh rose, hardly hoping that the panel would move, and indeed it did not; and he was about to seek for a secret spring among the lilies, when he perceived that one of the doors wrought with these had opened itself a little. So he passed through it and closed it after him.

"I must guard my treasures," he said. But when he had passed through the door and closed it, and put out his hand to raise the tattered tapestry that covered it from without, his hand met the empty air, and he knew that he had not come out by the door through which he had entered.

When the lantern was lighted, it showed him a vaulted passage, whose floor and whose walls were stone, and there was a damp air and a mouldering scent in it, as of a cellar long unopened. He was cold now, and the room with the wine and the treasures seemed long ago and far away, though but a door and a moment divided him from it, and though some of the wine was in his body, and some of the treasure in his hands. He set about to find the way to the quiet night outside, for this seemed to him a haven and a safeguard since, with the closing of that door, he had shut away warmth, and light, and companionship. He was enclosed in walls once more, and once more menaced by the invading silence that was almost a presence. Once more it seemed to him that he must creep softly, must hold his breath before he ventured to turn a corner – for always he felt that he was not alone, that near him was something, and that its breath, too, was held.

So he went by many passages and stairways, and could find no way out; and after a long time of searching he crept by another way back to come unawares on the door which shut him off from the room where the many lights were, and the wine and the treasure. Then terror leaped out upon him from the dark hush of the place, and he beat on the door with his hands and cried aloud, till the echo of his cry in the groined roof cowed him back into silence.

Again he crept stealthily by strange passages, and again could find no way except, after much wandering, back to the door where he had begun.

And now the fear of death beat in his brain with blows like a hammer. To die here like a rat in a trap, never to see the sun alight again, never to climb in at a window, or see brave jewels shine under his lantern, but to wander, and wander, and wander between these inexorable walls till he died, and the rats, admitting him to their brotherhood, swarmed round the dead body of him.

"I had better have been born a fool," said the thief.

Then once more he went through the damp and the blackness of the vaulted passages, tremulously searching for some outlet, but in vain.

Only at last, in a corner behind a pillar, he found a very little door and a stair that led down. So he followed it, to wander among other corridors and cellars, with the silence heavy about him, and despair growing thick and cold like a fungus about his heart, and in his brain the fear of death beating like a hammer.

It was quite suddenly in his wanderings, which had grown into an aimless frenzy, having now less of search in it than of flight from the insistent silence, that he saw at last a light – and it was the light of day coming through an open door. He stood at the door and breathed the air of the morning. The sun had risen and touched the tops of the towers of the house with white radiance; the birds were singing loudly. It was morning, then, and he was a free man.

He looked about him for a way to come at the park, and thence to the broken wall and the white road, which he had come by a very long time before. For this door opened on an inner enclosed courtyard, still in damp shadow, though the sun above struck level across it – a courtyard where tall weeds grew thick and dank. The dew of the night was heavy on them.

As he stood and looked, he was aware of a low, buzzing sound that came from the other side of the courtyard. He pushed through the weeds towards it; and the sense of a presence in the silence came upon him more than ever it had done in the darkened house, though now it was day, and the birds sang all gaily, and the good sun shone so bravely overhead.

As he thrust aside the weeds which grew waist-high, he trod on something that seemed to writhe under his feet like a snake. He started back and looked down. It was the long, firm, heavy plait of a woman's hair. And just beyond lay the green gown of a woman, and a woman's hands, and her golden head, and her eyes; all about the place where she lay was the thick buzzing of flies, and the black swarming of them.

The thief saw, and he turned and he fled back to his doorway, and down the steps and through the maze of vaulted passages – fled in the dark, and empty-handed, because when he had come into the presence that informed that house with silence, he had dropped lantern and treasure, and fled wildly, the horror in his soul driving him before it. Now fear is more wise than cunning, so, whereas he had sought for hours with his lantern and with all his thief's craft to find the way out, and had sought in vain, he now, in the dark and blindly, without thought or will, without pause or let, found the one way that led to a door, shot back the bolts, and fled through the awakened rose garden and across the dewy park.

He dropped from the wall into the road, and stood there looking eagerly to right and left. To the right the road wound white and sinuous, like a twisted ribbon over the great, grey shoulder of the hill; to the left the road curved down towards the river. No least black fly of a figure stirred on it. There are no travellers on such a road at such an hour.

The Downs

Amyas Northcote

I AM VENTURING to set down the following personal experience, inconclusive as it is, as I feel that it may interest those who have the patience to study the phenomena of the unseen world around us. It was my first experience of a psychical happening and its events are accordingly indelibly imprinted on my memory.

The date was, alas, a good many years ago, when I was still a young man and at the time was engaged in reading hard for a certain examination. My friend J. was in similar plight to myself and together we decided to abjure home and London life and seek a quiet country spot, where we might devote ourselves to our work amidst pleasant and congenial surroundings.

J. knew of such a place: a farm belonging to a Mr. Harkness, who was a distant connection of his own by marriage. Mr. Harkness was a childless widower and lived much to himself at Branksome Farm, attended to only by an elderly housekeeper and one or two servants. Although he called himself a farmer and did in fact farm fairly extensively, he was a man of cultivated and even learned tastes, widely read and deeply versed in the history and folklore of his neighbourhood. At the same time, although good-natured, he was the most reserved and taciturn man I ever met, and appeared to have a positive horror of communicating his very considerable fund of local knowledge to outsiders like ourselves. However, he was glad to welcome us as paying guests for the sake of his relationship to J., and he and his housekeeper certainly took great care to make us comfortable and happy.

Branksome Farm is a large old-fashioned house, surrounded by the usual farm buildings and situated in a valley winding its way among the Downs. The situation is beautiful and remote, and it would astonish many of our City dwellers to know that within two or three hours' railway journey from London there still are vast stretches of open Downland on which one may walk for hours without sight of a human being, and traversed only by winding roads which run from one small town or hamlet to another, linking a few lonely cottages or farms to civilisation on their route. Behind the house Branksome Down, the highest in the neighbourhood, rises steeply, and beyond it at a distance of about three miles is Willingbury, the nearest town, whence the railway runs to London.

It is necessary to describe the geography of the country between Willingbury and Branksome a little more closely. The two places lie, as is usually the case in the Down country, in valleys between the hills, and by road are distant from each other about six to seven miles, being separated by the long ridge of Branksome Down. But actually the distance between them does not exceed three miles across the Down: the path from Branksome, a mere sheep-track, leading up to the top of Branksome Down whence the wanderer sees before him a wide shallow dip in the Down, nearly circular, about three-quarters of a mile across and at the other side sloping up to another gentle ridge. Arrived at the summit of this second elevation the traveller gazes down on the Willingbury-Overbury road and following another sheep-track down the hillside he reaches the road about a mile outside Willingbury.

The whole Down is covered with sweet, short turf, unbroken by trees or shrubs and, at the time of my story, was unmarred by fencing of any form. Flocks of sheep tended by shepherds and their watchful dogs were almost its sole inhabitants, save for the shy, wild life that clings to all natural shelters. Of the beauty of this Down and, in fact, of the whole neighbourhood it is useless to speak. To anyone who has once felt the fascination of a walk in the fresh, pure air, over the springy and centuries-old turf, and who has allowed his eyes to wander over the miles and miles of open Down, studded here and there with rare belts of trees, and has watched the shifting lights play over the near and distant hills, it is needless to speak, and to anyone who has never yet been fortunate enough to find himself in Downland in fine weather one can hardly make its fascination clear in words, and one can only advise him to go and explore its beauties for himself.

Well, it was at Branksome Farm that J. and I took up our abode and commenced a course of steady reading, tempered and varied by long walks about the country. Our time passed pleasantly and profitably, and we discovered one day with regret that more than half of it had elapsed.

Dismayed at this discovery we began to set our wits to work to find an excuse for prolonging our stay at Branksome, when suddenly an event happened which entirely altered our plans.

Returning one day from our accustomed walk, J. found a telegram waiting for him, which called him to London without delay and the contents of which appeared to indicate the probability of his being unable to return to Branksome. No time was to be lost in making a start if he was to catch the afternoon train at Willingbury and, as it was really quicker to walk across the Down than to drive round the roads behind Mr. Harkness' rather slow old mare, he threw a few clothes hastily into a bag and departed for the station. I accompanied him to see him off and we made the best possible speed to Willingbury. But we had miscalculated the time; the afternoon train had gone, and we found on inquiry that there would be no other until the night mail for London, which passed through Willingbury shortly before 11 p.m.

J. urged me not to wait for this but to leave him at the little inn and go back to Branksome before dark, but I was anxious to keep him company and cheer up his rather depressed spirits, so finally we agreed to dine together at the Blue Lion and spend the evening there until the train left.

I was perfectly confident in my ability to find my way back over the Down to Branksome at night, as the path was very familiar to us, and I expected to be aided by the light of the moon which would rise about ten o'clock. In due course the train arrived, and having seen J. safely on his way to London I turned my steps towards the Willingbury Overbury road and its junction with the Branksome sheeptrack.

It was a little after 11 p.m. when I left Willingbury on my homeward way, and I was disappointed to find that the moon had failed me, being completely hidden behind a thick canopy of cloud. The night was profoundly still as well as being very dark, but I was confident in my powers of finding my way and I strode contentedly along the road till I reached the point where it was necessary I should diverge on to the Down. I found the commencement of the sheep-track without difficulty, as my eyes were now accustomed to the surrounding obscurity, and set myself to climbing the Down as quickly as possible.

I must make it clear that up to the present time I had been in my usual state of health and spirits, although the latter were somewhat depressed at J.'s sudden departure and the break-up of our pleasant association together. Up to this night, also, I had never in the least suspected that I was possessed of any special psychic intelligence. It is true that I had known that I was in the habit of occasionally dreaming very vividly and consecutively, but I had never given this faculty a serious thought, nor, like most young men in their twenties, had I ever given any consideration to psychic matters. It must be remembered also that I am writing of nearly forty years ago, when an intelligent interest in the potentialities of unseen beings and kindred topics was far less common than it is today.

Well, I commenced my ascent of the hill, and I had not gone very far when I became aware of a certain peculiar change taking place in myself. I fear I shall find it very difficult to describe my sensations in a fashion intelligible to those who have never experienced anything similar, whilst to those who have undergone psychic ordeals my description will probably appear bald and inadequate.

I seemed to be in some mysterious fashion divided into a dual personality. One, the familiar one, was myself, my body, which continued to walk up the sheep-track, keenly alive to the need to keep a sharp look out against losing my way or stumbling over some obstruction. This personality also felt loneliness and a certain degree of nervousness. The darkness, silence and immensity of the empty country round me were oppressive. I feared something, I was not quite sure what, and I anxiously wished I was at the end of my journey with the farm lights shining out to welcome me. My other personality was more vague and ill-defined; it seemed to be separated from my body and from my outer consciousness and to be floating in a region where there was neither space nor time. It seemed to be aware of another world, a world surrounding and intermingling with this one, in which all that is or was or will be was but one moment and in which all places near or far, the Down and the remotest of the invisible stars, were but one spot.

All was instantaneous and all was eternal. I am not clear how long this mood lasted, but it was probably only a few minutes before my earthly self was brought or appeared to be brought into entire control of my personality by a sudden shock.

As I walked I became aware that I was not alone. There was a man moving parallel with me on my right at the distance of some four or five yards. So suddenly and so silently had he appeared that he seemed to have risen from the earth. He was walking quite quietly at my own pace abreast of me, but apparently taking no notice of me, and I observed that his footsteps made no sound on the soft turf. The dim light made it difficult to see him at all distinctly, but he was evidently a tall, powerfully-built fellow, dressed in a long cloak, which, partly covering his face, fell nearly to his feet. On his head he wore a queer-shaped, three-cornered hat and in his hand he carried what appeared to be a short, heavy bludgeon.

I was greatly startled. I am a small and by no means robust man and the apparition of this odd-looking stranger on these lonely Downs was disquieting. What did he want? Had he followed me down the road from Willingbury, and, if so, for what purpose? However, I decided it was best not to appear alarmed and after taking another glance at the man, I wished him good evening.

He took not the faintest notice of my salutation, which he appeared not even to have heard, but continued to advance up the hill by my side in dead silence.

After a few moments I spoke again; and this time my voice sounded strange in my own ears, as if it did not come from my lips, but from somewhere far away.

"A dark night," I said.

And now he answered. In a slow, measured voice, but one in which there sounded a note of hopelessness and misery, he said:

"It is dark to you. It is darker for me."

I scarcely knew what to reply, but I felt that my courage was at an ebb and that I must maintain it by endeavouring to keep up a conversation, difficult though this might prove. Accordingly I went on:

"This is a strange place to walk in at night. Have you far to go?"

He did not turn his head or look at me.

"Your way is short and easy, but mine is long and hard. How long, O Lord, how long?" he cried. As he uttered the last words his voice rose to a cry and he tossed his arms above his head, letting them fall to his side with a gesture of despair.

We had now almost reached the top of the Down, and as we neared the summit I became aware that the wind was rising. At the moment we were sheltered from it by the brow of the hill, but I could hear its distant roaring, and as we reached the summit it broke upon us with a rush.

With it and mingled in its sounds came other sounds, the sounds of human voices, of many voices, in many keys. There were sounds of wailing, of shouting, of chanting, of sobbing, even at times of laughter. The great, shallow bowl of Branksome Down was alive with sounds. I could see nothing, save my strange companion, who continued to move steadily forward; and I, dreading his company and yet dreading even more to be left alone, accompanied him. The night was still profoundly dark and, though as I advanced the voices often sounded quite near, I saw nothing until after we had passed the centre of the depression and were mounting the opposite slope. At that moment the wind tore aside the clouds and the moon streamed down full upon the Downs. By her light I saw a marvellous and a terrifying sight. The whole of Branksome Down was alive with people hurrying hither and thither, some busy and absorbed in their occupations, whatever they might be, others roaming aimlessly and tossing their arms into the air with wild and tragic gesticulations. The crowd appeared to be of all sorts and conditions and to be dressed in the fashions of all the ages, though ancient costumes seemed to predominate. Here I saw a group of persons clothed apparently in the priestly robes of ancient Britain; there walked a soldier wearing the eagle-crested helmet of Rome. Other groups there were in dresses of later date, the steel-clad knight of the Middle Ages, the picturesque dress and flowing hair of a cavalier of the Seventeenth Century. But it was impossible to fix the shifting crowd. As I gazed, absorbed, at one figure, it melted and was gone and another took its place, to fade likewise as I watched.

My companion paid no heed to the throng. Steadily he passed on towards the crest of the hill, at intervals raising his arms and letting them fall with his old gesture of despair and uttering at the same time his mournful cry of "How long, how long?"

We passed onward and upward and reached the top of the Down, my companion now a few yards in front of me. As he reached the crest of the hill, he stopped and, lifting his arms above his head, stood motionless. Suddenly he wavered, his figure expanded, its lines became vague and blurred against the background, it faded and was gone. As it vanished the wind dropped suddenly, the sound of human voices ceased and gazing round me I saw the plain bare and still in the moonlight.

I was now at the top of the hill, and looking downwards I saw a light burning in a window of Branksome Farm. I stumbled down the hill in haste, and as I approached the house saw Mr. Harkness standing at the open door. He looked at me strangely as I entered.

"Have you come across Branksome Down tonight," he exclaimed, "tonight of all the nights in the year?"

"Yes," I replied.

"I should have warned you," he said, "but I expected you back before dark. Branksome Down is an ill place tonight and men have vanished upon it before now and never been heard of again. No shepherd will set foot upon it tonight, for this is the night in the year when, folk say, all those that ever died violent deaths upon the Downs come back to seek their lost rest."

The Undying Thing

Barry Pain

Chapter I

UP AND DOWN the oak-panelled dining hall of Mansteth the master of the house walked restlessly. At formal intervals down the long severe table were placed four silver candlesticks, but the light from these did not serve to illuminate the whole of the surroundings. It just touched the portrait of a fair-haired boy with a sad and wistful expression that hung at one end of the room; it sparkled on the lid of a silver tankard. As Sir Edric passed to and fro it lit up his face and figure. It was a bold and resolute face with a firm chin and passionate, dominant eyes. A bad past was written in the lines of it. And yet every now and then there came over it a strange look of very anxious gentleness that gave it some resemblance to the portrait of the fair-haired boy. Sir Edric paused a moment before the portrait and surveyed it carefully, his strong brown hands locked behind him, his gigantic shoulders thrust a little forward.

"Ah, what I was!" he murmured to himself – "what I was!"

Once more he commenced pacing up and down. The candles, mirrored in the polished wood of the table, had burnt low. For hours Sir Edric had been waiting, listening intently for some sound from the room above or from the broad staircase outside. There had been sounds – the wailing of a woman, a quick abrupt voice, the moving of rapid feet. But for the last hour he had heard nothing. Quite suddenly he stopped and dropped on his knees against the table:

"God, I have never thought of Thee. Thou knowest that – Thou knowest that by my devilish behaviour and cruelty I did veritably murder Alice, my first wife, albeit the physicians did maintain that she died of a decline – a wasting sickness. Thou knowest that all here in Mansteth do hate me, and that rightly. They say, too, that I am mad; but that they say not rightly, seeing that I know how wicked I am. I always knew it, but I never cared until I loved – oh, God, I never cared!"

His fierce eyes opened for a minute, glared round the room, and closed again tightly. He went on:

"God, for myself I ask nothing; I make no bargaining with Thee. Whatsoever punishment Thou givest me to bear I will bear it; whatsoever Thou givest me to do I will do it. Whether Thou killest Eve or whether Thou keepest her in life – and never have I loved but her – I will from this night be good. In due penitence will I receive the holy Sacrament of Thy Body and Blood. And my son, the one child that I had by Alice, I will fetch back again from Challonsea, where I kept him in order that I might not look upon him, and I will be to him a father in deed and very truth. And in all things, so far as in me lieth, I will make restitution and atonement. Whether Thou hearest me or whether Thou hearest me not, these things shall be. And for my prayer, it is but this: of Thy loving kindness, most merciful God, be Thou with Eve and make her happy; and after these great pains and perils of childbirth send her Thy peace. Of Thy loving-kindness. Thy merciful loving-kindness, O God!"

Perhaps the prayer that is offered when the time for praying is over is more terribly pathetic than any other. Yet one might hesitate to say that this prayer was unanswered.

Sir Edric rose to his feet. Once more he paced the room. There was a strange simplicity about him, the simplicity that scorns an incongruity. He felt that his lips and throat were parched and dry. He lifted the heavy silver tankard from the table and raised the lid; there was still a good draught of mulled wine in it with the burnt toast, cut heart-shape, floating on the top.

"To the health of Eve and her child," he said aloud, and drained it to the last drop.

Click, click! As he put the tankard down he heard distinctly two doors opened and shut quickly, one after the other. And then slowly down the stairs came a hesitating step. Sir Edric could bear the suspense no longer. He opened the dining-room door, and the dim light strayed out into the dark hall beyond.

"Dennison," he said, in a low, sharp whisper, "is that you?"

"Yes, yes. I am coming, Sir Edric."

A moment afterwards Dr. Dennison entered the room. He was very pale; perspiration streamed from his forehead; his cravat was disarranged. He was an old man, thin, with the air of proud humility. Sir Edric watched him narrowly.

"Then she is dead," he said, with a quiet that Dr. Dennison had not expected.

"Twenty physicians – a hundred physicians could not have saved her. Sir Edric. She was ——" He gave some details of medical interest.

"Dennison," said Sir Edric, still speaking with calm and restraint, "why do you seem thus indisposed and panic-stricken? You are a physician; have you never looked upon the face of death before? The soul of my wife is with God—"

"Yes," murmured Dennison, "a good woman, a perfect, saintly woman."

"And," Sir Edric went on, raising his eyes to the ceiling as though he could see through it, "her body lies in great dignity and beauty upon the bed, and there is no horror in it. Why are you afraid?"

"I do not fear death, Sir Edric."

"But your hands – they are not steady. You are evidently overcome. Does the child live?"

"Yes, it lives."

"Another boy – a brother for young Edric, the child that Alice bore me?"

"There – there is something wrong. I do not know what to do. I want you to come upstairs. And, Sir Edric, I must tell you, you will need your self-command."

"Dennison, the hand of God is heavy upon me; but from this time forth until the day of my death I am submissive to it, and God send that that day may come quickly! I will follow you and I will endure."

He took one of the high silver candlesticks from the table and stepped towards the door. He strode quickly up the staircase, Dr. Dennison following a little way behind him.

As Sir Edric waited at the top of the staircase he heard suddenly from the room before him a low cry. He put down the candlestick on the floor and leaned back against the wall listening. The cry came again, a vibrating monotone ending in a growl.

"Dennison, Dennison!"

His voice choked; he could not go on.

"Yes," said the doctor, "it is in there. I had the two women out of the room, and got it here. No one but myself has seen it. But you must see it, too."

He raised the candle and the two men entered the room – one of the spare bedrooms. On the bed there was something moving under cover of a blanket. Dr. Dennison paused for a moment and then flung the blanket partially back.

They did not remain in the room for more than a few seconds. The moment they got outside, Dr. Dennison began to speak.

"Sir Edric, I would fain suggest somewhat to you. There is no evil, as Sophocles hath it in his 'Antigone', for which man hath not found a remedy, except it be death, and here—"

Sir Edric interrupted him in a husky voice.

"Downstairs, Dennison. This is too near."

It was, indeed, passing strange. When once the novelty of this – this occurrence had worn off, Dr. Dennison seemed no longer frightened. He was calm, academic, interested in an unusual phenomenon. But Sir Edric, who was said in the village to fear nothing in earth, or heaven, or hell, was obviously much moved.

When they had got back to the dining room. Sir Edric motioned the doctor to a seat.

"Now, then," he said, "I will hear you. Something must be done – and tonight."

"Exceptional cases," said Dr. Dennison, "demand exceptional remedies. Well, it lies there upstairs and is at our mercy. We can let it live, or, placing one hand over the mouth and nostrils, we can—"

"Stop," said Sir Edric. "This thing has so crushed and humiliated me that I can scarcely think. But I recall that while I waited for you I fell upon my knees and prayed that God would save Eve. And, as I confessed unto Him more than I will ever confess unto man, it seemed to me that it were ignoble to offer a price for His favour. And I said that whatsoever punishment I had to bear, I would bear it; and whatsoever He called upon me to do, I would do it; and I made no conditions."

"Well?"

"Now my punishment is of two kinds. Firstly, my wife, Eve, is dead. And this I bear more easily because I know that now she is numbered with the company of God's saints, and with them her pure spirit finds happier communion than with me; I was not worthy of her. And yet she would call my roughness by gentle, pretty names. She gloried, Dennison, in the mere strength of my body, and in the greatness of my stature. And I am thankful that she never saw this – this shame that has come upon the house. For she was a proud woman, with all her gentleness, even as I was proud and bad until it pleased God this night to break me even to the dust. And for my second punishment, that, too, I must bear. This thing that lies upstairs, I will take and rear; it is bone of my bone and flesh of my flesh; only, if it be possible, I will hide my shame so that no man but you shall know of it."

"This is not possible. You cannot keep a living being in this house unless it be known. Will not these women say, 'Where is the child?'"

Sir Edric stood upright, his powerful hands linked before him, his face working in agony; but he was still resolute.

"Then if it must be known, it shall be known. The fault is mine. If I had but done sooner what Eve asked, this would not have happened. I will bear it."

"Sir Edric, do not be angry with me, for if I did not say this, then I should be but an ill counsellor. And, firstly, do not use the word shame. The ways of nature are past all explaining; if a woman be frail and easily impressed, and other circumstances concur, then in some few rare cases a thing of this sort does happen. If there be shame, it is not upon you but upon nature – to whom one would not lightly impute shame. Yet it is true that common and uninformed people might think that this shame was yours. And herein lies the great trouble – the shame would rest also on her memory."

"Then," said Sir Edric, in a low, unfaltering voice, "this night for the sake of Eve I will break my word, and lose my own soul eternally."

About an hour afterwards Sir Edric and Dr. Dennison left the house together. The doctor carried a stable lantern in his hand. Sir Edric bore in his arms something wrapped in a blanket. They went through the long garden, out into the orchard that skirts the north side of the park, and then across a field to a small dark plantation known as Hal's Planting. In the very heart of Hal's Planting there are some curious caves: access to the innermost chamber of them is exceedingly difficult and dangerous, and only possible to a climber of exceptional skill and courage. As they returned from these caves, Sir Edric no longer carried his burden. The dawn was breaking and the birds began to sing.

"Could not they be quiet just for this morning?" said Sir Edric wearily.

There were but few people who were asked to attend the funeral of Lady Vanquerest and of the baby which, it was said, had only survived her by a few hours. There were but three people who knew that only one body – the body of Lady Vanquerest – was really interred on that occasion. These three were Sir Edric Vanquerest, Dr. Dennison, and a nurse whom it had been found expedient to take into their confidence.

During the next six years Sir Edric lived, almost in solitude, a life of great sanctity, devoting much of his time to the education of the younger Edric, the child that he had by his first wife. In the course of this time some strange stories began to be told and believed in the neighbourhood with reference to Hal's Planting, and the place was generally avoided.

When Sir Edric lay on his deathbed the windows of the chamber were open, and suddenly through them came a low cry. The doctor in attendance hardly regarded it, supposing that it came from one of the owls in the trees outside. But Sir Edric, at the sound of it, rose right up in bed before anyone could stay him, and flinging up his arms cried, "Wolves! Wolves! Wolves!" Then he fell forward on his face, dead.

And four generations passed away.

Chapter II

TOWARDS the latter end of the nineteenth century, John Marsh, who was the oldest man in the village of Mansteth, could be prevailed upon to state what he recollected. His two sons supported him in his old age; he never felt the pinch of poverty, and he always had money in his pocket; but it was a settled principle with him that he would not pay for the pint of beer which he drank occasionally in the parlour of The Stag. Sometimes Farmer Wynthwaite paid for the beer; sometimes it was Mr. Spicer from the post office; sometimes the landlord of The Stag himself would finance the old man's evening dissipation. In return, John Marsh was prevailed upon to state what he recollected; this he would do with great heartiness and strict impartiality, recalling the intemperance of a former Wynthwaite and the dishonesty of some ancestral Spicer while he drank the beer of their direct descendants. He would tell you, with two tough old fingers crooked round the handle of the pewter that you had provided, how your grandfather was a poor thing, "fit for nowt but to brak steeans by ta rord-side." He was so disrespectful that it was believed that he spoke truth. He was particularly disrespectful when he spoke of that most devilish family, the Vanquerests; and he never tired of recounting the stories that from generation to generation had grown up about them. It would be objected, sometimes, that the present Sir Edric, the last surviving member of the race, was a pleasant-spoken young man, with none of the family wildness and hot temper. It was for no sin of his that Hal's Planting was haunted – a thing which everyone in Mansteth, and many beyond it, most devoutly believed. John Marsh would hear no apology for him, nor for any of his ancestors; he recounted the prophecy that an old mad woman had made of the family before her strange death, and hoped, fervently, that he might live to see it fulfilled.

The third baronet, as has already been told, had lived the latter part of his life, after his second wife's death, in peace and quietness. Of him John Marsh remembered nothing, of course, and could only recall the few fragments of information that had been handed down to him. He had been told that this Sir Edric, who had travelled a good deal, at one time kept wolves, intending to train them to serve as dogs; these wolves were not kept under proper restraint, and became a kind of terror to the neighbourhood. Lady Vanquerest, his second wife, had asked him frequently to destroy these beasts; but Sir Edric, although it was said that he loved his second wife even more than he hated the first, was obstinate when any of his whims were crossed, and put her off with promises. Then one day Lady Vanquerest herself was attacked by the wolves; she was not bitten, but she was badly frightened. That filled Sir Edric with remorse, and, when it was too late, he went out into the yard where the wolves were kept and shot them all. A few months afterwards Lady Vanquerest died in childbirth. It was a queer thing John Marsh noted, that it was just at this time that Hal's Planting began to get such a bad name. The fourth baronet was, John Marsh considered, the worst of the race; it was to him that the old mad woman had made her prophecy, an incident that Marsh himself had witnessed in his childhood and still vividly remembered.

The baronet, in his old age, had been cast up by his vices on the shores of melancholy; heavy-eyed, grey-haired, bent, he seemed to pass through life as in a dream. Every day he would go out on horseback, always at a walking pace, as though he were following the funeral of his past self. One night he was riding up the village street as this old woman came down it. Her name was Ann Ruthers; she had a kind of reputation in the village, and although all said that she was mad, many of her utterances were remembered, and she was treated with respect. It was growing dark, and the village street was almost empty; but just at the lower end was the usual group of men by the door of The Stag, dimly illuminated by the light that came through the quaint windows of the old inn. They glanced at Sir Edric as he rode slowly past them, taking no notice of their respectful salutes. At the upper end of the street there were two persons. One was Ann Ruthers, a tall, gaunt old woman, her head wrapped in a shawl; the other was John Marsh. He was then a boy of eight, and he was feeling somewhat frightened. He had been on an expedition to a distant and fetid pond, and in the black mud and clay about its borders he had discovered live newts; he had three of them in his pocket, and this was to some extent a joy to him, but his joy was damped by his knowledge that he was coming home much too late, and would probably be chastised in consequence. He was unable to walk fast or to run, because Ann Ruthers was immediately in front of him, and he dared not pass her, especially at night. She walked on until she met Sir Edric, and then, standing still, she called him by name. He pulled in his horse and raised his heavy eyes to look at her. Then in loud clear tones she spoke to him, and John Marsh heard and remembered every word that she said; it was her prophecy of the end of the Vanquerests. Sir Edric never answered a word. When she had finished, he rode on, while she remained standing there, her eyes fixed on the stars above her. John Marsh dared not pass the mad woman; he turned round and walked back, keeping close to Sir Edric's horse. Quite suddenly, without a word of warning, as if in a moment of ungovernable irritation, Sir Edric wheeled his horse round and struck the boy across the face with his switch.

On the following morning John Marsh – or rather, his parents – received a handsome solatium in coin of the realm; but sixty-five years afterwards he had not forgiven that blow, and still spoke of the Vanquerests as a most devilish family, still hoped and prayed that he might see the prophecy fulfilled. He would relate, too, the death of Ann Ruthers, which occurred either later on the night of her prophecy or early on the following day. She would often roam about the country all night, and on this particular night she left the main road to wander over the Vanquerest lands, where trespassers, especially at night, were not welcomed. But no one saw her, and it seemed that she had made her way to a part where no one was likely to see her; for none of the keepers would have entered Hal's Planting by night. Her body was found there at noon on the following day, lying under the tall bracken, dead, but without any mark of violence upon it. It was considered that she had died in a fit. This naturally added to the ill-repute of Hal's Planting. The woman's death caused considerable sensation in the village. Sir Edric sent a messenger to the married sister with whom she had lived, saying that he wished to pay all the funeral expenses. This offer, as John Marsh recalled with satisfaction, was refused.

Of the last two baronets he had but little to tell. The fifth baronet was credited with the family temper, but he conducted himself in a perfectly conventional way, and did not seem in the least to belong to romance. He was a good man of business, and devoted himself to making up, as far as he could, for the very extravagant expenditure of his predecessors. His son, the present Sir Edric, was a fine young fellow and popular in the village. Even John Marsh could find nothing to say against him; other people in the village were interested in him. It was said that he had chosen a wife in London – a Miss Guerdon – and would shortly be back to see that Mansteth Hall was put in proper order for her before his marriage at the close of the season. Modernity kills ghostly romance. It was difficult to associate this modern and handsome Sir Edric, bright and spirited, a good sportsman and a good fellow, with the doom that had been foretold for the Vanquerest family. He himself knew the tradition and laughed at it. He wore clothes made by a London tailor, looked healthy, smiled cheerfully, and, in a vain attempt to shame his own head-keeper, had himself spent a night alone in Hal's Planting. This last was used by Mr. Spicer in argument, who would ask John Marsh what he made of it. John Marsh replied, contemptuously, that it was "nowt". It was not so that the Vanquerest family was to end; but when the thing, whatever it was, that lived in Hal's Planting, left it and came up to the house, to Mansteth Hall itself, then one would see the end of the Vanquerests. So Ann Ruthers had prophesied. Sometimes Mr. Spicer would ask the pertinent question, how did John Marsh know that there really was anything in Hal's Planting? This he asked, less because he disbelieved, than because he wished to draw forth an account of John's personal experiences. These were given in great detail, but they did not amount to very much. One night John Marsh had been taken by business – Sir Edric's keepers would have called the business by hard names – into the neighbourhood of Hal's Planting. He had there been suddenly startled by a cry, and had run away as though he were running for his life. That was all he could tell about the cry – it was the kind of cry to make a man lose his head and run. And then it always happened that John Marsh was urged by his companions to enter Hal's Planting himself, and discover what was there. John pursed his thin lips together, and hinted that that also might be done one of these days. Whereupon Mr. Spicer looked across his pipe to Farmer Wynthwaite, and smiled significantly.

Shortly before Sir Edric's return from London, the attention of Mansteth was once more directed to Hal's Planting, but not by any supernatural occurrence. Quite suddenly, on a calm day, two trees there fell with a crash; there were caves in the centre of the plantation, and it seemed as if the roof of some big chamber in these caves had given way.

They talked it over one night in the parlour of The Stag. There was water in these caves. Farmer Wynthwaite knew it; and he expected a further subsidence. If the whole thing collapsed, what then?

"Ay," said John Marsh. He rose from his chair, and pointed in the direction of the Hall with his thumb. "What then?"

He walked across to the fire, looked at it meditatively for a moment, and then spat in it. "A trewly wun'ful owd mon," said Farmer Wynthwaite as he watched him.

Chapter III

IN THE SMOKING-ROOM at Mansteth Hall sat Sir Edric with his friend and intended brother-in-law, Dr. Andrew Guerdon. Both men were on the verge of middle-age; there was hardly a year's difference between them. Yet Guerdon looked much the older man; that was, perhaps, because he wore a short, black beard, while Sir Edric was clean-shaven. Guerdon was thought to be an enviable man. His father had made a fortune in the firm of Guerdon, Guerdon and Bird; the old style was still retained at the bank, although there was no longer a Guerdon in the firm. Andrew Guerdon had a handsome allowance from his father, and had also inherited money through his mother. He had taken the degree of Doctor of Medicine; he did not practise, but he was still interested in science, especially in out-of-the-way science. He was unmarried, gifted with perpetually good health, interested in life, popular. His friendship with Sir Edric dated from their college days. It had for some years been almost certain that Sir Edric would marry his friend's sister, Ray Guerdon, although the actual betrothal had only been announced that season.

On a bureau in one corner of the room were spread a couple of plans and various slips of paper. Sir Edric was wrinkling his brows over them, dropping cigar ash over them, and finally getting angry over them. He pushed back his chair irritably, and turned towards Guerdon.

"Look here, old man!" he said. "I desire to curse the original architect of this house – to curse him in his down-sitting and his uprising."

"Seeing that the original architect has gone to where beyond these voices there is peace, he won't be offended. Neither shall I. But why worry yourself? You've been rooted to that blessed bureau all day, and now, after dinner, when every self-respecting man chucks business, you return to it again – even as a sow returns to her wallowing in the mire."

"Now, my good Andrew, do be reasonable. How on earth can I bring Ray to such a place as this? And it's built with such ingrained malice and vexatiousness that one can't live in it as it is, and can't alter it without having the whole shanty tumble down about one's ears. Look at this plan now. That thing's what they're pleased to call a morning room. If the window had been *here* there would have been an uninterrupted view of open country. So what does this forsaken fool of an architect do? He sticks it *there*, where you see it on the plan, looking straight on to a blank wall with a stable yard on the other side of it. But that's a trifle. Look here again—"

"I won't look any more. This place is all right. It was good enough for your father and mother and several generations before them until you arose to improve the world; it was good enough for you until you started to get married. It's a picturesque place, and if you begin to alter it you'll spoil it." Guerdon looked round the room critically. "Upon my word," he said, "I don't know of any house where I like the smoking-room as well as I like this. It's not too big, and yet it's fairly lofty; it's got those comfortable-looking oak-panelled walls. That's the right kind of fireplace, too, and these corner cupboards are handy."

"Of course this won't *remain* the smoking-room. It has the morning sun, and Ray likes that, so I shall make it into her boudoir. It *is* a nice room, as you say."

"That's it, Ted, my boy," said Guerdon bitterly; "take a room which is designed by nature and art to be a smoking-room and turn it into a boudoir. Turn it into the very deuce of a boudoir with the morning sun laid on for ever and ever. Waste the twelfth of August by getting married on it. Spend the winter in foreign parts, and write letters that you can breakfast out of doors, just as if you'd created the mildness of the climate yourself. Come back in the spring and spend the London season in the country in order to avoid seeing anybody who wants to see you. That's the way to do it; that's the way to get yourself generally loved and admired!"

"That's chiefly imagination," said Sir Edric. "I'm blest if I can see why I should not make this house fit for Ray to live in."

"It's a queer thing: Ray was a good girl, and you weren't a bad sort yourself. You prepare to go into partnership, and you both straightway turn into despicable lunatics. I'll have a word or two with Ray. But I'm serious about this house. Don't go tinkering it; it's got a character of its own, and you'd better leave it. Turn half Tottenham Court Road and the culture thereof – Heaven help it! – into your town house if you like, but leave this alone."

"Haven't got a town house – yet. Anyway I'm not going to be unsuitable; I'm not going to feel myself at the mercy of a big firm. I shall supervise the whole thing myself. I shall drive over to Challonsea tomorrow afternoon and see if I can't find some intelligent and fairly conscientious workmen."

"That's all right; you supervise them and I'll supervise you. You'll be much too new if I don't look after you. You've got an old legend, I believe, that the family's coming to a bad end; you must be consistent with it. As you are bad, be beautiful. By the way, what do you yourself think of the legend?"

"It's nothing," said Sir Edric, speaking, however, rather seriously. "They say that Hal's Planting is haunted by something that will not die. Certainly an old woman, who for some godless reason of her own made her way there by night, was found there dead on the following morning; but her death could be, and was, accounted for by natural causes. Certainly, too, I haven't a man in my employ who'll go there by night now."

"Why not?"

"How should I know? I fancy that a few of the villagers sit boozing at The Stag in the evening, and like to scare themselves by swopping lies about Hal's Planting. I've done my best to stop it. I once, as you know, took a rug, a revolver and a flask of whisky and spent the night there myself. But even that didn't convince them."

"Yes, you told me. By the way, did you hear or see anything?"

Sir Edric hesitated before he answered. Finally he said:

"Look here, old man, I wouldn't tell this to anyone but yourself. I did think that I heard something. About the middle of the night I was awakened by a cry; I can only say that it was the kind of cry that frightened me. I sat up, and at that moment I heard some great, heavy thing go swishing through the bracken behind me at a great rate. Then all was still; I looked about, but I could find nothing. At last I argued as I would argue now that a man who is just awake is only half awake, and that his powers of observation, by hearing or any other sense, are not to be trusted. I even persuaded myself to go to sleep again, and there was no more disturbance. However, there's a real danger there now. In the heart of the plantation there are some eaves and a subterranean spring; lately there has been some slight subsidence there, and the same sort of thing will happen again in all probability. I wired today to an expert to come and look at the place; he has replied that he will come on Monday. The legend says that when the thing that lives in Hal's Planting comes up to the Hall the Vanquerests will be ended. If I cut down the trees and then break up the place with a charge of dynamite I shouldn't wonder if I spoiled that legend."

Guerdon smiled.

"I'm inclined to agree with you all through. It's absurd to trust the immediate impressions of a man just awakened; what you heard was probably a stray cow."

"No cow," said Sir Edric impartially. "There's a low wall all round the place – not much of a wall, but too much for a cow."

"Well, something else – some equally obvious explanation. In dealing with such questions, never forget that you're in the nineteenth century. By the way, your man's coming on Monday. That reminds me today's Friday, and as an indisputable consequence tomorrow's Saturday, therefore, if you want to find your intelligent workmen it will be of no use to go in the afternoon."

"True," said Sir Edric, "I'll go in the morning." He walked to a tray on a side table and poured a little whisky into a tumbler. "They don't seem to have brought any seltzer water," he remarked in a grumbling voice.

He rang the bell impatiently.

"Now why don't you use those corner cupboards for that kind of thing? If you kept a supply there, it would be handy in case of accidents."

"They're full up already."

He opened one of them and showed that it was filled with old account-books and yellow documents tied up in bundles. The servant entered.

"Oh, I say, there isn't any seltzer. Bring it, please."

He turned again to Guerdon.

"You might do me a favour when I'm away tomorrow, if there's nothing else that you want to do. I wish you'd look through all these papers for me. They're all old. Possibly some of them ought to go to my solicitor, and I know that a lot of them ought to be destroyed. Some few may be of family interest. It's not the kind of thing that I could ask a stranger or a servant to do for me, and I've so much on hand just now before my marriage—"

"But of course, my dear fellow, I'll do it with pleasure."

"I'm ashamed to give you all this bother. However, you said that you were coming here to help me, and I take you at your word. By the way, I think you'd better not say anything to Ray about the Hal's Planting story."

"I may be some of the things that you take me for, but really I am not a common ass. Of course I shouldn't tell her."

"I'll tell her myself, and I'd sooner do it when I've got the whole thing cleared up. Well, I'm really obliged to you."

"I needn't remind you that I hope to receive as much again. I believe in compensation. Nature always gives it and always requires it. One finds it everywhere, in philology and onwards."

"I could mention omissions."

"They are few, and make a belief in a hereafter to supply them logical."

"Lunatics, for instance?"

"Their delusions are often their compensation. They argue correctly from false premises. A lunatic believing himself to be a millionaire has as much delight as money can give."

"How about deformities or monstrosities?"

"The principle is there, although I don't pretend that the compensation is always adequate. A man who is deprived of one sense generally has another developed with unusual acuteness. As for monstrosities of at all a human type one sees none; the things exhibited in fairs are, almost without exception, frauds. They occur rarely, and one does not know enough about them. A really good textbook on the subject would be interesting. Still, such stories as I have heard would bear out my theory – stories of their superhuman strength and cunning, and of the extraordinary prolongation of life that has been noted, or is said to have been noted, in them.

But it is hardly fair to test my principle by exceptional cases. Besides, anyone can prove anything except that anything's worth proving."

"That's a cheerful thing to say. I wouldn't like to swear that I could prove how the Hal's Planting legend started; but I fancy, do you know, that I could make a very good shot at it."

"Well?"

"My great-grandfather kept wolves – I can't say why. Do you remember the portrait of him? – not the one when he was a boy, the other. It hangs on the staircase. There's now a group of wolves in one corner of the picture. I was looking carefully at the picture one day and thought that I detected some over-painting in that corner; indeed, it was done so roughly that a child would have noticed it if the picture had been hung in a better light. I had the over-painting removed by a good man, and underneath there was that group of wolves depicted. Well, one of these wolves must have escaped, got into Hal's Planting, and scared an old woman or two; that would start a story, and human mendacity would do the rest."

"Yes," said Guerdon meditatively, "that doesn't sound improbable. But why did your great-grandfather have the wolves painted out?"

Chapter IV

SATURDAY MORNING was fine, but very hot and sultry. After breakfast, when Sir Edric had driven off to Challonsea, Andrew Guerdon settled himself in a comfortable chair in the smoking-room. The contents of the corner cupboard were piled up on a table by his side. He lit his pipe and began to go through the papers and put them in order. He had been at work about a quarter of an hour when the butler entered rather abruptly, looking pale and disturbed.

"In Sir Edric's absence, sir, it was thought that I had better come to you for advice. There's been an awful thing happened."

"Well?"

"They've found a corpse in Hal's Planting about half an hour ago. It's the body of an old man, John Marsh, who used to live in the village. He seems to have died in some kind of a fit. They were bringing it here, but I had it taken down to the village where his cottage is. Then I sent to the police and to a doctor."

There was a moment or two's silence before Guerdon answered.

"This is a terrible thing. I don't know of anything else that you could do. Stop; if the police want to see the spot where the body was found, I think that Sir Edric would like them to have every facility."

"Quite so, sir."

"And no one else must be allowed there."

"No, sir. Thank you."

The butler withdrew.

Guerdon arose from his chair and began to pace up and down the room

"What an impressive thing a coincidence is!" he thought to himself. "Last night the whole of the Hal's Planting story seemed to me not worth consideration. But this second death there – it can be only coincidence. What else could it be?"

The question would not leave him. What else could it be? Had that dead man seen something there and died in sheer terror of it? Had Sir Edric really heard something when he spent that night there alone? He returned to his work, but he found that he got on with it but slowly. Every now and then his mind wandered back to the subject of Hal's Planting. His doubts annoyed him. It was unscientific and unmodern of him to feel any perplexity, because a natural and rational explanation was possible; he was annoyed with himself for being perplexed.

After luncheon he strolled round the grounds and smoked a cigar. He noticed that a thick bank of dark, slate-coloured clouds was gathering in the west. The air was very still. In a remote corner of the garden a big heap of weeds was burning; the smoke went up perfectly straight. On the top of the heap light flames danced; they were like the ghosts of flames in the strange light. A few big drops of rain fell. The small shower did not last for five seconds. Guerdon glanced at his watch. Sir Edric would be back in an hour, and he wanted to finish his work with the papers before Sir Edric's return, so he went back into the house once more.

He picked up the first document that came to hand. As he did so, another, smaller, and written on parchment, which had been folded in with it, dropped out. He began to read the parchment; it was written in faded ink, and the parchment itself was yellow and in many places stained. It was the confession of the third baronet – he could tell that by the date upon it. It told the story of that night when he and Dr. Dennison went together carrying a burden through the long garden out into the orchard that skirts the north side of the park, and then across a field to a small, dark plantation. It told how he made a vow to God and did not keep it. These were the last words of the confession:

Already upon me has the punishment fallen, and the devil's wolves do seem to hunt me in my sleep nightly. But I know that there is worse to come. The thing that I took to Hal's Planting is dead. Yet will it come back again to the Hall, and then will the Vanquerests be at an end. This writing I have committed to chance, neither showing it nor hiding it, and leaving it to chance if any man shall read it.

Underneath there was a line written in darker ink, and in quite a different handwriting. It was dated fifteen years later, and the initials R.D. were appended to it:

It is not dead. I do not think that it will ever die.

When Andrew Guerdon had finished reading this document, he looked slowly round the room. The subject had got on his nerves, and he was almost expecting to see something. Then he did his best to pull himself together. The first question he put to himself was this: "Has Ted ever seen this?" Obviously he had not. If he had, he could not have taken the tradition of Hal's Planting so lightly, nor have spoken of it so freely. Besides, he would either have mentioned the document to Guerdon, or he would have kept it carefully concealed. He would not have allowed him to come across it casually in that way. "Ted must never see it," thought Guerdon to himself. He then remembered the pile of weeds he had seen burning in the garden. He put the parchment in his pocket, and hurried out. There was no one about. He spread the parchment on the top of the pile, and waited until it was entirely consumed. Then he went back to the smoking-room; he felt easier now.

"Yes," thought Guerdon, "if Ted had first of all heard of the finding of that body, and then had read that document, I believe that he would have gone mad. Things that come near us affect us deeply."

Guerdon himself was much moved. He clung steadily to reason; he felt himself able to give a natural explanation all through, and yet he was nervous. The net of coincidence had closed in around him; the mention in Sir Edric's confession of the prophecy which had suubsequently become traditional in the village alarmed him. And what did that last line mean? He supposed that R.D. must be the initials of Dr. Dennison. What did he mean by saying that the thing was not dead? Did he mean that it had not really been killed, that it had been gifted with some preternatural strength and vitality and had survived, though Sir Edric did not know it? He recalled what he had said about the prolongation of the lives of such things. If it still survived, why had it never been seen? Had it joined to the wild hardiness of the beast a cunning that was human – or more than human? How could it have lived? There was water in the caves, he reflected, and food could have been secured – a wild beast's food. Or did Dr. Dennison mean that though the thing itself was dead, its wraith survived and haunted the place? He wondered how the doctor had found Sir Edric's confession, and why he had written that hue at the end of it. As he sat thinking, a low rumble of thunder in the distance startled him. He felt a touch of panic – a sudden impulse to leave Mansteth at once and, if possible, to take Ted with him. Ray could never live there. He went over the whole thing in his mind again and again, at one time calm and argumentative about it, and at another shaken by blind horror.

Sir Edric, on his return from Challonsea a few minutes afterwards, came straight to the smoking-room where Guerdon was. He looked tired and depressed. He began to speak at once:

"You needn't tell me about it – about John Marsh. I heard about it in the village."

"Did you? It's a painful occurrence, although, of course—"

"Stop. Don't go into it. Anything can be explained – I know that."

"I went through those papers and account-books while you were away. Most of them may just as well be destroyed; but there are a few – I put them aside there – which might be kept. There was nothing of any interest."

"Thanks; I'm much obliged to you."

"Oh, and look here, I've got an idea. I've been examining the plans of the house, and I'm coming round to your opinion. There are some alterations which should be made, and yet I'm afraid that they'd make the place look patched and renovated. It wouldn't be a bad thing to know what Ray thought about it."

"That's impossible. The workmen come on Monday, and we can't consult her before then. Besides, I have a general notion what she would like."

"We could catch the night express to town at Challonsea, and—"

Sir Edric rose from his seat angrily and hit the table.

"Good God! Don't sit there hunting up excuses to cover my cowardice, and making it easy for me to bolt. What do you suppose the villagers would say, and what would my own servants say, if I ran away tonight? I am a coward – I know it. I'm horribly afraid. But I'm not going to act like a coward if I can help it."

"Now, my dear chap, don't excite yourself. If you are going to care at all – to care as much as the conventional damn – for what people say, you'll have no peace in life. And I don't believe you're afraid. What are you afraid of?"

Sir Edric paced once or twice up and down the room, and then sat down again before replying.

"Look here, Andrew, I'll make a clean breast of it. I've always laughed at the tradition; I forced myself, as it seemed at least, to disprove it by spending a night in Hal's Planting; I took the pains even to make a theory which would account for its origin. All the time I had a sneaking, stifled belief in it. With the help of my reason I crushed that; but now my reason has thrown up the job, and I'm afraid. I'm afraid of the Undying Thing that is in Hal's Planting. I heard it that night. John Marsh saw it last night – they took me to see the body, and the face was awful; and I believe that one day it will come from Hal's Planting—"

"Yes," interrupted Guerdon, "I know. And at present I believe as much. Last night we laughed at the whole thing, and we shall live to laugh at it again, and be ashamed of ourselves for a couple of superstitious old women. I fancy that beliefs are affected by weather – there's thunder in the air."

"No," said Sir Edric, "my belief has come to stay."

"And what are you going to do?"

"I'm going to test it. On Monday I can begin to get to work, and then I'll blow up Hal's Planting with dynamite. After that we shan't need to believe – we shall *know*. And now let's dismiss the subject. Come down into the billiard room and have a game. Until Monday I won't think of the thing again."

Long before dinner. Sir Edric's depression seemed to have completely vanished. At dinner he was boisterous and amused. Afterwards he told stories and was interesting.

* * *

It was late at night; the terrific storm that was raging outside had awoke Guerdon from sleep. Hopeless of getting to sleep again, he had arisen and dressed, and now sat in the window seat watching the storm. He had never seen anything like it before; and every now and then the sky seemed to be torn across as if by hands of white fire. Suddenly he heard a tap at his door, and looked round. Sir Edric had already entered; he also had dressed. He spoke in a curious, subdued voice.

"I thought you wouldn't be able to sleep through this. Do you remember that I shut and fastened the dining-room window?"

"Yes, I remember it."

"Well, come in here."

Sir Edric led the way to his room, which was immediately over the dining room. By leaning out of window they could see that the dining-room window was open wide.

"Burglar," said Guerdon meditatively.

"No," Sir Edric answered, still speaking in a hushed voice. "It is the Undying Thing – it has come for me."

He snatched up the candle, and made towards the staircase; Guerdon caught up the loaded revolver which always lay on the table beside Sir Edric's bed and followed him. Both men ran down the staircase as though there were not another moment to lose. Sir Edric rushed at the dining-room door, opened it a little, and looked in. Then he turned to Guerdon, who was just behind him.

"Go back to your room," he said authoritatively.

"I won't," said Guerdon. "Why? What is it?"

Suddenly the corners of Sir Edric's mouth shot outward into the hideous grin of terror.

"It's there! It's there!" he gasped.

"Then I come in with you."

"Go back!"

With a sudden movement, Sir Edric thrust Guerdon away from the door, and then, quick as light, darted in, and locked the door behind him.

Guerdon bent down and listened. He heard Sir Edric say in a firm voice:

"Who are you? What are you?"

Then followed a heavy, snorting breathing, a low, vibrating growl, an awful cry, a scuffle.

Then Guerdon flung himself at the door. He kicked at the lock, but it would not give way. At last he fired his revolver at it. Then he managed to force his way into the room. It was perfectly empty. Overhead he could hear footsteps; the noise had awakened the servants; they were standing, tremulous, on the upper landing.

Through the open window access to the garden was easy. Guerdon did not wait to get help; and in all probability none of the servants could have been persuaded to come with him. He climbed out alone, and, as if by some blind impulse, started to run as hard as he could in the direction of Hal's Planting. He knew that Sir Edric would be found there.

But when he got within a hundred yards of the plantation, he stopped. There had been a great flash of lightning, and he saw that it had struck one of the trees. Flames darted about the plantation as the dry bracken caught. Suddenly, in the light of another flash, he saw the whole of the trees fling their heads upwards; then came a deafening crash, and the ground slipped under him, and he was flung forward on his face. The plantation had collapsed, fallen through into the caves beneath it. Guerdon slowly regained his feet; he was surprised to find that he was unhurt. He walked on a few steps, and then fell again; this time he had fainted away.

The Haunted Dragoon

Arthur Quiller-Couch

BESIDE the Plymouth road, as it plunges downhill past Ruan Lanihale church towards Ruan Cove, and ten paces beyond the lych-gate – where the graves lie level with the coping, and the horseman can decipher their inscriptions in passing, at the risk of a twisted neck – the base of the churchyard wall is pierced with a low archway, festooned with toad-flax and fringed with the hart's-tongue fern. Within the archway bubbles a well, the water of which was once used for all baptisms in the parish, for no child sprinkled with it could ever be hanged with hemp. But this belief is discredited now, and the well neglected: and the events which led to this are still a winter's tale in the neighbourhood. I set them down as they were told me, across the blue glow of a wreck-wood fire, by Sam Tregear, the parish bedman. Sam himself had borne an inconspicuous share in them; and because of them Sam's father had carried a white face to his grave.

My father and mother (said Sam) married late in life, for his trade was what mine is, and 'twasn't till her fortieth year that my mother could bring herself to kiss a gravedigger. That accounts, maybe, for my being born rickety and with other drawbacks that only made father the fonder. Weather permitting, he'd carry me off to churchyard, set me upon a flat stone, with his coat folded under, and talk to me while he delved. I can mind, now, the way he'd settle lower and lower, till his head played hidey-peep with me over the grave's edge, and at last he'd be clean swallowed up, but still discoursing or calling up how he'd come upon wonderful towns and kingdoms down underground, and how all the kings and queens there, in dyed garments, was offering him meat for his dinner every day of the week if he'd only stop and hobbynob with them – and all such gammut. He prettily doted on me – the poor old ancient!

But there came a day – a dry afternoon in the late wheat harvest – when we were up in the churchyard together, and though father had his tools beside him, not a tint did he work, but kept travishing back and forth, one time shading his eyes and gazing out to sea, and then looking far along the Plymouth road for minutes at a time. Out by Bradden Point there stood a little dandy-rigged craft, tacking lazily to and fro, with her mains'le all shiny-yellow in the sunset. Though I didn't know it then, she was the Preventive boat, and her business was to watch the Hauen: for there had been a brush between her and the *Unity* lugger, a fortnight back, and a Preventive man shot through the breast-bone, and my mother's brother Philip was hiding down in the town. I minded, later, how that the men across the vale, in Farmer Tresidder's wheat-field, paused every now and then, as they pitched the sheaves, to give a look up towards the churchyard, and the gleaners moved about in small knots, causeying and glancing over their shoulders at the cutter out in the bay; and how, when all the field was carried, they waited round the last load, no man offering to cry the *Neck*, as the fashion was, but lingering till sun was near down behind the slope and the long shadows stretching across the stubble.

"Sha'n't thee go underground today, father?" says I, at last.

He turned slowly round, and says he, "No, sonny. Reckon us'll climb skywards for a change."

And with that, he took my hand, and pushing abroad the belfry door began to climb the stairway. Up and up, round and round we went, in a sort of blind-man's-holiday full of little glints of light and whiffs of wind where the open windows came; and at last stepped out upon the leads of the tower and drew breath.

"There's two-an'-twenty parishes to be witnessed from where we're standin', sonny – if ye've got eyes," says my father.

Well, first I looked down towards the harvesters and laughed to see them so small: and then I fell to counting the church-towers dotted across the high-lands, and seeing if I could make out two-and-twenty. 'Twas the prettiest sight – all the country round looking as if 'twas dusted with gold, and the Plymouth road winding away over the hills like a long white tape. I had counted thirteen churches, when my father pointed his hand out along this road and called to me:

"Look'ee out yonder, honey, an' say what ye see!"

"I see dust," says I.

"Nothin' else? Sonny boy, use your eyes, for mine be dim."

"I see dust," says I again, "an' suthin' twinklin' in it, like a tin can—"

"Dragooners!" shouts my father; and then, running to the side of the tower facing the harvest-field, he put both hands to his mouth and called:

"*What have 'ee? What have 'ee?*" – very loud and long.

"*A neck – a neck!*" came back from the field, like as if all shouted at once – dear, the sweet sound! And then a gun was fired, and craning forward over the coping I saw a dozen men running across the stubble and out into the road towards the Hauen; and they called as they ran, "*A neck – a neck!*"

"Iss," says my father, "'tis a neck, sure 'nuff. Pray God they save en! Come, sonny—"

But we dallied up there till the horsemen were plain to see, and their scarlet coats and armour blazing in the dust as they came. And when they drew near within a mile, and our limbs ached with crouching – for fear they should spy us against the sky – father took me by the hand and pulled hot foot down the stairs. Before they rode by he had picked up his shovel and was shovelling out a grave for his life.

Forty valiant horsemen they were, riding two-and-two (by reason of the narrowness of the road) and a captain beside them – men broad and long, with hairy top-lips, and all clad in scarlet jackets and white breeches that showed bravely against their black war-horses and jet-black holsters, thick as they were wi' dust. Each man had a golden helmet, and a scabbard flapping by his side, and a piece of metal like a half-moon jingling from his horse's cheek-strap. 12 D was the numbering on every saddle, meaning the Twelfth Dragoons.

Tramp, tramp! they rode by, talking and joking, and taking no more heed of me – that sat upon the wall with my heels dangling above them – than if I'd been a sprig of stonecrop. But the captain, who carried a drawn sword and mopped his face with a handkerchief so that the dust ran across it in streaks, drew rein, and looked over my shoulder to where father was digging.

"Sergeant!" he calls back, turning with a hand upon his crupper; "didn't we see a figger like this a-top o' the tower, some way back?"

The sergeant pricked his horse forward and saluted. He was the tallest, straightest man in the troop, and the muscles on his arm filled out his sleeve with the three stripes upon it – a handsome red-faced fellow, with curly black hair.

Says he, "That we did, sir – a man with sloping shoulders and a boy with a goose neck." Saying this, he looked up at me with a grin.

"I'll bear it in mind," answered the officer, and the troop rode on in a cloud of dust, the sergeant looking back and smiling, as if 'twas a joke that he shared with us. Well, to be short, they rode down into the town as night fell. But 'twas too late, Uncle Philip having had fair warning and plenty of time to flee up towards the little secret hold under Mabel Down, where none but two families knew how to find him. All the town, though, knew he was safe, and lashins of women and children turned out to see the comely soldiers hunt in vain till ten o'clock at night.

The next thing was to billet the warriors. The captain of the troop, by this, was pesky cross-tempered, and flounced off to the 'Jolly Pilchards' in a huff. "Sergeant," says he, "here's an inn, though a damned bad 'un, an' here I means to stop. Somewheres about there's a farm called Constantine, where I'm told the men can be accommodated. Find out the place, if you can, an' do your best: an' don't let me see yer face till tomorra," says he.

So Sergeant Basket – that was his name – gave the salute, and rode his troop up the street, where – for his manners were mighty winning, notwithstanding the dirty nature of his errand – he soon found plenty to direct him to Farmer Noy's, of Constantine; and up the coombe they rode into the darkness, a dozen or more going along with them to show the way, being won by their martial bearing as well as the sergeant's very friendly way of speech.

Farmer Noy was in bed – a pock-marked, lantern-jawed old gaffer of sixty-five; and the most remarkable point about him was the wife he had married two years before – a young slip of a girl but just husband-high. Money did it, I reckon; but if so, 'twas a bad bargain for her. He was noted for stinginess to such a degree that they said his wife wore a brass wedding-ring, weekdays, to save the genuine article from wearing out. She was a Ruan woman, too, and therefore ought to have known all about him. But woman's ways be past finding out.

Hearing the hoofs in his yard and the sergeant's *stram-a-ram* upon the door, down comes the old curmudgeon with a candle held high above his head.

"What the devil's here?" he calls out. Sergeant Basket looks over the old man's shoulder; and there, halfway up the stairs, stood Madam Noy in her night rail – a high-coloured ripe girl, languishing for love, her red lips parted and neck all lily-white against a loosened pile of dark-brown hair.

"Be cussed if I turn back!" said the sergeant to himself; and added out loud:

"Forty souldjers, in the King's name!"

"Forty devils!" says old Noy.

"They're devils to eat," answered the sergeant, in the most friendly manner; "an', begad, ye must feed an' bed 'em this night – or else I'll search your cellars. Ye are a loyal man – eh, farmer? An' your cellars are big, I'm told."

"Sarah," calls out the old man, following the sergeant's bold glance, "go back an' dress yersel' dacently this instant! These here honest souldjers – forty damned honest gormandisin' souldjers – be come in his Majesty's name, forty strong, to protect honest folks' rights in the intervals of eatin' 'em out o' house an' home. Sergeant, ye be very welcome i' the King's name. Cheese an' cider ye shall have, an' I pray the mixture may turn your forty stomachs."

In a dozen minutes he had fetched out his stable-boys and farm-hands, and, lantern in hand, was helping the sergeant to picket the horses and stow the men about on clean straw in the outhouses. They were turning back to the house, and the old man was turning over in his mind that the sergeant hadn't yet said a word about where he was to sleep, when by the door they found Madam Noy waiting, in her wedding gown, and with her hair freshly braided.

Now, the farmer was mortally afraid of the sergeant, knowing he had thirty ankers and more of contraband liquor in his cellars, and minding the sergeant's threat. Nonetheless his jealousy got the upper hand.

"Woman," he cries out, "to thy bed!"

"I was waiting," said she, "to say the Cap'n's bed—"

"Sergeant's," says the dragoon, correcting her.

"—Was laid i' the spare room."

"Madam," replies Sergeant Basket, looking into her eyes and bowing, "a soldier with my responsibility sleeps but little. In the first place, I must see that my men sup."

"The maids be now cuttin' the bread an' cheese and drawin' the cider."

"Then, Madam, leave me but possession of the parlour, and let me have a chair to sleep in."

By this they were in the passage together, and her gaze devouring his regimentals. The old man stood a pace off, looking sourly. The sergeant fed his eyes upon her, and Satan got hold of him.

"Now if only," said he, "one of you could play cards!"

"But I must go to bed," she answered; "though I can play cribbage, if only you stay another night."

For she saw the glint in the farmer's eye; and so Sergeant Basket slept bolt upright that night in an armchair by the parlour fender. Next day the dragooners searched the town again, and were billeted all about among the cottages. But the sergeant returned to Constantine, and before going to bed – this time in the spare room – played a game of cribbage with Madam Noy, the farmer smoking sulkily in his armchair.

"Two for his heels!" said the rosy woman suddenly, halfway through the game. "Sergeant, you're cheatin' yoursel' an' forgettin' to mark. Gi'e me the board; I'll mark for both."

She put out her hand upon the board, and Sergeant Basket's closed upon it. 'Tis true he had forgot to mark; and feeling the hot pulse in her wrist, and beholding the hunger in her eyes, 'tis to be supposed he'd have forgot his own soul.

He rode away next day with his troop: but my uncle Philip not being caught yet, and the Government set on making an example of him, we hadn't seen the last of these dragoons. 'Twas a time of fear down in the town. At dead of night or at noonday they came on us – six times in all: and for two months the crew of the *Unity* couldn't call their souls their own, but lived from day to day in secret closets and wandered the country by night, hiding in hedges and straw-houses. All that time the revenue men watched the Hauen, night and day, like dogs before a rat-hole.

But one November morning 'twas whispered abroad that Uncle Philip had made his way to Falmouth, and slipped across to Guernsey. Time passed on, and the dragooners were seen no more, nor the handsome devil-may-care face of Sergeant Basket. Up at Constantine, where he had always contrived to billet himself, 'tis to be thought pretty Madam Noy pined to see him again, kicking his spurs in the porch and smiling out of his gay brown eyes; for her face fell away from its plump condition, and the hunger in her eyes grew and grew. But a more remarkable fact was that her old husband – who wouldn't have yearned after the dragoon, ye'd have thought – began to dwindle and fall away too. By the New Year he was a dying man, and carried his doom on his face. And on New Year's Day he straddled his mare for the last time, and rode over to Looe, to Doctor Gale's.

"Goody-losh!" cried the doctor, taken aback by his appearance – "What's come to ye, Noy?"

"Death!" says Noy. "Doctor, I hain't come for advice, for before this day week I'll be a clay-cold corpse. I come to ax a favour. When they summon ye, before lookin' at my body – that'll be past help – go you to the little left-top corner drawer o' my wife's bureau, an' there ye'll find a packet. You're my executor," says he, "and I leaves ye to deal wi' that packet as ye thinks fit."

With that, the farmer rode away home-along, and the very day week he went dead.

The doctor, when called over, minded what the old chap had said, and sending Madam Noy on some pretence to the kitchen, went over and unlocked the little drawer with a duplicate key, that the farmer had unhitched from his watch-chain and given him. There was no parcel of letters, as he looked to find, but only a small packet crumpled away in the corner. He pulled it out and gave a look, and a sniff, and another look: then shut the drawer, locked it, strode straight downstairs to his horse and galloped away.

In three hours' time, pretty Madam Noy was in the constables' hands upon the charge of murdering her husband by poison.

They tried her, next Spring Assize, at Bodmin, before the Lord Chief Justice. There wasn't evidence enough to put Sergeant Basket in the dock alongside of her – though 'twas freely guessed he knew more than anyone (saving the prisoner herself) about the arsenic that was found in the little drawer and inside the old man's body. He was subpoena'd from Plymouth, and cross-examined by a great hulking King's Counsel for three-quarters of an hour. But they got nothing out of him. All through the examination the prisoner looked at him and nodded her white face, every now and then, at his answers, as much as to say, "That's right – that's right: they shan't harm thee, my dear." And the love-light shone in her eyes for all the court to see. But the sergeant never let his look meet it. When he stepped down at last she gave a sob of joy, and fainted bang-off.

They roused her up, after this, to hear the verdict of *Guilty* and her doom spoken by the judge. "Pris'ner at the bar," said the Clerk of Arraigns, "have ye anything to say why this court should not pass sentence o' death?"

She held tight of the rail before her, and spoke out loud and clear:

"My Lord and gentlemen all, I be a guilty woman; an' I be ready to die at once for my sin. But if ye kill me now, ye kill the child in my body – an' he is innocent."

Well, 'twas found she spoke truth; and the hanging was put off till after the time of her delivery. She was led back to prison, and there, about the end of June, her child was born, and died before he was six hours old. But the mother recovered, and quietly abode the time of her hanging.

I can mind her execution very well; for father and mother had determined it would be an excellent thing for my rickets to take me into Bodmin that day, and get a touch of the dead woman's hand, which in those times was considered an unfailing remedy. So we borrowed the parson's manure-cart, and cleaned it thoroughly, and drove in together.

The place of the hangings, then, was a little door in the prison wall, looking over the bank where the railway now goes, and a dismal piece of water called Jail-pool, where the townsfolk drowned most of the dogs and cats they'd no further use for. All the bank under the gallows was that thick with people you could almost walk upon their heads; and my ribs were squeezed by the crowd so that I couldn't breathe freely for a month after. Back across the pool, the fields along the side of the valley were lined with booths and sweet-stalls and standings – a perfect Whitsun-fair; and a din going up that cracked your ears.

But there was the stillness of death when the woman came forth, with the sheriff and the chaplain reading in his book, and the unnamed man behind – all from the little door. She wore a strait black gown, and a white kerchief about her neck – a lovely woman, young and white and tearless.

She ran her eye over the crowd and stepped forward a pace, as if to speak; but lifted a finger and beckoned instead; and out of the people a man fought his way to the foot of the scaffold. 'Twas the dashing sergeant, that was here upon sick-leave. Sick he was, I believe. His face above his shining regimentals was grey as a slate; for he had committed perjury to save his skin, and on the face of the perjured no sun will ever shine.

"Have you got it?" the doomed woman said, many hearing the words.

He tried to reach, but the scaffold was too high, so he tossed up what was in his hand, and the woman caught it – a little screw of tissue-paper.

"I must see that, please!" said the sheriff, laying a hand upon her arm.

"'Tis but a weddin' ring, sir" – and she slipped it over her finger. Then she kissed it once, under the beam, and, lookin' into the dragoon's eyes, spoke very slow:

"Husband, our child shall go wi' you; an' when I want you he shall fetch you."

– and with that turned to the sheriff, saying:

"I be ready, sir."

The sheriff wouldn't give father and mother leave for me to touch the dead woman's hand; so they drove back that evening grumbling a good bit. 'Tis a sixteen-mile drive, and the ostler in at Bodmin had swindled the poor old horse out of his feed, I believe; for he crawled like a slug. But they were so taken up with discussing the day's doings, and what a mort of people had been present, and how the sheriff might have used milder language in refusing my father, that they forgot to use the whip. The moon was up before we got halfway home, and a star to be seen here and there; and still we never mended our pace.

'Twas in the middle of the lane leading down to Hendra Bottom, where for more than a mile two carts can't pass each other, that my father pricks up his ears and looks back.

"Hullo!" says he; "there's somebody gallopin' behind us."

Far back in the night we heard the noise of a horse's hoofs, pounding furiously on the road and drawing nearer and nearer.

"Save us!" cries father; "whoever 'tis, he's comin' down th' lane!" And in a minute's time the clatter was close on us and someone shouting behind.

"Hurry that crawlin' worm o' yourn – or draw aside in God's name, an' let me by!" the rider yelled.

"What's up?" asked my father, quartering as well as he could. "Why! Hullo! Farmer Hugo, be that you?"

"There's a mad devil o' a man behind, ridin' down all he comes across. A's blazin' drunk, I reckon – but 'tisn' *that* – 'tis the horrible voice that goes wi' en – Hark! Lord protect us, he's turn'd into the lane!"

Sure enough, the clatter of a second horse was coming down upon us, out of the night and with it the most ghastly sounds that ever creamed a man's flesh. Farmer Hugo pushed past us and sent a shower of mud in our faces as his horse leapt off again, and 'way-to-go down the hill. My father stood up and lashed our old grey with the reins, and down we went too, bumpity-bump for our lives, the poor beast being taken suddenly like one possessed. For the screaming behind was like nothing on earth but the wailing and sobbing of a little child – only tenfold louder. 'Twas just as you'd fancy a baby might wail if his little limbs was being twisted to death.

At the hill's foot, as you know, a stream crosses the lane – that widens out there a bit, and narrows again as it goes up t'other side of the valley. Knowing we must be overtaken further on – for the screams and clatter seemed at our very backs by this – father jumped out here into the stream and backed the cart well to one side; and not a second too soon.

The next moment, like a wind, this thing went by us in the moonlight – a man upon a black horse that splashed the stream all over us as he dashed through it and up the hill. 'Twas the scarlet dragoon with his ashen face; and behind him, holding to his cross-belt, rode a little shape that tugged and wailed and raved. As I stand here, sir, 'twas the shape of a naked babe!

Well, I won't go on to tell how my father dropped upon his knees in the water, or how my mother fainted off. The thing was gone, and from that moment for eight years nothing was seen or heard of Sergeant Basket. The fright killed my mother. Before next spring she fell into a decline, and early next fall the old man – for he was an old man now – had to delve her grave. After this he went feebly about his work, but held on, being wishful for me to step into his shoon, which I began to do as soon as I was fourteen, having outgrown the rickets by that time.

But one cool evening in September month, father was up digging in the yard alone: for 'twas a small child's grave, and in the loosest soil, and I was off on a day's work, thatching Farmer Tresidder's stacks. He was digging away slowly when he heard a rattle at the lych-gate, and looking over the edge of the grave, saw in the dusk a man hitching his horse there by the bridle.

'Twas a coal-black horse, and the man wore a scarlet coat all powdered with pilm; and as he opened the gate and came over the graves, father saw that 'twas the dashing dragoon. His face was still a slaty-grey, and clammy with sweat; and when he spoke, his voice was all of a whisper, with a shiver therein.

"Bedman," says he, "go to the hedge and look down the road, and tell me what you see."

My father went, with his knees shaking, and came back again.

"I see a woman," says he, "not fifty yards down the road. She is dressed in black, an' has a veil over her face; an' she's comin' this way."

"Bedman," answers the dragoon, "go to the gate an' look back along the Plymouth road, an' tell me what you see."

"I see," says my father, coming back with his teeth chattering, "I see, twenty yards back, a naked child comin'. He looks to be callin', but he makes no sound."

"Because his voice is wearied out," says the dragoon. And with that he faced about, and walked to the gate slowly.

"Bedman, come wi' me an' see the rest," he says, over his shoulder.

He opened the gate, unhitched the bridle and swung himself heavily up in the saddle.

Now from the gate the bank goes down pretty steep into the road, and at the foot of the bank my father saw two figures waiting. 'Twas the woman and the child, hand in hand; and their eyes burned up like coals: and the woman's veil was lifted, and her throat bare.

As the horse went down the bank towards these two, they reached out and took each a stirrup and climbed upon his back, the child before the dragoon and the woman behind. The man's face was set like a stone. Not a word did either speak, and in this fashion they rode down the hill towards Ruan sands. All that my father could mind, beyond, was that the woman's hands were passed round the man's neck, where the rope had passed round her own.

No more could he tell, being a stricken man from that hour. But Aunt Polgrain, the housekeeper up to Constantine, saw them, an hour later, go along the road below the town-place; and Jacobs, the smith, saw them pass his forge towards Bodmin about midnight. So the tale's true enough. But since that night no man has set eyes on horse or riders.

Bites

Aeryn Rudel

"HERE'S your stop," Katelyn said, pulling the Prius up to the curb. She turned and smiled at her passenger, hoping he might use Uber's tip option.

The balding middle-aged guy in the back seat did not put down his iPhone when he mumbled, "Uh huh," and exited the vehicle.

"Asshole," Katelyn said as the door closed. She'd been an Uber driver for a year, and most of her passengers were pleasant enough. The occasional creep was part of the job, sure, but the casual dismissal shown by her last client always got under her skin.

She picked up her phone and gave the guy three stars. Probably not enough to bring his passenger rating down much but enough for a petty rush of satisfaction.

A muffled buzz sounded from her glovebox. Katelyn opened it and took out her *other* phone. A message on the screen said 'Order Up' in a black bubble tinged with red. She touched the bubble and it expanded, revealing an address, a name, Lucas Wills, and an order preference: male, under forty.

Katelyn frowned. She hadn't had a new client through Bites in weeks. Still, if Mr. Wills used the app, the company would have cleared him, and a new client meant another three grand in her pocket, maybe on a regular basis. She put the phone down on the passenger seat and took a deep breath. Guilt washed over her, as it always did with a new Bites order. It would pass, and when the money hit her account and she paid her rent and student loans and, hell, maybe had enough left over to go to a fucking movie or something, she'd rationalize it away.

"Okay, Mr. Wills, what's on the menu today?" She put the Bites phone back in the glovebox and picked up her regular phone. There was no shortage of people looking for an Uber driver in downtown Seattle. Katelyn scrolled through the various requests until she came to one that looked promising. By his profile pic, Mark Harrison appeared young and healthy, probably in good shape, and close by. She accepted the request, put the Prius in gear, and drove off.

* * *

Mark Harrison waited on the sidewalk in front of the Pacific Place mall. He waved as Katelyn pulled up, a tall, good-looking guy with kind eyes and a broad, slightly goofy smile beneath a Mariner's baseball cap. She parked at the curb and unlocked the door. He got in, and she caught a whiff of his cologne, subtle and pleasant.

"Hi, Katelyn," Mark said, his voice smooth and deep. He remembered her name from the app. A little thing, but she liked him immediately, and that brought another sharp pang of guilt. Fuck. This would be easier if he was an asshole.

"Mariners fan, huh?" She would be taking him to Safeco Field after a slight detour.

His grin widened. "Yeah, *big* fan. You?"

"Nah, I prefer the Sounders," Katelyn said and pulled out into traffic.

"Ugh, soccer. So Seattle. I never could get into the sport."

"Well, I played in high school and college," She was enjoying the rhythm of the conversation. More than that, there was something genuine about Mark she found endearing.

"Oh, yeah, an athlete, huh?" he said. "Were you any good?"

Katelyn shrugged. "Good enough for a couple of scholarships, not good enough to avoid getting myself in debt up to my eyeballs." She waved a hand at the interior of the car. "Obviously."

"Well, that's further than I got with my favorite sport. No athletic ability. Hell, I was a benchwarmer in little league."

She laughed. The guy had charm, and he seemed sincere and kind. Her stomach churned. He almost certainly didn't deserve what she was about to do to him.

The phone in the glove compartment buzzed again. She needed to get to business. "Hey, would you like a mint?" she said. "They're in the side pocket on the door."

"Is my breath that bad?" She sensed the smile in his words.

"Nah, just standard friendly Uber driver protocol."

"Sure, I'll have one." She heard him rummaging around in the door compartment, then the crinkling of wax paper as he removed the wrapper. Finally, the tiny click of the mint hitting his teeth as he popped the candy into his mouth.

Katelyn checked the time on her phone. He should be out cold in five minutes.

"Hey, this is good," he said. "I can't quite put my finger on the flavor though."

"Yeah, I buy them at Whole Foods," Katelyn said and grinned into the rearview so he could see her. The 'flavor' he tasted was sodium thiopental. Well, something similar and a lot stronger. At least that's what the folks at Bites told her.

He was quiet for a few minutes as she drove, likely trying to figure out why he suddenly felt so tired. "Hey, I'm feeling...weird," he said. His voice was thick, the words halting. "Can you, uh, stop and let me out?"

"Are you sure?" she said, worried he might be a little too healthy, healthy enough the drug wouldn't take full effect. There was a tranquilizer gun in the center console for emergencies, but she hoped it wouldn't come to that. "We're almost at T-Mobile Park."

"I...think there's something..." She heard a soft thump and looked in the rearview. He'd slumped back in his seat, mouth hanging open, out cold.

"Oh, thank Christ." The drug would keep him out and quiet for about two hours. She retrieved the other phone from the glovebox and put it in the cradle on her dash. With a touch of the screen, a GPS map to Lucas Wills' house popped up. She made a U-turn before the freeway onramp that would have taken her to T-Mobile and headed off to make her delivery.

* * *

Lucas Wills lived in Belltown in one of the Bites-approved high-rise condominiums. That meant a separate garage Bites drivers could enter without the building's regular occupants seeing them.

Katelyn turned the Prius into an alley behind the building, drove up to a small garage door, and punched Lucas' number into her phone. It rang once before he answered it.

"Uh, hello? Is this Bites?"

Jesus, he sounded young. His voice even cracked a little. "Yes, Mr. Wills," she said. "This is Katelyn with your delivery. Can you let me in?"

"Oh, right." She heard rustling and thumping on the other end of the line, and then the garage door rose in front of her.

"Thanks," she said. "Just meet me down here."

"I'll be right down." He was excited now. That worried her a little.

Katelyn parked the Prius in one of the designated spots with the Bites symbol – a red uppercase B inside a black circle – painted on the asphalt. There were no other cars in the parking deck. She rarely crossed paths with other Bites drivers on duty.

She got out and opened the rear passenger door. Mark sat with head lolling against the seat, still unconscious. She put her fingers against his neck, checking for a pulse. It was strong and steady, as she expected, but it was standard operating procedure to check.

A door opened behind Katelyn. She turned, saw her client, and stifled a groan. Everything about Lucas Wills screamed 'new vampire'. He appeared to be in his late thirties – at least that's how old he'd been before becoming a monster – and sported what looked like a newbie vamp uniform: tight black jeans, black T-shirt, and a black leather jacket. He'd dyed his hair black and wore black eyeliner and lipstick. His complexion was milky pale, and she had a feeling it had been that way before he became one of the undead. He looked like a reject from a black metal band.

"Uh, hi." He offered her a shaky smile. He hadn't learned to keep his lips together to hide his fangs. How the hell did this guy get through the Bites client-approval process? Most of her clients had been living the nightlife for twenty years or more. They were subtle, discreet, and didn't dress like walking advertisements for undeath.

Putting on her best smile, Katelyn said, "Hello, Mr. Wills. I have your delivery right here." She opened the car door wider to give him a look.

His eyes bulged, and he licked his lips. "Oh, wow, good one. Conrad said you guys were fantastic."

That name rang a bell. One of the other Bites drivers had a client named Conrad, an old vamp and one of Bites' first clients. This must be a recommendation. That made her feel a little better.

"You know the rules, right?"

"The rules?" He stared at Mark like a starving man admires a Thanksgiving turkey.

"Yes, the rules. The rules you read, agreed to, and signed when you were vetted for this service."

"Oh, right. I can't kill him."

Katelyn frowned. "Mr. Wills, you're making me nervous. The rules are important. They are for your safety and the safety of the delivery."

"I'm sorry." He moved a few steps closer. His eyes were pink; he hadn't fed in a while. She realized she was alone in a parking garage with a starving vampire. "I'm just hungry. Not thinking straight."

Katelyn stepped back and held up her hands. "Let's slow down, okay." Her thoughts turned to the emergency kit in the glovebox. Every Bites driver had one in case a client found the driver more to their liking than the delivery. That kind of thing didn't happen often, though. Most of the vamps who used the service enjoyed its benefits and did not want to fuck up a good thing. Still, bad shit happened, and the emergency kit served as a Bites driver's last line of defense.

Maybe realizing he creeped her out, Lucas stopped moving toward her. He might still be human enough for that to register. She'd worked her way around to the other side of the Prius, keeping the car between her and her client.

"I'm sorry," he said. "I'm really hungry, and I let it go too long." He gathered himself. "The rules, right. I can't kill him. I can't take more than one pint of blood. There can be no visible wounds. I have to take what I need in thirty minutes."

She relaxed a little. "Good. I just need you to authorize payment, and then I'll turn the delivery over to you." Katelyn pulled out her phone and a stylus. Touch commands didn't work for vampires; their bodies didn't generate the small electric charge most phones worked off. She opened the Bites app to the payment screen. "Just sign on the line and hit accept."

He approached slowly, signed, and tapped the accept button. He did not, she noticed, tap the gratuity option. That sucked, but she would still get three grand wired to her bank account once she delivered Mark Harrison to his destination safe and sound.

Katelyn glanced at the backseat of the Prius. Mark was still out cold. "Okay, he's all yours."

Lucas smiled, his canines poking over his bottom lip. He dragged Mark out of the back seat and flung all two hundred pounds of him over his shoulder as easily as a man might hoist a bag of groceries. Katelyn sometimes forgot how strong vampires were, even the young ones. Would this rank newb be able to control that strength when he fed?

"I'm going to wait here." Normally, she might take another Uber call while waiting for one of her Bites clients to finish up. Not this time. She wanted to collect her three grand, sure, but she also wanted to make sure Mark came back in one piece.

Lucas had already started toward the door. There would be a private elevator beyond. All Bites-approved condos had to have separate elevators for their special residents. Couldn't have the humans seeing their vampire neighbors carting comatose bodies up the stairs. He looked over his shoulder. "Yeah, yeah. Thirty minutes."

Katelyn waited until Lucas left the parking garage before she pulled out her phone and set the timer.

* * *

Thirty minutes went quick. Then five more. That made Lucas Wills late and constituted a serious violation of the rules. Katelyn cursed herself for not going with her gut. Bites drivers could refuse delivery, and, sure, that was dangerous when dealing with a hungry monster, but the safety of the delivery was vitally important. When they ended up dead or missing, people asked questions, and no one – not Bites, not their drivers, and certainly not their clientele – wanted that kind of scrutiny.

The fact the deliveries survived unharmed was how she slept at night. Well, that and because her Bites fees were one of the few things standing between her and crippling debt. You also had to buy into the Bites spiel to not feel like a complete piece of shit. During her orientation, they'd impressed on her that working *with* vampires, providing them with meals they could enjoy in privacy and safety, *saved* lives. She'd seen enough to believe it.

Protocol demanded she call Lucas before doing anything else. Shit happened, even to vampires, and a late client didn't necessarily mean anything nefarious.

Katelyn dialed the number, and it rang once, twice, and then Lucas picked up.

"Hello, Mr. Wills? This is Katelyn. You're late."

Silence on the other end. She couldn't hear breathing, well, because vampires didn't breathe.

"Mr. Wills, you are currently in violation of Bites regulations, and are in danger of losing access to our service. In addition—"

"Uh, we have a problem." Lucas' voice came through the phone high and reedy.

She covered the phone's speaker with her hand. "Fuck, fuck, fuck." Then to Lucas, "What kind of problem, Mr. Wills? I need you to tell me."

"I'm new to this, and sometimes, well, I forget I can't take too much."

A chill ran up Katelyn's spine, followed by crushing guilt. She'd delivered Mark Harrison into the clutches of the vampire equivalent of an adolescent moron. "Is he dead?"

"I…I don't know. Can you come up and check? I'm not good at this."

She knew she should call this in, let the company know what had happened, then get the fuck out of Dodge. Bites employed a team of hard-ass vamp killers to deal with problem clients. Drivers had the right to defend themselves, but they weren't supposed to go all Wesley Snipes on a vamp if they could avoid it. But she had *liked* Mark Harrison. She'd liked him, and she'd done her job anyway.

"Okay, I'm coming up. Stay away from the delivery until I get there. Do you understand?"

"Yeah, he's in the bedroom. I'll keep out of there."

"What's your apartment number?"

"806. I'll leave the door unlocked. You can just come in."

Katelyn had more questions, but Lucas ended the call.

"Fuck," she said under her breath, then made a quick and no doubt foolish decision. She sat in the driver's seat of the Prius, opened the glovebox, and removed a nondescript black case: the driver emergency kit. Inside she found holy water in plastic ampoules (easy to crush), a six-inch silver cross, garlic mace (pepper spray for vampires), and for when things really went tits-up, a bolt gun.

The bolt gun looked like a small power drill and was designed for humanely killing cattle. It propelled a rod at high speed through a spring mechanism and compressed air, strong enough to pierce the thick skull of a cow. The ones Bites drivers carried had an ironwood stake in place of the steel rod.

Katelyn took a deep breath and removed two of the holy water ampoules and the bolt gun. She put the holy water in her pants pocket and the gun in her jacket. She only knew of one Bites driver ever having to use the emergency kit, and it didn't end well. The guy actually got close enough to stake his client but not before the enraged vampire ripped his arm clean off.

Katelyn got out of the Prius and walked to the door Lucas had emerged from. The lobby beyond held two elevators. She hit the up arrow on the first, and it slid open. She punched in the eighth floor and rode toward a monster's lair to the soothing sounds of Kenny G.

* * *

Music reverberated through Lucas Will's door and Katelyn couldn't control a groan and eye roll. The droning notes of Marilyn Manson's cover of *Sweet Dreams* drifted through the thick wood. It was exactly the kind of music a new vampire thought other vampires listened to.

Katelyn opened the door to a dark foyer that led to a large open room. It was still daylight outside, and Lucas had closed heavy steel shutters over the windows to keep the sun at bay. A few candles burned on a wrought-iron candelabra near the TV, shedding enough light to see.

Lucas' choice in furnishing didn't surprise her. Black leather everywhere with hints of silver and brass. He'd confined his taste in art to framed posters of rock bands: The Cure, Concrete Blonde, and, of course, Marilyn Manson. Between the posters for Concrete Blonde's *Bloodletting* (of course) and Manson's *Antichrist Superstar* (natch), he'd mounted a pair of swords on the wall: a katana and a wakizashi in black lacquered scabbards. It was like Lucas had read from some manual on how to be a vampire in 1994. Where the fuck was his maker? Someone had to have made him, and why would that person allow their spawn to have such awful goddamn taste?

There was no sign of Lucas, though a closed door to Katelyn's right probably led to the bedroom. She put her hand on the bolt gun in her pocket and palmed one of the holy water ampoules with the other. "Mr. Wills?" she called out.

Noise from behind the closed door and the muffled sound of footsteps. The door opened a crack, and Lucas Wills slithered out. The pale complexion had disappeared, giving way to something a bit more human. He'd recently fed and fed well. At least he wouldn't go into a hunger frenzy, though that didn't mean good things for Mark.

"Hey," he said. "I think I have this under control now." He didn't move from the doorway; in fact, he seemed to be guarding it.

"Where is the delivery," Katelyn said. "I need to see if he needs medical attention."

Lucas shook his head. "No, that won't be necessary. He's, uh, fine now."

The word *fine* spiked her guts with cold dread. "What do you mean he's fine?"

"I mean you can go now. There's something on the coffee table for you."

Katelyn glanced over at a manila envelope on the brushed steel surface of Lucas' table. A few hundred dollar bills jutted artfully from the open top. She sighed. "Look, man, I don't care about the money. I need to check the delivery and make sure he's okay. Otherwise, I have to call this in. You do *not* want that."

Lucas' eyes widened. Maybe he did know enough about the rules to understand the threat. "Whatever, but I'm telling you he's okay." He opened the door behind him. She could see more candlelight beyond.

"You go first, please," she said.

He nodded and walked through. Katelyn followed a few paces behind, hand clenched around the butt of the bolt gun.

A massive four-poster bed dominated Lucas' bedroom. She'd half expected an actual coffin. Black satin sheets covered the bed, and the black faux-fur covers were on the ground. Mark Harrison lay in the center of the bed, stripped to the waist. His complexion glowed milky pale in the candlelight. Not good.

Lucas stood on one side of the bed, so she went to the other. "Don't move." Katelyn leaned over Mark. She couldn't tell if he was breathing, so she put her fingers on his neck to check for a pulse. His skin was cool to the touch, the heartbeat nonexistent.

"You killed him," Katelyn said, sorrow and anger surging through her brain. "You fucking moron. Do you know what happens now?"

"Wait, wait, wait." Lucas held his hands out. "Look, I fixed it. He's gonna be fine. He just has to stay here and, uh, we need to keep this between us."

"Keep *what* between us? I have to—" Then she saw it. A crimson stain around Mark's mouth. The dread in her belly turned to outright terror. "No, no, no, you colossal fucking idiot. You didn't."

Lucas started to come around the bed, and she drew the bolt gun from her pocket and pointed it at him. You had to be right on top of someone to use it, but he didn't know that. "You stay right fucking there," she said. "Killing a delivery is one thing, but turning one? Oh, dude, Bites is gonna bring the fucking hammer down on you." *And probably me too.*

Katelyn edged toward the door, still pointing the bolt gun at Lucas. He grimaced at her, showing his fangs, and his hands curled into fists. She could see he was thinking shit over, thinking about how he could cover his ass, and he would eventually arrive at the one and only way to do that.

During her orientation as a Bites driver, a very nice old man who claimed to be descended from the semi-mythical Abraham Van Helsing, had outlined all the crazy, scary shit vampires could do when they got pissed off. This covered the gamut from super strength and turning into a bat to creepier things like mind control. Lucas showed her another.

Katelyn didn't see him move. One moment he was ten feet away, the next he'd batted the bolt gun out of her grasp, wrapped a hand around her throat, and hoisted her a full three feet in the air. Her breathing shut off like someone had fastened a c-clamp to her windpipe.

"You aren't telling anyone anything," he hissed up at her, lips skinned back from his fangs. "In fact, I think junior might need a bite to eat when he wakes up."

Lucas Wills might have been strong and supernaturally gifted, but he wasn't smart or particularly perceptive. He didn't notice the holy water ampoule in her left hand until she smashed it against his face.

Lucas dropped her, and she hit the ground hard, knocking the breath from her lungs. The vampire screamed and clutched his face, foul-smelling smoke rose from the scorched flesh. He stumbled away, howling.

Katelyn climbed to her feet, still struggling to breathe and picked up the bolt gun from the floor. She charged Lucas in a shuffling run, hitting him in clumsy tackle and knocking him to the ground. She fell on top of him, and his hands came away from his face and fastened around her neck. His eyes blazed with fury, and he squeezed.

The bolt gun was pinned between them, its barrel flush against the vampire's chest. Her vision grayed as Lucas throttled the life out of her, but she had enough strength and wits left to pull the trigger. The gun made a muffled popping sound and the wooden stake lanced into Lucas' body. His eyes bulged as the ironwood stake pierced his heart and his hands fell away from her throat.

She rolled off him, choking and gasping. When she could breathe again, she stood and cocked the bolt gun for another shot. There was no need. Lucas Wills lay motionless on the floor, a thin trickle of blood running from the hole in his chest. She wasn't done, though. Staking would only paralyze him for a short time; she needed to take more drastic measures to truly end the fledgling vampire.

Katelyn shuffled back into the living room and took the katana from the wall. She drew the blade from its scabbard. It had good weight and looked sharp. Well, at least the idiot had good taste in swords.

* * *

Mark Harrison was coming around when Katelyn finished disposing of Lucas. She'd dragged the body and head into the other room and opened the shutters. The sun did the rest.

He sat up in bed when she walked in, a look of surprise and horror on his face, and something else. Hunger. She'd prepared for the latter. Katelyn pushed a mug into his hands before he could ask any questions.

"Look, I'm gonna tell you everything that's happened," she said, trying to keep her voice from shaking. "But you gotta drink this now."

"I don't…oh, wow, that smells good." He lifted the mug to his lips and took a sip, then tipped it back and drained it. "Is there more?"

She'd taken as much blood from Lucas Wills' corpse as she could. Sure, some it was Mark's own blood, but it would keep him from going mad with hunger. "Yeah, and I'll get you some, but you need to listen now."

"Where am I?" he asked, his eyes gaining focus and clarity as his wits returned. "Wait, you're my Uber driver. What the fuck is going on?"

Katelyn drew in a deep breath. "Let me just start by saying I'm really, really sorry, and, uh, you're not gonna make that Mariners game."

Gabriel-Ernest

Saki

"THERE IS a wild beast in your woods," said the artist Cunningham, as he was being driven to the station. It was the only remark he had made during the drive, but as Van Cheele had talked incessantly his companion's silence had not been noticeable.

"A stray fox or two and some resident weasels. Nothing more formidable," said Van Cheele. The artist said nothing.

"What did you mean about a wild beast?" said Van Cheele later, when they were on the platform.

"Nothing. My imagination. Here is the train," said Cunningham.

That afternoon Van Cheele went for one of his frequent rambles through his woodland property. He had a stuffed bittern in his study, and knew the names of quite a number of wild flowers, so his aunt had possibly some justification in describing him as a great naturalist. At any rate, he was a great walker. It was his custom to take mental notes of everything he saw during his walks, not so much for the purpose of assisting contemporary science as to provide topics for conversation afterwards. When the bluebells began to show themselves in flower he made a point of informing everyone of the fact; the season of the year might have warned his hearers of the likelihood of such an occurrence, but at least they felt that he was being absolutely frank with them.

What Van Cheele saw on this particular afternoon was, however, something far removed from his ordinary range of experience. On a shelf of smooth stone overhanging a deep pool in the hollow of an oak coppice a boy of about sixteen lay asprawl, drying his wet brown limbs luxuriously in the sun. His wet hair, parted by a recent dive, lay close to his head, and his light-brown eyes, so light that there was an almost tigerish gleam in them, were turned towards Van Cheele with a certain lazy watchfulness. It was an unexpected apparition, and Van Cheele found himself engaged in the novel process of thinking before he spoke. Where on earth could this wild-looking boy hail from? The miller's wife had lost a child some two months ago, supposed to have been swept away by the mill-race, but that had been a mere baby, not a half-grown lad.

"What are you doing there?" he demanded.

"Obviously, sunning myself," replied the boy.

"Where do you live?"

"Here, in these woods."

"You can't live in the woods," said Van Cheele.

"They are very nice woods," said the boy, with a touch of patronage in his voice.

"But where do you sleep at night?"

"I don't sleep at night; that's my busiest time."

Van Cheele began to have an irritated feeling that he was grappling with a problem that was eluding him.

"What do you feed on?" he asked.

"Flesh," said the boy, and he pronounced the word with slow relish, as though he were tasting it.

"Flesh! What Flesh?"

"Since it interests you, rabbits, wild-fowl, hares, poultry, lambs in their season, children when I can get any; they're usually too well locked in at night, when I do most of my hunting. It's quite two months since I tasted child-flesh."

Ignoring the chaffing nature of the last remark Van Cheele tried to draw the boy on the subject of possible poaching operations.

"You're talking rather through your hat when you speak of feeding on hares." (Considering the nature of the boy's toilet the simile was hardly an apt one.) "Our hillside hares aren't easily caught."

"At night I hunt on four feet," was the somewhat cryptic response.

"I suppose you mean that you hunt with a dog?" hazarded Van Cheele.

The boy rolled slowly over on to his back, and laughed a weird low laugh, that was pleasantly like a chuckle and disagreeably like a snarl.

"I don't fancy any dog would be very anxious for my company, especially at night."

Van Cheele began to feel that there was something positively uncanny about the strange-eyed, strange-tongued youngster.

"I can't have you staying in these woods," he declared authoritatively.

"I fancy you'd rather have me here than in your house," said the boy.

The prospect of this wild, nude animal in Van Cheele's primly ordered house was certainly an alarming one.

"If you don't go. I shall have to make you," said Van Cheele.

The boy turned like a flash, plunged into the pool, and in a moment had flung his wet and glistening body halfway up the bank where Van Cheele was standing. In an otter the movement would not have been remarkable; in a boy Van Cheele found it sufficiently startling. His foot slipped as he made an involuntarily backward movement, and he found himself almost prostrate on the slippery weed-grown bank, with those tigerish yellow eyes not very far from his own. Almost instinctively he half raised his hand to his throat. The boy laughed again, a laugh in which the snarl had nearly driven out the chuckle, and then, with another of his astonishing lightning movements, plunged out of view into a yielding tangle of weed and fern.

"What an extraordinary wild animal!" said Van Cheele as he picked himself up. And then he recalled Cunningham's remark "There is a wild beast in your woods."

Walking slowly homeward, Van Cheele began to turn over in his mind various local occurrences which might be traceable to the existence of this astonishing young savage.

Something had been thinning the game in the woods lately, poultry had been missing from the farms, hares were growing unaccountably scarcer, and complaints had reached him of lambs being carried off bodily from the hills. Was it possible that this wild boy was really hunting the countryside in company with some clever poacher dogs? He had spoken of hunting 'four-footed' by night, but then, again, he had hinted strangely at no dog caring to come near him, 'especially at night'. It was certainly puzzling. And then, as Van Cheele ran his mind over the various depredations that had been committed during the last month or two, he came suddenly to a dead stop, alike in his walk and his speculations. The child missing from the mill two months ago – the accepted theory was that it had tumbled into the mill-race and been swept away; but the mother had always declared she had heard a shriek on the hillside of the house, in the opposite direction from the water. It was unthinkable, of course, but he wished that the boy had not made that uncanny remark about child-flesh eaten two months ago. Such dreadful things should not be said even in fun.

Van Cheele, contrary to his usual wont, did not feel disposed to be communicative about his discovery in the wood. His position as a parish councillor and justice of the peace seemed somehow compromised by the fact that he was harbouring a personality of such doubtful repute on his property; there was even a possibility that a heavy bill of damages for raided lambs and poultry might be laid at his door. At dinner that night he was quite unusually silent.

"Where's your voice gone to?" said his aunt. "One would think you had seen a wolf."

Van Cheele, who was not familiar with the old saying, thought the remark rather foolish; if he *had* seen a wolf on his property his tongue would have been extraordinarily busy with the subject.

At breakfast next morning Van Cheele was conscious that his feeling of uneasiness regarding yesterday's episode had not wholly disappeared, and he resolved to go by train to the neighbouring cathedral town, hunt up Cunningham, and learn from him what he had really seen that had prompted the remark about a wild beast in the woods. With this resolution taken, his usual cheerfulness partially returned, and he hummed a bright little melody as he sauntered to the morning room for his customary cigarette. As he entered the room the melody made way abruptly for a pious invocation. Gracefully asprawl on the ottoman, in an attitude of almost exaggerated repose, was the boy of the woods. He was drier than when Van Cheele had last seen him, but no other alteration was noticeable in his toilet.

"How dare you come here?" asked Van Cheele furiously.

"You told me I was not to stay in the woods," said the boy calmly.

"But not to come here. Supposing my aunt should see you!"

And with a view to minimising that catastrophe, Van Cheele hastily obscured as much of his unwelcome guest as possible under the folds of a *Morning Post*. At that moment his aunt entered the room.

"This is a poor boy who has lost his way – and lost his memory. He doesn't know who he is or where he comes from," explained Van Cheele desperately, glancing apprehensively at the waif's face to see whether he was going to add inconvenient candour to his other savage propensities.

Miss Van Cheele was enormously interested.

"Perhaps his underlinen is marked," she suggested.

"He seems to have lost most of that, too," said Van Cheele, making frantic little grabs at the *Morning Post* to keep it in its place.

A naked homeless child appealed to Miss Van Cheele as warmly as a stray kitten or derelict puppy would have done.

"We must do all we can for him," she decided, and in a very short time a messenger, dispatched to the rectory, where a page-boy was kept, had returned with a suit of pantry clothes, and the necessary accessories of shirt, shoes, collar, etc. Clothed, clean, and groomed, the boy lost none of his uncanniness in Van Cheele's eyes, but his aunt found him sweet.

"We must call him something till we know who he really is," she said. "Gabriel-Ernest, I think; those are nice suitable names."

Van Cheele agreed, but he privately doubted whether they were being grafted on to a nice suitable child. His misgivings were not diminished by the fact that his staid and elderly spaniel had bolted out of the house at the first incoming of the boy, and now obstinately remained shivering and yapping at the farther end of the orchard, while the canary, usually as vocally industrious as Van Cheele himself, had put itself on an allowance of frightened cheeps. More than ever he was resolved to consult Cunningham without loss of time.

As he drove off to the station his aunt was arranging that Gabriel-Ernest should help her to entertain the infant members of her Sunday-school class at tea that afternoon.

Cunningham was not at first disposed to be communicative.

"My mother died of some brain trouble," he explained, "so you will understand why I am averse to dwelling on anything of an impossibly fantastic nature that I may see or think that I have seen."

"But what *did* you see?" persisted Van Cheele.

"What I thought I saw was something so extraordinary that no really sane man could dignify it with the credit of having actually happened. I was standing, the last evening I was with you, half hidden in the hedge-growth by the orchard gate, watching the dying glow of the sunset. Suddenly I became aware of a naked boy, a bather from some neighbouring pool, I took him to be, who was standing out on the bare hillside also watching the sunset. His pose was so suggestive of some wild faun of Pagan myth that I instantly wanted to engage him as a model, and in another moment I think I should have hailed him. But just then the sun dipped out of view, and all the orange and pink slid out of the landscape, leaving it cold and grey. And at the same moment an astounding thing happened – the boy vanished too!"

"What! Vanished away into nothing?" asked Van Cheele excitedly.

"No; that is the dreadful part of it," answered the artist; "on the open hillside where the boy had been standing a second ago, stood a large wolf, blackish in colour, with gleaming fangs and cruel, yellow eyes. You may think—"

But Van Cheele did not stop for anything as futile as thought. Already he was tearing at top speed towards the station. He dismissed the idea of a telegram. 'Gabriel-Ernest is a werewolf' was a hopelessly inadequate effort at conveying the situation, and his aunt would think it was a code message to which he had omitted to give her the key. His one hope was that he might reach home before sundown. The cab which he chartered at the other end of the railway journey bore him with what seemed exasperating slowness along the country roads, which were pink and mauve with the flush of the sinking sun. His aunt was putting away some unfinished jams and cake when he arrived.

"Where is Gabriel-Ernest?" he almost screamed.

"He is taking the little Toop child home," said his aunt. "It was getting so late, I thought it wasn't safe to let it go back alone. What a lovely sunset, isn't it?"

But Van Cheele, although not oblivious of the glow in the western sky, did not stay to discuss its beauties. At a speed for which he was scarcely geared he raced along the narrow lane that led to the home of the Toops. On one side ran the swift current of the mill stream, on the other rose the stretch of bare hillside. A dwindling rim of red sun showed still on the skyline, and the next turning must bring him in view of the ill-assorted couple he was pursuing. Then the colour went suddenly out of things, and a grey light settled itself with a quick shiver over the landscape. Van Cheele heard a shrill wail of fear, and stopped running.

Nothing was ever seen again of the Toop child or Gabriel-Ernest, but the latter's discarded garments were found lying in the road so it was assumed that the child had fallen into the water, and that the boy had stripped and jumped in, in a vain endeavour to save it. Van Cheele and some workmen who were nearby at the time testified to having heard a child scream loudly just near the spot where the clothes were found. Mrs. Toop, who had eleven other children, was decently resigned to her bereavement, but Miss Van Cheele sincerely mourned her lost foundling. It was on her initiative that a memorial brass was put up in the parish church to 'Gabriel-Ernest, an unknown boy, who bravely sacrificed his life for another.'

Van Cheele gave way to his aunt in most things, but he flatly refused to subscribe to the Gabriel-Ernest memorial.

Chaneke

David Schmidt

MASSIVE conifer trees loomed over the bus as it lumbered uphill on the one lane highway. Thick bunches of Spanish moss hung from their branches, lending an ominous gloom to the scene outside my window. Even my reflection looked distorted, otherworldly. Though the face was my own – curly, black hair, bronze skin, the indigenous features of my ancestors – this high up the mountain, it all seemed to belong to someone else.

I was on my way to the village of Santa Isabel, in the remote mountains of the State of Oaxaca, Mexico. In my backpack, I carried my grandmother's ashes.

The bus had been lurching uphill for hours, pulling further and further away from the stability and comforts of Mexico City, deep into the wild southeast of my Mexican homeland. An hour before we reached the city of Huautla de Jiménez, I pressed my face against the cold glass window and stared until I saw the sign that announced my grandmother's home town: *SANTA ISABEL*. I collected my things and asked the driver to leave me by the roadside. I hopped onto the gravel road, and watched the creaky bus roll off into the foggy distance.

This was my first time seeing the town that Grandma Carmen had told me so many stories about. A light drizzle fell as I walked up the dirt path. On one arm, I carried my heavy backpack, loaded with photographic equipment and anthropology books. The other shoulder held the padded bag with my grandmother's urn.

In the soft glow of twilight, a broad constellation of lights twinkled on the hillside above me, the kerosene lamps that glowed inside thirty-odd adobe houses and tin shacks. I was headed to the home of Uncle Marcos, one of my few relatives who never left Santa Isabel for the prosperity of the capital. As I walked down the wet cobblestones of Santa Isabel's main street, an elderly man hobbled past me, wearing a worn, wide-brimmed hat and tired *huarache* sandals. I greeted him in Spanish.

"I'm Enrique, the grandson of Doña Carmen. This is my first time in town. I'm looking for the home of my uncle, Marcos."

He stared at me and shook his head. Like many of the elderly residents of such rural communities, he spoke no Spanish. The man replied in the indigenous Mixtec language, in soft and melodious tones. While I never learned the language of my ancestors, it always struck me as beautifully sonorous, a fluid river of sounds, water quietly running over the smooth stones of a brook, a rainy evening in the forest.

When I repeated the name of Uncle Marcos, the old man's eyes lit up, and he gestured up to a hill behind the old colonial church. I hiked up through the grass and brush, past ancient pine trees, to the house the man had indicated. It was a one-room cinder block structure, standing beside an older kitchen made of adobe.

I knocked on the creaky, wooden door of the kitchen. My uncle was waiting for me, heating tortillas over an open fire. He looked to be in his late fifties, with ample smile lines, his skin a shade darker than mine, and a bushy, gray moustache. In heavily-accented Spanish, he welcomed me to my family's hometown.

"Thank you for bringing your *abuela's* ashes back to Santa Isabel, Enrique," he said with gravity. "I can tell you loved her very much. Tomorrow we will celebrate Mass for her in the church. Then we will bury her."

What Uncle Marcos didn't know was my other motive for visiting this village. I was not only here to bury my *abuela's* ashes – I had also come to search for the *chanekes*.

* * *

Grandma Carmen was the first member of our family to leave Santa Isabel. She was only ten when she moved to Mexico City. Ever since I was a little boy, visiting Grandma Carmen at her house on the outskirts of the capital, she would tell me stories of the *chanekes*. The mythical Little People lived deep in the wilderness of southern Mexico, she told me, tiny gnomes who lived in the forest. Sometimes, the chanekes came down the mountain and played tricks on the humans of Santa Isabel. They would steal food, frighten housewives, and occasionally even kidnap children from the village.

As a child, the stories thrilled and terrified me. As I worked my way through secondary school, then preparatory, then university, I learned to scoff at them. Simple country superstitions, I thought, imaginative fancies of a primitive people. Then I began my doctoral studies of anthropology at the National Autonomous University of Mexico City, and I revisited those old stories. I now suspect that they may have been more than just stories.

I believe the chanekes may be real.

In my studies, I came across accounts from the remote island of Flores, Indonesia. The natives of Flores used to tell similar stories of Little People. When the first European explorers reached the island and heard the tales of the *ebu gogo*, 'the ugly uncle', they laughed at the natives' primitive superstitions. Then an American anthropologist discovered the fossils of an *ebu gogo* in 2004. The natives had been right all along: they shared the island with a distant human ancestor, a humanoid species now known as *Homo floresiensis*.

I suspect that the same could be true of the chanekes right here in Mexico.

Grandma Carmen told me that she encountered them several times as a child. She would see them perched in the trees, hiding in the forest. She remembers the chilling call of the chanekes as they cried out at dusk: *Squaliú, squaliú, squaliuá…* Her stories were devoid of any magic or mysticism – they were very matter-of-fact, eyewitness accounts of a strange creature in the wilderness. Why could the chaneke not be simply another species on this planet?

If this is the case, someone has yet to discover it. That someone could be me.

Over the past several months, as my academic career has floundered – lacking a topic for my doctoral thesis, mocked by my peers, failing to thrive in the competitive doctoral program – I have been consumed by thoughts of the chanekes. If such a hominid actually existed, if I could even find a few fossils, my future in the field of anthropology would be transformed.

And so I offered to carry my grandmother's ashes to Santa Isabel. To honour her memory, of course, but more importantly, to search for a missing human ancestor. There was only one problem, though – I could find nobody in the village willing to talk about the chanekes.

After Uncle Marcos and I buried Grandma Carmen's ashes in the old cemetery, I spent the next couple weeks familiarizing myself with the town of my ancestors. Bit by bit, I asked the residents of Santa Isabel if they had heard stories of the chanekes.

A few people shared stories from some distant past, legends full of magical and supernatural elements. I heard tales of chanekes that appeared and disappeared at will, masters of shapeshifting that could transform into any living human. Years ago, they said, a woman came home to find her husband asleep on the floor. She suspected that something was wrong. When she pressed an icon of the Virgin of Guadalupe to his face, he transformed back into a chaneke and crawled out into the woods.

"But what about you?" I asked the townsfolk. "Have you ever seen a chaneke?"

The response to this question was universal – every single person would turn away, avoid my gaze, and whisper, "No, Enrique. Those things don't happen here anymore."

Two weeks in Santa Isabel, and I was coming up dry. Zero personal accounts of the mysterious Little People. I was preparing to pack my bags, say farewell to Uncle Marcos, and return to university with my tail between my legs.

Then I met a survivor: a man who had been kidnapped by the chanekes.

* * *

I saw him one dark, cloudy day, after I had gone into the mountains with my uncle to chop firewood. As we walked our burro back to town, I noticed an elderly man standing by the general store, swaying back and forth. His appearance was squalid: clothing dirty and torn, straw hat askew. He was one of the few men in town who wore a full beard, white and scraggly.

Uncle Marcos and I stood at a distance, watching as the man chatted in Mixtec with Don Bartolo, the owner of the general store. He gesticulated wildly, slurring his words, while he threw back swallows of the homemade liquor that Don Bartolo sold. His earlobes hung low and wiggled when he spoke. At one point, he raised his voice, pulled off his old gray shirt and threw it on the ground.

"Oh, dear," my uncle chuckled. "Mardonio is about to get naked again."

"Pardon?"

"Mardonio here, every time he gets drunk on *aguardiente,* he takes off all his clothes and stomps on them. He says that the chanekes don't wear clothes, so he doesn't want to wear clothes either."

I stared at my uncle. "The chanekes, you say?"

"When Mardonio was a little boy, the chanekes took him. They stole him away from town and carried him off into the mountains. That is why he drinks so much."

The following day, I returned to the general store. I stood by the entrance for several hours, chatting with the store owner about the weather, this year's crop of corn, and the old traditions of Santa Isabel. He told me that our families were distantly related, through a great-great-grandfather who had been a traditional healer. Around dusk, when most townsfolk were heading home from their cornfields, a hunched figure approached the store. It was Mardonio.

I offered to buy him a drink of *aguardiente.* He gladly accepted. When I smelled his breath, I suspected that he hadn't stopped drinking since the previous evening. After we had shared three glasses of liquor, he smiled widely at me, holding onto my shoulder for balance. I broached the subject of the chanekes.

"Don Mardonio," I whispered, "I hear that you met the chanekes."

He told me the story in a slurred mix of Spanish and Mixtec. From the fragments I was able to understand, I pieced together the following:

When he was seven years old, Mardonio went to play in the forest alone. The chanekes found him. They emerged from the woods, surrounded him on all sides and grabbed him. With otherworldly force, they lifted him above their heads and carried him far from Santa Isabel, all the way to a cave high in the mountains.

"That cave is their *vi'i*, their house," he said gravely. "That is where the chanekes live. I spent many months with them. I even learned their language."

I longed to ask him so many questions, but my time was running short – by this point, Mardonio was a couple drinks away from becoming incoherent. I skipped straight to my most pressing question:

"Do you remember where that cave is?"

He nodded and took a drink from the unmarked bottle. He explained that the chanekes' cave was uphill from town, a two hours' hike to the northwest, near a natural spring called *Agua del Español*.

"The entrance is in a cliff just behind that spring."

"And do you think you could take me there?" I asked.

Mardonio spit on the ground and shook his head vehemently, his earlobes wiggling back and forth. It would have been comical, were it not for the absolute terror that shone through his eyes.

"I am never going back to that cave, Enrique. Never."

If I wanted to explore the chaneke's cave, I would need to go alone.

* * *

I convinced Uncle Marcos to take me to the cave, on the pretext of visiting the natural spring.

"My mother asked me to bring her some water from *Agua del Español*," I said the next morning as we ate our breakfast of black beans, tortillas and coffee. "She says it has medicinal properties, and wants me to bring her a couple bottles of it."

We left Santa Isabel early that afternoon and hiked uphill, into the steep mountains that overshadowed the town. My uncle warned me to not stray far from the path, as these woods were infested with poisonous snakes. I asked if there were any human settlements this high up.

"No, Enrique, nobody lives up here. This country is… It is not good for people."

Perfect, I thought. *If any undiscovered species existed in these mountains, this would be the ideal place to survive.*

As I checked the battery of my camera, a strange sound rang out in the trees. "*Uuu… Uuu…*"

"What was that?" I asked with alarm. "Is somebody else here?"

"Calm down, son. It's nothing but a *tikukuu*. An owl."

"But aren't owls nocturnal? Why would it be hooting during the daytime?"

"Nobody's perfect," he chuckled. "Even owls make mistakes."

We reached the spring, a trickle of water that bubbled out of the rocks. I stared up at the dark, cloudy sky, then surveyed my surroundings. Just as Mardonio had said, a rocky cliff stood behind the spring, on the other side of a small ravine. On the face of the cliff, I saw it: a dark shadow in the rocks, framed on all sides by the thick brush. The cave.

"You had better hurry up and fill your bottles." Uncle Marcos stared at the dark sky with furrowed brow. "It's about to rain any minute."

I filled two plastic bottles, then pulled out a third one. "Wait for me here, uncle. I heard of another spring down here past the ravine."

"No, Enrique. Don't go down there." His voice trembled slightly. "Nobody goes over there."

"Why not, uncle?"

"Because there are… Snakes. They might bite you."

"I'll be careful, uncle. Don't worry about me."

I hiked downhill, clearing the brush with my machete every few steps. Again, I heard that cry: "*Uuu... Uuu...*" The confused owl must have followed us here. Perhaps the dark clouds made it think that night-time was near. I came to a creek in the ravine and stared up at the rocky cliff. The entrance to the cave was some two hundred meters overhead. I checked the batteries in my flashlight and made sure I had empty space in my backpack.

At the very least, I'll be taking samples of the rocks and earth around the cave. But hopefully... Hopefully, I'll find something much more worthwhile. I held my breath at the thought. *Bones. Remains. The remains of an undiscovered species.*

As I reached the bank of the creek, a voice suddenly cried out. "Enrique! Enrique! Help me!"

It was Uncle Marcos. He was somewhere to my right, down in the ravine.

How did he get down here so quickly? Did he fall down the hillside?

"Where are you, uncle?" I shouted. "Are you hurt?"

"Come here, Enrique, please!"

He sounded desperate. I ran alongside the creek, splashing water and soaking my boots. It began to drizzle. Raindrops drew rippling rings across the surface of the water.

"Uncle! Where are you!" I reached the point where his voice had come from, but there was no sign of him. "Uncle!"

"Enrique! Help me!" I shook my head. The voice was now *above* me.

"Uncle! How did you get all the way up there?" I stared upwards. The rocks on the cliff shone with the fresh rain, now falling in full force. It looked steep and treacherously slippery. "Uncle! We need to go back to town!"

Silence. No sound but the rain pouring down on the leaves of the trees and the creek murmuring across the stones. Thunder rolled in the distance.

"Uncle Marcos!"

I started to climb the rocky cliffs, grabbing roots and plants with care, checking my footing slowly. The owl hooted again in some nearby tree. "*Uuu... Uuu...*"

"Enrique! I'm up here!"

There was an echo to his voice this time. He must have gone inside the cave, taking refuge from the rain. I climbed as quickly as I could, slipping now and again, until I reached the top.

"I'm on my way, uncle!"

A different owl cried out at the opposite end of the ravine behind me.

"*Uuu... Uuu...*"

I turned my head. There was something strange in its cry. When it sang again, its cry was drawn out and distorted.

"*Uuu... Uuu... Squaliú, squaliú...*"

Another voice responded from the bottom of the ravine. "*Squaliú, squaliú, squaliuá... "*

I had never heard such an alien, blood-chilling sound in my life. I ran to the entrance of the cave and shouted into the darkness. "Uncle! Are you in there?"

"Down here, Enrique! Come on down!"

A second later, I heard that strange cry in the forest behind me. "*Squaliú, squaliú, squaliuá...*" It was closer now. I rushed into the cave and turned on my flashlight.

It was silent as a graveyard, the only sound a rhythmic *drip, drip, drip* of rainwater that seeped in from the soil above. I slowly edged forward across the flat, stony ground which sloped gradually downhill. I shone the flashlight downwards – the floor of the cave was free of dust. No footprints.

"Uncle?"

My voice echoed inside the cavern. I observed my surroundings. I was descending down a rocky tunnel, narrow on both sides but stretching high up above me. I called out for my uncle again. My voice rang out in the empty underground chamber for several seconds. *Could he be hurt? What if he fell down a sinkhole?*

As I crept deeper into the cave, a terrible stench surrounded me. Something between a dead animal and a person who hasn't bathed in weeks. Out of nowhere, a vivid memory invaded my mind: my first fight in secondary school.

Nicolás had been the tallest boy in my class, since he had failed sixth grade three times. Some of us suspected he was the tallest teenager in all of Mexico City. He was stocky, wore his hair cut short, and always had stains and holes in his uniform. One day, he demanded my bus money. I refused. As we were leaving school, he grabbed me in a bear hug and rained blows down on my kidneys. With his flabby chest pressed against my face, slowly suffocating me, I was overcome with a terrible, predatory stench. It was more than the body odor of Nicolás, more than his pubescent armpits – this was the smell of violent hormones, of an ancient instinct of aggression.

The same smell now filled the cave. All my muscles tensed as I walked forward.

"Uncle! If you're down here, answer me, please!"

I heard a shuffle inside the cave. I froze. The sound was behind me.

Something was crawling down the tunnel through which I had entered. It moved quickly, scuttling across the gravel. Two, four, six, countless feet pattered across the rocks, with a sound like claws scratching the stone walls.

Then I heard the voices.

They no longer cried out. The call of *"squaliú, squaliuá"* would have sounded positively comforting in the solitude of that cave. At least that cry was something similar to human language, something that could be transcribed with the International Phonetic Alphabet. The voices inside the cave whispered with a series of clicks and tics and tocs, of guttural growls and grunts, vowels that sounded like an unnatural inhalation. Far from the Mixtec language of my ancestors, far from the entire Otomanguean linguistic family, these voices were nothing human at all.

I panicked and started running down the tunnel at a breakneck speed, holding the flashlight out to light the way. A massive fissure appeared in the ground up ahead. I had to hold the flashlight between my teeth and grasp the rocky walls, carefully spider-crawling over the fissure. One false step and I would drop into the chasm beneath me. As I edged forward, those horrible, otherworldly voices echoed throughout the cave.

The tunnel finally emptied into a wide, open cavern. A cloud of bats swirled about a high, arched ceiling, circling the stalactites. I paused to catch my breath, and the beam of my flashlight fell upon a massive rock formation. In the darkness, it looked like a hooded, cloaked figure holding a scythe. *La Santa Muerte,* I thought. The image of 'Holy Death', the dark goddess of the underworld invoked by the witches and warlocks of Mexico City. *No,* I tried to convince myself. *It's nothing but a natural formation, the accumulation of minerals over thousands of years. It's an illusion,* pareidolia, *my imagination.*

Meanwhile, my heart told me: *No, Enrique, your instinct is correct. The spectre of death haunts this place.*

I jogged through the broad cavern. As I passed beneath the statuesque formation, a horrid voice rang out in the tunnel behind me. It laughed, if you could call that perverse, unhuman giggle a laugh, that cruel falsetto that echoed throughout the cavern. It sounded more like a recording of laughter played backwards, inhaling, rising and falling unnaturally. *"A-h, a-h, a-h, a-h."*

I broke into a sprint.

I ran like mad across the cavern as the bats reacted to my natural tension, swooping down from the vaulted ceiling, swirling around me, tangling their claws in my thick black hair and scratching my scalp, and still I ran without looking back.

At the far end of the cavern, my flashlight illuminated a large, rectangular stone half a metre high, like a great stone table, with strange forms carved on the edges. I didn't even stop to examine it. I didn't even take a photograph. Archaeology be damned. My mind was consumed with whatever horrors pursued me. I ran past the table and ducked into another tunnel, hoping to God that it would not be a dead end.

I was running for my life. No, more than that – my soul, my *ser,* the essence of my being was threatened. I suddenly recalled a Bible verse from my days of childhood catechism: *Fear not them which kill the body, but are not able to kill the soul, but rather fear him which is able to destroy both soul and body in Sheol...*

I was in Sheol, the kingdom of the dead. The tunnel pressed further downhill, deeper and deeper into the bowels of the earth, into Hades, into Xibalbá, the Mayan underworld.

I lost all sense of time and direction, and I had no idea how long I had running down that dark tunnel, or in which direction. At one point, I could have sworn that my feet ran along the roof of the tunnel, as if gravity obeyed different rules altogether.

Then the air suddenly changed. The suffocating stench was gone, and I perceived the clean, fresh aroma of ocote pine trees and rich vegetation. I turned my flashlight off for one second, and saw a soft light glowing in the distance.

A way out.

I ran with all my strength, wheezing, drenched in sweat, toward that small piece of sky, that patch of light, a circle of stars, larger and larger, until it grew into an opening one metre across. I ducked and crawled through it. I was outside at last.

The lights I had seen were not stars at all, but the lights of Santa Isabel, the kerosene lanterns and fires burning in a dozen homes and adobe kitchens. The tunnel had led me to a small hill overlooking the town. I was safe.

I breathed a sigh of relief and made my way down the wooded hillside. One of the first houses I passed was Mardonio's, the man whose story had led me to that cursed cave in the first place. The old man peeked out through the window. I greeted him. He stared at me, wide-eyed, and ducked his head back inside.

I must be a horrid sight right now – covered in mud, hair disheveled. Like some caveman emerging from an interdimensional portal, stepping out into the modern day.

All the terror I felt in that cave evaporated in the cool, fresh air of the night. I must have been starved for oxygen and imagined those voices: my uncle's cries, the otherworldly laughter, the call of the chanekes. There are strange gases in those caves that could cause anyone to hallucinate.

My relief was perfected when I reached Uncle Marcos's house and saw the light on inside the adobe kitchen. I laughed to myself. He had beat me back to town.

Of course. He knows these mountains better than I ever could. He got a head start and made it home long before I emerged from the cave.

I felt foolish for giving in to the power of suggestion. A combination of claustrophobia, the unfamiliar surroundings, and memories of Grandma Carmen's stories, and I had panicked. But here I was, back at Uncle Marcos's adobe kitchen.

I sauntered up to the wooden door. From a distance, I could smell the fresh coffee and tortillas, the smoke from the open fire that billowed out the gap in the roof. I peered in through the window and saw his shadow dancing over the adobe walls, flickering in the firelight.

No, this wasn't right. Someone else was in there. It was not Uncle Marcos.

The person was too tall, too thin. *Must be a neighbor or relative.* I squinted to get a better look. In the dim light of the fire, He stood next to the woodpile with his back turned to me. I gently tapped on the windowpane to get his attention.

He turned toward me. The flashlight fell from my hand and rolled down the hillside, into the brush wet with fresh rain. My blood ran cold and all the terror of the cave returned tenfold, every childhood nightmare and phobia come to life. I knew those eyes that stared at me through the window, reflecting the flickering firelight.

They were my eyes. It was me inside the kitchen.

He smiled, sly and malicious. He reached his hand slowly up before his face. And he pulled the curtain shut.

Hunting the Howler

Cody Schroeder

TREVOR tugged the zipper on his coat all the way up to keep the wind off his neck and squinted as the cows neared the barn. His father rode behind them on his ATV, driving them across the snowy field.

He blinked snowflakes from his eyes and counted heads as they filed past, shuffling into the barn with plenty of grunting, lowing, and far too much farting. When the last one passed through the door, he pulled the doors shut behind them.

"Get 'em all?" his father asked, pulling up behind him.

"I only counted forty-nine."

His father frowned. "You sure?"

"Yes, sir."

"Damn." His father bounced his hand off the steering wheel. "Well, come on. Let's go see if we missed one."

The windscreen blocked the wind well enough, but didn't keep the cold out as they bounced across the field, searching for the cow they had somehow missed.

"I did a last lap before I headed back to the barn," his father said over the roar of the motor and the rush of the wind. "Didn't see any strays."

"Maybe one got out or wandered into the woods?"

His father shook his head. "Checked the fence last night, didn't see any gaps or breaks."

Trevor spotted the missing cow as they swung by the back southern corner of the field. It already looked more like a lumpy mound of snow than a cow.

"Ain't a good sign," his father said. "Must be something wrong for it to lay there and let the snow cover it."

They spotted the problem the instant they pulled up beside the fallen beast. Half of its body was gone. Guts and innards spilled over the ground, steaming in the cold air. A trail of gore led into the woods beyond the field.

"Son of a bitch," his father whispered, though he'd been thinking the same himself. "This must have just happened. The body is still steaming."

Trevor leaned closer for a better look. The cow had been torn apart. Long slashes marked the half that remained, deep cuts made by sharp claws. Big ones too.

"What in the world could have done this, Dad?"

His father sighed a tiny cloud. "Beats the hell out of me, boy. Never seen nothing like it. Ain't nothing in these woods could carry off even half a cow. Must weigh a few hundred pounds."

"Mountain lion? A black bear? Coyotes?"

"Not likely. Only spotted a couple mountain lions around here and a single bear. They've never come this close before and never bothered the cattle. Coyotes might, but I don't see enough tracks."

There was just one set of tracks where whatever attacked the cow dragged it back into the trees. Any prints left behind had been ruined.

Trevor looked to his father. "What do we do?"

His father reached back into the ATV. "We find the damn thing and kill it, before it kills another of our cows."

Trevor glanced to the overcast sky. "Can't we wait until the snow stops?"

"Nah, by then the thing will be cozy in its lair and the snow will have covered the trail. Come on, don't be a wimp."

"Yes, sir."

They both grabbed their rifles from the ATV's rack and trudged into the woods. Thankfully, the trees blocked most of the wind. Snow fell in uneven patches between trees who had dropped their leaves and evergreens who sheltered the ground beneath them.

The trail of blood made the predator easy to follow.

Convenient, since it appeared to have dragged the half-a-cow deep into the woods. They went half a mile or more before the blood began to thin, making the trail harder to follow.

The wind died down, but the snow picked up. Fat, fluffy flakes fell in a steady stream. The whole thing might have been beautiful if not for the trail of blood before them.

They paused under a tall cedar to catch their breath and warm up for a moment.

"Shit," his father uttered, leaning against the tree. "If I'd known we'd be hiking a mile into the damn hills, we would've waited. Or at least brought the thermos of coffee with us."

Trevor grinned behind the scarf covering the bottom of his face. "I did suggest putting the cows in the barn last night, but someone was too tired. You said we'd have plenty of time before the snow started."

"Idiot weatherman on channel six said it wouldn't start 'til after lunch." He rolled his sleeve back to check his watch. "This look like 'after lunch' to you?"

His watch displayed four minutes after ten.

"We'll know better next time."

"Screw next time. I need me a cushy office job. I'm too old for this."

Trevor managed half a laugh. His dad had been pulling the 'too old for this' card for over a decade, but every time he did, the complaint was a little more true. He'd be sixty in a couple months. Maybe he was right, maybe it was time to hang up his cowboy hat.

Trevor held his gloves to his face and blew a breath into his cupped hands. "Come on. The longer we stand here groaning, the longer it'll take to find this thing."

His father nodded and pulled his own scarf up over the bottom of his face. "You got a point. Let's get back to it."

They followed the trail deeper, into thicker trees. Only the odd hunter or meth maker ventured this deep into the woods.

The trail crossed a narrow, trickle of a stream ahead of them. Too wide to easily jump, but not wide enough to make them turn back.

Trevor took a running start and vaulted across.

"Show-off," his father said.

"Come on old man. You can make it. Or are you a wimp?"

"Don't make me shoot you boy. That's a lot of paperwork for me."

He stepped back, got up to what passed for a run for him, and jumped. He landed on the other side in front of Trevor and flailed, almost falling back into the water.

Trevor caught him and yanked him forward. They tumbled back into the snow.

His father pushed himself back up, laughing. "Aren't we the pair of idiots? Going to get ourselves a good case of hypothermia if we're not careful."

He held out a hand to help Trevor up. Trevor took it. He made it halfway up when a howl rang out over the hills. Long, loud, and low. A bit like a wolf's with something else thrown in. Something bigger from the sound of it.

"The hell was that?" his father asked, both of them back on their feet.

"Coyotes?"

"Didn't sound anything like a coyote. More like a wolf, but different."

"Think it's what got our cow?"

His father shrugged. "Could be. We'll have to find it and see."

They followed the trail up the hill on the other side of the stream. The land flattened out, but the trees grew bigger and closer together. What little sun came through the clouds didn't make it through the limbs, giving the woods a twilight feel. What snow had fallen seemed to glow on the ground.

The trail of blood continued on, though thinner than before.

Another howl issued through the shadowy trees. A chill that had nothing to do with the cold coursed down his spine.

"Sounds close."

His father nodded and kept going.

Not a dozen yards further ahead, his father stuck out an arm to stop him.

Trevor halted. "What?"

"Look there."

His father pointed a small hill ahead of them. The trail of blood led right to it and into a hole dug into the hill.

"Some kind of burrow you think?"

His father held his rifle ready. "Don't know. Let's find out."

Trevor flexed his fingers on his gun. He hadn't realized how tight he had been gripping it. He let out a cloudy breath as they stalked closer to the hole in the hillside.

Another howl rent the quiet air, definitely coming from inside the hole.

The howl went on so long and loud, it seemed to rattle his bones. He noticed his father shiver at the noise as well.

As they crept closer, another sound reached his ears. A deep, guttural growl. The sort of sound a dog makes to warn others away from its food, though deeper and throatier. If the creature making the sound was a dog, it had to be a damn big one.

Images of black hounds from movies filled his imagination. The great hounds of death from all manner of legends and stories. Beasts as big as bears, more than enough to drag a cow, let alone a man, back to its lair and feast on him.

His father reached the hole in the hill a step before him. He knelt in front of the hole and drew a flashlight from his coat pocket. With a click, bright LED lights shined into the dark, illuminating a rough tunnel.

"Huh."

"What?" Trevor asked.

His father shined the light around the tunnel. "If I didn't know better, I'd say this was dug recently." He leaned further into the tunnel. "And by something with claws."

"Right." Trevor took a step back. "How about we head back then? We know where the thing lives now."

"Come on, Trev. We didn't hike all the way out here to turn around and go home."

The growling grew louder. His father stilled, listening to the sound.

Then he turned back. "Let's find this thing and put it down before it gets any more of our cows."

"Or us," he muttered.

"Whatcha say?"

"Nothing Dad. What are we going to do?"

His father tried to angle the beam of light deeper into the burrow but the tunnel curved. The light showed only a patch of dirt wall with torn roots sticking out of it. Drops of blood shone in the light.

"Could try to lure it out?" his father suggested.

"Doubt it's going to come out if it has half a cow to chew on. What would we use to bait it out?"

His father grumbled.

A good sign.

He rubbed his gloved hands together and blew into them again. The barrel of his gun drooped toward the ground.

"Come on, Dad. Let's go back. This thing isn't going anywhere soon. The herd is safe in the barn."

"Good point. Guess one of us will have to crawl in there and take a look."

His mouth fell open while his ears tried to process his father's words and their meaning. Surely he hadn't said what it sounded like he did.

His father knelt down with a grunt and plenty of groans. His knees popped.

"Come on Dad, don't. This is nuts. You can't crawl in there. You won't fit."

"Making a crack about my weight?"

"Dad, seriously. You can't crawl in there after this thing. It tore a cow apart. What do you think it will do to you?"

He nodded to his rifle. "I'll take it down before it has a chance. Put one in its face while it's eating."

"And if it gets to you first?"

"Bah."

He spread out on his stomach and crawled into the hole.

Trevor grabbed the back of his coat. "Dad."

"Damn it, Trevor, let go of me. I ain't screwing around here."

The thing inside the burrow growled again, longer and lower than before.

"It already knows we're here."

His father jerked away from him. "I'll go in there and kill it and be done with this nonsense. It's just a hole with a critter in it. Done this a hundred times."

Trevor had to literally bite his tongue to not say something about his father's age. He'd heard stories since childhood about his father and his buddies scaring bears out of caves to shoot them, or fishing for catfish with their bare hands, not to mention a thousand other idiotic ideas.

He recalled a line his grandmother often used about the Good Lord protecting babies, drunkards, and fools. His father fell into at least one of those categories.

"Dad, please."

His father didn't respond this time. Instead, he wiggled deeper into the hole, his head and shoulders disappearing.

Another growl issued forth.

Trevor knelt in front of the hole as his father's knees vanished inside. His rifle trembled in his hands. He took a deep breath to steady them. It did him no good.

"Holy shit!"

A gunshot rang out of the hole.

Trevor fumbled with his own gun, trying to aim into the shadows, praying he wouldn't hit his dad.

His father flailed backwards out of the hole, covered in dirt and mud.

Another growl erupted out at them, almost a roar. A howl followed it. The sound reverberated into his bones. His legs shook worse than his hands.

His father staggered back past him, slipping. "Come on, Trevor!" He grabbed Trevor's coat and jerked him along.

He fell into a clumsy retreat as a black head emerged from the hole in the hillside. Fur black and sleek as oil, eyes gleaming like obsidian, and teeth as long as his fingers. An amalgamation of features, part-lion, part-hound, it raised its head and howled again. The very sound chased them through the trees as they fled.

Trevor slipped on patches of snow and fallen leaves and needles. His father fought for breath beside him, most of three decades older and eighty pounds heavier.

The monster howled again, too close behind them. Heavy footfalls joined their own.

He chanced a glance over his right shoulder and wished he hadn't. The creature, its body the size and shape of a hulking bear, bounded after them, closing the gap with every step.

They couldn't outrun it.

"Dad," he said, between breaths, dodging around a tree.

"I know."

He heard the creature's breathing right behind him, felt its footfalls between his own.

"Dad!"

"I know!"

His father vanished. Dropped out of sight.

Trevor skidded to a stop, barely missed plowing headlong into a tree, and turned. Then he screamed as he had never screamed before.

The creature stood on his father's back, its head tearing into him. Not with its teeth, but with the horns that curled from the sides of its head, thick and sharp like a ram's. His father's blood dripped from the horns.

Trevor didn't think. He didn't have time. He raised his rifle and fired at the monster.

The gunshot left his ears ringing, but hit the thing's left front shoulder near its ear. It jerked back, startled, and lifted its gaze to him, growling and bearing its teeth.

His father moaned on the ground. He scraped at the dirt with his fingers, trying to pry himself out from under the beast.

It noticed his struggle and rammed its horns into his spine again, wrenching them around.

Trevor screamed again and fired off another shot. This one struck the creature's right ear. He'd been aiming for its forehead.

Its shriek ripped through the trees, enough to hurt his ears, even with them ringing. He'd hurt it, but not enough, it seemed, to scare it away or draw it off his father.

This time, while staring him straight in the face, it raised a paw the size of hubcap and slammed it down on his father.

He screamed in pain, his head arched back, his eyes stretched wide, the muscles in his neck taught and bulging.

The thing dug into him with its paw. Claws scraped on bone and ripped flesh.

"Run, Trevor," his father uttered, his face almost as white as the snow. "Run, son!"

Trevor lifted his rifle again to line up another shot. His whole body shook so bad it was all he could do to aim at the monster.

"Run!" his father screamed one last time before he collapsed in the snow, limp and silent.

"Dad?"

The creature ignored him. Now it bit into his father's back, tearing a hunk of bloody meat out of his right side.

"Dad?"

It stared at him while it chewed, mocking and taunting.

Trevor, trembling, aimed his rifle.

The monster dropped the gore in its mouth and growled.

He slid his left foot back a couple inches, turning as he did.

It lowered its head, its shoulders hunched, its growl deeper.

He fired, but didn't wait to see where or even if he hit it. The instant the explosion went off beside his ear, Trevor bolted back toward the house.

He ran harder and faster than ever before, trees mere blurs whipping past. At some point, he started crying. The tears blurred his vision, but it didn't matter.

It seemed only seconds before the trees vanished altogether and he stumbled into the open field, not far from the mutilated cow and the trail of blood.

Still, he didn't stop. He pushed himself on toward the house, ignoring the ATV. He threw himself into the house and slammed the back door behind him. Locking it, he dropped into a kitchen chair, the strap on his rifle the only thing keeping it from falling out of his cold and quivering hands.

He gasped for breath, his chest on fire. His lungs couldn't decide to sob or draw breath and tried to do both. He slipped to the floor on his knees, clutching his chest, tears pouring hot and fast down his face.

"Daaaad!" he cried, his voice breaking, his throat raw. The pitiful sound echoed through the empty house.

Trevor clutched himself, leaning forward onto the tile. Despite the warmth inside the house, he shivered.

And he cried.

He cried until his body could no longer, until his eyes burned, his head ached, and his chest felt too tight to breathe.

By the time he lifted himself from the floor, using the chair as a crutch, clouds had gathered outside, turning the sky the dark gray of old dryer lint. Snow fell again in heavy flakes.

He couldn't see past the barn a hundred yards from the house, and it was early afternoon. The clock over the mantle in the living room showed ten after two. They'd been hours in the woods.

Trevor set his rifle on the kitchen table, along with his gloves and hat. He went into the living room, grabbed the phone from the table by his father's recliner, and dialed the sheriff's number. Rather than Jessie, the usual receptionist, a shrill, robotic recording played in his ear.

This certainly qualified as an emergency, so he pressed zero and waited while elevator music droned out of the phone. He shivered worse with every passing second, no matter how much he warmed up.

Minutes dragged on while the music played.

"Come on, come on," he whispered into the plastic covered speaker.

More minutes passed, his heart pounding in time with every tick of the clock.

At the ten-minute mark, he swore and threw the phone into his father's chair. Music still issued out of it.

Trevor snatched it up, fought down the urge to throw it into the fireplace, and mashed the END button. He pushed TALK, and dialed 911 this time.

Only to hear another message informing him that all circuits were busy and to try his call again later.

"Fucking fuck!"

The phone missed the gaping maw of the fireplace and smashed against the old bricks above it, exploding into plastic confetti.

He clenched his fists so hard his nails dug into his palms and screamed, filling the house with his rage.

The power went out.

Lights winked out, the refrigerator ceased its humming, and the dull roar of the furnace's blower fell silent.

Damn snow. Probably a limb on a line somewhere.

Trevor fell to his knees again. A thousand whispered swears crossed his lips, but none made him feel the least bit better.

He couldn't call for help. Couldn't go for help either. His car wouldn't get up the driveway in this snow and a glance to the key hooks by the door showed his father's keys were missing. In his pocket back in the woods, most likely.

He sat back on the floor, his back against his father's chair. Cold crept into the dark house as the hours ticked by and more snow fell. Every now and then, one of the cows in the barn made its presence known.

They'll be fine, he told himself. Probably warmer in there anyway.

A few minutes after five, a howl rose out of the woods behind the house. It started low and built up the longer it went on. Even through the walls and windows, he heard it loud and clear.

The howl of no mere animal. This was the monster who killed his father and ripped him apart.

Trevor lifted his gaze to the picture over the fireplace. An old picture of him as a child, in his best clothes, taken at Christmas many years ago. His mother and father stood on either side of him smiling, posing in front of a Christmas tree for a photographer. The only such photo they had made before his mother passed.

He looked away from the lying smiles.

"Now Dad is gone too."

Another howl sang over the winter wind.

Without realizing it, Trevor rose and went to the back door, grabbing his rifle as he did. He flung the door open and stepped onto the short porch.

In the growing darkness, he stepped off the porch into snow that rose over his ankles. He strode past the barn and grumbling cows, stopping when he reached the fence. The field spread out below him.

A dark shape, shorter than a cow by inches, but thicker, lurked near the snow-covered ATV. It wrestled with the half of the cow left behind, working to drag it into the trees.

Trevor, devoid of conscious thought, vaulted over the fence and charged at the thing, his rifle ready.

It spotted him and retreated into the woods.

He didn't stop though. The wind whipping at his exposed ears and face didn't matter anymore. The chill in his bare fingers didn't matter anymore. All that mattered, was killing the howling monster.

Trevor ran at a steady pace, not the frantic fleeing of before. He recognized landmarks as he drew closer to the thing's lair. He readied himself, replaying the last seconds of his father's life over and over again in his mind, steeling himself to kill the monster or die trying.

He stopped when he reached the spot. His father's body was gone, dragged away from the look of the ground nearby. Another bloody trail led back toward the hole in the hill.

Did it rip him in half too? he wondered, clutching his rifle tighter, ignoring the numbness in his fingers.

Walking now, he found the hole again with ease. Growling issued forth from it again. The sounds of the creature devouring his father.

But he wouldn't make the same mistake. He wouldn't crawl into the hole after it, give the howler the advantage. He paced back and forth in front of the hole, shouting and making as much noise as possible to draw his prey out.

It growled again, but didn't emerge. Seemed to reserve that for those foolish enough to stray right into its territory and challenge it personally.

More growling and a loud crunch.

Trevor halted, imagining it crushing his father's skull with its claws, or punching through his chest with its teeth, biting his spine in two.

He shook his head and shivered. Full dark reigned over the woods now and still the snow fell thick and fast. Glistening in the light of a half-moon. He tightened his hood around his face as much as he could without hindering his vision.

If he didn't do something soon, the cold would kill him before the creature had a chance to.

It howled from its hole, as if challenging him to come inside.

Trevor stared at the hole for several minutes, reliving the conversation with his father that seemed years ago instead of hours, begging him not to do what he himself was about to do.

"Hope you're watching Dad," he said, getting down on his knees before the mouth of the burrow. "Let you know your boy is every bit as stupid as you are."

He crawled forward on his elbows, his rifle in his hands, some slim shield between him and the monster within. Darkness swallowed him in seconds, but enough moonlight came through from the outside to show him a black animal gnawing at something it held between its front paws.

Except, there were two, no three of them. Smaller ones. He spotted a larger one behind them, curled against the back wall of the burrow, the smaller ones huddled against it. Eyes of obsidian stared back in the light and growled. Not one of them had horns.

The larger creature howled, filling his skull with the sound.

Trevor scurried back, away from the mother and her cubs. Behind him, another howl called, growing louder and closer as it did. He lifted his head from the tunnel and turned to see the howler who killed his father charging right at him. Blood still on its horns.

Protecting its family.

He fumbled with his rifle, all the while thinking, Holy shit, indeed.

Waking the Monster

Shana Scott

THE WINTER NIGHT was cold and wet, ice pelting the windows of the small Dutch cottage. In the hearth the glowing remnants of the fire slowly crumbled to ash, offering little heat to the cooling home. Rembrandt held Lena under the quilts she'd sewn all summer in preparation, their bodies warming each other into comfortable slumber.

Lena murmured in a sleep-heavy voice as a baby's cry woke them. Rembrandt squeezed her hand and shooed her back to sleep. "I'll check on her," he said as he tossed the quilt aside, goose bumps prickling up over his skin. "She's probably just cold."

With his eyes still mostly closed, Rembrandt sat up, a hiss escaping him as his foot landed on the flat side of a metal ax blade. He'd brought it in for safety; there were rumors of bandits on the road coming close to town. Setting the ax back up against the wall, he stood far more awake than before and headed for the crib, carved by his own hand, sitting close to the dying fire.

He didn't see the figure standing over her crib at first, eyes still adjusting. Soon enough the lean body of their guest came into focus, the soft, almost feminine angle of his face beneath neat brown hair. No doubt when he turned around, Rembrandt would see the same gentle smile that had come calling on them that night seeking refuge from the sleet and snow.

"Hector," he called out to the other man, "I'm sorry Anne woke you. Please, return to sleep. She's probably just cold, I'll take her to bed with us."

Hector's fair face turned, revealing in a faded light thin lips pulled tight over teeth too long to be human. His eyes, which had been disarmingly weak, now stared at Rembrandt red with hunger. "No need. I like a little life in my meal."

* * *

Rembrandt couldn't breathe; there was too much pressure, too much weight pressing down atop him. Yet his lungs didn't throb with the need to swell with air and his heart didn't struggle to beat from the lack of it. He felt...still.

Opening his eyes, there was nothing but darkness. Darkness and the smell of mint mixed with freshly turned earth. It was Lena, Rembrandt knew, because she always saved a few leaves of mint to mix with the balm she used to keep her skin from cracking in the winter. He reached out into the heavy darkness to find her, his hand sliding between a cloth surrounding him. After a moment he felt a finger, then another, then the lace ruffle at her wrist. He grasped Lena's hand like a lifeline in a sea of confusion. Whatever was happening, she was there with him.

But she was cold. She did not move. And the same weight pressed down on her as it did him. Rembrandt stroked the inside of her palm, trying to coax some small measure of life to the limp hand. None came.

Panic began to rise in his throat. Rembrandt tried to bring his other arm up to push off whatever pressed down on him when a sound came from above, so soft and faint he wasn't sure he heard it at first. He moved his arm again, and this time he felt something tugging at his wrist each time the noise came. It was a ringing, that of a bell, but muffled as if a pillow were placed over it. Or, more precisely, placed over him with the bell above.

Rembrandt listened to the quick tinkling of the bell, trying desperately not to understand what was coming all too soon as the truth. The bell, the dark pressure, his wife's icy, unresponsive hand. He was buried – a dead ringer.

Terror overwhelmed any other thought or reason as Rembrandt pushed against the ground above him. He clawed through the burial cloth, the wet dirt falling onto his face and sticking between his fingers, but he kept moving until enough loose soil had fallen for Rembrandt to pull himself up. Again and again, he dug and pulled, dug and pulled, until earth turned to snow and snow to air.

Frozen soil clumped in Rembrandt's brown hair as he hauled himself out of the ground. It was night, but the sky was clear and bright with a waxing gibbous moon. Behind him he found a wooden cross with three names staring back at him, a nightmare crafted by an artisan's hand: *Rembrandt, Lena, and Anne.* He looked at it, unbelieving. Then the memory returned. The blood, the screams, his baby girl torn apart in front of his eyes.

"This can't be real," Rembrandt whispered. His fingers traced the script immortalizing his death and he marveled at the smooth, unmarred skin. He remembered running for the ax, taking it up only to have it ripped from his hands and turned on him. The blade sliced deep in his arm, slicing through bone and muscle alike. Yet now not even a scar remained as proof of that night.

"Sleep well?" said a voice from behind. It sounded like sandpaper on stone. Rembrandt would never forget that voice.

Hector leaned against the gnarled trunk of a winter-bare white birch tree, the aged black bark rising up in tendril fingers to greet him. A cloak hid most of his features, but Rembrandt remembered those eyes, red and feral as the devil himself.

The rage at the sight of those vile eyes burned away any questions he'd had about crawling out of his own grave. All he could think of was Anne laying lifeless in her crib, and Lena with tears clearing a path down her face through the blood. Rembrandt ran. Ran with all the hatred boiling inside him. Ran with the strength of a demon of the dead. Ran with a blood haze blinding him. He ran straight for the monster he let into his home.

The only move Hector made to protect himself was to point to the ground. "Stop and kneel."

Rembrandt's body dropped to the ground the moment Hector spoke, his head inches from the frozen mud in front of the monster's feet. He trembled in the ache to move, but not even his rage broke Hector's enthrallment. Why couldn't he kill the creature that slaughtered his family when he was mere inches away?

"What have you done to me?"

A dirty leather boot snaked out and tucked under Rembrandt's chin until he stared up into those devil eyes. "I've made you just like me. You should be honored. It's been so long since I last made a companion."

"Why?" he whispered, for the first time realizing the voice that spoke was no longer his own. It was thicker and crackled like gravel in his ears.

The boot slid up so that the tip stretched Rembrandt's chin as far as he could lift, and Hector observed him, appraising the supplicant at his feet. "Why not? It's not often someone is actually brave enough to threaten to chase me in life or death. By the time I finish my fun with their families, most beg for their own pathetic lives. They don't deserve to live. The ones that beg for death are far more fun. I enjoy watching them slowly decay within until they do to themselves what I wouldn't.

"But you. I decided to give you your wish. You now have the strength to kill me and an eternity to try, though those gifts come at a price." He tapped Rembrandt's chin. "I am your father now, and like the good book says, children must obey their fathers. I wonder how long it will take for you to call me god and beg for death. I'm so very curious."

Was this his hell? The cold stung his skin. The tears that clouded his strange vision darkened the muck on the creature's boot. Rembrandt could still smell his wife lingering on his burial clothes. The world was real – *he* was real – but no matter how hard he tried, he couldn't stand up. The muscles in his hands burned hot with controlled tension, ready to move but immobile. If he couldn't move a hand without that monster's permission, how could he ever kill him?

The monster smiled, a handsome lie to hide his true nature. "Come along, Rembrandt, let us get you cleaned up. You must be hungry and we can't have you walking around looking like you just crawled out of a grave."

Rembrandt's body moved without his consent and hung a step behind Hector on puppet strings. He was led to the edge of the graveyard where a young body lay pale and shredded from cheek to neck. In a move that was wholly his own, Rembrandt knelt down next to the man barely more than a boy and turned him to see the unspoiled side of his face.

"Pieter, oh God." Rembrandt's gaze fell on the broken string still tied to his wrist.

Pieter acted as the village's grave watcher. He would have waited on the first night of a burial to listen for the bell of the buried alive.

Hector licked his lips as if searching for a few last crumbs to taste. "My apologies. He was supposed to be yours, but I got bored waiting."

Rembrandt didn't know what sickened him more, that he was happy to be spared being ordered to kill Pieter himself, or the blood staining Pieter's clothes, which drew him closer to the boy's body like a will-o'-the-wisp in the darkness. A new sensation built up inside him. Not hunger the way he knew it. It was instinct. Need. Mere inches from Pieter's face, Rembrandt turned him back to the blood-stained side and breathed in the delectable scent, muted in death but still there, like the smell of venison after it's cooled.

"Leave him, Rembrandt, we have much to do tonight."

Hector's voice broke the spell Pieter's body cast on him. Rembrandt stared at his fingers almost touching his tongue to taste the flakes of dry, frozen blood now stuck to his skin. What was he doing? Rembrandt dropped Pieter like he was fire in his hands and held his breath, partly to hold down the sickness crawling up his throat, but mostly to keep from breathing in anything about the boy again. His body trembled from so much more than the cold as he sat in the graveyard.

"Rembrandt, come."

He obeyed without question, if only to get away from that body and what it did to him. They walked the empty dirt road heading toward town without worry of being seen. The townspeople didn't travel after dark anymore, not since reports of bandits filtered from the neighboring villages. If only they knew the true threat hunting them, they'd know staying at home wasn't any safer. It hadn't been for him.

They stopped at a small stream and Rembrandt washed himself. The ice-glazed water should have had him shaking the moment he dipped his hands in, but though he felt the bitter bite against his skin, his movements were strong and even. In the glassy reflection of the stream, eyes like the monster who made him stared back from his face. Rembrandt closed his demon eyes and turned away. He couldn't bear to see it any longer.

Once cleaned up, Hector gave Rembrandt his cloak to hide his face. Uncovered, Rembrandt saw that the monster had turned back to a man. His eyes still showed venom, but the blood red color had softened to a dark brown that matched his neat hair. He was disgustingly favorable, with the same disarming smile that had beguiled his way into Rembrandt's home. The devil truly found an innocent disguise in this creature.

The dirt soon turned to cobblestone under their feet, and Hector's smile grew dark with delight. "You will not speak until I say so," he ordered. "You will not move except to follow me. You will not interfere with anything I do."

The command spread like fire on oil through Rembrandt's body, every muscle taut with the desire to escape, to fight, to do something more than walk as a mutt at its master's heels. Unable to disobey, Rembrandt pulled the hood of the cloak as far over his face as he could, not wanting to see what kind of horrors Hector was planning for him. Not wanting to know the truth.

They headed toward the central square of the town. His town. His home. Where Rembrandt was dead. All he wanted was to run from this place and leave these people to grieve in peace without ever discovering the monster Hector had turned him into, but trudging was the closest thing to resistance Rembrandt could produce. A few people he once called friends walked the streets nearby, offering curious glances at the pair of strangers entering their town. The need he'd felt with Pieter grew stronger the more people they encountered. He could hear their hearts beating yards away, tempting him to follow. If not for Hector's command, Rembrandt wasn't certain he could have resisted. Hector paid them little attention, walking through the narrow streets with the confidence of a native.

Once they entered the town square, Rembrandt knew where they were going and – bound to silence as he was – he wordlessly prayed to God, should God be listening to whatever he was now. The townspeople were close to one another. After a burial, many would gather together to be with the bereaved family. Rembrandt's terrified gaze watched the torchlight flicker behind the tavern's windows, casting dancing shadows across the faces of people he loved – people who loved him enough to mourn his family's deaths.

Rembrandt kept a hand on the hood of his cloak as they entered the tavern, the tender warmth of the fireplace greeting his death-cold skin. There would have been drinking and laughter filling the tavern on a normal night, but tonight the atmosphere was somber and all eyes fell on them as they moved through the crowd. Once again the need within him swelled. What had been a temptation with Pieter now screamed a siren's song all around him. The warmth coursing through these living bodies, the life. He needed the blood as much as those hearts needed to beat.

But he remained as ordered, not speaking, not moving other than to follow Hector to a table next to a group of somber-faced people. Rembrandt examined two of the faces with horror. His parents sat close while the rest of the group attended to them with tender care. Kristof, like many in the town, had brown hair and strong northern features that drew his face to hard edges. In comparison, Nicia was exotic with dark olive skin and green eyes now clouded with age. If the people could see Rembrandt, they'd find those hard edges on his own face and that olive skin. He wanted to hold his parents close and comfort them, but his presence would be no blessing, and Hector's evil couldn't have chosen that table at random.

Hector presented the group around Rembrandt's parents his lying smile. "Quite a dour place tonight. Has it been a hard winter here?"

"You're lucky to have found us, stranger," Willem, Rembrandt's childhood friend, said. Willem had slaughtered his best hog when Anne was born – to celebrate. "Bandits are doing what the cold isn't. They took an entire family from us only days ago. Best to stay close to town until daylight."

"How tragic," Hector said and gave the table a consoling nod. "My own companion just lost his family as well."

A primal noise tore from Rembrandt's throat, guttural and inhuman and filled with all the hate in hell, which caused all those nearby to move away.

Rather than being upset by Rembrandt's interruption, Hector's lips twisted up with sinister glee. "Still so hard on him. Come now, why don't you join them and drink your woes away together," he cooed, then reached back to pull away Rembrandt's only protection.

Kristof pulled his wife from her chair and retreated to the far wall; his unbelieving gaze never wavered. "It can't be," he hissed.

Like a string wound too tight and suddenly cut, the chair toppling to the floor broke the solemn quiet of the room as the townspeople gawked on in confusion, terror, and – most painful to Rembrandt – revulsion. A few tried to run, but Hector leapt faster than a whip crack to block the tavern door. All illusion fled from his face and everyone found the beast lurking within him. "Now, now, is that any way to greet an old friend?"

Rembrandt couldn't speak or he would've begged a thousand times over for his parents not to look on him like he was the same as that monster. He wanted to believe that he was more than the undeniable need clawing within him, but when they stared back he found the demon reflected in their faces. And when he closed his eyes, the quick beat of their hearts beckoned to him in a way he tried to deny.

"My son is dead," Kristof said.

"Yes," Hector stretched the word into a playful note, "but that doesn't mean he's not also sitting before you right now."

Nicia clenched her husband's arm. "Rembrandt?"

Hector chuckled and a chill settled over the room. "Go ahead, Rembrandt, not many get the chance to speak with the people they love after death."

What could he say? His fingers scratched the top of the knotted wood table, following the dark lines trying to find the words to prove he was still himself. "I'm sorry I couldn't protect Lena and Anne. Please make sure they don't become like me. Make sure they rest."

Kristof and Nicia clung to each other to resist the urge to touch their son. "We shouldn't listen to one who is dead," Kristof said, looking desperately like all he wanted to do was to bring Rembrandt into their shaking embrace.

"Poor child," Hector sang, "parents so cruel should be punished. Don't you agree, Rembrandt?"

"No," Rembrandt pleaded. He'd already lost his wife and daughter; he couldn't also watch Hector kill his parents, too.

"But they should. Parents are supposed to provide for their children, and you must be so very hungry right now," Hector said, and Rembrandt felt the creature's power over him wane. Without that forced control, the need flooded his body – cold and desperate – urging him forward over the table to the closest living body.

"No, Rembrandt, only one of your parents. Let's not be greedy."

Despite the hunger fighting against his humanity, Rembrandt grasped the table so hard his fingers dug into the thick wood. "I won't. I won't hurt them."

The monster took a deep breath through his nose as if savoring the aroma of a luscious meal. "That's your choice, but I'll be quite bored without my entertainment. If you don't do something to keep my attention, I'll be forced to find my pleasures with the rest of these fine people here. And I believe you know what pleases me."

The blood and screams of his wife filled Rembrandt's mind. He had to choose to kill one of his parents or release the monster onto everyone in the tavern. To witness that depravity again or become it. Become the monster.

"Be quick," Hector warned, "Pieter knows I don't like waiting."

Rembrandt bowed his head to the table, his knuckles white as he kept the unnatural need from moving him. Tears dampened the dark wood. He couldn't choose between the last people he loved and so many innocents.

"Kristof." Nicia's voice, barely more than a whisper, seemed to echo in the silence.

No one breathed while Kristof approached his dead son. The only other movement was from Willem taking Nicia's crying form into his arms. Kristof looked long into the scarlet eyes the creature gave his son. Rembrandt couldn't remember the last time he'd seen his father cry, but tears now tracked down those hard northern edges of his face to disappear into the gray tangle of his beard.

"Rembrandt." Kristof yanked his son hard and fast against him, hands curled tight in Rembrandt's dark hair. "I absolve you, my son. I don't know if God will, but I absolve you."

Once more Rembrandt felt his body move without his consent, this time at his father's forgiveness. His head dipped into the curve of his father's aged neck, eyes closing as he felt instinct take hold and his mouth found the beating pulse. In his ear his father recited the Lord's Prayer in a slow monotone that made Rembrandt feel like a child again.

He whispered an unheard apology before fangs he didn't have a moment before pierced Kristof's flesh and he suckled the life bubbling from the wound. The iron tang of his blood was the sweetest ambrosia, and with one taste Rembrandt needed more, so much more. The gentleness that his shame and horror had incited disappeared under the monster's desire to satisfy his hunger. He bit in again and again, red life staining them both as he drank greedily. His father was gone, he was gone, and all that remained was beast and prey.

After the blood haze faded, Rembrandt pulled away and attempted to wipe the blood from his mouth. His father's once strong and robust body – the body of a carpenter – slumped limply in his arms. He'd killed his father...and savored it.

Rembrandt laid the body on the table with loving care. As he looked down at his father, at his mother weeping against those holding her – those who didn't want to die – Rembrandt licked the smeared blood from his lips. He was so hungry still.

He wanted to die.

"Wonderful, Rembrandt." Hector shrieked with laughter. "The first should always be special."

Rembrandt's crimson gaze settled on Hector. No, he wanted to be the monster. He *needed* to be the monster.

Only a monster could kill a demon.

Where Their Fire Is Not Quenched

May Sinclair

THERE WAS NOBODY in the orchard. Harriott Leigh went out, carefully, through the iron gate into the field. She had made the latch slip into its notch without a sound.

The path slanted widely up the field from the orchard gate to the stile under the elder tree. George Waring waited for her there.

Years afterwards, when she thought of George Waring she smelt the sweet, hot, wine-scent of the elder flowers. Years afterwards, when she smelt elder flowers she saw George Waring, with his beautiful, gentle face, like a poet's or a musician's, his black-blue eyes, and sleek, olive-brown hair. He was a naval lieutenant.

Yesterday he had asked her to marry him and she had consented. But her father hadn't, and she had come to tell him that and say goodbye before he left her. His ship was to sail the next day.

He was eager and excited. He couldn't believe that anything could stop their happiness, that anything he didn't want to happen could happen.

"Well?" he said.

"He's a perfect beast, George. He won't let us. He says we're too young."

"I was twenty last August," he said, aggrieved.

"And I shall be seventeen in September."

"And this is June. We're quite old, really. How long does he mean us to wait?"

"Three years."

"Three years before we can be engaged even— Why, we might be dead."

She put her arms round him to make him feel safe. They kissed; and the sweet, hot, wine-scent of the elder flowers mixed with their kisses. They stood, pressed close together, under the elder tree.

Across the yellow fields of charlock they heard the village clock strike seven. Up in the house a gong clanged.

"Darling, I must go," she said.

"Oh stay – stay *five* minutes."

He pressed her close. It lasted five minutes, and five more. Then he was running fast down the road to the station, while Harriott went along the field-path, slowly, struggling with her tears.

"He'll be back in three months," she said. "I can live through three months."

But he never came back. There was something wrong with the engines of his ship, the *Alexandra*. Three weeks later she went down in the Mediterranean, and George with her.

Harriott said she didn't care how soon she died now. She was quite sure it would be soon, because she couldn't live without him.

Five years passed.

* * *

The two lines of beech trees stretched on and on, the whole length of the Park, a broad green drive between. When you came to the middle they branched off right and left in the form of a cross, and at the end of the right arm there was a white stucco pavilion with pillars and a three-cornered pediment like a Greek temple. At the end of the left arm, the west entrance to the Park, double gates and a side door.

Harriott, on her stone seat at the back of the pavilion, could see Stephen Philpotts the very minute he came through the side door.

He had asked her to wait for him there. It was the place he always chose to read his poems aloud in. The poems were a pretext. She knew what he was going to say. And she knew what she would answer.

There were elder bushes in flower at the back of the pavilion, and Harriott thought of George Waring. She told herself that George was nearer to her now than he could ever have been, living. If she married Stephen she would not be unfaithful, because she loved him with another part of herself. It was not as though Stephen were taking George's place. She loved Stephen with her soul, in an unearthly way.

But her body quivered like a stretched wire when the door opened and the young man came towards her down the drive under the beech trees.

She loved him; she loved his slenderness, his darkness and sallow whiteness, his black eyes lighting up with the intellectual flame, the way his black hair swept back from his forehead, the way he walked, tiptoe, as if his feet were lifted with wings.

He sat down beside her. She could see his hands tremble. She felt that her moment was coming; it had come.

"I wanted to see you alone because there's something I must say to you. I don't quite know how to begin…"

Her lips parted. She panted lightly.

"You've heard me speak of Sybill Foster?"

Her voice came stammering, "N-no, Stephen. Did you?"

"Well, I didn't mean to, till I knew it was all right. I only heard yesterday."

"Heard what?"

"Why, that she'll have me. Oh, Harriott – do you know what it's like to be terribly happy?"

She knew. She had known just now, the moment before he told her. She sat there, stone-cold and stiff, listening to his raptures; listening to her own voice saying she was glad.

Ten years passed.

* * *

Harriott Leigh sat waiting in the drawing room of a small house in Maida Vale. She had lived there ever since her father's death two years before.

She was restless. She kept on looking at the clock to see if it was four, the hour that Oscar Wade had appointed. She was not sure that he would come, after she had sent him away yesterday.

She now asked herself, why, when she had sent him away yesterday, she had let him come today. Her motives were not altogether clear. If she really meant what she had said then, she oughtn't to let him come to her again. Never again.

She had shown him plainly what she meant. She could see herself, sitting very straight in her chair, uplifted by a passionate integrity, while he stood before her, hanging his head, ashamed and beaten; she could feel again the throb in her voice as she kept on saying that she couldn't, she couldn't; he must see that she couldn't; that no, nothing would make her change her mind; she couldn't forget he had a wife; that he must think of Muriel.

To which he had answered savagely: "I needn't. That's all over. We only live together for the look of the thing."

And she, serenely, with great dignity: "And for the look of the thing, Oscar, we must leave off seeing each other. Please go."

"Do you mean it?"

"Yes. We must never see each other again."

And he had gone then, ashamed and beaten.

She could see him, squaring his broad shoulders to meet the blow. And she was sorry for him. She told herself she had been unnecessarily hard. Why shouldn't they see each other again, now he understood where they must draw the line? Until yesterday the line had never been very clearly drawn. Today she meant to ask him to forget what he had said to her. Once it was forgotten, they could go on being friends as if nothing had happened.

It was four o'clock. Half-past. Five. She had finished tea and given him up when, between the half-hour and six o'clock, he came.

He came as he had come a dozen times, with his measured, deliberate, thoughtful tread, carrying himself well braced, with a sort of held-in arrogance, his great shoulders heaving. He was a man of about forty, broad and tall, lean-flanked and short-necked, his straight, handsome features showing small and even in the big square face and in the flush that swamped it. The close-clipped, reddish-brown moustache bristled forwards from the pushed-out upper lip. His small, flat eyes shone, reddish-brown, eager and animal.

She liked to think of him when he was not there, but always at the first sight of him she felt a slight shock. Physically, he was very far from her admired ideal. So different from George Waring and Stephen Philpotts.

He sat down, facing her.

There was an embarrassed silence, broken by Oscar Wade.

"Well, Harriott, you said I could come." He seemed to be throwing the responsibility on her.

"So I suppose you've forgiven me," he said.

"Oh, yes, Oscar, I've forgiven you."

He said she'd better show it by coming to dine with him somewhere that evening.

She could give no reason to herself for going. She simply went.

He took her to a restaurant in Soho. Oscar Wade dined well, even extravagantly, giving each dish its importance. She liked his extravagance. He had none of the mean virtues.

It was over. His flushed, embarrassed silence told her what he was thinking. But when he had seen her home he left her at her garden gate. He had thought better of it.

She was not sure whether she were glad or sorry. She had had her moment of righteous exaltation and she had enjoyed it. But there was no joy in the weeks that followed it. She had given up Oscar Wade because she didn't want him very much; and now she wanted him furiously, perversely, because she had given him up. Though he had no resemblance to her ideal, she couldn't live without him.

She dined with him again and again, till she knew Schnebler's Restaurant by heart, the white panelled walls picked out with gold; the white pillars, and the curling gold fronds of their capitals; the Turkey carpets, blue and crimson, soft under her feet; the thick crimson velvet cushions, that clung to her skirts; the glitter of silver and glass on the innumerable white circles of the tables. And the faces of the diners, red, white, pink, brown, grey and sallow, distorted and excited; the curled mouths that twisted as they ate; the convoluted electric bulbs pointing,

pointing down at them, under the red, crinkled shades. All shimmering in a thick air that the red light stained as wine stains water.

And Oscar's face, flushed with his dinner. Always, when he leaned back from the table and brooded in silence she knew what he was thinking. His heavy eyelids would lift; she would find his eyes fixed on hers, wondering, considering.

She knew now what the end would be. She thought of George Waring, and Stephen Philpotts, and of her life, cheated. She hadn't chosen Oscar, she hadn't really wanted him; but now he had forced himself on her she couldn't afford to let him go. Since George died no man had loved her, no other man ever would. And she was sorry for him when she thought of him going from her, beaten and ashamed.

She was certain, before he was, of the end. Only she didn't know when and where and how it would come. That was what Oscar knew.

It came at the close of one of their evenings when they had dined in a private sitting room. He said he couldn't stand the heat and noise of the public restaurant.

She went before him, up a steep, red-carpeted stair to a white door on the second landing.

From time to time they repeated the furtive, hidden adventure. Sometimes she met him in the room above Schnebler's. Sometimes, when her maid was out, she received him at her house in Maida Vale. But that was dangerous, not to be risked too often.

Oscar declared himself unspeakably happy. Harriott was not quite sure. This was love, the thing she had never had, that she had dreamed of, hungered and thirsted for; but now she had it she was not satisfied. Always she looked for something just beyond it, some mystic, heavenly rapture, always beginning to come, that never came. There was something about Oscar that repelled her. But because she had taken him for her lover, she couldn't bring herself to admit that it was a certain coarseness. She looked another way and pretended it wasn't there. To justify herself, she fixed her mind on his good qualities, his generosity, his strength, the way he had built up his engineering business. She made him take her over his works and show her his great dynamos. She made him lend her the books he read. But always, when she tried to talk to him, he let her see that *that* wasn't what she was there for.

"My dear girl, we haven't time," he said. "It's a waste of our priceless moments."

She persisted. "There's something wrong about it all if we can't talk to each other."

He was irritated. "Women never seem to consider that a man can get all the talk he wants from other men. What's wrong is our meeting in this unsatisfactory way. We ought to live together. It's the only sane thing. I would, only I don't want to break up Muriel's home and make her miserable."

"I thought you said she wouldn't care."

"My dear, she cares for her home and her position and the children. You forget the children."

Yes. She had forgotten the children. She had forgotten Muriel. She had left off thinking of Oscar as a man with a wife and children and a home.

He had a plan. His mother-in-law was coming to stay with Muriel in October and he would get away. He would go to Paris, and Harriott should come to him there. He could say he went on business. No need to lie about it; he *had* business in Paris.

He engaged rooms in a hotel in the rue de Rivoli. They spent two weeks there.

For three days Oscar was madly in love with Harriott and Harriott with him. As she lay awake she would turn on the light and look at him as he slept at her side. Sleep made him beautiful and innocent; it laid a fine, smooth tissue over his coarseness; it made his mouth gentle; it entirely hid his eyes.

In six days reaction had set in. At the end of the tenth day, Harriott, returning with Oscar from Montmartre, burst into a fit of crying. When questioned, she answered wildly that the Hotel Saint Pierre was too hideously ugly it was getting on her nerves. Mercifully Oscar explained her state as fatigue following excitement. She tried hard to believe that she was miserable because her love was purer and more spiritual than Oscar's; but all the time she knew perfectly well she had cried from pure boredom. She was in love with Oscar, and Oscar bored her. Oscar was in love with her, and she bored him. At close quarters, day in and day out, each was revealed to the other as an incredible bore.

At the end of the second week she began to doubt whether she had ever been really in love with him.

* * *

Her passion returned for a little while after they got back to London. Freed from the unnatural strain which Paris had put on them, they persuaded themselves that their romantic temperaments were better fitted to the old life of casual adventure.

Then, gradually, the sense of danger began to wake in them. They lived in perpetual fear, face to face with all the chances of discovery. They tormented themselves and each other by imagining possibilities that they would never have considered in their first fine moments. It was as though they were beginning to ask themselves if it were, after all, worthwhile running such awful risks, for all they got out of it. Oscar still swore that if he had been free he would have married her. He pointed out that his intentions at any rate were regular. But she asked herself: Would I marry *him*? Marriage would be the Hotel Saint Pierre all over again, without any possibility of escape. But, if she wouldn't marry him, was she in love with him? That was the test. Perhaps it was a good thing he wasn't free. Then she told herself that these doubts were morbid, and that the question wouldn't arise.

One evening Oscar called to see her. He had come to tell her that Muriel was ill.

"Seriously ill?"

"I'm afraid so. It's pleurisy. May turn to pneumonia. We shall know one way or another in the next few days."

A terrible fear seized upon Harriott. Muriel might die of her pleurisy; and if Muriel died, she would have to marry Oscar. He was looking at her queerly, as if he knew what she was thinking, and she could see that the same thought had occurred to him and that he was frightened too.

Muriel got well again; but their danger had enlightened them. Muriel's life was now inconceivably precious to them both; she stood between them and that permanent union, which they dreaded and yet would not have the courage to refuse.

After enlightenment the rupture.

It came from Oscar, one evening when he sat with her in her drawing room.

"Harriott," he said, "do you know I'm thinking seriously of settling down?"

"How do you mean, settling down?"

"Patching it up with Muriel, poor girl… Has it never occurred to you that this little affair of ours can't go on forever?"

"You don't want it to go on?"

"I don't want to have any humbug about it. For God's sake, let's be straight. If it's done, it's done. Let's end it decently."

"I see. You want to get rid of me."

"That's a beastly way of putting it."

"Is there any way that isn't beastly? The whole thing's beastly. I should have thought you'd have stuck to it now you've made it what you wanted. When I haven't an ideal, I haven't a single illusion, when you've destroyed everything you didn't want."

"What didn't I want?"

"The clean, beautiful part of it. The part *I* wanted."

"My part at least was real. It was cleaner and more beautiful than all that putrid stuff you wrapped it up in. You were a hypocrite, Harriott, and I wasn't. You're a hypocrite now if you say you weren't happy with me."

"I was never really happy. Never for one moment. There was always something I missed. Something you didn't give me. Perhaps you couldn't."

"No. I wasn't spiritual enough," he sneered.

"You were not. And you made me what you were."

"Oh, I noticed that you were always very spiritual *after* you'd got what you wanted."

"What I wanted?" she cried. "Oh, my God—"

"If you ever knew what you wanted."

"What – I – wanted," she repeated, drawing out her bitterness.

"Come," he said, "why not be honest? Face facts. I was awfully gone on you. You were awfully gone on me – once. We got tired of each other and it's over. But at least you might own we had a good time while it lasted."

"A good time?"

"Good enough for me."

"For you, because for you love only means one thing. Everything that's high and noble in it you dragged down to that, till there's nothing left for us but that. *That's* what you made of love."

Twenty years passed.

* * *

It was Oscar who died first, three years after the rupture. He did it suddenly one evening, falling down in a fit of apoplexy.

His death was an immense relief to Harriott. Perfect security had been impossible as long as he was alive. But now there wasn't a living soul who knew her secret.

Still, in the first moment of shock Harriott told herself that Oscar dead would be nearer to her than ever. She forgot how little she had wanted him to be near her, alive. And long before the twenty years had passed she had contrived to persuade herself that he had never been near to her at all. It was incredible that she had ever known such a person as Oscar Wade. As for their affair, she couldn't think of Harriott Leigh as the sort of woman to whom such a thing could happen. Schnebler's and the Hotel Saint Pierre ceased to figure among prominent images of her past. Her memories, if she had allowed herself to remember, would have clashed disagreeably with the reputation for sanctity which she had now acquired.

For Harriott at fifty-two was the friend and helper of the Reverend Clement Farmer, Vicar of St. Mary the Virgin's, Maida Vale. She worked as a deaconess in his parish, wearing the uniform of a deaconess, the semi-religious gown, the cloak, the bonnet and veil, the cross and rosary, the holy smile. She was also secretary to the Maida Vale and Kilburn Home for Fallen Girls.

Her moments of excitement came when Clement Farmer, the lean, austere likeness of Stephen Philpotts, in his cassock and lace-bordered surplice, issued from the vestry, when he mounted the pulpit, when he stood before the altar rails and lifted up his arms in the

Benediction; her moments of ecstasy when she received the Sacrament from his hands. And she had moments of calm happiness when his study door closed on their communion. All these moments were saturated with a solemn holiness.

And they were insignificant compared with the moment of her dying.

She lay dozing in her white bed under the black crucifix with the ivory Christ. The basins and medicine bottles had been cleared from the table by her pillow; it was spread for the last rites. The priest moved quietly about the room, arranging the candles, the Prayer Book and the Holy Sacrament. Then he drew a chair to her bedside and watched with her, waiting for her to come up out of her doze.

She woke suddenly. Her eyes were fixed upon him. She had a flash of lucidity. She was dying, and her dying made her supremely important to Clement Farmer.

"Are you ready?" he asked.

"Not yet. I think I'm afraid. Make me not afraid."

He rose and lit the two candles on the altar. He took down the crucifix from the wall and stood it against the foot-rail of the bed.

She sighed. That was not what she had wanted.

"You will not be afraid now," he said.

"I'm not afraid of the hereafter. I suppose you get used to it. Only it may be terrible just at first."

"Our first state will depend very much on what we are thinking of at our last hour."

"There'll be my – confession," she said.

"And after it you will receive the Sacrament. Then you will have your mind fixed firmly upon God and your Redeemer... Do you feel able to make your confession now, Sister? Everything is ready."

Her mind went back over her past and found Oscar Wade there. She wondered: Should she confess to him about Oscar Wade? One moment she thought it was possible; the next she knew that she couldn't. She could not. It wasn't necessary. For twenty years he had not been part of her life. No. She wouldn't confess about Oscar Wade. She had been guilty of other sins.

She made a careful selection.

"I have cared too much for the beauty of this world... I have failed in charity to my poor girls. Because of my intense repugnance to their sin... I have thought, often, about – people I love, when I should have been thinking about God."

After that she received the Sacrament.

"Now," he said, "there is nothing to be afraid of."

"I won't be afraid if – if you would hold my hand."

He held it. And she lay still a long time, with her eyes shut. Then he heard her murmuring something. He stooped close.

"This – is – dying. I thought it would be horrible. And it's bliss... Bliss."

The priest's hand slackened, as if at the bidding of some wonder. She gave a weak cry.

"Oh – don't let me go."

His grasp tightened.

"Try," he said, "to think about God. Keep on looking at the crucifix."

"If I look," she whispered, "you won't let go my hand?"

"I will not let you go."

He held it till it was wrenched from him in the last agony.

* * *

She lingered for some hours in the room where these things had happened.

Its aspect was familiar and yet unfamiliar, and slightly repugnant to her. The altar, the crucifix, the lighted candles, suggested some tremendous and awful experience the details of which she was not able to recall. She seemed to remember that they had been connected in some way with the sheeted body on the bed; but the nature of the connection was not clear; and she did not associate the dead body with herself. When the nurse came in and laid it out, she saw that it was the body of a middle-aged woman. Her own living body was that of a young woman of about thirty-two.

Her mind had no past and no future, no sharp-edged, coherent memories, and no idea of anything to be done next.

Then, suddenly, the room began to come apart before her eyes, to split into shafts of floor and furniture and ceiling that shifted and were thrown by their commotion into different planes. They leaned slanting at every possible angle; they crossed and overlaid each other with a transparent mingling of dislocated perspectives, like reflections fallen on an interior seen behind glass.

The bed and the sheeted body slid away somewhere out of sight. She was standing by the door that still remained in position.

She opened it and found herself in the street, outside a building of yellowish-grey brick and freestone, with a tall slated spire. Her mind came together with a palpable click of recognition. This object was the Church of St. Mary the Virgin, Maida Vale. She could hear the droning of the organ. She opened the door and slipped in.

She had gone back into a definite space and time, and recovered a certain limited section of coherent memory. She remembered the rows of pitch-pine benches, with their Gothic peaks and mouldings; the stone-coloured walls and pillars with their chocolate stencilling; the hanging rings of lights along the aisles of the nave; the high altar with its lighted candles, and the polished brass cross, twinkling. These things were somehow permanent and real, adjusted to the image that now took possession of her.

She knew what she had come there for. The service was over. The choir had gone from the chancel; the sacristan moved before the altar, putting out the candles. She walked up the middle aisle to a seat that she knew under the pulpit. She knelt down and covered her face with her hands. Peeping sideways through her fingers, she could see the door of the vestry on her left at the end of the north aisle. She watched it steadily.

Up in the organ loft the organist drew out the Recessional, slowly and softly, to its end in the two solemn, vibrating chords.

The vestry door opened and Clement Farmer came out, dressed in his black cassock. He passed before her, close, close outside the bench where she knelt. He paused at the opening. He was waiting for her. There was something he had to say.

She stood up and went towards him. He still waited. He didn't move to make way for her. She came close, closer than she had ever come to him, so close that his features grew indistinct. She bent her head back, peering, short-sightedly, and found herself looking into Oscar Wade's face.

He stood still, horribly still, and close, barring her passage.

She drew back; his heaving shoulders followed her. He leaned forward, covering her with his eyes. She opened her mouth to scream and no sound came.

She was afraid to move lest he should move with her. The heaving of his shoulders terrified her.

One by one the lights in the side aisles were going out. The lights in the middle aisle would go next. They had gone. If she didn't get away she would be shut up with him there, in the appalling darkness.

She turned and moved towards the north aisle, groping, steadying herself by the book ledge. When she looked back, Oscar Wade was not there.

Then she remembered that Oscar Wade was dead. Therefore, what she had seen was not Oscar; it was his ghost. He was dead; dead seventeen years ago. She was safe from him forever.

* * *

When she came out on to the steps of the church she saw that the road it stood in had changed. It was not the road she remembered. The pavement on this side was raised slightly and covered in. It ran under a succession of arches. It was a long gallery walled with glittering shop windows on one side; on the other a line of tall grey columns divided it from the street.

She was going along the arcades of the rue de Rivoli. Ahead of her she could see the edge of an immense grey pillar jutting out. That was the porch of the Hotel Saint Pierre. The revolving glass doors swung forward to receive her; she crossed the grey, sultry vestibule under the pillared arches. She knew it. She knew the porter's shining, wine-coloured mahogany pen on her left, and the shining wine-coloured mahogany barrier of the clerk's bureau on her right; she made straight for the great grey carpeted staircase; she climbed the endless flights that turned round and round the caged-in shaft of the well, past the latticed doors of the lift, and came up on to a landing that she knew, and into the long, ash-grey, foreign corridor lit by a dull window at one end.

It was there that the horror of the place came on her. She had no longer any memory of St. Mary's Church, so that she was unaware of her backward course through time. All space and time were here.

She remembered she had to go to the left, the left. But there was something there; where the corridor turned by the window; at the end of all the corridors. If she went the other way she would escape it.

The corridor stopped there. A blank wall. She was driven back past the stairhead to the left.

At the corner, by the window, she turned down another long ash-grey corridor on her right, and to the right again where the night light sputtered on the table-flap at the turn.

This third corridor was dark and secret and depraved. She knew the soiled walls and the warped door at the end. There was a sharp-pointed streak of light at the top. She could see the number on it now, 107.

Something had happened there. If she went in it would happen again.

Oscar Wade was in the room waiting for her behind the closed door. She felt him moving about in there. She leaned forward, her ear to the keyhole, and listened. She could hear the measured, deliberate, thoughtful footsteps. They were coming from the bed to the door.

She turned and ran; her knees gave way under her; she sank and ran on, down the long grey corridors and the stairs, quick and blind, a hunted beast seeking for cover, hearing his feet coming after her.

The revolving doors caught her and pushed her out into the street.

* * *

The strange quality of her state was this, that it had no time. She remembered dimly that there had once been a thing called time; but she had forgotten altogether what it was like. She was aware of things happening and about to happen; she fixed them by the place they occupied, and measured their duration by the space she went through.

So now she thought: If I could only go back and get to the place where it hadn't happened. To get back farther—

She was walking now on a white road that went between broad grass borders. To the right and left were the long raking lines of the hills, curve after curve, shimmering in a thin mist.

The road dropped to the green valley. It mounted the humped bridge over the river. Beyond it she saw the twin gables of the grey house pricked up over the high, grey garden wall. The tall iron gate stood in front of it between the ball-topped stone pillars.

And now she was in a large, low-ceilinged room with drawn blinds. She was standing before the wide double bed. It was her father's bed. The dead body, stretched out in the middle under the drawn white sheet, was her father's body.

The outline of the sheet sank from the peak of the upturned toes to the shin bone, and from the high bridge of the nose to the chin.

She lifted the sheet and folded it back across the breast of the dead man. The face she saw then was Oscar Wade's face, stilled and smoothed in the innocence of sleep, the supreme innocence of death. She stared at it, fascinated, in a cold, pitiless joy.

Oscar was dead.

She remembered how he used to lie like that beside her in the room in the Hotel Saint Pierre, on his back with his hands folded on his waist, his mouth half open, his big chest rising and falling. If he was dead, it would never happen again. She would be safe.

The dead face frightened her, and she was about to cover it up again when she was aware of a light heaving, a rhythmical rise and fall. As she drew the sheet up tighter, the hands under it began to struggle convulsively, the broad ends of the fingers appeared above the edge, clutching it to keep it down. The mouth opened; the eyes opened; the whole face stared back at her in a look of agony and horror.

Then the body drew itself forwards from the hips and sat up, its eyes peering into her eyes; he and she remained for an instant motionless, each held there by the other's fear.

Suddenly she broke away, turned and ran, out of the room, out of the house.

She stood at the gate, looking up and down the road, not knowing by which way she must go to escape Oscar. To the right, over the bridge and up the hill and across the downs she would come to the arcades of the rue de Rivoli and the dreadful grey corridors of the hotel. To the left the road went through the village.

If she could get further back she would be safe, out of Oscar's reach. Standing by her father's deathbed she had been young, but not young enough. She must get back to the place where she was younger still, to the Park and the green drive under the beech trees and the white pavilion at the cross. She knew how to find it. At the end of the village the high road ran right and left, east and west, under the Park walls; the south gate stood there at the top, looking down the narrow street.

She ran towards it through the village, past the long grey barns of Goodyer's farm, past the grocer's shop, past the yellow front and blue sign of the 'Queen's Head', past the post office, with its one black window blinking under its vine, past the church and the yew trees in the churchyard, to where the south gate made a delicate black pattern on the green grass.

These things appeared insubstantial, drawn back behind a sheet of air that shimmered over them like thin glass. They opened out, floated past and away from her; and instead of the high road and park walls she saw a London street of dingy white façades, and instead of the south gate the swinging glass doors of Schnebler's Restaurant.

* * *

The glass doors swung open and she passed into the restaurant. The scene beat on her with the hard impact of reality: the white and gold panels, the white pillars and their curling gold capitals, the white circles of the tables, glittering, the flushed faces of the diners, moving mechanically.

She was driven forward by some irresistible compulsion to a table in the corner, where a man sat alone. The table napkin he was using hid his mouth, and jaw, and chest; and she was not sure of the upper part of the face above the straight, drawn edge. It dropped; and she saw Oscar Wade's face. She came to him, dragged, without power to resist; she sat down beside him, and he leaned to her over the table; she could feel the warmth of his red, congested face; the smell of wine floated towards her on his thick whisper.

"I knew you would come."

She ate and drank with him in silence, nibbling and sipping slowly, staving off the abominable moment it would end in.

At last they got up and faced each other. His long bulk stood before her, above her; she could almost feel the vibration of its power.

"Come," he said. "Come."

And she went before him, slowly, slipping out through the maze of the tables, hearing behind her Oscar's measured, deliberate, thoughtful tread. The steep, red-carpeted staircase rose up before her.

She swerved from it, but he turned her back.

"You know the way," he said.

At the top of the flight she found the white door of the room she knew. She knew the long windows guarded by drawn muslin blinds; the gilt looking-glass over the chimney-piece that reflected Oscar's head and shoulders grotesquely between two white porcelain babies with bulbous limbs and garlanded loins, she knew the sprawling stain on the drab carpet by the table, the shabby, infamous couch behind the screen.

They moved about the room, turning and turning in it like beasts in a cage, uneasy, inimical, avoiding each other.

At last they stood still, he at the window, she at the door, the length of the room between.

"It's no good your getting away like that," he said. "There couldn't be any other end to it – to what we did."

"But that *was* ended."

"Ended there, but not here."

"Ended for ever. We've done with it for ever."

"We haven't. We've got to begin again. And go on. And go on."

"Oh, no. No. Anything but that."

"There isn't anything else."

"We can't. We can't. Don't you remember how it bored us?"

"Remember? Do you suppose I'd touch you if I could help it...? That's what we're here for. We must. We must."

"No. No. I shall get away – now."

She turned to the door to open it.

"You can't," he said. "The door's locked."

"Oscar – what did you do that for?"

"We always did it. Don't you remember?"

She turned to the door again and shook it; she beat on it with her hands.

"It's no use, Harriott. If you got out now you'd only have to come back again. You might stave it off for an hour or so, but what's that in an immortality?"

"Immortality?"

"That's what we're in for."

"Time enough to talk about immortality when we're dead…Ah—"

They were being drawn towards each other across the room, moving slowly, like figures in some monstrous and appalling dance, their heads thrown back over their shoulders, their faces turned from the horrible approach. Their arms rose slowly, heavy with intolerable reluctance; they stretched them out towards each other, aching, as if they held up an overpowering weight. Their feet dragged and were drawn.

Suddenly her knees sank under her; she shut her eyes; all her being went down before him in darkness and terror.

* * *

It was over. She had got away, she was going back, back, to the green drive of the Park, between the beech trees, where Oscar had never been, where he would never find her. When she passed through the south gate her memory became suddenly young and clean. She forgot the rue de Rivoli and the Hotel Saint Pierre; she forgot Schnebler's Restaurant and the room at the top of the stairs. She was back in her youth. She was Harriott Leigh going to wait for Stephen Philpotts in the pavilion opposite the west gate. She could feel herself, a slender figure moving fast over the grass between the lines of the great beech trees. The freshness of her youth was upon her.

She came to the heart of the drive where it branched right and left in the form of a cross. At the end of the right arm the white Greek temple, with its pediment and pillars, gleamed against the wood.

She was sitting on their seat at the back of the pavilion, watching the side door that Stephen would come in by.

The door was pushed open; he came towards her, light and young, skimming between the beech trees with his eager, tiptoeing stride. She rose up to meet him. She gave a cry.

"Stephen!"

It had been Stephen. She had seen him coming. But the man who stood before her between the pillars of the pavilion was Oscar Wade.

And now she was walking along the field-path that slanted from the orchard door to the stile; further and further back, to where young George Waring waited for her under the elder tree. The smell of the elder flowers came to her over the field. She could feel on her lips and in all her body the sweet, innocent excitement of her youth.

"George, oh, George!"

As she went along the field-path she had seen him. But the man who stood waiting for her under the elder tree was Oscar Wade.

"I told you it's no use getting away, Harriott. Every path brings you back to me. You'll find me at every turn."

"But how did you get *here?*"

"As I got into the pavilion. As I got into your father's room, on to his deathbed. Because I *was* there. I am in all your memories."

"My memories are innocent. How could you take my father's place, and Stephen's, and George Waring's? You."

"Because I did take them."

"Never. My love for *them* was innocent."

"Your love for me was part of it. You think the past affects the future. Has it never struck you that the future may affect the past? In your innocence there was the beginning of your sin. You *were* what you *were to be*."

"I shall get away," she said.

"And, this time, I shall go with you."

The stile, the elder tree, and the field floated away from her. She was going under the beech trees down the Park drive towards the south gate and the village, slinking close to the right-hand row of trees. She was aware that Oscar Wade was going with her under the left-hand row, keeping even with her, step by step, and tree by tree. And presently there was grey pavement under her feet and a row of grey pillars on her right hand. They were walking side by side down the rue de Rivoli towards the hotel.

They were sitting together now on the edge of the dingy white bed. Their arms hung by their sides, heavy and limp, their heads drooped, averted. Their passion weighed on them with the unbearable, unescapable boredom of immortality.

"Oscar – how long will it last?"

"I can't tell you. I don't know whether *this* is one moment of eternity, or the eternity of one moment."

"It must end some time," she said. "Life doesn't go on for ever. We shall die."

"Die? We *have* died. Don't you know what this is? Don't you know where you are? This is death. We're dead, Harriott. We're in hell."

"Yes. There can't be anything worse than this."

"This isn't the worst. We're not quite dead yet, as long as we've life in us to turn and run and get away from each other; as long as we can escape into our memories. But when you've got back to the farthest memory of all and there's nothing beyond it – when there's no memory but this—

"In the last hell we shall not run away any longer; we shall find no more roads, no more passages, no more open doors. We shall have no need to look for each other.

"In the last death we shall be shut up in this room, behind that locked door, together. We shall lie here together, forever and ever, joined so fast that even God can't put us asunder. We shall be one flesh and one spirit, one sin repeated forever, and ever; spirit loathing flesh, flesh loathing spirit; you and I loathing each other."

"Why? Why?" she cried.

"Because that's all that's left us. That's what you made of love."

* * *

The darkness came down swamping, it blotted out the room. She was walking along a garden path between high borders of phlox and larkspur and lupin. They were taller than she was, their flowers swayed and nodded above her head. She tugged at the tall stems and had no strength to break them. She was a little thing.

She said to herself then that she was safe. She had gone back so far that she was a child again; she had the blank innocence of childhood. To be a child, to go small under the heads of the lupins, to be blank and innocent, without memory, was to be safe.

The walk led her out through a yew hedge on to a bright green lawn. In the middle of the lawn there was a shallow round pond in a ring of rockery cushioned with small flowers, yellow and white and purple. Goldfish swam in the olive-brown water. She would be safe when she saw the goldfish swimming towards her. The old one with the white scales would come up first, pushing up his nose, making bubbles in the water.

At the bottom of the lawn there was a privet hedge cut by a broad path that went through the orchard. She knew what she would find there; her mother was in the orchard. She would lift her up in her arms to play with the hard red balls of the apples that hung from the tree. She had got back to the farthest memory of all; there was nothing beyond it.

There would be an iron gate in the wall of the orchard. It would lead into a field.

Something was different here, something that frightened her. An ash-grey door instead of an iron gate.

She pushed it open and came into the last corridor of the Hotel Saint Pierre.

The Conquering Will

Harriet Prescott Spofford

THERE WAS NO DOUBT that he was a masterful man. He ruled everyone on shore as he had ruled everyone at sea. His wife had never meant to marry him; but she did. When the fleet went into Asiatic waters she had declared she would not follow; but she did. When the child died she had wished to clothe herself in black; but she didn't. Wherever he was Captain Gilbert's will was the only will. Whenever she resisted him she felt like a wave shattering itself to foam against a rock in the mid-seas.

Sometimes she wondered if there were any hypnotic quality about him. Her mother had said she was possessed. But she really knew better. So far as she was concerned, she knew that the reason the Captain had his own way was simply because she loved him. And so far as everyone else was concerned, she was glad he did have his own way.

She had at first admired Captain Gilbert more than she loved him – admired his superb and stalwart figure of the large, heroic type; his Greek head, ringed over with short, yellow curls; his bold features, his eyes, that had in them the blue of the skies but also the glance of the eagle; his commanding air. And moreover, his manner, when he chose, had an inexpressible charm that carried all before it. No one dared contend with him – and then no one wished to do so. No wonder he was a masterful man. He was never resisted; and the habit had become nature.

Indeed, his wife hardly knew, after a while, when she had a wish other than her husband's. It is true she thought blue more becoming, but he liked to see her in pink, and she always went about like a lovely blush rose. It was also true that there had been a time when she cared for dancing; but Captain Gilbert would not endure the familiarity of the waltz, and so she never waltzed – when Captain Gilbert was looking. It is true she enjoyed the theatre; but Captain Gilbert prepared to go to church, and she went to church, and felt afterward very righteous and content.

But on the other hand, she loved riding; and the Captain kept her provided with a mount that was the envy of all the other women in the field. He himself rode like a centaur, and she never admired him more than in the saddle. She was fond of sea bathing, and he took for her every Summer a little place by the seaside, and none of the mer-people ever disported themselves with more sense of possession of the deep sea caves than they did. She would have enjoyed land travel; but Captain Gilbert preferred seafaring, so that she never saw any other world than the world of waters. She recovered from her seasickness after a few days, and then took keenest pleasure in the bounding and soaring from billow to billow, as if she were a seagull sitting on the wave or flying over it. Alone, too, in the vast region of sunlit sky and sea, or when night carried space into dark infinity, or when they rode triumphant over storm, and every man on the yacht was a machine moved by the Captain's will, he seemed to her each time a more positive potency than before.

But if the Captain had his own way in the outside things of life his way was usually right. It was because he said that it simply should be done that the salary of Dr. Saintly was raised to living limit. It was he who, when the rest of the town where he lived when off-duty frowned down an embezzling bank officer who had served his term in prison, insisted that the man should be helped to work and to respect again. It was he who brought home a forsaken woman of the place, and required civility for her so long as she did right. "If there is one thing certain," said the Captain, "it is that love is the best thing in the world. And I mean, Fanny, that you and I shall be as much at one with this great spirit filling the universe as holding the helpful hand to all can make us."

Perhaps, however, the Captain would not have carried things so before him if all his little world had not known of certain splendid achievements in the sea fights, giving him, in a measure, the right to his own way, giving him also the wounds that enforced his retirement and shortened his life. Wherever they were, people turned to look at him and to approve, and it gratified Mrs. Gilbert as much as when they turned to look at her – she was the woman whom this wonder among men had chosen out of all the women on the earth. But they always found it well worth their while to look at her. "The Lord may have thought He made the most beautiful thing possible when He made this rose," the Captain said to her once, stooping to a wayside bramble, "but I think He made the most beautiful thing when He made a woman. And you are a woman and a rose, too!"

"You make me blush," said Mrs. Gilbert; "and here, on the street!" They were going home from church across the fields.

"Yes, I should wonder why I was given such a wife if it were not that she has such a husband," he added, laughing. And when Captain Gilbert laughed Mrs. Gilbert felt that the world went well, and she laughed, too. And she never looked prettier than when her red lips curved apart over the rice-pearl teeth, and disclosed ravishing little dimples in either velvet cheek.

But possibly Captain Gilbert could not have so completely dominated his wife if she had not felt in him a fine superiority to the small things of life and had not had a fearsome joy in sometimes following his thought out into what he called the Fourth Dimension. "This earth and its envelopings are beautiful," he said, "but when I remember that there are colors we cannot see, sounds too fine for our ears, I know we are only spelling the alphabet of all we shall find – out there. Nights when I have walked the deck, virtually alone, and have seen the stars sentineling the great courts of space beyond space, I have felt sure they were made for no idleness – that there were reasons for their being; and in some form or other we shall tread their mazes and come out upon the reason for all things." She did not entirely understand him; but it may be that she admired him all the more on that account.

But there was one thing in which Captain Gilbert failed to have his own way. One thing? – two things! He could not hinder men from staring at Mrs. Gilbert, and he could not hinder Mrs. Gilbert from showing – in the mildest mannered way – that she was conscious of the gaze and possibly not unpleased. "I am sure I can't help their looking at me," she pouted, turning away from the window.

"You can help making eyes at them!" he replied.

"Captain Gilbert! What language!"

"Suiting the word to the action."

"And as if I could help my eyes!" the tears making them like live jewels.

"I know they're beautiful eyes!" said the Captain, remorsefully. "But they're my eyes! They don't belong to every fool going by."

"I never knew such a tyrant! You're like the man in the *Morte d'Arthur* who wanted his wife hideous before the court, but beautiful when alone with him."

"Precisely," said Captain Gilbert, laughing. "And I wish we had those days back – days when a man owned his wife, like any other precious thing, till a stronger took her—"

"It's always a stronger that takes her, one way or another."

"He'll be stronger than the laws of the universe if he takes you, that's all," said the Captain, lifting her in his arms and walking down the room with her as if she had been a child; "for by all the laws of the universe you are mine! And mine you will be forever, alive or dead!" And, to her troubled amazement, he was sobbing. "Fanny," he cried, "if you married another man after I died – after I died – if I were in the farthest star of the farthest heavens I should come back and punish him!"

"Oh!" cried Mrs. Gilbert. Then, through her own tears: "Why not leave that to me?"

Mrs. Gilbert was one of the women with whom this brigand-like way of making love is effective. And when, shortly afterward, Captain Gilbert betook himself to the farthest star and left her widowed, she missed the excitations and the raptures and the sense of being adored, even if tyrannized over; and she was not at all consoled by the fact that she looked charming in black, which there was no one now to forbid her.

But a little time works wonders. Mrs. Gilbert one day woke to the fact that she was free, with no one to say her nay; free as a bird in the air. At least, she would have been free if she had had any money to be free with. But Captain Gilbert's half-pay had stopped with his breath, and there was a delay about pension business and about other money, during which Mrs. Gilbert found herself so hard-pressed as to be almost in despair about ways and means. And when Mr. Mercer proposed that she share a million with him, she was in more minds than one about accepting the idea, and she actually asked for time. Captain Gilbert, she reasoned, would never want her to be put about this way for money – her mourning was positively shabby. And she thought of it very seriously – it might do – Mr. Mercer was a gentleman. But when he called for his reply she came down, white to her lips, so white that she was ghastly, and said it was impossible.

It was the same way with Dr. Vaughn. It seemed so eminently respectable, so altogether what the gossips would have called too good a chance to lose, she would be so well cared for – and she was just on the point of yielding. But after a night's reflection she wrote that it was out of the question, her hand shaking so that her script looked like a field of wheat bowed in the wind.

And after that she went for a while so sedately, so demurely, so entirely as the fond and faithful widow should, that who but the rector should be acknowledging her fascination? And she knew in her heart that she would be a capital wife for a clergyman, that she might have the parish under her little thumb – she, a helpmeet better than the best! She said to herself it was a pity if she could not do as she pleased; she smiled on him; she came near giving him her hand to kiss in token of the ring it might wear presently. And then she sent him in his turn the hurried note that laid all hope low.

Captain Gilbert had been lost to the breathing world almost half a dozen years, and his wife was as much like a lovely blooming rose as ever, when John Mowbray crossed her path. And he not only crossed it, but he obstructed it. The years had passed quietly; her affairs had adjusted themselves; although she could have spent more, she was no longer in need of money. She had almost forgotten Mr. Mercer and his successors in misfortune. And John Mowbray was a man of an unfamiliar and engaging type. He loved music, the opera, Wagner; she had never had enough of music in her life. He was more or less of a student, acquainted with books, a haunter of libraries; it seemed to her that he held the gates open to a fair and inviting plaisance. Well-born and well-bred, he had the air, without having traveled much, of knowing men and manners and the world; but to travel was his intention – and she saw the gates open to a life of infinitely wider interest than this small daily round. He was on the sunny side, as she was; with a most agreeable personality, with a delightful courtesy, and as she began to suspect, with a sincere affection for herself.

He had come to see her, that snowy night, through all the storm, bringing her an armful of great red roses. There was something very pleasant about his coming in; it gave her a feeling of protection, emphasized the idea of shelter. She heaped the fire and presently the ruddy flames danced over the room and the flowers, and over the pretty woman disposing them in their bowls and jars, till it all seemed to John Mowbray, still warming his hands at the blaze, the ideal of a home. What a place to come to every night! What a place never to go away from! What a dream!

She knew what was coming very well. Some subtle instinct made her try to fortify herself against it. She sat down behind a table and leaned forward, rearranging with twinkling fingers the roses in the vase that nearly hid her face. And then in another moment he was half-kneeling beside her, and he was murmuring, "Fanny, Fanny! Let it be real – this dream. I am dreaming! Tell me not to wake! Say, dear, say that you love me!" And before she knew it the strong arms were about her, and she was hiding her face on his shoulder.

What an evening of deep, serene happiness it was! Side by side they looked into the future, and its glow shed a light over them. "It is too much, too much happiness," she said, as they parted. "Something will hinder. I – I shall not be allowed—" And she grew very pale.

"Thank heaven, there is no one to allow or to disallow," said John Mowbray. "You are not now the young girl to be dominated, but the woman whose beautiful nature has developed the power to choose, and I am crowned and blessed by your choice!"

"I am afraid – I am afraid—" she said, as he bade her goodnight.

"Of what, my love?" he asked her.

"Oh, of nothing, of nothing, so long as you are here!" she said, clinging to him more closely. And "I am afraid!" she repeated again, as she went upstairs, though trembling with joy.

She had half a mind to sit up that night and not go to sleep at all. She dropped the curtain quickly as she saw the stars sparkling in the sky from which the snow clouds were already blowing away. The thought of that farthest star would come back and make her shiver. But she was tired out with emotion – with hope and joy and fear – and she fell asleep in the big armchair just as Captain Gilbert came into the room, strong, stalwart, mighty, and looking like the hero of some Viking legend.

The wind had blown a fine color into his face; his curls were sprayed with the melted snow, his eyes were as dazzlingly blue as a noonday sky. "I have come a long way to see you, my wife," he said, and the old familiar tone rang sweetly through all the chambers of her heart. "And I never saw you lovelier. How dear, how beautiful you are! How long we have belonged to each other! Do you remember the night by the gate under the honeysuckles, when you reached out your hand in the dark, uncertain if I was there, and suddenly I clasped it? Dear hand! I have never, never let it go! I never will! I saw a sapphire as blue as Lyra on my way here. I will have it for this little hand – only the band is so slight, the sapphire is so heavy. How quiet it is here – it is always quiet about you, my wife – you are so serene, and your husband is so stormy! Here is the smell of roses that always hovers about you – oh, how sweet, how sweet you are! Up, and let me sit down and hold you in my arms, you featherweight! There, rest the dear head. What makes you shiver so? It is warm. I am here – your husband. Warm? I am warm to my marrow, being with you, holding you, living again the delicious life we used to live. Oh, what life will be again with you, most perfect of women, most faithful of wives! I have been so cold, so far off, so longing for you! What ways I have traversed, what have I encountered, just for this hour! And it is worth it all. There are great things in store for us, little woman. Lean your cheek on mine how velvet soft, how warm – you are mine, mine, mine—"

She heard, she remembered no more, but woke with the sun pouring into the window and streaming over her through the crimson warmth of the geraniums, and all her heart expanded with the old affection.

Suffused still with the mood of the night, she made her toilette and went down, thoughtless, reckless, almost gay – and met John Mowbray coming through the door, his sleigh-bells still jangling at the gate – he had come to take her sleighing. But at the first sight of his eager, expectant face she stopped. All her bloom fell away, she shook like a leaf; and he sprang forward, thinking she was about to fall. "No, no, no!" she cried. "Forget last night! Forget everything! It is impossible! It is out of the question. I am Captain Gilbert's wife still. Captain Gilbert – will not – will not allow it."

And then she dropped fainting into his arms.

She did not, however, lose consciousness entirely. She knew very well that John Mowbray was covering her face with kisses while carrying her to the sofa. The blood surged over her forehead in a conviction of guilt, and then she turned her face to the wall.

"What does this mean?" cried John Mowbray.

"He – he has been here," she faltered.

"Who has been here?" he demanded.

"Captain Gilbert."

"What – what is it you say?" he exclaimed, springing to his feet.

"He was here last night – I am not out of my head. Oh, no, I am not beside myself! He has been here before – the same way – whenever – Oh, see how unworthy I am!"

And she covered her face with her hands.

He seated himself on the edge of the sofa and took down the two hands, holding them in his own.

"You mean you dreamed last night," he said.

"Oh, no, no! Dreamed? Oh, it was too real! Dreamed? I don't know— Do you suppose it could be just a dream? Always the same dream, only with differences? And he so all he used to be when he was best and tenderest, making me feel that he was my husband forever and ever, that I— Oh, you see I love him still!"

"I should be ashamed of you if you didn't!" said John Mowbray, sternly. "But you love me, too! You know you do!"

"How can I love two men at once?" cried Fanny.

"You don't. One of us is an angel in heaven. I shall never have the least jealousy of your affection for him. You and I are on the earth. And when we are as the angels in heaven we shall never marry or be given in marriage. Come, you need the air. Where is your thick cloak, your furs, a hood? Here is the sleigh at the gate. We will drive up the river. On the way we will stop at the rectory—"

"But – but—"

"Not a but about it. I shall have the right then to shield my wife in her dreams and from her dreams. And I don't believe anyone will come where I am to challenge him!" And Fanny Gilbert had found again the power that surrounded her like a fortress and the will that was perhaps as strong as Captain Gilbert's will.

It seemed that John Mowbray must have been right. After the sleigh ride and the brief ceremony at the rector's he took his wife away and into a round of gaieties that gave her no time to reflect. And then came the voyage overseas and the travel that should so fill thought and memory as to leave no room for the past. Under all the novelty and pleasure and excitement, and Mr. Mowbray's constant presence and care, she became a new creature.

Blooming with fresh being, enlarged to the larger life, her prettiness became beauty, her liveliness sparkling, and her sweetness, to John Mowbray, enchanting. His pride in her was equal to his passion. It was with pleasure that he saw men's eyes follow her, and women's, too. When she rode, her trim grace and dauntless spirit hung afterward before his own eyes, as if he had seen Dian and her train pass by. At the opera, as she stood a moment, easy, gracious, dropping off her cloak and revealing a dazzle of jewels and gleaming tissues, of eyes like jewels, too, of roses, cream and blush, and of smiles, and when he saw her breathless, rapt in the music and the play, he felt a joy of possession that was like a pain; but with the emotion came a vague fear of its evanescence.

The premonition was not felt at once, however. There was a season of unassailed rapture before he noticed that Mrs. Mowbray had become very restless, seeking perpetually some new object, and so absent-minded that he sometimes spoke twice or thrice before she heard him. Glowing with color and life and happiness in the evening, in the morning she would be as pale and sad and languid as if she had danced all night with witches, so that he wondered if she slept at all. She ate almost nothing, started at every sound, laughed nervously at nothing, and her eyes filled with tears likewise at nothing. She began to grow very thin. Suddenly he perceived that she was wasting away before his eyes.

Like Asa of old, Mr. Mowbray had recourse to the physicians, and that without loss of time. But as she persisted that nothing ailed her, and had no symptoms to present other than those they saw, they could do little beyond administering tonics, which were as idle as spring water.

"My dear one," he said to her at last, "tell me – what is it? There is something you hide from me. My precious one, my wife, tell me; are you unhappy?"

"Oh, yes, yes, yes!" she cried, lifting her hands passionately. "I am wretched! I am wretched!" He turned as white as she. "Fanny!" he cried.

"Oh, not the way you think!" she cried. "But, oh! I cannot tell you!"

He sat down beside her and took her in his arms. "Whatever it is, you must tell me," he said, gently. "You are my one thought in life. I can do nothing to serve you if I am in the dark."

"It is I! – It is I who am in the dark!" she wept.

"Tell me what you mean, my darling," he urged her.

"I – I don't know if I am your darling!" she exclaimed. "I don't know who I am!"

"Fanny, dearest, I don't understand. Be reasonable, my little wife, let me know."

"Am I your wife? Or am I his?"

"Dearest!"

"I don't know. He comes – he has come every night—"

He clasped her convulsively in his arms. "I live a double life," she said, moving herself feebly yet resistingly. "All day I am yours. All night I am his!"

"Dear child! Dear little one! You are ill. You are letting a dream—"

"It is not like any dream—"

"But, dream or not, it is when all your powers are submerged in sleep, when you are not fully yourself—"

"Oh, but in the daylight—"

"Yes, in the daylight, when you are you, then – then you are only mine!"

"I am afraid – I am afraid," she sighed. "Every night when I go to sleep – I don't know what may happen. Some night, some night, he will take me!" And her voice died to a whisper.

"Never!" he cried. "Never, while I am beside you."

At that moment, as she lay in his arms, they both were possessed by a great shuddering and fear. It was dark all about them, as if it were already night. A wind seemed to fill the room and then to hold its breath, a wind that might have been blowing from nowhere to nowhere, but hanging now still and chill.

"Hold me, hold me fast, John!" she murmured. "He has come for me!" Her arms fell, her head drooped nerveless over his arm.

"Oh, John, I love—"

The lips, wide open, said no more. And in the instant of that last sigh John Mowbray knew, by some other than the sense of sight, that Captain Gilbert, masterful, laughing, debonair, towered like a shaft of sunlight before him.

"You are wronged of nothing," a voice that had no sound was ringing in his ears. "The bindweed falls that leans upon a straw. You would have made her happy if you might. But you could not conquer the unconquerable will. And I have come for my own!"

"As a destroying force – destroying joy, destroying life!" cried John Mowbray. "And I defy you! For though you carry her beyond your farthest star, she loves me best, and I will follow you!"

"Spirit to spirit, flesh to flesh, John Mowbray. She is mine!"

There was a flutter of the purple-veined eyelids in the face that had fallen from his arm, a tremor of the lips, a long, slow, bubbling sigh. Slipping, slipping from his grasp, a lifeless heap lay on the floor – and by all the avenues through which the viewless thing may reach the soul, John Mowbray saw Captain Gilbert fading into an intenser light, his wife held close beside him. And then, though it was broad noonday, the world was black and still.

The Strange Case of Dr. Jekyll and Mr. Hyde

Robert Louis Stevenson

Story of the Door

MR. UTTERSON the lawyer was a man of a rugged countenance that was never lighted by a smile; cold, scanty and embarrassed in discourse; backward in sentiment; lean, long, dusty, dreary and yet somehow lovable. At friendly meetings, and when the wine was to his taste, something eminently human beaconed from his eye; something indeed which never found its way into his talk, but which spoke not only in these silent symbols of the after-dinner face, but more often and loudly in the acts of his life. He was austere with himself; drank gin when he was alone, to mortify a taste for vintages; and though he enjoyed the theatre, had not crossed the doors of one for twenty years. But he had an approved tolerance for others; sometimes wondering, almost with envy, at the high pressure of spirits involved in their misdeeds; and in any extremity inclined to help rather than to reprove. "I incline to Cain's heresy," he used to say quaintly: "I let my brother go to the devil in his own way." In this character, it was frequently his fortune to be the last reputable acquaintance and the last good influence in the lives of downgoing men. And to such as these, so long as they came about his chambers, he never marked a shade of change in his demeanour.

No doubt the feat was easy to Mr. Utterson; for he was undemonstrative at the best, and even his friendship seemed to be founded in a similar catholicity of good nature. It is the mark of a modest man to accept his friendly circle ready-made from the hands of opportunity; and that was the lawyer's way. His friends were those of his own blood or those whom he had known the longest; his affections, like ivy, were the growth of time, they implied no aptness in the object. Hence, no doubt the bond that united him to Mr. Richard Enfield, his distant kinsman, the well-known man about town. It was a nut to crack for many, what these two could see in each other, or what subject they could find in common. It was reported by those who encountered them in their Sunday walks, that they said nothing, looked singularly dull and would hail with obvious relief the appearance of a friend. For all that, the two men put the greatest store by these excursions, counted them the chief jewel of each week, and not only set aside occasions of pleasure, but even resisted the calls of business, that they might enjoy them uninterrupted.

It chanced on one of these rambles that their way led them down a by-street in a busy quarter of London. The street was small and what is called quiet, but it drove a thriving trade on the weekdays. The inhabitants were all doing well, it seemed, and all emulously hoping to do better still, and laying out the surplus of their grains in coquetry; so that the shop fronts stood along that thoroughfare with an air of invitation, like rows of smiling saleswomen. Even on Sunday, when it veiled its more florid charms and lay comparatively empty of passage, the street shone out in contrast to its dingy neighbourhood, like a fire in a forest; and with its freshly painted shutters, well-polished brasses, and general cleanliness and gaiety of note, instantly caught and pleased the eye of the passenger.

Two doors from one corner, on the left hand going east the line was broken by the entry of a court; and just at that point a certain sinister block of building thrust forward its gable on the street. It was two storeys high; showed no window, nothing but a door on the lower storey and a blind forehead of discoloured wall on the upper; and bore in every feature, the marks of prolonged and sordid negligence. The door, which was equipped with neither bell nor knocker, was blistered and distained. Tramps slouched into the recess and struck matches on the panels; children kept shop upon the steps; the schoolboy had tried his knife on the mouldings; and for close on a generation, no one had appeared to drive away these random visitors or to repair their ravages.

Mr. Enfield and the lawyer were on the other side of the by-street; but when they came abreast of the entry, the former lifted up his cane and pointed.

"Did you ever remark that door?" he asked; and when his companion had replied in the affirmative, "It is connected in my mind," added he, "with a very odd story."

"Indeed?" said Mr. Utterson, with a slight change of voice, "and what was that?"

"Well, it was this way," returned Mr. Enfield: "I was coming home from some place at the end of the world, about three o'clock of a black winter morning, and my way lay through a part of town where there was literally nothing to be seen but lamps. Street after street and all the folks asleep – street after street, all lighted up as if for a procession and all as empty as a church – till at last I got into that state of mind when a man listens and listens and begins to long for the sight of a policeman. All at once, I saw two figures: one a little man who was stumping along eastward at a good walk, and the other a girl of maybe eight or ten who was running as hard as she was able down a cross street. Well, sir, the two ran into one another naturally enough at the corner; and then came the horrible part of the thing; for the man trampled calmly over the child's body and left her screaming on the ground. It sounds nothing to hear, but it was hellish to see. It wasn't like a man; it was like some damned Juggernaut. I gave a few halloa, took to my heels, collared my gentleman, and brought him back to where there was already quite a group about the screaming child. He was perfectly cool and made no resistance, but gave me one look, so ugly that it brought out the sweat on me like running. The people who had turned out were the girl's own family; and pretty soon, the doctor, for whom she had been sent put in his appearance. Well, the child was not much the worse, more frightened, according to the sawbones; and there you might have supposed would be an end to it. But there was one curious circumstance. I had taken a loathing to my gentleman at first sight. So had the child's family, which was only natural. But the doctor's case was what struck me. He was the usual cut and dry apothecary, of no particular age and colour, with a strong Edinburgh accent and about as emotional as a bagpipe. Well, sir, he was like the rest of us; every time he looked at my prisoner, I saw that sawbones turn sick and white with the desire to kill him. I knew what was in his mind, just as he knew what was in mine; and killing being out of the question, we did the next best. We told the man we could and would make such a scandal out of this as should make his name stink from one end of London to the other. If he had any friends or any credit, we undertook that he should lose them. And all the time, as we were pitching it in red hot, we were keeping the women off him as best we could for they were as wild as harpies. I never saw a circle of such hateful faces; and there was the man in the middle, with a kind of black sneering coolness – frightened too, I could see that – but carrying it off, sir, really like Satan. 'If you choose to make capital out of this accident,' said he, 'I am naturally helpless. No gentleman but wishes to avoid a scene,' says he. 'Name your figure.' Well, we screwed him up to a hundred pounds for the child's family; he would have clearly liked to stick out; but there was something about the lot of us that meant mischief, and at last he struck. The next thing was to get the money; and where do you think he carried us but to that place with the door? – whipped out a key, went in, and presently came back with the matter of ten pounds in gold and a cheque for the balance on Coutts's, drawn payable to bearer and signed with a name that I can't mention, though it's one of the points of my story, but it was a name at least very well known and often printed. The figure was stiff; but the signature was good for more than that if it was only genuine. I took the liberty of pointing out to my gentleman that the whole business looked apocryphal, and that a man does not, in real life, walk into a cellar door at four in the morning and come out with another man's cheque for close upon a hundred pounds. But he was quite easy and sneering. 'Set your mind at rest,' says he, 'I will stay with you till the banks open and cash the cheque myself.' So we all set off, the doctor, and the child's father, and our friend and myself, and passed the rest of the night in my chambers; and next day, when we had breakfasted, went in a body to the bank. I gave in the cheque myself, and said I had every reason to believe it was a forgery. Not a bit of it. The cheque was genuine."

"Tut-tut!" said Mr. Utterson.

"I see you feel as I do," said Mr. Enfield. "Yes, it's a bad story. For my man was a fellow that nobody could have to do with, a really damnable man; and the person that drew the cheque is the very pink of the proprieties, celebrated too, and (what makes it worse) one of your fellows who do what they call good. Blackmail, I suppose; an honest man paying through the nose for some of the capers of his youth. Black Mail House is what I call the place with the door, in consequence. Though even that, you know, is far from explaining all," he added, and with the words fell into a vein of musing.

From this he was recalled by Mr. Utterson asking rather suddenly: "And you don't know if the drawer of the cheque lives there?"

"A likely place, isn't it?" returned Mr. Enfield. "But I happen to have noticed his address; he lives in some square or other."

"And you never asked about the – place with the door?" said Mr. Utterson.

"No, sir; I had a delicacy," was the reply. "I feel very strongly about putting questions; it partakes too much of the style of the day of judgment. You start a question, and it's like starting a stone. You sit quietly on the top of a hill; and away the stone goes, starting others; and presently some bland old bird (the last you would have thought of) is knocked on the head in his own back garden and the family have to change their name. No sir, I make it a rule of mine: the more it looks like Queer Street, the less I ask."

"A very good rule, too," said the lawyer.

"But I have studied the place for myself," continued Mr. Enfield. "It seems scarcely a house. There is no other door, and nobody goes in or out of that one but, once in a great while, the gentleman of my adventure. There are three windows looking on the court on the first floor; none below; the windows are always shut but they're clean. And then there is a chimney which is generally smoking; so somebody must live there. And yet it's not so sure; for the buildings are so packed together about the court, that it's hard to say where one ends and another begins."

The pair walked on again for a while in silence; and then "Enfield," said Mr. Utterson, "that's a good rule of yours."

"Yes, I think it is," returned Enfield.

"But for all that," continued the lawyer, "there's one point I want to ask. I want to ask the name of that man who walked over the child."

"Well," said Mr. Enfield, "I can't see what harm it would do. It was a man of the name of Hyde."

"Hm," said Mr. Utterson. "What sort of a man is he to see?"

"He is not easy to describe. There is something wrong with his appearance; something displeasing, something downright detestable. I never saw a man I so disliked, and yet I scarce know why. He must be deformed somewhere; he gives a strong feeling of deformity, although I couldn't specify the point. He's an extraordinary looking man, and yet I really can name nothing out of the way. No, sir; I can make no hand of it; I can't describe him. And it's not want of memory; for I declare I can see him this moment."

Mr. Utterson again walked some way in silence and obviously under a weight of consideration. "You are sure he used a key?" he inquired at last.

"My dear sir..." began Enfield, surprised out of himself.

"Yes, I know," said Utterson; "I know it must seem strange. The fact is, if I do not ask you the name of the other party, it is because I know it already. You see, Richard, your tale has gone home. If you have been inexact in any point you had better correct it."

"I think you might have warned me," returned the other with a touch of sullenness. "But I have been pedantically exact, as you call it. The fellow had a key; and what's more, he has it still. I saw him use it not a week ago."

Mr. Utterson sighed deeply but said never a word; and the young man presently resumed. "Here is another lesson to say nothing," said he. "I am ashamed of my long tongue. Let us make a bargain never to refer to this again."

"With all my heart," said the lawyer. "I shake hands on that, Richard."

Search for Mr. Hyde

THAT EVENING Mr. Utterson came home to his bachelor house in sombre spirits and sat down to dinner without relish. It was his custom of a Sunday, when this meal was over, to sit close by the fire, a volume of some dry divinity on his reading desk, until the clock of the neighbouring church rang out the hour of twelve, when he would go soberly and gratefully to bed. On this night however, as soon as the cloth was taken away, he took up a candle and went into his business room. There he opened his safe, took from the most private part of it a document endorsed on the envelope as Dr. Jekyll's Will and sat down with a clouded brow to study its contents. The will was holograph, for Mr. Utterson though he took charge of it now that it was made, had refused to lend the least assistance in the making of it; it provided not only that, in case of the decease of Henry Jekyll, M.D., D.C.L., L.L.D., F.R.S., etc., all his possessions were to pass into the hands of his 'friend and benefactor Edward Hyde', but that in case of Dr. Jekyll's 'disappearance or unexplained absence for any period exceeding three calendar months', the said Edward Hyde should step into the said Henry Jekyll's shoes without further delay and free from any burthen or obligation beyond the payment of a few small sums to the members of the doctor's household. This document had long been the lawyer's eyesore. It offended him both as a lawyer and as a lover of the sane and customary sides of life, to whom the fanciful was the immodest. And hitherto it was his ignorance of Mr. Hyde that had swelled his indignation; now, by a sudden turn, it was his knowledge. It was already bad enough when the name was but a name of which he could learn no more. It was worse when it began to be clothed upon with detestable attributes; and out of the shifting, insubstantial mists that had so long baffled his eye, there leaped up the sudden, definite presentment of a fiend.

"I thought it was madness," he said, as he replaced the obnoxious paper in the safe, "and now I begin to fear it is disgrace."

With that he blew out his candle, put on a greatcoat, and set forth in the direction of Cavendish Square, that citadel of medicine, where his friend, the great Dr. Lanyon, had his house and received his crowding patients. "If anyone knows, it will be Lanyon," he had thought.

The solemn butler knew and welcomed him; he was subjected to no stage of delay, but ushered direct from the door to the dining room where Dr. Lanyon sat alone over his wine. This was a hearty, healthy, dapper, red-faced gentleman, with a shock of hair prematurely white, and a boisterous and decided manner. At sight of Mr. Utterson, he sprang up from his chair and welcomed him with both hands. The geniality, as was the way of the man, was somewhat theatrical to the eye; but it reposed on genuine feeling. For these two were old friends, old mates both at school and college, both thorough respectors of themselves and of each other, and what does not always follow, men who thoroughly enjoyed each other's company.

After a little rambling talk, the lawyer led up to the subject which so disagreeably preoccupied his mind.

"I suppose, Lanyon," said he, "you and I must be the two oldest friends that Henry Jekyll has?"

"I wish the friends were younger," chuckled Dr. Lanyon. "But I suppose we are. And what of that? I see little of him now."

"Indeed?" said Utterson. "I thought you had a bond of common interest."

"We had," was the reply. "But it is more than ten years since Henry Jekyll became too fanciful for me. He began to go wrong, wrong in mind; and though of course I continue to take an interest in him for old sake's sake, as they say, I see and I have seen devilish little of the man. Such unscientific balderdash," added the doctor, flushing suddenly purple, "would have estranged Damon and Pythias."

This little spirit of temper was somewhat of a relief to Mr. Utterson. "They have only differed on some point of science," he thought; and being a man of no scientific passions (except in the matter of conveyancing), he even added: "It is nothing worse than that!" He gave his friend a few seconds to recover his composure, and then approached the question he had come to put. "Did you ever come across a *protégé* of his – one Hyde?" he asked.

"Hyde?" repeated Lanyon. "No. Never heard of him. Since my time."

That was the amount of information that the lawyer carried back with him to the great, dark bed on which he tossed to and fro, until the small hours of the morning began to grow large. It was a night of little ease to his toiling mind, toiling in mere darkness and besieged by questions.

Six o'clock struck on the bells of the church that was so conveniently near to Mr. Utterson's dwelling, and still he was digging at the problem. Hitherto it had touched him on the intellectual side alone; but now his imagination also was engaged, or rather enslaved; and as he lay and tossed in the gross darkness of the night and the curtained room, Mr. Enfield's tale went by before his mind in a scroll of lighted pictures. He would be aware of the great field of lamps of a nocturnal city; then of the figure of a man walking swiftly; then of a child running from the doctor's; and then these met, and that human Juggernaut trod the child down and passed on regardless of her screams. Or else he would see a room in a rich house, where his friend lay asleep, dreaming and smiling at his dreams; and then the door of that room would be opened, the curtains of the bed plucked apart, the sleeper recalled, and lo! there would stand by his side a figure to whom power was given, and even at that dead hour, he must rise and do its bidding. The figure in these two phases haunted the lawyer all night; and if at any time he dozed over, it was but to see it glide more stealthily through sleeping houses, or move the more swiftly and still the more swiftly, even to dizziness, through wider labyrinths of lamplighted city, and at every street corner crush a child and leave her screaming. And still the figure had no face by which he might know it; even in his dreams, it had no face, or one that baffled him and melted before his eyes; and thus it was that there sprang up and grew apace in the lawyer's mind a singularly strong, almost an inordinate, curiosity to behold the features of the real Mr. Hyde. If he could but once set eyes on him, he thought the mystery would lighten and perhaps roll altogether away, as was the habit of mysterious things when well examined. He might see a reason for his friend's strange preference or bondage (call it which you please) and even for the startling clause of the will. At least it would be a face worth seeing: the face of a man who was without bowels of mercy: a face which had but to show itself to raise up, in the mind of the unimpressionable Enfield, a spirit of enduring hatred.

From that time forward, Mr. Utterson began to haunt the door in the by-street of shops. In the morning before office hours, at noon when business was plenty and time scarce, at night under the face of the fogged city moon, by all lights and at all hours of solitude or concourse, the lawyer was to be found on his chosen post.

"If he be Mr. Hyde," he had thought, "I shall be Mr. Seek."

And at last his patience was rewarded. It was a fine dry night; frost in the air; the streets as clean as a ballroom floor; the lamps, unshaken by any wind, drawing a regular pattern of light and shadow. By ten o'clock, when the shops were closed, the by-street was very solitary and, in spite of the low growl of London from all round, very silent. Small sounds carried far; domestic sounds out of the houses were clearly audible on either side of the roadway; and the rumour of the approach of any passenger preceded him by a long time. Mr. Utterson had been some minutes at his post, when he was aware of an odd light footstep drawing near. In the course of his nightly patrols, he had long grown accustomed to the quaint effect with which the footfalls of a single person, while he is still a great way off, suddenly spring out distinct from the vast hum and clatter of the city. Yet his attention had never before been so sharply and decisively arrested; and it was with a strong, superstitious prevision of success that he withdrew into the entry of the court.

The steps drew swiftly nearer, and swelled out suddenly louder as they turned the end of the street. The lawyer, looking forth from the entry, could soon see what manner of man he had to deal with. He was small and very plainly dressed and the look of him, even at that distance, went somehow strongly against the watcher's inclination. But he made straight for the door, crossing the roadway to save time; and as he came, he drew a key from his pocket like one approaching home.

Mr. Utterson stepped out and touched him on the shoulder as he passed. "Mr. Hyde, I think?"

Mr. Hyde shrank back with a hissing intake of the breath. But his fear was only momentary; and though he did not look the lawyer in the face, he answered coolly enough: "That is my name. What do you want?"

"I see you are going in," returned the lawyer. "I am an old friend of Dr. Jekyll's – Mr. Utterson of Gaunt Street – you must have heard of my name; and meeting you so conveniently, I thought you might admit me."

"You will not find Dr. Jekyll; he is from home," replied Mr. Hyde, blowing in the key. And then suddenly, but still without looking up, "How did you know me?" he asked.

"On your side," said Mr. Utterson "will you do me a favour?"

"With pleasure," replied the other. "What shall it be?"

"Will you let me see your face?" asked the lawyer.

Mr. Hyde appeared to hesitate, and then, as if upon some sudden reflection, fronted about with an air of defiance; and the pair stared at each other pretty fixedly for a few seconds. "Now I shall know you again," said Mr. Utterson. "It may be useful."

"Yes," returned Mr. Hyde, "It is as well we have met; and *à propos*, you should have my address." And he gave a number of a street in Soho.

"Good God!" thought Mr. Utterson, "can he, too, have been thinking of the will?" But he kept his feelings to himself and only grunted in acknowledgment of the address.

"And now," said the other, "how did you know me?"

"By description," was the reply.

"Whose description?"

"We have common friends," said Mr. Utterson.

"Common friends," echoed Mr. Hyde, a little hoarsely. "Who are they?"

"Jekyll, for instance," said the lawyer.

"He never told you," cried Mr. Hyde, with a flush of anger. "I did not think you would have lied."

"Come," said Mr. Utterson, "that is not fitting language."

The other snarled aloud into a savage laugh; and the next moment, with extraordinary quickness, he had unlocked the door and disappeared into the house.

The lawyer stood awhile when Mr. Hyde had left him, the picture of disquietude. Then he began slowly to mount the street, pausing every step or two and putting his hand to his brow like a man in mental perplexity. The problem he was thus debating as he walked, was one of a class that is rarely solved. Mr. Hyde was pale and dwarfish, he gave an impression of deformity without any nameable malformation, he had a displeasing smile, he had borne himself to the lawyer with a sort of murderous mixture of timidity and boldness, and he spoke with a husky, whispering and somewhat broken voice; all these were points against him, but not all of these together could explain the hitherto unknown disgust, loathing and fear with which Mr. Utterson regarded him. "There must be something else," said the perplexed gentleman. "There *is* something more, if I could find a name for it. God bless me, the man seems hardly human! Something troglodytic, shall we say? Or can it be the old story of Dr. Fell? Or is it the mere radiance of a foul soul that thus transpires through, and transfigures, its clay continent? The last, I think; for, O my poor old Harry Jekyll, if ever I read Satan's signature upon a face, it is on that of your new friend."

Round the corner from the by-street, there was a square of ancient, handsome houses, now for the most part decayed from their high estate and let in flats and chambers to all sorts and conditions of men; map-engravers, architects, shady lawyers and the agents of obscure enterprises. One house, however, second from the corner, was still occupied entire; and at the door of this, which wore a great air of wealth and comfort, though it was now plunged in darkness except for the fanlight, Mr. Utterson stopped and knocked. A well-dressed, elderly servant opened the door.

"Is Dr. Jekyll at home, Poole?" asked the lawyer.

"I will see, Mr. Utterson," said Poole, admitting the visitor, as he spoke, into a large, low-roofed, comfortable hall paved with flags, warmed (after the fashion of a country house) by a bright, open fire, and furnished with costly cabinets of oak. "Will you wait here by the fire, sir? or shall I give you a light in the dining room?"

"Here, thank you," said the lawyer, and he drew near and leaned on the tall fender. This hall, in which he was now left alone, was a pet fancy of his friend the doctor's; and Utterson himself was wont to speak of it as the pleasantest room in London. But tonight there was a shudder in his blood; the face of Hyde sat heavy on his memory; he felt (what was rare with him) a nausea and distaste of life; and in the gloom of his spirits, he seemed to read a menace in the flickering of the firelight on the polished cabinets and the uneasy starting of the shadow on the roof.

He was ashamed of his relief, when Poole presently returned to announce that Dr. Jekyll was gone out.

"I saw Mr. Hyde go in by the old dissecting room, Poole," he said. "Is that right, when Dr. Jekyll is from home?"

"Quite right, Mr. Utterson, sir," replied the servant. "Mr. Hyde has a key."

"Your master seems to repose a great deal of trust in that young man, Poole," resumed the other musingly.

"Yes, sir, he does indeed," said Poole. "We have all orders to obey him."

"I do not think I ever met Mr. Hyde?" asked Utterson.

"O, dear no, sir. He never *dines* here," replied the butler. "Indeed we see very little of him on this side of the house; he mostly comes and goes by the laboratory."

"Well, goodnight, Poole."

"Goodnight, Mr. Utterson."

And the lawyer set out homeward with a very heavy heart. "Poor Harry Jekyll," he thought, "my mind misgives me he is in deep waters! He was wild when he was young; a long while ago to be sure; but in the law of God, there is no statute of limitations. Ay, it must be that; the ghost of some old sin, the cancer of some concealed disgrace: punishment coming, *pede claudo*, years after memory has forgotten and self-love condoned the fault." And the lawyer, scared by the thought, brooded a while on his own past, groping in all the corners of memory, least by chance some Jack-in-the-Box of an old iniquity should leap to light there. His past was fairly blameless; few men could read the rolls of their life with less apprehension; yet he was humbled to the dust by the many ill things he had done, and raised up again into a sober and fearful gratitude by the many he had come so near to doing yet avoided. And then by a return on his former subject, he conceived a spark of hope. "This Master Hyde, if he were studied," thought he, "must have secrets of his own; black secrets, by the look of him; secrets compared to which poor Jekyll's worst would be like sunshine. Things cannot continue as they are. It turns me cold to think of this creature stealing like a thief to Harry's bedside; poor Harry, what a wakening! And the danger of it; for if this Hyde suspects the existence of the will, he may grow impatient to inherit. Ay, I must put my shoulders to the wheel – if Jekyll will but let me," he added, "if Jekyll will only let me." For once more he saw before his mind's eye, as clear as transparency, the strange clauses of the will.

Dr. Jekyll Was Quite at Ease

A FORTNIGHT LATER, by excellent good fortune, the doctor gave one of his pleasant dinners to some five or six old cronies, all intelligent, reputable men and all judges of good wine; and Mr. Utterson so contrived that he remained behind after the others had departed. This was no new arrangement, but a thing that had befallen many scores of times. Where Utterson was liked, he was liked well. Hosts loved to detain the dry lawyer, when the light-hearted and loose-tongued had already their foot on the threshold; they liked to sit a while in his unobtrusive company, practising for solitude, sobering their minds in the man's rich silence after the expense and strain of gaiety. To this rule, Dr. Jekyll was no exception; and as he now sat on the opposite side of the fire – a large, well-made, smooth-faced man of fifty, with something of a stylish cast perhaps, but every mark of capacity and kindness – you could see by his looks that he cherished for Mr. Utterson a sincere and warm affection.

"I have been wanting to speak to you, Jekyll," began the latter. "You know that will of yours?"

A close observer might have gathered that the topic was distasteful; but the doctor carried it off gaily. "My poor Utterson," said he, "you are unfortunate in such a client. I never saw a man so distressed as you were by my will; unless it were that hide-bound pedant, Lanyon, at what he called my scientific heresies. O, I know he's a good fellow – you needn't frown – an excellent fellow, and I always mean to see more of him; but a hide-bound pedant for all that; an ignorant, blatant pedant. I was never more disappointed in any man than Lanyon."

"You know I never approved of it," pursued Utterson, ruthlessly disregarding the fresh topic.

"My will? Yes, certainly, I know that," said the doctor, a trifle sharply. "You have told me so."

"Well, I tell you so again," continued the lawyer. "I have been learning something of young Hyde."

The large handsome face of Dr. Jekyll grew pale to the very lips, and there came a blackness about his eyes. "I do not care to hear more," said he. "This is a matter I thought we had agreed to drop."

"What I heard was abominable," said Utterson.

"It can make no change. You do not understand my position," returned the doctor, with a certain incoherency of manner. "I am painfully situated, Utterson; my position is a very strange – a very strange one. It is one of those affairs that cannot be mended by talking."

"Jekyll," said Utterson, "you know me: I am a man to be trusted. Make a clean breast of this in confidence; and I make no doubt I can get you out of it."

"My good Utterson," said the doctor, "this is very good of you, this is downright good of you, and I cannot find words to thank you in. I believe you fully; I would trust you before any man alive, ay, before myself, if I could make the choice; but indeed it isn't what you fancy; it is not as bad as that; and just to put your good heart at rest, I will tell you one thing: the moment I choose, I can be rid of Mr. Hyde. I give you my hand upon that; and I thank you again and again; and I will just add one little word, Utterson, that I'm sure you'll take in good part: this is a private matter, and I beg of you to let it sleep."

Utterson reflected a little, looking in the fire.

"I have no doubt you are perfectly right," he said at last, getting to his feet.

"Well, but since we have touched upon this business, and for the last time I hope," continued the doctor, "there is one point I should like you to understand. I have really a very great interest in poor Hyde. I know you have seen him; he told me so; and I fear he was rude. But I do sincerely take a great, a very great interest in that young man; and if I am taken away, Utterson, I wish you to promise me that you will bear with him and get his rights for him. I think you would, if you knew all; and it would be a weight off my mind if you would promise."

"I can't pretend that I shall ever like him," said the lawyer.

"I don't ask that," pleaded Jekyll, laying his hand upon the other's arm; "I only ask for justice; I only ask you to help him for my sake, when I am no longer here."

Utterson heaved an irrepressible sigh. "Well," said he, "I promise."

The Carew Murder Case

NEARLY A YEAR LATER, in the month of October, 18—, London was startled by a crime of singular ferocity and rendered all the more notable by the high position of the victim. The details were few and startling. A maid servant living alone in a house not far from the river, had gone upstairs to bed about eleven. Although a fog rolled over the city in the small hours, the early part of the night was cloudless, and the lane, which the maid's window overlooked, was brilliantly lit by the full moon. It seems she was romantically given, for she sat down upon her box, which stood immediately under the window, and fell into a dream of musing. Never (she used to say, with streaming tears, when she narrated that experience), never had she felt more at peace with all men or thought more kindly of the world. And as she so sat she became aware of an aged beautiful gentleman with white hair, drawing near along the lane; and advancing to meet him, another and very small gentleman, to whom at first she paid less attention. When they had come within speech (which was just under the maid's eyes) the older man bowed and accosted the other with a very pretty manner of politeness. It did not seem as if the subject of his address were of great importance; indeed, from his pointing, it sometimes appeared as if he were only inquiring his way; but the moon shone on his face as he spoke, and the girl was pleased to watch it, it seemed to breathe such an innocent and old-world kindness of disposition, yet with something high too, as of a well-founded self-content. Presently her eye wandered to the other, and she was surprised to recognise in him a certain Mr. Hyde, who had once visited her master and for whom she had conceived a dislike. He had in his hand a heavy cane, with which he was trifling; but he answered never a word, and seemed to listen with an ill-contained impatience. And then all of a sudden he broke out in a great flame of anger, stamping with his foot, brandishing the cane, and carrying on (as the maid described it) like a madman. The old gentleman took a step back, with the air of one very much surprised and a trifle hurt; and at that Mr. Hyde broke out of all bounds and clubbed him to the earth. And next moment, with ape-like fury, he was trampling his victim under foot and hailing down a storm of blows, under which the bones were audibly shattered and the body jumped upon the roadway. At the horror of these sights and sounds, the maid fainted.

It was two o'clock when she came to herself and called for the police. The murderer was gone long ago; but there lay his victim in the middle of the lane, incredibly mangled. The stick with which the deed had been done, although it was of some rare and very tough and heavy wood, had broken in the middle under the stress of this insensate cruelty; and one splintered half had rolled in the neighbouring gutter – the other, without doubt, had been carried away by the murderer. A purse and gold watch were found upon the victim: but no cards or papers, except a sealed and stamped envelope, which he had been probably carrying to the post, and which bore the name and address of Mr. Utterson.

This was brought to the lawyer the next morning, before he was out of bed; and he had no sooner seen it and been told the circumstances, than he shot out a solemn lip. "I shall say nothing till I have seen the body," said he; "this may be very serious. Have the kindness to wait while I dress." And with the same grave countenance he hurried through his breakfast and drove to the police station, whither the body had been carried. As soon as he came into the cell, he nodded.

"Yes," said he, "I recognise him. I am sorry to say that this is Sir Danvers Carew."

"Good God, sir," exclaimed the officer, "is it possible?" And the next moment his eye lighted up with professional ambition. "This will make a deal of noise," he said. "And perhaps you can help us to the man." And he briefly narrated what the maid had seen, and showed the broken stick.

Mr. Utterson had already quailed at the name of Hyde; but when the stick was laid before him, he could doubt no longer; broken and battered as it was, he recognised it for one that he had himself presented many years before to Henry Jekyll.

"Is this Mr. Hyde a person of small stature?" he inquired.

"Particularly small and particularly wicked-looking, is what the maid calls him," said the officer.

Mr. Utterson reflected; and then, raising his head, "If you will come with me in my cab," he said, "I think I can take you to his house."

It was by this time about nine in the morning, and the first fog of the season. A great chocolate-coloured pall lowered over heaven, but the wind was continually charging and routing these embattled vapours; so that as the cab crawled from street to street, Mr. Utterson beheld a marvelous number of degrees and hues of twilight; for here it would be dark like the back-end of evening; and there would be a glow of a rich, lurid brown, like the light of some strange conflagration; and here, for a moment, the fog would be quite broken up, and a haggard shaft of daylight would glance in between the swirling wreaths. The dismal quarter of Soho seen under these changing glimpses, with its muddy ways, and slatternly passengers, and its lamps, which had never been extinguished or had been kindled afresh to combat this mournful reinvasion of darkness, seemed, in the lawyer's eyes, like a district of some city in a nightmare. The thoughts of his mind, besides, were of the gloomiest dye; and when he glanced at the companion of his drive, he was conscious of some touch of that terror of the law and the law's officers, which may at times assail the most honest.

As the cab drew up before the address indicated, the fog lifted a little and showed him a dingy street, a gin palace, a low French eating house, a shop for the retail of penny numbers and twopenny salads, many ragged children huddled in the doorways, and many women of many different nationalities passing out, key in hand, to have a morning glass; and the next moment the fog settled down again upon that part, as brown as umber, and cut him off from his blackguardly surroundings. This was the home of Henry Jekyll's favourite; of a man who was heir to a quarter of a million sterling.

An ivory-faced and silvery-haired old woman opened the door. She had an evil face, smoothed by hypocrisy: but her manners were excellent. Yes, she said, this was Mr. Hyde's, but he was not at home; he had been in that night very late, but he had gone away again in less than an hour; there was nothing strange in that; his habits were very irregular, and he was often absent; for instance, it was nearly two months since she had seen him till yesterday.

"Very well, then, we wish to see his rooms," said the lawyer; and when the woman began to declare it was impossible, "I had better tell you who this person is," he added. "This is Inspector Newcomen of Scotland Yard."

A flash of odious joy appeared upon the woman's face. "Ah!" said she, "he is in trouble! What has he done?"

Mr. Utterson and the inspector exchanged glances. "He don't seem a very popular character," observed the latter. "And now, my good woman, just let me and this gentleman have a look about us."

In the whole extent of the house, which but for the old woman remained otherwise empty, Mr. Hyde had only used a couple of rooms; but these were furnished with luxury and good taste. A closet was filled with wine; the plate was of silver, the napery elegant; a good picture hung upon the walls, a gift (as Utterson supposed) from Henry Jekyll, who was much of a connoisseur; and the carpets were of many plies and agreeable in colour. At this moment, however, the rooms bore every mark of having been recently and hurriedly ransacked; clothes lay about the floor, with their pockets inside out; lock-fast drawers stood open; and on the hearth there lay a pile of grey ashes, as though many papers had been burned. From these embers the inspector disinterred the butt end of a green cheque book, which had resisted the action of the fire; the other half of the stick was found behind the door; and as this clinched his suspicions, the officer declared himself delighted. A visit to the bank, where several thousand pounds were found to be lying to the murderer's credit, completed his gratification.

"You may depend upon it, sir," he told Mr. Utterson: "I have him in my hand. He must have lost his head, or he never would have left the stick or, above all, burned the cheque book. Why, money's life to the man. We have nothing to do but wait for him at the bank, and get out the handbills."

This last, however, was not so easy of accomplishment; for Mr. Hyde had numbered few familiars – even the master of the servant maid had only seen him twice; his family could nowhere be traced; he had never been photographed; and the few who could describe him differed widely, as common observers will. Only on one point were they agreed; and that was the haunting sense of unexpressed deformity with which the fugitive impressed his beholders.

Incident of the Letter

IT WAS LATE in the afternoon, when Mr. Utterson found his way to Dr. Jekyll's door, where he was at once admitted by Poole, and carried down by the kitchen offices and across a yard which had once been a garden, to the building which was indifferently known as the laboratory or dissecting rooms. The doctor had bought the house from the heirs of a celebrated surgeon; and his own tastes being rather chemical than anatomical, had changed the destination of the block at the bottom of the garden. It was the first time that the lawyer had been received in that part of his friend's quarters; and he eyed the dingy, windowless structure with curiosity, and gazed round with a distasteful sense of strangeness as he crossed the theatre, once crowded with eager students and now lying gaunt and silent, the tables laden with chemical apparatus, the floor strewn with crates and littered with packing straw, and the light falling dimly through the foggy cupola. At the further end, a flight of stairs mounted to a door covered with red baize; and through this, Mr. Utterson was at last received into the doctor's cabinet. It was a large room fitted round with glass presses, furnished, among other things, with a cheval-glass and a business table, and looking out upon the court by three dusty windows barred with iron. The fire burned in the grate; a lamp was set lighted on the chimney shelf, for even in the houses the fog began to lie thickly; and there, close up to the warmth, sat Dr. Jekyll, looking deathly sick. He did not rise to meet his visitor, but held out a cold hand and bade him welcome in a changed voice.

"And now," said Mr. Utterson, as soon as Poole had left them, "you have heard the news?"

The doctor shuddered. "They were crying it in the square," he said. "I heard them in my dining room."

"One word," said the lawyer. "Carew was my client, but so are you, and I want to know what I am doing. You have not been mad enough to hide this fellow?"

"Utterson, I swear to God," cried the doctor, "I swear to God I will never set eyes on him again. I bind my honour to you that I am done with him in this world. It is all at an end. And indeed he does not want my help; you do not know him as I do; he is safe, he is quite safe; mark my words, he will never more be heard of."

The lawyer listened gloomily; he did not like his friend's feverish manner. "You seem pretty sure of him," said he; "and for your sake, I hope you may be right. If it came to a trial, your name might appear."

"I am quite sure of him," replied Jekyll; "I have grounds for certainty that I cannot share with anyone. But there is one thing on which you may advise me. I have – I have received a letter; and I am at a loss whether I should show it to the police. I should like to leave it in your hands, Utterson; you would judge wisely, I am sure; I have so great a trust in you."

"You fear, I suppose, that it might lead to his detection?" asked the lawyer.

"No," said the other. "I cannot say that I care what becomes of Hyde; I am quite done with him. I was thinking of my own character, which this hateful business has rather exposed."

Utterson ruminated awhile; he was surprised at his friend's selfishness, and yet relieved by it. "Well," said he, at last, "let me see the letter."

The letter was written in an odd, upright hand and signed 'Edward Hyde': and it signified, briefly enough, that the writer's benefactor, Dr. Jekyll, whom he had long so unworthily repaid for a thousand generosities, need labour under no alarm for his safety, as he had means of escape on which he placed a sure dependence. The lawyer liked this letter well enough; it put a better colour on the intimacy than he had looked for; and he blamed himself for some of his past suspicions.

"Have you the envelope?" he asked.

"I burned it," replied Jekyll, "before I thought what I was about. But it bore no postmark. The note was handed in."

"Shall I keep this and sleep upon it?" asked Utterson.

"I wish you to judge for me entirely," was the reply. "I have lost confidence in myself."

"Well, I shall consider," returned the lawyer. "And now one word more: it was Hyde who dictated the terms in your will about that disappearance?"

The doctor seemed seized with a qualm of faintness; he shut his mouth tight and nodded.

"I knew it," said Utterson. "He meant to murder you. You had a fine escape."

"I have had what is far more to the purpose," returned the doctor solemnly: "I have had a lesson— O God, Utterson, what a lesson I have had!" And he covered his face for a moment with his hands.

On his way out, the lawyer stopped and had a word or two with Poole. "By the bye," said he, "there was a letter handed in today: what was the messenger like?" But Poole was positive nothing had come except by post; "and only circulars by that," he added.

This news sent off the visitor with his fears renewed. Plainly the letter had come by the laboratory door; possibly, indeed, it had been written in the cabinet; and if that were so, it must be differently judged, and handled with the more caution. The newsboys, as he went, were crying themselves hoarse along the footways: "Special edition. Shocking murder of an M.P." That was the funeral oration of one friend and client; and he could not help a certain apprehension lest the good name of another should be sucked down in the eddy of the scandal. It was, at least, a ticklish decision that he had to make; and self-reliant as he was by habit, he began to cherish a longing for advice. It was not to be had directly; but perhaps, he thought, it might be fished for.

Presently after, he sat on one side of his own hearth, with Mr. Guest, his head clerk, upon the other, and midway between, at a nicely calculated distance from the fire, a bottle of a particular old wine that had long dwelt unsunned in the foundations of his house. The fog still slept on the wing above the drowned city, where the lamps glimmered like carbuncles; and through the muffle and smother of these fallen clouds, the procession of the town's life was still rolling in through the great arteries with a sound as of a mighty wind. But the room was gay with firelight. In the bottle the acids were long ago resolved; the imperial dye had softened with time, as the colour grows richer in stained windows; and the glow of hot autumn afternoons on hillside vineyards, was ready to be set free and to disperse the fogs of London. Insensibly the lawyer melted. There was no man from whom he kept fewer secrets than Mr. Guest; and he was not always sure that he kept as many as he meant. Guest had often been on business to the doctor's; he knew Poole; he could scarce have failed to hear of Mr. Hyde's familiarity about the house;

he might draw conclusions: was it not as well, then, that he should see a letter which put that mystery to right? And above all since Guest, being a great student and critic of handwriting, would consider the step natural and obliging? The clerk, besides, was a man of counsel; he could scarce read so strange a document without dropping a remark; and by that remark Mr. Utterson might shape his future course.

"This is a sad business about Sir Danvers," he said.

"Yes, sir, indeed. It has elicited a great deal of public feeling," returned Guest. "The man, of course, was mad."

"I should like to hear your views on that," replied Utterson. "I have a document here in his handwriting; it is between ourselves, for I scarce know what to do about it; it is an ugly business at the best. But there it is; quite in your way: a murderer's autograph."

Guest's eyes brightened, and he sat down at once and studied it with passion. "No sir," he said: "not mad; but it is an odd hand."

"And by all accounts a very odd writer," added the lawyer.

Just then the servant entered with a note.

"Is that from Dr. Jekyll, sir?" inquired the clerk. "I thought I knew the writing. Anything private, Mr. Utterson?"

"Only an invitation to dinner. Why? Do you want to see it?"

"One moment. I thank you, sir"; and the clerk laid the two sheets of paper alongside and sedulously compared their contents. "Thank you, sir," he said at last, returning both; "it's a very interesting autograph."

There was a pause, during which Mr. Utterson struggled with himself. "Why did you compare them, Guest?" he inquired suddenly.

"Well, sir," returned the clerk, "there's a rather singular resemblance; the two hands are in many points identical: only differently sloped."

"Rather quaint," said Utterson.

"It is, as you say, rather quaint," returned Guest.

"I wouldn't speak of this note, you know," said the master.

"No, sir," said the clerk. "I understand."

But no sooner was Mr. Utterson alone that night, than he locked the note into his safe, where it reposed from that time forward. "What!" he thought. "Henry Jekyll forge for a murderer!" And his blood ran cold in his veins.

Incident of Dr. Lanyon

TIME RAN ON; thousands of pounds were offered in reward, for the death of Sir Danvers was resented as a public injury; but Mr. Hyde had disappeared out of the ken of the police as though he had never existed. Much of his past was unearthed, indeed, and all disreputable: tales came out of the man's cruelty, at once so callous and violent; of his vile life, of his strange associates, of the hatred that seemed to have surrounded his career; but of his present whereabouts, not a whisper. From the time he had left the house in Soho on the morning of the murder, he was simply blotted out; and gradually, as time drew on, Mr. Utterson began to recover from the hotness of his alarm, and to grow more at quiet with himself. The death of Sir Danvers was, to his way of thinking, more than paid for by the disappearance of Mr. Hyde. Now that that evil influence had been withdrawn, a new life began for Dr. Jekyll. He came out of his seclusion, renewed relations with his friends, became once more their familiar guest and entertainer; and whilst he had always been known for charities, he was now no less distinguished for religion. He was busy, he was much in the open air, he did good; his face seemed to open and brighten, as if with an inward consciousness of service; and for more than two months, the doctor was at peace.

On the 8th of January Utterson had dined at the doctor's with a small party; Lanyon had been there; and the face of the host had looked from one to the other as in the old days when the trio were inseparable friends. On the 12th, and again on the 14th, the door was shut against the lawyer. "The doctor was confined to the house," Poole said, "and saw no one." On the 15th, he tried again, and was again refused; and having now been used for the last two months to see his friend almost daily, he found this return of solitude to weigh upon his spirits. The fifth night he had in Guest to dine with him; and the sixth he betook himself to Dr. Lanyon's.

There at least he was not denied admittance; but when he came in, he was shocked at the change which had taken place in the doctor's appearance. He had his death-warrant written legibly upon his face. The rosy man had grown pale; his flesh had fallen away; he was visibly balder and older; and yet it was not so much these tokens of a swift physical decay that arrested the lawyer's notice, as a look in the eye and quality of manner that seemed to testify to some deep-seated terror of the mind. It was unlikely that the doctor should fear death; and yet that was what Utterson was tempted to suspect. "Yes," he thought; "he is a doctor, he must know his own state and that his days are counted; and the knowledge is more than he can bear." And yet when Utterson remarked on his ill looks, it was with an air of great firmness that Lanyon declared himself a doomed man.

"I have had a shock," he said, "and I shall never recover. It is a question of weeks. Well, life has been pleasant; I liked it; yes, sir, I used to like it. I sometimes think if we knew all, we should be more glad to get away."

"Jekyll is ill, too," observed Utterson. "Have you seen him?"

But Lanyon's face changed, and he held up a trembling hand. "I wish to see or hear no more of Dr. Jekyll," he said in a loud, unsteady voice. "I am quite done with that person; and I beg that you will spare me any allusion to one whom I regard as dead."

"Tut, tut!" said Mr. Utterson; and then after a considerable pause, "Can't I do anything?" he inquired. "We are three very old friends, Lanyon; we shall not live to make others."

"Nothing can be done," returned Lanyon; "ask himself."

"He will not see me," said the lawyer.

"I am not surprised at that," was the reply. "Some day, Utterson, after I am dead, you may perhaps come to learn the right and wrong of this. I cannot tell you. And in the meantime, if you can sit and talk with me of other things, for God's sake, stay and do so; but if you cannot keep clear of this accursed topic, then in God's name, go, for I cannot bear it."

As soon as he got home, Utterson sat down and wrote to Jekyll, complaining of his exclusion from the house, and asking the cause of this unhappy break with Lanyon; and the next day brought him a long answer, often very pathetically worded, and sometimes darkly mysterious in drift. The quarrel with Lanyon was incurable. "I do not blame our old friend," Jekyll wrote, "but I share his view that we must never meet. I mean from henceforth to lead a life of extreme seclusion; you must not be surprised, nor must you doubt my friendship, if my door is often shut even to you. You must suffer me to go my own dark way. I have brought on myself a punishment and a danger that I cannot name. If I am the chief of sinners, I am the chief of sufferers also. I could not think that this earth contained a place for sufferings and terrors so unmanning; and you can do but one thing, Utterson, to lighten this destiny, and that is to respect my silence."

Utterson was amazed; the dark influence of Hyde had been withdrawn, the doctor had returned to his old tasks and amities; a week ago, the prospect had smiled with every promise of a cheerful and an honoured age; and now in a moment, friendship, and peace of mind, and the whole tenor of his life were wrecked. So great and unprepared a change pointed to madness; but in view of Lanyon's manner and words, there must lie for it some deeper ground.

A week afterwards Dr. Lanyon took to his bed, and in something less than a fortnight he was dead. The night after the funeral, at which he had been sadly affected, Utterson locked the door of his business room, and sitting there by the light of a melancholy candle, drew out and set before him an envelope addressed by the hand and sealed with the seal of his dead friend. "PRIVATE: for the hands of G.J. Utterson ALONE, and in case of his predecease *to be destroyed unread*," so it was emphatically superscribed; and the lawyer dreaded to behold the contents. "I have buried one friend today," he thought: "what if this should cost me another?" And then he condemned the fear as a disloyalty, and broke the seal. Within there was another enclosure, likewise sealed, and marked upon the cover as "not to be opened till the death or disappearance of Dr. Henry Jekyll." Utterson could not trust his eyes. Yes, it was disappearance; here again, as in the mad will which he had long ago restored to its author, here again were the idea of a disappearance and the name of Henry Jekyll bracketted. But in the will, that idea had sprung from the sinister suggestion of the man Hyde; it was set there with a purpose all too plain and horrible. Written by the hand of Lanyon, what should it mean? A great curiosity came on the trustee, to disregard the prohibition and dive at once to the bottom of these mysteries; but professional honour and faith to his dead friend were stringent obligations; and the packet slept in the inmost corner of his private safe.

It is one thing to mortify curiosity, another to conquer it; and it may be doubted if, from that day forth, Utterson desired the society of his surviving friend with the same eagerness. He thought of him kindly; but his thoughts were disquieted and fearful. He went to call indeed; but he was perhaps relieved to be denied admittance; perhaps, in his heart, he preferred to speak with Poole upon the doorstep and surrounded by the air and sounds of the open city, rather than to be admitted into that house of voluntary bondage, and to sit and speak with its inscrutable recluse. Poole had, indeed, no very pleasant news to communicate. The doctor, it appeared, now more than ever confined himself to the cabinet over the laboratory, where he would sometimes even sleep; he was out of spirits, he had grown very silent, he did not read; it seemed as if he had something on his mind. Utterson became so used to the unvarying character of these reports, that he fell off little by little in the frequency of his visits.

Incident at the Window

IT CHANCED on Sunday, when Mr. Utterson was on his usual walk with Mr. Enfield, that their way lay once again through the by-street; and that when they came in front of the door, both stopped to gaze on it.

"Well," said Enfield, "that story's at an end at least. We shall never see more of Mr. Hyde."

"I hope not," said Utterson. "Did I ever tell you that I once saw him, and shared your feeling of repulsion?"

"It was impossible to do the one without the other," returned Enfield. "And by the way, what an ass you must have thought me, not to know that this was a back way to Dr. Jekyll's! It was partly your own fault that I found it out, even when I did."

"So you found it out, did you?" said Utterson. "But if that be so, we may step into the court and take a look at the windows. To tell you the truth, I am uneasy about poor Jekyll; and even outside, I feel as if the presence of a friend might do him good."

The court was very cool and a little damp, and full of premature twilight, although the sky, high up overhead, was still bright with sunset. The middle one of the three windows was halfway open; and sitting close beside it, taking the air with an infinite sadness of mien, like some disconsolate prisoner, Utterson saw Dr. Jekyll.

"What! Jekyll!" he cried. "I trust you are better."

"I am very low, Utterson," replied the doctor drearily, "very low. It will not last long, thank God."

"You stay too much indoors," said the lawyer. "You should be out, whipping up the circulation like Mr. Enfield and me. (This is my cousin – Mr. Enfield – Dr. Jekyll.) Come now; get your hat and take a quick turn with us."

"You are very good," sighed the other. "I should like to very much; but no, no, no, it is quite impossible; I dare not. But indeed, Utterson, I am very glad to see you; this is really a great pleasure; I would ask you and Mr. Enfield up, but the place is really not fit."

"Why, then," said the lawyer, good-naturedly, "the best thing we can do is to stay down here and speak with you from where we are."

"That is just what I was about to venture to propose," returned the doctor with a smile. But the words were hardly uttered, before the smile was struck out of his face and succeeded by an expression of such abject terror and despair, as froze the very blood of the two gentlemen below. They saw it but for a glimpse for the window was instantly thrust down; but that glimpse had been sufficient, and they turned and left the court without a word. In silence, too, they traversed the by-street; and it was not until they had come into a neighbouring thoroughfare, where even upon a Sunday there were still some stirrings of life, that Mr. Utterson at last turned and looked at his companion. They were both pale, and there was an answering horror in their eyes.

"God forgive us, God forgive us," said Mr. Utterson.

But Mr. Enfield only nodded his head very seriously, and walked on once more in silence.

The Last Night

MR. UTTERSON was sitting by his fireside one evening after dinner, when he was surprised to receive a visit from Poole.

"Bless me, Poole, what brings you here?" he cried; and then taking a second look at him, "What ails you?" he added; "is the doctor ill?"

"Mr. Utterson," said the man, "there is something wrong."

"Take a seat, and here is a glass of wine for you," said the lawyer. "Now, take your time, and tell me plainly what you want."

"You know the doctor's ways, sir," replied Poole, "and how he shuts himself up. Well, he's shut up again in the cabinet, and I don't like it, sir – I wish I may die if I like it. Mr. Utterson, sir, I'm afraid."

"Now, my good man," said the lawyer, "be explicit. What are you afraid of?"

"I've been afraid for about a week," returned Poole, doggedly disregarding the question, "and I can bear it no more."

The man's appearance amply bore out his words; his manner was altered for the worse; and except for the moment when he had first announced his terror, he had not once looked the lawyer in the face. Even now, he sat with the glass of wine untasted on his knee, and his eyes directed to a corner of the floor. "I can bear it no more," he repeated.

"Come," said the lawyer, "I see you have some good reason, Poole; I see there is something seriously amiss. Try to tell me what it is."

"I think there's been foul play," said Poole, hoarsely.

"Foul play!" cried the lawyer, a good deal frightened and rather inclined to be irritated in consequence. "What foul play! What does the man mean?"

"I daren't say, sir," was the answer; "but will you come along with me and see for yourself?"

Mr. Utterson's only answer was to rise and get his hat and greatcoat; but he observed with wonder the greatness of the relief that appeared upon the butler's face, and perhaps with no less, that the wine was still untasted when he set it down to follow.

It was a wild, cold, seasonable night of March, with a pale moon, lying on her back as though the wind had tilted her, and flying wrack of the most diaphanous and lawny texture. The wind made talking difficult, and flecked the blood into the face. It seemed to have swept the streets unusually bare of passengers, besides; for Mr. Utterson thought he had never seen that part of London so deserted. He could have wished it otherwise; never in his life had he been conscious of so sharp a wish to see and touch his fellow creatures; for struggle as he might, there was borne in upon his mind a crushing anticipation of calamity. The square, when they got there, was full of wind and dust, and the thin trees in the garden were lashing themselves along the railing. Poole, who had kept all the way a pace or two ahead, now pulled up in the middle of the pavement, and in spite of the biting weather, took off his hat and mopped his brow with a red pocket-handkerchief. But for all the hurry of his coming, these were not the dews of exertion that he wiped away, but the moisture of some strangling anguish; for his face was white and his voice, when he spoke, harsh and broken.

"Well, sir," he said, "here we are, and God grant there be nothing wrong."

"Amen, Poole," said the lawyer.

Thereupon the servant knocked in a very guarded manner; the door was opened on the chain; and a voice asked from within, "Is that you, Poole?"

"It's all right," said Poole. "Open the door."

The hall, when they entered it, was brightly lighted up; the fire was built high; and about the hearth the whole of the servants, men and women, stood huddled together like a flock of sheep. At the sight of Mr. Utterson, the housemaid broke into hysterical whimpering; and the cook, crying out "Bless God! It's Mr. Utterson," ran forward as if to take him in her arms.

"What, what? Are you all here?" said the lawyer peevishly. "Very irregular, very unseemly; your master would be far from pleased."

"They're all afraid," said Poole.

Blank silence followed, no one protesting; only the maid lifted her voice and now wept loudly.

"Hold your tongue!" Poole said to her, with a ferocity of accent that testified to his own jangled nerves; and indeed, when the girl had so suddenly raised the note of her lamentation, they had all started and turned towards the inner door with faces of dreadful expectation. "And now," continued the butler, addressing the knife-boy, "reach me a candle, and we'll get this through hands at once." And then he begged Mr. Utterson to follow him, and led the way to the back garden.

"Now, sir," said he, "you come as gently as you can. I want you to hear, and I don't want you to be heard. And see here, sir, if by any chance he was to ask you in, don't go."

Mr. Utterson's nerves, at this unlooked-for termination, gave a jerk that nearly threw him from his balance; but he recollected his courage and followed the butler into the laboratory building through the surgical theatre, with its lumber of crates and bottles, to the foot of the stair. Here Poole motioned him to stand on one side and listen; while he himself, setting down the candle and making a great and obvious call on his resolution, mounted the steps and knocked with a somewhat uncertain hand on the red baize of the cabinet door.

"Mr. Utterson, sir, asking to see you," he called; and even as he did so, once more violently signed to the lawyer to give ear.

A voice answered from within: "Tell him I cannot see anyone," it said complainingly.

"Thank you, sir," said Poole, with a note of something like triumph in his voice; and taking up his candle, he led Mr. Utterson back across the yard and into the great kitchen, where the fire was out and the beetles were leaping on the floor.

"Sir," he said, looking Mr. Utterson in the eyes, "Was that my master's voice?"

"It seems much changed," replied the lawyer, very pale, but giving look for look.

"Changed? Well, yes, I think so," said the butler. "Have I been twenty years in this man's house, to be deceived about his voice? No, sir; master's made away with; he was made away with eight days ago, when we heard him cry out upon the name of God; and *who's* in there instead of him, and *why* it stays there, is a thing that cries to Heaven, Mr. Utterson!"

"This is a very strange tale, Poole; this is rather a wild tale my man," said Mr. Utterson, biting his finger. "Suppose it were as you suppose, supposing Dr. Jekyll to have been – well, murdered, what could induce the murderer to stay? That won't hold water; it doesn't commend itself to reason."

"Well, Mr. Utterson, you are a hard man to satisfy, but I'll do it yet," said Poole. "All this last week (you must know) him, or it, whatever it is that lives in that cabinet, has been crying night and day for some sort of medicine and cannot get it to his mind. It was sometimes his way – the master's, that is – to write his orders on a sheet of paper and throw it on the stair. We've had nothing else this week back; nothing but papers, and a closed door, and the very meals left there to be smuggled in when nobody was looking. Well, sir, every day, ay, and twice and thrice in the same day, there have been orders and complaints, and I have been sent flying to all the wholesale chemists in town. Every time I brought the stuff back, there would be another paper telling me to return it, because it was not pure, and another order to a different firm. This drug is wanted bitter bad, sir, whatever for."

"Have you any of these papers?" asked Mr. Utterson.

Poole felt in his pocket and handed out a crumpled note, which the lawyer, bending nearer to the candle, carefully examined. Its contents ran thus: "Dr. Jekyll presents his compliments to Messrs. Maw. He assures them that their last sample is impure and quite useless for his present purpose. In the year 18—, Dr. J. purchased a somewhat large quantity from Messrs. M. He now begs them to search with most sedulous care, and should any of the same quality be left, forward it to him at once. Expense is no consideration. The importance of this to Dr. J. can hardly be exaggerated." So far the letter had run composedly enough, but here with a sudden splutter of the pen, the writer's emotion had broken loose. "For God's-sake," he added, "find me some of the old."

"This is a strange note," said Mr. Utterson; and then sharply, "How do you come to have it open?"

"The man at Maw's was main angry, sir, and he threw it back to me like so much dirt," returned Poole.

"This is unquestionably the doctor's hand, do you know?" resumed the lawyer.

"I thought it looked like it," said the servant rather sulkily; and then, with another voice, "But what matters hand of write?" he said. "I've seen him!"

"Seen him?" repeated Mr. Utterson. "Well?"

"That's it!" said Poole. "It was this way. I came suddenly into the theatre from the garden. It seems he had slipped out to look for this drug or whatever it is; for the cabinet door was open, and there he was at the far end of the room digging among the crates. He looked up when I came in, gave a kind of cry, and whipped upstairs into the cabinet. It was but for one minute that I saw him, but the hair stood upon my head like quills. Sir, if that was my master, why had he a mask upon his face? If it was my master, why did he cry out like a rat, and run from me? I have served him long enough. And then..." The man paused and passed his hand over his face.

"These are all very strange circumstances," said Mr. Utterson, "but I think I begin to see daylight. Your master, Poole, is plainly seized with one of those maladies that both torture and deform the sufferer; hence, for aught I know, the alteration of his voice; hence the mask and the avoidance of his friends; hence his eagerness to find this drug, by means of which the poor soul retains some hope of ultimate recovery – God grant that he be not deceived! There is my explanation; it is sad enough, Poole, ay, and appalling to consider; but it is plain and natural, hangs well together, and delivers us from all exorbitant alarms."

"Sir," said the butler, turning to a sort of mottled pallor, "that thing was not my master, and there's the truth. My master" – here he looked round him and began to whisper – "is a tall, fine build of a man, and this was more of a dwarf." Utterson attempted to protest. "O, sir," cried Poole, "do you think I do not know my master after twenty years? Do you think I do not know where his head comes to in the cabinet door, where I saw him every morning of my life? No, sir, that thing in the mask was never Dr. Jekyll – God knows what it was, but it was never Dr. Jekyll; and it is the belief of my heart that there was murder done."

"Poole," replied the lawyer, "if you say that, it will become my duty to make certain. Much as I desire to spare your master's feelings, much as I am puzzled by this note which seems to prove him to be still alive, I shall consider it my duty to break in that door."

"Ah, Mr. Utterson, that's talking!" cried the butler.

"And now comes the second question," resumed Utterson: "Who is going to do it?"

"Why, you and me, sir," was the undaunted reply.

"That's very well said," returned the lawyer; "and whatever comes of it, I shall make it my business to see you are no loser."

"There is an axe in the theatre," continued Poole, "and you might take the kitchen poker for yourself."

The lawyer took that rude but weighty instrument into his hand, and balanced it. "Do you know, Poole," he said, looking up, "that you and I are about to place ourselves in a position of some peril?"

"You may say so, sir, indeed," returned the butler.

"It is well, then that we should be frank," said the other. "We both think more than we have said; let us make a clean breast. This masked figure that you saw, did you recognise it?"

"Well, sir, it went so quick, and the creature was so doubled up, that I could hardly swear to that," was the answer. "But if you mean, was it Mr. Hyde? – why, yes, I think it was! You see, it was much of the same bigness; and it had the same quick, light way with it; and then who else could have got in by the laboratory door? You have not forgot, sir, that at the time of the murder he had still the key with him? But that's not all. I don't know, Mr. Utterson, if you ever met this Mr. Hyde?"

"Yes," said the lawyer, "I once spoke with him."

"Then you must know as well as the rest of us that there was something queer about that gentleman – something that gave a man a turn – I don't know rightly how to say it, sir, beyond this: that you felt in your marrow kind of cold and thin."

"I own I felt something of what you describe," said Mr. Utterson.

"Quite so, sir," returned Poole. "Well, when that masked thing like a monkey jumped from among the chemicals and whipped into the cabinet, it went down my spine like ice. O, I know it's not evidence, Mr. Utterson; I'm book-learned enough for that; but a man has his feelings, and I give you my bible-word it was Mr. Hyde!"

"Ay, ay," said the lawyer. "My fears incline to the same point. Evil, I fear, founded – evil was sure to come – of that connection. Ay truly, I believe you; I believe poor Harry is killed; and I believe his murderer (for what purpose, God alone can tell) is still lurking in his victim's room. Well, let our name be vengeance. Call Bradshaw."

The footman came at the summons, very white and nervous.

"Pull yourself together, Bradshaw," said the lawyer. "This suspense, I know, is telling upon all of you; but it is now our intention to make an end of it. Poole, here, and I are going to force our way into the cabinet. If all is well, my shoulders are broad enough to bear the blame. Meanwhile, lest anything should really be amiss, or any malefactor seek to escape by the back, you and the boy must go round the corner with a pair of good sticks and take your post at the laboratory door. We give you ten minutes to get to your stations."

As Bradshaw left, the lawyer looked at his watch. "And now, Poole, let us get to ours," he said; and taking the poker under his arm, led the way into the yard. The scud had banked over the moon, and it was now quite dark. The wind, which only broke in puffs and draughts into that deep well of building, tossed the light of the candle to and fro about their steps, until they came into the shelter of the theatre, where they sat down silently to wait. London hummed solemnly all around; but nearer at hand, the stillness was only broken by the sounds of a footfall moving to and fro along the cabinet floor.

"So it will walk all day, sir," whispered Poole; "ay, and the better part of the night. Only when a new sample comes from the chemist, there's a bit of a break. Ah, it's an ill conscience that's such an enemy to rest! Ah, sir, there's blood foully shed in every step of it! But hark again, a little closer – put your heart in your ears, Mr. Utterson, and tell me, is that the doctor's foot?"

The steps fell lightly and oddly, with a certain swing, for all they went so slowly; it was different indeed from the heavy creaking tread of Henry Jekyll. Utterson sighed. "Is there never anything else?" he asked.

Poole nodded. "Once," he said. "Once I heard it weeping!"

"Weeping? How that?" said the lawyer, conscious of a sudden chill of horror.

"Weeping like a woman or a lost soul," said the butler. "I came away with that upon my heart, that I could have wept too."

But now the ten minutes drew to an end. Poole disinterred the axe from under a stack of packing straw; the candle was set upon the nearest table to light them to the attack; and they drew near with bated breath to where that patient foot was still going up and down, up and down, in the quiet of the night.

"Jekyll," cried Utterson, with a loud voice, "I demand to see you." He paused a moment, but there came no reply. "I give you fair warning, our suspicions are aroused, and I must and shall see you," he resumed; "if not by fair means, then by foul – if not of your consent, then by brute force!"

"Utterson," said the voice, "for God's sake, have mercy!"

"Ah, that's not Jekyll's voice – it's Hyde's!" cried Utterson. "Down with the door, Poole!"

Poole swung the axe over his shoulder; the blow shook the building, and the red baize door leaped against the lock and hinges. A dismal screech, as of mere animal terror, rang from the cabinet. Up went the axe again, and again the panels crashed and the frame bounded; four times the blow fell; but the wood was tough and the fittings were of excellent workmanship; and it was not until the fifth, that the lock burst and the wreck of the door fell inwards on the carpet.

The besiegers, appalled by their own riot and the stillness that had succeeded, stood back a little and peered in. There lay the cabinet before their eyes in the quiet lamplight, a good fire glowing and chattering on the hearth, the kettle singing its thin strain, a drawer or two open, papers neatly set forth on the business table, and nearer the fire, the things laid out for tea; the quietest room, you would have said, and, but for the glazed presses full of chemicals, the most commonplace that night in London.

Right in the middle there lay the body of a man sorely contorted and still twitching. They drew near on tiptoe, turned it on its back and beheld the face of Edward Hyde. He was dressed in clothes far too large for him, clothes of the doctor's bigness; the cords of his face still moved with a semblance of life, but life was quite gone; and by the crushed phial in the hand and the strong smell of kernels that hung upon the air, Utterson knew that he was looking on the body of a self-destroyer.

"We have come too late," he said sternly, "whether to save or punish. Hyde is gone to his account; and it only remains for us to find the body of your master."

The far greater proportion of the building was occupied by the theatre, which filled almost the whole ground storey and was lighted from above, and by the cabinet, which formed an upper storey at one end and looked upon the court. A corridor joined the theatre to the door on the by-street; and with this the cabinet communicated separately by a second flight of stairs. There were besides a few dark closets and a spacious cellar. All these they now thoroughly examined. Each closet needed but a glance, for all were empty, and all, by the dust that fell from their doors, had stood long unopened. The cellar, indeed, was filled with crazy lumber, mostly dating from the times of the surgeon who was Jekyll's predecessor; but even as they opened the door they were advertised of the uselessness of further search, by the fall of a perfect mat of cobweb which had for years sealed up the entrance. Nowhere was there any trace of Henry Jekyll, dead or alive.

Poole stamped on the flags of the corridor. "He must be buried here," he said, hearkening to the sound.

"Or he may have fled," said Utterson, and he turned to examine the door in the by-street. It was locked; and lying near by on the flags, they found the key, already stained with rust.

"This does not look like use," observed the lawyer.

"Use!" echoed Poole. "Do you not see, sir, it is broken? Much as if a man had stamped on it."

"Ay," continued Utterson, "and the fractures, too, are rusty." The two men looked at each other with a scare. "This is beyond me, Poole," said the lawyer. "Let us go back to the cabinet."

They mounted the stair in silence, and still with an occasional awestruck glance at the dead body, proceeded more thoroughly to examine the contents of the cabinet. At one table, there were traces of chemical work, various measured heaps of some white salt being laid on glass saucers, as though for an experiment in which the unhappy man had been prevented.

"That is the same drug that I was always bringing him," said Poole; and even as he spoke, the kettle with a startling noise boiled over.

This brought them to the fireside, where the easy-chair was drawn cosily up, and the tea things stood ready to the sitter's elbow, the very sugar in the cup. There were several books on a shelf; one lay beside the tea things open, and Utterson was amazed to find it a copy of a pious work, for which Jekyll had several times expressed a great esteem, annotated, in his own hand with startling blasphemies.

Next, in the course of their review of the chamber, the searchers came to the cheval-glass, into whose depths they looked with an involuntary horror. But it was so turned as to show them nothing but the rosy glow playing on the roof, the fire sparkling in a hundred repetitions along the glazed front of the presses, and their own pale and fearful countenances stooping to look in.

"This glass has seen some strange things, sir," whispered Poole.

"And surely none stranger than itself," echoed the lawyer in the same tones. "For what did Jekyll" – he caught himself up at the word with a start, and then conquering the weakness – "what could Jekyll want with it?" he said.

"You may say that!" said Poole.

Next they turned to the business table. On the desk, among the neat array of papers, a large envelope was uppermost, and bore, in the doctor's hand, the name of Mr. Utterson. The lawyer unsealed it, and several enclosures fell to the floor. The first was a will, drawn in the same eccentric terms as the one which he had returned six months before, to serve as a testament in case of death and as a deed of gift in case of disappearance; but in place of the name of Edward Hyde, the lawyer, with indescribable amazement read the name of Gabriel John Utterson. He looked at Poole, and then back at the paper, and last of all at the dead malefactor stretched upon the carpet.

"My head goes round," he said. "He has been all these days in possession; he had no cause to like me; he must have raged to see himself displaced; and he has not destroyed this document."

He caught up the next paper; it was a brief note in the doctor's hand and dated at the top. "O Poole!" the lawyer cried, "he was alive and here this day. He cannot have been disposed of in so short a space; he must be still alive, he must have fled! And then, why fled? And how? and in that case, can we venture to declare this suicide? O, we must be careful. I foresee that we may yet involve your master in some dire catastrophe."

"Why don't you read it, sir?" asked Poole.

"Because I fear," replied the lawyer solemnly. "God grant I have no cause for it!" And with that he brought the paper to his eyes and read as follows:

> *My dear Utterson, – When this shall fall into your hands, I shall have disappeared, under what circumstances I have not the penetration to foresee, but my instinct and all the circumstances of my nameless situation tell me that the end is sure and must be early. Go then, and first read the narrative which Lanyon warned me he was to place in your hands; and if you care to hear more, turn to the confession of*
> *Your unworthy and unhappy friend,*
> *HENRY JEKYLL.*

"There was a third enclosure?" asked Utterson.

"Here, sir," said Poole, and gave into his hands a considerable packet sealed in several places.

The lawyer put it in his pocket. "I would say nothing of this paper. If your master has fled or is dead, we may at least save his credit. It is now ten; I must go home and read these documents in quiet; but I shall be back before midnight, when we shall send for the police."

They went out, locking the door of the theatre behind them; and Utterson, once more leaving the servants gathered about the fire in the hall, trudged back to his office to read the two narratives in which this mystery was now to be explained.

Dr. Lanyon's Narrative

ON THE NINTH of January, now four days ago, I received by the evening delivery a registered envelope, addressed in the hand of my colleague and old school companion, Henry Jekyll. I was a good deal surprised by this; for we were by no means in the habit of correspondence; I had seen the man, dined with him, indeed, the night before; and I could imagine nothing in our intercourse that should justify formality of registration. The contents increased my wonder; for this is how the letter ran:

10th December, 18—.

Dear Lanyon, – You are one of my oldest friends; and although we may have differed at times on scientific questions, I cannot remember, at least on my side, any break in our affection. There was never a day when, if you had said to me, 'Jekyll, my life, my honour, my reason, depend upon you,' I would not have sacrificed my left hand to help you. Lanyon, my life, my honour, my reason, are all at your mercy; if you fail me tonight, I am lost. You might suppose, after this preface, that I am going to ask you for something dishonourable to grant. Judge for yourself.

I want you to postpone all other engagements for tonight – ay, even if you were summoned to the bedside of an emperor; to take a cab, unless your carriage should be actually at the door; and with this letter in your hand for consultation, to drive straight to my house. Poole, my butler, has his orders; you will find him waiting your arrival with a locksmith. The door of my cabinet is then to be forced; and you are to go in alone; to open the glazed press (letter E) on the left hand, breaking the lock if it be shut; and to draw out, with all its contents as they stand, the fourth drawer from the top or (which is the same thing) the third from the bottom. In my extreme distress of mind, I have a morbid fear of misdirecting you; but even if I am in error, you may know the right drawer by its contents: some powders, a phial and a paper book. This drawer I beg of you to carry back with you to Cavendish Square exactly as it stands.

That is the first part of the service: now for the second. You should be back, if you set out at once on the receipt of this, long before midnight; but I will leave you that amount of margin, not only in the fear of one of those obstacles that can neither be prevented nor foreseen, but because an hour when your servants are in bed is to be preferred for what will then remain to do. At midnight, then, I have to ask you to be alone in your consulting room, to admit with your own hand into the house a man who will present himself in my name, and to place in his hands the drawer that you will have brought with you from my cabinet. Then you will have played your part and earned my gratitude completely. Five minutes afterwards, if you insist upon an explanation, you will have understood that these arrangements are of capital importance; and that by the neglect of one of them, fantastic as they must appear, you might have charged your conscience with my death or the shipwreck of my reason.

Confident as I am that you will not trifle with this appeal, my heart sinks and my hand trembles at the bare thought of such a possibility. Think of me at this hour, in a strange place, labouring under a blackness of distress that no fancy can exaggerate, and yet well aware that, if you will but punctually serve me, my troubles will roll away like a story that is told. Serve me, my dear Lanyon and save
Your friend,
H.J.

P.S. – I had already sealed this up when a fresh terror struck upon my soul. It is possible that the post office may fail me, and this letter not come into your hands until tomorrow morning. In that case, dear Lanyon, do my errand when it shall be most convenient for you in the course of the day; and once more expect my messenger at midnight. It may then already be too late; and if that night passes without event, you will know that you have seen the last of Henry Jekyll.

Upon the reading of this letter, I made sure my colleague was insane; but till that was proved beyond the possibility of doubt, I felt bound to do as he requested. The less I understood of this farrago, the less I was in a position to judge of its importance; and an appeal so worded could not be set aside without a grave responsibility. I rose accordingly from table, got into a hansom, and drove straight to Jekyll's house. The butler was awaiting my arrival; he had received by the same post as mine a registered letter of instruction, and had sent at once for a locksmith and a carpenter. The tradesmen came while we were yet speaking; and we moved in a body to old Dr. Denman's surgical theatre, from which (as you are doubtless aware) Jekyll's private cabinet is most conveniently entered. The door was very strong, the lock excellent; the carpenter avowed he would have great trouble and have to do much damage, if force were to be used; and the locksmith was near despair. But this last was a handy fellow, and after two hour's work, the door stood open. The press marked E was unlocked; and I took out the drawer, had it filled up with straw and tied in a sheet, and returned with it to Cavendish Square.

Here I proceeded to examine its contents. The powders were neatly enough made up, but not with the nicety of the dispensing chemist; so that it was plain they were of Jekyll's private manufacture; and when I opened one of the wrappers I found what seemed to me a simple crystalline salt of a white colour. The phial, to which I next turned my attention, might have been about half full of a blood-red liquor, which was highly pungent to the sense of smell and seemed to me to contain phosphorus and some volatile ether. At the other ingredients I could make no guess. The book was an ordinary version book and contained little but a series of dates. These covered a period of many years, but I observed that the entries ceased nearly a year ago and quite abruptly. Here and there a brief remark was appended to a date, usually no more than a single word: 'double' occurring perhaps six times in a total of several hundred entries; and once very early in the list and followed by several marks of exclamation, 'total failure!!!' All this, though it whetted my curiosity, told me little that was definite. Here were a phial of some salt, and the record of a series of experiments that had led (like too many of Jekyll's investigations) to no end of practical usefulness. How could the presence of these articles in my house affect either the honour, the sanity, or the life of my flighty colleague? If his messenger could go to one place, why could he not go to another? And even granting some impediment, why was this gentleman to be received by me in secret? The more I reflected the more convinced I grew that I was dealing with a case of cerebral disease; and though I dismissed my servants to bed, I loaded an old revolver, that I might be found in some posture of self-defence.

Twelve o'clock had scarce rung out over London, ere the knocker sounded very gently on the door. I went myself at the summons, and found a small man crouching against the pillars of the portico.

"Are you come from Dr. Jekyll?" I asked.

He told me 'yes' by a constrained gesture; and when I had bidden him enter, he did not obey me without a searching backward glance into the darkness of the square. There was a policeman not far off, advancing with his bull's eye open; and at the sight, I thought my visitor started and made greater haste.

These particulars struck me, I confess, disagreeably; and as I followed him into the bright light of the consulting room, I kept my hand ready on my weapon. Here, at last, I had a chance of clearly seeing him. I had never set eyes on him before, so much was certain. He was small, as I have said; I was struck besides with the shocking expression of his face, with his remarkable combination of great muscular activity and great apparent debility of constitution, and – last but not least – with the odd, subjective disturbance caused by his neighbourhood. This bore some resemblance to incipient rigour, and was accompanied by a marked sinking of the pulse. At the time, I set it down to some idiosyncratic, personal distaste, and merely wondered at the acuteness of the symptoms; but I have since had reason to believe the cause to lie much deeper in the nature of man, and to turn on some nobler hinge than the principle of hatred.

This person (who had thus, from the first moment of his entrance, struck in me what I can only describe as a disgustful curiosity) was dressed in a fashion that would have made an ordinary person laughable; his clothes, that is to say, although they were of rich and sober fabric, were enormously too large for him in every measurement – the trousers hanging on his legs and rolled up to keep them from the ground, the waist of the coat below his haunches, and the collar sprawling wide upon his shoulders. Strange to relate, this ludicrous accoutrement was far from moving me to laughter. Rather, as there was something abnormal and misbegotten in the very essence of the creature that now faced me – something seizing, surprising and revolting – this fresh disparity seemed but to fit in with and to reinforce it; so that to my interest in the man's nature and character, there was added a curiosity as to his origin, his life, his fortune and status in the world.

These observations, though they have taken so great a space to be set down in, were yet the work of a few seconds. My visitor was, indeed, on fire with sombre excitement.

"Have you got it?" he cried. "Have you got it?" And so lively was his impatience that he even laid his hand upon my arm and sought to shake me.

I put him back, conscious at his touch of a certain icy pang along my blood. "Come, sir," said I. "You forget that I have not yet the pleasure of your acquaintance. Be seated, if you please." And I showed him an example, and sat down myself in my customary seat and with as fair an imitation of my ordinary manner to a patient, as the lateness of the hour, the nature of my preoccupations, and the horror I had of my visitor, would suffer me to muster.

"I beg your pardon, Dr. Lanyon," he replied civilly enough. "What you say is very well founded; and my impatience has shown its heels to my politeness. I come here at the instance of your colleague, Dr. Henry Jekyll, on a piece of business of some moment; and I understood..." He paused and put his hand to his throat, and I could see, in spite of his collected manner, that he was wrestling against the approaches of the hysteria – "I understood, a drawer..."

But here I took pity on my visitor's suspense, and some perhaps on my own growing curiosity.

"There it is, sir," said I, pointing to the drawer, where it lay on the floor behind a table and still covered with the sheet.

He sprang to it, and then paused, and laid his hand upon his heart; I could hear his teeth grate with the convulsive action of his jaws; and his face was so ghastly to see that I grew alarmed both for his life and reason.

"Compose yourself," said I.

He turned a dreadful smile to me, and as if with the decision of despair, plucked away the sheet. At sight of the contents, he uttered one loud sob of such immense relief that I sat petrified. And the next moment, in a voice that was already fairly well under control, "Have you a graduated glass?" he asked.

I rose from my place with something of an effort and gave him what he asked.

He thanked me with a smiling nod, measured out a few minims of the red tincture and added one of the powders. The mixture, which was at first of a reddish hue, began, in proportion as the crystals melted, to brighten in colour, to effervesce audibly, and to throw off small fumes of vapour. Suddenly and at the same moment, the ebullition ceased and the compound changed to a dark purple, which faded again more slowly to a watery green. My visitor, who had watched these metamorphoses with a keen eye, smiled, set down the glass upon the table, and then turned and looked upon me with an air of scrutiny.

"And now," said he, "to settle what remains. Will you be wise? Will you be guided? Will you suffer me to take this glass in my hand and to go forth from your house without further parley? Or has the greed of curiosity too much command of you? Think before you answer, for it shall be done as you decide. As you decide, you shall be left as you were before, and neither richer nor wiser, unless the sense of service rendered to a man in mortal distress may be counted as a kind of riches of the soul. Or, if you shall so prefer to choose, a new province of knowledge and new avenues to fame and power shall be laid open to you, here, in this room, upon the instant; and your sight shall be blasted by a prodigy to stagger the unbelief of Satan."

"Sir," said I, affecting a coolness that I was far from truly possessing, "you speak enigmas, and you will perhaps not wonder that I hear you with no very strong impression of belief. But I have gone too far in the way of inexplicable services to pause before I see the end."

"It is well," replied my visitor. "Lanyon, you remember your vows: what follows is under the seal of our profession. And now, you who have so long been bound to the most narrow and material views, you who have denied the virtue of transcendental medicine, you who have derided your superiors – behold!"

He put the glass to his lips and drank at one gulp. A cry followed; he reeled, staggered, clutched at the table and held on, staring with injected eyes, gasping with open mouth; and as I looked there came, I thought, a change – he seemed to swell – his face became suddenly black and the features seemed to melt and alter – and the next moment, I had sprung to my feet and leaped back against the wall, my arms raised to shield me from that prodigy, my mind submerged in terror.

"O God!" I screamed, and "O God!" again and again; for there before my eyes – pale and shaken, and half fainting, and groping before him with his hands, like a man restored from death – there stood Henry Jekyll!

What he told me in the next hour, I cannot bring my mind to set on paper. I saw what I saw, I heard what I heard, and my soul sickened at it; and yet now when that sight has faded from my eyes, I ask myself if I believe it, and I cannot answer. My life is shaken to its roots; sleep has left me; the deadliest terror sits by me at all hours of the day and night; and I feel that my days are numbered, and that I must die; and yet I shall die incredulous. As for the moral turpitude that man unveiled to me, even with tears of penitence, I cannot, even in memory, dwell on it without a start of horror. I will say but one thing, Utterson, and that (if you can bring your mind to credit it) will be more than enough. The creature who crept into my house that night was, on Jekyll's own confession, known by the name of Hyde and hunted for in every corner of the land as the murderer of Carew.

HASTIE LANYON.

Henry Jekyll's Full Statement of the Case

I WAS BORN in the year 18— to a large fortune, endowed besides with excellent parts, inclined by nature to industry, fond of the respect of the wise and good among my fellowmen, and thus, as might have been supposed, with every guarantee of an honourable and distinguished future. And indeed the worst of my faults was a certain impatient gaiety of disposition, such as has made the happiness of many, but such as I found it hard to reconcile with my imperious desire to carry my head high, and wear a more than commonly grave countenance before the public. Hence it came about that I concealed my pleasures; and that when I reached years of reflection, and began to look round me and take stock of my progress and position in the world, I stood already committed to a profound duplicity of life. Many a man would have even blazoned such irregularities as I was guilty of; but from the high views that I had set before me, I regarded and hid them with an almost morbid sense of shame. It was thus rather the exacting nature of my aspirations than any particular degradation in my faults, that made me what I was, and, with even a deeper trench than in the majority of men, severed in me those provinces of good and ill which divide and compound man's dual nature. In this case, I was driven to reflect deeply and inveterately on that hard law of life, which lies at the root of religion and is one of the most plentiful springs of distress. Though so profound a double-dealer, I was in no sense a hypocrite; both sides of me were in dead earnest; I was no more myself when I laid aside restraint and plunged in shame, than when I laboured, in the eye of day, at the furtherance of knowledge or the relief of sorrow and suffering. And it chanced that the direction of my scientific studies, which led wholly towards the mystic and the transcendental, reacted and shed a strong light on this consciousness of the perennial war among my members. With every day, and from both sides of my intelligence, the moral and the intellectual, I thus drew steadily nearer to that truth, by whose partial discovery I have been doomed to such a dreadful shipwreck: that man is not truly one, but truly two. I say two, because the state of my own knowledge does not pass beyond that point. Others will follow, others will outstrip me on the same lines; and I hazard the guess that man will be ultimately known for a mere polity of multifarious, incongruous and independent denizens. I, for my part, from the nature of my life, advanced infallibly in one direction and in one direction only. It was on the moral side, and in my own person, that I learned to recognise the thorough and primitive duality of man; I saw that, of the two natures that contended in the field of my consciousness, even if I could rightly be said to be either, it was only because I was radically both; and from an early date, even before the course of my scientific discoveries had begun to suggest the most naked possibility of such a miracle, I had learned to dwell with pleasure, as a beloved daydream, on the thought of the separation of these elements. If each, I told myself, could be housed in separate identities, life would be relieved of all that was unbearable; the unjust might go his way, delivered from the aspirations and remorse of his more upright twin; and the just could walk steadfastly and securely on his upward path, doing the good things in which he found his pleasure, and no longer exposed to disgrace and penitence by the hands of this extraneous evil. It was the curse of mankind that these incongruous faggots were thus bound together – that in the agonised womb of consciousness, these polar twins should be continuously struggling. How, then were they dissociated?

I was so far in my reflections when, as I have said, a side light began to shine upon the subject from the laboratory table. I began to perceive more deeply than it has ever yet been stated, the trembling immateriality, the mistlike transience, of this seemingly so solid body in which we walk attired. Certain agents I found to have the power to shake and pluck back that fleshly vestment, even as a wind might toss the curtains of a pavilion. For two good reasons, I will not enter deeply into this scientific branch of my confession. First, because I have been made to learn that the doom and burthen of our life is bound forever on man's shoulders, and when the attempt is made to cast it off, it but returns upon us with more unfamiliar and more awful pressure. Second, because, as my narrative will make, alas! too evident, my discoveries were incomplete. Enough then, that I not only recognised my natural body from the mere aura and effulgence of certain of the powers that made up my spirit, but managed to compound a drug by which these powers should be dethroned from their supremacy, and a second form and countenance substituted, none the less natural to me because they were the expression, and bore the stamp of lower elements in my soul.

I hesitated long before I put this theory to the test of practice. I knew well that I risked death; for any drug that so potently controlled and shook the very fortress of identity, might, by the least scruple of an overdose or at the least inopportunity in the moment of exhibition, utterly blot out that immaterial tabernacle which I looked to it to change. But the temptation of a discovery so singular and profound at last overcame the suggestions of alarm. I had long since prepared my tincture; I purchased at once, from a firm of wholesale chemists, a large quantity of a particular salt which I knew, from my experiments, to be the last ingredient required; and late one accursed night, I compounded the elements, watched them boil and smoke together in the glass, and when the ebullition had subsided, with a strong glow of courage, drank off the potion.

The most racking pangs succeeded: a grinding in the bones, deadly nausea, and a horror of the spirit that cannot be exceeded at the hour of birth or death. Then these agonies began swiftly to subside, and I came to myself as if out of a great sickness. There was something strange in my sensations, something indescribably new and, from its very novelty, incredibly sweet. I felt younger, lighter, happier in body; within I was conscious of a heady recklessness, a current of disordered sensual images running like a millrace in my fancy, a solution of the bonds of obligation, an unknown but not an innocent freedom of the soul. I knew myself, at the first breath of this new life, to be more wicked, tenfold more wicked, sold a slave to my original evil; and the thought, in that moment, braced and delighted me like wine. I stretched out my hands, exulting in the freshness of these sensations; and in the act, I was suddenly aware that I had lost in stature.

There was no mirror, at that date, in my room; that which stands beside me as I write, was brought there later on and for the very purpose of these transformations. The night however, was far gone into the morning – the morning, black as it was, was nearly ripe for the conception of the day – the inmates of my house were locked in the most rigorous hours of slumber; and I determined, flushed as I was with hope and triumph, to venture in my new shape as far as to my bedroom. I crossed the yard, wherein the constellations looked down upon me, I could have thought, with wonder, the first creature of that sort that their unsleeping vigilance had yet disclosed to them; I stole through the corridors, a stranger in my own house; and coming to my room, I saw for the first time the appearance of Edward Hyde.

I must here speak by theory alone, saying not that which I know, but that which I suppose to be most probable. The evil side of my nature, to which I had now transferred the stamping efficacy, was less robust and less developed than the good which I had just deposed. Again, in the course of my life, which had been, after all, nine tenths a life of effort, virtue and control, it had been much less exercised and much less exhausted. And hence, as I think, it came about that Edward Hyde was so much smaller, slighter and younger than Henry Jekyll. Even as good shone upon the countenance of the one, evil was written broadly and plainly on the face of the other. Evil besides (which I must still believe to be the lethal side of man) had left on that body an imprint of deformity and decay. And yet when I looked upon that ugly idol in the glass, I was conscious of no repugnance, rather of a leap of welcome. This, too, was myself. It seemed natural and human. In my eyes it bore a livelier image of the spirit, it seemed more express and single, than the imperfect and divided countenance I had been hitherto accustomed to call mine. And in so far I was doubtless right. I have observed that when I wore the semblance of Edward Hyde, none could come near to me at first without a visible misgiving of the flesh. This, as I take it, was because all human beings, as we meet them, are commingled out of good and evil: and Edward Hyde, alone in the ranks of mankind, was pure evil.

I lingered but a moment at the mirror: the second and conclusive experiment had yet to be attempted; it yet remained to be seen if I had lost my identity beyond redemption and must flee before daylight from a house that was no longer mine; and hurrying back to my cabinet, I once more prepared and drank the cup, once more suffered the pangs of dissolution, and came to myself once more with the character, the stature and the face of Henry Jekyll.

That night I had come to the fatal crossroads. Had I approached my discovery in a more noble spirit, had I risked the experiment while under the empire of generous or pious aspirations, all must have been otherwise, and from these agonies of death and birth, I had come forth an angel instead of a fiend. The drug had no discriminating action; it was neither diabolical nor divine; it but shook the doors of the prison house of my disposition; and like the captives of Philippi, that which stood within ran forth. At that time my virtue slumbered; my evil, kept awake by ambition, was alert and swift to seize the occasion; and the thing that was projected was Edward Hyde. Hence, although I had now two characters as well as two appearances, one was wholly evil, and the other was still the old Henry Jekyll, that incongruous compound of whose reformation and improvement I had already learned to despair. The movement was thus wholly toward the worse.

Even at that time, I had not conquered my aversions to the dryness of a life of study. I would still be merrily disposed at times; and as my pleasures were (to say the least) undignified, and I was not only well known and highly considered, but growing towards the elderly man, this incoherency of my life was daily growing more unwelcome. It was on this side that my new power tempted me until I fell in slavery. I had but to drink the cup, to doff at once the body of the noted professor, and to assume, like a thick cloak, that of Edward Hyde. I smiled at the notion; it seemed to me at the time to be humourous; and I made my preparations with the most studious care. I took and furnished that house in Soho, to which Hyde was tracked by the police; and engaged as a housekeeper a creature whom I knew well to be silent and unscrupulous. On the other side, I announced to my servants that a Mr. Hyde (whom I described) was to have full liberty and power about my house in the square; and to parry mishaps, I even called and made myself a familiar object, in my second character. I next drew up that will to which you so much objected; so that if anything befell me in the person of Dr. Jekyll, I could enter on that of Edward Hyde without pecuniary loss. And thus fortified, as I supposed, on every side, I began to profit by the strange immunities of my position.

Men have before hired bravos to transact their crimes, while their own person and reputation sat under shelter. I was the first that ever did so for his pleasures. I was the first that could plod in the public eye with a load of genial respectability, and in a moment, like a schoolboy, strip off these lendings and spring headlong into the sea of liberty. But for me, in my impenetrable mantle, the safety was complete. Think of it – I did not even exist! Let me but escape into my laboratory door, give me but a second or two to mix and swallow the draught that I had always standing ready; and whatever he had done, Edward Hyde would pass away like the stain of breath upon a mirror; and there in his stead, quietly at home, trimming the midnight lamp in his study, a man who could afford to laugh at suspicion, would be Henry Jekyll.

The pleasures which I made haste to seek in my disguise were, as I have said, undignified; I would scarce use a harder term. But in the hands of Edward Hyde, they soon began to turn toward the monstrous. When I would come back from these excursions, I was often plunged into a kind of wonder at my vicarious depravity. This familiar that I called out of my own soul, and sent forth alone to do his good pleasure, was a being inherently malign and villainous; his every act and thought centered on self; drinking pleasure with bestial avidity from any degree of torture to another; relentless like a man of stone. Henry Jekyll stood at times aghast before the acts of Edward Hyde; but the situation was apart from ordinary laws, and insidiously relaxed the grasp of conscience. It was Hyde, after all, and Hyde alone, that was guilty. Jekyll was no worse; he woke again to his good qualities seemingly unimpaired; he would even make haste, where it was possible, to undo the evil done by Hyde. And thus his conscience slumbered.

Into the details of the infamy at which I thus connived (for even now I can scarce grant that I committed it) I have no design of entering; I mean but to point out the warnings and the successive steps with which my chastisement approached. I met with one accident which, as it brought on no consequence, I shall no more than mention. An act of cruelty to a child aroused against me the anger of a passer-by, whom I recognised the other day in the person of your kinsman; the doctor and the child's family joined him; there were moments when I feared for my life; and at last, in order to pacify their too just resentment, Edward Hyde had to bring them to the door, and pay them in a cheque drawn in the name of Henry Jekyll. But this danger was easily eliminated from the future, by opening an account at another bank in the name of Edward Hyde himself; and when, by sloping my own hand backward, I had supplied my double with a signature, I thought I sat beyond the reach of fate.

Some two months before the murder of Sir Danvers, I had been out for one of my adventures, had returned at a late hour, and woke the next day in bed with somewhat odd sensations. It was in vain I looked about me; in vain I saw the decent furniture and tall proportions of my room in the square; in vain that I recognised the pattern of the bed curtains and the design of the mahogany frame; something still kept insisting that I was not where I was, that I had not wakened where I seemed to be, but in the little room in Soho where I was accustomed to sleep in the body of Edward Hyde. I smiled to myself, and in my psychological way, began lazily to inquire into the elements of this illusion, occasionally, even as I did so, dropping back into a comfortable morning doze. I was still so engaged when, in one of my more wakeful moments, my eyes fell upon my hand. Now the hand of Henry Jekyll (as you have often remarked) was professional in shape and size; it was large, firm, white and comely. But the hand which I now saw, clearly enough, in the yellow light of a mid-London morning, lying half shut on the bedclothes, was lean, corded, knuckly, of a dusky pallor and thickly shaded with a swart growth of hair. It was the hand of Edward Hyde.

I must have stared upon it for near half a minute, sunk as I was in the mere stupidity of wonder, before terror woke up in my breast as sudden and startling as the crash of cymbals; and bounding from my bed I rushed to the mirror. At the sight that met my eyes, my blood was changed into something exquisitely thin and icy. Yes, I had gone to bed Henry Jekyll, I had awakened Edward Hyde. How was this to be explained? I asked myself; and then, with another bound of terror – how was it to be remedied? It was well on in the morning; the servants were up; all my drugs were in the cabinet – a long journey down two pairs of stairs, through the back passage, across the open court and through the anatomical theatre, from where I was then standing horror-struck. It might indeed be possible to cover my face; but of what use was that, when I was unable to conceal the alteration in my stature? And then with an overpowering sweetness of relief, it came back upon my mind that the servants were already used to the coming and going of my second self. I had soon dressed, as well as I was able, in clothes of my own size: had soon passed through the house, where Bradshaw stared and drew back at seeing Mr. Hyde at such an hour and in such a strange array; and ten minutes later, Dr. Jekyll had returned to his own shape and was sitting down, with a darkened brow, to make a feint of breakfasting.

Small indeed was my appetite. This inexplicable incident, this reversal of my previous experience, seemed, like the Babylonian finger on the wall, to be spelling out the letters of my judgment; and I began to reflect more seriously than ever before on the issues and possibilities of my double existence. That part of me which I had the power of projecting, had lately been much exercised and nourished; it had seemed to me of late as though the body of Edward Hyde had grown in stature, as though (when I wore that form) I were conscious of a more generous tide of blood; and I began to spy a danger that, if this were much prolonged, the balance of my nature might be permanently overthrown, the power of voluntary change be forfeited, and the character of Edward Hyde become irrevocably mine. The power of the drug had not been always equally displayed. Once, very early in my career, it had totally failed me; since then I had been obliged on more than one occasion to double, and once, with infinite risk of death, to treble the amount; and these rare uncertainties had cast hitherto the sole shadow on my contentment. Now, however, and in the light of that morning's accident, I was led to remark that whereas, in the beginning, the difficulty had been to throw off the body of Jekyll, it had of late gradually but decidedly transferred itself to the other side. All things therefore seemed to point to this; that I was slowly losing hold of my original and better self, and becoming slowly incorporated with my second and worse.

Between these two, I now felt I had to choose. My two natures had memory in common, but all other faculties were most unequally shared between them. Jekyll (who was composite) now with the most sensitive apprehensions, now with a greedy gusto, projected and shared in the pleasures and adventures of Hyde; but Hyde was indifferent to Jekyll, or but remembered him as the mountain bandit remembers the cavern in which he conceals himself from pursuit. Jekyll had more than a father's interest; Hyde had more than a son's indifference. To cast in my lot with Jekyll, was to die to those appetites which I had long secretly indulged and had of late begun to pamper. To cast it in with Hyde, was to die to a thousand interests and aspirations, and to become, at a blow and forever, despised and friendless. The bargain might appear unequal; but there was still another consideration in the scales; for while Jekyll would suffer smartingly in the fires of abstinence, Hyde would be not even conscious of all that he had lost. Strange as my circumstances were, the terms of this debate are as old and commonplace as man; much the same inducements and alarms cast the die for any tempted and trembling sinner; and it fell out with me, as it falls with so vast a majority of my fellows, that I chose the better part and was found wanting in the strength to keep to it.

Yes, I preferred the elderly and discontented doctor, surrounded by friends and cherishing honest hopes; and bade a resolute farewell to the liberty, the comparative youth, the light step, leaping impulses and secret pleasures, that I had enjoyed in the disguise of Hyde. I made this choice perhaps with some unconscious reservation, for I neither gave up the house in Soho, nor destroyed the clothes of Edward Hyde, which still lay ready in my cabinet. For two months, however, I was true to my determination; for two months, I led a life of such severity as I had never before attained to, and enjoyed the compensations of an approving conscience. But time began at last to obliterate the freshness of my alarm; the praises of conscience began to grow into a thing of course; I began to be tortured with throes and longings, as of Hyde struggling after freedom; and at last, in an hour of moral weakness, I once again compounded and swallowed the transforming draught.

I do not suppose that, when a drunkard reasons with himself upon his vice, he is once out of five hundred times affected by the dangers that he runs through his brutish, physical insensibility; neither had I, long as I had considered my position, made enough allowance for the complete moral insensibility and insensate readiness to evil, which were the leading characters of Edward Hyde. Yet it was by these that I was punished. My devil had been long caged, he came out roaring. I was conscious, even when I took the draught, of a more unbridled, a more furious propensity to ill. It must have been this, I suppose, that stirred in my soul that tempest of impatience with which I listened to the civilities of my unhappy victim; I declare, at least, before God, no man morally sane could have been guilty of that crime upon so pitiful a provocation; and that I struck in no more reasonable spirit than that in which a sick child may break a plaything. But I had voluntarily stripped myself of all those balancing instincts by which even the worst of us continues to walk with some degree of steadiness among temptations; and in my case, to be tempted, however slightly, was to fall.

Instantly the spirit of hell awoke in me and raged. With a transport of glee, I mauled the unresisting body, tasting delight from every blow; and it was not till weariness had begun to succeed, that I was suddenly, in the top fit of my delirium, struck through the heart by a cold thrill of terror. A mist dispersed; I saw my life to be forfeit; and fled from the scene of these excesses, at once glorying and trembling, my lust of evil gratified and stimulated, my love of life screwed to the topmost peg. I ran to the house in Soho, and (to make assurance doubly sure) destroyed my papers; thence I set out through the lamplit streets, in the same divided ecstasy of mind, gloating on my crime, light-headedly devising others in the future, and yet still hastening and still hearkening in my wake for the steps of the avenger. Hyde had a song upon his lips as he compounded the draught, and as he drank it, pledged the dead man. The pangs of transformation had not done tearing him, before Henry Jekyll, with streaming tears of gratitude and remorse, had fallen upon his knees and lifted his clasped hands to God. The veil of self-indulgence was rent from head to foot. I saw my life as a whole: I followed it up from the days of childhood, when I had walked with my father's hand, and through the self-denying toils of my professional life, to arrive again and again, with the same sense of unreality, at the damned horrors of the evening. I could have screamed aloud; I sought with tears and prayers to smother down the crowd of hideous images and sounds with which my memory swarmed against me; and still, between the petitions, the ugly face of my iniquity stared into my soul. As the acuteness of this remorse began to die away, it was succeeded by a sense of joy. The problem of my conduct was solved. Hyde was thenceforth impossible; whether I would or not, I was now confined to the better part of my existence; and O, how I rejoiced to think of it! With what willing humility I embraced anew the restrictions of natural life! With what sincere renunciation I locked the door by which I had so often gone and come, and ground the key under my heel!

The next day, came the news that the murder had not been overlooked, that the guilt of Hyde was patent to the world, and that the victim was a man high in public estimation. It was not only a crime, it had been a tragic folly. I think I was glad to know it; I think I was glad to have my better impulses thus buttressed and guarded by the terrors of the scaffold. Jekyll was now my city of refuge; let but Hyde peep out an instant, and the hands of all men would be raised to take and slay him.

I resolved in my future conduct to redeem the past; and I can say with honesty that my resolve was fruitful of some good. You know yourself how earnestly, in the last months of the last year, I laboured to relieve suffering; you know that much was done for others, and that the days passed quietly, almost happily for myself. Nor can I truly say that I wearied of this beneficent and innocent life; I think instead that I daily enjoyed it more completely; but I was still cursed with my duality of purpose; and as the first edge of my penitence wore off, the lower side of me, so long indulged, so recently chained down, began to growl for licence. Not that I dreamed of resuscitating Hyde; the bare idea of that would startle me to frenzy: no, it was in my own person that I was once more tempted to trifle with my conscience; and it was as an ordinary secret sinner that I at last fell before the assaults of temptation.

There comes an end to all things; the most capacious measure is filled at last; and this brief condescension to my evil finally destroyed the balance of my soul. And yet I was not alarmed; the fall seemed natural, like a return to the old days before I had made my discovery. It was a fine, clear, January day, wet underfoot where the frost had melted, but cloudless overhead; and the Regent's Park was full of winter chirrupings and sweet with spring odours. I sat in the sun on a bench; the animal within me licking the chops of memory; the spiritual side a little drowsed, promising subsequent penitence, but not yet moved to begin. After all, I reflected, I was like my neighbours; and then I smiled, comparing myself with other men, comparing my active goodwill with the lazy cruelty of their neglect. And at the very moment of that vainglorious thought, a qualm came over me, a horrid nausea and the most deadly shuddering. These passed away, and left me faint; and then as in its turn faintness subsided, I began to be aware of a change in the temper of my thoughts, a greater boldness, a contempt of danger, a solution of the bonds of obligation. I looked down; my clothes hung formlessly on my shrunken limbs; the hand that lay on my knee was corded and hairy. I was once more Edward Hyde. A moment before I had been safe of all men's respect, wealthy, beloved – the cloth laying for me in the dining room at home; and now I was the common quarry of mankind, hunted, houseless, a known murderer, thrall to the gallows.

My reason wavered, but it did not fail me utterly. I have more than once observed that in my second character, my faculties seemed sharpened to a point and my spirits more tensely elastic; thus it came about that, where Jekyll perhaps might have succumbed, Hyde rose to the importance of the moment. My drugs were in one of the presses of my cabinet; how was I to reach them? That was the problem that (crushing my temples in my hands) I set myself to solve. The laboratory door I had closed. If I sought to enter by the house, my own servants would consign me to the gallows. I saw I must employ another hand, and thought of Lanyon. How was he to be reached? How persuaded? Supposing that I escaped capture in the streets, how was I to make my way into his presence? And how should I, an unknown and displeasing visitor, prevail on the famous physician to rifle the study of his colleague, Dr. Jekyll? Then I remembered that of my original character, one part remained to me: I could write my own hand; and once I had conceived that kindling spark, the way that I must follow became lighted up from end to end.

Thereupon, I arranged my clothes as best I could, and summoning a passing hansom, drove to an hotel in Portland Street, the name of which I chanced to remember. At my appearance (which was indeed comical enough, however tragic a fate these garments covered) the driver could not conceal his mirth. I gnashed my teeth upon him with a gust of devilish fury; and the smile withered from his face – happily for him – yet more happily for myself, for in another instant I had certainly dragged him from his perch. At the inn, as I entered, I looked about me with so black a countenance as made the attendants tremble; not a look did they exchange in my presence; but obsequiously took my orders, led me to a private room, and brought me wherewithal to write. Hyde in danger of his life was a creature new to me; shaken with inordinate anger, strung to the pitch of murder, lusting to inflict pain. Yet the creature was astute; mastered his fury with a great effort of the will; composed his two important letters, one to Lanyon and one to Poole; and that he might receive actual evidence of their being posted, sent them out with directions that they should be registered. Thenceforward, he sat all day over the fire in the private room, gnawing his nails; there he dined, sitting alone with his fears, the waiter visibly quailing before his eye; and thence, when the night was fully come, he set forth in the corner of a closed cab, and was driven to and fro about the streets of the city. He, I say – I cannot say, I. That child of Hell had nothing human; nothing lived in him but fear and hatred. And when at last, thinking the driver had begun to grow suspicious, he discharged the cab and ventured on foot, attired in his misfitting clothes, an object marked out for observation, into the midst of the nocturnal passengers, these two base passions raged within him like a tempest. He walked fast, hunted by his fears, chattering to himself, skulking through the less frequented thoroughfares, counting the minutes that still divided him from midnight. Once a woman spoke to him, offering, I think, a box of lights. He smote her in the face, and she fled.

When I came to myself at Lanyon's, the horror of my old friend perhaps affected me somewhat: I do not know; it was at least but a drop in the sea to the abhorrence with which I looked back upon these hours. A change had come over me. It was no longer the fear of the gallows, it was the horror of being Hyde that racked me. I received Lanyon's condemnation partly in a dream; it was partly in a dream that I came home to my own house and got into bed. I slept after the prostration of the day, with a stringent and profound slumber which not even the nightmares that wrung me could avail to break. I awoke in the morning shaken, weakened, but refreshed. I still hated and feared the thought of the brute that slept within me, and I had not of course forgotten the appalling dangers of the day before; but I was once more at home, in my own house and close to my drugs; and gratitude for my escape shone so strong in my soul that it almost rivalled the brightness of hope.

I was stepping leisurely across the court after breakfast, drinking the chill of the air with pleasure, when I was seized again with those indescribable sensations that heralded the change; and I had but the time to gain the shelter of my cabinet, before I was once again raging and freezing with the passions of Hyde. It took on this occasion a double dose to recall me to myself; and alas! six hours after, as I sat looking sadly in the fire, the pangs returned, and the drug had to be re-administered. In short, from that day forth it seemed only by a great effort as of gymnastics, and only under the immediate stimulation of the drug, that I was able to wear the countenance of Jekyll. At all hours of the day and night, I would be taken with the premonitory shudder; above all, if I slept, or even dozed for a moment in my chair, it was always as Hyde that I awakened. Under the strain of this continually impending doom and by the sleeplessness to which I now condemned myself, ay, even beyond what I had thought possible to man, I became, in my own person, a creature eaten up and emptied by fever, languidly weak both in body and mind, and solely occupied by one thought: the horror of my other self. But when I slept, or when the virtue of the medicine wore off, I would leap almost without transition (for the pangs of transformation grew daily less marked) into the possession of a fancy brimming with images of terror, a soul boiling with causeless hatreds, and a body that seemed not strong enough to contain the raging energies of life. The powers of Hyde seemed to have grown with the sickliness of Jekyll. And certainly the hate that now divided them was equal on each side. With Jekyll, it was a thing of vital instinct. He had now seen the full deformity of that creature that shared with him some of the phenomena of consciousness, and was co-heir with him to death: and beyond these links of community, which in themselves made the most poignant part of his distress, he thought of Hyde, for all his energy of life, as of something not only hellish but inorganic. This was the shocking thing; that the slime of the pit seemed to utter cries and voices; that the amorphous dust gesticulated and sinned; that what was dead, and had no shape, should usurp the offices of life. And this again, that that insurgent horror was knit to him closer than a wife, closer than an eye; lay caged in his flesh, where he heard it mutter and felt it struggle to be born; and at every hour of weakness, and in the confidence of slumber, prevailed against him, and deposed him out of life. The hatred of Hyde for Jekyll was of a different order. His terror of the gallows drove him continually to commit temporary suicide, and return to his subordinate station of a part instead of a person; but he loathed the necessity, he loathed the despondency into which Jekyll was now fallen, and he resented the dislike with which he was himself regarded. Hence the ape-like tricks that he would play me, scrawling in my own hand blasphemies on the pages of my books, burning the letters and destroying the portrait of my father; and indeed, had it not been for his fear of death, he would long ago have ruined himself in order to involve me in the ruin. But his love of life is wonderful; I go further: I, who sicken and freeze at the mere thought of him, when I recall the abjection and passion of this attachment, and when I know how he fears my power to cut him off by suicide, I find it in my heart to pity him.

It is useless, and the time awfully fails me, to prolong this description; no one has ever suffered such torments, let that suffice; and yet even to these, habit brought – no, not alleviation – but a certain callousness of soul, a certain acquiescence of despair; and my punishment might have gone on for years, but for the last calamity which has now fallen, and which has finally severed me from my own face and nature. My provision of the salt, which had never been renewed since the date of the first experiment, began to run low. I sent out for a fresh supply and mixed the draught; the ebullition followed, and the first change of colour, not the second; I drank it and it was without efficiency. You will learn from Poole how I have had London ransacked; it was in vain; and I am now persuaded that my first supply was impure, and that it was that unknown impurity which lent efficacy to the draught.

About a week has passed, and I am now finishing this statement under the influence of the last of the old powders. This, then, is the last time, short of a miracle, that Henry Jekyll can think his own thoughts or see his own face (now how sadly altered!) in the glass. Nor must I delay too long to bring my writing to an end; for if my narrative has hitherto escaped destruction, it has been by a combination of great prudence and great good luck. Should the throes of change take me in the act of writing it, Hyde will tear it in pieces; but if some time shall have elapsed after I have laid it by, his wonderful selfishness and circumscription to the moment will probably save it once again from the action of his ape-like spite. And indeed the doom that is closing on us both has already changed and crushed him. Half an hour from now, when I shall again and forever reindue that hated personality, I know how I shall sit shuddering and weeping in my chair, or continue, with the most strained and fearstruck ecstasy of listening, to pace up and down this room (my last earthly refuge) and give ear to every sound of menace. Will Hyde die upon the scaffold? Or will he find courage to release himself at the last moment? God knows; I am careless; this is my true hour of death, and what is to follow concerns another than myself. Here then, as I lay down the pen and proceed to seal up my confession, I bring the life of that unhappy Henry Jekyll to an end.

The Secret of the Growing Gold

Bram Stoker

WHEN Margaret Delandre went to live at Brent's Rock the whole neighbourhood awoke to the pleasure of an entirely new scandal. Scandals in connection with either the Delandre family or the Brents of Brent's Rock, were not few; and if the secret history of the county had been written in full both names would have been found well represented. It is true that the status of each was so different that they might have belonged to different continents – or to different worlds for the matter of that – for hitherto their orbits had never crossed. The Brents were accorded by the whole section of the country a unique social dominance, and had ever held themselves as high above the yeoman class to which Margaret Delandre belonged, as a blue-blooded Spanish hidalgo out-tops his peasant tenantry.

The Delandres had an ancient record and were proud of it in their way as the Brents were of theirs. But the family had never risen above yeomanry; and although they had been once well-to-do in the good old times of foreign wars and protection, their fortunes had withered under the scorching of the free trade sun and the 'piping times of peace'. They had, as the elder members used to assert, 'stuck to the land', with the result that they had taken root in it, body and soul. In fact, they, having chosen the life of vegetables, had flourished as vegetation does – blossomed and thrived in the good season and suffered in the bad. Their holding, Dander's Croft, seemed to have been worked out, and to be typical of the family which had inhabited it. The latter had declined generation after generation, sending out now and again some abortive shoot of unsatisfied energy in the shape of a soldier or sailor, who had worked his way to the minor grades of the services and had there stopped, cut short either from unheeding gallantry in action or from that destroying cause to men without breeding or youthful care – the recognition of a position above them which they feel unfitted to fill. So, little by little, the family dropped lower and lower, the men brooding and dissatisfied, and drinking themselves into the grave, the women drudging at home, or marrying beneath them – or worse. In process of time all disappeared, leaving only two in the Croft, Wykham Delandre and his sister Margaret. The man and woman seemed to have inherited in masculine and feminine form respectively the evil tendency of their race, sharing in common the principles, though manifesting them in different ways, of sullen passion, voluptuousness and recklessness.

The history of the Brents had been something similar, but showing the causes of decadence in their aristocratic and not their plebeian forms. They, too, had sent their shoots to the wars; but their positions had been different and they had often attained honour – for without flaw they were gallant, and brave deeds were done by them before the selfish dissipation which marked them had sapped their vigour.

The present head of the family – if family it could now be called when one remained of the direct line – was Geoffrey Brent. He was almost a type of worn out race, manifesting in some ways its most brilliant qualities, and in others its utter degradation. He might be fairly compared with some of those antique Italian nobles whom the painters have preserved to us with their courage, their unscrupulousness, their refinement of lust and cruelty – the voluptuary actual with the fiend potential. He was certainly handsome, with that dark, aquiline, commanding beauty which women so generally recognise as dominant. With men he was distant and cold; but such a bearing never deters womankind. The inscrutable laws of sex have so arranged that even a timid woman is not afraid of a fierce and haughty man. And so it was that there was hardly a woman of any kind or degree, who lived within view of Brent's Rock, who did not cherish some form of secret admiration for the handsome wastrel. The category was a wide one, for Brent's Rock rose up steeply from the midst of a level region and for a circuit of a hundred miles it lay on the horizon, with its high old towers and steep roofs cutting the level edge of wood and hamlet, and far-scattered mansions.

So long as Geoffrey Brent confined his dissipations to London and Paris and Vienna – anywhere out of sight and sound of his home – opinion was silent. It is easy to listen to far off echoes unmoved, and we can treat them with disbelief, or scorn, or disdain, or whatever attitude of coldness may suit our purpose. But when the scandal came close home it was another matter; and the feelings of independence and integrity which is in people of every community which is not utterly spoiled, asserted itself and demanded that condemnation should be expressed. Still there was a certain reticence in all, and no more notice was taken of the existing facts than was absolutely necessary. Margaret Delandre bore herself so fearlessly and so openly – she accepted her position as the justified companion of Geoffrey Brent so naturally that people came to believe that she was secretly married to him, and therefore thought it wiser to hold their tongues lest time should justify her and also make her an active enemy.

The one person who, by his interference, could have settled all doubts was debarred by circumstances from interfering in the matter. Wykham Delandre had quarrelled with his sister – or perhaps it was that she had quarrelled with him – and they were on terms not merely of armed neutrality but of bitter hatred. The quarrel had been antecedent to Margaret going to Brent's Rock. She and Wykham had almost come to blows. There had certainly been threats on one side and on the other; and in the end Wykham, overcome with passion, had ordered his sister to leave his house. She had risen straightway, and, without waiting to pack up even her own personal belongings, had walked out of the house. On the threshold she had paused for a moment to hurl a bitter threat at Wykham that he would rue in shame and despair to the last hour of his life his act of that day. Some weeks had since passed; and it was understood in the neighbourhood that Margaret had gone to London, when she suddenly appeared driving out with Geoffrey Brent, and the entire neighbourhood knew before nightfall that she had taken up her abode at the Rock. It was no subject of surprise that Brent had come back unexpectedly, for such was his usual custom. Even his own servants never knew when to expect him, for there was a private door, of which he alone had the key, by which he sometimes entered without anyone in the house being aware of his coming. This was his usual method of appearing after a long absence.

Wykham Delandre was furious at the news. He vowed vengeance – and to keep his mind level with his passion drank deeper than ever. He tried several times to see his sister, but she contemptuously refused to meet him. He tried to have an interview with Brent and was refused by him also. Then he tried to stop him in the road, but without avail, for Geoffrey was not a man to be stopped against his will. Several actual encounters took place between the two men, and many more were threatened and avoided. At last Wykham Delandre settled down to a morose, vengeful acceptance of the situation.

Neither Margaret nor Geoffrey was of a pacific temperament, and it was not long before there began to be quarrels between them. One thing would lead to another, and wine flowed freely at Brent's Rock. Now and again the quarrels would assume a bitter aspect, and threats would be exchanged in uncompromising language that fairly awed the listening servants. But such quarrels generally ended where domestic altercations do, in reconciliation, and in a mutual respect for the fighting qualities proportionate to their manifestation. Fighting for its own sake is found by a certain class of persons, all the world over, to be a matter of absorbing interest, and there is no reason to believe that domestic conditions minimise its potency. Geoffrey and Margaret made occasional absences from Brent's Rock, and on each of these occasions Wykham Delandre also absented himself; but as he generally heard of the absence too late to be of any service, he returned home each time in a more bitter and discontented frame of mind than before.

At last there came a time when the absence from Brent's Rock became longer than before. Only a few days earlier there had been a quarrel, exceeding in bitterness anything which had gone before; but this, too, had been made up, and a trip on the Continent had been mentioned before the servants. After a few days Wykham Delandre also went away, and it was some weeks before he returned. It was noticed that he was full of some new importance – satisfaction, exaltation – they hardly knew how to call it. He went straightway to Brent's Rock, and demanded to see Geoffrey Brent, and on being told that he had not yet returned, said, with a grim decision which the servants noted:

"I shall come again. My news is solid – it can wait!" and turned away. Week after week went by, and month after month; and then there came a rumour, certified later on, that an accident had occurred in the Zermatt valley. Whilst crossing a dangerous pass the carriage containing an English lady and the driver had fallen over a precipice, the gentleman of the party, Mr. Geoffrey Brent, having been fortunately saved as he had been walking up the hill to ease the horses. He gave information, and search was made. The broken rail, the excoriated roadway, the marks where the horses had struggled on the decline before finally pitching over into the torrent – all told the sad tale. It was a wet season, and there had been much snow in the winter, so that the river was swollen beyond its usual volume, and the eddies of the stream were packed with ice. All search was made, and finally the wreck of the carriage and the body of one horse were found in an eddy of the river. Later on the body of the driver was found on the sandy, torrent-swept waste near Täsch; but the body of the lady, like that of the other horse, had quite disappeared, and was – what was left of it by that time – whirling amongst the eddies of the Rhone on its way down to the Lake of Geneva.

Wykham Delandre made all the enquiries possible, but could not find any trace of the missing woman. He found, however, in the books of the various hotels the name of 'Mr. and Mrs. Geoffrey Brent'. And he had a stone erected at Zermatt to his sister's memory, under her married name, and a tablet put up in the church at Bretten, the parish in which both Brent's Rock and Dander's Croft were situated.

There was a lapse of nearly a year, after the excitement of the matter had worn away, and the whole neighbourhood had gone on its accustomed way. Brent was still absent, and Delandre more drunken, more morose, and more revengeful than before.

Then there was a new excitement. Brent's Rock was being made ready for a new mistress. It was officially announced by Geoffrey himself in a letter to the Vicar, that he had been married some months before to an Italian lady, and that they were then on their way home. Then a small army of workmen invaded the house; and hammer and plane sounded, and a general air of size and paint pervaded the atmosphere. One wing of the old house, the south, was entirely re-done; and then the great body of the workmen departed, leaving only materials for the doing of the old hall when Geoffrey Brent should have returned, for he had directed that the decoration was only to be done under his own eyes. He had brought with him accurate drawings of a hall in the house of his bride's father, for he wished to reproduce for her the place to which she had been accustomed. As the moulding had all to be re-done, some scaffolding poles and boards were brought in and laid on one side of the great hall, and also a great wooden tank or box for mixing the lime, which was laid in bags beside it.

When the new mistress of Brent's Rock arrived the bells of the church rang out, and there was a general jubilation. She was a beautiful creature, full of the poetry and fire and passion of the South; and the few English words which she had learned were spoken in such a sweet and pretty broken way that she won the hearts of the people almost as much by the music of her voice as by the melting beauty of her dark eyes.

Geoffrey Brent seemed more happy than he had ever before appeared; but there was a dark, anxious look on his face that was new to those who knew him of old, and he started at times as though at some noise that was unheard by others.

And so months passed and the whisper grew that at last Brent's Rock was to have an heir. Geoffrey was very tender to his wife, and the new bond between them seemed to soften him. He took more interest in his tenants and their needs than he had ever done; and works of charity on his part as well as on his sweet young wife's were not lacking. He seemed to have set all his hopes on the child that was coming, and as he looked deeper into the future the dark shadow that had come over his face seemed to die gradually away.

All the time Wykham Delandre nursed his revenge. Deep in his heart had grown up a purpose of vengeance which only waited an opportunity to crystallise and take a definite shape. His vague idea was somehow centred in the wife of Brent, for he knew that he could strike him best through those he loved, and the coming time seemed to hold in its womb the opportunity for which he longed. One night he sat alone in the living room of his house. It had once been a handsome room in its way, but time and neglect had done their work and it was now little better than a ruin, without dignity or picturesqueness of any kind. He had been drinking heavily for some time and was more than half stupefied. He thought he heard a noise as of someone at the door and looked up. Then he called half savagely to come in; but there was no response. With a muttered blasphemy he renewed his potations. Presently he forgot all around him, sank into a daze, but suddenly awoke to see standing before him someone or something like a battered, ghostly edition of his sister. For a few moments there came upon him a sort of fear. The woman before him, with distorted features and burning eyes seemed hardly human, and the only thing that seemed a reality of his sister, as she had been, was her wealth of golden hair, and this was now streaked with grey. She eyed her brother with a long, cold stare; and he, too, as he looked and began to realise the actuality of her presence, found the hatred of her which he had had, once again surging up in his heart. All the brooding passion of the past year seemed to find a voice at once as he asked her:

"Why are you here? You're dead and buried."

"I am here, Wykham Delandre, for no love of you, but because I hate another even more than I do you!" A great passion blazed in her eyes.

"Him?" he asked, in so fierce a whisper that even the woman was for an instant startled till she regained her calm.

"Yes, him!" she answered. "But make no mistake, my revenge is my own; and I merely use you to help me to it." Wykham asked suddenly:

"Did he marry you?"

The woman's distorted face broadened out in a ghastly attempt at a smile. It was a hideous mockery, for the broken features and seamed scars took strange shapes and strange colours, and queer lines of white showed out as the straining muscles pressed on the old cicatrices.

"So you would like to know! It would please your pride to feel that your sister was truly married! Well, you shall not know. That was my revenge on you, and I do not mean to change it by a hair's breadth. I have come here tonight simply to let you know that I am alive, so that if any violence be done me where I am going there may be a witness."

"Where are you going?" demanded her brother.

"That is my affair! And I have not the least intention of letting you know!" Wykham stood up, but the drink was on him and he reeled and fell. As he lay on the floor he announced his intention of following his sister; and with an outburst of splenetic humour told her that he would follow her through the darkness by the light of her hair, and of her beauty. At this she turned on him, and said that there were others beside him that would rue her hair and her beauty too. "As he will," she hissed; "for the hair remains though the beauty be gone. When he withdrew the lynch-pin and sent us over the precipice into the torrent, he had little thought of my beauty. Perhaps his beauty would be scarred like mine were he whirled, as I was, among the rocks of the Visp, and frozen on the ice pack in the drift of the river. But let him beware! His time is coming!" and with a fierce gesture she flung open the door and passed out into the night.

* * *

Later on that night, Mrs. Brent, who was but half asleep, became suddenly awake and spoke to her husband:

"Geoffrey, was not that the click of a lock somewhere below our window?"

But Geoffrey – though she thought that he, too, had started at the noise – seemed sound asleep, and breathed heavily. Again Mrs. Brent dozed; but this time awoke to the fact that her husband had arisen and was partially dressed. He was deadly pale, and when the light of the lamp which he had in his hand fell on his face, she was frightened at the look in his eyes.

"What is it, Geoffrey? What dost thou?" she asked.

"Hush! Little one," he answered, in a strange, hoarse voice. "Go to sleep. I am restless, and wish to finish some work I left undone."

"Bring it here, my husband," she said; "I am lonely and I fear when thou art away."

For reply he merely kissed her and went out, closing the door behind him. She lay awake for a while, and then nature asserted itself, and she slept.

Suddenly she started broad awake with the memory in her ears of a smothered cry from somewhere not far off. She jumped up and ran to the door and listened, but there was no sound. She grew alarmed for her husband, and called out: "Geoffrey! Geoffrey!"

After a few moments the door of the great hall opened, and Geoffrey appeared at it, but without his lamp.

"Hush!" he said, in a sort of whisper, and his voice was harsh and stern. "Hush! Get to bed! I am working, and must not be disturbed. Go to sleep, and do not wake the house!"

With a chill in her heart – for the harshness of her husband's voice was new to her – she crept back to bed and lay there trembling, too frightened to cry, and listened to every sound. There was a long pause of silence, and then the sound of some iron implement striking muffled blows! Then there came a clang of a heavy stone falling, followed by a muffled curse. Then a dragging sound, and then more noise of stone on stone. She lay all the while in an agony of fear, and her heart beat dreadfully. She heard a curious sort of scraping sound; and then there was silence. Presently the door opened gently, and Geoffrey appeared. His wife pretended to be asleep; but through her eyelashes she saw him wash from his hands something white that looked like lime.

In the morning he made no allusion to the previous night, and she was afraid to ask any question.

From that day there seemed some shadow over Geoffrey Brent. He neither ate nor slept as he had been accustomed, and his former habit of turning suddenly as though someone were speaking from behind him revived. The old hall seemed to have some kind of fascination for him. He used to go there many times in the day, but grew impatient if anyone, even his wife, entered it. When the builder's foreman came to inquire about continuing his work Geoffrey was out driving; the man went into the hall, and when Geoffrey returned the servant told him of his arrival and where he was. With a frightful oath he pushed the servant aside and hurried up to the old hall. The workman met him almost at the door; and as Geoffrey burst into the room he ran against him. The man apologised:

"Beg pardon, sir, but I was just going out to make some enquiries. I directed twelve sacks of lime to be sent here, but I see there are only ten."

"Damn the ten sacks and the twelve too!" was the ungracious and incomprehensible rejoinder.

The workman looked surprised, and tried to turn the conversation.

"I see, sir, there is a little matter which our people must have done; but the governor will of course see it set right at his own cost."

"What do you mean?"

"That 'ere 'arth-stone, sir: Some idiot must have put a scaffold pole on it and cracked it right down the middle, and it's thick enough you'd think to stand hanythink." Geoffrey was silent for quite a minute, and then said in a constrained voice and with much gentler manner:

"Tell your people that I am not going on with the work in the hall at present. I want to leave it as it is for a while longer."

"All right sir. I'll send up a few of our chaps to take away these poles and lime bags and tidy the place up a bit."

"No! No!" said Geoffrey, "leave them where they are. I shall send and tell you when you are to get on with the work." So the foreman went away, and his comment to his master was:

"I'd send in the bill, sir, for the work already done. 'Pears to me that money's a little shaky in that quarter."

Once or twice Delandre tried to stop Brent on the road, and, at last, finding that he could not attain his object rode after the carriage, calling out:

"What has become of my sister, your wife?" Geoffrey lashed his horses into a gallop, and the other, seeing from his white face and from his wife's collapse almost into a faint that his object was attained, rode away with a scowl and a laugh.

That night when Geoffrey went into the hall he passed over to the great fireplace, and all at once started back with a smothered cry. Then with an effort he pulled himself together and went away, returning with a light. He bent down over the broken hearth-stone to see if the moonlight falling through the storied window had in any way deceived him. Then with a groan of anguish he sank to his knees.

There, sure enough, through the crack in the broken stone were protruding a multitude of threads of golden hair just tinged with grey!

He was disturbed by a noise at the door, and looking round, saw his wife standing in the doorway. In the desperation of the moment he took action to prevent discovery, and lighting a match at the lamp, stooped down and burned away the hair that rose through the broken stone. Then rising nonchalantly as he could, he pretended surprise at seeing his wife beside him.

For the next week he lived in an agony; for, whether by accident or design, he could not find himself alone in the hall for any length of time. At each visit the hair had grown afresh through the crack, and he had to watch it carefully lest his terrible secret should be discovered. He tried to find a receptacle for the body of the murdered woman outside the house, but someone always interrupted him; and once, when he was coming out of the private doorway, he was met by his wife, who began to question him about it, and manifested surprise that she should not have before noticed the key which he now reluctantly showed her. Geoffrey dearly and passionately loved his wife, so that any possibility of her discovering his dread secrets, or even of doubting him, filled him with anguish; and after a couple of days had passed, he could not help coming to the conclusion that, at least, she suspected something.

That very evening she came into the hall after her drive and found him there sitting moodily by the deserted fireplace. She spoke to him directly.

"Geoffrey, I have been spoken to by that fellow Delandre, and he says horrible things. He tells to me that a week ago his sister returned to his house, the wreck and ruin of her former self, with only her golden hair as of old, and announced some fell intention. He asked me where she is – and oh, Geoffrey, she is dead, she is dead! So how can she have returned? Oh! I am in dread, and I know not where to turn!"

For answer, Geoffrey burst into a torrent of blasphemy which made her shudder. He cursed Delandre and his sister and all their kind, and in especial he hurled curse after curse on her golden hair.

"Oh, hush! Hush!" she said, and was then silent, for she feared her husband when she saw the evil effect of his humour. Geoffrey in the torrent of his anger stood up and moved away from the hearth; but suddenly stopped as he saw a new look of terror in his wife's eyes. He followed their glance, and then he too, shuddered – for there on the broken hearth-stone lay a golden streak as the point of the hair rose though the crack.

"Look, look!" she shrieked. "Is it some ghost of the dead! Come away – come away!" and seizing her husband by the wrist with the frenzy of madness, she pulled him from the room.

That night she was in a raging fever. The doctor of the district attended her at once, and special aid was telegraphed for to London. Geoffrey was in despair, and in his anguish at the danger of his young wife almost forgot his own crime and its consequences. In the evening the doctor had to leave to attend to others; but he left Geoffrey in charge of his wife. His last words were:

"Remember, you must humour her till I come in the morning, or till some other doctor has her case in hand. What you have to dread is another attack of emotion. See that she is kept warm. Nothing more can be done."

Late in the evening, when the rest of the household had retired, Geoffrey's wife got up from her bed and called to her husband.

"Come!" she said. "Come to the old hall! I know where the gold comes from! I want to see it grow!"

Geoffrey would fain have stopped her, but he feared for her life or reason on the one hand, and lest in a paroxysm she should shriek out her terrible suspicion, and seeing that it was useless to try to prevent her, wrapped a warm rug around her and went with her to the old hall. When they entered, she turned and shut the door and locked it.

"We want no strangers amongst us three tonight!" she whispered with a wan smile.

"We three! Nay we are but two," said Geoffrey with a shudder; he feared to say more.

"Sit here," said his wife as she put out the light. "Sit here by the hearth and watch the gold growing. The silver moonlight is jealous! See, it steals along the floor towards the gold – our gold!" Geoffrey looked with growing horror, and saw that during the hours that had passed the golden hair had protruded further through the broken hearth-stone. He tried to hide it by placing his feet over the broken place; and his wife, drawing her chair beside him, leant over and laid her head on his shoulder.

"Now do not stir, dear," she said; "let us sit still and watch. We shall find the secret of the growing gold!" He passed his arm round her and sat silent; and as the moonlight stole along the floor she sank to sleep.

He feared to wake her; and so sat silent and miserable as the hours stole away.

Before his horror-struck eyes the golden hair from the broken stone grew and grew; and as it increased, so his heart got colder and colder, till at last he had not power to stir, and sat with eyes full of terror watching his doom.

* * *

In the morning when the London doctor came, neither Geoffrey nor his wife could be found. Search was made in all the rooms, but without avail. As a last resource the great door of the old hall was broken open, and those who entered saw a grim and sorry sight.

There by the deserted hearth Geoffrey Brent and his young wife sat cold and white and dead. Her face was peaceful, and her eyes were closed in sleep; but his face was a sight that made all who saw it shudder, for there was on it a look of unutterable horror. The eyes were open and stared glassily at his feet, which were twined with tresses of golden hair, streaked with grey, which came through the broken hearth-stone.

Rusalka

Anna Taborska

Full fathom five thy father lies;
Of his bones are coral made;
Those are pearls that were his eyes:
Nothing of him that doth fade,
But doth suffer a sea-change
Into something rich and strange.
Sea-nymphs hourly ring his knell:
Hark! now I hear them – Ding-dong, bell.

William Shakespeare

I ALWAYS LOVED Shakespeare at school. Never went on to college. I guess the possibility just didn't figure on anybody's radar. Once I turned sixteen and school was over, I went straight back to work on my parents' farm. But I didn't stop reading. The number of times my father caught me stretched out under the oak tree at the far end of the north field with a copy of *Macbeth* or *King Lear*… Once, in a fit of rage, he swore he'd cut the old tree down, and he did too. But don't think that my father was a bad man – not at all. He just worried that he would die and leave my mother with no-one to take care of her. He loved my mother, you see – loved her like a man possessed. He wouldn't let her sew at night lest she strain her eyes; he wouldn't let her help in the fields so she wouldn't become all hunched over and sore-backed like the other women in the village. He wouldn't even let her milk the cow in case she got cow pox and her dainty little hands grew blistered and calloused. Very delicate she was – my mother. Pale-skinned and raven-haired, with haunted green eyes. My father always said that she'd married beneath her, and that he was the luckiest man in the world.

But my father shouldn't have worried; it was my mother who died first. Cancer, the doctors said. Her cheeks grew gaunt and her whole face appeared to recede until her huge frightened eyes seemed to be all that was left, like a pair of emerald moons shining brightest before their eclipse. Her slender body shrivelled away to nothing. And her raven locks became streaked with white, then fell from her scalp after the hospital treatment – like discarded angel-hair once the festive season is over and Christmas trees are thrown on the compost heap to rot. My father's cries were pitiful to hear. His violent episodes became more frequent as his drinking increased; my mother – the only thing that had stood between him and his baser nature – was gone. He didn't hit me – as even through the veil of cheap whiskey he must have remembered my mother's screams the one time he'd laid a hand on me – but he found my books and burned them. *Coriolanus, Hamlet, As You Like It*, all the tattered copies of the Histories and Tragedies I had acquired from second-hand bookstores in the nearest town with the pennies my mother had slipped me out of her housekeeping money. All gone up in smoke. Only *The Tempest* escaped annihilation. I think my father simply hadn't seen it – for there is no other explanation as to its survival. It was as if Prospero had come out of retirement and conjured up a supernatural mist – shrouding the small volume and rendering it invisible for five long minutes while my father rampaged through my tiny room. Or some such thing. When my father finally fell asleep on the kitchen table, tears in his eyes and an empty bottle in his hand, I picked up *The Tempest* and left. I never saw my father again.

* * *

Four years later, aged twenty-two now and having worked my way across Europe doing odd jobs, I found myself in Eastern Poland. I'd wanted to come here for some time, as my mother had mentioned that her mother came from a village in this part of the world. I hadn't pushed her on the subject, as it always seemed to make her sad; I gather that the family had fled some pogrom or other when the Russians occupied the region. But I regretted not having asked exactly which village it was…

The country was beginning to recover from forty-five years of communism, but nobody had told the peasants in its easternmost areas. Here people still scratched a meagre living from the difficult soil.

I'd saved some money working as a hotel receptionist in Lublin, and I knocked around the countryside, half-heartedly looking for my grandmother's village, and whole-heartedly enjoying the exotic landscape of ramshackle settlements and unspoilt forests.

I fell in love with the little village of Switeziec at once, and took up temporary residence with an old lady who let rooms and cooked a great breakfast. To my delight, her grandson Piotr – a friendly young man of eighteen or so – knew a little English; and what he didn't know, he made up for in enthusiasm, expansive gestures and an easy laugh, which always seemed to be bubbling just under the surface, ready to erupt.

"They start to teach English in school as soon as compulsory Russian was kicked out," laughed Piotr when I expressed my surprise at his linguistic skills. I couldn't help but think that Piotr made a nice change from the serious, somewhat gloomy majority of young Polish men I'd come across so far. Young men who reminded me too much of… well… me. Yes, I realised that laughter was something that didn't come easily to me, and I often chided myself for my inability to kick back and have fun.

"You come to Switeziec at good time," Piotr flashed a full set of healthy-looking teeth at me. "We have big party tonight." I waited for Piotr to continue, then realised that he was awaiting my response.

"Oh, I see. Well. Thanks for mentioning it, Piotr, but I've got to get an early start tomorrow if I'm going to get to the next village…" Piotr blinked uncomprehendingly. "You remember what we spoke about? – I'm trying to find the village my grandmother's family came from?"

"Oh, I see." Piotr looked crestfallen for a moment, but the teeth were out again soon enough. "But tonight is very special night. It's… longest day. Very special."

"Oh. Midsummer's Eve?… So it is."

"Yes. We have very special party. It's tradition. We have fire and the girls make… out of flowers… and light candles… and put them on river, and the boys have to catch them."

"What?"

"I not explain well…" Piotr's frustration was painful to watch. "It's tradition… You will like… Please, you come with me." Whether it was a chance to practise his English, or to show off his foreign friend to the other villagers, or just his innate friendliness and desire to be a great host that rendered my presence so seemingly important to him, I don't know, but when Piotr's smile started to waver, I gave in. And so later that evening I found myself following him and a group of his friends to the river that flowed west of the village.

* * *

Twilight had been slow in coming. Beyond the various shades of grey, an orange glow emanated from the riverbank. As we got closer, the sounds of singing and laughter steadily grew. There was a large bonfire on the nearside. Young men sat around, drinking beers and talking excitedly. On the far bank, and about fifty metres upriver, was another bonfire.

"The girls are making... erm... out of flowers," Piotr tried to explain, following my gaze. "Like this." He used both hands to draw a circle in the air.

"Wreaths?" I suggested.

"Yes, wreaths... Normally you put on head, like this," Piotr demonstrated by lifting the invisible circle and placing it on his head, "but today they put candles in them and put them on river." I nodded, doing my best to understand.

"The boys catch the... wreaths. And when a boy catch the wreath, he can kiss the girl who made it."

"I see... But how do you know whose wreath you've fished out?"

"Oh, I think the boys – they just kiss the girl they like."

"That sounds like cheating to me," I quipped.

Piotr looked at me, worked out that I was joking, and started to laugh.

There was a flurry of giggling and exited shrieks from the far side of the river.

"Look!" cried Piotr, "Girls put wreaths on water!" And sure enough, a dozen or so little lights came floating in our direction. Some went out almost immediately, others sank without a trace, but a few continued to float and burn, carried downriver by the strong current.

Piotr's friends giggled no less than the girls, and rushed down the bank with the other youths.

"Come on!" Piotr called out as he hurried after the others, who were already braving the freezing water to intercept those wreaths that hadn't already drowned.

I followed cautiously, afraid of slipping and falling in. I'd always been scared of water; even before the time when my father had tried to teach me to swim. He'd used the same method his father had used on him: he'd rowed us out to the middle of the lake near our farm, and pushed me out of the boat. I don't remember much after that, except that he'd had to fish me out himself; his anger at having to get wet tempered by the fear that he'd actually drowned me and that the shock would kill my mother. He never gave me another swimming lesson, evidently deciding that having a pathetic runt of a son was better than having a dead one.

The mirth on the riverbank was infectious, and I couldn't help but smile as Piotr beat his friend to a wreath and pulled it out of the water, waving it in the air and whooping in triumph. Then I saw something that stopped the breath in my lungs.

She was standing between the willows on the far bank, a little aside from the other girls. The light from the bonfire seemed to die before it reached her, and she was bathed in shadow. At first I thought that one of the willows had moved, and I felt startled and disorientated. As I peered into the gloom, my eyes adjusted, and then I saw her quite plainly — no, 'plainly' is the wrong word – for there was nothing plain about her at all. The bonfire, the singing, the shouts and laughter – everything subsided and disappeared for a moment. All I was aware of was the girl on the other side of the river. She was tall and slender; her dress as pale as her delicate features. Her waist-long hair was so fair it seemed to glow blue in the twilight. As I stared, the girl turned to face me, and I finally understood what people meant when they said that their heart had skipped a beat. I paused, steadying myself, and inhaled deeply. She smiled at me and, despite the distance and the scant light, I could tell that her lips were the colour of coral. Every detail of her form was etched into my memory from that moment on, forever. The only strange thing was – perhaps because she tilted her head down shyly, perhaps because a strand of flaxen hair fell across her face – I couldn't see her eyes.

The girl waved at me; her hand small, with long, tapering fingers. I looked around to see whether she could be waving at someone else, but there was no one behind or next to me. Hesitantly, I waved back, and she waved again, beckoning me to join her on the far bank. My heart beat so fast I could hardly breathe.

"Piotr!" I ran up to the boy and grabbed his arm.

"Hey," he turned towards me and grinned. "Look! I have a wreath."

"Where can I cross the river?"

"Huh?"

"Where's the nearest place I can cross the river?" I slowed my words right down, articulating each one as clearly as I could.

"Just there, to the right," Piotr's confusion was replaced by mere surprise, and he pointed downriver. I peered into the darkness, but saw nothing. "There are logs put on river. About twenty metres that way," continued Piotr, adding: "Hey, why do you want to go to girls' side anyway?" Then he grinned, "It's cheating!"

"The girl," was all I managed by way of an explanation.

"It's cheating," Piotr repeated, laughing. "You're supposed to catch a wreath first… Anyway, which girl it is you like?"

"The girl," I pointed across the water, but she was gone. An indescribable, overwhelming feeling of loss and longing came over me; I felt like I'd been kicked in the stomach and I figured I must be having a panic attack of some sort.

"What girl?" laughed Piotr, then stopped laughing as he saw the look on my face.

"The blonde girl," I tried to explain, my eyes scouring the opposite bank. "Look, Piotr, thanks," I stammered. "I've got to go."

I staggered off in the direction of the makeshift bridge, leaving a perplexed Piotr muttering to his friends – something about the lovelorn foreigner, no doubt.

Soon I was standing next to the bridge – a couple of logs thrown over the fast flowing river. I stared down into the murky water.

Full fathom five thy father lies;

If I had any chance at all of finding the girl, I'd have to get a move on. I placed my right foot on one of the logs, then, checking to make sure there was nobody watching, I got down on my hands and knees, tested the logs and started to crawl along them; one hand and knee on one log, one on the other.

The gushing noise of the current made me feel giddy. I determined to crawl straight over to the other side, without looking down. I made it about halfway across, but then I caught sight of something white in the water to my left.

Of his bones are coral made;

I came to an unsteady halt. I could hear my breath coming in short gasps and my heart beating – a blessing, I thought, as it seemed to drown out the hideous hiss of the river. Holding onto the rough bark of the logs, I glanced down to my left.

Nothing: only blackness and the rushing, hissing water. I took a deep breath and moved off slowly. It came again: a silvery flash in the water, caught out of the corner of my eye.

I jerked my head in the direction of whatever it was, digging my fingers into the wood and flattening myself against the logs for fear of falling in. And I saw it: a pale shape floating just beneath the surface of the inky water. In my fear, I thought I could make out a human face, and for a moment I believed I was looking at a corpse.

Those are pearls that were his eyes:

But then the thing disappeared upriver, apparently swimming against the strong current. Once I stopped trembling, I crawled as quickly as I dared to the far side. I stood up shakily and looked upriver. Nothing there. As my heartbeat returned to normal, I told myself that I'd imagined everything; that my innate fear of death by water had conjured up visions of corpse-like monsters to torment me.

Then I remembered the girl, and that unbearable feeling of sadness and yearning returned. I hurried up the bank, unnerved by the willows, which looked like frozen human forms in the half-light, and headed upriver.

As I approached the girls' bonfire, I looked in vain for the girl with the flaxen hair. The other girls didn't notice me at first, but as my search grew more desperate, a couple of them spotted me. They approached, giggling, and searched me for any sign of a wreath, telling me off and shooing me away amicably when they found no sign of one. I stumbled past the bonfire and into the forest beyond.

* * *

The forest was a frightening place at night. The darkness was full of noises – rustling and scuttling, as startled animals fled before me into the undergrowth. Never for a moment did I stop to think about what I was doing. I only knew that if I didn't find the girl, my heart would break – indeed, it was breaking already.

"Hello?" I called out, peering between the ancient trees. "Are you there?" Only the wind answered, sighing in the branches. For a moment I thought I glimpsed something white flitting in between the trees nearest the river. "Hey!" I called out, and tried to run, but tripped on a root and almost fell. I righted myself by grabbing hold of a tree, scratching my hand painfully in the process. When I looked up again, there was nothing between the trees but shadow. I stumbled on in this inept and idiotic way, imagining from time to time that I could see a wisp of blue-white hair ahead of me, stopping only when the dawn chorus broke through my desperate reveries and a rosy glimmer appeared in the east. Defeated and exhausted, I turned around and headed back along the river.

The shouts and laughter, and glow of the bonfire, reached me before I broke clear of the tree line. I was surprised to find the young villagers still partying. The boys and girls had largely paired off, and were holding hands and leaping across the fairly feisty remains of the fire. Had I been in a fit state to appreciate what was going on around me, I would no doubt have concluded that their stamina and party spirit was something to be admired, even if the local vodka was a contributing factor.

"Hey!" someone called, and then Piotr was patting me on the back and laughing – a relieved kind of laugh. "Where have you been? I been worried for you!"

"I'm sorry, Piotr," I muttered gloomily.

"Where you were?"

"I was looking for the girl," I told him, but didn't expect to make him understand.

"What girl? All the girls are here…" I must have looked as shattered and distressed as I was feeling, because Piotr put his arm around my shoulders and said, "Come on, my friend, we go home." I protested weekly, mumbling something about having to look for the girl. "Come on, man," Piotr steered me in a friendly, but firm manner away from the river. "You look terrible. You need sleep."

"But…"

"I help you look for girl tomorrow… or actually, later today." Piotr winked at a cute red-headed girl and whispered something to her which made her smile, then led me back to his grandmother's house.

* * *

I fell into an exhausted sleep – punctuated by dreams of floating corpses, dark forests, and the girl disappearing among the trees – and woke at lunchtime. I got dressed and sloped downstairs, presumably looking awful, as a worried look appeared on Piotr's grandmother's face when she saw me. She asked Piotr a question and he shrugged her off, in a not unfriendly manner. He pushed an empty chair away from the table, inviting me to sit down. I forced myself to sit, but every nerve in my body was crying out to get back outside and look for the girl.

Piotr's grandmother busied herself at the stove, and moments later set a bowl of hot hunter's stew down in front of me, along with a small basket of fresh rye bread. I hadn't eaten since the previous evening and yet, when Piotr's grandmother gestured for me to eat, I found that I couldn't.

"I'm sorry," I said, feeling miserable and ungrateful.

"You feel bad?" asked Piotr, the concern in his face echoing that in his grandmother's.

"The girl," I said. "I have to find her." I rose swiftly, apologised again to Piotr's grandmother, and headed for the door.

"Wait!" Piotr got up and ran after me. "I come with you!"

* * *

A couple of hours later, Piotr persuaded me to return to the house for fear that I would pass out. Reluctantly I succumbed, drinking a cup of sweet tea and packing a chunk of bread, before heading back out, much to the chagrin of Piotr's grandmother.

"I come with you," said Piotr, somewhat less enthusiastically than earlier.

"No," I insisted. "You stay here; your grandmother looks worried." I left quickly, hearing Piotr and his grandmother arguing as I walked away.

I spent the rest of the day following the Swita River first one way, then the other. Once or twice I thought I saw something pale shimmering in the water, but when I turned to look, it was gone. When my feet grew too sore to keep walking, I returned to the house and tried to sleep. I tossed and turned, and attempted to free my mind of thoughts, but whenever I closed my eyes, I saw the girl waving to me from the row of willows. The terrible yearning and hopelessness gnawed away at me, and I'm ashamed to say that I cried into my pillow. I finally dozed off a little before dawn, and got up late again.

As I entered the kitchen, Piotr's grandmother eyed me with unease.

"*Piotrusiu!*" she called, and a moment later Piotr appeared, smiling at me in a worried way that I was coming to dislike. There was a brief exchange between the two of them, during which the look on the old woman's face became progressively more alarmed. She said something to Piotr, who laughed, causing her to brandish a wooden spoon at him in a less than friendly gesture. She cast me an extremely troubled glance, then returned her attention to the frying pan.

"Are you okay?" asked Piotr.

"I'm fine," I said, forcing myself to smile at the old lady as she set a plate of ham and eggs down in front of me before sitting down opposite and staring at me intently.

"What you are going to do today?" questioned Piotr with feigned cheerfulness; then added doubtfully, "You are going to look for your grandmother's village?"

"No."

"You are going to look for girl?"

"Yes."

Piotr's grandmother evidently asked Piotr what I'd said. The boy translated, and the old lady leapt up from the table, glanced at me, then let out a tirade at her grandson, who was looking more and more embarrassed.

"What did she say?" I asked.

"Nothing," said Piotr.

"Tell me, please."

"It's rubbish. Stupid story."

"Piotr!" I pleaded, and the old lady interjected on my behalf.

"Okay," Piotr finally gave in. "My grandmother says your girl is Rusalka."

"Who?"

"Rusalka. A bad spirit."

"What do you mean?"

"It's an old story that the peasants tell."

"Go on."

"They say that if a girl dies... violent death, or kill herself... she becomes Rusalka. A bad spirit. They live in water and in trees."

"Like nymphs?" If I hadn't been in such a sorry state, I probably would have found Piotr's story entertaining.

"Yes... Stupid story."

"Yes," I agreed. Then I noticed Piotr's grandmother still staring at me and nodding her head gravely. "But please tell your grandmother not to worry. The girl I saw isn't a... Rusalka. She's a girl, and I'm worried that something might have happened to her. I need to find her." I got up and headed out, stopping Piotr from following me with a staying hand gesture.

The day passed much as the previous one, except that the sadness and feeling I can only describe as emptiness was even stronger than before. It was as though I'd lost a limb, but could still feel intense pain where it had once been.

I went home when it got dark, and went to bed without speaking to Piotr. I couldn't face his questions or his grandmother's look of concern. I lay awake for a long time, looking at the ceiling. When I finally closed my eyes, the full moon rose outside my window, its light unnerving me even through closed lids. I could swear I heard someone whispering my name, and I turned to the window. The moonlight was silver-blue, like the girl's hair. The whispering came again and the sighing of the wind in the branches of the tree outside. Eventually I could lie there no longer. I got dressed, crept as quietly as I could along the creaky wooden floor, and headed for the river.

* * *

The fields were a pale grey, and beyond them the river sparkled silver. I planned to start at the makeshift bridge, then work my way upriver and into the forest. I walked along distractedly and didn't notice that I was approaching the water a little upriver of my chosen starting point. In fact, it wasn't until I was at the river's edge that I noticed I'd come out amidst the willows – in almost the same place as I'd seen the girl. Startled out of my stupor by that thought, I looked across to where she'd stood. I thought I heard my name whispered on the wind, and then I saw a willow move in the pale light. No, not a willow – her! Standing on the opposite side of the river, now as she had the first time I'd seen her, but even more beautiful in the moonlight, even more heart-stopping. A shiver ran down my spine and goose bumps appeared on my skin despite the warm June night. The girl's hair was so pale that it glowed blue in the moon's rays, and her lips were the colour of coral. I tried, but I couldn't see her eyes. She smiled at me and waved, beckoning me to join her on the other side of the river. Mesmerised, I took a step forward, then stopped as my foot slipped on the soft mud of the riverbank and I nearly lost my footing. I looked down at the rushing, roaring current and felt dizzy. But I had to get to her somehow.

"Wait!" I pleaded. "I'll cross over the bridge!" But she was already moving off in the opposite direction. "Wait, please!" I ran a few steps towards the bridge, then turned quickly and ran after the girl, keeping track of her across the river as she moved in and out of the willows, smiling and waving to me. Each time her slim form disappeared from my field of vision, it was like a stab to my heart. I'd missed my opportunity to cross the bridge to her side of the river, but I wouldn't let her out of my sight for more than a split-second.

"Hey, slow down! Please!" I followed her upriver. The solitary willows gave way to clusters of birch, oak and pine, and soon we were in the forest; the river between us all the while. She was the most beautiful thing one could imagine; she was a silvery-blue angel, shining among the dark monoliths of the trees. I panicked as she disappeared from view, and quickened my pace.

"Where are you?" I practically begged, hurrying deeper and deeper into the forest. "Please! Where are you?" Light-headed with anxiety, I stopped and peered across the river. For a moment all was still and I was alone with my own heartbeat once again. A stab of fear and that overpowering sense of loss assaulted me for a moment, and then I saw her. She moved from behind a tree and stood directly opposite me on the far side of the river. Naked. The moonlight reflected off her lily-white skin and blue-blonde hair. Her body was perfection, and she stood quite still, gazing at me, frozen like the alabaster statue of a goddess. I heard my name whispered in the air, and the girl moved so gracefully that she seemed to float down to the water's edge. She waved to me, beckoning me to approach the river on my side. I got as close to the water as I dared, then stopped and watched the girl go in.

"No!" I called out in alarm. "Don't." But the girl merely laughed and immersed herself in the river; the water covering her nakedness. She waved to me to join her, and I waved back, pleading with her to come to my side. The girl laughed and swam over to my side, then swam leisurely back to the middle of the river and floated there. The ease with which she swam and floated in that rushing water made me wonder whether perhaps the current was less strong than it looked and sounded. Perhaps the water wasn't as deep as I'd thought.

The girl beckoned me again and I shook my head, indicating for her to swim to me and come out. I held a hand out to her, and eventually she swam towards me, stopping just a little out of my reach. I extended my hand out further, and she pushed herself up from the water and reached out to me. As she did so, the drops of water on her breasts sparkled like diamonds. I couldn't take my eyes off her. She moved away again and I lost my balance, toppling into the icy water.

Fear – all the more dreadful for its long-forgotten familiarity – seized me as the dark waters closed over my head. I flailed my arms wildly, managing somehow to right myself and get my head above the surface. Eyes screwed shut against the lashing current, I coughed up water and finally managed to scream for help. Then I felt arms around me – arms colder than the river against which I fought.

"Help me," I begged through the roar of the raging water – water that no longer looked silver, but black and threatening. I felt the brush of wet hair on my face and of icy lips against my ear – lips colder than the spray that blinded me. The girl whispered my name, and her voice was the sigh of the wind and the murmur of the sea. For a moment I remembered my mother and how she would hold a large shell to my ear when I was little, and say, "Listen, my love, it's the sound of the sea."

The girl's grip on me tightened and I prayed that she would save me, but the water closed over my head once more.

* * *

I try to draw breath, but swallow river water instead. I don't understand. I kick and writhe, but cold hands pull me down and hold me firm.

Gradually I weaken and stop fighting. My terror subsides and I open my eyes. In the blackness, the girl's face looms white before my own. She lifts her heavy lids and I see her eyes clearly for the first time. Fear seizes me once more; the last of my air escapes in a flurry of bubbles as I panic. She holds onto me and smiles, gazing at me with those eyes – a corpse's eyes: milky, opaque… like pearls.

My lungs swell with water. A strange calm descends on me and I stop struggling for the last time. The girl cradles me in her arms.

I wonder if the current will carry me down to the sea…

The Tarn

Hugh Walpole

Chapter I

AS FOSTER MOVED unconsciously across the room, bent towards the bookcase, and stood leaning forward a little, choosing now one book, now another, with his eyes, his host, seeing the muscles of the back of his thin, scraggy neck stand out above his low flannel collar, thought of the ease with which he could squeeze that throat, and the pleasure, the triumphant, lustful pleasure, that such an action would give him.

The low, white-walled, white-ceilinged room was flooded with the mellow, kindly Lakeland sun. October is a wonderful month in the English Lakes, golden, rich, and perfumed, slow suns moving through apricot-tinted skies to ruby evening glories; the shadows lie then thick about that beautiful country, in dark purple patches, in long web-like patterns of silver gauze, in thick splotches of amber and grey. The clouds pass in galleons across the mountains, now veiling, now revealing, now descending with ghost-like armies to the very breast of the plains, suddenly rising to the softest of blue skies and lying thin in lazy languorous colour.

Fenwick's cottage looked across to Low Fells; on his right, seen through side windows, sprawled the hills above Ullswater.

Fenwick looked at Foster's back and felt suddenly sick, so that he sat down, veiling his eyes for a moment with his hand. Foster had come up there, come all the way from London, to explain. It was so like Foster to want to explain, to want to put things right. For how many years had he known Foster? Why, for twenty at least, and during all those years Foster had been forever determined to put things right with everybody. He could never bear to be disliked; he hated that anyone should think ill of him; he wanted everyone to be his friends. That was one reason, perhaps, why Foster had got on so well, had prospered so in his career; one reason, too, why Fenwick had not.

For Fenwick was the opposite of Foster in this. He did not want friends, he certainly did not care that people should like him – that is people for whom, for one reason or another, he had contempt – and he had contempt for quite a number of people.

Fenwick looked at that long, thin, bending back and felt his knees tremble. Soon Foster would turn round and that high, reedy voice would pipe out something about the books. "What jolly books you have, Fenwick!" How many, many times in the long watches of the night, when Fenwick could not sleep, had he heard that pipe sounding close there – yes, in the very shadows of his bed! And how many times had Fenwick replied to it: "I hate you! You are the cause of my failure in life! You have been in my way always. Always, always, always! Patronising and pretending, and in truth showing others what a poor thing you thought me, how great a failure, how conceited a fool! I know. You can hide nothing from me! I can hear you!"

For twenty years now Foster had been persistently in Fenwick's way. There had been that affair, so long ago now, when Robins had wanted a sub-editor for his wonderful review, the *Parthenon*, and Fenwick had gone to see him and they had had a splendid talk. How magnificently Fenwick had talked that day; with what enthusiasm he had shown Robins (who was blinded by his own conceit, anyway) the kind of paper the *Parthenon* might be; how Robins had caught his own enthusiasm, how he had pushed his fat body about the room, crying: "Yes, yes, Fenwick – that's fine! That's fine indeed!" – and then how, after all, Foster had got that job.

The paper had only lived for a year or so, it is true, but the connection with it had brought Foster into prominence just as it might have brought Fenwick!

Then, five years later, there was Fenwick's novel, *The Bitter Aloe* – the novel upon which he had spent three years of blood-and-tears endeavour – and then, in the very same week of publication, Foster brings out *The Circus*, the novel that made his name; although, Heaven knows, the thing was poor enough sentimental trash. You may say that one novel cannot kill another – but can it not? Had not *The Circus* appeared would not that group of London know-alls – that conceited, limited, ignorant, self-satisfied crowd, who nevertheless can do, by their talk, so much to affect a book's good or evil fortunes – have talked about *The Bitter Aloe* and so forced it into prominence? As it was, the book was stillborn and *The Circus* went on its prancing, triumphant way.

After that there had been many occasions – some small, some big – and always in one way or another that thin, scraggy body of Foster's was interfering with Fenwick's happiness.

The thing had become, of course, an obsession with Fenwick. Hiding up there in the heart of the Lakes, with no friends, almost no company, and very little money, he was given too much to brooding over his failure. He was a failure and it was not his own fault. How could it be his own fault with his talents and his brilliance? It was the fault of modern life and its lack of culture, the fault of the stupid material mess that made up the intelligence of human beings – and the fault of Foster.

Always Fenwick hoped that Foster would keep away from him. He did not know what he would not do did he see the man. And then one day, to his amazement, he received a telegram:

Passing through this way. May I stop with you Monday and Tuesday? – Giles Foster.

Fenwick could scarcely believe his eyes, and then – from curiosity, from cynical contempt, from some deeper, more mysterious motive that he dared not analyse – he had telegraphed – *Come.*

And here the man was. And he had come – would you believe it? – to 'put things right'. He had heard from Hamlin Eddis that Fenwick was hurt with him, had some kind of grievance.

"I didn't like to feel that, old man, and so I thought I'd just stop by and have it out with you, see what the matter was, and put it right."

Last night after supper Foster had tried to put it right. Eagerly, his eyes like a good dog's who is asking for a bone that he knows he thoroughly deserves, he had held out his hand and asked Fenwick to 'say what was up'.

Fenwick simply had said that nothing was up, Hamlin Eddis was a damned fool.

"Oh, I'm glad to hear that!" Foster had cried, springing up out of his chair and putting his hand on Fenwick's shoulder. "I'm glad of that, old man. I couldn't bear for us not to be friends. We've been friends so long."

Lord! How Fenwick hated him at that moment!

Chapter II

"WHAT A JOLLY lot of books you have!" Foster turned round and looked at Fenwick with eager, gratified eyes. "Every book here is interesting! I like your arrangement of them, too, and those open bookshelves – it always seems to me a shame to shut up books behind glass!"

Foster came forward and sat down quite close to his host. He even reached forward and laid his hand on his host's knee. "Look here! I'm mentioning it for the last time – positively! But I do want to make quite certain. There *is* nothing wrong between us, is there, old man? I know you assured me last night, but I just want…"

Fenwick looked at him and, surveying him, felt suddenly an exquisite pleasure of hatred. He liked the touch of the man's hand on his knee; he himself bent forward a little and, thinking how agreeable it would be to push Foster's eyes in, deep, deep into his head, crunching them, smashing them to purple, leaving the empty, staring, bloody sockets, said:

"Why, no. Of course not. I told you last night. What could there be?"

The hand gripped the knee a little more tightly.

"I *am* so glad! That's splendid! Splendid! I hope you won't think me ridiculous, but I've always had an affection for you ever since I can remember. I've always wanted to know you better. I've admired your talent so greatly. That novel of yours – the – the – the one about the aloe—"

"*The Bitter Aloe?*"

"Ah yes, that was it. That was a splendid book. Pessimistic, of course, but still fine. It ought to have done better. I remember thinking so at the time."

"Yes, it ought to have done better."

"Your time will come, though. What I say is that good work always tells in the end."

"Yes, my time will come."

The thin, piping voice went on:

"Now, I've had more success than I deserved. Oh yes, I have. You can't deny it. I'm not falsely modest. I mean it. I've got some talent, of course, but not so much as people say. And you! Why, you've got so *much* more than they acknowledge. You have, old man. You have indeed. Only – I do hope you'll forgive my saying this – perhaps you haven't advanced quite as you might have done. Living up here, shut away here, closed in by all these mountains, in this wet climate – always raining – why, you're out of things! You don't see people, don't talk and discover what's really going on. Why, look at me!"

Fenwick turned round and looked at him.

"Now, I have half the year in London, where one gets the best of everything, best talk, best music, best plays; and then I'm three months abroad, Italy or Greece or somewhere, and then three months in the country. Now, that's an ideal arrangement. You have everything that way."

Italy or Greece or somewhere!

Something turned in Fenwick's breast, grinding, grinding, grinding. How he had longed, oh, how passionately, for just one week in Greece, two days in Sicily! Sometimes he had thought that he might run to it, but when it had come to the actual counting of the pennies… And how this fool, this fat-head, this self-satisfied, conceited, patronising…

He got up, looking out at the golden sun.

"What do you say to a walk?" he suggested. "The sun will last for a good hour yet."

Chapter III

AS SOON AS the words were out of his lips he felt as though someone else had said them for him. He even turned half round to see whether anyone else were there. Ever since Foster's arrival on the evening before he had been conscious of this sensation. A walk? Why should he take Foster for a walk, show him his beloved country, point out those curves and lines and hollows, the broad silver shield of Ullswater, the cloudy purple hills hunched like blankets about the knees of some recumbent giant? Why? It was as though he had turned round to someone behind him and had said: "You have some further design in this."

They started out. The road sank abruptly to the lake, then the path ran between trees at the water's edge. Across the lake tones of bright yellow light, crocus-hued, rode upon the blue. The hills were dark.

The very way that Foster walked bespoke the man. He was always a little ahead of you, pushing his long, thin body along with little eager jerks, as though, did he not hurry, he would miss something that would be immensely to his advantage. He talked, throwing words over his shoulder to Fenwick as you throw crumbs of bread to a robin.

"Of course I was pleased. Who would not be? After all, it's a new prize. They've only been awarding it for a year or two, but it's gratifying – really gratifying – to secure it. When I opened the envelope and found the cheque there – well, you could have knocked me down with a feather. You could, indeed. Of course, a hundred pounds isn't much. But it's the honour...."

Whither were they going? Their destiny was as certain as though they had no free will. Free will? There is no free will. All is Fate. Fenwick suddenly laughed aloud.

Foster stopped.

"Why, what is it?"

"What's what?"

"You laughed."

"Something amused me."

Foster slipped his arm through Fenwick's.

"It *is* jolly to be walking along together like this, arm in arm, friends. I'm a sentimental man. I won't deny it. What I say is that life is short and one must love one's fellow beings, or where is one? You live too much alone, old man." He squeezed Fenwick's arm. "That's the truth of it."

It was torture, exquisite, heavenly torture. It was wonderful to feel that thin, bony arm pressing against his. Almost you could hear the beating of that other heart. Wonderful to feel that arm and the temptation to take it in your hands and to bend it and twist it and then to hear the bones crack... crack... crack.... Wonderful to feel that temptation rise through one's body like boiling water and yet not to yield to it. For a moment Fenwick's hand touched Foster's. Then he drew himself apart.

"We're at the village. This is the hotel where they all come in the summer. We turn off at the right here. I'll show you my tarn."

Chapter IV

"YOUR TARN?" asked Foster. "Forgive my ignorance, but what is a tarn exactly?"

"A tarn is a miniature lake, a pool of water lying in the lap of the hill. Very quiet, lovely, silent. Some of them are immensely deep."

"I should like to see that."

"It is some little distance – up a rough road. Do you mind?"

"Not a bit. I have long legs."

"Some of them are immensely deep – unfathomable – nobody touched the bottom – but quiet, like glass, with shadows only—"

"Do you know, Fenwick, I have always been afraid of water – I've never learnt to swim. I'm afraid to go out of my depth. Isn't that ridiculous? But it is all because at my private school, years ago, when I was a small boy, some big fellows took me and held me with my head under the water and nearly drowned me. They did indeed. They went farther than they meant to. I can see their faces."

Fenwick considered this. The picture leapt to his mind. He could see the boys – large, strong fellows, probably – and this skinny thing like a frog, their thick hands about his throat, his legs like grey sticks kicking out of the water, their laughter, their sudden sense that something was wrong, the skinny body all flaccid and still....

He drew a deep breath.

Foster was walking beside him now, not ahead of him, as though he were a little afraid and needed reassurance. Indeed, the scene had changed. Before and behind them stretched the uphill path, loose with shale and stones. On their right, on a ridge at the foot of the hill, were some quarries, almost deserted, but the more melancholy in the fading afternoon because a little work still continued there; faint sounds came from the gaunt listening chimneys, a stream of water ran and tumbled angrily into a pool below, once and again a black silhouette, like a question mark, appeared against the darkening hill.

It was a little steep here, and Foster puffed and blew.

Fenwick hated him the more for that. So thin and spare and still he could not keep in condition! They stumbled, keeping below the quarry, on the edge of the running water, now green, now a dirty white-grey, pushing their way along the side of the hill.

Their faces were set now towards Helvellyn. It rounded the cup of hills, closing in the base and then sprawling to the right.

"There's the tarn!" Fenwick exclaimed; and then added, "The sun's not lasting as long as I had expected. It's growing dark already."

Foster stumbled and caught Fenwick's arm.

"This twilight makes the hills look strange – like living men. I can scarcely see my way."

"We're alone here," Fenwick answered. "Don't you feel the stillness? The men will have left the quarry now and gone home. There is no one in all this place but ourselves. If you watch you will see a strange green light steal down over the hills. It lasts for but a moment and then it is dark.

"Ah, here is my tarn. Do you know how I love this place, Foster? It seems to belong especially to me, just as much as all your work and your glory and fame and success seem to belong to you. I have this and you have that. Perhaps in the end we are even, after all. Yes....

"But I feel as though that piece of water belonged to me and I to it, and as though we should never be separated – yes... Isn't it black?

"It is one of the deep ones. No one has ever sounded it. Only Helvellyn knows, and one day I fancy that it will take me, too, into its confidence, will whisper its secrets—"

Foster sneezed.

"Very nice. Very beautiful, Fenwick. I like your tarn. Charming. And now let's turn back. That is a difficult walk beneath the quarry. It's chilly, too."

"Do you see that little jetty there?" Fenwick led Foster by the arm. "Someone built that out into the water. He had a boat there, I suppose. Come and look down. From the end of the little jetty it looks so deep and the mountains seem to close round."

Fenwick took Foster's arm and led him to the end of the jetty. Indeed, the water looked deep here. Deep and very black. Foster peered down, then he looked up at the hills that did indeed seem to have gathered close around him. He sneezed again.

"I've caught a cold, I am afraid. Let's turn homewards, Fenwick, or we shall never find our way."

"Home, then," said Fenwick, and his hands closed about the thin, scraggy neck. For the instant the head half turned, and two startled, strangely childish eyes stared; then, with a push that was ludicrously simple, the body was impelled forward, there was a sharp cry, a splash, a stir of something white against the swiftly gathering dusk, again and then again, then far-spreading ripples, then silence.

Chapter V

THE SILENCE extended. Having enwrapped the tarn, it spread as though with finger on lip to the already quiescent hills. Fenwick shared in the silence. He luxuriated in it. He did not move at all. He stood there looking upon the inky water of the tarn, his arms folded, a man lost in intensest thought. But he was not thinking. He was only conscious of a warm, luxurious relief, a sensuous feeling that was not thought at all.

Foster was gone – that tiresome, prating, conceited, self-satisfied fool! Gone, never to return. The tarn assured him of that. It stared back into Fenwick's face approvingly as though it said: "You have done well – a clean and necessary job. We have done it together, you and I. I am proud of you."

He was proud of himself. At last he had done something definite with his life. Thought, eager, active thought, was beginning now to flood his brain. For all these years he had hung around in this place doing nothing but cherish grievances, weak, backboneless – now at last there was action. He drew himself up and looked at the hills. He was proud – and he was cold. He was shivering. He turned up the collar of his coat. Yes, there was that faint green light that always lingered in the shadows of the hills for a brief moment before darkness came. It was growing late. He had better return.

Shivering now so that his teeth chattered, he started off down the path, and then was aware that he did not wish to leave the tarn. The tarn was friendly – the only friend he had in all the world. As he stumbled along in the dark this sense of loneliness grew. He was going home to an empty house. There had been a guest in it last night. Who was it? Why, Foster, of course – Foster with his silly laugh and amiable, mediocre eyes. Well, Foster would not be there now. No, he never would be there again.

And suddenly Fenwick started to run. He did not know why, except that, now that he had left the tarn, he was lonely. He wished that he could have stayed there all night, but because it was cold he could not, and so now he was running so that he might be at home with the lights and the familiar furniture – and all the things that he knew to reassure him.

As he ran the shale and stones scattered beneath his feet. They made a tit-tattering noise under him, and someone else seemed to be running too. He stopped, and the other runner also stopped. He breathed in the silence. He was hot now. The perspiration was trickling down his cheeks. He could feel a dribble of it down his back inside his shirt. His knees were pounding. His heart was thumping. And all around him the hills were so amazingly silent, now like india-rubber clouds that you could push in or pull out as you do those india-rubber faces, grey against the night sky of a crystal purple, upon whose surface, like the twinkling eyes of boats at sea, stars were now appearing.

His knees steadied, his heart beat less fiercely, and he began to run again. Suddenly he had turned the corner and was out at the hotel. Its lamps were kindly and reassuring. He walked then quietly along the lake-side path, and had it not been for the certainty that someone was treading behind him he would have been comfortable and at his ease. He stopped once or twice and looked back, and once he stopped and called out, "Who's there?" Only the rustling trees answered.

He had the strangest fancy, but his brain was throbbing so fiercely that he could not think, that it was the tarn that was following him, the tarn slipping, sliding along the road, being with him so that he should not be lonely. He could almost hear the tarn whisper in his ear: "We did that together, and so I do not wish you to bear all the responsibility yourself. I will stay with you, so that you are not lonely."

He climbed down the road towards home, and there were the lights of his house. He heard the gate click behind him as though it were shutting him in. He went into the sitting room, lighted and ready. There were the books that Foster had admired.

The old woman who looked after him appeared.

"Will you be having some tea, sir?"

"No, thank you, Annie."

"Will the other gentleman be wanting any?"

"No; the other gentleman is away for the night."

"Then there will be only one for supper?"

"Yes, only one for supper."

He sat in the corner of the sofa and fell instantly into a deep slumber.

Chapter VI

HE WOKE when the old woman tapped him on the shoulder and told him that supper was served. The room was dark save for the jumping light of two uncertain candles. Those two red candlesticks – how he hated them up there on the mantelpiece! He had always hated them, and now they seemed to him to have something of the quality of Foster's voice – that thin, reedy, piping tone.

He was expecting at every moment that Foster would enter, and yet he knew that he would not. He continued to turn his head towards the door, but it was so dark there that you could not see. The whole room was dark except just there by the fireplace, where the two candlesticks went whining with their miserable twinkling plaint.

He went into the dining room and sat down to his meal. But he could not eat anything. It was odd – that place by the table where Foster's chair should be. Odd, naked, and made a man feel lonely.

He got up once from the table and went to the window, opened it and looked out. He listened for something, A trickle as of running water, a stir, through the silence, as though some deep pool were filling to the brim. A rustle in the trees, perhaps. An owl hooted; Sharply, as though someone had spoken unexpectedly behind his shoulder, he closed the windows and looked back, peering under his dark eyebrows into the room.

Later on he went up to his bed.

Chapter VII

HAD HE BEEN sleeping, or had he been lying lazily, as one does, half dozing, half luxuriously not thinking? He was wide awake now, utterly awake, and his heart was beating with apprehension. It was as though someone had called him by name. He slept always with his window a little open and the blind up. Tonight the moonlight shadowed in sickly fashion the objects in his room. It was not a flood of light nor yet a sharp splash, silvering a square, a circle, throwing the rest into ebony darkness. The light was dim, a little green, perhaps, like the shadow that comes over the hills just before dark.

He stared at the window, and it seemed to him that something moved there. Within, or rather against, the green-grey light, something silver-tinted glistened. Fenwick stared. It had the look, exactly, of slipping water.

Slipping water! He listened, his head up, and it seemed to him that from beyond the window he caught the stir of water, not running, but rather welling up and up, gurgling with satisfaction as it filled and filled.

He sat up higher in bed, and then saw that down the wallpaper beneath the window water was undoubtedly trickling. He could see it lurch to the projecting wood of the sill, pause, and then slip, slither down the incline. The odd thing was that it fell so silently.

Beyond the window there was that odd gurgle, but in the room itself absolute silence. Whence could it come? He saw the line of silver rise and fall as the stream on the window-ledge ebbed and flowed.

He must get up and close the window. He drew his legs above the sheets and blankets and looked down.

He shrieked. The floor was covered with a shining film of water. It was rising. As he looked it had covered half the short stumpy legs of the bed. It rose without a wink, a bubble, a break! Over the sill it poured now in a steady flow, but soundless. Fenwick sat up in the bed, the clothes gathered up to his chin, his eyes blinking, the Adam's apple throbbing like a throttle in his throat.

But he must do something, he must stop this. The water was now level with the seats of the chairs, but still was soundless. Could he but reach the door!

He put down his naked foot, then cried again. The water was icy cold. Suddenly, leaning, staring at its dark, unbroken sheen, something seemed to push him forward. He fell. His head, his face was under the icy liquid; it seemed adhesive and, in the heart of its ice, hot like melting wax. He struggled to his feet. The water was breast-high. He screamed again and again. He could see the looking-glass, the row of books, the picture of Dürer's 'Horse', aloof, impervious. He beat at the water, and flakes of it seemed to cling to him like scales of fish, clammy to his touch. He struggled, ploughing his way towards the door.

The water now was at his neck. Then something had caught him by the ankle. Something held him. He struggled, crying: "Let me go! Let me go! I tell you to let me go! I hate you! I hate you! I will not come down to you! I will not—"

The water covered his mouth. He felt that someone pushed in his eyeballs with bare knuckles. A cold hand reached up and caught his naked thigh.

Chapter VIII

IN THE MORNING the little maid knocked and, receiving no answer, came in, as was her wont, with his shaving-water. What she saw made her scream. She ran for the gardener.

They took the body with its staring, protruding eyes, its tongue sticking out between the clenched teeth, and laid it on the bed.

The only sign of disorder was an overturned water jug. A small pool of water stained the carpet.

It was a lovely morning. A twig of ivy idly, in the little breeze, tapped the pane.

Restless Natives

D.A. Watson

IN THE ACHTRIOCHTAN Police Station, a tiny stone building so small and homely looking you could mistake it for one of the twenty or so other houses that made up the village, Special Constable Bruce McLister sat behind his desk, fully engrossed in the high seas derring do of a Wilbur Smith novel.

That was the thing about rural policing; most of the time there just wasn't a whole lot of policing to do, and here, three hours north of Fort William, in the deepest, most remote parts of the western highlands, was about as rural as you could get. Not that he minded. He had a nice heat from the open fireplace in the corner, a mug of sweet milky coffee on his desk, a saucer of chocolate Hobnobs, a good book in his hands, and no pressing appointments.

He was just getting into the climactic sword fight on the last few pages of *Birds of Prey* when the phone rang. Sighing, McLister put the book aside and picked up. "Achtriochtan Police Station."

"Bruce. It's MacIain."

Ewan MacIain. A farmer who owned a sizeable portion of land outside the village. "Hello, Ewan," McLister said. "What can I do for you?"

"There's an abandoned car out by the loch."

McLister leant forward in his chair, tapping computer keys and bringing up the national crime bulletins for that morning. "Sure there's no one around?"

"Not a soul," MacIain said. "Might be nothing, but I thought you should know."

"Aye," McLister said as he clicked icons, filtering the bulletin list to show news from the Highlands and Islands division. An assault up in Wick. A house breaking in Dornoch. A sexual assault in Inverness. And an armed robbery of a mobile bank near Fort William. Three fatalities, and three suspects, still at large, who'd made off with close to fifty grand.

"Thanks for letting me know, Ewan," McLister said. "I'll check it out."

"Aye," MacIain said, *"Na dèan cron sam bith."*

"Na dèan cron sam bith," he returned, and hung up.

* * *

The loch sat by a single track road just three miles outside Achtriochtan. Ringed by trees, shaped like a ragged comma, it was a small body of water, barely a quarter of a mile in length, less than two hundred metres across at its widest point. As MacIain has reported, the vehicle, a nondescript pale blue Fiat Punto, sat by the roadside, the rear driver's side door lying open. McLister pulled in twenty yards behind it, killed the engine and just sat looking at it for a moment. No hazard lights on. No visible damage. Nothing moving in the car's shadowy interior.

McLister jotted the registration down in his notebook, then stepped out onto the road and approached the car. As he already knew, there was no one there. Leaning inside, the inside of the Punto contained only a few empty sandwich wrappers, a stale smell of old fast food and cigarettes, and a rucksack lying in the passenger side footspace of the back seat. Snapping a pair of disposable Nitrile gloves onto his hands, McLister carefully opened the rucksack's zip a few inches. Enough to reveal the wrapped bundles of banknotes crammed inside. He closed the zip again, went to the rear of the vehicle and checked inside the boot, where he found three sawn off shotguns, the serial numbers filed off.

Turning from the car, he examined the grassy verge and tarmac of the single track road in the immediate vicinity, but found nothing out of place. He crossed to the verge on the lochside, where he searched carefully amid the weeds and long grass of the embankment that led down to a thick grove of willows on the bank of the loch.

It was here that McLister found a mobile phone lying amid a bramble patch. He picked it up, checked it and found the battery dead. He searched along the trees and underbrush of the lochside for a few more minutes, finding nothing, then trudged back up the embankment and returned to his patrol vehicle.

Back in the four-by-four, he reached into the back seat and grabbed a laptop bag, from which he took his personal MacBook and a small rectangular device with a wire at one end. He powered up the laptop and plugged in the rectangular device via a USB port. Taking the mobile he'd found, he opened the casing and retrieved the SIM card. This he slipped into a slot on the device, then clicked icons on the MacBook screen, initialising the SIM cracking software. He'd been surprised, and a little perturbed, at how easy it'd been to find and purchase the illegal decryption gear online. Sign of the times, he guessed. It was of course a flagrant breach of standard operating procedure, but Special Constable McLister knew that sometimes the rules had to be bent for the greater good.

* * *

A ghostly pale face appears on the screen. White male, mid-twenties, dark close cropped hair, three-day stubble. Partially visible tattoo on the right side of his neck, a small v-shaped scar above the bridge of his nose which is canted to the left, an old break not healed straight. The light from the mobile recording the video is enough to show that he's in the back of a car, lying prone across the rear seat, his head propped against the interior of the rear passenger side door.

He's all wide staring eyes, flaring nostrils and wet, twitchy lips. It's the face of a very badly frightened young man.

He begins speaking. A strained, urgent whisper with a Glaswegian twang. "Ma name's William Graham Murphy. Date of birth twelfth of May nineteen ninety-four. Ah stay at seventeen Bargeddie Way in Possil." The lad pauses a moment, squeezing his eyes closed, tears spilling down into the scraggly stubble of his jaw. "Ah want tae confess," he whispers, opening his eyes again, and McLister has rarely seen such a haunted man. "Ah think Ahm gonnae die here the night, an Ah want tae confess. Ah wis involved in the robbery at the RBS mobile bank in Grianain yesterday mornin. Me, a guy called Frankie Reid, an… ma brother. Brian Michael Murphy. Date of birth third of March eighty-nine." More tears spill from his eyes. He takes a shuddering breath and continues.

"Ah'm no trying tae shift the blame tae anybody else. Ah wis there, an Ah did what Ah did, but it wis Frankie's idea. Ah'd never met the guy till a few days ago. Mate of ma brother. They shared a cell in Barlinnie jail last year when Brian was in for assault. Frankie was daein time for burglary. He got in touch wi Brian a couple weeks ago aboot the job. Brian knew Ah wis strugglin for cash, an they needed a third man. He asked me if Ah wanted in. Ah sais aye, nae bother. We met up wi Frankie, an he made it sound like a pure canter. Had it aw planned oot. The job wis wan of they mobile bank trucks that go out tae the villages in the middle of naewhere so punters can make deposits an withdrawals an that. Frankie sais there wis wan that stopped in at a wee village up in the hills past Fort William. Pure remote as fuck. Just two staff in the van. A teller and the driver slash security guy. No many customers, an mainly auld folk. As saft a target as you could get, far as stick ups go. Said he'd had a tip aff fae a guy he knew who worked in the bank's security. The wee vans toured all over the place, an the cash drawers got stocked up wi notes once a week, fifty grand at a time, an we were gonnae hit it on their first stop eftir the delivery. Plan wis tae go in, frighten the fuck oot them, get the cash, then take aff intae the hills before the polis showed up. Just like in that auld film *Restless Natives*. Frankie had a couple of dirt bikes awready stashed in a garage roon the corner. Said we could take aff into the hills on the trails where polis motors couldnae come eftir us. He'd another car planked at an auld cabin in the middle of a forest a few miles away. Totally covered fae above, so nae polis choppers tae worry aboot. Plan wis to stay in the cabin that night, then head oot the next day in this motor an drive north on shady wee B roads up tae another place he had ready, way up in the wilds past Kyle of Lochlash where we'd hide oot for a few mair days. He'd been planning it for ages, he said. Had the shotguns, masks, gloves, rucksacks, bike helmets, aw sorted. He said it'd be easier than usin a fuckin cash machine."

The lad, William, pauses in his confession as more tears fill his eyes. "It wis aw goin fine," he says, his voice almost a whine. "We drove up in another car Frankie had, parked it in a layby ootside the village, an walked in. The bank van wis right where he said it'd be, parked by the wee inn an post office. Nae cunt aboot. We just marched up, masks on, guns oot, an in we went.

"The driver security guy wis inside, but Frankie knocked him oot wi the shotgun butt before he could even blink. Brian went tae the teller, gun in her face, telt her tae fill the rucksack he gave her, an… Ah covered the customers. Wis just a lassie there. Just a young lassie wi her wean. Wee girl, must've been aboot two. Ah just shouted at them *get doon, don't fuckin move,* covered them wi my gun. The teller wis nae bother, stuffin Brian's rucksack fae the cash drawers while Frankie watched the door. We got the cash, oot we went, done and dusted, then that fuckin eejit ootside had tae get involved. Just some random guy walkin past. Big beardy cunt in a farmer's jumper an wellies. Fuckin tackled me. Tried tae grab ma gun, an we're staggering aboot on the pavement fightin for it… and the lassie wi the wean comes oot the van and tries tae make a run for it… the… gun went aff as she ran by us… an… an she wis holdin her wee girl…"

Watching, McLister feels his jaw tighten as a slow, cold surge of sadness and anger swells inside him. On the video, young William's voice breaks and he starts sobbing. "Ah swear tae fuck Ah didnae mean it… it wis an accident… Ah just stood there… lookin at them lyin facedoon on the pavement… no movin… the big hole in her back… blood runnin oot fae under them intae the gutter… then the big farmer bastard knocked me on ma arse an booted ma gun away… then he grabs me and pins me doon, shoutin for some cunt tae phone the polis… but then… Brian runs over and just fuckin blasts him… then he's pullin me up and we're sprintin away roon the corner… Frankie's already got the trail bikes oot the garage an he jumps on one an me and Brian jump on the other, me on the back, and fuckin *whoosh*… we're away aff the street onto a wee dirt trail just like Frankie said… away intae the hills…"

He pauses for breath, trying to compose himself. He sits up briefly and checks the windows, but apparently sees nothing outside. He slouches low on the back seat again. "We stayed in the cabin last night like we planned. Got intae this motor late yesterday afternoon and drove north. Were in the car for maybe three hours an it wis startin tae get dark… then it just died. We'd plenty of petrol, an Frankie swore blind he'd had the car checked before the job an it was tip top. But it just conked oot. Engine died, headlights went aff, dashboard went dark an we just rolled tae a stop. Here. By this wee loch."

"Aboot an hour ago," he continues, and McLister is aware of a new tremor that now creeps into his voice, "we were sittin here in the motor wonderin what the fuck we were gonnae dae. It was pitch black ootside, an we were in the arse end of naewhere, at least ten miles fae the last village we'd passed. Nae phone signal. We were startin tae talk aboot hikin oot, even though none of us wis dressed for the weather, an it wis fuckin baltic even *inside* the car. That's when Frankie said he heard a voice ootside."

He falls silent again, a pleading look in his eyes, chin trembling, lips pressed tight. McLister feels a prickling sensation in his palms. "Me an Brian didnae hear anythin, but Frankie was sure he'd heard someone, an he bounces oot the motor an runs across the road tae the embankment. Brian gets oot as well, tells me tae stay wi the car so Ah can guide them back if they get lost, then goes eftir him. Ah gets oot an staunds there by the car. It's freezing cauld, pure pitch black, an Ah hear Brian somewhere in the trees on the other side of the road, callin oot for Frankie. Then it aw goes quiet. Ah calls oot for Brian, an he goes *aye, Ah'm here*, an Ah'm like *whit the fuck's happenin* an he goes *haud oan there's something...* Then there's this mad... *sloshin* sound, an Ah hears Brian goin *oh jesus fuck*, an Ah then can hear him runnin back tae the road, crashin aboot in the trees. So Ah runs tae the embankment an Ah'm shoutin *here man here* an A've got ma phone's torch on tae gie him a light tae head for. Ah see him as he comes oot the trees an he's just pure screamin at me goin *run just fuckin run Billy get back tae the car* so Ah turns and bolts back across the road, pile intae the motor an Ah look back... an Ah saw... somethin chasin him."

"Ah don't... know whit it wis," he says after a very shaky beat. "Ah only saw it behind Brian for a second in the light fae ma phone... but it wis... big... pale... kinda like a person but... wrong... aw... bent in the wrong places... an the way it *moved*... it... it wisane human. It... took Brian. Fuckin plucked him up aff the road and yanked him back intae the dark. Ah just... just sat there in the motor... couldnae move... Ah could hear him screamin... could hear him gettin dragged through the trees... screamin ma name... screamin for me tae help him... then... then Ah heard splashin again... and that wis it. He wis gone."

Again his face clenches up. Eyes squeezing tears, jaw shuddering as he chokes back a sob. "Ah'm so fuckin sorry," he whimpers. "For everythin. Ah've fucked up so many times... Ah don't know where tae begin. But Ah'm sorry for it aw." He looks away from the camera, shaking his head. "Ah don't want tae die," he whispers brokenly, "but Ah think... this... thing... that took Brian an Frankie... it's gonnae come for me as well... an... Ah just wanted tae confess before..."

His words end in a short, breathy scream as the car suddenly rocks and groans. The shaky camera angle shows William, his jaw hanging agape, looking upwards as something moves on the roof of the car. There's a low metallic groan, and William's terrified eyes are now aimed just above the lens, like he's staring at something outside the rear driver's side window. "*Ohhh Jesus... oh fuuuuuuuck...*" he moans.

Watching, McLister's mouth goes dry, sudden sweat beading along his receding grey hairline.

There's the soft clunk and squeak of a car door opening, and William's breath rushes out as if he's been punched in the gut. Then, out of shot, comes a second voice. Rasping. Ancient. And wet.

"*Mèirleach,*" it hisses. "*Murtair. Peacach.*"

William, his eyes just about bugging out of their sockets now, begins to scream, long and loud. Then the picture rolls and sways showing a confused series of images, and McLister's stomach swoops with vertigo as the camera starts *moving*, the footage showing the interior of the car, then a ground level shot of the tarmac of the road outside sliding past at close range, the Pale blue Punto receding behind it, then long grass and weeds fill the screen as the camera crosses into the undergrowth of the embankment, and all the while, as he's dragged from the car and into the brush, the lad, William, screams his throat raw.

The camera angle swoops again, and for just a second, the video shows a few frames of something tall, pale and leathery, moving through the undergrowth on long, oddly angled limbs, a ghostly white appendage like a clawed tentacle coiled round the lad's ankle.

Then the footage rolls and jerks and comes to a stop. McLister's laptop screen fills with a close up view of the brambles where he'd found the mobile. Out of shot, William Graham Murphy continues to shriek and beg, his panicked, spiralling cries dwindling in volume. Then comes a distant splashing and William's screams become choked desperate splutters. There's one final drawn-out wail of such hopelessness and terror that McLister feels his blood turn to slush, a final *splash*, and then silence.

McLister sits watching the screen for several more minutes, but there's just the silent bug's eye view of the bramble bush. Reaching out a badly trembling hand, he uses the laptop's mousepad to move the playback cursor along the timeline, skipping the footage forward. But there's nothing else. The video ends undramatically in a black screen as the mobile's battery finally dies.

* * *

McLister takes a minute to gather himself, then returns the memory card to the mobile and snaps the phone's casing closed again. He steps out of the patrol car, and on shaky legs, makes his way back down the embankment to the lochside. There, he rears back and hurls the mobile as far as he can, watching it arc up into the air, drop, and hit the dark surface with a small *splosh*.

Only then does he return to his vehicle and radio HQ, reporting the discovery of a suspicious abandoned vehicle containing three shotguns and a rucksack full of cash.

* * *

Later that afternoon, the lonely single track road by the loch is a hive of activity. Detectives, patrolmen, forensic officers and technicians scuttle to and fro on the road, photographing, measuring and examining everything in sight. A helicopter buzzes overhead as a search team with sniffer dogs – who do little but run in circles, baying anxiously, tails between their legs – search the area.

McLister makes his report to the detective in charge, DS Simpson from the Major Investigations Team. A thin, intense woman with intelligent eyes and dark hair scraped back in a severe ponytail. She tells him the banknotes have been traced to a mobile bank robbery two days before. He offers no more than he reported over the radio, and suggests only the simplest explanation for what might have occurred. The robbers thought to hide out in the most remote area they could find, but their car broke down, and they'd foolishly tried to make it out on foot. Bad idea up here, he says. Dangerous land. Unpredictable weather. Even if they'd followed the road, in the dark it'd be easy to wander off the path and get lost in the vastness of the moors and mountains, where there was no shortage of peat bogs, rock slides and hidden drop-offs. Even experienced, fully equipped hikers and climbers went missing fairly regularly this far north. Three city dwellers without the proper clothing and equipment and presumably no outdoors experience? They wouldn't have made it far. They'll turn up eventually, maybe, he says, but the land up here was unforgiving, and had a way of disappearing the unwary sometimes. Could be they'd never be found. Wouldn't be the first time.

DS Simpson nods, but wonders aloud why the thieves hadn't taken the guns and rucksack full of cash with them, or even bothered to try and hide them somewhere nearby. McLister merely shrugs. Folks in dire situations panic and often aren't thinking straight, he says, and who knows what goes through the minds of such animals? DS Simpson seems unconvinced, but thanks him for his input, dismisses him, then returns to the pale blue Punto where a technician is dusting the dashboard for prints.

* * *

Driving back into the village, McLister wonders if DS Simpson from the MIT will eventually link the disappearance of the three bank robbers to the others that have occurred in the area. That banker and his wife five years back, vanished while driving through the area during a campervan holiday. A few years before that, there'd been that hiker that disappeared. Doing a little digging, McLister had found that the banker and his wife were under investigation for fraud and were awaiting a court date. The missing hiker had done three years in Saughton for the attempted rape of a nine-year-old girl.

Over the forty plus years McLister had lived and worked in Achtriochtan, there'd been others. Not a lot, but more than a couple. As he'd told DS Simpson, missing hikers in the wilds of the west highlands weren't that uncommon, which is why, he supposed, no one had ever looked too deeply into the occasional disappearances in the area. The fact was, no one but McLister – and the other thirty-seven residents of Achtriochtan – knew that those who vanished in the area had the stain of a grievous sin on their soul.

And sinners didn't do well up here.

When he'd been posted to Achtriochtan all those years ago, taking over from the previous Special Constable who'd dropped dead of a heart attack at his desk one day at the age of seventy-three, McLister had been bemused by the little subculture of paganism he'd found in the village. A simple way of life centred around respecting and worshipping nature, and living life according to one simple rule. *Na dèan cron sam bith.* Do no harm. And he'd enjoyed hearing the local folk tales. Stories of the *Cirein-cròin*. A creature of the faery world that legend said lived in a nearby loch and protected the village from evildoers. The *Cirein-cròin*, the locals whispered, could smell the blood of sinners from miles away, and roamed the land hereabouts after sunset, snatching the unworthy and spiriting them back to its loch, never to be seen again.

McLister thinks of that brief glance in the video of something tall and pale and oddly jointed, dragging the screaming William Graham Murphy away into the night. And he thinks of that voice. Gravelly and wet and so very *old*.

Mèirleach. Murtair. Peacach.
Thief. Murderer. Sinner.

* * *

The sun is just beginning to slip behind the hills when McLister pulls up outside his little cottage on the village outskirts, the western sky a herringbone pattern of stormy grey and blood red, the lengthening shadows cast by the mountains washing the land below in eastward creeping darkness.

At his front door, McLister takes a penknife from his pocket and makes a small cut on the tip of his right index finger. Whispering a few words in the old tongue, words of thanksgiving and protection, he daubs a bloody runic symbol on the doorframe. Then he goes inside, and in his cramped but cosy living room, picks up the phone and dials Ewan MacIain. The farmer, as if expecting his call, picks up after the first ring.

"Hello?"

"Aye," McLister says. "Tell the others to make their mark. *Na dèan cron sam bith.*"

"Aye," Ewan replies. *"Na dèan cron sam bith."*

The Lady Maid's Bell

Edith Wharton

Chapter I

IT WAS the autumn after I had the typhoid. I'd been three months in hospital, and when I came out I looked so weak and tottery that the two or three ladies I applied to were afraid to engage me. Most of my money was gone, and after I'd boarded for two months, hanging about the employment-agencies, and answering any advertisement that looked any way respectable, I pretty nearly lost heart, for fretting hadn't made me fatter, and I didn't see why my luck should ever turn. It did though – or I thought so at the time. A Mrs. Railton, a friend of the lady that first brought me out to the States, met me one day and stopped to speak to me: she was one that had always a friendly way with her. She asked me what ailed me to look so white, and when I told her, "Why, Hartley," says she, "I believe I've got the very place for you. Come in tomorrow and we'll talk about it."

The next day, when I called, she told me the lady she'd in mind was a niece of hers, a Mrs. Brympton, a youngish lady, but something of an invalid, who lived all the year round at her country-place on the Hudson, owing to not being able to stand the fatigue of town life.

"Now, Hartley," Mrs. Railton said, in that cheery way that always made me feel things must be going to take a turn for the better – "now understand me; it's not a cheerful place I'm sending you to. The house is big and gloomy; my niece is nervous, vaporish; her husband – well, he's generally away; and the two children are dead. A year ago, I would as soon have thought of shutting a rosy active girl like you into a vault; but you're not particularly brisk yourself just now, are you? And a quiet place, with country air and wholesome food and early hours, ought to be the very thing for you. Don't mistake me," she added, for I suppose I looked a trifle downcast; "you may find it dull, but you won't be unhappy. My niece is an angel. Her former maid, who died last spring, had been with her twenty years and worshipped the ground she walked on. She's a kind mistress to all, and where the mistress is kind, as you know, the servants are generally good-humored, so you'll probably get on well enough with the rest of the household. And you're the very woman I want for my niece: quiet, well-mannered, and educated above your station. You read aloud well, I think? That's a good thing; my niece likes to be read to. She wants a maid that can be something of a companion: her last was, and I can't say how she misses her. It's a lonely life… Well, have you decided?"

"Why, ma'am," I said, "I'm not afraid of solitude."

"Well, then, go; my niece will take you on my recommendation. I'll telegraph her at once and you can take the afternoon train. She has no one to wait on her at present, and I don't want you to lose any time."

I was ready enough to start, yet something in me hung back; and to gain time I asked, "And the gentleman, ma'am?"

"The gentleman's almost always away, I tell you," said Mrs. Ralston, quick-like – "and when he's there," says she suddenly, "you've only to keep out of his way."

I took the afternoon train and got out at D— station at about four o'clock. A groom in a dog-cart was waiting, and we drove off at a smart pace. It was a dull October day, with rain hanging close overhead, and by the time we turned into the Brympton Place woods the daylight was almost gone. The drive wound through the woods for a mile or two, and came out on a gravel court shut in with thickets of tall black-looking shrubs. There were no lights in the windows, and the house *did* look a bit gloomy.

I had asked no questions of the groom, for I never was one to get my notion of new masters from their other servants: I prefer to wait and see for myself. But I could tell by the look of everything that I had got into the right kind of house, and that things were done handsomely. A pleasant-faced cook met me at the back door and called the house-maid to show me up to my room. "You'll see madam later," she said. "Mrs. Brympton has a visitor."

I hadn't fancied Mrs. Brympton was a lady to have many visitors, and somehow the words cheered me. I followed the house-maid upstairs, and saw, through a door on the upper landing, that the main part of the house seemed well-furnished, with dark panelling and a number of old portraits. Another flight of stairs led us up to the servants' wing. It was almost dark now, and the house-maid excused herself for not having brought a light. "But there's matches in your room," she said, "and if you go careful you'll be all right. Mind the step at the end of the passage. Your room is just beyond."

I looked ahead as she spoke, and halfway down the passage, I saw a woman standing. She drew back into a doorway as we passed, and the house-maid didn't appear to notice her. She was a thin woman with a white face, and a darkish stuff gown and apron. I took her for the housekeeper and thought it odd that she didn't speak, but just gave me a long look as she went by. My room opened into a square hall at the end of the passage. Facing my door was another which stood open: the house-maid exclaimed when she saw it.

"There – Mrs. Blinder's left that door open again!" said she, closing it.

"Is Mrs. Blinder the housekeeper?"

"There's no housekeeper: Mrs. Blinder's the cook."

"And is that her room?"

"Laws, no," said the house-maid, cross-like. "That's nobody's room. It's empty, I mean, and the door hadn't ought to be open. Mrs. Brympton wants it kept locked." She opened my door and led me into a neat room, nicely furnished, with a picture or two on the walls; and having lit a candle she took leave, telling me that the servants'-hall tea was at six, and that Mrs. Brympton would see me afterward.

I found them a pleasant-spoken set in the servants' hall, and by what they let fall I gathered that, as Mrs. Railton had said, Mrs. Brympton was the kindest of ladies; but I didn't take much notice of their talk, for I was watching to see the pale woman in the dark gown come in. She didn't show herself, however, and I wondered if she ate apart; but if she wasn't the housekeeper, why should she? Suddenly it struck me that she might be a trained nurse, and in that case her meals would of course be served in her room. If Mrs. Brympton was an invalid it was likely enough she had a nurse. The idea annoyed me, I own, for they're not always the easiest to get on with, and if I'd known, I shouldn't have taken the place. But there I was, and there was no use pulling a long face over it; and not being one to ask questions, I waited to see what would turn up.

When tea was over, the house-maid said to the footman: "Has Mr. Ranford gone?" and when he said yes, she told me to come up with her to Mrs. Brympton.

Mrs. Brympton was lying down in her bedroom. Her lounge stood near the fire and beside it was a shaded lamp. She was a delicate-looking lady, but when she smiled I felt there was nothing

I wouldn't do for her. She spoke very pleasantly, in a low voice, asking me my name and age and so on, and if I had everything I wanted, and if I wasn't afraid of feeling lonely in the country.

"Not with you I wouldn't be, madam," I said, and the words surprised me when I'd spoken them, for I'm not an impulsive person; but it was just as if I'd thought aloud.

She seemed pleased at that, and said she hoped I'd continue in the same mind; then she gave me a few directions about her toilet, and said Agnes the house-maid would show me next morning where things were kept.

"I am tired tonight, and shall dine upstairs," she said. "Agnes will bring me my tray, that you may have time to unpack and settle yourself; and later you may come and undress me."

"Very well, ma'am," I said. "You'll ring, I suppose?"

I thought she looked odd.

"No – Agnes will fetch you," says she quickly, and took up her book again.

Well – that was certainly strange: a lady's maid having to be fetched by the house-maid whenever her lady wanted her! I wondered if there were no bells in the house; but the next day I satisfied myself that there was one in every room, and a special one ringing from my mistress's room to mine; and after that it did strike me as queer that, whenever Mrs. Brympton wanted anything, she rang for Agnes, who had to walk the whole length of the servants' wing to call me.

But that wasn't the only queer thing in the house. The very next day I found out that Mrs. Brympton had no nurse; and then I asked Agnes about the woman I had seen in the passage the afternoon before. Agnes said she had seen no one, and I saw that she thought I was dreaming. To be sure, it was dusk when we went down the passage, and she had excused herself for not bringing a light; but I had seen the woman plain enough to know her again if we should meet. I decided that she must have been a friend of the cook's, or of one of the other women-servants: perhaps she had come down from town for a night's visit, and the servants wanted it kept secret. Some ladies are very stiff about having their servants' friends in the house overnight. At any rate, I made up my mind to ask no more questions.

In a day or two, another odd thing happened. I was chatting one afternoon with Mrs. Blinder, who was a friendly disposed woman, and had been longer in the house than the other servants, and she asked me if I was quite comfortable and had everything I needed. I said I had no fault to find with my place or with my mistress, but I thought it odd that in so large a house there was no sewing-room for the lady's maid.

"Why," says she, "there *is* one; the room you're in is the old sewing room."

"Oh," said I; "and where did the other lady's maid sleep?"

At that she grew confused, and said hurriedly that the servants' rooms had all been changed about last year, and she didn't rightly remember.

That struck me as peculiar, but I went on as if I hadn't noticed: "Well, there's a vacant room opposite mine, and I mean to ask Mrs. Brympton if I mayn't use that as a sewing-room."

To my astonishment, Mrs. Blinder went white, and gave my hand a kind of squeeze. "Don't do that, my dear," said she, trembling-like. "To tell you the truth, that was Emma Saxon's room, and my mistress has kept it closed ever since her death."

"And who was Emma Saxon?"

"Mrs. Brympton's former maid."

"The one that was with her so many years?" said I, remembering what Mrs. Railton had told me.

Mrs. Blinder nodded.

"What sort of woman was she?"

"No better walked the earth," said Mrs. Blinder. "My mistress loved her like a sister."

"But I mean – what did she look like?"

Mrs. Blinder got up and gave me a kind of angry stare. "I'm no great hand at describing," she said; "and I believe my pastry's rising." And she walked off into the kitchen and shut the door after her.

Chapter II

I HAD BEEN near a week at Brympton before I saw my master. Word came that he was arriving one afternoon, and a change passed over the whole household. It was plain that nobody loved him below stairs. Mrs. Blinder took uncommon care with the dinner that night, but she snapped at the kitchen-maid in a way quite unusual with her; and Mr. Wace, the butler, a serious, slow-spoken man, went about his duties as if he'd been getting ready for a funeral. He was a great Bible-reader, Mr. Wace was, and had a beautiful assortment of texts at his command; but that day he used such dreadful language that I was about to leave the table, when he assured me it was all out of Isaiah; and I noticed that whenever the master came Mr. Wace took to the prophets.

About seven, Agnes called me to my mistress's room; and there I found Mr. Brympton. He was standing on the hearth; a big fair bull-necked man, with a red face and little bad-tempered blue eyes: the kind of man a young simpleton might have thought handsome, and would have been like to pay dear for thinking it.

He swung about when I came in, and looked me over in a trice. I knew what the look meant, from having experienced it once or twice in my former places. Then he turned his back on me, and went on talking to his wife; and I knew what *that* meant, too. I was not the kind of morsel he was after. The typhoid had served me well enough in one way: it kept that kind of gentleman at arm's-length.

"This is my new maid, Hartley," says Mrs. Brympton in her kind voice; and he nodded and went on with what he was saying.

In a minute or two he went off, and left my mistress to dress for dinner, and I noticed as I waited on her that she was white, and chill to the touch.

Mr. Brympton took himself off the next morning, and the whole house drew a long breath when he drove away. As for my mistress, she put on her hat and furs (for it was a fine winter morning) and went out for a walk in the gardens, coming back quite fresh and rosy, so that for a minute, before her color faded, I could guess what a pretty young lady she must have been, and not so long ago, either.

She had met Mr. Ranford in the grounds, and the two came back together, I remember, smiling and talking as they walked along the terrace under my window. That was the first time I saw Mr. Ranford, though I had often heard his name mentioned in the hall. He was a neighbor, it appeared, living a mile or two beyond Brympton, at the end of the village; and as he was in the habit of spending his winters in the country he was almost the only company my mistress had at that season. He was a slight tall gentleman of about thirty, and I thought him rather melancholy-looking till I saw his smile, which had a kind of surprise in it, like the first warm day in spring. He was a great reader, I heard, like my mistress, and the two were forever borrowing books of one another, and sometimes (Mr. Wace told me) he would read aloud to Mrs. Brympton by the hour, in the big dark library where she sat in the winter afternoons. The servants all liked him, and perhaps that's more of a compliment than the masters suspect. He had a friendly word for every one of us, and we were all glad to think that Mrs. Brympton had a pleasant companionable gentleman like that to keep her company when the master was away. Mr. Ranford seemed on excellent terms with Mr. Brympton too; though I couldn't but wonder that two gentlemen so unlike each other should be so friendly. But then I knew how the real quality can keep their feelings to themselves.

As for Mr. Brympton, he came and went, never staying more than a day or two, cursing the dullness and the solitude, grumbling at everything, and (as I soon found out) drinking a deal more than was good for him. After Mrs. Brympton left the table he would sit half the night over the old Brympton port and madeira, and once, as I was leaving my mistress's room rather later than usual, I met him coming up the stairs in such a state that I turned sick to think of what some ladies have to endure and hold their tongues about.

The servants said very little about their master; but from what they let drop I could see it had been an unhappy match from the beginning. Mr. Brympton was coarse, loud and pleasure-loving; my mistress quiet, retiring, and perhaps a trifle cold. Not that she was not always pleasant-spoken to him: I thought her wonderfully forbearing; but to a gentleman as free as Mr. Brympton I daresay she seemed a little offish.

Well, things went on quietly for several weeks. My mistress was kind, my duties were light, and I got on well with the other servants. In short, I had nothing to complain of; yet there was always a weight on me. I can't say why it was so, but I know it was not the loneliness that I felt. I soon got used to that; and being still languid from the fever, I was thankful for the quiet and the good country air. Nevertheless, I was never quite easy in my mind. My mistress, knowing I had been ill, insisted that I should take my walk regular, and often invented errands for me: a yard of ribbon to be fetched from the village, a letter posted, or a book returned to Mr. Ranford. As soon as I was out of doors my spirits rose, and I looked forward to my walks through the bare moist-smelling woods; but the moment I caught sight of the house again my heart dropped down like a stone in a well. It was not a gloomy house exactly, yet I never entered it but a feeling of gloom came over me.

Mrs. Brympton seldom went out in winter; only on the finest days did she walk an hour at noon on the south terrace. Excepting Mr. Ranford, we had no visitors but the doctor, who drove over from D— about once a week. He sent for me once or twice to give me some trifling direction about my mistress, and though he never told me what her illness was, I thought, from a waxy look she had now and then of a morning, that it might be the heart that ailed her. The season was soft and unwholesome, and in January we had a long spell of rain. That was a sore trial to me, I own, for I couldn't go out, and sitting over my sewing all day, listening to the *drip, drip* of the eaves, I grew so nervous that the least sound made me jump. Somehow, the thought of that locked room across the passage began to weigh on me. Once or twice, in the long rainy nights, I fancied I heard noises there; but that was nonsense, of course, and the daylight drove such notions out of my head. Well, one morning Mrs. Brympton gave me quite a start of pleasure by telling me she wished me to go to town for some shopping. I hadn't known till then how low my spirits had fallen. I set off in high glee, and my first sight of the crowded streets and the cheerful-looking shops quite took me out of myself. Toward afternoon, however, the noise and confusion began to tire me, and I was actually looking forward to the quiet of Brympton, and thinking how I should enjoy the drive home through the dark woods, when I ran across an old acquaintance, a maid I had once been in service with. We had lost sight of each other for a number of years, and I had to stop and tell her what had happened to me in the interval. When I mentioned where I was living she rolled up her eyes and pulled a long face.

"What! The Mrs. Brympton that lives all the year at her place on the Hudson? My dear, you won't stay there three months."

"Oh, but I don't mind the country," says I, offended somehow at her tone. "Since the fever I'm glad to be quiet."

She shook her head. "It's not the country I'm thinking of. All I know is she's had four maids in the last six months, and the last one, who was a friend of mine, told me nobody could stay in the house."

"Did she say why?" I asked.

"No – she wouldn't give me her reason. But she says to me, *Mrs. Ansey*, she says, *if ever a young woman as you know of thinks of going there, you tell her it's not worthwhile to unpack her boxes.*"

"Is she young and handsome?" said I, thinking of Mr. Brympton.

"Not her! She's the kind that mothers engage when they've gay young gentlemen at college."

Well, though I knew the woman was an idle gossip, the words stuck in my head, and my heart sank lower than ever as I drove up to Brympton in the dusk. There *was* something about the house – I was sure of it now...

When I went in to tea I heard that Mr. Brympton had arrived, and I saw at a glance that there had been a disturbance of some kind. Mrs. Blinder's hand shook so that she could hardly pour the tea, and Mr. Wace quoted the most dreadful texts full of brimstone. Nobody said a word to me then, but when I went up to my room Mrs. Blinder followed me.

"Oh, my dear," says she, taking my hand, "I'm so glad and thankful you've come back to us!"

That struck me, as you may imagine. "Why," said I, "did you think I was leaving for good?"

"No, no, to be sure," said she, a little confused, "but I can't a-bear to have madam left alone for a day even." She pressed my hand hard, and, "Oh, Miss Hartley," says she, "be good to your mistress, as you're a Christian woman." And with that she hurried away, and left me staring.

A moment later Agnes called me to Mrs. Brympton. Hearing Mr. Brympton's voice in her room, I went round by the dressing-room, thinking I would lay out her dinner-gown before going in. The dressing-room is a large room with a window over the portico that looks toward the gardens. Mr. Brympton's apartments are beyond. When I went in, the door into the bedroom was ajar, and I heard Mr. Brympton saying angrily: "One would suppose he was the only person fit for you to talk to."

"I don't have many visitors in winter," Mrs. Brympton answered quietly.

"You have *me!*" he flung at her, sneering.

"You are here so seldom," said she.

"Well – whose fault is that? You make the place about as lively as a family vault—"

With that I rattled the toilet-things, to give my mistress warning and she rose and called me in.

The two dined alone, as usual, and I knew by Mr. Wace's manner at supper that things must be going badly. He quoted the prophets something terrible, and worked on the kitchen-maid so that she declared she wouldn't go down alone to put the cold meat in the ice-box. I felt nervous myself, and after I had put my mistress to bed I was half tempted to go down again and persuade Mrs. Blinder to sit up awhile over a game of cards. But I heard her door closing for the night, and so I went on to my own room. The rain had begun again, and the *drip, drip, drip* seemed to be dropping into my brain. I lay awake listening to it, and turning over what my friend in town had said. What puzzled me was that it was always the maids who left...

After a while I slept; but suddenly a loud noise wakened me. My bell had rung. I sat up, terrified by the unusual sound, which seemed to go on jangling through the darkness. My hands shook so that I couldn't find the matches. At length I struck a light and jumped out of bed. I began to think I must have been dreaming; but I looked at the bell against the wall, and there was the little hammer still quivering.

I was just beginning to huddle on my clothes when I heard another sound. This time it was the door of the locked room opposite mine softly opening and closing. I heard the sound distinctly, and it frightened me so that I stood stock still. Then I heard a footstep hurrying down the passage toward the main house. The floor being carpeted, the sound was very faint, but I was quite sure it was a woman's step. I turned cold with the thought of it, and for a minute or two I dursn't breathe or move. Then I came to my senses.

"Alice Hartley," says I to myself, "someone left that room just now and ran down the passage ahead of you. The idea isn't pleasant, but you may as well face it. Your mistress has rung for you, and to answer her bell you've got to go the way that other woman has gone."

Well – I did it. I never walked faster in my life, yet I thought I should never get to the end of the passage or reach Mrs. Brympton's room. On the way I heard nothing and saw nothing: all was dark and quiet as the grave. When I reached my mistress's door the silence was so deep that I began to think I must be dreaming, and was half-minded to turn back. Then a panic seized me, and I knocked.

There was no answer, and I knocked again, loudly. To my astonishment the door was opened by Mr. Brympton. He started back when he saw me, and in the light of my candle his face looked red and savage.

"*You!*" he said, in a queer voice. "*How many of you are there, in God's name?*"

At that I felt the ground give under me; but I said to myself that he had been drinking, and answered as steadily as I could: "May I go in, sir? Mrs. Brympton has rung for me."

"You may all go in, for what I care," says he, and, pushing by me, walked down the hall to his own bedroom. I looked after him as he went, and to my surprise I saw that he walked as straight as a sober man.

I found my mistress lying very weak and still, but she forced a smile when she saw me, and signed to me to pour out some drops for her. After that she lay without speaking, her breath coming quick, and her eyes closed. Suddenly she groped out with her hand, and "*Emma*," says she, faintly.

"It's Hartley, madam," I said. "Do you want anything?"

She opened her eyes wide and gave me a startled look.

"I was dreaming," she said. "You may go, now, Hartley, and thank you kindly. I'm quite well again, you see." And she turned her face away from me.

Chapter III

THERE WAS NO more sleep for me that night, and I was thankful when daylight came.

Soon afterward, Agnes called me to Mrs. Brympton. I was afraid she was ill again, for she seldom sent for me before nine, but I found her sitting up in bed, pale and drawn-looking, but quite herself.

"Hartley," says she quickly, "will you put on your things at once and go down to the village for me? I want this prescription made up—" here she hesitated a minute and blushed, "—and I should like you to be back again before Mr. Brympton is up."

"Certainly, madam," I said.

"And – stay a moment—" she called me back as if an idea had just struck her, "—while you're waiting for the mixture, you'll have time to go on to Mr. Ranford's with this note."

It was a two-mile walk to the village, and on my way I had time to turn things over in my mind. It struck me as peculiar that my mistress should wish the prescription made up without Mr. Brympton's knowledge; and, putting this together with the scene of the night before, and with much else that I had noticed and suspected, I began to wonder if the poor lady was weary of her life, and had come to the mad resolve of ending it. The idea took such hold on me that I reached the village on a run, and dropped breathless into a chair before the chemist's counter. The good man, who was just taking down his shutters, stared at me so hard that it brought me to myself.

"Mr. Limmel," I says, trying to speak indifferent, "will you run your eye over this, and tell me if it's quite right?"

He put on his spectacles and studied the prescription.

"Why, it's one of Dr. Walton's," says he. "What should be wrong with it?"

"Well – is it dangerous to take?"

"Dangerous – how do you mean?"

I could have shaken the man for his stupidity.

"I mean – if a person was to take too much of it – by mistake of course—" says I, my heart in my throat.

"Lord bless you, no. It's only lime-water. You might feed it to a baby by the bottleful."

I gave a great sigh of relief, and hurried on to Mr. Ranford's. But on the way another thought struck me. If there was nothing to conceal about my visit to the chemist's, was it my other errand that Mrs. Brympton wished me to keep private? Somehow, that thought frightened me worse than the other. Yet the two gentlemen seemed fast friends, and I would have staked my head on my mistress's goodness. I felt ashamed of my suspicions, and concluded that I was still disturbed by the strange events of the night. I left the note at Mr. Ranford's – and, hurrying back to Brympton, slipped in by a side door without being seen, as I thought.

An hour later, however, as I was carrying in my mistress's breakfast, I was stopped in the hall by Mr. Brympton.

"What were you doing out so early?" he says, looking hard at me.

"Early – me, sir?" I said, in a tremble.

"Come, come," he says, an angry red spot coming out on his forehead, "didn't I see you scuttling home through the shrubbery an hour or more ago?"

I'm a truthful woman by nature, but at that a lie popped out ready-made. "No, sir, you didn't," said I, and looked straight back at him.

He shrugged his shoulders and gave a sullen laugh. "I suppose you think I was drunk last night?" he asked suddenly.

"No, sir, I don't," I answered, this time truthfully enough.

He turned away with another shrug. "A pretty notion my servants have of me!" I heard him mutter as he walked off.

Not till I had settled down to my afternoon's sewing did I realize how the events of the night had shaken me. I couldn't pass that locked door without a shiver. I knew I had heard someone come out of it, and walk down the passage ahead of me. I thought of speaking to Mrs. Blinder or to Mr. Wace, the only two in the house who appeared to have an inkling of what was going on, but I had a feeling that if I questioned them they would deny everything, and that I might learn more by holding my tongue and keeping my eyes open. The idea of spending another night opposite the locked room sickened me, and once I was seized with the notion of packing my trunk and taking the first train to town; but it wasn't in me to throw over a kind mistress in that manner, and I tried to go on with my sewing as if nothing had happened.

I hadn't worked ten minutes before the sewing-machine broke down. It was one I had found in the house, a good machine, but a trifle out of order: Mrs. Blinder said it had never been used since Emma Saxon's death. I stopped to see what was wrong, and as I was working at the machine a drawer which I had never been able to open slid forward and a photograph fell out. I picked it up and sat looking at it in a maze. It was a woman's likeness, and I knew I had seen the face somewhere – the eyes had an asking look that I had felt on me before. And suddenly I remembered the pale woman in the passage.

I stood up, cold all over, and ran out of the room. My heart seemed to be thumping in the top of my head, and I felt as if I should never get away from the look in those eyes. I went straight to Mrs. Blinder. She was taking her afternoon nap, and sat up with a jump when I came in.

"Mrs. Blinder," said I, "who is that?" And I held out the photograph.

She rubbed her eyes and stared.

"Why, Emma Saxon," says she. "Where did you find it?"

I looked hard at her for a minute. "Mrs. Blinder," I said, "I've seen that face before."

Mrs. Blinder got up and walked over to the looking-glass. "Dear me! I must have been asleep," she says. "My front is all over one ear. And now do run along, Miss Hartley, dear, for I hear the clock striking four, and I must go down this very minute and put on the Virginia ham for Mr. Brympton's dinner."

Chapter IV

TO ALL APPEARANCES, things went on as usual for a week or two. The only difference was that Mr. Brympton stayed on, instead of going off as he usually did, and that Mr. Ranford never showed himself. I heard Mr. Brympton remark on this one afternoon when he was sitting in my mistress's room before dinner.

"Where's Ranford?" says he. "He hasn't been near the house for a week. Does he keep away because I'm here?"

Mrs. Brympton spoke so low that I couldn't catch her answer.

"Well," he went on, "two's company and three's trumpery; I'm sorry to be in Ranford's way, and I suppose I shall have to take myself off again in a day or two and give him a show." And he laughed at his own joke.

The very next day, as it happened, Mr. Ranford called. The footman said the three were very merry over their tea in the library, and Mr. Brympton strolled down to the gate with Mr. Ranford when he left.

I have said that things went on as usual; and so they did with the rest of the household; but as for myself, I had never been the same since the night my bell had rung. Night after night I used to lie awake, listening for it to ring again, and for the door of the locked room to open stealthily. But the bell never rang, and I heard no sound across the passage. At last the silence began to be more dreadful to me than the most mysterious sounds. I felt that *someone* were cowering there, behind the locked door, watching and listening as I watched and listened, and I could almost have cried out, "Whoever you are, come out and let me see you face to face, but don't lurk there and spy on me in the darkness!"

Feeling as I did, you may wonder I didn't give warning. Once I very nearly did so; but at the last moment something held me back. Whether it was compassion for my mistress, who had grown more and more dependent on me, or unwillingness to try a new place, or some other feeling that I couldn't put a name to, I lingered on as if spell-bound, though every night was dreadful to me, and the days but little better.

For one thing, I didn't like Mrs. Brympton's looks. She had never been the same since that night, no more than I had. I thought she would brighten up after Mr. Brympton left, but though she seemed easier in her mind, her spirits didn't revive, nor her strength either. She had grown attached to me, and seemed to like to have me about; and Agnes told me one day that, since Emma Saxon's death, I was the only maid her mistress had taken to. This gave me a warm feeling for the poor lady, though after all there was little I could do to help her.

After Mr. Brympton's departure, Mr. Ranford took to coming again, though less often than formerly. I met him once or twice in the grounds, or in the village, and I couldn't but think there was a change in him too; but I set it down to my disordered fancy.

The weeks passed, and Mr. Brympton had now been a month absent. We heard he was cruising with a friend in the West Indies, and Mr. Wace said that was a long way off, but though you had the wings of a dove and went to the uttermost parts of the earth, you couldn't get away from the Almighty. Agnes said that as long as he stayed away from Brympton, the Almighty might have him and welcome; and this raised a laugh, though Mrs. Blinder tried to look shocked, and Mr. Wace said the bears would eat us.

We were all glad to hear that the West Indies were a long way off, and I remember that, in spite of Mr. Wace's solemn looks, we had a very merry dinner that day in the hall. I don't know if it was because of my being in better spirits, but I fancied Mrs. Brympton looked better too, and seemed more cheerful in her manner. She had been for a walk in the morning, and after luncheon she lay down in her room, and I read aloud to her. When she dismissed me I went to my own room feeling quite bright and happy, and for the first time in weeks walked past the locked door without thinking of it. As I sat down to my work I looked out and saw a few snowflakes falling. The sight was pleasanter than the eternal rain, and I pictured to myself how pretty the bare gardens would look in their white mantle. It seemed to me as if the snow would cover up all the dreariness, indoors as well as out.

The fancy had hardly crossed my mind when I heard a step at my side. I looked up, thinking it was Agnes.

"Well, Agnes—" said I, and the words froze on my tongue; for there, in the door, stood Emma Saxon.

I don't know how long she stood there. I only know I couldn't stir or take my eyes from her. Afterward I was terribly frightened, but at the time it wasn't fear I felt, but something deeper and quieter. She looked at me long and long, and her face was just one dumb prayer to me – but how in the world was I to help her? Suddenly she turned, and I heard her walk down the passage. This time I wasn't afraid to follow – I felt that I must know what she wanted. I sprang up and ran out. She was at the other end of the passage, and I expected her to take the turn toward my mistress's room; but instead of that she pushed open the door that led to the backstairs. I followed her down the stairs, and across the passageway to the back door. The kitchen and hall were empty at that hour, the servants being off duty, except for the footman, who was in the pantry. At the door she stood still a moment, with another look at me; then she turned the handle, and stepped out. For a minute I hesitated. Where was she leading me to? The door had closed softly after her, and I opened it and looked out, half expecting to find that she had disappeared. But I saw her a few yards off, hurrying across the courtyard to the path through the woods. Her figure looked black and lonely in the snow, and for a second my heart failed me and I thought of turning back. But all the while she was drawing me after her; and catching up an old shawl of Mrs. Blinder's I ran out into the open.

Emma Saxon was in the wood-path now. She walked on steadily, and I followed at the same pace, till we passed out of the gates and reached the high-road. Then she struck across the open fields to the village. By this time the ground was white, and as she climbed the slope of a bare hill ahead of me I noticed that she left no footprints behind her. At sight of that, my heart shrivelled up within me, and my knees were water. Somehow, it was worse here than indoors. She made the whole countryside seem lonely as the grave, with none but us two in it, and no help in the wide world.

Once I tried to go back; but she turned and looked at me, and it was as if she had dragged me with ropes. After that I followed her like a dog. We came to the village, and she led me through it, past the church and the blacksmith's shop, and down the lane to Mr. Ranford's. Mr. Ranford's house stands close to the road: a plain old-fashioned building, with a flagged path leading to the door between box-borders. The lane was deserted, and as I turned into it, I saw Emma Saxon pause under the old elm by the gate. And now another fear came over me. I saw that we had reached the end of our journey, and that it was my turn to act. All the way from Brympton I had been asking myself what she wanted of me, but I had followed in a trance, as it were, and not till I saw her stop at Mr. Ranford's gate did my brain begin to clear itself. It stood a little way off in the snow, my heart beating fit to strangle me, and my feet frozen to the ground; and she stood under the elm and watched me.

I knew well enough that she hadn't led me there for nothing. I felt there was something I ought to say or do – but how was I to guess what it was? I had never thought harm of my mistress and Mr. Ranford, but I was sure now that, from one cause or another, some dreadful thing hung over them. *She* knew what it was; she would tell me if she could; perhaps she would answer if I questioned her.

It turned me faint to think of speaking to her; but I plucked up heart and dragged myself across the few yards between us. As I did so, I heard the house-door open, and saw Mr. Ranford approaching. He looked handsome and cheerful, as my mistress had looked that morning, and at sight of him the blood began to flow again in my veins.

"Why, Hartley," said he, "what's the matter? I saw you coming down the lane just now, and came out to see if you had taken root in the snow." He stopped and stared at me. "What are you looking at?" he says.

I turned toward the elm as he spoke, and his eyes followed me; but there was no one there. The lane was empty as far as the eye could reach.

A sense of helplessness came over me. She was gone, and I had not been able to guess what she wanted. Her last look had pierced me to the marrow; and yet it had not told me! All at once, I felt more desolate than when she had stood there watching me. It seemed as if she had left me all alone to carry the weight of the secret I couldn't guess. The snow went round me in great circles, and the ground fell away from me...

A drop of brandy and the warmth of Mr. Ranford's fire soon brought me to, and I insisted on being driven back at once to Brympton. It was nearly dark, and I was afraid my mistress might be wanting me. I explained to Mr. Ranford that I had been out for a walk and had been taken with a fit of giddiness as I passed his gate. This was true enough; yet I never felt more like a liar than when I said it.

When I dressed Mrs. Brympton for dinner she remarked on my pale looks and asked what ailed me. I told her I had a headache, and she said she would not require me again that evening, and advised me to go to bed.

It was a fact that I could scarcely keep on my feet; yet I had no fancy to spend a solitary evening in my room. I sat downstairs in the hall as long as I could hold my head up; but by nine I crept upstairs, too weary to care what happened if I could but get my head on a pillow. The rest of the household went to bed soon afterward; they kept early hours when the master was away, and before ten I heard Mrs. Blinder's door close, and Mr. Wace's soon after.

It was a very still night, earth and air all muffled in snow. Once in bed I felt easier, and lay quiet, listening to the strange noises that come out in a house after dark. Once I thought I heard a door open and close again below: it might have been the glass door that led to the gardens. I got up and peered out of the window; but it was in the dark of the moon, and nothing visible outside but the streaking of snow against the panes.

I went back to bed and must have dozed, for I jumped awake to the furious ringing of my bell. Before my head was clear I had sprung out of bed, and was dragging on my clothes. *It is going to happen now*, I heard myself saying; but what I meant I had no notion. My hands seemed to be covered with glue – I thought I should never get into my clothes. At last I opened my door and peered down the passage. As far as my candle-flame carried, I could see nothing unusual ahead of me. I hurried on, breathless; but as I pushed open the baize door leading to the main hall my heart stood still, for there at the head of the stairs was Emma Saxon, peering dreadfully down into the darkness.

For a second I couldn't stir; but my hand slipped from the door, and as it swung shut the figure vanished. At the same instant there came another sound from below stairs – a stealthy mysterious sound, as of a latch-key turning in the house-door. I ran to Mrs. Brympton's room and knocked.

There was no answer, and I knocked again. This time I heard someone moving in the room; the bolt slipped back and my mistress stood before me. To my surprise I saw that she had not undressed for the night. She gave me a startled look.

"What is this, Hartley?" she says in a whisper. "Are you ill? What are you doing here at this hour?"

"I am not ill, madam; but my bell rang."

At that she turned pale, and seemed about to fall.

"You are mistaken," she said harshly; "I didn't ring. You must have been dreaming." I had never heard her speak in such a tone. "Go back to bed," she said, closing the door on me.

But as she spoke I heard sounds again in the hall below: a man's step this time; and the truth leaped out on me.

"Madam," I said, pushing past her, "there is someone in the house—"

"Someone—?"

"Mr. Brympton, I think – I hear his step below—"

A dreadful look came over her, and without a word, she dropped flat at my feet. I fell on my knees and tried to lift her: by the way she breathed I saw it was no common faint. But as I raised her head there came quick steps on the stairs and across the hall: the door was flung open, and there stood Mr. Brympton, in his travelling clothes, the snow dripping from him. He drew back with a start as he saw me kneeling by my mistress.

"What the devil is this?" he shouted. He was less high-colored than usual, and the red spot came out on his forehead.

"Mrs. Brympton has fainted, sir," said I.

He laughed unsteadily and pushed by me. "It's a pity she didn't choose a more convenient moment. I'm sorry to disturb her, but—"

I raised myself up, aghast at the man's action.

"Sir," said I, "are you mad? What are you doing?"

"Going to meet a friend," said he, and seemed to make for the dressing-room.

At that my heart turned over. I don't know what I thought or feared; but I sprang up and caught him by the sleeve.

"Sir, sir," said I, "for pity's sake look at your wife!"

He shook me off furiously.

"It seems that's done for me," says he, and caught hold of the dressing-room door.

At that moment I heard a slight noise inside. Slight as it was, he heard it too, and tore the door open; but as he did so he dropped back. On the threshold stood Emma Saxon. All was dark behind her, but I saw her plainly, and so did he. He threw up his hands as if to hide his face from her; and when I looked again she was gone.

He stood motionless, as if the strength had run out of him; and in the stillness my mistress suddenly raised herself, and opening her eyes fixed a look on him. Then she fell back, and I saw the death-flutter pass over her...

We buried her on the third day, in a driving snowstorm. There were few people in the church, for it was bad weather to come from town, and I've a notion my mistress was one that hadn't many near friends. Mr. Ranford was among the last to come, just before they carried her up the aisle. He was in black, of course, being such a friend of the family, and I never saw a gentleman so pale. As he passed me, I noticed that he leaned a trifle on a stick he carried; and I fancy Mr. Brympton noticed it too, for the red spot came out sharp on his forehead, and all through the service he kept staring across the church at Mr. Ranford, instead of following the prayers as a mourner should.

When it was over and we went out to the graveyard, Mr. Ranford had disappeared, and as soon as my poor mistress's body was underground, Mr. Brympton jumped into the carriage nearest the gate and drove off without a word to any of us. I heard him call out, "To the station," and we servants went back alone to the house.

You Think You Are Safe

Nemma Wollenfang

YOU THINK you are safe. That's the reason you stay, I'm certain of it. But how can you be so sure? I'm not. And I should know. I've never understood the faith you have in me.

"It's alright, Ruby. Easy, *easy…*"

Double-wrapped chain; padlock fastened; cage secure. Tingles roll beneath my skin, it has already begun. Our eyes meet. "Ethan… *Leave…*"

A spike of pain has me curving forward. Bones crackle.

Why do you never flinch when you see me… *this way*? Elongating limbs cording with muscle, coarse black hair as adamantine as wire. And it gets worse. That wrinkled snout, those razor-edged fangs. Claws like talons – curved for hooking. Meant to maim and disembowel.

Agile, lethal, *terrifying* – so you say. It's not like I remember the full effect once it takes hold; that cool brush of oblivion wipes away every vestige of the woman you love.

"LEAVE!" I slam into the bars, rattling metal.

No reaction. You don't even wince.

"Alright. I'm going." Pocketing the key you back up. Spine straight, eyes up, *maintaining* contact. No hint of supplication. Good, good. Rule number one: show no weakness.

Nevertheless, I don't understand your calm demeanor. I never have. Appearance in itself should trigger some survival instinct, should make you shy away. And what of the danger? Its carnivorous appetite? There's always blood. Always. Prey is prey and it doesn't differentiate. Once it wakes, everything is fair game. Yet here you remain… my steadfast ally against the darkness. Lover, protector, jailor – without regret you've championed all three roles.

I suppose it's because while you've been close, you've never been *that* close. There's always been some kind of barrier between us – whether it's ten-inch glass or a steel cell door. Back at the labs they took every precaution. One cell was reinforced with five feet of solid brick. It was safer that way, not like now. Free, the world is at my mercy. Because despite our efforts at containment, every attempt so far has proved utterly futile. But you've said it's better this way, that you could no longer stand to watch what they did to me, those men in white coats.

That sets it off; the reminder of past pain. I squeeze too hard and the bar just *snaps*. Six-inch steel reduced to dust. Useless – the cage is never going to hold.

"*Run…*"

There's nothing left of me in the gravelly command – only danger wrapped in velvet.

* * *

It comes in threes: every three months, for three nights, lasting three hours. Like clockwork. You know the routine now, you've lived it long enough. You even timed it, once.

That's why you're always there, awaiting my return the morning after.

You're the Jekyll to my Hyde. All understanding empathy as I stagger from the woods into our backyard, barefoot and freezing, grotesque in ragged jammies with twigs in my hair and blood on my hands. The cage didn't work; as expected. I'd feared the worst until I saw you.

"Ethan…" My voice is my own again, quaky though it is.

Glints of sunrise catch in your hair like gold. Such beauty, such opposing clean normality, is grounding. Opening your coat, you gently wrap me up, conceal the glaring evidence of my nocturnal crimes, and smile as you wipe a stray red smear from my lips.

"Hey there, beautiful girl."

That's you. Not a trace of judgement or horror.

One side of me loves you utterly for that. The other… well…

Even when the mailman went missing last year you stuck by my side. Knowing, already knowing the heinous truth and accepting what could not be undone. You've become my sanity, my anchor. You deal with this, my changeling nature, telling me that we will overcome, that it will not happen again. Only five repetitions later does it begin to sound like a lie…

Usually it's not so bad: a missing pet here, some savaged livestock there. No one calls the police over one mutilated sheep, no matter how grisly the carcass. Coyotes, people conclude. Maybe mountain lions? And that's that. We plow past and carry on.

There are rumors, of course, that it may be something more… but no one ever looks to our door. After all, no neighbor could be capable of such atrocious savagery.

Lately, though, it's been getting worse. Kills are increasing, the ferocity escalating. The human death toll racks up while animals see a decline. *Unparalleled brutality* one reporter calls it. Another goes as far as 'Reign of Terror!' Chalk that melodrama up to low viewing figures and hopes of a promotion. It's over-embellishment, if you ask me. After all, none of it has made the national news, yet. But it highlights a major issue. Why the escalation? It worries me…

Perhaps it's just a progression of my condition. Perhaps it's because of your prodding and poking. Let's admit it – it's not wise to jab a hibernating beast. It's gonna get mad. The scholar in you can't help it, though. He is hard at work, deducing and speculating, in search of that ever elusive cure, and that requires some *jabbing*. You've burned through tomes of research already, exhausted books on lore, those spectacles sliding down the bridge of your nose while you read. Whenever you discover something new you light up like a firefly. It's adorable, how excitable you get. Professor of Parapsychology, you earned the title at twenty-five. That's how we met. I was your first subject. *Volunteer*, let's use the right word. At least I was willing, in the beginning. And even then, even seeing the worst of me, you never beheld me with dread. Your sole ambition has always been to help me, to rectify my… ailment.

Were, you told me back then, but *were*-what? Wolf?! *No.* My inclinations have always leant more towards the feline than the canine. Something to do with sinuousness, the sleek grace of feeling. Organza satin, plush fur rugs, fresh laundry, hmmm… Once you found me in a textile factory, curled amongst their most luscious silks. I'd broken in during a nightly rampage. Luckily you got there before the security guards did. That could have been bad – naked girl, found dozing in the stock, covered in blood. Front page news, anyone? But no, there is nothing of the wolf in me, I'm certain. Dogs don't luxuriate in fine fabrics quite the same way that cats do. Those dull, plodding creatures have little wit when it comes to such appreciations.

"Lycanthropy *is* still the most viable explanation," you insist, even now. The argument is your old stand-by. "And the vocal recording supports that theory."

"Ah, yes. The infamous recording." During my last lunar cycle, when I got out again – we don't talk about that – you braved the night to catch this. But it's poor quality; the sound grainy.

"Distinctly lupine." You nod at the distorted yowl that plays. But I am unconvinced.

"How can you be so sure that's me? It could have been anything." Fouler monsters than I lurk about during those heinous nights, I'm certain of it. Hunting in the gloom.

You don't look at me, fiddling with the recorder. "Perhaps I can accompany you next time you break-out. Make sure the sample is valid?" The request is so simple, blasé, as if you're asking for nothing more than to tag along to the local store. You think you are safe and that's why you ask. It's a poor excuse, flimsy in the extreme. There's no compromise in my tone when I say, "You should never get that close." In the grim quiet that follows you don't argue.

Your *'were* theory' doesn't weigh up against silver – I've never had a problem with that, and you've performed enough tests – but the full moon? Now *that's* a different story. During that third cycle I can feel its pull; the lunar eddies and flows. It's like it reaches deep inside and squeezes something hidden, something feral and visceral, and reels it slashing to the surface.

Other proof supports it too; traits indicative of classic folklore. Bristles beneath the tongue, curved nails, a stare that can *paralyse* – that only happened once, though, and neither of us was certain of the young grad-student's truthfulness. He'd stunk of rancid yellow.

Wolfsbane has a noticeable effect, and that perennial has always been associated with lycanthrope legends. When I was a volunteer, the men in lab-coats prepared a tincture, to see its effects. Which were *bad*. Burning, swelling, numbness of the face. The abdominal cramps sent me screaming to the floor. I hadn't known what they'd given me, and with tear-stained vision I'd begged for help, not understanding why they stood over me, impassive, writing on their boards while I writhed on the floor, choking on vomit, blind to shame. That was when you broke rank and knelt by my side, cradling my sweat-dappled face as the lines of consciousness blurred.

"*Aconitum* is known as the 'Queen of all Poisons' for a reason," you'd spat, red-faced with fury. "It kills a human just as easily, so that test proved nothing!" They'd been unmoved. But I overcame it; you nursed me back to health. That was the moment, though, the moment when you'd had enough. The moment when you began to plan our escape…

You've disregarded texts on satanic sorcery or divine punishment as a means for metamorphosis. Most cases document a survivor of an attack becoming infected. But I was born, not bitten. I've suffered this affliction my whole life. So a genetic predisposition, perhaps? Thing is, most lore is superstition, supposition. Not fact, only unreliable fiction. Myths in the guise of fancy tales designed to explain unexplainable horrors. The scientist in you riles at such drivel, you say nonsense obscures truth. Markers in my blood, though, differentiations in genes, cannot lie. All you have to do is find them. So far, no luck. But that's no surprise. The equipment you use is limited. If we'd been back at the university perhaps you would have learnt more, having access to better facilities. But that would mean sterile white labs and the constant pierce of needles. No rest, no reprieve. No end to the experiments. We forsook that life, risking it on our own. And if they knew where we were, we wouldn't retain what freedom we have for long.

* * *

Neighborhood animals have never liked me, on two legs or four – that's something that has you fascinated. Walking too close sends them into frenzies. Snarling, snapping, hissing. They recognize the threat, you've said, the presence of a superior predator. An apex.

On our daily excursions it happens sometimes – inevitable collisions with dog-walkers.

"I'm so sorry," Mrs. Blake from No. 2 says one day, as she struggles to rein in her tiny Pomeranian. "Murphy's usually so sweet. I don't know what's come over him. Stop that, boy!"

The little mutt barely notices as she yanks its leash. Lips quivering against its snarl, it tries to decide its play: attack and defend its mistress, or flee? A trickle of urine runs down its leg. With the change so close, mere hours away, that's all it takes. One simple trigger.

"Something must've spooked him," you say fluidly as I hold myself in check. With fear peppering the air it's hard. Weakness smells like rancid yellow and it *saturates* the pup.

When she turns away the urge grows too strong. I bare my teeth in a silent snarl, relishing its high-pitched yelp. You steer me away – your arm a shackle around my waist, not an embrace. And when I turn on you, ready to launch, your glower pins me down.

"Ruby! No!" A growl, a domineering rumble that crawls beneath skin...

The key is not to show weakness, you've told me. Predators sense it, hone in on it. A limp, old age, a flinch, *urination*. The mailman had been a paraplegic. Signs of easy prey attract my inner monster like catnip. Sometimes it's hard to rein me in but, this time, your primal posturing is a show of strength that brings me to heel. You quell the beast with authority.

There's never any rancid yellow in your scent, not a trace of it.

* * *

You should be leaving. Tonight's a full moon and we never risk it – not since my first break-out. We can't trust the basement cage, whatever its reinforcements. But you're too busy. Playing with your chemicals. "Just five more minutes," you say. "*Nearly* done."

"Ethan..." You wave away my warning, so I slouch against a beam and wait. Cement floors, rough stone walls. The one window – a sliver near the ceiling – is boarded up, and the space is lit by harsh halogen bulbs. In one dark corner lies my flimsy cage – at least we *try*. Beside it, shelved jars of photosensitive chemicals glow like jewels. This is where you hide away, my Dr. Frankenstein. Working on your remedies. We've already tried so many.

Most were devised by medieval practitioners; their violence equivalent to their uselessness, but the Ancient Greeks prescribed long periods of exertion to purge the malady and you saw merit in this. Halt the carnage by rendering the beast too weak to rise. *Exhaust* it.

Shame it didn't work, or the hypnotherapy. Tranquilizers are a no-no too; I've had enough to drop an elephant. But you say you have something new.

"Yes!" You hold the test-tube up like a prize. Whatever's inside shimmers like liquid sapphires. "I've done it, Ruby. I've finally done it! I'm sure of it!"

"What is it?" A formula? To counteract the beastliness?

"It'll keep you calm tonight," you assure, chasing away the syringe's sting with a caress to my cheek. "You'll sleep right through the change, I guarantee it. This will make you better!"

And your eyes are so bright, so sure, that there's no room for doubt.

* * *

It doesn't make it better. It makes it worse. So much worse.

Tearing through the undergrowth, snapping ferns and branches and ripping out great clods of turf, I bulldoze through the forest. Fury drives me, sears my blood, stoking it beyond comprehension. Fiery, blistering, frothing. Never have I felt such all-consuming rage!

There's not much left of me, only a vague recollection. You never understood that – how completely it takes over. A coup of body and mind and soul.

Sounds: a crunch of leaves, a snap of twigs. Footfalls amongst the trees. My body turns, redirecting, powerful limbs pump with speed. Closer, closer... Bursting through some shrubs I collide with a solid mass. Muscle caves beneath grinding teeth and with a thrash and a gurgle – quickly muted – a familiar iron tang flavors my tongue, spiced with the bite of adrenaline and fear and rancid yellow. The growl resonates as I clamp down harder. Bones crunch, sinews rip, more blood floods in. Hot and glutinous and thick. It coats my maw, congeals fur, as I glut on stinking viscera. The stench is delicious and sickening all at once.

Whatever it was, it never stood a chance.

When I stumble from the woods at sunrise, numbed by ice and drenched in gore, it's you who runs from the house with a blanket, you who covers my nakedness and draws me close, you who holds me as hiccupping sobs overwhelm and my knees buckle, slamming into grass.

It's you who keeps me sane and cleans up the mess.

Seated in the kitchen, cradling a hot cup of cocoa, I stare at nothing. There's a news report playing in the background, something about a wild animal attack. A grizzly, perhaps? No, a wolf-pack... A rabid cougar? And this close to the suburbs? That poor, *poor* girl.

I killed a human. A late-night jogger. Purposefully I ignore the pretty profile image, staring at the pristine snow outside until my eyes sting. I don't want to know who.

Words catch my attention at random. *Disemboweled... partially devoured...* Reports of sightings include descriptions of *slavering fangs* and *luminous eyes*. They've passed into the realm of monster now, with no other way to fathom the savagery. The 'Reign of Terror!' reporter is no longer being scoffed at. Whispers surround her of wendigoes and loogaroos; even the infamous *chupacabra* gets a mention. We aren't far from the Mexican border. Sightings have been reported this far north before. People are scared – as they should be – and minds are running amok. My focus is transient, though, mainly on you while you dust away the tracks in the snow that lead to our back door. I watch the way you examine each paw-print, whipping out your phone as you record and catalogue. No doubt they'll make the archives.

Even in the chill, sweat dapples your sun-kissed skin and your arms bulge with muscle, with *strength*. You need it with me – to display, to use. Not that it seems to bother you. With those high cheekbones and that lovely straight nose, you're the epitome of charm – something I've never possessed. Those slightly arching eyebrows, always amused, frame such gentle eyes. A beacon of joy, even in the grimmest times, you're the light to my darkness. Everything I'm not. You could've had any girl and yet you're here, bound to me. This wretched deadly thing.

Why do you do it? Why do you stay and comfort me so sweetly?

You can't possibly comprehend the blackness in my heart; the beast that claws away within. Whatever cage I build, however I stack my defenses, it always breaks through. It's only ever a matter of time. You are yet to understand, or perhaps accept, that.

The cocoa is drugged; I can taste the herbal tang. I swill it gratefully until calm is a cozy veil, coating me in blissful uncaring warmth. I head to bed early and let it pull me under.

Night encroaches and it doesn't take long for the change to begin. The first shivers ripple outwards as the moon meets its zenith, stinging my mind into wakefulness. It's cold and methodical; a kind of black, sneering coolness that creeps underneath the skin...

A rustle of bedsheets, a brush of a leg. Oh! My eyes bulge as I flip over. What are you doing here?! You should've left hours ago! Being in the same house is bad enough but I'm not even in my cage! The words won't form, all I can do is grit my teeth as the ripples intensify.

"*L-leave*," I gasp, riding waves of cracking agony – the breaking and reshaping of bone.

In the darkness you shake your head, you *stupid man*. And reaching out, your fingers caress a cheek. The budding barbs there abrade your soft pads – like needles, drawing blood.

"Last night was my mistake," you say, suppressing a wince. "*Mine* not yours."

I gulp air in pants, white-knuckling the sheets, straining so hard to hold the viciousness at bay that I barely hear you. Your eyes glint in the shadows – twin flints of resolve.

"I'm staying to help you through this. I know what I'm doing." There's no indecision but we both taste the lie. You have absolutely no idea.

My sanity, my anchor. I can't lose you to this.

One particularly ferocious spike makes me cry out, arching off the bed. The attempt at restraint is making it worse. More wild, more rabid. Like a caged panther.

"I love you, Ruby," you rasp. "Hold onto that. Hold onto *us*!"

I can't! The beast craves blood and carnage.

As I writhe, struggling to suppress it, your face looms over me in the gloom. Features set with determination, you pin my arms. Nails drive into skin.

"Fight it, Ruby! You're stronger than this. Fight it! *Push it back*."

My groan turns deep; frustration leeks into a growl. The change is taking hold fast. I can feel it. The tiny bones in my hands shiver and crack, reshaping into something stronger. Your face becomes clearer, its contours sharper. Your heart sings such a wild, frantic, fragile song.

You're a wide-eyed coney and nothing more; a gregarious, frolicking, *naïve* creature. It can scent that, taste that. Beneath the surface I feel it stretching. Testing. Reaching out...

I do the only thing I can think of.

I kiss you, hard. Because perhaps the love in you can calm the beast in me.

With your cologne in my nostrils and your chest crushing mine, we thrash in the sheets like wolves in the undergrowth. It's reminiscent of the hunt, the kill, and more...

Something primitive. Something carnal.

Inside, the beast's rage subdues. As if it's hesitating, reconsidering.

Love, loathe; despise, desire. Animal and human both.

Our battle slows. You pause, indecisive as we hang on the precipice. Those eyes of yours bore deep; black with the thinnest rings of color. Perhaps mine isn't the only beast here.

"Ruby?" you say. Hoarse now, low and gravelly.

There's more than one type of hunger and you can sate either one or the other. For a heartbeat I'm not sure which. Then your lips crash into mine and the decision is made.

* * *

That was foolish, what you did, and I plan to tell you so, berate you over bagels and coffee. But I'm not as upset as I should be – in fact, I'm brimming with excitement – because last night was different. Blood did not saturate the earth. Last night you changed the game.

I grin as I descend the stairs to the sizzling bacon smell of breakfast. I have a theory I want to share with you. The beast sees you as dominant, its Alpha, something stronger without fear. That's why it capitulates. Logically I know this isn't true. Logically I know it could shred you like tissue paper. But the monster seems unaware of this. Which means you have control.

The TV is on, news coverage still on the recent attack, and with your back to the door and the noise on-screen you do not hear my approach.

"Morning, love."

Spine going rigid you turn, tacking on a hasty grin. My sunny smile fades, because in that instant, that microsecond before you faced me, I saw it.

A flinch.

Barely perceptible but it speaks volumes.

You fear me.

You... *fear me*.

The realization is jarring, earth-shattering. Even from across the room I can scent it; the twinge of dread that spices your blood, however quickly snuffed. Minute fissures are hair-lining you, my pillar of strength, cracking their way through your marble resolve in tiny but ever more definable branches. Beneath my skin the beast unfurls, scenting the new aroma...

I shake my head to clear it. "You shouldn't have flinched."

* * *

There was a reason they locked me up, and I think now you're beginning to realize it, to finally comprehend the true magnitude of the peril you face. It tears at my heart, knowing how easily you could grow to despise me. It's a silent fear I live with every day.

You're still there later, a stoic sentinel snoring at my side. Even though it's the third night, even though you know what will happen... Likely because of it. You're going to try and restrain me again, aren't you? So confident, my gallant warrior, so ready to prove your mettle. I can't let you risk it, though, not again. It won't work a second time. That's why I slip from the sheets, my stealth masked in fluid satin, and leave the house before the moon rises too high.

Once the cool air caresses my skin, I feel it. The change. The thing that awakes within.

Muscles tighten and protrude, prickly hair sprouts from every pore as I hunch forward. It stretches out, invading every limb like it's climbing into a suit. Until I am not me anymore.

Senses hone to a glaring new spectrum. The chirp of insects, the pulse of blood, vibrate in the red rhythm of the woodland. Not even fully succumbed it finds a target. Padded feet slam into a quarry. The kill is easy. All I register is that it's large. The 'what' has no meaning, neither do its feeble bleats. Flesh cleaves, an arterial spray coats my muzzle, and I exult in the saltiness of it. The earthy tang of fear, how the life-form struggles and writhes. Strong, then weaker... and weaker... I bear down, crushing, until finally it falls still. Then I stand atop – Huntress Triumphant – and throw my head back to howl at the sky!

It's fresh and clean, the euphoria of the kill – an expanse of time without conscience or shame when I can indulge in the gloriousness before reality takes hold.

There's time enough yet. Time enough to gorge—

A snap. Branch or twig. I whip around, a snarl on my lips...

You should never have followed me. You know this. I see it in the whites of your eyes as you're reminded of it now. The danger is vast, the risk too great, but you came anyway because you believe you are safe, you always do. You believe that you, above every other human, are somehow exempt. The same confidence that saved you before may well kill you this time.

Hands up, you edge closer. Slow, like a stalking lion. "Ruby, it's me. Your Ethan."

Hackles rise. Lips peel back from teeth. Your understanding is *abhorrent*, your empathy a lie. Both wither to ash. Bitter realization strikes as I understand what I misinterpreted before. It's not love I see in your gaze but *pity*. Something so much worse than a flinch.

Clouds float past to reveal the full moon; uncannily bright. Beams splash the foliage with silver, driving what love I hold for you far, *far* away. It's so much worse under unfiltered light. Tendrils of shadow crawl up, threatening to smother what awareness I have, what little control I wield. As the full majesty of the beast uncoils, it fills my body, my mind, my soul, with glittering onyx madness. It is a nightmare to many. It will become yours too.

"*Go*..." The low rumble bares no hint of mercy; only rolls of hate and wrath.

The urge to hurt you is overwhelming. I want to carve into your bones! Rip you to bloody ribbons! Your warm flesh, slithering between my claws, will shimmer like wet silk.

Yet you stand your ground.

"No, I'm not going anywhere," you say. "Look, Ruby. I'm not flinching."

Breath leaves me in an angry rush. Suddenly it makes sense. I know why you're here – to prove yourself, to ratify your bravery. I'll hand it to you, you *do* have courage. Even as my nasal bones snap and elongate, even as my nails harden into scythe-like claws, you hold your bladder. Show no weakness. *Rule number one.* But will it be enough?

A scream rips from my throat as new teeth break through – razor-sharp enamel meant to ravage and tear. The transformation is nearly complete. If you don't run, it'll be too late. It may already be. I don't know how long I can–

Clammy palms grab my cheeks and your lips slam into mine.

A kiss; firm and demanding. I understand why. It worked before.

But I'm too far gone this time, already overtaken. All the kiss does is slice your delicate skin, wetting both our mouths with blood. Besides, the beast does not want you anymore. Not in that way. Sanity? Anchoring? No. It wants to burst free in an explosion of wild fury, and battling against it unleashes an agony that threatens to crack my body in two.

For you, I try to hold out.

You think you are safe. And that's why you don't let go. That's why you try to restrain me. *It.* I'm hardly even here anymore. The edges of perception dim as fluid ebony seeps in and the monster takes control. I whine, knowing it's useless, knowing the fight is lost. Saltwater stings my vision, blurring it further, blurring *you*. Blackness coils, wiping my sight completely and, finally, as I lose my grip and tumble into the lulling obsidian nothingness – so pure, so calm, like the deepest of sleeps – the barest hint of rancid yellow alights on my tongue.

You think you are safe?

You're not. You never were.

He Will Hear Us Coming

Anna Ziegelhof

IN MY MEMORY my father's hall had not been quite so desolate. When I returned after four years, the house lay dark in the middle of the brown wintery meadow. The piercing wind from the North Sea tore at me when I was led inside, held tightly by the gruff housekeeper on one side and my stepmother on the other. My stepmother had chattered pleasant nonsense throughout the journey, but I had seen the disdain she was trying to hide from me. I had seen it in the tight lines around her mouth, in the distracted flitting of her eyes as the landscape outside the carriage had grown more rural.

Somebody had begun to heat the ancestral hall by the sea, but the warmth was still helpless against years of disuse. I was shown to my room as if I couldn't remember the way. Rest had been recommended, but in this room? The room from which I had been carried four years ago, screaming in terror?

My silly pictures were still there. My dolls were there. Their empty cheerful faces were still staring into the void. The four-poster bed had been made up for me. Only the books had been cleared off the shelves. They had left ghostly marks in the dust. That stranger who had intruded into my life nearly unbeknownst to me during my absence, my father's new wife, my stepmother, had clearly followed orders.

I had been diagnosed with an active imagination. Reading, they had said all along, was too strenuous. It would upset my injured mind. That's where all those noises had come from, they said: from my active imagination. After I had learned to keep quite still and to say exactly what they wanted to hear, they discharged me from the institution and not even my father's well-meaning protest could change their verdict: I was cured. For the first time in four years I went home to my father's neglected hall by the sea.

My stepmother reminded me to rest – my father would join us for dinner – and then I was left alone in that terrible room. Of course, a story about a little girl left alone in a haunted room came back to me. I shook it off. I was, after all, an eighteen year-old woman, not a little girl, but that only reminded me of yet another story – "this atrocious nursery!"

And so, the stories shouted at me. In me, a tight ball of rage formed and came out as a suppressed grunt. I swallowed it quickly and spent the afternoon gazing out of the window across the soggy meadow from which that infernal, eternal fog rose.

* * *

My father sat down with us for dinner in the large wood-paneled dining room that, like everything else, seemed to have shrunk slightly in the years of my absence. He boomed anecdotes of travel and business through the room and then he announced his departure for France the next morning, leaving his problem – me – as an occupation for his new wife.

I had learned a lot during my time in the hospital: to observe, to contain violence, to smile, to be docile. I had learned everything about fear– not even fear of the noises in the walls, but fear of repercussions for honesty. So I smiled and said thank you.

* * *

The wintery evening drew on, my stepmother observing me between stitches of her needle, and as bedtime drew closer, I realized that four years of absence had not relativized my memories of the reason I had been sent away in the first place: there was a violent presence that haunted my father's cliff-top hall and I had little hope that it had given up and left. I expected that it would continue its attacks on me. It would finally drag me down into its hellish haunts. I grew more and more certain of it as the evening drew on.

Of course, I had been taught, it had all been in my head. A hysterical reaction to the death of my mother. I had been taught to recite that explanation meekly. I had recited it so often and so convincingly that I was discharged with only a recommendation for rest, despite my father's outspoken doubt about my recovery.

My reluctant stepmother, grudgingly following her orders, walked me back up to my childhood room after an appropriate amount of time had been spent by us, silently occupied with needlework in the drawing room.

Exhausted, not from travel but from holding a strained smile, from the thought of inactivity and boredom and aimlessness, I fell asleep in my old bed, its curtains drawn.

I started from first delirious slumber to the familiar rustling sound.

The mice in the walls!

I had known that it was going to be back, because I knew it had never been in my head. All those lovely stories that my mother had always shared with me had nothing at all to do with it.

The mice in the walls, I had been taught to say to myself. Little had they known that I had recited their lines and nodded diligently without even once believing them. In the dark, in my familiarly haunted room, I grinned to myself and put quotation marks around the mice in the walls.

The second sound came next. I expected it. I had told the police and the doctors all about it. I had been eloquent about it, as eloquent as a fourteen-year-old could be:

"In those moments of first slumber," I had explained to them in a very rational tone, "I awaken again because of a noise. A soft rustling at first, not as even as the wind, much closer. It grows to a scratching. And next, predictably, the scraping sound of fingernails against wood."

"And this was inside the wall behind your bed?" the men in their dark uniforms or white coats had asked me with eyebrows raised in amusement at the silly fourteen-year-old who was taking the death of her mother too hard.

"Yes," I had responded. "Somebody is walking around inside the wall and they are scratching the panels with their fingernails. There," I had pointed to the headboard of my four-poster bed.

I was young then. I had not yet learned to read the expressions of arrogant patronization and amused belittlement. Silly me, I had shared so eagerly, thinking somebody had finally come to help me with my abject fear in those nights after my mother's death.

Four years later I found that the reflex for fear was still in me, but it had become an old familiar, and I had learned things during my absence. I now knew how to control myself, to check myself, to put on an act even while scared, angry, or desperate. And so I was able to listen to the sounds in the dark with a calm mind for the first time.

First, the rustling. Mice they had said. Wrong. It was the scratching of long talons along the board behind my bed. The creature in the walls had never left, even while I had been gone. It had missed me. It had waited for me.

I knew what would come next. I braced for it. I was unable to hide under my covers, to cry, or to shiver. I was frozen in my childhood bed. And then, there it came. The sound I was able to describe too well. It was the sound of footsteps. Four years ago, it had sent me into crying fits in the middle of the night. I had fled from my room every night and my agonized screams roused my father, my teacher, the servants, every breathing being in the house.

"A man's footfall?" the people who had been called in to help when my father still pretended to believe me had asked with their patronizing sneers.

"No," I had been eager to explain, feeling listened to, "softer. Like a person who is not wearing shoes."

"You are reporting somebody on bare feet pattering around inside the wall behind your bed?"

Maybe that was the moment I had started to realize that I was not being listened to, that I was already merely being checked for symptoms of some illness of the mind.

I can now imagine how they may have said to each other, "vivid imagination. Didn't the girl get a glimpse of her mother's body? A drowned body, that's a sight that even some grown men might not digest easily." I imagined their sonorous laughter before their conversation would have moved on to more entertaining matters.

Now, older and wiser, I lay awake in my bed again waiting for the distinct sound of bare, wet feet in my wall. This time, I was not going to flee. I was going to meet this evil thing. I needed to see it with my own eyes. I sneered. I felt my upper lip lifting, baring my teeth, like an animal.

I knew with certainty what was in my wall. It was whatever malevolent presence had possessed my mother to take her own life in those dark and angry waves. They could take away my books to cure my active imagination, but they could never take away the stories I created in my head. And now, I thought, triumphantly, it was coming for me. It would walk me down to the water, and then they would see that I had attempted to tell the truth all along. And whoever would see my body, bloated, gnawed by fish, white and blue and green, would be haunted, too.

I lay there in my dark room, immobile and sneering with anticipation or terror, as the sounds of the wet footsteps inside the wall grew louder and ever louder, closer, so close now. The curtain around my bed did nothing to alleviate the freezing cold of the North Sea waters that had intruded. The demon was there now, in the room, just like I had always feared. Two more taps of those wet paws on the wooden floor. The bed curtain moved as if by a breeze brought in from the sea. It billowed slightly, then sagged again. The demon moved around me to check for the best way to get to me, to access my soul. It had grown brave in the past four years, but I had grown less frightened, too.

"They never believed me," I hissed under my breath and finally I was able to reach for the bed curtain. With all my weak might I tore the curtain away to face the haunting presence.

The creature's hollow, waxen face glared at me and there was a fire in its dead eyes that I hadn't seen there back when I found her, washed up on the beach, not far from the cliff from which she had flung herself. The wax-like eyes of my mother's dead body had haunted me the most. A passionate fury burnt in those eyes now, as if she had wandered the seas of Europe and brought back a glow of Baltic amber. She glared and opened her frayed mouth, gnawed wider by fishes, and let out a moan so chilling that it nearly sent me back into my frightened paralysis. But I kept my eyes open, I kept my body unmoving, just like I had practiced for four years, and I looked at her distorted, destroyed face. Her hair, icy-white from the wintery seas and laced with seaweed, hung in wet rags to her waist. She was still in her nightgown, that white lace nightgown. Her chilly fingers reached out to me. They dripped a wet trail on my bed, on me, so cold it burnt. I wanted to grasp her dear, dear hands in mine to breathe warmth on her, to warm her up again after all those years in the icy sea and all those years haunting this icy house. But my hands passed through her as if through water.

"Mother," I said, glad, nevertheless.

"Dear," her voice came hoarse and gurgling, a painful strain. I could hear the effort it took. "You," she brought out word by hissing and rolling word, "came back."

I nodded next to her frozen presence.

"But why did *you*?" I asked and a new emotion rolled through me: one of bottomless grief and pain.

"To tell you," the ocean in her crashed and gurgled, "that he killed me."

I gasped. I was shivering now. She tried to withdraw. She didn't want to cause me pain. She had had to deliver her message. I had always been too frightened to listen.

"To," she began again, with renewed strength after her first confession, "tell *her* that he will kill again."

"To," it pained me to hear her struggle so much, "tell you that this house is not haunted by me but by him."

I couldn't help myself then, and I cried.

All those condescending doctors and along with them, ready to agree, inconvenienced, dismissive, always, my father. My father, always abroad, always traveling. Always interested in the more delicate, the more modern, the younger.

"You've come to warn her?" I repeated.

When she moved her head from side to side, shaking her head, ocean spray speckled my face.

"I can only haunt you," she said, sounding stronger by the minute, "but I've come to ask you to take revenge for me and to rescue her."

There was not a doubt on my mind. I slipped out of my bed. I led the icy presence of my long-dead mother through the halls of the house. I stepped quietly so as not to disturb anyone except for the right person.

I found my stepmother in the study adjacent to her bedroom. She sat at her desk by lamplight. Her forehead was cradled in her hand. I recognized a shudder of a stifled sob, followed by a shudder caused by the cold sea wind that had suddenly entered her room.

She dissolved her posture of tired despair and turned around to me. Seemliness dictated that she clean herself up and not let her tears show to her frail stepdaughter.

"Oh," she sighed. It took her a moment to pull herself together before she managed to scold me for roaming the hallways late at night when I was under strict orders to rest.

"Mother," I said and meant the woman who had died, not the woman who had risen from her writing desk, disturbed in her distress and helpless against my late-night rebellion.

When the icy sea breeze drew closer and the fraying specter entered her study, I witnessed my stepmother blanch. I witnessed her every reaction and I sneered again, relieved to see my own terror of years finally reflected in someone else's visceral reaction to the haunting injustice.

"This is my mother," I introduced them, calmly. My stepmother had shrunk away. She was whimpering now, her back to her desk. As unable as I had been to tear my eyes away from the drowned body, my stepmother's eyes, huge and brimming with tears, were fixed on the ghost who was a steadying presence behind me.

"We have come to save your life," I said, the power behind me making me feel strong for the first time in my life.

My stepmother's lip began to quiver. Her hands that had been clasped tight under her chin loosened. Her posture sagged.

"He killed you," she said to my mother's presence, evenly now. She was a smart woman, I thought. She had collected clues, I assumed, over the past four years. "He killed you because he wanted me."

"Will you join us?" I invited her.

I recognized a liberating grin, probably similar to my own, on my stepmother's face when she agreed.

"But wear your heavy boots," the ghost of my mother spoke. "Just like he did that night when he took me out to the cliff. So he will hear us coming. He will know we are coming for him."

Biographies & Sources

A.J. Alan

My Adventure in Norfolk

(Originally Broadcast on BBC Radio, 1924; transcript collected in *Good Evening, Everyone!*, 1928)

Born in Nottingham, Leslie Harrison Lambert (1883–1941), who wrote under the name A.J. Alan, trained as a surveyor before taking up conjuring – first as a hobby; then as a professional. An enthusiast for radio in the very infancy of broadcasting, he worked in signals intelligence during World War I. In January 1924, he read the first of a series of hugely successful stories on the BBC – all carefully crafted to have an easy, extemporised air. A radio star, he was nevertheless able to fade from view with the start of World War II, which he spent with the government's secret codebreaking service at Bletchley Park.

Dr. Emily Alder

Foreword: Footsteps in the Dark Short Stories

Dr. Emily Alder is lecturer in literature and culture at Edinburgh Napier University, where she teaches and writes about her obsessions with weird and fantastic genre fictions and their intersections with science and the natural environment. She has written essays and articles on nineteenth-century weird and science fiction, children's picture-books, Nautical Gothic, and EcoGothic, and has written a book: *Weird Fiction and Science at the Fin de Siècle*. Emily edits the journal *Gothic Studies*.

Gertrude Atherton

Death and the Woman

(Originally Published in *Vanity Fair*, 1892)

Gertrude Atherton (1857–1948), who also wrote under the pseudonyms 'Frank Lin' and 'Asmodeus', was born in California. She wrote her first novel while living with her husband in the Atherton Mansion in San Francisco. Her family disapproved of her writing, which often featured independent, driven women. After her husband died at sea she moved to New York, and travelled in Europe. Her novel *Black Oxen* (1923) was made into a silent film, and her other supernatural tales include 'The Striding Place', 'The Foghorn' and 'The Bell in the Fog'.

E.F. Benson

Mrs. Amworth

(Originally Published in *Hutchinson's Magazine*, 1922)

Edward Frederic ('E.F.') Benson (1867–1940) was born at Wellington College in Berkshire, England, where his father, the future Archbishop of Canterbury Edward White Benson, was headmaster. Benson is widely known for being a writer of reminiscences, fiction, satirical novels, biographies and autobiographical studies. His first published novel, *Dodo*, initiated his success, followed by a series of comic novels such as *Queen Lucia* and *Trouble for Lucia*. Later in life, Benson moved to Rye where he was elected mayor. It was here that he was inspired to write several macabre ghost story and supernatural collections and novels, including *Paying Guests* and *Mrs. Ames*.

Ambrose Bierce
The Eyes of the Panther
(Originally Published in *The San Francisco Examiner*, 1897)
Ambrose Bierce (1842–*c.* 1914) was born in Meigs County, Ohio. He was a famous journalist and author known for writing *The Devil's Dictionary*. After fighting in the American Civil War, Bierce used his combat experience to write stories based on the war, such as in 'An Occurrence at Owl Creek Bridge'. Following the separate deaths of his ex-wife and two of his three children he gained a sardonic view of human nature and earned the name 'Bitter Bierce'. His disappearance at the age of 71 on a trip to Mexico remains a great mystery and continues to spark speculation.

Rhoda Broughton
The Man with the Nose
(Originally Published in *Temple Bar*, 1872)
Rhoda Broughton (1840–1920) was born in Denbigh, North Wales. She was raised in an Elizabethan manor house and given a classical education, which influenced her later writing. Broughton quickly established herself as a writer of controversially frank portrayals of female sexuality. Despite the consternation at her subject matter her novels were very popular and widely read. She also became known as a society wit that even intimidated Oscar Wilde.

Ramsey Campbell
The Long Way
(Originally Published by PS Publishing in 2008, © Ramsey Campbell)
The Oxford Companion to English Literature describes Ramsey Campbell as 'Britain's most respected living horror writer'. He has been given more awards than any other writer in the field, including the Grand Master Award of the World Horror Convention, the Lifetime Achievement Award of the Horror Writers Association, the Living Legend Award of the International Horror Guild and the World Fantasy Lifetime Achievement Award. In 2015 he was made an Honorary Fellow of Liverpool John Moores University for outstanding services to literature. Among his novels available from Flame Tree Press are *Thirteen Days by Sunset Beach*, *Think Yourself Lucky*, and *The Wise Friend*.

Ralph Adams Cram
The White Villa
(Originally Published in *Black Spirits and White*, 1895)
Ralph Adams Cram (1863–1942) was born in Hampton Falls, New Hampshire, United States. He wrote a number of fiction stories and was praised by H.P. Lovecraft for his horror. In addition to his work as a writer, Cram was also one of the foremost architects of the Gothic revival in the United States. His influence helped to establish Gothic as the standard style of the period for American college and university buildings.

Dick Donovan
A Night of Horror
(Originally Published in *Tales of Terror*, 1899)
Dick Donovan (1843–1934) was the pseudonym of J.E. Preston Muddock. Born near Southampton, England, Muddock became a journalist and travelled the globe. 'Dick Donovan' was the name of Muddock's fictional Glasgow detective – a character who so rivalled the popularity of Sherlock Holmes that Muddock later chose Donovan as his own pen name. This

technique of using a fictional detective as a pseudonym was used later by Ellery Queen and Nick Carter. He was incredibly prolific in crime and horror genres in particular, and some theorise that the origin of the term 'Dick' to mean an American private detective may be linked back to him.

Amelia B. Edwards

A Night on the Borders of the Black Forest

(Originally Published in *A Night on the Borders of the Black Forest*, 1874)

Amelia B. Edwards (1831–92) was born in London, England. Enjoying a rich and varied career as a writer, journalist and Egyptologist, Edwards was a precocious talent, as her first poem was published when she was only seven years old. Her most successful works included the short story 'The Phantom Coach' – one of her many ghost stories, and the novels *Barbara's History* and *Lord Brackenbury*, alongside her Egyptian travelogue *A Thousand Miles up the Nile*, which detailed her extensive 1873–74 voyage through the country.

Joseph Sheridan Le Fanu

The Familiar

(Originally Published in *In a Glass Darkly*, 1872)

The remarkable father of Victorian ghost stories Joseph Thomas Sheridan Le Fanu (1814–73) was born in Dublin, Ireland. His gothic tales and mystery novels led to him become a leading ghost story writer of the nineteenth century. Three oft-cited works of his are *Uncle Silas, Carmilla* and *The House by the Churchyard*, which all are assumed to have influenced Bram Stoker's *Dracula*. Le Fanu wrote his most successful and productive works after his wife's tragic death and he remained a relatively strong writer up until his own death. An earlier version of 'The Familiar' was titled 'The Watcher' and appeared in *Ghost Stories and Tales of Mystery* in 1851.

P.G. Galalis

Knock, Knock, Wolf

(First Publication)

P.G. Galalis lives with his family near Boston, Massachusetts, where he teaches high school English and writes fiction. When he used to vacation throughout his youth in the Adirondack Mountains of upstate New York, his imagination would bloom wildly with the folk magic and myth that he just knew must live in such places. That same impulse inspires much of his writing today. His other stories have appeared in *Galaxy's Edge Magazine* and *Diabolical Plots*.

Kevin J.J. Gallivan

Mrs. Courcy's Folly

(Originally Published in *All Hallows*, 2002)

Kevin J.J. Gallivan, a former Los Angeles, CA resident, presently resides in a suburb of Buffalo, NY, his native city. He lives with his wife, daughter and dog. He is an avid fan of classic supernatural fiction from Poe to Stoker to E.F. Benson and M.R. James. While stationed in East Anglia, 'the Witch Country', with the U.S. Air Force more than forty years ago, he indulged in some ghost hunting. He has written essays and pastiches on Sherlock Holmes that have appeared in Sherlockian periodicals and been footnoted in Leslie S. Klinger's *New Annotated Sherlock Holmes*.

Théophile Gautier, and Lafcadio Hearn (translator)
Clarimonde
(Originally Published as 'La Morte amoureuse' in *La Chronique de Paris*, 1836; this version uses the 1908 translation by Lafcadio Hearn)
Born in Tarbes, in southwest France, Théophile Gautier (1811–72) was brought up in Paris. He was a school-friend of Gérard de Nerval (1808–55), the Romantic poet. Through him he met Victor Hugo (1802–85), who would be his mentor. Gautier became a fixture on the Paris literary scene, a friend to many of the leading artists and intellectuals of his day. A poet, novelist, essayist and travel writer of immense distinction, Gautier had a particular interest in ballet. It was he who wrote the scenario for *Giselle* (1841). Of Anglo-Irish and Greek extraction, translator Patrick Lafcadio Hearn (1850–1904) was a literary force in his own right, with a longstanding interest in the supernatural. Much of his more scholarly interest was focused on the mythology and traditions of Japan (though he also wrote on Louisiana Creole culture). Along with Gautier's *One of Cleopatra's Nights, and Other Fantastic Romances*, he translated works by Anatole France, Gustave Flaubert, Émile Zola and Guy de Maupassant.

Nikolai Gogol, and Claud Field (translator)
The Viy
(Originally Published in *Mirgorod*, 1835; the English translation here is from *The Mantle and Other Stories*, c. 1916)
Nikolai Gogol (1809–52) was a famous Russian writer born in Sorochyntsi, Ukraine. Gogol is responsible for creating the foundation of the nineteenth century tradition of Russian Realism, a term used to describe, for example, his novel *Dead Souls* and his short story 'The Overcoat'. His later writings evolved from a fundamentally romantic sensibility to Surrealism and the Grotesque. Influenced by his Ukrainian childhood, his horror stories developed into great works such as his play *The Government Inspector*, which is now globally recognised. Claud Field (1863–1941) translated a number of Gogol's works, and also translated texts from Arabic for authors including Abu Hamid al-Ghazali. He was also an author and editor in his own right, with books including *Persian Literature* and *The Charm of India*.

Ali Habashi
The Blackdamp
(First Publication)
Ali Habashi graduated from the University of St. Andrews, Scotland, with a degree in English and Management, and currently works in Boston at an academic publisher. When not at work she can usually be found drinking coffee and stressing about a self-inflicted creative project involving monsters or witches. Her short stories have been featured on *The Other Stories* horror podcast, *The NoSleep Podcast* and several anthologies including *The Corona Book of Ghost Stories*. She is the winner of the Creature Feature category for *The Asterisk Anthology Vol II*. Learn more by visiting her website at alihabashi.com.

Maria Haskins
It's Easy to Shoot a Dog
(Originally Published in *Beneath Ceaseless Skies #260*, 2018)
Maria Haskins is a Swedish-Canadian writer and reviewer of speculative fiction. She debuted as a writer in Sweden, but currently lives just outside Vancouver with a husband, two kids, and a very large black dog. Her work has appeared in *Fireside Fiction*, *Beneath*

Ceaseless Skies, PseudoPod, Flash Fiction Online, Shimmer, Cast of Wonders, and elsewhere. Find out more on her website mariahaskins.com, or follow her on Twitter where she tweets as @mariahaskins.

E.T.A. Hoffmann, and Major Alex. Ewing (translator)
The Mines of Falun
(Originally Published as 'Die Bergwerke zur Falun' in Volume 1 of *Die Serapions-Brüder* (The Serapion Brethren), 1819; the English translation here was published in *The Serapion Brethren*, 1886)
Ernst Theodor Amadeus Hoffmann (1776–1822) was a musician and a painter as well as a successful writer. Born in Germany and raised by his uncle, Hoffmann followed a legal career until his interests drew him to composing operas and ballets. He began to write richly imaginative stories that helped secure his reputation as an influential figure during the German Romantic movement, with many of his tales inspiring stage adaptations, such as *The Nutcracker* and *Coppélia*. Hoffmann's chilling tale 'The Sandman' has influenced many, including Neil Gaiman, whose popalular graphic novel series *The Sandman* also features a character who steals peoples' eyes. Alexander Ewing (1830–95) was a Scottish musical composer and translator. He translated works by Jean Paul as well as E.T.A. Hoffmann, but is perhaps most famous for composing the tune for the popular hymn 'Jerusalem the Golden'.

W.W. Jacobs
The Three Sisters
(Originally Published in *Night Watches*, 1914)
William Wymark ('W.W.') Jacobs (1863–1943) was born in London, England, and he is known for his deeply humorous and horrifying works. Drawing upon his childhood experiences, Jacobs wrote many works reflecting on his father's profession as a dockhand and wharf manager. His first volume of stories, *Many Cargoes,* was a great success and gave Jacobs the courage to publish other stories such as 'The Monkey's Paw' and 'The Toll-House'. Jacobs used realistic experiences as well as a combination of superstition, terror, exotic adventure and humour in each one of his famous tales.

M.R. James
Canon Alberic's Scrap-book
(Originally Published in *National Review*, 1895)
Montague Rhodes James (1862–1936), whose works are regarded as being at the forefront of the ghost story genre, was born in Kent, England. James dispensed with the traditional, predictable techniques of ghost story construction, instead using realistic contemporary settings for his works. He was also a British medieval scholar, so his stories tended to incorporate antiquarian elements. His stories often reflect his childhood in Suffolk and talented acting career, which both seem to have assisted in the build-up of tension and horror in his works.

Vernon Lee
Amour Dure
(Originally Published in *Hauntings: Fantastic Stories*, 1890)
Vernon Lee was a pseudonym for British writer Violet Paget (1856–1935) who was born in France but spent much of her time in Italy. She wrote essays on art, music and travel but is mostly remembered for her supernatural fiction. Lee was an active feminist and was involved in

an anti-militarist organisation during the First World War. Lee's short fiction was often themed around hauntings and she was first published in the well-known *The Yellow Book*. English writer Montague Summers referred to Lee as 'the greatest…of modern exponents of the supernatural in fiction'.

H.P. Lovecraft
The Beast in the Cave
(Originally Published in *The Vagrant*, 1918)
Master of weird fiction Howard Phillips Lovecraft (1890–1937) was born in Providence, Rhode Island. Featuring unknown and otherworldly creatures, his stories were one of the first to mix science fiction with horror. Plagued by nightmares from an early age, he was inspired to write his dark and strange fantasy tales; the isolation he must have experienced from suffering frequent illnesses can be felt as a prominent theme in his work. Lovecraft inspired many other authors, and his most famous story 'The Call of Cthulhu' has influenced many aspects of popular culture.

Frederick Marryat
The White Wolf of the Hartz Mountains
(Originally Published as part of *The Phantom Ship*, 1839, then published as a separate story excerpt under the title 'The White Wolf')
Frederick Marryat (1792–1848), who also used the name H.B. Marryat, was a merchant's son brought up in London. He is now best known for his historical novel *The Children of the New Forest* (1847), but much of his life – and most of his writing – was devoted to the sea. His early years in the Royal Navy were fictionalised in *Mr. Midshipman Easy* (1836), and he wrote several other maritime novels. He also developed an early system of flag-signalling for use at sea. His gothic novel *The Phantom Ship* was based on the legend of the Flying Dutchman but makes a foray ashore to include this classic werewolf story, considered the first appearance of a female werewolf in the history of werewolf fiction.

S.R. Masters
The Cure for Boredom
(First Publication)
S.R. Masters is an internationally published short story writer and novelist. His short fiction has appeared in venues such as *Shock Totem*, *Lamplight*, *The Fiction Desk*, and the *Press Start to Play* anthology. His debut novel, *The Killer You Know*, a coming-of-age murder mystery, was published in the UK by Sphere/Little, Brown, and in the US by Redhook/Hachette. His story 'A Cure for Boredom' was partly inspired by Walker Hamilton's *All the Little Animals*, which Masters read after a chance encounter with the late writer's wife while on holiday in North Wales. Masters keeps a website at www.sr-masters.com and occasionally tweets at @srmastersauthor.

Guy de Maupassant
The Wolf
(Originally Published under the title 'Le Loup' in *Le Gaulois*, 1882. This version originally published in a volume of Maupassant's *Complete Short Stories*, translated by Albert M.C. McMaster, A.E. Henderson, Mme. Quesada, and Others, 1880–93)
Henri René Albert Guy de Maupassant (1850–1893) was born at the Château de Miromesnil in France, and is considered the father of the modern short story. He is perhaps known best for his

short stories 'The Necklace' and 'Boule de Suif', which was inspired by his time serving during the Franco-Prussian War. Maupassant developed syphilis early on in his life, causing him to develop a mental disorder coupled with nightmarish visions, no doubt contributing to his skill in producing supernatural stories. He died in an asylum in 1893.

Damien Mckeating
Under Barrow Downs
(First Publication)
Damien Mckeating was born and a short time after that he developed a love of fantasy and the supernatural. He graduated with an MA in Screenwriting from Bournemouth University and worked for a time as a radio copywriter. He has short stories included in different anthologies, ranging from modern takes on Irish mythology to SF adventures for young readers. He is developing ideas for novels while raising a family and working as a primary school SEN teacher. He is fond of corvids, writes daily, and is currently the oldest he has ever been.

John Moralee
Cold, Wet Hands
(First Publication)
John Moralee lives in England, where his crime, horror and science fiction stories have been published in various magazines and anthologies, including *The Mammoth Book of Jack the Ripper Stories*, *The Mammoth Book of Future Cops*, *Crimewave*, *Switchblade: Tech Noir* and *Clockwork Cairo*. His published novels include the thriller *Acting Dead*, the zombie apocalypse story *Journal of the Living*, and the comic fantasy tale *Crowning Achievements: The Legend of King Arthur*. He is also the author of over two hundred short stories and a satirical collection of comic strips about writing.

Edith Nesbit
The House of Silence
(Originally Published in *Windsor Magazine*, 1906)
Edith Nesbit (1858–1924) was born in Kennington, England. Nesbit established herself as a successful author and poet, writing a variety of literature ranging from children's books to adult horror stories. She co-founded the Fabian Society and was also a strong political activist. Marrying young and frequently moving home, Nesbit made many friendships with other writers including H.G. Wells and George Bernard Shaw. Although she gained most of her success from her children's books, like the ever-popular *The Railway Children*, she was also a well-known horror writer, with such collections as *Something Wrong* and *Grim Tales*.

Amyas Northcote
The Downs
(Originally Published in *In Ghostly Company*, 1921)
A son of the Conservative politician Stafford Northcote (1818–87), Earl of Iddesleigh, Amyas Northcote (1864–1923) was born into the British ascendancy. But as his father's seventh son, his position was comparatively marginal – a fact reflected in the sketchiness of the biographical material that remains. Whilst he is known to have served as a magistrate in Buckinghamshire; he is believed to have lived in Chicago for a while, but few details are known. Like the ghosts he loved to write about (but did not *publish* until his very final years), his most vivid life seems to have been lived posthumously.

Barry Pain

The Undying Thing

(Originally Published in *Stories in the Dark*, 1901)

A regular contributor to *Punch* and other magazines, Cambridge-born Barry Pain (1864–1928) was renowned first and foremost as a comic writer. Like his friend and fellow-humourist Jerome K. Jerome (1859–1927), however, he had a longstanding interest in the supernatural and the gothic. His mad-scientist shocker *The Octave of Claudius* (1897) was to become a pioneering Hollywood Horror movie (*A Blind Bargain*, with Lon Chaney and Raymond McKee, 1922).

Arthur Quiller-Couch

The Haunted Dragoon

(Originally Published in *I Saw Three Ships and Other Winter's Tales*, 1892)

Sir Arthur Quiller-Couch (1863–1944) was born in Bodmin, Cornwall, England. He wrote under the pseudonym 'Q' and, despite publishing many works of fiction and verse, he is best remembered for editing *The Oxford Book of English Verse 1250–1900*. Quiller-Couch was a well-respected literary critic and professor at the University of Cambridge. Interestingly, Sir Arthur Quiller-Couch was said to be the inspiration for the character of Ratty in *The Wind in the Willows*.

Aeryn Rudel

Bites

(First Publication)

Aeryn Rudel is a freelance writer from Seattle, Washington. He is the author of the Acts of War novels published by Privateer Press, and his short fiction has appeared in *The Arcanist*, *The Molotov Cocktail*, and *Pseudopod*, among others. Aeryn is a notorious dinosaur nerd, a baseball fanatic, and knows far more about swords than is healthy or socially acceptable. He occasionally offers dubious advice on the subjects of writing and rejection (mostly rejection) at rejectomancy.com or Twitter @Aeryn_Rudel.

Saki

Gabriel-Ernest

(Originally Published in *The Westminster Gazette*, 1909)

Saki was the pen-name for Hector Hugh Munro (1870–1916). Born in British Burma, the son of an Inspector General of the Imperial Indian Police, Munro lost his mother early and was brought up by grandparents in England. He signed up for the Imperial Police himself, but was quickly invalided home. At a loose end in London, he wrote for newspapers and magazines. The theory always was that his witty, but frequently macabre, short stories were just a way of supporting him as he worked on serious studies of Russian history and politics. In practice, they were to become the basis of both his contemporary and his enduring fame.

David Schmidt

Chaneke

(First Publication)

David J. Schmidt is an author, podcaster, multilingual translator, and homebrewer who splits his time between Mexico City and San Diego, California. His English-language titles include such works of 'non-fiction horror' as *Three Nights in the Clown Motel* and *Holy Ghosts: True Tales from a Haunted Christian College*, as well as *The Tiny Staircase* series, devoted to the mysterious and the unexplained. His Spanish-language books *Más frío que la nieve: cuentos sobrenaturales de Rusia* and *Tunguska: luces en el cielo sobre Siberia* were published nationwide in Mexico. Schmidt is the co-host of the podcast *To Russia with Love*. He speaks twelve languages and has been to thirty-three countries. He received his B.A. in psychology from Point Loma Nazarene University. Find out more at holyghoststories.com.

Cody Schroeder

Hunting the Howler
(First Publication)
Cody Schroeder lives in Missouri, USA surrounded by books. He spends unreasonable amounts of time reading and writing about all manner of creepy, macabre, and fantastic things. He can be found on Twitter at @LordVoltrex, where he tweets about whatever happens to be distracting him. His published works include a short story, 'Clouds over Lichen Spire', in *The Literary Hatchet Issue 14*, 'Tracks in the Snow' in the *Supernatural Horror Short Stories* collection from Flame Tree Publishing, 'Storm Stones' published in *Occult Detective Quarterly Issue #5*, and 'Shadows in the Trees' published in *Horror* by Breaking Rules Publishing.

Shana Scott

Waking the Monster
(First Publication)
Shana Scott is a digital archivist and content specialist with a Master's degree in Professional Writing and Publishing, living in St. Louis, Missouri. She's a member of SFWA, and her work has been published in magazines, anthologies, and podcasts such as *Escape Pod*, *Agents & Spies Short Stories*, and *TulipTree Review*. Currently, she writes about the craft of world-building in her blog, womanintheredroom.com, and posts cute picture of her pomsky, Howl.

May Sinclair

Where Their Fire Is Not Quenched
(Originally Published in *The English Review*, 1922)
May Sinclair's (1863–1946) first fame was as a 'bluestocking': a literary critic and novelist of note, she was also prominent in the fight for women's suffrage. But her place among the intellectual aristocracy was hard-won. Born in Rock Ferry, Wirral, the daughter of a Liverpool shipowner, she had to move south with her family when his business failed. He fell into alcoholism and died soon after, leaving May struggling to support her sickly family, despite the fragility of her own health. Her writings on the supernatural show her working out atavistic anxieties against the unsettling insights of modern psychology and science.

Harriet Prescott Spofford

The Conquering Will
(Originally Published in *The Smart Set*, June 1901)
Harriet Prescott Spofford (1835–1921) was born in Maine, with the family moving to Massachusetts during her early life. From the age of seventeen she supported her family with her early published stories: her mother was an invalid and her father, one of the California Gold Rush Pioneers and a founder of Oregon City, suffered from paralysis. Spofford published over one hundred stories in the next few years, but it was her 1858 publication of 'In a Cellar' in The Atlantic Monthly that elevated her reputation and secured her future as a widely successful author.

Robert Louis Stevenson

The Strange Case of Dr. Jekyll and Mr. Hyde

(Originally Published in 1886)

Robert Louis Stevenson (1850–1894) was born in Edinburgh, Scotland. He became a well-known novelist, poet and travel writer, publishing the famous works *Treasure Island, Kidnapped* and *The Strange Case of Dr. Jekyll and Mr. Hyde*. All of his works were highly admired by many other artists, as he was a literary celebrity during his lifetime. Travelling a lot for health reasons and because of his family's business, Stevenson ended up writing many of his journeys into his stories and wrote works mainly related to children's literature and the horror genre.

Bram Stoker

The Secret of the Growing Gold

(Originally Published in *Black and White*, 1892)

Abraham 'Bram' Stoker (1847–1912) was born in Dublin, Ireland. Often ill during his childhood, he spent a lot of time in bed listening to his mother's grim stories, sparking his imagination. Striking up a friendship as an adult with the actor Henry Irving, Stoker eventually came to work and live in London, meeting notable authors such as Arthur Conan Doyle and Oscar Wilde. Stoker wrote several stories based on supernatural horror, such as the gothic masterpiece *Dracula* which has left an enduring and powerful impact on the genre, creating one of the most iconic figures that horror fiction has ever seen.

Anna Taborska

Rusalka

(Originally Published in *Exotic Gothic 4: #28/29: A Postscripts Anthology*, 2012)

Anna Taborska is a British filmmaker and horror writer. She has written and directed two short fiction films, two documentaries and an award-winning TV drama, and worked on over twenty other film and television productions. Anna's debut short story collection, *For Those Who Dream Monsters*, published by Mortbury Press in 2013, won the Dracula Society's Children of the Night Award and was nominated for a British Fantasy Award. Anna is a Bram Stoker Award nominee, and author of the cat-themed micro-collection *Shadowcats*. Her latest collection of novelettes and short stories, entitled *Bloody Britain*, will come out soon with Shadow Publishing.

Hugh Walpole

The Tarn

(Originally Published in *Success*, 1923)

Sir Hugh Walpole (1884–1941) was born in Auckland, New Zealand. He was incredibly popular and successful during his lifetime. As well as writing many novel and short stories, Walpole also conducted lecture tours of North America, and was invited to Hollywood to write scenarios for *David Copperfield* and *Little Lord Fauntleroy*. Walpole's reputation and popularity suffered after his death. Recently there has been a re-emergence in interest for the author.

D.A. Watson

Restless Natives

(First Publication)

D.A. Watson is the author of the novels *In the Devil's Name, The Wolves of Langabhat* and *Cuttin' Heads*, plus the collection of short stories and epic poetry, *Tales of the What the Fuck*. Nominated for a Pushcart Prize in the US and the People's Book Prize in the UK, his writing has appeared in several international anthologies and won competitions from Falkirk to New Zealand. Also a regular spoken word performer, he lives with his family on the west coast of Scotland. His fourth novel *Adonias Low* will be published in early 2021.

Edith Wharton

The Lady Maid's Bell

(Originally Published in *Scribner's Magazine*, 1902)

Edith Wharton (1862–1937), the Pulitzer Prize-winning writer of *The Age of Innocence*, was born in New York. As well as her talent as an American novelist, Wharton was also known for her short stories and designer career. Wharton was born into a controlled New York society where women were discouraged from achieving anything beyond a proper marriage. Defeating the norms, Wharton grew to become one of America's greatest writers. Writing numerous ghost stories and murderous tales such as 'Kerfol, 'Mr. Jones' and 'Afterward', Wharton is widely known for the ghost tours that now take place at her old home, The Mount.

Nemma Wollenfang

You Think You Are Safe

(First Publication)

Nemma Wollenfang is an MSc Postgraduate and prize-winning short story writer who lives in Northern England. Her stories have appeared in several venues, including: *Beyond the Stars*, *Abyss & Apex*, *Cossmass Infinities*, and *Chicken Soup for the Soul*, as well as previously in Flame Tree's Gothic Fantasy series. She is also a recipient of the Speculative Literature Foundation's Working Class Writers Grant for her in-progress novel, *I, Phoenix*. She can be found on Facebook, Twitter, and at her website: nemmawollenfang.co.uk.

Anna Ziegelhof

He Will Hear Us Coming

(First Publication)

Originally from Germany, Anna Ziegelhof now lives in the San Francisco Bay Area, where she works in tech by day and writes short fiction by night. She is the author of several horror and science fiction short stories, such as 'Dimenso-Yarn Ad Copy Draft' (*Shoreline of Infinity*), 'The Night Guard' (*Close the Gate* anthology), 'Hello, Funny Horse' (*Crimson Streets*), 'Little Grey Weirdos' (*The Future Fire*), and 'My Little Danger-Stranger' (*Daily Science Fiction*).

FLAME TREE PUBLISHING
Short Story Series
New & Classic Writing

Flame Tree's Gothic Fantasy books offer a carefully curated series of new titles, each with combinations of original and classic writing:

*Chilling Horror • Chilling Ghost • Science Fiction
Murder Mayhem • Crime & Mystery • Swords & Steam
Dystopia Utopia • Supernatural Horror • Lost Worlds
Time Travel • Heroic Fantasy • Pirates & Ghosts • Agents & Spies
Endless Apocalypse • Alien Invasion • Robots & AI • Lost Souls
Haunted House • Cosy Crime • American Gothic
Urban Crime • Epic Fantasy • Detective Mysteries
Detective Thrillers • A Dying Planet • Bodies in the Library*

**Also, new companion titles offer rich collections of
classic fiction, myths and tales in the gothic fantasy tradition:**

*H.G. Wells • Lovecraft • Sherlock Holmes
Edgar Allan Poe • Bram Stoker • Mary Shelley
Charles Dickens Supernatural • Heroes & Heroines Myths & Tales
African Myths & Tales • Celtic Myths & Tales • Greek Myths & Tales
Norse Myths & Tales • Chinese Myths & Tales • Japanese Myths & Tales
Irish Fairy Tales • King Arthur & The Knights of the Round Table
Alice's Adventures in Wonderland • The Divine Comedy
Hans Christian Andersen Fairy Tales • Brothers Grimm
The Wonderful Wizard of Oz • The Age of Queen Victoria*

Available from all good bookstores, worldwide, and online at
flametreepublishing.com

See our new fiction imprint
FLAME TREE PRESS | FICTION WITHOUT FRONTIERS
New and original writing in Horror, Crime, SF and Fantasy

And join our monthly newsletter with offers and more stories:
FLAME TREE FICTION NEWSLETTER
flametreepress.com

GOTHIC FANTASY

For our books, calendars, blog
and latest special offers please see:
flametreepublishing.com